It wou~~ld...~~ be ~~...~~ t~~...~~
the Executioner had been
forced to rethink a mission

The chill draft caused by the train's motion buffeted him and pulled at his clothing. From the tracks the ground fell away in a long grassy slope. Some way ahead he could see clusters of lights, indicating some habitation. A town. That meant people and maybe the chance to gain some other kind of transportation.

The sudden shriek of the train's whistle alerted him. The train reduced its speed somewhat. He watched the ground some feet below. It still seemed to be moving by at a dangerous speed.

He figured it wasn't going to get better than this. He was about to take a calculated risk—one that might leave him injured. But if he decided to stay on the train he could find himself in the hands of the authorities and his freedom might become a thing of the past. Bolan swung around so he faced the way the train was moving, waited for the clearest patch of slope and went for it.

MACK BOLAN ®
The Executioner

The Don Pendleton's®
Executioner®
DESPERATE CARGO

A GOLD EAGLE BOOK FROM
W🦅RLDWIDE.

TORONTO • NEW YORK • LONDON
AMSTERDAM • PARIS • SYDNEY • HAMBURG
STOCKHOLM • ATHENS • TOKYO • MILAN
MADRID • WARSAW • BUDAPEST • AUCKLAND

If you purchased this book without a cover you should be aware
that this book is stolen property. It was reported as "unsold and
destroyed" to the publisher, and neither the author nor the
publisher has received any payment for this "stripped book."

Recycling programs
for this product may
not exist in your area.

First edition April 2010

ISBN-13: 978-0-373-64377-6

Special thanks and acknowledgment to
Mike Linaker for his contribution to this work.

DESPERATE CARGO

Copyright © 2010 by Worldwide Library.

All rights reserved. Except for use in any review, the
reproduction or utilization of this work in whole or in part
in any form by any electronic, mechanical or other means,
now known or hereafter invented, including xerography,
photocopying and recording, or in any information storage
or retrieval system, is forbidden without the written permission
of the publisher, Worldwide Library, 225 Duncan Mill Road,
Don Mills, Ontario, Canada M3B 3K9.

This is a work of fiction. Names, characters, places and incidents are
either the product of the author's imagination or are used fictitiously,
and any resemblance to actual persons, living or dead, business
establishments, events or locales is entirely coincidental.

® and TM are trademarks of the publisher. Trademarks indicated
with ® are registered in the United States Patent and Trademark
Office, the Canadian Trade Marks Office and in other countries.

Printed in U.S.A.

It is easy to be brave behind a castle wall.
—Welsh proverb

The men who hide behind their wealth and pretend to
be brave will pay the ultimate price.
—Mack Bolan

THE
MACK BOLAN
LEGEND

Nothing less than a war could have fashioned the destiny of the man called Mack Bolan. Bolan earned the Executioner title in the jungle hell of Vietnam.

But this soldier also wore another name—Sergeant Mercy. He was so tagged because of the compassion he showed to wounded comrades-in-arms and Vietnamese civilians.

Mack Bolan's second tour of duty ended prematurely when he was given emergency leave to return home and bury his family, victims of the Mob. Then he declared a one-man war against the Mafia.

He confronted the Families head-on from coast to coast, and soon a hope of victory began to appear. But Bolan had broken society's every rule. That same society started gunning for this elusive warrior—to no avail.

So Bolan was offered amnesty to work within the system against terrorism. This time, as an employee of Uncle Sam, Bolan became Colonel John Phoenix. With a command center at Stony Man Farm in Virginia, he and his new allies—Able Team and Phoenix Force—waged relentless war on a new adversary: the KGB.

But when his one true love, April Rose, died at the hands of the Soviet terror machine, Bolan severed all ties with Establishment authority.

Now, after a lengthy lone-wolf struggle and much soul-searching, the Executioner has agreed to enter an "arm's-length" alliance with his government once more, reserving the right to pursue personal missions in his Everlasting War.

Prologue

During its long, slow voyage from Thailand, the *Orient Venturer* made a number of calls into friendly ports. Sometimes it was to take on more cargo, or to unload. It refueled and during those stays in port the captain played host to officials who marked his cargo as legitimate and departed the ship with considerably more cash in their pockets than they'd had when they boarded.

The *Orient Venturer*'s voyage was one it had made a number of times. In its hold, or in the steel seagoing containers secured to its rusting and scarred deck plates, it carried the mixed cargo that marked it as a ship of all trades. The cargo—mainly clothing and electrical goods, manufactured in Asian sweatshops—would find its way into stores and retail outlets spread across Europe. Cheaply made, the goods would be sold at marked-up prices for Western consumers. These items brought a fair profit for the company that owned the ship.

One container, however, held cargo that would net an even greater profit for the men behind the *Orient Venturer.*

The special cargo was stowed in a special container. A close inspection would have shown that the container had been altered to facilitate its cargo.

In the roof were a number of vented grilles to allow air to travel in and out of the steel box. This was necessary in order to keep the cargo of young Thai women and children alive.

The eldest woman was twenty-two, the youngest twelve. They were all kidnap victims, intended for sale when they reached their destination. They had no choice in the matter because they were virtual slaves. They'd been stolen from their homes for induction into the twilight world of human trafficking. At journey's end they would be passed along to their new masters. Some would be forced into the garment industry where they would work endless hours for starvation wages. Others would be moved into prostitution, the sex industry, or they would go as personal playthings for wealthy clients. The younger and prettier a girl, the more likely she would be bought for sexual gratification.

Business was thriving. The *Orient Venturer* made regular trips delivering the cargo to mainland Europe and the United Kingdom. The men behind the business were based in Rotterdam and London. The organization conducted business globally, procuring assets for clients in the Middle East and the United States. It was well run, protected because of weak legislation and the inability of legal forces to act without absolute and watertight cases. One slip, one word or phrase, on a document, and the whole case could be thrown out of court. Proof positive was almost an impossibility, and although a dedicated effort was being made, no indictments had yet been achieved. Government task forces working together had their hands tied. They struggled for months to concentrate their investigations only to find that their superiors, sensitive to the demands of the courts, would shake their heads and demand even more proof.

The task forces looked for ways to gather their evidence and took the decision to insert undercover agents into the organization in an effort to obtain what they needed.

Dean Turner and Ron Bentley were seasoned agents, working for the joint task force. When they had been asked to take on a covert assignment to infiltrate the trafficking group in Rotterdam they didn't need to be asked twice. Once assigned they distanced themselves from the main group, setting themselves up to watch suspected members of the trafficking organization. Over a couple of months they concentrated on the Rotterdam group, looking for any members who seemed to be vulnerable to turning, and finally fixed on a single individual who expressed some vocal dissatisfaction with his position within the organization.

The initial contact went well. Their man seemed to have a grievance against his employers and a tendency to complain about them to the American undercover agents. They spent time with him, sympathizing with his complaints, and slowly reeled him into their confidence. In the end he agreed to provide them with evidence that would give the task force solid evidence into the workings of the trafficking group.

However, when the agents made the rendezvous to meet their contact they were ambushed, disarmed and taken to an isolated location.

They were told they were going to be made examples of—used to show the task force that further efforts to break the organization were useless. The traffickers wanted the international task force to know powerful forces ranged against them. The organization had high-profile protection. They could not be touched. No one could harm them. The agents would be used to make the task force realize they were simply wasting their time.

For three days the agents were savagely tortured, their naked bodies abused and broken. Photographs were taken to be sent to the task force and a final message stated where the bodies could be found.

The stark warning, showing the brazen contempt the traffickers had for the task force, had its effect. After the bodies had been located and removed, the task force was ordered to stand back and reassess its operational method. There was a need to regroup—by no means to admit defeat, but the clear message to the task force from the traffickers had got through, and it was realized that the enemy had the upper hand.

1

From the window of his hotel room Mack Bolan could see the distant configuration of Rotterdam Port, the night sky ablaze with lights. He saw a vast sprawl of warehouse units, cranes and endless rows of steel cargo containers. He was seeing the vista through the sheeting rain covering the city, blown in from the cold swells of the North Sea. Across the stretch of water was England, the secondary target of Bolan's mission.

The Executioner's presence in Rotterdam was down to intel he received during a briefing with Hal Brognola back in Washington. That clandestine meeting between the man from Justice and Bolan had kick-started the Executioner's journey to Europe. After touching down at Schiphol Airport, Bolan had ridden a local train to Rotterdam and his prebooked room. The weather had been rough for most of the flight and stayed the course while Bolan had transferred to his hotel. It was midevening, the sky already dark. Bolan had a rendezvous with a contact the next day, so he figured he would have an early meal and turn in. The turbulent weather during the flight had denied him sleep, so a solid night's rest was advisable.

Bolan turned from the window when he heard a tap on his door. He crossed the room and opened up. A trolley was wheeled inside carrying the meal he had ordered. Bolan handed the service girl a tip, then closed and locked the door after she left. Bolan was on alert. He wasn't the paranoid type who saw threats lurking in every corner. Even so, past experience had taught him never to leave anything to chance.

He took off the covers and checked the meal. It was exactly what he had ordered. A steak, potatoes, salad. He pulled up a chair and settled down to eat. The food was good. Only when he was done did he activate his tri-band cell phone and tap the speed-dial number that would connect him with Hal Brognola. The connection hummed and buzzed, then the big Fed's voice reached Bolan.

"So how is Rotterdam?"

"Cold. It's raining like it's in for the duration. I'm fine. You have any updates for me?"

"No. Status hasn't changed much since we talked and you flew out. The operation is stalled. The heads are talking. Trying to come up with a fresh way of moving on, but as of now it's a no-go. Those two agents getting killed has hit hard. You know why. Suspicions there was a mole inside the task force appear to have been proved. Turner and Bentley were betrayed and the fact we have someone operating inside the group and capable of passing along information makes everyone suspicious of the man next to him. No one is going to commit to anything."

"Let's hope my meeting in the morning throws up something useful," the Executioner said.

Brognola hesitated before he replied.

"Tread carefully with this man Bickell. Hasn't been proved he was the one who turned Turner and Bentley over to the opposition but he was the only man who had access to them. The more I think about it, the less I'm in favor of you using him."

"Right now we don't have anything else. I'm not about to go into this meet blind."

"Striker, these people are bad. You saw what they did to our two mans. They work a business that treats human beings like so much merchandise. Don't believe they won't do the same to you given the chance."

"Understood, pal, now quit worrying and give me some good news."

"Your Brit buddy," Brognola said, referring to David McCarter, the Phoenix Force commander, "has a contact for you in London. He can set you up with specialist equipment. I'm sending a photo over your phone for identification. And I'll text a name and phone number to set up your meet. This man is supposed to be good. He'll sort out anything you want. Anything else you need right now?"

"Just a good night's sleep," Bolan said. "I'll be in touch."

Bolan checked the information Brognola had sent to him. A half hour later he turned in, clicking off the light. He lay staring at the rain-flecked window, his mind still active as he reviewed the past couple of days and the events that had brought him to Rotterdam and his upcoming meeting with a man who might turn out to be a Judas.

Two Days Earlier, Washington

DRESSED IN CASUAL clothing he might have been just another tourist taking in the sights of the nation's capital.

But Mack Bolan was a world away from being just that. As he strolled around in the pale sunlight, observing the scene around him, Hal Brognola fell into step beside him.

"Looking good as ever," Brognola said lightly. "Your life-style must suit you."

"You didn't call me just to boost my confidence, Hal."

"Would you believe I need your help on a problem?"

"Go ahead."

"A joint US-UK-European task force has been compromised by the deaths of two of its undercover agents. Dean Turner and Ron Bentley. They had gotten close to the group the task force was investigating. Human trafficking on a big scale. Working out of Europe and serving the needs of clients in Europe and the U.S. Striker, this is as nasty as it gets. These people are running a virtual slave trade. Men, women and even kids." Brognola pointed at the slim briefcase he was carrying. "I have the whole dossier in here. Details the perps. Their locations. Right now the operation has stalled because there's some concern how deep infiltration might have gone. The whole thing is on hold. And while that happens the suspects are still operating. Evidence against them is all suspicion but no substance. Nowhere near enough to even haul anyone in. It's a big organization. Run by an influential head honcho with top-class protection. Hugo Canfield. British citizen. He has a hotshot lawyer with an impeccable record standing behind him. Dutch man called Ludwig van Ryden. And he uses that man every time one of his clients even gets a parking ticket."

"What do you need, Hal?"

"Someone without ties to any part of the task force. A clean slate. No allegiances. Nothing that connects." The big Fed paused. "And someone who can leave the book of rules at home."

Brognola opened his case and extracted a thick folder. He handed it to Bolan. "We can see the end result of this business, Striker. What those bastards do to people. I want to reach the head and cut it off. The task force has its hands tied right now and I'm damn tired of the restrictions holding us back. If I had my way I'd go in all guns blazing but I'd have to fight bureaucracy first and last. I need a lever. Something I can use to force the game into the open."

"Where would I start?"

"Our dead agents had an informant. Part of the organization but he convinced our mans he wanted to quit and was willing to cooperate. Name of Wilhelm Bickell. Based in Rotterdam, where the traffickers are said to have what Bickell called a distribution point. We don't know if that's true because our mans were killed before they got that information to us. All we have is a cell phone contact number for him."

"It's thin," Bolan said. "But I've started with less." He weighed the folder in his hand. "I'll need credentials. Anything else you can conjure up."

Brognola nodded. "No problem." He tapped the folder. "The phrase *read it and weep* applies pretty well here, Striker."

THE EXECUTIONER SPENT most of the day going through the contents of the explicit data. It covered suspects, the trafficking group known as Venturer Exports and its head, Hugo Canfield. Its grip on human trafficking was widespread and from the text of the reports Bolan became aware of the callous indifference of the people running the enterprise. The hub for Venturer Exports was mainland Europe and the U.K. Its market was worldwide and even Mack Bolan, well versed in the evil manifested through man's indifference to human suffering, was forced to sit back and take a moment's respite. It appeared that the practice of slavery was still thriving. From his reading it seemed that the majority of victims involved came from those ravaged parts of the world where recent conflicts had created rich hunting grounds for the traffickers. They scavenged through Asian and Eastern European countries, snatching people off the streets, collecting them from holding camps. The countless numbers of displaced people were seldom missed. Officials were paid off, heads turned and no questions asked. The victims were bundled into containers and taken by road, across borders where money replaced transit visas, and the human cargo was waved through without an inspection. The final destination of the converging containers appeared to be Rotterdam, and from there the merchandise was sent to whichever market placed its order.

The slaves provided cheap labor for sweatshops, for service industries, where the employers held the workers illegally.

They were in foreign countries without proper papers, earning little money and constantly under the threat of violence if they made any kind of protest. Young women, chosen for their good looks, were channeled into the many-tentacled sex industry, from making adult movies to working the streets. And there was the ever-present shadow of the drug business in the background. The data Brognola had provided included photographs that emphasized the ever-present dangers encroaching on the lives of the traffickers' victims. The sick, the dying and the dead. Drug affliction. The punishment meted out to a victim who had rebelled. Or those who simply succumbed to the pitiful life forced on them.

Read it and weep.

Brognola's words had not been far from the truth. Venturer Exports and the men profiting from it had to be stopped. The Executioner was onboard.

2

Wilhelm Bickell, average height, near-bald head glistening from the rain, hunched his shoulders beneath the long raincoat. Bolan recognized him from the photograph in the folder Brognola had provided. The image had been taken from a distance, but it was not difficult to identify the man. Bickell had an extraordinarily plain face. His outstanding feature was his large, crooked nose supporting a pair of heavy eyeglasses. According to the intelligence relating to the man, Bickell was a fixer for Venturer Exports. The detail provided by Turner and Bentley had him down as dissatisfied with his position. A disgruntled employee passed over by his superiors, tired of being treated as mere hired help. He was supposedly ready to turn against them for the simple emotion of revenge. The two agents had nurtured his feelings, fueling his resentment. They had been preparing Bickell as an aide in gaining possession of evidence that might have turned the task-force investigation to a positive outcome. That hope died after they had been lured into a meeting, taken captive and tortured savagely before being killed.

The Executioner kept those thoughts in mind as he stepped away from the café door and crossed the sidewalk to where Bickell was standing.

"Wilhelm Bickell? I'm Cooper."

Bickell nodded.

Bolan took his hand from his coat pocket and palmed the leather wallet holding the U.S. Justice Department badge

Brognola had supplied. Next to the badge, beneath a plastic cover was a laminated card with Bolan's picture and cover name on it.

Bickell's eyes, magnified by the lenses of his glasses, examined the big American's face. The only contact he had had with Bolan was over the phone, arranging the meet. He recognized the voice.

"This is not a very satisfactory way for us to meet, you understand. *Ja?*"

"Under the circumstances I was given little choice. Turner and Bentley didn't leave much in the way of contact details. You remember them, don't you?"

Bickell visibly stiffened. Red spots colored his pale cheeks.

"Of course I remember them. We were working together. Am I under suspicion concerning their deaths? Perhaps you are not aware of the risk I took even associating with them. My own life is in danger now."

"We're all in a risky position, Bickell. I came to Rotterdam to try and pick up where the others left off. Are you willing to continue cooperating?"

"Of course," Bickell said. "I am ready to help any way I can."

A little too quickly, Bolan thought. Slow down, Bickell, you're making yourself obvious.

"We should walk," Bickell suggested. "I really feel I am being watched. You understand? *Ja?*"

"Let's go," Bolan said.

Bickell led the way along the sidewalk. The rain and the early hour had reduced the number of pedestrians. They walked for a few hundred feet before Bickell paused at the mouth of a side street. His hesitation warned Bolan, but for the present he played along.

"There is a quiet coffee shop down here," Bickell said. "We can talk in private. *Ja?*"

Bolan fell in alongside the man and they walked along the

street. The tall buildings on either side reduced the rain to a slight mist. They also cut the intrusion of sound and it enabled Bolan to pick up the soft murmur of a car engine and the sound of wet tires rolling along the street. From the corner of his eye Bolan saw Bickell's shoulders hunch under his coat. The sound of his footsteps sharpened as he began to walk faster.

"We running out of time?" Bolan asked.

Bickell said something Bolan couldn't catch. But he understood the threat offered by the pistol that emerged from the right-hand pocket of the man's coat. The muzzle aimed at Bolan.

"Over there," Bickell snapped, gesturing with the pistol.

The Executioner saw they were at the entrance to an empty delivery yard, the gates standing open, the adjoining building deserted and quiet. Bickell's gun hand gestured again and Bolan walked ahead, the Dutchman following. As Bolan turned to face Bickell, the car he had heard turned in through the open gateway and rolled to a stop. A tall man climbed out and pushed the wooden gates shut, dropping a metal bar in place. He moved to stand a few feet behind Bickell, hands thrust deep in the pockets of his thick coat. A moment later he was joined by the man who had been behind the wheel of the car.

"Tell me, *Mijnheer* Cooper, are you so trusting it never occurred to you that something like this might happen? Or are you simply stupid?" Bickell asked.

"Look at it from where I'm standing. I only arrived last night and it appears I have already been betrayed by the man who set up Turner and Bentley for execution."

Bickell didn't like the inference, but shrugged it off.

"That was so easy it was almost embarrassing. Those two were so naive they deserved to die. Like so many Americans they believed in trust and loyalty. It was like shooting fish in a barrel."

Bickell said something in Dutch to his two companions. It drew a round of laughter.

"So, Cooper, they sent you in like the Lone Ranger to deal with the bad mans. *Ja?*"

Bickell raised his left hand to wipe at the rain spots on his glasses. It created a thin window of opportunity. It was enough for Bolan to bunch his right hand into a big fist that struck out at Bickell's face. Bolan hit him twice. The blows were powerfully brutal. They slammed into Bickell's mouth and nose, jerking his head around and toppling him against the side of the parked car. Bickell slid across the rain-slick surface, his legs going from under him. He hit the ground on his knees, head dropping. Blood spilled from his battered face.

"For Turner and Bentley," Bolan said softly. "Consider it a down payment."

The pair behind Bickell came alive, producing handguns. They covered Bolan, who had already stepped back, his hands raised in surrender. When they saw he was not going to do anything one of them moved to where Bickell knelt. He reached out a hand and dragged Bickell to his feet, pushing him against the side of the car. He also retrieved the pistol Bickell had dropped. Then he moved up to Bolan and expertly checked him for weapons. Satisfied the American was not armed he rejoined his partner.

Bickell, hands pressed to his bloody face, stared at Bolan. The left lens of his glasses had cracked when Bolan hit him and the single eye left visible blazed with undisguised anger.

"Bastaard." The invective was muffled but there was enough force for Bolan to understand the feeling behind it.

The man who had searched Bolan moved to open the passenger door and roughly hustled Bickell inside. He slammed the door and walked around to the driver's door. He barked a command to his partner, who moved to reopen the gate. Then he gestured at Bolan.

"In the back, Cooper."

Bolan did as he was told. With the gate open the second man

climbed in beside Bolan, covering him. The car started and reversed out onto the street. It was driven to the far end, then picked up a wider street that wound through the city. The thought struck Bolan that no one had made any move to prevent him seeing the way they were going. Their ultimate destination looked to be an intended one-way trip for Bolan. He sat back, taking in the scenery, his agile mind working on that fact. His captors wanted him alive for the present. His future was another matter. Once the opposition had decided how much— or how little—he knew about their operation, his usefulness would end. These people had already shown how little they cared when it came to disposing of unwanted baggage.

With that in mind Bolan prepared himself for what might come. He had no illusions. What waited for him at the end of this drive would be far from pleasant if he failed to make use of any opportunity presenting itself. He was not being driven to a barbecue. Pain and suffering were the only items liable to be on any menu put before Bolan.

He concentrated on his captors. The damage he had inflicted on Bickell would keep the man out of any hard action. His injuries would divert his attention away from Bolan. Not a great victory but at least it had cut the opposition by a third. Until they arrived at their destination Bolan wasn't going to know by how much that percentage might rise. He had assessed the two men accompanying Bickell as solid professionals. It appeared that their orders had been to bring Bolan in alive and unharmed, and they were doing that. Bickell had let his mouth run away with himself and had received the necessary chiding to shut him up temporarily. From the brief time he had been able to watch the others Bolan had seen they were strongly built, capable of handling themselves. And both were armed. Bickell was unarmed, his fallen pistol having been retrieved by the man behind the wheel.

The Executioner sank back in the soft leather seat,

watching the wet streets of Rotterdam slip by. As they eased through the narrow streets Bolan caught glimpses of the river that ran through the city. Cranes and warehouses began to dominate the skyline. They were heading in the direction of the port. The car made some sharp turns, moving along narrower streets that edged the main port facility. There were businesses along this section. Distribution warehouses. Service industries. Private vehicles were replaced by vans and trucks. The car made a sharp right turn that took it along a narrow road that paralleled the water before swinging in through open gates into a freight yard that had a large warehouse structure at the far end.

There didn't appear to be much activity around the yard. Bolan noticed a number of large steel containers, some stacked three high. There was a car parked near the warehouse. They drove over the yard's rutted surface and through a high doorway into the warehouse. As the car came to a stop inside Bolan heard the metallic rattle behind them as a metal roller door was lowered.

Bolan's minder produced his pistol, gesturing. "Get out."

With the pair of minders flanking him Bolan was walked across to an office block against one wall. The door was opened and he was pushed inside. Bolan sized up the man awaiting his arrival.

Well dressed. A sober suit and tie. Expensive. The cold expression on his face did nothing to endear him to Bolan. He had a fine look to him. Almost delicate. His skin was silky, lips colorless, pale blond hair. Rimless glasses with lightly tinted lenses shaded his gray eyes. He was observing Bolan with an intensity that could have been intimidating to anyone with less confidence.

"Where's Bickell?" the man asked.

Bolan picked up the English accent.

The minder who had driven the car wagged a thumb in Bolan's direction.

"There was some aggravation. Willi came off worse," he explained in his heavily accented English. "He's never learned to keep his mouth closed. He's in the car."

The blond Brit leaned forward a little, stroking the tip of his narrow chin.

"I was surprised when you contacted Bickell. Obviously the example of your dead friends failed as the deterrent it was intended to be."

"Did you expect us to ignore it?" Bolan said.

"Had it not occurred to your superiors that Bickell might have been the one who turned on your friends?" The man adjusted the hang of his jacket.

"We guessed. It was decided to draw him out. Give him a chance to repent his misdeeds."

"A sense of humor. I like that in a man. But it isn't going to save you."

"I wasn't expecting it to. I just wanted to get a look at the kind of people who would kill so readily."

"Look, Cooper…is that correct? *Cooper?* Turner and Bentley, or whatever their real names, were dealt with as part of a tactical maneuver." He smiled. "Sounds bloody pretentious, doesn't it? But they were getting a little too close to us at a busy time. Couldn't afford to have them snooping around like that."

Bolan stayed silent, watching the man. He was playing it light, but there was intelligence in those eyes.

"You can't avoid it," Bolan said. "Sooner or later your organization is going to come down. Killing Turner and Bentley shows you're getting scared because the investigation is closing in."

The Brit smiled. Not from bravado. It was clearly from the security that he felt.

"It will never happen, Cooper. Turner and Bentley were blundering around like a pair of blind men. They had no idea

what they were taking on. Just like your bloody task force."
He held up a single finger. "You can't touch us. Understand.
You cannot touch us. Keep sending your sad little agents and
we will get rid of them just like Turner and Bentley. And
you, *Cooper.*"

He turned aside to speak to Bickell's heavies. The conversation was brief, words muffled. Then he glanced back at Bolan.

"Now?" asked the man who had driven the car.

"Yes. We get rid of him. No time to play games this time.
Just kill him and dispose of the body." The Brit barely glanced
at Bolan as he made for the door. "Your trip here was a waste
of time. Pity you won't even get to see the sights."

As he passed through the office door the driver attracted
his attention.

"What about Bickell, Mr. Chambers? He *is* becoming a li-
ability. Since we dealt with those Americans he's become
nervous. Scared. He could break. We don't think he should
be trusted any longer."

Chambers stopped in his tracks, turning to face the driver.
His pale face showed twin red blotches on his cheeks.

"What are my orders about using my name? Tell me."

"Never to mention it. I apologize for my error, sir."

The Brit glanced across at Bolan.

The big American shrugged.

"I'm not going to be telling anyone. Am I, Mr. Chambers?"

A thin smile curled Chambers's lips.

"Very true, Cooper. Very true." He turned to the driver.
"Make sure they are *both* taken care of. We can't afford any
more of Bickell's nerves."

Chambers stepped out of the office.

The driver perched on the edge of the office desk. His
partner moved for the first time since they had entered the
office. "Willi?" he asked.

"Bring him in here. Give Chambers a minute to get clear.

You know he prefers not to be around at times like these," the driver said.

"He has no stomach."

"It's what we are paid for."

As the partner left the office Bolan glanced at the driver. "Is the English for my benefit?" he asked.

The driver grinned, seeming to enjoy the question. "Rotterdam can be a very hospitable city. But not exactly so in your case."

"And there I was hoping you might show me around."

The sound of a car engine rose as Chambers drove away, the noise fading quickly. Bolan heard the scrape of shoe leather on the concrete outside the office. The door was pushed open to admit Bickell and the driver's partner. The lower part of Bickell's face was swollen and bloody. The moment he saw Bolan he erupted into a wild verbal assault.

The driver yelled at him. Bickell ignored him, still screaming. Without warning he launched himself at Bolan, arms flailing wildly.

The driver's partner reached out to grab Bickell. He had both hands free, having put his pistol away.

Bolan allowed Bickell to get within a foot or so, then launched himself into action. He caught hold of Bickell's coat, swinging the man off balance, and used him as a battering ram against the driver. Bolan's contained energy lifted Bickell off his feet and he was catapulted into the driver. Locked briefly together the pair tumbled back over the desk, sliding across the smooth surface and over the far edge.

The moment he released Bickell, Bolan swung about and met the driver's partner head-on. Before the man could put up any defense Bolan slammed into him, hitting him in the face with a crippling elbow smash. The man grunted, stunned, briefly stalled, blood gushing from his crushed nose. Bolan hit him again, then caught his shoulders and spun the man around, wrapping his arms around the man's neck. Bolan applied pressure, twisting, until he heard the crunch of crushed vertebrae. He felt the man shudder, body going into spasm, before it became dead weight. Bolan's right hand moved down and located the pistol in the deep pocket of the man's coat. He reached in and hauled the heavy automatic pistol clear. It was a SIG-Sauer P-226. The Executioner knew the weapon well. As he swung the gun up, turning, he let the dead man slip from his grasp. The weapon's muzzle lined up on the desk as the driver struggled upright, head and shoulders coming into view. Bolan's fingers stroked the trigger and released a trio of fast shots into the driver. The slugs cored in through the target's chest. The driver fell back and slammed against the wall, a stunned expression on his face.

As the driver slid sideways, blood smearing the wall, Bickell lurched upright, hands grabbing for the pistol still in the dead man's hand. He snatched it free and turned the muzzle toward Bolan, his finger jerking back on the trigger in a moment of frantic zeal.

The bullet hit the wall behind Bolan. The Executioner returned fire, his double shot blowing through Bickell's upper body and dumping him on the floor. Bickell hunched up in fetal curl.

"Not the way I wanted this to end," Bolan muttered.

The Executioner moved from body to body, checking pockets and placing the contents on the desk. He had three handguns and extra magazines. He took a cell phone from Bickell and one from the driver. Wallets offered banknotes and credit cards. The only one with identification was the driver. It gave his name as Rik Vandergelt. Bolan kept that. He also took the banknotes. Cash money was always useful. He pocketed the cell phones.

The Executioner searched the office. He wasn't expecting hard evidence to directly point the finger at the trafficking business. He was just hoping to find something to work with. The desk yielded little of interest. He moved on to the battered wooden filing cabinets standing against one wall. The first held not much more than office stationary. The second had three drawers. Two were empty. The top one had a couple of folders stuffed with invoices. They were all from a company in the U.K. The company, South East Containers, was based near a coastal town that served as a conduit for the container business with Europe. The invoices were dated as far back as a couple of years. Bolan was about to leave the invoices when his attention was caught by the name of the company's director, printed in a small box at the top of the invoice.

In itself the name wouldn't mean very much. A legitimate-sounding company. Legitimate-sounding director.

Except that he had just ordered Mack Bolan's death before walking out of the office.

The director was Paul Chambers.

Bolan folded one of the invoices and slid it into a pocket. As he placed the stack of papers back in the drawer a pale cream envelope he hadn't noticed slipped from the documents. He picked it up and took a look at the address. It was to the same one that the invoices had been sent. The postmark showed it was at least three months old and mailed from Amsterdam. The envelope held a single sheet of good-quality notepaper. The same color as the envelope, the paper was heavy and embossed. The heading showed it was from a law firm in Rotterdam. The brief text in a smart font was in Dutch. One line indicated a time and date a week earlier. Bolan stared at the note, his eyes checking out the printed name at the bottom of the text.

Ludwig van Ryden. The lawyer Brognola's information had named.

Small beginnings.

Bolan had long ago learned never to ignore any lead, no matter the initial insignificance. The letter went into his pocket next to the invoice.

Bolan took the SIG-Sauer and the extra magazines. Leaving the office he crossed to the car that had transported him to the warehouse. He made a quick search that netted him nothing. The car was clean. He debated whether to use the vehicle, making a quick decision to leave it where it was. The car might be fitted with a manufacturer's tracking chip, allowing the opposition pick him up once they realized the vehicle was missing. Bolan decided he would be better off hiring a vehicle himself.

He walked away. It was still raining, the morning overcast. The weather was the least of his concerns. It took him twenty minutes to retrace the route the car had taken. Back on a main thoroughfare he managed to catch a passing cab and asked to be returned to his hotel. Back in his room he stripped off his damp clothing and took a hot shower. Clad in a thick bathrobe he rang room service and ordered a pot of coffee. It arrived quickly and Bolan filled a cup. He had the company invoice and the letter from the man called van Ryden in front of him. He took the pair of cell phones and switched them on. Bickell's phone listed more than two dozen incoming calls, the majority from the same number. Vandergelt's phone showed a couple of calls from the same number. The number matched the one on van Ryden's letterhead.

Bolan activated his phone and called Brognola. His friend's voice was slurry from sleep when he answered. "You get a kick waking me up?"

"Hal, if you insist on going to bed every night, what can I do?"

The big Fed laughed. Bolan heard him moving around before he spoke again.

"How did the meeting with Bickell go?"

"Interesting. You can scratch him off the list. He *was* the one who drew your mans into a trap. Had me walk into a setup with a couple of his Dutch buddies. We went to a rendezvous with a Brit named Chambers. He wasn't too happy with me. Seems your task force was getting close to Venturer Exports. So the hit on your mans was ordered."

"You mentioned Bickell in the past tense."

"After Chambers ordered his local heavies to feed me to the fishes matters got a little heated. Venturer Exports is down three employees."

"Understood. Did you gain any intel?"

"Couple of things. I want you to check into a U.K. company called South East Containers. Director is Paul Chambers. Has to be the same one who wanted me dead. I also found a connection with your lawyer Ludwig van Ryden. Another name for you—Rik Vandergelt. He was one of Chambers's enforcers. See if there's anything on the database."

"Okay. I'll get right on to it. Striker, you need anything else?"

"Right now, no."

"Expect a call," Brognola said.

"I may be on the move."

"No surprise there."

BOLAN DRESSED in one of the suits he had brought with him. He tucked the SIG-Sauer in his belt and buttoned his jacket. From a leather case he took a couple of printed business cards Brognola had provided. They showed Bolan as an executive from a computer software company based in Maryland. It was a fictitious company located at a nonexistent address. The telephone and e-mail contacts would route any caller to an automatic response that would accept the call and promise a return response. Bolan placed the cards in his wallet. He called the front desk and asked for a cab to take him to the *Hofpoort* district of the city. It was in the business center of Rotterdam. Ludwig van Ryden's office was located there.

Bolan dropped his damp clothes into a plastic bag and took them down with him, asking for them to be cleaned and pressed. His cab was already waiting when he emerged from the hotel. The weather had brightened, the rain had stopped. The Executioner settled back for the journey, planning ahead for his anticipated rendezvous with Ludwig van Ryden.

THE OFFICE BLOCK was one of a number in the neat plaza. The notice board outside told him van Ryden occupied a suite on the sixth floor. Bolan made his way toward the entrance, pausing briefly to switch off his phone. Brognola had called during the cab ride to inform him that Ludwig van Ryden was one of the key names on the task-force database. His association with individuals within the trafficking business was known to the force, but they had nothing they could move on with certainty. The man was sharp. His reputation as a lawyer who worked very closely with human rights groups made it difficult to nail. The slightest hint of any possible move against him brought instant and vociferous agitation from influential members of the Dutch establishment. The big Fed provided information that van Ryden had made a number of visits to the U.K. where he had meetings with Paul Chambers and Hugo Canfield.

"Rik Vandergelt is known to Interpol. He served a couple of prison terms a few years back. Since his last incarceration he's managed to stay out of jail. Seems he got himself a hotshot lawyer. Name of van Ryden."

"Keeping it in the family," Bolan said.

The Executioner stepped through the glass doors of the office block, hearing them swish shut behind him. He crossed the art-deco lobby and smiled pleasantly at the young woman behind the expansive reception desk.

"Do I need to sign in?" he asked, placing his hands on the marble-topped counter. "My first visit to Rotterdam. I guess I'm still finding my way around."

The receptionist observed the tall, good-looking man, noting the intense blue eyes and the genuine smile. His voice was deep and a little unsettling. His steady gaze, appreciating her blond beauty, took her by surprise. She was not accustomed to such intimate scrutiny. The sensation was not unpleasant.

"Have you an appointment with anyone?"

Bolan shook his head. He took out one of his business cards and slid it across the counter for the young woman to read.

"I only got in last night. Haven't had the chance to make formal arrangements yet. Would have done it this morning but my meetings went on longer than I expected. Next thing I received a call from my CEO to catch the evening flight to Paris, but to call in and say hello to Mr. van Ryden. We're hoping to meet up with him soon to negotiate some long-term representation with our company." He increased his smile. "Help, please."

She returned his smile and picked up her phone, tapping

in a number. When it was answered she spoke quietly, her eyes never once leaving Bolan's face. When she was finished she replaced the receiver.

"Mr. van Ryden will see you immediately," she said. "He has a meeting in half an hour but says he can spare some time." She directed Bolan to the bank of elevators across the lobby. "Sixth floor. Suite thirty-two."

"If I wasn't leaving in a few hours I would invite you out for dinner."

"If you were not going away I would accept."

"Maybe next time."

"Yes. Maybe next time." She watched him walk to the elevator, giving a sigh before she returned to her duties.

Definitely next time.

BOLAN STEPPED OUT of the elevator, checking the wallboard for directions. Suite thirty-two was to his left. He pushed open the pale wood door and stepped inside. An outer office contained a desk and another attractive young woman. The Dutch seemed to have got it right, Bolan decided.

"Mr. Connor?" the woman asked, pushing to her feet. She was strikingly tall. She guided him to double doors and knocked, pushing open one of the doors to let him enter. It closed firmly behind Bolan.

Ludwig van Ryden's office was wide, spacious, furnished expensively. The man's desk looked large enough to host a dinner party. There was an open laptop computer in the center. The office was a mix of pale wood, glass, stainless steel. Hidden lights illuminated a collection of slender glass sculptures housed in wall cabinets. A half-open door showed a private washroom. Underfoot the carpet was thick and soft.

The lawyer rose from behind his desk to meet Bolan. He was in his forties. A tall, leanly fit man wearing a suit that had probably cost a small fortune. His thick brown hair fell to the collar of his jacket. He came around the desk to take Bolan's hand, his smile showing even white teeth.

"Please sit down, Mr. Connor. Would you like a drink?"

"Thanks, no." Bolan sat in one of the cream leather chairs, watching van Ryden fill a heavy tumbler with whiskey. "You might want to make that a double, van Ryden," he said quietly.

The lawyer half turned, an amused smile on his lips. Then he saw the pistol Bolan was pointing in his direction. For a moment he froze, glass in his hand.

"I don't understand. What is this?"

"*This* is a gun. Taken earlier from a friend of yours. Rik Vandergelt." Bolan saw the color drain from van Ryden's face. The name had meant something to him. "I see I have your attention now."

"I do not know what you mean. The name means nothing to me."

"Right. So you've forgotten that you represented him legally? I'm sure he could have done with your advice a couple of hours ago. Then we have Paul Chambers. And Wilhelm Bickell. I don't suppose you know them, either?"

"Of course not."

"So you'll be even more surprised if I tell you my name isn't Connor. It's Cooper."

The lawyer flinched at the mention of the name. He recovered enough to move the whiskey glass, raising it to his lips and swallowing the liquid in a single gulp. Bolan saw it as a simple ploy to allow van Ryden time to gather himself. When the man returned his gaze to Bolan he had composed himself.

"We could spend the next hour playing word games," van Ryden said. "But that would be a waste of your time and mine, *Mr. Cooper.* So, what is it you want?"

"American agents Turner and Bentley were both murdered

by your associates. Bickell arranged for the same to happen to me. It didn't happen as planned. Bickell is dead. So is Vandergelt," the Executioner said.

"If I knew these people, what am I supposed to understand from what you have told me?"

"It's simple enough. You and your associates are involved up to your necks in human trafficking. I'm here to serve notice. Nothing fancy wrapped up in legal terms. Time is up for all of you. I'm going to close you down. All the way. Mark it in your diary, van Ryden."

The lawyer took a moment to absorb Bolan's words. He looked like a man who couldn't decide whether he had heard the truth, or been fed a line. He ran a hand across his mouth, then wagged a finger in Bolan's direction.

"A joke. This is a bad joke. *Ja?*"

"Call your associate Chambers. Ask him about Cooper. We were face-to-face this morning. Maybe he'll see the funny side. And don't waste time denying any involvement with Chambers. It's on record you've had meetings with him in the U.K. And with Hugo Canfield."

The lawyer sobered up suddenly, accepting that the stranger in his office was deadly serious. He glanced at the black muzzle of the pistol. At Bolan's unflinching gaze. He realized he was in a risky position. He became a lawyer again, relying on his bargaining skills.

"You have virtually admitted killing Bickell and Vandergelt. You're an American in a foreign country. You represent the U.S. government. How do you think the Dutch police will view this? Add the fact you have walked into my office and threatened me with a gun?"

"I'm sure you're going to make it clear for me."

"Cooper, you cannot win. Everything is against you. So I admit I am working with Chambers. There are others. Far too powerful for you to influence. I am a respected member of the community. Who do think they will side with? *You?* I do not think so."

"Let me think about that. In the meantime I need to make sure you don't raise the alarm when I leave." Bolan pressed the muzzle of the pistol against van Ryden's forehead. "Take off your belt," he ordered.

"Why?"

Bolan waggled the pistol. "Humor me. I'm an American in a strange town and it's been difficult to say the least. So I'm allowed to act oddly. Now do it."

The lawyer did as he was told. Bolan made him face the desk, hands behind his back. He used the thin belt to strap the lawyer's wrists together, tightly. Pushing the man around the desk Bolan shoved him into his chair. He yanked out the telephone cable and circled van Ryden's neck, drawing it around the seat's headrest. Bolan pulled it tight enough to be uncomfortable.

"Don't struggle against it. The knot I've tied will pull tighter if you put pressure on it," the Executioner said.

Bolan was lying but van Ryden didn't know that. His face was shiny with sweat and his eyes showed real fear.

The big American crossed the office and stepped into the well-appointed washroom, grabbing a couple of towels. He used one to blindfold van Ryden. The other he partially stuffed into van Ryden's mouth, muffling any sound the man might make. Bolan spun the leather seat and pushed it away from the desk, leaving it facing the window.

Bolan checked the open laptop on the desk. The lawyer had been composing an e-mail. It was addressed to Paul Chambers. In English. It was advising the arrival of cargo that night at a place called *Noosen Hag* and told Chambers that distribution would take place within a few days. He was to expect his consignment then. Bolan memorized the location details. He would follow it up after he left van Ryden's office.

Unsure what was happening van Ryden began to use his

feet to turn his chair around. Bolan waited, then moved in close, bending to whisper in the man's ear.

"I said don't move. Try that again and I'll tighten that cord around your neck myself."

Bolan rolled the chair across the office and into the washroom. He flicked off the light and closed the door on van Ryden.

Bolan let himself out of the main office, pausing to say goodbye to van Ryden for the benefit of his secretary. He closed the door, turning to smile at the young woman.

"Mr. van Ryden said to tell you he's making a private call and doesn't want to be disturbed. He'll call when he's done."

The secretary nodded. "Thank you."

Bolan stepped into the corridor and made for the elevator. On the ground floor he walked calmly out of the building, raising a hand to the girl he'd spoken to earlier. Outside he walked along the street until he was around the corner from the building before he hailed a cab to take him back to his hotel and a call he needed to make to Washington.

4

Bolan's call to Brognola had resulted in the man coming back to him with details on the location. The big Fed had gone into the task-force database and it had provided Bolan with enough intel to hire a vehicle and drive along the coast to the isolated promontory where *Noosen Hag,* the former oil storage depot, stood. Brognola's check had revealed that the depot, closed down for three years, had been leased through a shell company fronting for a consortium proposing to regenerate the site. It turned out that the consortium had connections with business-men allied, through shadowy links to South East Containers, in turn tied to Venturer Exports. The various connections were all carefully concealed by setups and financial maneuvering in attempts to hide who was really at the helm. But as Brognola had pointed out *all roads led to Rome.* In this instance Hugo Canfield's name kept popping up. Distanced from the everyday workings of the multilayered companies, his presence kept re-vealing itself. Still vague enough to prevent any interference by the legally bound task force, leaving them looking on, unable to act against him. Brognola offered the information to his loose cannon, knowing full well that Bolan would act on it.

The defunct oil refinery was having a busy night. From his vantage point Bolan could see a number of parked vehicles. Panel vans. Private cars. There was some activity on the concrete jetty built to serve vessels belonging to the oil company. Powerful spotlights, powered by a portable generator, illuminated the area.

Bolan had made his way to the site in the Toyota SUV he had rented earlier in the day. He'd covered the twenty-five miles in ample time and parked at a safe distance to go in on foot for the final distance. Crouching in shadow behind a scrap heap of rusting steel edging the jetty, only yards from the activity, Bolan watched as a crane hoisted a large steel container onto the trailer of a low-loader rig. He had watched the container being off-loaded from the small container ship that was now making its way back out to sea after delivering the container to the waiting handling crew. The turnaround time had been fast. No delays. The container ship would be back on its original course within a half hour.

He had counted six in the crew on the jetty. Only two were showing weapons—H&K MP-5s. That didn't mean the rest were unarmed. Bolan had the SIG-Sauer P-226. It held a full 15-round magazine and he had three more as backup. Unless he could pick up additional weaponry the pistol was going to have to earn its keep. Time was against Bolan, as well. It wouldn't be long before the container was opened and its cargo released. That was a relative term. The people inside the container would simply be exchanging one form of captivity for another. Steel container to panel truck. Not a great exchange, thinking ahead to where the unfortunate passengers might finally end up.

Someone on the jetty crew started to call out orders. Bolan saw figures move to the front of the container and begin to unseal the doors.

As the container doors swung open, the gunmen standing guard, one of the crew hauled himself into the opening. From where he crouched Bolan could hear his barked orders. Moments later shuffling figures appeared at the opening of the container. They reacted when they saw the weapons aimed at them, but there was nowhere for them to go. One by one they began to drop to the ground, huddling together out of instinct. Bolan saw mostly women and young girls. When one held back she was pushed forward, stumbling to her knees. The muzzle of a submachine gun was jammed into her spine. The gunman took hold of the girl's long dark hair and dragged her to her feet. He was yelling at her as he slapped her across the face. He raised his weapon and took aim.

He didn't get a chance to fire. Bolan tracked in with his weapon and put a single shot through the back of the man's skull. The gunman pitched forward onto his face, blood pooling around him.

The jetty crew panicked. The Executioner took advantage of the chaos. He targeted the men wielding weapons, the SIG-Sauer cracking steadily. The men carrying the guns were down on the jetty before they were able to pinpoint the hidden shooter. Bolan changed position, moving around the scrap metal and emerging near the container. He met one of the remaining three crewmen face-on. The man was dragging a pistol from beneath his jacket when Bolan slammed the SIG-Sauer across the side of the man's skull. The man grunted, stumbling, and Bolan helped him down with a bone-crunching second blow. The man hit the jetty facedown.

The Executioner crouched briefly to take charge of the man's pistol. He heard someone yelling in English. He ducked around the end of the container where the captives were scattering along the jetty. He caught a glimpse of others still inside the container, shrinking back from the chaos outside. The crewman who had climbed inside the container was still there. He had a gun in his hand as he leaned cautiously from the opening. He failed to see Bolan until it was too late. The SIG-Sauer cracked, driving two 9 mm slugs into the man's torso. He tumbled from the container onto the hard concrete. His skull bounced against the jetty.

As Bolan checked the far side of the container he saw the sixth man making a run for the parked cars. Bolan hit him with a few 9 mm slugs to the legs, taking him down in an uncoordinated sprawl.

"Anyone speak English?" Bolan asked the women in the container. Two of the young woman acknowledged his question.

"Get them to calm down. Tell them they are going to be freed."

Bolan walked to where the leg-shot man lay. The man had rolled onto his back, sitting up and staring at his shattered limbs. Bolan kept his pistol in clear sight as he approached the man. He spotted the man's dropped weapon and kicked it across the jetty and into the water.

"Must hurt like hell," Bolan said.

The man swore in English, his brittle British accent exaggerated by the pain from his wounds. He dragged himself to the container trailer and pushed his back against one of the rear wheels.

"I'll bet you're the bastard who took down Bickell and his minders. Right, am I? They told us to watch out in case you showed."

"Lucky for me you didn't pay too much attention," the Executioner said.

"Fuck you, Yank. My legs hurt, you bleeder."

"Can't you see the tears in my eyes?"

"What are you going to do to him?" A woman's voice came from behind Bolan.

He turned. It was the young woman he had spoken to. Her gaze was fixed on the wounded crewman. There was no pity in her eyes as she stared down at him. She was attractive, but right then her face was a hardened mask of sharp angles, pale and bloodless.

"What does he deserve?" Bolan asked.

She turned her gaze on Bolan, searching his face, seeing someone who would treat her respectfully. Despite her drawn, pale features the Executioner could see she was a determined young woman. He glanced beyond her to the rest of the "cargo" from the container. They were all exhibiting the ravages of their ordeal but they were far from being defeated.

"He deserves the worst we could do to him," the young woman said. Her soft voice bore traces of an Eastern European accent. "But if we did that, then we become as bad as they are."

The crewman glanced at her, unsure how to take the remark. He had the sense to stay silent, concentrating on his wounds.

Bolan drew the woman aside, looking over her shoulder so he could keep the wounded Brit in sight. "What do I call you?"

"Lucky?" She reached out to touch his arm, a simple gesture that expressed her feelings. "My mother was always telling me my humor would get me into trouble. My name is Majira."

"Where did they pick you all from?"

"Pristina. Off the streets. My own fault for walking home alone after dark. But what was I supposed to do? Never go out? Lose my job? I had heard about the traffickers. How they grab people and send them abroad. I never imagined I would be one of their victims. Nor would any of the others." She took a breath, her voice breaking slightly. "It is the children who would suffer worst. We all understand what would happen to them. Sold to…to soulless monsters who would abuse them."

"Not his time, Majira."

"You are American. Why are you doing this?"

"Long story. Let's say I'm trying to shut this group down."

"Are you a policeman? One of the good mans?"

Bolan nodded. "I'll go with that. The name is Cooper, by the way."

"So, Cooper, tell me, what happens now?"

Bolan looked at the huddled figures. He turned, checking out the darkened buildings at the landward end of the jetty.

"Take everyone to those buildings. At least you'll have shelter while I organize things. Do it now, Majira."

She nodded, turned quickly and spoke to the group. Her voice persuaded them to follow her. Bolan watched the uneven line moving away, the older women comforting the children. He waited until they had vanished inside one of the buildings before turning his attention to his captive.

"What's bloody well going on?" the Brit asked.

"I feel more comfortable without witnesses," Bolan said, standing over the downed man and staring at him.

The Brit watched him, short-lived defiance showing through his pain. He wasn't sure how to perceive the tall, black-clad American. One thing he did know. The man was serious. The way he had taken down the crew had been an eye-opener. Once he had his opening he had taken out the opposition with ruthless efficiency. Being the sole survivor might not turn out to be the greatest blessing.

"What?" the Brit asked. "Christ, if you're going to kill me get on with it. Standing there saying nothing. It's creepy." His remark was said more out of bravado than anything else. In truth he was scared.

"Tell me about the two Americans you killed."

"Now you wait a minute. I had nothing to do with that. It was down to Willi Bickell and the blokes who run things. No shit, mate, they did it. I'm just hired help."

Loyalty never flew the coop so fast, Bolan thought.

"Chambers is the head man around here?"

A frantic nod. The Brit looked eager to talk, hopeful it would go toward extending his life span. The man was no different to anyone else. His first thoughts were of his own survival.

Bolan made a show of ejecting the pistol's magazine and snapping in a fresh one. He dropped the ejected mag into his pocket, moving round the prone man on the ground.

"What the fuck are you doing?"

Bolan glanced at the man. "I can't afford loose ends."

"You can't. You people don't go round executing people."

"People like me?" Bolan said.

"You're a cop. And bloody cops don't—"

"I think we need to clear something up. I never said I was a cop. I don't have a rule book."

"Look, fuck this game. You can't just shoot me like this."

"No?"

"Can we deal?" the man pleaded.

"Maybe you don't have anything I want."

"Try me. But we make a deal first or I don't say a thing."

"My word good enough?"

"I have to trust you? Big risk for me."

"You're still alive."

The Brit considered his situation. He wasn't going to get a written guarantee, and he was in no shape to play hard to get.

"So what do you need to know?"

"Tell me about van Ryden?"

"He fixes things. Has connections here. Arranges for people to look the other way so we can get cargo in and out. He works with the top level in the U.K., as well. Yeah, well, Chambers does the hiring and firing here and at the U.K. base, but Hugo Canfield is the real man in charge. Chambers is second fiddle, really. He likes to throw his weight about. Canfield is the man. But you wouldn't want to tangle with him. He's too big. Can't be interfered with. The man has a cop in his pocket. An Interpol agent. Probably even customs officers. Hell, maybe even higher than that. He runs in serious circles. No shit, mate, Canfield is bad news. I'd sooner sit naked in a crate of fuckin' rattlesnakes than cross Canfield."

"What about a database? Names and locations?"

"Even if I told you, there isn't anything you can do."

"So what have you got to lose?"

"Only my balls. If they find out I gave them up what they did to your undercover men will be like a slap on the wrist."

"One way or another you're going to tell me. I can walk away and let you bleed to death, or end it with a bullet behind the ear. Believe me when I say I don't give a damn one way or another. It's your choice. Your buddies took the hard way. That can be arranged for you."

"What about protection? I've cooperated. You can get me protection."

Bolan took out his cell phone.

"I can make the call from right here if you give me what I need."

"I did hear van Ryden has a database on his computer. It's supposed to have details on everyone who works for Venturer. Means they can keep tabs on us all. Hold on to all our unsavory little secrets. Keeps it at his home outside the city. Place is watched over by armed security. Only other thing I can tell you about is the farm they use to house people while trade is done. I can give you a location for both places."

Bolan made his call minutes later. When Brognola came on Bolan briefed him on the status of the mission.

"If the task force wasn't wrapped up in protocols and red tape, maybe they could have gotten further," Brognola grumbled. "So tell me again about these people you found."

"Women and children. One I spoke to said she was snatched in Pristina so I'm guessing this group came from that area. Offloaded from a container ship. I arrived in time to prevent them being moved off the dock and sent to God knows where. Hal, do you still have people on the ground hereabouts?"

"Part of the task force is cooling their heels in Amsterdam. You need their help?"

"The women and kids need looking after. Somewhere they'll be secure until a decision can be made about them. I also have a survivor from the crew who were going to ship them out. He's wounded. Needs medical assistance and protection. Your task force might be able to get more info out of him."

"I expect you've already got what you need?"

"We exchanged mutual considerations."

"I'm sure. Striker, let me talk to our people out there. I'll come back to you ASAP."

Bolan spent time collecting weapons from the dead crewmen. He placed his small arsenal just inside the open container. He kept one of the MP-5s and extra magazines for his own use. He checked out the cab of the big tractor-trailer unit and located a first-aid box under the passenger seat. Using the contents he bound up the Brit's legs, applying pressure pads to slow any further blood loss.

"First you shoot me, now you bandage me up. What next? A mug of hot sweet tea?"

"What do you think?"

"Sounds like I'm a dead man either way."

"Redemption can go a long way to keeping you alive."

"Meaning what exactly?"

"You gave me what I needed. So I'll keep my word. You'll be taken into protective custody."

"Don't I have a say about all this?"

The hardness that etched itself across the big American's face told the man he had said the wrong thing. The blue eyes were suddenly like chips of ice. He could almost feel the chill emanating from them.

"I'd be justified to shoot you right now after what I've seen tonight. You people are crawling in the gutter. You sleep well at night? Seeing those young kids and knowing the life you're sending them to? Have you looked at pictures showing how those perverts treat them?"

"Look, I just work on this part of the business. Collection and distribution. Never seen where they go."

"That clear your conscience?"

"Mate, I've been struggling for years to do that. Probably too late for me. I'm just trying to earn a living. Bloody hell, aren't we all?"

Bolan didn't answer. He had all too often heard the

excuses, the self-justification, the criminal element came up with to whitewash their activities. He didn't believe a word of it. He dismissed it as he always did, because if he digested it and analyzed the pathetic reasons he might have turned his gun on them out of sheer disgust.

Reasoning platitudes were the get-out clauses from the mouths of criminals through the decades. From mass murderers to raving dictators who slaughtered thousands, there was always an excuse. A smiling word that was supposed to wash away the bloodlust and the wanton elimination of entire cultures. The perpetrators never considered they had done anything wrong. It was always the rest of the world that was out of step. That did not understand why a particular horror had been committed. Some odd quirk lodged deep in the homicidal, deranged minds of the despots allowed them to excuse away what they had done. If they explained it they self-purged their conscience. They became heroes instead of maniacal villains. And in many instances they often convinced others to see the justification.

In Mack Bolan's eyes a bloody-handed butcher was just that. There was no redemption. No vainglorious explanation that wiped away the needless deaths of men, women and children. Evil was evil. It would never be reconciled as far as he was concerned. It was why the Executioner existed. Why he stood against the monsters.

Someone had to.

Because if he didn't, who would?

5

Hugo Canfield was having lunch at his London club when the maître d' brought him the telephone. He plugged it into one of the sockets, then placed the instrument on the table for Canfield.

"The caller said it was quite urgent, Mr. Canfield."

Canfield nodded. "Thank you, Enright." He waited until the man had withdrawn before picking up the receiver.

"Canfield."

"This is van Ryden. Is it convenient?"

Canfield allowed himself a slight smile. The club dining room was exceptionally quiet. Only two other diners were seated together on the far side of the opulent room. All Canfield could hear was the low murmur of their voices and the click of knives and forks as they ate.

"It will cease to be if my roast beef gets cold."

"There has been a problem with the latest cargo due for delivery. I thought you should know."

"Explain 'problem,' Ludwig."

There was a slight pause before van Ryden spoke. "The problem occurred at the delivery location and the cargo was lost."

"I'll be going back to my office after lunch. Use the jet. I want you in London before the end of the day."

"Of course, Hugo."

Canfield ended the call. He beckoned for Enright to remove the phone, then returned to his meal. He found his appetite a little soured at the news. Hugo Canfield did not enjoy being told that one of his shipments had been lost. He knew the details of the particular cargo that had been expected in Rotterdam. He had invested time and money, as he always did, and if it had been lost, then that meant he was going to be down a considerable sum. Not only that but he was going to have to disappoint important clients. They would not be pleased, which meant Canfield would not be pleased. Client satisfaction was something he prided himself on. It was one of the reasons his organization was the best. He allowed no slackening in standards. He would not tolerate failure.

He smiled suddenly at the thought of van Ryden sitting in the comfort of the Learjet as it crossed from Rotterdam to London. The man would not enjoy the flight. His churning stomach would not be put down to air sickness. He would be worrying. He would not realize that Canfield was not about to lay the blame on him. The lawyer was responsible for the legal part of the operation and logistics. He also dealt with finance. He was not a field operative.

Let the man worry, Canfield decided. It would not do him any harm. It paid to keep his people on their toes, to shoulder their responsibilities.

Canfield finished his meal, called for his car to be brought to the entrance and strolled to the reception desk where he collected his coat and hat. He made an imposing figure. Just over six feet tall, athletically built—he kept himself fit—and expensively dressed. Women found him excitingly attractive and he played on that. His aloof demeanor toward those he considered below him made others step back when confronted. He *was* powerful. He exercised immense control and had no hesitation when it came to using his influence.

When he stepped outside, shielded from the London rain by the doorman's umbrella, his year-old, top-of-the-range Bentley was already at the curb. The doorman opened the rear door and Canfield slid onto the soft leather seat.

"Back to the office, sir?" asked Gantley, his driver and minder. Gantley was a former British Army military policeman. A big man. Solid and tough. Above his hard face he wore his hair close-cropped. He had worked for Canfield for eight years, was loyal and had a fearsome reputation for brutal violence. "Bloody day, sir. Global warming obviously hasn't reached London yet."

"Always the pessimist, Sergeant Gantley."

"That's me, sir. So, the office?"

"The office. No rush now. Mr. van Ryden is flying in from Rotterdam so there's plenty of time."

"Way the traffic's building up he'll more than likely be there before us."

LUDWIG VAN RYDEN WAS shown into Canfield's spacious Canary Wharf office just before five o'clock. Watching from behind his executive desk Canfield was barely able to refrain from smiling at the concern on van Ryden's face.

"Sit down, Ludwig." Canfield caught the attention of his secretary, who had shown the Dutchman in. "Jane, please arrange some fresh coffee for us. Or would you like something stronger, Ludwig?"

"Coffee will be fine."

As the door closed behind the young woman, Canfield pushed to his feet and stood at the wide window that overlooked Canary Wharf. He never failed to enjoy the view. It excited him.

This was *his* pinnacle.

It had taken him a long time to build his organization—taking it from humble beginnings all the way to an empire that spanned the globe. On his way to the top Canfield had honed his skills on the backs of others. Weaker men failed to spot the quiet ambition of the younger man in their employ. Canfield had been a good pupil. Always watching and listening, gathering his strength by exploiting others. When he was ready he struck.

During his climb to absolute power he left behind a trail of dead bodies. Literally. But Canfield always covered his tracks. There were rumors about the way he worked, but Canfield was sharp enough never to leave evidence that might point the finger his way. Each time he took out rivals he absorbed the operations they had been running, slowly and carefully creating his own. Now he controlled a powerful criminal network that had its hand in a number of illegal operations, the most lucrative was his human trafficking.

It had not taken Canfield long to realize the potential of the trade in people. From the very young to adults, the slave business was thriving.

The suite of offices at Canary Wharf, the prestigious docklands business complex, housed Canfield Enterprises. Day to day it carried on the legitimate side of the business. Finance and development. It acted as a cover for Canfield's murkier business dealings. The majority of the people working there knew nothing of Canfield's other enterprises. The legitimate business earned him a lot of money and contacts he made from that part of his empire were icing on the cake.

His illicit enterprise had recently brought Canfield's organization under the close scrutiny of a multination task force. The goal of the task force was to gather enough evidence to allow the law to close him down. That was the plain and simple fact. The intent was there but the task force, though it had its suspicions, was unable to garner the hard evidence that would lead to Canfield's conviction. The task force worked within the constrictions of lawful intent. They had to follow the rules. Canfield was under no such regulation. He worked by his own set of rules. There were no limits in his world of business. As long as he made his money and increased his power, then he was satisfied. He was already ultrawealthy and making more money by the day. He was a well-known businessman. He had, over the years, cultivated many relationships with respectable people in positions of power. Some of those individuals were also under his patronage because Canfield had something on them. He disliked the word *blackmail,* preferring to see the associations as a mutual understanding between friends. He protected them by keeping their guilty secrets hidden away, suggesting that reciprocating gestures from them would retain the status quo. Within his circle of friends Canfield had government ministers, cops, wealthy individuals who moved in high circles.

Hugo Canfield felt very secure in his world.

The recent events in Rotterdam, namely the disposal of the two American agents who had managed to penetrate his organization, had been a means of announcing to the task force that they were ineffective. That nothing they could do would ever touch him. It showed that he, Hugo Canfield, had the power to do such a thing without fear of reprisal. The task force knew what had happened, but there had not been a thing they could do about it. Proof positive did not exist. If they had arrested Canfield, or any of his people, it would have ended up with them all walking free because there was not the slightest shred of evidence against him. Or the people who had carried out the torture and murder. His legal team would refute any and all charges against him as being without basis. The task force would have one chance to take Canfield down and one chance only. They needed proof absolute. To the last detail. Evidence both documentary and verbal. Witnesses. They would need enough backup to fill a courtroom. The task force knew that and so did Canfield. Despite the international members of the task force they had nothing they could use against Hugo Canfield. With his contacts he would be able to buy, destroy or wipe out anything the task force threatened him with.

"Wait until the coffee arrives, then we can talk," he said over his shoulder to van Ryden.

The lawyer was in no hurry to get to the reason he was in London. He had been debating the matter with himself during the flight in Canfield's jet. Whenever he had flown before he had always immersed himself in the luxury of the executive aircraft. Canfield had ordered many custom additions to the airplane during its construction. It was equipped with the most comfortable seats van Ryden had ever sat in. It had a communications system that would have cast a shadow over Air Force One. Onboard entertainment played to perfection and the cabin crew were able to serve up practically anything a passenger wanted. On this particular flight van Ryden had found he couldn't face anything except for a couple of glasses of whiskey. Even they failed to quell the queasy sensation growing stronger in his stomach the closer he got to London.

The office door opened and the young secretary wheeled in a burnished steel trolley. It held the coffee Canfield had ordered.

"Would you like me to pour, sir?" Jane asked.

"We'll be fine," Canfield said. "And, Jane, no interruptions until I say. No exceptions."

She nodded and withdrew, quietly closing the double doors.

Canfield moved to the trolley and poured two cups of coffee. He handed one to van Ryden, then resumed his seat behind his desk.

"Bring me up-to-date, Ludwig. I have some details but I need clarification."

The lawyer explained the occurrences from the meeting between Wilhelm Bickell and the American, Cooper, to the strike against the freshly delivered cargo at the former oil dock. His delivery was detailed and precise. He felt as if he was in a courtroom at that moment, though for once it felt as if he was on the witness stand himself.

Canfield listened without comment, drinking his coffee, his

eyes fixed on van Ryden throughout. When the lawyer finished and took a long swallow from his own cup, Canfield waited for a few moments before he responded.

"Do we assume that it was this man, Cooper, who carried out the attack at the dock?"

"Who else would it be? He dealt with Bickell and his men. He is obviously a man who believes in direct action. As the strike at the dock showed."

"What do we know about this man? Apart from the obvious fact he knows his job."

"All searches have failed to bring up anything about him. His initial contact with Bickell suggested he was involved with the task force. He isn't on any databases I had our people check. It's as if he doesn't exist."

"His actions are certainly real, Ludwig. The bullets he used killed my people, his ability to have the cargo taken into care was certainly real. I'll have my sources look into who this bastard is. Someone, somewhere, must know about him."

"He fooled Bickell into believing he was genuine."

"Bickell was an incompetent idiot. He should have contacted me before he went ahead and arranged that meeting. What the bloody hell did he think he was doing? Did he imagine that every time he was confronted by someone from the task force all he had to do was kill them? The removal of Turner and Bentley was a single, clearly defined warning to the task force that they were on dangerous ground. I was not advocating open season."

When van Ryden appeared reluctant to say any more Canfield realized he hadn't been told the whole story. He refilled his coffee cup, sat again and asked the lawyer outright what else he had to say.

"He came to my office, Hugo," van Ryden said. "Tricked his way in as a potential client, then made it clear his intentions are to bring us down."

He detailed what had happened from the moment the man named Cooper had entered his office.

Canfield laughed. "If nothing else he has a bloody nerve. Whoever he is, this man doesn't sound like your everyday task-force agent. He must be some specialist. I don't suppose he gave anything away we could use?"

"Hugo, I was scared. He tied me up, blindfolded and gagged me and shut me in my own washroom. I'm no hero. The man terrified me. I admit that. He was serious. He proved that by the attack at the dock. For all I knew he had come to my office to kill me. And before you ask, I did not divulge any information. He already knew of my association with you."

"Now that is interesting," Canfield said. "The man has background details on our operation. Has information about us. What does that suggest?"

"That he does have some kind of contact with the task force."

"They haven't advertised their investigations to the media. Cooper must have been fed intel to get him on track."

"But he is only one man."

"He's shown us that one man can do a lot of damage. He doesn't follow any kind of rule book. Works instinctively and just goes for his targets." Canfield sat back, considering the options open to him. "Time for some of our resources to earn their retainers. The problem with a wild card like Cooper is not knowing where he's going to show up next."

He reached out and tapped a button on the office intercom. "Jane, get me Paul Chambers. Tell him to drop everything and get here immediately. ASAP. Any objections just put him directly through to me. I'll deal with him."

"Yes, Mr. Canfield. Does that mean you'll be staying over?"

"I won't be going anywhere until I've spoken to him."

"I'll arrange for a meal to be delivered later. What would you prefer this evening?"

"I leave that in your capable hands, Jane. And make the meal enough for two. Mr. van Ryden will be joining me."

"Will you need me to stay?"

"That won't be necessary, my dear. You just make the arrangements, then you can go home as normal."

Canfield spent the next hour discussing with van Ryden the need for damage control over the missing cargo. Client satisfaction meant a great deal to Hugo Canfield. He had a good record and the thought of that record becoming tarnished did not sit well.

"We need to arrange with Timor to gather another cargo to be ready to ship out when I give the word. I'll have to smooth things over with our clients about the delay. I think a discounted rate should make them happy. Everybody likes a price drop."

"I am sure *they* won't lower the charges when they move the merchandise on."

Canfield shrugged. "What they do with the cargo once they have bought and paid for it is their business. As long as we receive our fee I don't give a damn."

"What can I do to help?" van Ryden asked, eager to please his employer.

"In the morning you get back to Rotterdam. Speak to De-Chambre first, then arrange for him to contact me. He's been damned quiet since he fingered those American agents. Perhaps I'm being too soft with him. Then you go home and lay low for a few days. Relax. Stay away from your office. Keep your security crew on hand."

"I will contact DeChambre as soon as I get back."

"Make sure he is aware I am not happy. My God, the man is an Interpol inspector. Wouldn't you expect him to have at least a suspicion the Americans had sent someone else over after the deaths of Turner and Bentley? Tell DeChambre I want some answers, or his monthly retainer might suddenly dry up. That should kick-start his French arse. Now, loosen your tie, Ludwig, and don't stay so uptight." A wide grin crossed Canfield's face and he leaned forward to clap van Ryden on the shoulder. "God, I would have given a fortune to have seen your expression when Cooper walked into your office and poked a gun in your face."

The lawyer still paled when he recalled the incident. He failed to see what was even faintly amusing about it. "Hugo, I think I will take that drink now, please."

Canfield poured him a large whiskey.

"Here, get that down, then we can go over the details of this Russian drug deal. We need to work on our distribution list."

6

Harass the enemy. If there's no opportunity to confront him in a full-on attack because he has an overwhelming force, the next best thing is to hit and run. Strike here, then fall back, move on and hit somewhere else. Keep the enemy guessing. Don't allow him to take a breath before you strike somewhere else. Take him down piece by piece.

It was a strategy the Executioner had employed many times before. He worked more often than not as a single entity without the privilege of a large supporting team behind him. His lonely war gave him no other option. Bolan had adapted to this over the years and he felt no disadvantage in having to operate without backup. On the reverse side of the card, working alone meant he could concentrate fully during an attack without having the burden of allies on his mind—no worries whether they were safe, whether they had been compromised. He only had to concentrate on himself. Responsibility came with its own shackles. When the need arose Bolan shouldered responsibility without thought, but when he was moving into a lone combat situation his mind could focus on the mission full-time.

He had liaised with Stony Man Farm. Aaron "the Bear" Kurtzman had assigned his cyber team to run a detailed check on Ludwig van Ryden's background. Especially his home. By the time Bolan was in full receipt of the information he knew enough about the lawyer's house to walk around it in the dark. He wasn't even surprised that Kurtzman had come up with detailed architect's drawing for the place.

When Bolan had staked out the property initially it quickly became evident that van Ryden was not at home. The house stood empty, no vehicle evident on the paved driveway. A call back to the Farm to run a check on van Ryden's whereabouts gave Bolan the answer to his query. An innocent telephone call to his office came back with the information that Mr. van Ryden was out of the country on business for a couple of days. So the Executioner had to wait. He did it by taking in the sights of Rotterdam he had almost missed on his arrival. He rested up for the battle to come.

When Bolan took up his surveillance again he still spent a fruitless stakeout. But on the second morning circumstances changed for the better.

The van Ryden residence stood in well-landscaped tranquility. The low-rise house was at least a quarter of a mile from the road, fronted by the curving driveway lined by slender trees and cultivated bushes. At the rear sweeping lawns reached to a high fence that encircled the acreage. A paved patio jutting out from the back of the house had a large swimming pool and a stepped terrace that allowed observers to look down on the pool.

Bolan had climbed the fence during the early morning hours and was concealed in the dense foliage of the garden that occupied the northeast corner of the property. From his vantage point he was able to watch the back of the house without being seen himself. He used the powerful binoculars he had purchased to maintain a solid watch over the house, and during the couple of hours he had been in position he had spotted the appearance of van Ryden's security team. It consisted of a pair of armed men, dressed in suits and ties, who made regular patrols around the property. Bringing them into detailed closeup Bolan saw the sentries wore lightweight headsets that allowed them to communicate with each other, and maybe an internal control, as they patrolled the grounds. The paved driveway now held three expensive cars.

At 7:30 a.m. van Ryden, dressed in bathing shorts, stepped out through French doors. He hit the water and for the next twenty minutes swam up and down the length of the pool. He finally emerged and picked up the towel he had brought out with him.

Bolan watched him walk back inside the house, picked up the MP-5 he had brought with him from the dock mission and began to work his way through the foliage in the direction of the house. He reached the north corner, staying in the cover provided by the heavily bushed garden and waited until the sentry appeared. The man had an MP-5 hanging by a strap from his left shoulder, his hand resting lightly on the weapon. He walked past Bolan's hiding place with feet to spare. Once he had his back to him Bolan rose silently, stepped up behind the man and took him in a blood choke hold, applying instant pressure to carotid and jugular.

Starved of blood the sentry had little chance to fight back. As soon as he felt the man's legs weaken Bolan followed him down, keeping up the pressure until the sentry lost consciousness. With the sentry on the ground Bolan disabled the comset and stripped it clear. He threw it aside, into the tangle of bushes. From his back pocket Bolan pulled out a couple of the plastic ties. He looped one around the sentry's ankles, another to bind his hands behind him. Aware that the man could recover quickly Bolan took off the guard's tie, balled it up and stuffed it into the man's mouth. He took the magazine out of the man's MP-5 and threw both items deep into the undergrowth. He located a handgun, holstered under the man's coat. Bolan disassembled the weapon and scattered the parts.

The Executioner had studied the routes the pair of sentries had taken. He fell in behind the second man, trailing silently in his shadow until he was walking the paved path that ran down the side of the house's double garage. It was the ideal spot to deal with the man. Bolan moved up, ready to strike.

The sentry stopped suddenly, reaching up to check his comset, speaking into the microphone. Bolan didn't understand the words, but he picked up the urgent tone when the man failed to get a response from his partner. The sentry turned about, ready to retrace his steps. The first thing he saw was Bolan, poised only feet away. The sentry responded swiftly, snatching at his shoulder-hung weapon. Bolan closed in quickly, his left hand grasping the barrel of the submachine gun, forcing it skyward. His right hand snapped forward, closing around the sentry's throat, pushing him hard against the garage wall. The back of the man's skull slammed against the brickwork, the impact stunning him briefly and allowing Bolan the opportunity to lean in closer, turning and dragging the man's gun arm down across his shoulder. The sentry's resistance lasted only for as long as it took for his arm to snap. The MP-5 slipped from splayed fingers.

Bolan spun, braced himself and launched a full-on right fist that connected with the sentry's jaw. The impact threw the man to his knees, spitting blood. Bolan slammed his foot between his shoulders and hammered him to the ground, the man's face crunching against the concrete. As he bent to relieve the man of his handgun Bolan picked up radio chatter. He pulled off the guard's headset and listened closely. Someone was demanding a response in Dutch. Even though he couldn't understand the language Bolan recognized the urgency in the challenge.

Had his recon been spotted?

Whatever the reason for the agitation Bolan wasn't about to back off. He was too close to his target now.

He checked the handgun. It held a full magazine. He slung his MP-5 across his back. Turning he made his way around to the back of the house again, heading for the French doors

van Ryden had used. The glass doors opened at his touch and
Bolan slipped inside, pausing to check out the well-appointed
room. Even his cursory examination told Bolan that everything in the room spoke of expensive taste. Recalling the
detail Kurtzman had supplied this was the main living area.
He knew van Ryden's study was directly through the arch
ahead of him and to the right.

From somewhere beyond the room he heard a murmur of
voices and footsteps on hardwood floors. Bolan moved to the
far side of the room. If anyone came in they would be forced
to take time to locate him. Maybe only for brief seconds but
that would allow him the advantage.

Bolan spotted movement on the far side of the arch.

A tall, dark-haired man edged into the room. He carried
the obligatory MP-5, the muzzle arcing back and forth as he
surveyed what seemed to be an empty room. When he saw
Bolan's dark figure against the end wall he tracked his weapon
around, finger pulling back on the trigger. Slugs chunked into
the wall, filling the air with plaster chips and dust.

Bolan's acquired auto pistol rapped out a fast trio of
shots that hit the man in the chest. He stumbled back, a
sharp cry bursting from his lips, and banged against the
wall. As he did his finger held its trigger pull, sending 9 mm
slugs into the wall above Bolan's head. More plaster dust
erupted in white spouts. The shot man slipped to the floor,
face contorted into a snarl of anger and he attempted to pull
his submachine gun back on line. A fourth shot from Bolan
caught him above the left eye, blowing a chunk of bone out
of the back of his skull, spattering bloody debris on the door
behind him.

Moving quickly Bolan crossed the room and stepped over
the body, turning to scan the open hall and the doors beyond.
He caught a flicker of movement ahead. He saw a figure
emerge from an open door, pistol in hand. The man opened

fire the moment he saw Bolan, then ran in a semicrouch across the open space, still triggering shots. Bolan heard the slugs thud into the wall. He stepped forward, dropping, holding the pistol double-handed as he picked up on the moving gunner. The Executioner fired off half the magazine, spent casings hitting the floor around him. The moving figure paused, lost coordination and crashed to the polished floor, skidding across the surface. The man rolled on his side, hauling his pistol around and fired again, not allowing himself time to lock on his target.

Bolan centered his weapon and returned fire, his slugs catching the gunman in the torso. The man let out a long gasp as he rolled slowly on his back and lay still. Bolan pushed to his feet and loped across to where the man lay. He kicked the dropped gun across the hall, threw aside the pistol that had locked on an empty chamber and drew the SIG-Sauer.

The house had fallen silent around him.

Four down.

Was that van Ryden's complete security complement?

Bolan figured that two on the outside, two more inside, would have been adequate under normal circumstances. Unless van Ryden recently felt he needed more. Bolan remained on full alert. Assumption could never replace caution. Complacency invited trouble. And Mack Bolan had never accepted complacency as a companion.

He picked up sounds from behind a closed door on the far side of the wide hall. He knew that was the study. Someone was speaking. Bolan flattened against the wall and picked up a voice he recognized.

It was van Ryden.

The conversation sounded one-sided. Bolan figured van Ryden was on the phone.

Calling in help?

The Executioner eased the door handle, pushing the door

open. The room was large and airy. He saw book-lined shelves, a large desk, a picture window showing the grounds.

He spotted the hunched figure of the lawyer with a phone to his ear, free hand waving to emphasize his conversation. He had his back to Bolan. He did not hear him enter. Or close the door and engage the lock. He made a final plea, then slammed the phone down. As he straightened up his senses warned him he was not alone. There was a handgun on the desk next to the phone and van Ryden's hand made a tentative move toward it.

"Not advisable," Bolan cautioned.

The lawyer turned to face him. His face had lost its color. Right then he looked far from his smart public image. His hair, still damp from his swim, hung limply across his scalp and he needed a shave. He was dressed in a gray tracksuit and running shoes. And he was visibly distressed.

"You cannot do this," he said. "Invade my home. Attack my house staff."

Bolan shrugged.

"Are all domestics in Holland expected to walk around carrying machine guns and pistols? Hell of a way to greet visitors."

A burst of defiance flared. "You are not a guest in my house. You are an invader. Have you forgotten who I am? A respected member of the legal profession. My name is known in high circles. I can have you arrested for breaching my human rights."

"Words, van Ryden. Coming from a scum who trades in human lives. I haven't forgotten what you are. You forfeited your rights when you took up your business. Remember what I told you in your office? I'm going to bring you and rest of your associates down. No hiding behind your *respectable* name."

The lawyer snapped. Eyes widening with a reckless gleam, a scream of rage burst from his lips as he snatched up a heavy paperweight from the desk and swung it at Bolan, ignoring the gun pointing at him. Bolan leaned back, feeling the disturbed air stroke his face as the paperweight curved past. The lunge pulled van Ryden closer to Bolan and before he could regain his balance the Executioner hit him across the jaw with the P-226, putting every ounce of strength into the blow. As bone crunched and blood flew from his open mouth van Ryden slammed down across the desk, scattering papers. The paperweight slipped from his grasp. His face thumped against the hard surface of the desk. As he struggled to push himself upright Bolan stepped in closer and slammed the pistol down hard against the back of van Ryden's skull. The lawyer groaned, his body becoming limp. Bolan stepped back as the lawyer slithered to the floor, sprawling on his back. His jaw was raw and bloody.

Putting the pistol away Bolan moved around the desk and sat down. He removed van Ryden's handgun. The computer sat in front of him. Bolan figured the lawyer would have data stored somewhere within the machine detailing the trafficking operation. In his capacity as the organization's facilitator he would need information. The problem was that the screen text Bolan was looking at was in Dutch. A language Bolan was unfamiliar with. Bolan took out his phone and keyed in the number to connect with Stony Man Farm.

"Striker," Aaron Kurtzman acknowledged when he came on.

"I need you to hack into a computer and download everything on it, then get the data translated into English."

"'Hacking,' as you put it, is for geeky amateurs. But I will electronically intrude into the hard drive and extract whatever is hidden there."

"Okay. Tell me what to do."

Bolan followed the concise instructions. With Kurtzman's program installed on van Ryden's computer it took less than ten minutes before the contents were transferred.

"I'll get everyone working on this. You need anything else?" Kurtzman asked.

"How about emptying this system? Wiping the memory? Give these bastards more to worry about."

"Sounds like someone has upset you, Striker."

"And some."

"A thought here. There could be backup to this data. Flash drives. I'll clear the hard drive and leave a little visitor. If they try to reinstall the data my little buddy will pick it up and fritz that, as well. How's that?"

"Pretty sneaky for a high-tech *hacker.*"

Kurtzman's booming laughter rumbled through Bolan's cell phone before he ended the call.

As the Executioner moved away from the desk the monitor screen began to flash with lines of rapidly scrolling codes. Kurtzman's wipeout program had started, methodically eating its way through the data embedded in the computer's hard drive.

The Executioner had reached the center of the room when he heard a rush of sound behind him. Bolan spun on his heel. He saw van Ryden halfway across the room, coming at him full-on. The lawyer's face was wet with blood, more of it making dark streaks down the front of his track suit, his mouth open as he let out a long, harsh scream of anger. Bolan saw the slim-bladed letter opener the man had snatched up off the desk. It was aimed in Bolan's direction. But van Ryden was no combat veteran. It was unlikely he had ever been in a violent situation in his life.

Bolan let the man get in close before he sidestepped, slamming a hard-edged hand across the knife wrist. As the blade spun from his nerveless fingers van Ryden squealed. In desperation he lashed out. Bolan caught the arm, turning it. He spun van Ryden in a half circle, then released his arm. The man's own weight carried him across the room. Out of control he crashed head-on into a glass-fronted display cabinet. His shout of fright was lost in the sound of shattering glass. Scattered porcelain figurines suddenly spattered with blood as van Ryden's severely gashed throat began to spurt. He fell to the floor, body going into spasm as his lifeblood began to spread in a wide, glistening pool from beneath his body.

"No more human rights for you to abuse, Mr. van Ryden," Bolan said as he left the room.

The phone call van Ryden had been making to his associates was more than likely to bring reinforcements. It was on Bolan's mind as he retraced his steps from the house, through the grounds and out to where he had parked his rented SUV. He slid the unused MP-5 beneath the seat. Climbing behind the wheel he started the engine and followed the narrow back road until he joined up with the main route.

7

Inspector Marcel DeChambre, Interpol, and joint task-force member, parked across the street from the hotel where the man known as Cooper was staying. He had made a telephone call a half hour earlier to be informed that Cooper was not at the hotel, and no, he had not checked out.

So where was he?

DeChambre's long fingers tapped impatiently against the steering wheel. He needed a result. The explicit order from Hugo Canfield had explained things very clearly. He expected DeChambre to come up with something that would identify Cooper. Canfield's message held a direct threat. He had not been paying DeChambre large amounts of money for the fun of it. He expected the Frenchman to earn his keep. If he didn't... There was no need for the sentence to be completed.

DeChambre understood. He had been associated with the Englishman long enough to have witnessed how Canfield dealt with those who let him down. Or betrayed him. De-Chambre had been present when the two American under-cover agents had been eliminated. The men DeChambre had betrayed when he informed on them to Canfield.

The extreme torture before the men were killed had con-vinced DeChambre that the man meant every word. Now he was under the spotlight. And there was no avoiding it. He served up Cooper, or paid the price for his own incompetence in not knowing the man had been sent to check out what had happened to Turner and Bentley.

Informing Canfield about the agents had been a good moment in his relationship with the man. It hadn't been a lasting moment. Canfield didn't concern himself about former successes. He lived in the moment and this particular moment was not boding too well for the trafficking group. The man named Cooper had already created enough problems. Apart from killing Bickell and his team, Cooper had brazenly walked into van Ryden's office and had presented the lawyer with his intentions to take down Venturer Exports. It had been a direct challenge, given by a man who plainly did not work within official rules. Cooper had then moved on to intercept a freshly arrived shipment, taking out the crew, freeing the cargo and getting them into the hands of the task force.

Canfield had been angry at this deliberately provocative act and it had been made crystal clear to DeChambre that he had to identify, locate and terminate Cooper.

No excuses.

No delays.

DeChambre's problems began when he made casual inquiries into the identity of the man who had handed the task-force information in the form of live evidence. No one had any idea who the man was. None of the agents working the case appeared to be worried about that. They were more concerned with what they could get from the freed people and the wounded crew member from the dock. DeChambre had not been able to discover where the man had been taken. The agents within the task force were staying silent on that matter and DeChambre stopped asking questions after a while, not wanting to make himself conspicuous.

Cooper had presented himself to Bickell as being from the same American department as Turner and Bentley. He had advertised his arrival time in Rotterdam and the hotel where he was staying. When DeChambre made a computer check of his own the search for Cooper came up blank. It was as if the man did not exist. That puzzled the Interpol agent even more. He made a deeper check, opening his search even wider. And still came up with nothing.

So he went looking for Cooper using old-fashioned policing methods. Sitting in his car across the street from the hotel, staring out through the rain-speckled windshield, he found his mind wandering away from Cooper to the subject of his own mortality. He had no doubt in his mind that if he failed to satisfy Hugo Canfield's demands, his life would end very quickly. He accepted the fact. Marcel DeChambre was a realist. No one had forced his hand when Canfield made him the offer to join his organization. If he had a weakness it was for money. His position within Interpol was never going to make him a rich man. By contrast his association with Venturer Exports had created opportunities DeChambre had never dreamed of. Canfield's extended influence brought DeChambre into contact with a number of the man's powerful friends in Rotterdam and throughout France. DeChambre's position within Interpol allowed him to work favors for these people. In return he received substantial financial rewards. DeChambre's nest egg had grown accordingly. He had hidden accounts, each holding extremely healthy balances. DeChambre wanted to be able to enjoy his money. That might not happen if he didn't locate and eliminate Cooper.

DeChambre felt the need for a cigarette. He thrust a hand into the pocket of his dark raincoat and pulled out a packet of *Gitanes*. The dark, extremely strong French cigarettes had been his favorite since his teenage years. His taste had never changed. With the current war on smoking—something DeChambre detested with a vengeance—*Gitanes* had ceased to be made in France. Ironically they were now manufactured in the Netherlands and DeChambre always kept a good supply in his apartment, bought from a small importer he knew. He lit one now, using a wooden match. He refused to pander to the trend for disposable gas lighters, convinced they ruined the flavor. Sitting back he drew deeply, inhaling the rich aroma. Wreaths of blue smoke drifted through the interior of the car. As he smoked he felt his mood ease a little. It was the effect of the tobacco, he knew. He was on his second cigarette when he recognized Cooper as the man alighted from a dark SUV. Cooper carried a bag with him as he went into the hotel.

DeChambre took out his cell phone, deciding he needed some of Canfield's backup crew. He saw that the phone was still switched off from the previous night. Still smarting from Canfield's demands he had forgotten to turn the damn thing on before leaving his Rotterdam apartment. As it powered up DeChambre saw a number of missed calls up and he recognized the caller's number.

Canfield.

He hit redial and sat waiting for his call to be picked up.

"Where the bloody hell have you been? What's the fucking point of a cell phone if you don't switch it on? What the hell am I paying you for, DeChambre?" Canfield shouted.

"Wait. I've spotted Cooper. He just walked back into his hotel. I've been sitting across the road for a few hours, but he's here now."

"Am I supposed to happy about that?" Canfield's voice rose an octave. "While you've been perched on your Gallic derriere Cooper has been busy. He turned up at van Ryden's house first thing this morning. Disabled the security crew—three of them are dead. And so is van Ryden. The bastard wiped the memory from his computer. Now I'm bloody certain he downloaded all the data on van Ryden's hard drive first. So understand why I'm not exactly wild with joy just because you've actually seen the bugger."

"I need some local backup and van Ryden should have given me a number to call—"

"He isn't exactly in any condition to give out numbers. And you don't have time to wait around for help. Christ, Marcel, you're a cop. Go into that hotel and arrest him. Drive to a deserted spot and put a bullet through him. The man is acting like a vigilante. No jurisdiction. Taking the law into his own hands. You arrested him and he tried to make a break. Make something up."

"Yes. I suppose I could do that."

"We can protect you. All I need to do is make a couple of calls. But I need that man out of the way. He's only been in the country five minutes and he's creating chaos. Just get it done." Canfield paused, then said, "I'll see what I can do with backup."

The call ended, leaving DeChambre holding a dead cell phone.

He stared at the hotel. The rain had increased again, dropping heavily from the leaden sky. The gloom only added to DeChambre's sullen mood. He lit another cigarette, drawing on it so hard the smoke stung the back of his throat. DeChambre decided he could have used a large tumbler of cognac to take away the taste.

He couldn't believe van Ryden was dead.

That was a shock. It was obvious that Cooper took no prisoners. Well, he wasn't going to find DeChambre so easy to dispose of.

He reached under his coat and eased out his pistol. A Glock 21.45 ACP. DeChambre checked the weapon and returned the 13-round magazine. He returned it to his shoulder rig, making sure the weapon hung right, then opened the car door and stepped out. He locked the vehicle and made a quick run across the road, depositing his cigarette in the gutter. In the lobby he shook the rain off his coat and crossed to the reception desk. Before the clerk could speak DeChambre showed his Interpol badge, leaning forward to speak quietly.

"It is important I check out a guest. May I see your register?"

The computer screen was turned so DeChambre could view the guest list. He located the name he was looking for and the room number.

"Thank you."

The clerk fingered his collar nervously. "Is there a problem?"

DeChambre shook his head. "Purely a routine check on a possible visa irregularity. Everything is fine."

As he walked away from the desk DeChambre glanced at the clerk. The man watched him for a few moments, then turned away, distracted by another inquiry. The moment the clerk's head was turned DeChambre turned and crossed the lobby, taking the stairs. Cooper was on the third floor. He took out his cell and this time deliberately turned it off. The last thing he needed was the phone ringing at the wrong moment.

As he climbed the stairs, DeChambre prepared himself. The Glock was drawn, thrust into the deep right-hand pocket of his topcoat. He kept his fingers curled around the grip of the pistol. DeChambre reached the third floor and paced along the carpeted corridor, counting off the room numbers until he reached Cooper's. The Frenchman paused. A slight sheen of sweat covered the palm of his hand holding the gun. It was not the first time DeChambre had needed to do something like this on his own. He breathed deeply, calming himself.

Damn Canfield.

The man could have made this easier by sending along some local backup. But Hugo Canfield was not in the business of making things easy for those in his employ. It was a part of the man's makeup. A need to show his authority. His utter strength and power. And no matter what DeChambre thought personally he would do what Canfield instructed, because the man owned him.

DeChambre raised his left hand and knocked on the door.

MACK BOLAN TURNED at the sound. The last thing he expected was a visitor. Though it might be a hotel employee with fresh towels or something of that nature he would never assume anything.

He picked up his pistol, pushing it into the waistband of his pants, against his spine. Crossing to the door he stood to one side.

"Yes?"

"Mr. Cooper, my name is DeChambre. Inspector Marcel DeChambre. Interpol. Liaison with the task force. I need to speak with you urgently."

Bolan's mind worked swiftly. As far as he knew, his location in Rotterdam had not been broadcast to anyone outside of Brognola's area of responsibility. No communication had been sent to any European agency, even though the task force had some interdepartmental links. His thoughts covered the facts even as he opened the door and faced DeChambre.

The man was tall, lean, his head of thick dark hair still damp from the rain. He had a strong beak of a nose above a wide mouth. He raised his left hand after dipping it into his coat pocket, showing Bolan the ID wallet with his Interpol credentials. A shadow of a friendly smile edged his lips. Bolan ignored that. His gaze settled on DeChambre's gray-blue eyes. There was no friendliness there. The eyes mirrored the cold enmity the Frenchman held.

"May I come in?" the man asked.

Polite. Exhibiting a professional courtesy that was intended to relax Bolan.

"Sure," the Executioner said.

Bolan kept himself to one side as DeChambre stepped into the room. The man's right hand remained inside his coat pocket. Bolan followed the contours of the cloth, the shape of DeChambre's hand. It was a hand that was gripping something solid, fingers curled around the object. Bolan pushed the door shut, then watched as DeChambre made a slow turn to face him.

"I was hoping I might get a chance to rest up," Bolan remarked, keeping his voice conversational. "One of the problems of having a superior like Dillon. That man is so on the fast-track for promotion he keeps us on the go 24/7."

Bolan gave DeChambre points for a quick reaction. His moment of blankness was smoothed over by a Gallic shrug. "It is the same with my own superiors."

In that moment he was thinking about Hugo Canfield. But only as a superior in control, certainly not in intellect. Canfield was nothing but a thug in expensive clothing. Wealthy and powerful, but basically a peasant.

"You must have heard the man at briefings. Holds the floor and won't shut up," Bolan said.

DeChambre hesitated, slightly thrown off stride. He had no knowledge of a man named Dillon. Had not heard him speak. Had never seen him. He had been hoping to deal with Cooper without any difficulty. The American faced him, hands at his sides, apparently comfortable with the way the conversation was going.

"I am not—" he began.

"Familiar with Dillon?"

Now the American's tone had altered, his words taking on a harder edge. And the way he was staring at him made DeChambre nervous.

"I understand that," Bolan said. "Seeing how Dillon doesn't exist."

Bolan saw the material of DeChambre's coat pocket move. Watched his arm draw back as the Frenchman began to take his hand out.

Bolan saw the dark metal of the pistol as it started to emerge from the pocket. He stepped forward, hands reaching out to catch hold of DeChambre's gun arm. DeChambre tensed, resisting, which was just how Bolan had expected him to react. The Executioner turned in, slamming into De-Chambre as he executed a fast hip throw that launched the Frenchman across the room.

DeChambre crashed down on the bed. The recoil from the thick mattress threw him onto the floor, breath gusting from his lungs as he hit. Bolan didn't allow him any chance. He saw DeChambre's right hand, fully clear of the pocket, still gripping the Glock. Bolan stamped down hard on DeChambre's hand. He heard bones crunch a split second before De-Chambre squealed in pain. Blood oozed from between the shattered fingers and Bolan kicked the pistol across the room. He bent and caught hold of DeChambre's coat lapels, hauling the man to his feet. DeChambre's face had turned ashen, thick hair falling over his eyes.

"You're the worst kind of man. A cop who betrays his own kind."

"They were American agents. I owed them nothing," De-Chambre said.

The Frenchman threw up his left arm, jamming his hand beneath Bolan's chin, forcing his head back. Ignoring his pain he used his right arm to hammer at Bolan's face. De-Chambre was no weakling. Bolan could feel the strength in his hard body as they briefly struggled for advantage. He felt the slam of DeChambre's knee against his thigh, absorbed the impact and retaliated with a savage head butt that rocked the Frenchman back on his heels. The stunning blow distracted DeChambre long enough for Bolan to circle his neck with one arm and twist the man off balance. As De-Chambre turned, Bolan punched him hard under his ribs, delivering a number of crippling blows that left the French-man choking for breath. Weakened, DeChambre offered no resistance when Bolan pushed him upright and slammed a fist into the French cop's jaw. DeChambre backpedaled, coming up short against the wall, and hit the floor in a bloody heap.

He was too stunned to offer any further resistance as Bolan bent over him and emptied his coat pockets while checking for additional weapons. He tossed the items onto the bed.

"Nothing worse than a crooked cop. And especially one who turns on his own kind and allows them to be killed."

"Turner and Bentley knew what they were doing. You carry the badge, you stand the risk. What should I do? Cry for them?"

For a cold, heart-shrinking moment DeChambre thought the big American was about to turn on him. His cocky attitude became a greasy lurch in the pit of his stomach. The expression on his opponent's face was truly frightening. Then the moment passed.

"Get on your feet. We're leaving soon," Bolan said.

"Where are we going?" DeChambre demanded.

"You're going to be delivered to some of your friends in the task force. The American contingent. They'll be really pleased to meet one of the men involved in the deaths of their buddies."

"You cannot do that."

"Give you odds I can," Bolan said.

He took out his cell and made contact with Brognola. He explained briefly that he had a gift for the U.S. agents on the task force. When he told Brognola who he had and what the man was involved with, the big Fed said he would make contact about a handover location.

"If I was you, DeChambre, I would wave goodbye to my Interpol pension," Bolan said.

The Frenchman made no reply. He seemed more concerned with nursing his damaged hand.

Brognola called back within ten minutes, offering Bolan a location where he could meet up with members of the U.S. task-force contingent.

"No questions asked," Brognola said. "Lead man is Neil

Youngman. Just deliver DeChambre and get on your way. Okay?"

"Thanks."

Bolan ended the call. He pulled on his jacket and gestured for DeChambre to move. He showed him the SIG-Sauer before he slid it just inside the jacket. DeChambre slid his damaged hand into his coat pocket.

"Out the door. Turn right. Left at the junction. We can go down the emergency stairs. No games, DeChambre. The jury is out on you at the moment, so don't play clever."

They negotiated the concrete steps to the ground floor, emerging through the fire door into the alley next to the hotel. Bolan stayed just behind DeChambre. The alley brought them to the main street. The sidewalk was close to being deserted. The rain was keeping people inside.

"My car is just beyond the main entrance. Straight to it and get in."

Bolan indicated the SUV and they moved in the direction of the vehicle. They had almost reached it when three men stepped out from the hotel entrance. One ranged in close behind and Bolan felt the hard press of a pistol muzzle against his spine. A second stood on Bolan's right, his own weapon visible under his coat. The third man confronted DeChambre, a thin smile on his lips.

"Good of you to bring him out to us," he said in English.

"Bertran, he has a gun under his jacket," DeChambre said, turning to face Bolan. DeChambre wagged a finger at the SUV. "We won't be riding in your vehicle, after all," he said. "We can go across the street and get into my friends' car. Is that going to be a problem, Mr. Cooper?"

"Not for me," Bolan said calmly.

The man facing Bolan took the SIG-Sauer from his hand. Bolan's pockets were searched and his cell phone was removed and it vanished inside the man's coat.

Bertran took out his own phone and dialed a number. He moved aside from the group as they began to cross the street, so his conversation couldn't be heard by the American.

"Valk, we have him. Where are you? On your way? Okay. Listen, we're taking Cooper to the site as arranged. Why don't you and Lucien wait outside the hotel. We'll handle this end. When we are done we'll join you and DeChambre can get us into Cooper's room. We need to check it for anything he might have about the organization. You may want to keep an eye on his vehicle too. Dark blue Toyota SUV. Parked at the curb outside the hotel." He quoted the license plate number. "Okay? We will see you later."

Bertran finished the call and nodded to DeChambre as he rejoined them.

"Time to go, then," DeChambre said.

8

"You're not as clever as you believed you were," DeChambre said. He nodded curtly at the men covering Bolan. "Your task-force friends are going to have a disappointing wait." He gestured impatiently. "Get him in the car. Let's get away from here before anyone becomes curious."

Bolan was pushed into the back of the elderly Citroën waiting by the opposite curb and flanked by a man on either side. De-Chambre climbed in beside the driver. The car moved off with a brief squeal of rubber against the road surface, taking the first corner fast. The man beside Bolan rolled with the sway of the car and the Executioner felt the hard outline of the pistol holstered against the man's right hip. He filed away the knowledge.

"You have upset too many people, Cooper. Cost us a great deal of money and caused much damage. Naturally you are not very popular with my employer," DeChambre said.

"That would be Hugo Canfield," Bolan replied. "Knowing that makes my day worthwhile."

DeChambre turned to face Bolan. The Frenchman's face was flushed with anger. Self-consciously he reached up to finger the bruises that spread across his face. He exposed his battered hand, staring at the livid, bloody flesh. He reached inside his coat and drew out a handkerchief. DeChambre wrapped it around his injured hand, wincing against the pain.

"Make all the clever jokes you want. Just be aware that you have very little time left. In fact, only for as long as this ride lasts.

When we reach our destination you are going to die. Simple as that. Dead simple. You see, even I can make clever remarks."

"They say the French have no sense of humor. I think you just proved it."

DeChambre's expression hardened. His good hand gripped the top of the seat, knuckles growing pale.

"Can't this thing go any faster?" he snapped at the driver.

The man shrugged, but responded by jamming his foot down hard on the pedal and the Citroën increased speed.

Bolan could see they were passing through an industrial area. Warehouses and buildings flashed by, the majority of them empty. Over to one side Bolan saw the tall cranes and machinery of construction sites. A redevelopment area. He understood why DeChambre had chosen this place for his intended disposal of his problem.

It was time, then, the Executioner decided, to make his play, because the window of opportunity was closing fast.

Without warning he slammed the point of his elbow into the throat of the man on his immediate left, hearing the soft crunch of cartilage. The man clutched at his throat, gagging nosily. The moment he struck, Bolan leaned forward and wrapped both arms around the driver's neck, applying severe pressure and wrenching the man's neck with enough force to snap the vertebra. The driver uttered a startled gasp, his body rising from his seat, control of the speeding car lost in an instant. The Citroën began to swerve back and forth across the road.

Bolan felt his second minder lunge at him, hands scrabbling for contact. With the driver incapacitated the Executioner swiveled to meet his attacker, slamming an open palm full into the man's face, the heel of his hand connecting with the nose. The man's head snapped back, blood starting to blossom and pour down over his mouth and chin. Bolan's follow-up punch failed to land as the driverless Citroën was still veering wildly from side to side, throwing the occupants around like loose sacks of grain. Bolan gained a handhold, grabbing one of the trailing seat belts and wrapping it around his wrist. He held on hard as the car hit the rough edge of the road, wheels climbing up the turned-earth bank. The car's weight and speed carried it along the bank for several yards, the vehicle tilted at an angle.

Suddenly the wild ride came to an abrupt end. The nose of the Citroën smashed into a large concrete block partially sunk into the edge of the road. It was a section of construction fabrication waiting for removal. The block was solid, reinforced with steel rods, and it barely moved under the impact. The effect on the car was extreme. The hood collapsed as the engine was pushed back into the passenger compartment. Steel buckled and glass showered the interior. Neither DeChambre nor the driver were wearing seatbelts and the driver was thrown forward into the steering wheel, then partway out through the windshield. DeChambre, with nothing to restrain him, was propelled out through the gap, his upper body slamming into the concrete block with enough force to crush his head to a bloody pulp and shatter bones.

If Bolan had not had the presence of mind to grab the nylon belt strap he might have ended up in the front of the car himself. He was thrown against the front seats, breath driven from his body. The two men with him, already immobilized, were battered by the effects of the crash. As the Citroën rocked to a halt Bolan had to push the limp forms off him before he could kick open a door and half tumble from the wrecked car. He hit the wet ground with a thump and lay sucking in harsh breaths. His chest hurt and his ribs ached. He lay still for a while until his breathing settled, then pushed to his feet, slumping against the side of the car.

Canfield's organization was persistent if little else. The man was fighting hard to preserve his business empire, and violent action appeared to be his hallmark. If that was what

he wanted Bolan was happy to respond. He was determined
to close down Canfield's sleazy operation. And he would
battle his way through Canfield's entire crew, if necessary.

The Executioner glanced around. The area still appeared
deserted and no one had come forward to check out the site
of the crash. It would be better for Bolan if he distanced
himself from the area before anyone did show up. He remembered that one of DeChambre's men had taken his gun. Bolan
pushed away from the side of the car and leaned in to locate
his weapon.

A slight movement warned him too late. The toe of a shoe
slammed across the side of his face. The blow shoved Bolan
back a couple of steps, pain flaring over his cheekbone. Bolan
saw a figure push out of the open door, blood covering the
lower half of his face.

The man whose nose he had broken.

The thug exited the car in a rush that carried him into
Bolan, slamming the tall American off balance. The man
wrapped both arms around Bolan's body, digging in his heels
as he increased the pressure. Bolan felt his ribs move. The man
was no weakling. He snuffled harshly through his shattered
nose, spraying blood. Bolan jammed both hands under the
man's chin and pushed hard, forcing the head back.

There was a momentary standoff, each man going for gold
until Bolan slammed one knee up between his opponent's
thighs. The man gave a screech of pain, his encircling arms
slackening off. Bolan gave a final push and the startled minder
was left open. A sledging fist slammed against the man's jaw,
flinging his head to the side, giving Bolan the chance to grab
a handful of thick hair. He swung hard, whacking the man's
skull against the edge of the Citroën's roof a couple of times.
The man went down without another sound.

Bolan searched the pockets of the man's coat and located
his cell phone, the SIG-Sauer and the spare magazines.

Jamming the gun back into his waistband Bolan pocketed everything else, then turned away from the scene, retracing the route to the main road.

It took him close to a half hour and it was getting near dusk by the time Bolan found himself walking back toward the city. For once the rain had reduced to a fine drizzle. It was a small thing but he was getting tired of Rotterdam's wet season. It was a couple of miles before he hit the outer city and found he had a signal again on his phone. He punched in Brognola's number and let it ring until his friend's voice came through.

"Call off the meet. I won't be delivering DeChambre. I had a little confrontation with him and some of his buddies. They wanted to take *me* for a one-way ride. It ended badly."

"I'll have the team advised. What's going on over there, Striker?"

"Everyone I meet wants me dead, Hal. These are seriously terminally minded jokers."

"You're upsetting their paradise. On the bright side I spoke to my task-force contact. They have all those women in secure placements. And some detail has been forthcoming. The women have identified photographs, picking out some of the people involved in snatching them off the streets. All that is going to help build up the files on Venturer Exports. But still not enough to move on it. That lawyer of Canfield's would be hopping all over the scene before we moved a stick of furniture."

"Canfield's favorite lawyer won't be serving any more writs. The man is dead."

"Score one for us? So what are you thinking now, Striker?"

"That the world has forgotten the difference between doing the right thing and standing by watching."

"Striker, we've had this conversation before. If the task force went in now and arrested everyone on Canfield's payroll who would benefit? His second-team lawyers would scream abuse of human rights, quoting every law on the books, and without every charge sheet being one-hundred-and-one-percent absolutely correct down to the last full stop, the whole crew would walk. Justice, here and in Europe would be slapped with writs, false-arrest accusations and claims for defamation. We'd have compensation claims being stuffed into every orifice. And Hugo Canfield would be sitting in his plush offices having a glass of champagne while he set up his next trafficking deal."

"You know how to cheer a man up, Hal."

"They are lousy, lower-than-low scumbags, Striker. Safe because they're having the last laugh at us. They know it. We know it."

"They may be laughing, Hal, but it won't be for long. Right now they're hurting and I aim to make them hurt even more. One more strike here in Rotterdam, then I'm going after Canfield and his U.K. setup."

"McCarter's man in London will have what you need. I'll look out for smoke rising over Big Ben."

After he ended the call Bolan looked around for a cruising taxi. He had had enough of walking around Rotterdam's rainy streets.

"IT'S BEEN TOO LONG," Valk said again, glancing at his watch. "They should be back by now."

"So where are they?" his partner asked.

"Try Bertran's cell again," Valk suggested.

Lucien nodded and dialed the number. He waited as the cell rang out, shaking his head.

Valk banged his fist on the steering wheel. "Why don't they answer?"

"You think maybe something went wrong?"

"Actually, yes."

"So what do we do?"

"One thing we don't do is call Canfield and admit our suspicions. You know what they do to the messenger with bad news."

Lucien managed a weak smile. Their employer's volatile moods were legend. No one ever wanted to get on Hugo Canfield's bad side. Or incur a visit from the man called Sergeant Gantley. He found himself reaching inside his coat for the pistol nestling in its shoulder holster. When his fingers touched the smooth steel it gave Lucien a sliver of comfort.

"This man. Cooper. He's no fool. Look what he did to van Ryden and his team. And at the landing dock. Valk, we should cover ourselves. Maybe he got away from Bertran and the others. Maybe we…"

Valk wasn't listening. He was staring out through the car window, past the rain spatter and the gloom. He was watching a tall figure emerging from a taxi that had just pulled up outside the hotel.

Tall.

Black hair.

An athletically built man dressed in black.

He paid the driver and moved down the sidewalk to an SUV parked at the curb. It was the vehicle that Bertran had identified as belonging to Cooper.

"I think that's him," Valk said. "Damn, it has to be him."

Lucien saw the man in question checking the SUV before turning and going into the hotel. He was about to ask what they should do, but when he saw that Valk had taken his own pistol from its holster, screwing on the threaded sound-suppressor, he knew he didn't need to ask.

"Let him get to his room," Valk said. "No fucking about, Lucien. I don't want this bastard playing any of his fancy tricks with us. We go in hard and shoot him. Plain and simple. It's past time for being polite."

"If that is Cooper—where are Bertran and the others?"

"If that *is* Cooper," Valk answered, "I think we already know where they are."

Lucien attached his own sound-suppressor. He slid the pistol back inside the holster, then ran the back of his hand across dry lips. He glanced at his partner and saw that Valk was wearing that expression he always displayed when he had worked himself into a killing mood.

"Let's do it," Valk said.

He was out of the car, striding across the street before Lucien could say a word. All he could do was step out himself and follow Valk to the hotel entrance.

They crossed the lobby and went to the desk where Valk caught the attention of the clerk.

"Hey, wasn't that the American, Cooper? The guy who just came in?" Valk had a wide grin on his face.

He turned to Lucien. "I said it was Cooper. Didn't he say he was staying here?" He turned back to the clerk. "I'm right? Cooper? We've been tracking him all day. Supposed to be going to a company celebration tonight, but he vanished earlier."

Valk lowered his voice to a conspiratorial whisper. "Sly guy—I think he met one of the saleswomen at the party last night and when we looked around he was gone." He glanced at his watch. "Only a couple of hours and he's supposed to be giving the big speech tonight. We don't get him there on time we'll be sweeping the streets tomorrow."

Lucien nodded, caught up in his partner's enthusiastic charade. "That's right. Help us out, friend. We need to get him all tidied up and daisy fresh. What's his room number?"

Valk had his cell phone out, tapping in a number. "Got to call our boss. Tell him everything's okay. Then see if we can drag Cooper back on form."

He went through the pantomime of talking to someone on the other end of the line. In fact, he had dialed his own home number and was speaking to his own phone, making up the dialog as he went along.

"We have him getting ready now, sir. What? No problem. We'll have him there on time. Yes, sir. My word, sir."

He closed the phone, glanced at his watch again. "Cooper? Room number? Please…"

The young clerk, looking from one man to the other, caught up in the excitement of the moment, blurted out the room number.

"Thanks, friend. You have saved our sanity and probably our jobs." Valk slapped Lucien on the shoulder. "Come on, let's go and get Cooper ready."

As the two headed for the elevator bank, Valk waved at the clerk. "Thanks, friend, you did us a real favor there."

The clerk watched the elevator doors close, frowning as the rush calmed down. He reached for the house phone and called the room occupied by the American named Cooper.

"*Mijnheer* Cooper? Reception. You have two visitors on their way up to you. They say they should be picking you up for a company social evening. Was I right in sending them up, sir? I hope I haven't disturbed you, only you did say you wanted a meal sent up because you were not going out again…"

The phone cut off abruptly and the clerk was left feeling that he had indeed disturbed the hotel guest.

BOLAN DROPPED THE PHONE back on its cradle and turned toward the door. He opened it and checked the deserted corridor. The elevator bank was to his left. He stepped out of the room and pulled the door closed behind him. He walked quickly and quietly to the far end of the corridor, reaching the junction a few doors along where the corridor made a right-angle turn in the direction of the emergency exit, the same one he had used to get DeChambre out of the hotel. He pressed against the wall, leaning slightly forward so he could watch the empty corridor.

Seconds later the elevator pinged and the doors slid open with a subdued hiss.

Bolan saw two men step out, checking the corridor before they walked briskly to his door. The way they moved told him they were anything but hotel guests, and when they each produced an automatic pistol, both fitted with sound-suppressors, he needed no more convincing. They stopped at his door, one turning to stand watch while the other reached to knock.

When there was no response the pair exchanged glances. The man who had knocked said something that Bolan was unable to pick up, then stepped back to give himself space. Bolan realized what the man was about to do even before he raised his right foot prior to launching a kick at the closed door.

Bolan slid around the corner and drew down on the man standing watch. He spotted Bolan the moment he stepped into view and called a warning to his partner. The man then extended his gun arm, the muzzle of his pistol sliding across his buddy's shoulder. The SIG-Sauer in Bolan's hand cracked twice. The first slug took a chunk out of the target's right shoulder, blowing a spray of blood and flesh from his jacket. The force of the slug twisted the man half around so that Bolan's second shot hit him in the throat and knocked him off his feet, gagging for air.

As the crack of the shots echoed in the second man's ears he spun on one foot, exceptionally fast, his pistol tracking in quickly. He fired on the move, his slug chugging from the muzzle and tearing a gouge of plaster from the corner of the wall an inch over Bolan's head.

The first man had barely hit the carpet when Bolan retuned fire from his one-knee position on the floor. He saw the gunman react to the slug that powered into his chest, knocking him back against the wall. As he rebounded from the impact the man took two more slugs from Bolan's weapon. They hit with tremendous force, shattering his spine. He faltered, surprise etched across his face as he fell face down on the carpet.

Bolan moved quickly, holstering his pistol, stepping over the bodies, and used his key card to open his door. In his room he picked up his bag. He always kept his belongings packed ready for a fast exit and right now that was what he wanted.

The thought crossed his mind that Canfield seemed determined to continue his attempts to get rid of him. How many more of his crew was he going to throw at Bolan?

Back in the corridor the Executioner turned and went for the emergency exit as he had done before, only this time he wouldn't be returning to his room. As he turned the corner of the corridor he realized that no one had come out of any of the rooms to check the disturbance. Either they hadn't heard the brief encounter because TV sets were playing, or the modern-day malady of minding their own business had struck once again. In a way he couldn't blame them. It was unfortunate that butting into the affairs of others often got the responsible individual into serious trouble, so people chose to stay behind their own closed doors.

As he descended the stairs Bolan knew that his luck would not hold for long. Sooner or later someone was going to find the bodies, and when they did, the missing Cooper was going to find himself the center of the Rotterdam police's attention.

He needed to distance himself from them quickly.

At street level he moved along the alley, reached the sidewalk and walked calmly to his waiting SUV. Bolan unlocked the vehicle and slid inside. He fired up the engine and eased away from the curb, merging with the traffic. He had no idea how long he might have before the cops picked up on his rental. In the time he did have he needed to lose the vehicle and get himself a fresh set of wheels.

HAL BROGNOLA WORKED his influence with the task force and arranged for Bolan to get his SUV off the streets. He parked in the basement garage of a derelict office block and left it for the task force to pick up. They had left a black BMW SUV for Bolan to take over. It had legitimate plates and no history that would attract attention from the local cops. The Toyota would be lifted by a recovery truck, concealed under a tarp and driven to a task-force safe house.

"You understand, buddy, that the task force will deny any association with you and your activities if questions are asked?" Brognola had told him.

Bolan had smiled at that.

"Hal, those words are like an old, familiar song."

"Off the record the team mans are high-fiving every time you hit Canfield's organization. On a secondary note the two mans at the hotel turned out to be a couple of local hitters allied to Canfield's group. Same as the ones who hijacked you along with DeChambre."

"Hal, stayed tuned. 'Radio Rotterdam' hasn't finished broadcasting yet."

9

The following day found Mack Bolan preparing for his planned hit on Canfield's main distribution site in Holland. The farm and the processing plant occupied a large area off the main route out of Rotterdam. The information the man at the dock had given him proved to be extremely accurate.

It took Bolan more than an hour to reach the location. He noticed that the area he had driven through was taken up by similar industry. This part of the country grew vast quantities of agricultural produce that was distributed all across Europe and into the U.K. There were constant streams of vehicles towing large containers that held fresh supplies of vegetables and dairy products heading for distribution points. A large percentage of these vehicles were on their way to Rotterdam. Bolan saw a number of South East Containers trucks arriving and leaving the Knookreising Farm.

He sat at the side of the road studying the layout of the farm. There was a wide turn leading off the road onto a paved strip that terminated in the large freight yard fronting the farm. There was an office block and, behind that, the sprawl of large greenhouses and open strips of planted fields. To one side were the processing and packing sheds. It was an impressive setup.

Bolan moved his powerful binoculars to the far distance where, his research had informed him, the original farm still remained. He spotted a large house built in the 1950s. Next to it were traditional Dutch barns and outhouses. Bolan saw a couple of South East Containers trucks parked nearby. According to the maps he had studied there was a minor road that ran along the back of the property, close to the original farm setup. It seemed to offer the best opportunity for him to check out the place.

He glanced at his watch. Midafternoon. Overhead the sky was heavy with dark clouds. It looked as if he really had chosen Holland's rainy season to make his visit. Bolan started the SUV and pulled back onto the road. He drove a couple of miles before he spotted the narrow road that skirted the eastern perimeter of the farmland. It took him almost twenty minutes before he found himself paralleling the main route. In that time he had encountered no traffic. The road he was on may have been the principal one when the original farm had been built, but the wider, faster main route had taken all the traffic. For Bolan's purpose that was ideal.

He pulled off the road, turning the BMW around before taking it down a rutted strip into the cover of tangled undergrowth. Out of sight Bolan was able to take his gear from the SUV's back and ready himself.

His intention was to dismantle Venturer Export's distribution base. Given the right equipment that would have been straightforward. But his access to specialist ordnance was virtually nil. Coming into the country unarmed and with no recourse to hardware meant the Executioner was winging his mission. Bolan didn't let that hold him back. He was just going to have to be a tad more creative. In the SUV he had the handguns confiscated from the opposition, plus the MP-5. The shoulder rig he had taken from one of the gunmen housed the SIG-Sauer. His second pistol was tucked behind his belt.

Before leaving Rotterdam Bolan had used some of the money taken from Canfield's people to outfit himself. A visit to a sporting goods store had offered him close substitutes for his combat gear. Combat-style pants, a thin sweater and a pair of sturdy walking boots—all in black. The photographer's jacket he had purchased at a store farther along the street provided pockets for his extra ammo clips. He slung the MP-5 across his back by the webbing sling and pulled on the dark cap he'd bought.

Exiting the vehicle Bolan eased along the bottom of the ditch and peered over the rim. A few lights were on in the farmhouse and buildings against the gloom of the afternoon and the overcast sky. He studied the layout. There would be adequate cover. He spotted parked farm machinery, stacks of crates and barrels. And he saw a few more people about than he might have expected on an old-fashioned farm. Bolan had a feeling they might be there because of him and the problems he had been creating for the traffickers. His appearance and interference had stirred them into defensive mode. Hit-and-run tactics had the effect of making the enemy nervous because they had no idea where or when he might strike again.

Look out, guys, I'm closer than you think.

The first drops of rain warned Bolan of the downpour about to come. He welcomed it. Rain would work more on his behalf than the opposition's. It would cover his approach. Deaden any sound. The rainfall began in earnest, heavy drops bouncing off the road. Bolan used the rain as his cue, pushing up to the road, crouching low as he went across it and through the tall grass to the perimeter fence. The outer fence was no more than a couple of feet high, a simple three-bar structure. From there Bolan wound his way across a hard packed-earth strip and dropped to a kneeling position behind an ancient, rusting trailer. Its tires were flat and cracked, the paintwork long faded and flaking. Bolan dropped flat and crawled beneath the chassis, working his way along the trailer until he was able to look out across the main yard.

The first man he saw might have been a farmhand. His clothes were nondescript, made for heavy work, and so were the thick boots on his feet. But the squat submachine gun he carried close to his body had no place on a working farm. The next figure moving into Bolan's line of vision, clad in a similar fashion to the first man, also had an automatic weapon. The two men came together, shoulders hunched against the rain, sharing their patrolling misery and the cigarettes they lit. Their collars were pulled up and caps pulled down against the rain.

Watching them convinced Bolan they were protecting something with a much higher value than the tomatoes being produced across the way.

Human cargo.

Somewhere in the distance thunder rumbled, low and deep. The intensity of the rainfall increased. The armed guards parted company, each moving in a different direction. As one man moved out of sight the other one moved in Bolan's general direction, flicking his cigarette butt to the ground as he tramped past the old trailer, cutting across the rear of the farm property. Bolan watched where he went and waited patiently until he returned minutes later. There was no military precision in the patrolling. The man simply wandered, the submachine gun pressed close to his side as if he was afraid getting it wet might render it inoperative. He walked past Bolan again, moving down the side of the farm building, then pausing to presumably check out his area of responsibility. He kept looking skyward, displeased at the weather, shaking his head a couple of times as he turned and resumed his restless patrolling. When the Executioner saw the man moving into a shadowed area, he slid out from beneath the trailer and fell in behind him.

Typical of old, long-established farms, there were tumbledown sheds and more abandoned machinery scattered around the property. The grass grew randomly, sprouting in defiant clumps between the rusting metal parts and cast-aside tires.

Bolan stalked his man until they were well to the back of

the old house. He moved up without warning, catching his un-suspecting quarry in a powerful neck lock. He dragged the man to the wet ground, ignoring the man's frantic struggle for his weapon, the hoarse gasp from a restricted throat. Slamming one knee into the guard's lower spine Bolan hauled back until he felt vertebrae snap. The man went soft in his grasp. Bolan released him and pushed to his feet, stepping back, catching a final shuddering spasm before the guard became still. The Executioner took the man's weapon and threw it into an untidy stack of old machinery. He slid the body out of sight under a trailer.

One less gunman to worry about.

Bolan wanted no surprises from guards coming in behind his back. No probe, whether hard or soft, guaranteed total security. Reducing that probability was Bolan's only safe-guard, though even he knew it wasn't going to shield him fully.

Flat against the end wall of the barnlike building, Bolan peered around the corner. The downed guard's partner was trudging up the slight incline, pulling up his coat collar and no doubt cursing the inclement weather. He slowed as he neared Bolan's position, looking around for his missing buddy, then continued on toward the corner of the barn.

Was he thinking his partner had stopped under cover for another cigarette? Maybe taking shelter from the downpour?

His casual movement gave the impression he was not alerted by any possible trouble.

Bolan let the man round the end of the barn, then used his right forearm to deliver a brutal throat strike. The guard's strangled cry was cut off before he could generate any warning sound. Trying to suck air through his crushed pas-sages the man offered little resistance to Bolan's follow-up maneuver. He caught hold of the guard's coat collar and pulled down, driving his knee up into the vulnerable face. The solid impact drove the guard up and back. He slammed against the wood wall of the barn, splintering a couple of the weathered slats, then pitched facedown on the rain-sodden ground. Bolan relieved him of his weapons, hurling them into the shadowed piles of machinery.

He was turning away from the barn when something caught his eye. A gleam of metal showing through the gap created by the broken wood slats. Bolan checked it out. Pulling away a length of wood he saw an inner lining of steel sheeting. Something was constructed within the wooden shell of the old barn. He didn't waste time speculating, though he didn't expect to find anything good.

He heard a rumbling sound. The rainfall was increasing. The ground under Bolan's feet was quickly becoming waterlogged, the disturbed earth sluicing down the gradual slope in brown rivulets. He crept around the side of the barn. Some twenty feet away the raw earth gave way to a concrete apron that provided hard standing for the vehicles that would draw up to the barn access. From his position Bolan could see that the sliding door had been rolled back. One of the South East Containers trucks had reversed up to the door and Bolan watched as the container doors at the back of the truck were opened. Figures clustered around the opening. One of them was gesturing, his raised voice reaching Bolan. Hesitant figures appeared at the edge of the container. One of the men reached up and caught an arm, dragging a young woman down out of the container. She stumbled as she landed on the concrete. Other hands reached out to steady her balance before pushing her roughly inside the barn. Bolan counted six more women being removed from the truck. The container doors were closed and secured. Someone banged on the side of the truck and it pulled away, moving down toward the main farm buildings.

The Executioner had his confirmation.

He pulled the MP-5's sling over his head, running a quick check to confirm the weapon was set for use.

There was one man lingering near the barn door. He was leaning against the frame as he spoke into a cell phone, his head nodding as he talked. He wore a long dark coat and a baseball cap.

Bolan edged along the wall of the barn, his eyes fixed on the man. The downpour muffled any sound he might have made and Bolan was standing directly behind the man by the time he completed his call and pushed his phone into a pocket. The webbing sling flipped over the man's head and Bolan twisted it, pulling it tight against flesh. He pulled the man back and down, jamming a knee into the spine as the squirming, panicked man struggled to reach for his gun. The powerful muscles in Bolan's arms were taut under the pressure he was applying. The frantic struggles weakened; the boot heels drumming against the concrete slowed, jerked into stillness. Bolan held his position for a few more seconds, then loosened his grip and drew the webbing strap over the man's head, dislodging the cap. He lowered the man to the wet concrete, caught hold of his collar and slid him away from the access door to the base of the barn wall.

With his MP-5 set for triple bursts Bolan edged around the access door, sparing a few seconds to assimilate the image.

The steel construction he had partially glimpsed through the broken barn slats was a twenty-foot-square lockbox, the front wall facing him, constructed of close-spaced bars with an inset door. Inside the box Bolan saw the group of young women from the container, some standing in listless poses, others sitting on the low cots that were bunched together at the far end of the box. Bolan's fingers tightened around the MP-5 as the image of the captive females registered. Herded into the steel box like so much cattle. Trapped, without hope, awaiting the next stage of their forced captivity.

On the far side of the barn were stored metal canisters and

Get FREE BOOKS and a FREE GIFT when you play the...

LAS VEGAS

GAME

Just scratch off the gold box with a coin. Then check below to see the gifts you get!

YES! I have scratched off the gold box. Please send me my **2 FREE BOOKS** and **gift for which I qualify.** I understand that I am under no obligation to purchase any books as explained on the back of this card.

▼ DETACH AND MAIL CARD TODAY! ▼

© 2009 WORLDWIDE LIBRARY. Printed in Canada.
® and ™ are trademarks owned and used by the trademark owner and/or its licensee.

366 ADL E4CE   166 ADL E4CE

FIRST NAME

LAST NAME

ADDRESS

APT.#

CITY

STATE/ PROV.

ZIP/POSTAL CODE

7 7 7	Worth TWO FREE BOOKS plus a BONUS Mystery Gift!
🍒🍒🍒	Worth TWO FREE BOOKS!
🔔🔔♣	TRY AGAIN!

Offer limited to one per household and not valid to current subscribers of Gold Eagle® books. All orders subject to approval. Please allow 4 to 6 weeks for delivery.

Your Privacy—Worldwide Library is committed to protecting your privacy. Our privacy policy is available online at www.ReaderService.com or upon request from the Reader Service. From time to time we make our lists of customers available to reputable third parties who may have a product or service of interest to you. If you would prefer for us not to share your name and address, please check here ☐. **Help us get it right**—We strive for accurate, respectful and relevant communications. To clarify or modify your communication preferences, visit us at www.ReaderService.com/consumerchoice.

The Reader Service — Here's how it works:

Accepting your 2 free books and free gift (gift valued at approximately $5.00) places you under no obligation to buy anything. You may keep the books and gift and return the shipping statement marked "cancel." If you do not cancel, about a month later we'll send you 6 additional books and bill you just $31.94* — that's a savings of 24% off the cover price of all 6 books! And there's no extra charge for shipping! You may cancel at any time, but if you choose to continue, every other month we'll send you 6 more books, which you may either purchase at the discount price or return to us and cancel your subscription.

*Terms and prices subject to change without notice. Price does not include applicable taxes. Sales tax applicable in N.Y. Canadian residents will be charged applicable provincial taxes and GST. Offer not vaid in Quebec. Credit or debit balances in a customer's account(s) may be offset by any other outstanding balance owed by or to the customer. Offer available while quantities last.

If offer card is missing write to: The Reader Service, P.O. Box 1867, Buffalo NY 14240-1867

BUSINESS REPLY MAIL
FIRST-CLASS MAIL   PERMIT NO. 717   BUFFALO, NY

POSTAGE WILL BE PAID BY ADDRESSEE

THE READER SERVICE
PO BOX 1867
BUFFALO NY 14240-9952

NO POSTAGE
NECESSARY
IF MAILED
IN THE
UNITED STATES

crates, some standing five high. There were also racks of wooden pallets and filled sacks.

In front of the stored goods were the men who currently dominated the frightening world the women had been forced into. The traffickers. Bolan had nothing but contempt for them as they talked and laughed, clustered around one of a number of desks holding a computer, the large monitor displaying pornographic images. Bolan counted five of them. They were intent on studying the screen images, oblivious to the Executioner's presence until one of them straightened to light a cigarette. He moved back from the main group, touching his lighter flame to the cigarette, casually glancing across the barn.

He saw Bolan.

His reaction was fast but not enough to allow himself and his partners clear space. The man shouted a warning, snatching at the handgun tucked behind his belt. He was still yelling when Bolan hit him with a 3-round burst that thudded into his chest, shoving him back against the edge of the desk. As the man arched back across the desk Bolan fed him three more slugs that shattered ribs and chewed at flesh.

The man's four colleagues scattered in a panic, reaching for weapons. A couple wore them in body holsters, the others grabbed at MP-5s on nearby desks.

By this time Bolan was on the move, angling in across the barn, his weapon up and firing, seeking targets. His mobility proved an asset. Bolan weaved about, laying down deadly fire that cut into the unprepared traffickers. His slugs punctured flesh, broke bone and caused bloody gouts and spurts. Only one of the crew got off retaliatory fire, yanking his own MP-5 around in a panicky sweep that sent gunfire ripping through the barn's timber walls. His action only lasted brief seconds before Bolan's strike continued. He stitched the man with a pair of triple bursts that slammed the trafficker back across the desk, dislodging the computer monitor and sending it crashing to the floor. The man rolled across the desk, arms thrown wide, his weapon spilling from his limp grasp.

Before he moved again Bolan exchanged the MP-5's magazine for a fresh one. It was time, mainly the lack of it, that dictated Bolan's actions. He crossed to the lockbox. The inset door was secured by a modern lock mechanism. He studied it, then heard a quiet voice. It came from one of the young women. He didn't understand the language and looked at her through the bars.

"English?" he asked.

She turned and gestured at one of the other girls, speaking to her.

"I understand a little," the young woman said. "There are…keys in drawer. I saw them put in there."

Bolan tracked her pointing finger and crossed to the desk she indicated.

"Yes. There."

He found a set of keys, took them back to the door and found the right one on the third attempt.

"Tell them to come out. We have to move quickly. Make them understand. Others may be coming because of the shooting," he said.

The woman nodded. She began to instruct the others and they responded without argument. They gathered at the barn door.

"That way," Bolan said. "You'll find a fence. A narrow road on the other side. Best I can do right now. Take them. *Go.*"

"What will you do?" the woman asked.

"Whatever needs doing. Now get out of here."

The young woman nodded. Before she followed the others she bent to retrieve one of the abandoned handguns. "They will not touch us again," she said.

Bolan followed her to the door and watched the small group as they moved up the slope, away from the barn. He picked up sound coming from below his position. Turning Bolan saw an open-backed 4x4 swinging into view and racing in his direction. His presence on the farm was well and truly acknowledged now.

Bolan stepped out from cover to take the battle to the enemy.

10

The driver of the 4x4 raised a warning as the tall, dark-clad figure stepped out of the barn, the submachine gun in his hands raised. Beyond him the women from the lockbox were running free and clear. At the driver's shout one of the men standing in the exposed rear of the vehicle swung his weapon on-line and opened fire. The slight bounce of the 4x4 took his aim off-line and the stream of 9 mm slugs chewed wood from the barn wall, spitting splinters into the air.

The shooter's partner, less reckless, called him an idiot. He told him to hold back until they were closer. It might have been sound advice but in this case it did little to gain them any advantage.

The Executioner broke into a hard run, weaving slightly as he approached them, then brought himself to a stop. The MP-5 in his steady hands settled on the 4x4. Flame winked at the muzzle. Glass shattered as the windshield blew apart. The driver screamed as he caught a face full of razor fragments and 9 mm slugs. He twisted away from the windshield, losing control of the 4x4. It lurched to the right, jerking as the lack of control brought about a stall.

The pair of shooters were thrown off balance for seconds that cost them dearly.

Bolan raised the MP-5 as he stepped to the side, clearing the cab as the vehicle came to a dead stop. The shooters in the back reached out to steady themselves by grabbing the rail at the rear of the cab. It was Bolan's opening. He took it without pause, his weapon spitting triple bursts as he closed in on the vehicle. The closest shooter jerked and twitched as he caught a triple tap, the force of the slugs turning him sideways, so that Bolan's second burst hit him in the ribs, splintering bone and coring through to his heart. His partner scrambled to the far side of the truck and jumped to the ground, hauling his own submachine gun into position for a fast response once he saw his target. He failed to see Bolan drop to the concrete and angle his MP-5 beneath the 4x4. The Executioner tracked the shooter as he moved the length of the truck, then triggered two 3-round bursts that shattered the man's ankles, dumping him screaming on the ground, blood squirting from his torn flesh and shattered bone. The shooter caught a quick glimpse of Bolan before the MP-5 crackled again and the shooter's head snapped back under the force of the 9 mm slugs.

Bolan yanked open the driver's door and hauled the body from the seat and climbed in. He dropped the MP-5 and dipped the clutch, turning the key to restart the stalled 4x4. As the engine burst into life Bolan put the vehicle into gear and slammed down on the gas pedal, sending the 4x4 into a rubber-scorching lurch forward. He spun the steering wheel and took the truck inside the barn, bringing it to a hard stop. Out of the cab he grabbed his weapon and some spare magazines, then stepped around to the side of the 4x4, crouched and raked the underside, puncturing the gas tank. Streams of gasoline began to spurt from the ragged holes. Bolan kept firing the MP-5 until the magazine was empty. The gas was spreading in a wide pool across the concrete floor of the barn.

Crossing to the desks Bolan searched the floor and found the lighter dropped by the first man he had shot. He scooped it up and ignited it. The lighter flared as Bolan turned up the butane. Bolan snatched up a discarded newspaper and formed it into a loose tube. He lit the paper and let it burn, then tossed the flaming torch into the spreading gasoline. Vapor caught the fire, sucking at it hungrily. It engulfed the 4x4 in a frantic surge, flame swelling up in a ravenous ball. Bolan retreated, snapping in a fresh magazine for the MP-5. He had just reached the door as the truck blew, the force of the blast slamming between his shoulders and almost knocking him off balance as he stumbled out into the cool of the rain.

Raised voices made him turn. Three armed figures were running in his direction. They opened fire the moment Bolan appeared, slugs hammering at the concrete. Bolan pulled back, flat against the wall of the barn, feeling the heat from the fire starting to penetrate the wood. He raised the MP-5 and tracked the closest of the approaching hostiles. He stroked the trigger and saw his target stumble. The man went down all the way when Bolan hit him with a second triple burst. The sight of their partner falling made the other two fall back, hesitating as they realized their own vulnerable positions. Bolan didn't hesitate. He put a burst into one of the men, the slugs tearing through his shoulder and spraying bloody bits of flesh and bone from the wound. The man dropped his weapon, clutching at his shoulder. In his haste to get away he lost his footing and crashed headlong to the concrete. Bolan heard the crackle of automatic fire from the remaining man, felt the snap of slugs as they burned the air around him. He felt the shock of a hit as a bullet clipped his right side, just above the hip. The force knocked him off balance. Bolan forced himself to absorb the pain as he swung his MP-5 toward the shooter. He saw the man go down hard, his weapon discharging into the sky.

Clamping a hand over his bleeding hip Bolan straightened, turning to head back up the slope to his waiting car.

Behind him flames were flaring from between the wooden slats as the barn fire expanded. Bolan heard soft explosions from within the blazing structure and remembered the stored canisters and packed sacks. He had no idea what they might have held but they seemed to be reacting to the intense heat. He had almost reached the low fence when a powerful explosion rocked the ground under his feet. When he looked back over his shoulder he witnessed a series of blasts that threw spiraling geysers of flame into the sky, tearing out the barn roof. He maintained his retreat from the farm as the explosions continued, the fireballs arcing across the farm grounds, raining down on the main buildings and parked vehicles. Whatever had been stored in the barn was proving to be highly flammable and was creating chaos on the traffickers' base.

Bolan stumbled over the fence, going to his knees on the rain-sodden ground, a sudden weakness starting to spread over him. Reaction to the bullet wound. The hand over the flesh gouge in his side was leaking blood between his fingers. He felt the ground shudder as one of the arcing fireballs hit the earth just yards away, spreading a burning mass of liquid flame. *Too close,* Bolan decided. He struggled to his feet and made for the road.

A rain-soaked figure appeared, hands reaching out to support him. Bolan blinked his watery eyes and recognized the young woman from the barn. The one who spoke some English.

"I can help. Come."

She let him lean against her. She was stronger than she looked. One arm around his body she led Bolan across the road and down the slope to his parked SUV. The rest of the women were crouching down behind the vehicle. They watched Bolan with wary expressions, faces lit by the rising flames in the gray afternoon.

"We need to move away from here," Bolan said, using his key to unlock the BMW. "Tell them to get in the vehicle. Now."

Before the woman had time to answer something caught her eye and she gripped Bolan's shoulder. "They come."

Bolan swung around. Saw the approaching bulk of a big

SUV. It was speeding up from the farm, bouncing over the rutted ground. It hit the concrete strip, swinging out from its direct path as it powered past the blazing barn.

"In the car," he yelled, bringing the MP-5 on-line.

Bolan fought back the rising pain from the bullet gouge, ignored the blood still seeping from the wound, as he pushed up to road level, facing the oncoming bulk of the SUV. He saw a dark figure lean out from the side window and level a weapon. The muzzle flared briefly as the weapon crackled. The ill-judged volley went wide. Bolan stood his ground and returned fire from his static position, and as the heavy vehicle smashed through the flimsy perimeter fence, his burst clattered in through the grille and into the radiator. Raising his weapon Bolan hit the hood and the windshield. The glass failed to break, the slugs ricocheting off, leaving starred cracks. The effect made the driver haul on the wheel, the big tires squealing as they ground into the paved surface of the road. The SUV slid sideways, swinging dangerously close to Bolan as it came around. He threw himself out of harm's way, the bulk of the vehicle missing him by inches before it righted itself and powered along the strip of the road.

Bolan tucked and rolled, biting back the flare of pain from his wounded hip as he slid across the rain-soaked ground. He scrambled to his knees, bringing the MP-5 back on track as the SUV jerked to a sliding stop, rear doors swinging open. Armed figures disgorged from the vehicle. Bolan opened fire before they had the chance to set themselves and caught one with a couple of tri-bursts that slammed him back against the open door. The man on Bolan's blind side made it to the rear of the SUV, searching for a target. He walked into Bolan's steady fire and went down with a harsh gurgle.

Bolan heard the roar of the SUV's motor as the driver decided to gain some distance. He ran forward, raising the MP-5 to shoulder height, angling the muzzle, firing into the vehicle at window level. The side glass shattered as repeated bursts riddled the interior. The SUV made a brief forward jerk, then stalled, the motor dying. Bolan cleared the magazine, ejected it and felt in a pocket for a fresh load. He clicked it in place. He jerked the weapon around as the driver's door clicked open. The driver slid sideways, pushing the door wide as he dropped from the seat onto the road, blood gleaming on his torn neck and from ragged wounds in his face and skull.

Bolan stood in the middle of the road, soaked from the heavy rain, hand clutched over his bloody side. The MP-5 dropped in his right hand. He didn't hear the woman step alongside. Only glanced around when she touched his arm.

"Now we go," she suggested.

Bolan stared at her.

"Before others come. Please."

He followed her back to the SUV. The other women were already crowded inside the vehicle. The woman slid onto the passenger seat and waited until Bolan climbed behind the wheel. He started the motor and got the SUV moving up out of the hollow and onto the road. He hit the wiper switch and the blades swept back and forth, clearing the rain from the windshield. As he followed the road on its curving path back to the main highway the farm came into view on their right. The blazing barn was in plain sight, other fires raging from the fallout created by the explosion of the material stored inside the building.

Beside Bolan the young woman, still clutching the pistol she had picked up, nodded to herself as she stared at the blaze.

Bolan kept the BMW rolling, slowing only when he reached the junction where the side road rejoined the main route. He swung the wheel and drove past the jam of vehicles starting to crowd the highway. Once he was clear Bolan increased his speed. Twice they saw emergency vehicles heading for the blaze site. Hugo Canfield's people were going to have to answer some serious questions once the police became involved. Bolan's hope was that the disruption to the trafficking operation would simply add more pressure to his actions. He was also aware that Canfield's involvement would be well camouflaged and any connection between himself and the operation would be hard to prove on a legal level.

Bolan's past experience had educated him in the complexities of the criminal mind-set. Men like Hugo Canfield operated on a different level. Distanced from the everyday exposure of his criminal activities by legal manipulation, the use of cover titles and companies operating under him but run by underlings. Canfield was far beyond the grasp of law enforcement. He was able to make his profits by proxy. He allowed others to take the risks and the falls from grace. That was why the task force had not been able to reach him. Canfield simply sidestepped all their efforts, using the law and its complex infrastructure to protect him, while at the same time giving it the finger.

Now he had a different hunter on his trail. One who moved outside the restrictions of such laws. Mack Bolan used a simple logic. He saw the crimes. He identified the perpetrators. He did not stand idly by and do nothing.

Bolan considered the huddled group of young women in the SUV. They were the victims. Taken by force from the streets they called home. Transported to a strange place by men who saw them as nothing more than merchandise. Objects with a price over their heads, to be bartered for and sold into lives of deprivation and humiliation. The traffickers dealt in human souls, without any thought for the innocents they preyed upon. Human trafficking, in Bolan's eyes, was one of the most despicable crimes man had ever devised. There was something especially evil when men could take others of their kind and sell them like so much cattle, indifferent to the suffering they caused.

Hugo Canfield made vast amounts of money via this sickening business. He collected his payments from the people he sold to, enriching his already privileged life with increasing amounts. While he lounged in comfort the nameless victims were forced into degrading occupations, where any kind of resistance would be rewarded with violence. Their new masters looked upon their purchases as simply that—*purchases*—objects they could treat how they wished. The objects had no rights. No redress against the treatment they received, and there was nowhere for them to escape. Owned body and soul by their masters they found that the only relief they could expect came through obedience. Total, unquestioning obedience.

Venturer Exports existed because of the protective umbrella spread over it. A formation of powerful individuals who used their positions to hide the activities of the traffickers beneath complex covers. Favors and money fueled the actions of these protectors. Canfield knew his people and he lavished his bounty on them, sucking them into his circle. It was a self-perpetuating monster. One that demanded more from everyone involved. Any threat against the safety of the collective would bring powerful responses because there was too much to lose. Money aside, there were reputations and careers to protect. The higher the profile the more they had to lose. Bolan had already witnessed the willingness of his enemies to hit back. As far as he was concerned the responses he was getting indicated his strikes were starting to bite.

He had no option but to maintain his offensive.

"I think we have company," the young woman at his side said, her body twisted around in the seat as she peered through the BMW's rear window.

Bolan checked his side mirror and spotted a big silver Mercedes barreling along behind them. It wasn't so much the car but the aggressive way it was being driven that was alarming.

Bolan saw the vehicle accelerate. Silver spray misted behind it from the rain-slick road. It drew closer to the SUV. The driver was pushing to the limit. The thought of engaging on this busy strip of highway didn't sit well with Bolan. He always did his best to avoid involving those he considered innocents. It was looking as if his opponents had no such scruples.

A figure leaned out from one of the car's windows, a pistol in his hand. The shooter held his position for a while but was unable to gain a solid shot and finally pulled back inside the car.

"We can't avoid them out here," Bolan said to the woman. "Tell everyone to hang on."

These mans don't give up, he thought. Well, neither do I.

He jammed his foot hard down on the gas, sending the SUV surging forward. Peering through the streaked windshield he saw a sign ahead, indicating a right turn onto what appeared to be a construction site. Bolan hauled the wheel at the last moment, feeling the heavy SUV rock on its suspension as it fought gravity in the sudden turn. For a moment the rear wheels felt as if they were about to lose traction. They held and the SUV bumped over the edge of the paved highway onto a wide strip of hard packed earth made slippery by the falling rain.

Bolan checked out the way ahead. The muddy track opened out on a wide expanse of graded terrain. There were scattered items of heavy earth-moving vehicles. All of them sat motionless at the moment. To their left steel girders thrust up from concrete bases. Stacks of buildings materials dotted the site. All that was missing were the construction workers. They had quit for the day, or had been forced to quit because of the weather. Bolan didn't fail to notice the pools of brown water that had gathered in the ground hollows. Even with its high suspension and deep-treaded tires the SUV was finding the loose surface hard work. Glancing in his rearview mirror Bolan saw the Mercedes still in sight, but making its way over the muddy terrain.

Okay, Bolan decided, let's do it the hard way.

He gunned the engine, swinging the wheel around and faced back the way he had come.

Beside him the young woman gasped. "What are you doing? This is crazy."

"You could be right," Bolan said. "But it's been that way the past few days."

He aimed the big SUV directly at the Mercedes, arcs of mud spraying up from beneath his wheels. He saw the car slide to a stop, then start to flounder as it sank in brown mud, the driver giving in to panic as he tried to apply full power to the wheels. All he did was dig the car in deeper.

"You will hit them," the woman said.

"Maybe, but not with this," Bolan said, taking his foot off the gas pedal and pressing the brake.

The SUV slowed, sliding sideways as Bolan let go of the wheel. He grabbed the MP-5, shoved open his door and jumped out. The ground was soft, slippery, underfoot. He leaned against the side of the stalled SUV and worked his way to the front.

The driver of the Mercedes shouted something to his partners as he saw the black-clad figure emerge from the SUV. One of the back doors opened and Bolan saw a raised weapon. He shouldered the MP-5, tracked the shooter and hit him with a burst that shattered the door window before reaching the target. The man stumbled back, clutching at his punctured chest.

Bolan half turned and jacked out more bursts, this time aimed at the driver behind the windshield. It took a couple of assaults before the glass starred and imploded. The driver's hand flew off the wheel, a reflex action as he caught slugs and glass that tore the flesh of his throat and face. The car jerked to a sudden stop as the engine stalled. Bolan moved out from cover, closing in on the Mercedes. He had seen movement at the rear of the vehicle. The far-side rear door being pushed open. He flicked the selector to full auto and riddled the car with 9 mm death. He maintained his forward motion, pausing only once to feed in a fresh magazine before continuing his attack. He took it to the logical conclusion.

The Executioner checked the interior of the car. The driver and the two men in the rear lay in bloody sprawls. The one man who had stepped out lay facedown in the mud.

Bolan turned back to the BMW, seeing the white, shocked faces of the young women pressed against the window glass. They watched him without saying a word as he climbed back inside, dropping the spent MP-5 on the floor. He started the engine and slowly drove back the way they had come until they reached the road again. He wasn't in a talkative mood himself. The wound in his hip was still hurting. He could feel warm blood drawing the blacksuit against his flesh. He should have done something about it but his main concern was getting the women as far away from the farm as possible. The authorities were going to have a great deal to sort out. It would keep them occupied for some time and he wanted to use that time to get well clear. At the earliest opportunity he needed to call Brognola again to have him liaise with the task force so the women could be taken care of.

Bolan needed to take some time for himself to deal with his wound, get some rest and prepare for the next phase of his operation.

It was time to leave Rotterdam and relocate to the U.K.

Hugo Canfield had his secondary operation there and that was the Executioner's next target.

He had a final request for Brognola. Bolan needed a flight out of Holland. One that would not involve him having to negotiate official channels. Bolan's Matt Cooper identity had been involved in too much action within Holland's borders. He wanted to get out quickly and quietly, and enter the U.K. in the same way.

11

Len Watts waited for the Executioner in a quiet pub in Pinner, a suburb of London. His appearance did not hint at his profession. Watts, a tall, athletically built man in his early forties, had the look of an academic. He wore beige corduroy slacks and a tweedy sports coat, an open-neck shirt and tan loafers. His dark hair was collar length. Yet his easy manner concealed the sharp mind of a man with his finger on the pulse of the covert world he worked in.

McCarter had given little away when he had sent along the details to Bolan concerning Watts. Reading between the lines Bolan's guess was that Len Watts not only provided ordnance, but knew how to use it, and most likely *had* used it.

Bolan showed up on time, parked the car he had rented and went into the pub. He spotted his man seated in a booth near the oak-beamed fireplace, identifying him from the photograph McCarter had sent over. Watts raised his pint glass in acknowledgment and Bolan joined him. There was a full pint of beer waiting for him.

Watts offered a hand as Bolan sat down. "I ordered a couple of ploughmen's," he said.

"Thanks," Bolan said. He took the glass and checked the beer. It was nicely chilled.

"So how is the old reprobate? Still a smart-arse?" Watts asked.

"You know him well, then?"

Watts chuckled. He took a swallow from his pint.

"Our relationship goes back a long way. Sometimes I think too long. But he and I have shared some hairy moments together." Watts paused as a server came with their food. Cheese, salad and pickle, with chunks of crusty fresh bread and rich butter. "Couple more pints, love."

They ate quietly for a while until Watts said, "I have what you asked for. It's outside in the boot of my car. When we leave I'll hand it over and we can go on our merry ways. I imagine with what you asked for your way isn't about to be all that merry."

"Something that needs to be done," was all Bolan said.

Watts nodded. He studied Bolan's face, picking up on a couple of healing marks in evidence.

"Fell over my skis," Bolan said.

"I understand they can be pretty aggressive at times," Watts said straight-faced.

As they stood to leave Bolan hesitated as the bullet gouge in his hip reminded him it was still there. He noticed Watts had seen the pause.

"Skiing again? Maybe you should think of quitting."

"Problem is it becomes an addiction. Hard to give it up."

Watts went to the bar to pay the tab, then led Bolan out of the pub. He pointed to a gleaming maroon Jaguar parked at the far corner of the parking lot. Bolan went to his car and reversed out of his spot, then drove across to stop behind the Jaguar. Watts opened the trunk and took out a heavy black bag. He opened the rear door of Bolan's vehicle and placed it on the floor behind the driver's seat.

"Everything you asked for," he said. "The explosive packs are already fitted with timed detonators. Just set them where you need and the handheld unit will do the rest."

Bolan shook the man's hand. "Thanks."

"You watch your back. And next time you see my buddy tell him not to stay away too long. He's a pain but he's a good friend. And there aren't many of those left these days."

Bolan raised a hand as he drove away, turning the car along the quiet road. He circled the outer road system that bypassed London and made for the coast. He had a room booked in a hotel that was no more than an hour's drive from the South East Containers offices.

South East Containers was the company Paul Chambers ran. The same company he had seen delivering human cargo to the farm outside Rotterdam. The Executioner had an appointment with the freight company. Initially it would be to reconnoiter the setup so he knew what he was up against when he made his full strike.

12

South East Containers occupied a large site ten miles inland from the ferry port where its vehicles maintained their schedules to and from Rotterdam Port. The freight business sat in near isolation, the closest village some eight miles along the road that ran west to east along the coastal area. The area around the site was timbered grassland, with some wide-spaced farms in the distance.

The location was ideal for Bolan's initial observation of the setup. He parked off the road, deep in a stand of trees and heavy bush. Dressed in casual clothing, with binoculars and a camera around his neck, he was prepared to check out the freight business and pass himself off as an enthusiastic photographer if anyone asked.

He had parked a half mile from the site, making his way through the greenery until he was able to scan South East Containers from concealment.

The frontage comprised of an expansive spread of concrete that allowed the large rigs to pull safely off the road. Large metal gates gave access to the freight yard itself and the whole property was enclosed behind sturdy metal fencing. Bolan could see cameras mounted strategically along the top of the fencing. Next to the access gates was a front office that housed security men. Bolan spent long hours watching the activity as South East Containers vehicles came and went, each checked when they arrived and again when they left.

At the far end of the freight yard was a long warehouse building with loading ramps and a number of roller-shutter doors at the rear of each bay. A concrete island in the yard held a number of fuel pumps where the drivers could fill up their diesel tanks.

Over the two days and nights Bolan observed the activity, he saw that South East Containers closed for trading by eight every night. Rigs were parked in the yard, the drivers taking their own cars and driving away, leaving the security team to watch over the site. As darkness fell powerful lights came into operation, covering the freight yard and the frontage. The cameras set on the metal fences rotated to cover both.

Bolan decided that if he was going to get into the freight yard and the warehouse the security facilities needed neutralizing first. And from what he had seen, the front office would be the place to start.

Day three was Saturday, and South East Containers closed for the weekend just after midday. Bolan watched the drivers park and leave in their own vehicles. He also saw the two security men hand over to a single man who arrived in a Land Rover. He parked inside the yard and they drove out. The gates were closed and the lone guard made his way into the site office.

Bolan saw the situation as his chance to make a closer inspection. It was necessary if he was going to carry out his planned strike.

He returned to his concealed car and drove back to his hotel, where he changed from his casual gear into a suit, complete with shirt, tie and polished shoes. Back in his car he returned to the South East Containers site, only this time he rolled his car off the road and across the concrete apron, parking. As Bolan stepped out of the car he could see the lone security man staring at him.

RAY KEPPLE FINISHED rolling his cigarette as he watched the tall, expensively dressed man climb out of the gleaming sedan and make his way across to the office. There was something about the man that aroused a nervous sensation in Kepple's stomach. He quickly stuck the thin cigarette between his lips and lit it, sucking smoke deep into his lungs.

The newcomer spotted him through the streaked office window and angled across to the door. He pushed it open, pausing in the frame. Kepple got an impression of a big man, physically fit under the suit. He had thick dark hair, his face tanned but showing some recent bruising. The eyes fixed on Kepple were of a startling blue, expressionless and cold. They unnerved Kepple.

"What can I do for you?" he asked.

Bolan had seen the name badge pinned to the man's shirt. "Ray Kepple. The man I came to see."

Kepple realized the man was plainly an American, his tone firm without being aggressive.

"Yes. Who are you?"

"I'm the man about to get you out of trouble."

"Eh?"

"You've heard about the problems in Rotterdam? Someone making a lot of noise? Upsetting business? It's making Mr. Canfield nervous."

Kepple rubbed the back of his neck, shifting uneasily from one foot to the other. "Well, I don't get involved in the operation over there. All I do is supervise things here."

"From what the boss man told me you're the main man here. Run this depot like clockwork. Keep the trucks moving on time and the merchandise turned around pretty fast."

"Canfield said that?" Kepple gave a nervous grin. "I like to think I do my job efficiently."

He didn't have that much authority around the place but someone seemed to believe he had, so why spoil their illusions.

"It hasn't gone unnoticed, Mr. Kepple. All the way to the top."

It was not very often Kepple received any praise for his work.

"Hey, you want a cup of tea? Coffee? I know you Yanks... Americans...prefer coffee."

"Yeah, why not, and the name's Ryan."

Kepple turned to the unit in the corner of the office where he kept the makings, switching on a plastic kettle. "Be a couple of minutes."

Bolan had settled himself by the desk, leaning against it. He appeared relaxed, studying the layout of the office. "Quiet around here."

"Oh, yeah," Kepple said. "Weekend, see. We don't operate weekends. Old traditions die hard in this part of the country. Half day Saturday. Sunday all day. Day of rest and all that stuff. We have to keep a low profile. Look suspicious to the locals if we didn't. And we don't want that, do we?"

"Hey, good thinking, Ray."

Kepple handed the visitor a mug of black coffee. The American took it, sampling the strong brew.

"Sorry it's instant. Don't run to fresh roast hereabouts. Yes, I keep my eye on the place. I mean, there's a lot of expensive vehicles back there in the yard. Mr. Chambers gets twitchy. Especially after all that bloody stuff in Holland. You understand."

"One of the reasons I've been sent over. No disrespect, Mr. Kepple, but there's a lot riding on keeping the operations running smooth. That's my job. Overseeing security. So I can report back to the man at the top and let him know he ain't got anything to worry about. If he's kept happy we can *all* be happy."

"Chambers said they're letting things cool for a while. No more shipments until we get the word again. Keep the place looking normal. No unnecessary activity."

"That's good," Bolan said. He placed his mug on the desk. "I need to let that cool. Now, you want to give me the guided tour? I can't see any problems here but we'd better do this right. You run a tight ship, Ray, I can see that." Kepple nodded. "Between you and me I just want to do my job and get back to London. Young lady waiting for me there and I wouldn't want to leave her standing, if you know what I mean."

"I understand."

"Look, just take me on a quick walk around the freight yard. I'll take a few pictures with my digital camera and report back when I get back to the city. Give you a good write-up."

Kepple stubbed out his cigarette, nodding enthusiastically. "Where do you want to start?"

"The yard is monitored? Cameras and stuff?"

"That's right."

Kepple led him through to the office, to another room where the security setup was housed. It was an air-conditioned control center where a bank of monitors relayed images from the freight yard. It was an expensive assembly.

"Digital cameras," Kepple explained. "Recorded so we can check back if we spot anything suspicious. Cameras are infrared so they can see in the dark. Bloody clever stuff."

"You said it, buddy. And you're the man in charge of all this? Impressive stuff, Ray."

"The freight yard is fenced all around. Steel embedded in concrete. There are even motion sensors on the gates and fences, so anyone trying to break in will set the alarms off. Now, in most cases the security system would be linked to the local cops. But it could prove embarrassing if they turned up and found *merchandise* on the premises. Chambers would go crazy if that happened. So would Canfield. We keep security in-house. If it's broken it's linked to the main office in London."

"Wise move, Ray."

Kepple led the way through a solid door at the back of the control center that opened on to the freight yard. The wide concrete area held a dozen of the distinctive South East Container rigs. All were locked. As they walked down the line of vehicles Bolan nodded his approval. He spent some time taking photographs with the compact camera he had produced from his suit jacket.

At the edge of the yard was the long, low-rise warehouse. "Your hospitality suite in there?" Bolan asked, grinning.

"Only ones who know are those involved in the business. Rest of the work staff are involved in packing and loading. We run a produce setup. Bring in stuff from Europe and ship throughout the U.K. The routine business, if you know what I mean. We have a five-star setup. Soundproof. Isolated. There's a false wall so that the day employees know nothing about it. The special deliveries are off-loaded at night when the day shift has gone."

He was warming to his subject now. Pleased to have someone around who seemed to appreciate what he did.

"Hell of a lot more fun than lugging crates of food around," the big American said.

"Well, I like to think of the merchandise as vegetables on legs," Kepple said, grinning expansively. "Expensive, but still bloody vegetables."

He wasn't looking at Bolan as he spoke, which was a good thing. If he had seen the ice-chip expression in the American's eyes he would have had doubts concerning his own life expectancy.

As they returned to the control room, Bolan walked beside Kepple.

"Great job you're doing here, Ray. When the big man gets my report he's liable to send you a bonus. I'm going to recommend that. I were you, though, I wouldn't let on to Chambers I said so. Don't want him grabbing all the glory when you're the man holding all this together. In fact Canfield said not to mention this visit to him at all. After what happened in Holland Chambers isn't what you'd call flavor of the month. You understand?"

"I know what you mean," Kepple said, inwardly pleased that Chambers was out of favor.

Bolan took a final look around, pretending to be suitably impressed. "If anyone did get in here could they disable the security system?" he asked.

"There's a master override that shuts the whole thing down, but it's in that box on the wall and it won't open unless I use my key."

"I hope you look after that key, Ray, my man."

"Always have it with me."

"So, you man the ship all night?"

"Today and Sunday. Never get any visitors over the weekend. Not even Chambers. He likes to live it up in London."

"Doesn't it get lonely?"

"I'm okay with that. I have my radio. That's all I need. My shift ends at 6:00 a.m. Monday Day crew comes on then. Drivers arrive at seven. Then I get to go home. Nice long break."

Back in the office Bolan picked up his mug and drank the rest of his coffee. He turned to Kepple and shook his hand. The American's big hand swamped Kepple's.

"Good job, Ray. I can tell the boss man things are running real smooth here. It's important right now. Lot of money at stake so it's reassuring to know the man in charge has it all tied down. You take it easy."

Kepple watched the American return to his car and drive away. As the vehicle coasted along the straight, flat road he rolled himself another cigarette, lit it and sat back behind his desk.

He wondered if the man had been telling the truth about a bonus. It would be nice if he did get something. He would keep that to himself. If Chambers learned about it he would moan and bitch. The man was a mean bastard. Liked to believe he was the smart one. Maybe this time it wouldn't be so.

Maybe this time it would be Ray Kepple who got the surprise.

13

Ray Kepple received his surprise far sooner than expected. And it was not in the form he had anticipated.

It came dressed in black. Armed. Carrying a heavy nylon bag, and made an appearance just after midnight.

Kepple, in the front office, had just fixed himself another mug of tea. From the control room behind him the plaintive wail of a female singer drifted through the open door. The lyrics told of her disappointment with her boyfriend who had run off with another woman, leaving her brokenhearted.

Give me ten minutes with you, love, and I'd change your mind, Kepple thought.

He chuckled at his own thoughts, picked up his steaming mug and crossed to the office door, unlocking it to step outside for a breath of fresh air. There was a full moon, casting pale light, and it was warm, surprisingly so for the late hour. Kepple knew he didn't make it any easier on himself with his constant smoking. The office reeked of stale tobacco. He had smoked since his fourteenth birthday, couldn't quit if he wanted to, but even he had to admit his habit did little to enhance the confined area in the office. He never smoked in the control room. He kept the place clean because Chambers would lose it if his precious, cutting-edge security system became tainted. And Kepple didn't like the chill, conditioned air. He had spent the past hour in the place, staring at monitors that never changed, and he decided he needed a mug of tea, a sandwich from his lunch box and a smoke.

He placed his mug on the office windowsill, pulled the makings from his pocket and proceeded to make a cigarette. As he wet the strip of paper something moved on his extreme left. It was only a fleeting shadow on the periphery of his vision. Kepple glanced in that direction and saw nothing but the sway of tall grass at the edge of the concrete apron near the road. He shrugged and returned to his cigarette. About to light it Kepple felt certain he saw something again.

"Bloody hell, son, you're jumping at shadows," he said out loud.

He lit the cigarette and took a deep pull on it. A moment later the smoke caught in his throat and he almost choked, coughing harshly. The cold press of hard metal against the side of his head was the cause. Kepple didn't need to be told what it was.

The muzzle of a gun was pressing hard enough to cause some discomfort.

"Ray, those cigarettes are not doing you any good," a soft voice said. "Are you carrying a weapon?"

"A what? A gun? No."

"Let's go back inside."

Kepple sucked frantically on the cigarette. He turned to walk back into the office. He stood just inside the office when he heard the door close and the lock click shut.

"Go sit down."

Before he turned around Kepple's suspicions were confirmed. He knew the voice.

Ryan.

The American who had visited him earlier. Supposedly one of Canfield's people. The man was a fraud. Nothing to do with the company and he had checked out the set up simply for a return visit.

The suit was gone. Now the big American was dressed all in black. He had a large black nylon bag dangling from his left hand.

"You bastard," Kepple said.

The American hefted the bag and dropped it on Kepple's desk.

"We were getting on well last time I was here, Ray. I thought we had something going on."

"I don't like being made to look a bloody fool. Jesus, Chambers will tear my bloody heart out if I let you—"

The big man gestured with the pistol. "Empty your pockets. Everything on the desk."

The Executioner watched Kepple turn out his pockets. He picked up the bunch of keys, weighing them in his hand.

"Sit down, Kepple." All friendliness was gone. "I want you to pass along a message to Chambers and Canfield. It's for both of them. Tell them their time is running out. Tell them it might be easier of they took the quick way out, because when I'm done there isn't going to be a damn thing left."

Slumped in his chair Kepple wondered what the American had planned for him. He understood now what the earlier visit had been for. The man had been checking the place out prior to this return visit. Learning how the security system worked, finding out how long Kepple would be on his own. And he, fooled by the man, had shown him around the control center, telling him exactly how to immobilize the system.

Kepple knew something else. This man was Cooper, the one who had been wreaking havoc around Rotterdam.

Bolan pressed the muzzle of the pistol against the side of Kepple's skull. With his free hand he produced plastic ties from a pocket of his blacksuit.

"Hands behind you," he said.

Bolan made sure Kepple's hands were threaded through the wooden slats in the chair, looped one of the ties over his wrists and pulled it tight. Then he secured Kepple's ankles to the chair legs.

"Hey, my wrists hurt," Kepple protested.

Bolan stood back, holstering his pistol. When he looked down at Kepple his face was impassive.

"If you were one of your 'vegetables on legs' you wouldn't feel a thing. Isn't that what you tell yourself?"

Kepple stayed silent this time. He had decided his survival was in his own hands. Antagonizing this man would not be a wise move. There was nothing he could do, so he kept his mouth shut.

The Executioner picked up the bag and moved into the control room. He checked the bunch of keys and selected one. It didn't fit the wall box. Bolan tried two more before the lock turned. He opened the door and checked the internal panel. Simple enough. He threw the cancel switch. When he turned to check the monitor bank the screens were blank. He moved to the telephone connections and pulled the lines from the wall sockets.

Kepple had said that the security system was linked to the London office. It wouldn't take long for someone to realize the link had gone down. Once that was certified, action would be taken. Before that happened Bolan would be long gone.

He pushed open the control-center door leading into the freight yard. His targets were the parked rigs and the warehouse behind. Bolan wasted little time. He moved along the line of vehicles, attaching a Semtex block to the underside of each of the trucks.

As Len Watts had told him the Semtex blocks were fitted with electronic detonators that would respond to the handheld activation unit he carried. As each block was fixed Bolan pressed the small button that primed the detonator, a red light winking to show it was ready.

From the trucks Bolan made his way to the warehouse building. One of the keys from Kepple's bunch opened the small side door. It didn't take Bolan long to find the "hospitality suite" at the far end of the building, concealed behind its false wall. Inside he found primitive living quarters equipped with basic wooden cots. The front wall was built from steel bars with a single door set in it. The place hadn't been cleaned for some time and Bolan could only imagine how the captive occupants must have felt. He placed one of his blocks through the bars, sliding it across the floor, then as he worked his way back to the exit he laid down his remaining explosive blocks. The final pack was placed near the fuel pumps. Dropping the nylon bag Bolan returned to where he had started, across the freight yard and through to the office where Kepple was making halfhearted attempts to free himself.

"You can't fucking do this," Kepple yelled. "Don't you realize how big Canfield is? The man will—"

"If he's half as smart as everyone keeps telling me, he'll cut and run. But I don't think he is all that smart," Bolan said.

"You really think you can get away with this?"

"Let's see," Bolan said. He walked out of the office.

At the point where the concrete apron met the road Bolan took the handheld unit from his pocket. The first key he pressed powered the unit. The second activated the detonation units fixed to the Semtex blocks, and the third started the timers. Bolan had set them for four minutes. Enough for him to get well clear.

He'd parked his rental car a hundred yards down the road. The Executioner pulled on the jacket he had dropped on the seat, fired up the engine and swung the car around, starting his drive back toward his hotel. The roads were quiet. Bolan saw no other vehicles as he cruised steadily away from South East Containers.

The explosions rocked the countryside. They detonated almost in unison, some after a microsecond delay. Overall it was like a single, massive blast that rippled and echoed. Bright fireballs rose into the night sky, expanding and shooting fire and smoke into the sky. Bolan slowed, leaning out of his window to look back as the destruction of Canfield's fleet took place. He felt the aftershock of the explosions rock his vehicle. Seconds later he heard the patter of debris fall to earth. The rumble of the blasts went on for some time, fading as Bolan drove on.

He settled back in the seat, his mind already locked on to the next phase in his systematic takedown of Venturer Exports.

14

"Tell me something positive," Hugo Canfield raged, facing the men sitting across the conference table. "I do not want an itemized list of the vehicles that were destroyed. Or an estimate of the damned cost."

No one spoke because they had no positive input to deliver.

"One man. One fucking man. And he is making fools of us all. The operation in Holland has been severely compromised. Now our transport was blown to hell while we were sitting back doing nothing."

From the end of the conference table someone spoke up. "Ray Kepple wasn't injured…"

The speaker's voice trailed off into an embarrassed silence as he realized the ineffectual content of his remark, and it became very quiet in the room.

"The fact that Kepple wasn't injured tends to make me think he wasn't doing his job properly. Think back to the fact that he took Cooper on a guided tour of the freight yard only hours before the bastard came back and blew it up." Canfield slammed his hand down on the table. "How did that happen? Cooper just walks in and presents himself as part of our operation and Kepple falls for it. Someone please tell me where we get these people?"

"Chambers hired him," one of Canfield's lieutenants, a lean, eager-faced young man named Travis said. "Kepple oversaw the site on weekends."

"Why is it every time I hear that name just lately I get a

queasy feeling. It was Chambers who screwed up trying to take care of Cooper in Rotterdam. Now his operation here goes up in smoke. Tell me where that walking disaster is right now."

"We, er, well, we can't seem to locate him, sir," Travis admitted. "He's somewhere in the city."

Canfield didn't speak for a while, leaving the gathering in uncomfortable silence until Travis spoke up again.

"I'll get some people on that right away, Mr. Canfield."

Canfield cleared his throat. "Do that. When you get your hands on him I want him here. I want it done discreetly. Make him realize this isn't a request, it's a fucking order. And I also want Kepple taken care of. He is superfluous to requirements and stupidity of the degree he's shown requires stamping on. The thought crossed my mind that the local police may be conducting a detailed investigation and they might be liaising with that bloody task force. If Kepple sees an opportunity to make a deal he might decide to cooperate to save his own bloody skin." Canfield let the words sink in. "Are we clear on this? It only takes a small stone to create ever-widening ripples."

"Are we still going to slow operations down?" Travis asked.

"I'm debating that. This Cooper seems to be concentrating his attention on Europe and now the U.K. Until we sort out this mess I'm considering stopping our trade here. The U.S. and Asia haven't been targeted yet so let's maintain those areas."

In Canfield's mind he was hearing the message Cooper had instructed Kepple to pass along.

Tell Canfield his time is running low. He should take the easy way out.

He couldn't wipe it away and it irritated him.

"One more thing, sir," Travis said. "There is a shipment due to arrive from Thailand. On the *Orient Venturer.* It will dock tomorrow afternoon unless we act."

Canfield sat back, gently drumming his fingers on the conference table. "I need some time to decide on matters. This meeting is adjourned," he said while nodding at Travis.

Everyone stood and filed out. Travis got as far as the door before closing it and turning back into the office.

"Sit down, Clive," Canfield said. "Glad you mentioned that incoming shipment. I think we need to do something about it fairly quickly."

"It came to me, sir, that because of what this man Cooper has been doing, the authorities may be renewing their interest in our business. Even if we got word to our man in the local customs-and-excise division he might not be able to prevent the ship being searched."

"Precisely, Clive. Of course, if they did make a search and there was nothing but the regular cargo on board…"

"No special cargo, no proof."

"Pity to have to lose that consignment. The Thai girls are high earners."

Travis shrugged. "There's a plentiful supply, sir."

"Exactly."

Travis crossed to a framed map on the wall. He tapped it with his finger.

"Pretty deep water where the ship is right now."

"Wouldn't be the first time a container got lost at sea," Canfield said.

"No time like the present, sir," Travis said reaching for the satellite phone on the table. He tapped in a number and waited until the call was answered.

Canfield took the phone, acknowledging the identification of the ship's captain.

"Canfield," he said. "Are you running to schedule? Good. I heard you've had troubled waters. All clear now? That's fine, Captain Muren. I hope the rest of your trip goes well. Goodbye." Replacing the phone Canfield returned to sit behind his own desk. "Problem solved, Clive."

AFTER TRAVIS HAD GONE Canfield smiled to himself.

Troubled waters.

Two simple words. In this case it was a prearranged signal that told whoever received it to dispose of any special cargo they were carrying. Venturer Exports had used the order a number of times when unexpected problems came up. There were no exceptions to the rule. If a threat appeared and there was time to implement the command it was issued quickly. The loss of cargo, financially, was to be avoided if possible, but if circumstances deemed so it was put into action without further thought.

There's a plentiful supply, sir.

Travis had put it plain and simple. In Canfield's business the supply of human fodder was limitless—and so, too, were the customers.

15

Ray Kepple shook his head in frustration, trying to work out where the contents of the bottle had gone. He brought it closer, staring at it with blurred eyes. He couldn't recall having downed the half bottle so quickly. Despite his condition he decided that he must have drunk the stuff. The problem was he could remember *why* he had been drinking.

The freight yard and the warehouse. Those bloody awful explosions after the man called Cooper had gone, leaving him tied to his office chair. The blasts, seeming to go on forever, had destroyed the fleet of trucks and reduced the warehouse to rubble. The force of the blast had demolished most of the control center and had blown Kepple's chair, with him tied to it, across the office. He had lain there, stunned, clothing and skin scorched, deafened by the blasts, barely able to move. Following the explosions and the rain of debris falling back to earth there was a lot of smoke. It drifted into his office and Kepple could smell the acrid tang. As his hearing returned he picked up the crackling of flames.

Cooper had done a real number on the yard.

Kepple was able to see why the man had been so effective in Holland, running rings around everyone. He wasn't held back by rules and regulations. He chose his targets, checked them out and went directly for them. Not like the cops and their pals on the task force. Cooper, whoever he was, got results.

When Paul Chambers turned up to inspect the damage he

had exploded with rage. His mood ranged from disbelief to incandescent fury. Ray Kepple was his main target. He blamed him for everything, including the weather. When Kepple pointed out that it had been Chambers's idea to keep the place low-key over the weekend the man almost lost it. He had to be careful because the police and fire crews were still around, poking and prying, asking questions. It had been a difficult time. Chambers had maintained that the explosions had been the work of a rival group who wanted to take over the business. The cops were skeptical, but when Canfield's lawyers arrived, backed up by orders from on high, the local authorities had to back off. Canfield, as usual, had used his influence to have the investigation stalled. It wouldn't last forever, but any delay would give Canfield and his backers time to negotiate themselves out from under. Even so it was a nervous time for Chambers and Kepple.

Later, when they were alone, Chambers had turned on Kepple again. He raged back and forth, venting his anger, and continued his verbal attack on Kepple until the man, driven to fighting back, told Chambers what he and Canfield could do with his job if they didn't like what had happened. He delivered Cooper's message with relish, enjoying the look on Chambers's face. Then he walked away from Chambers with a final wild threat that suggested if anyone did come asking questions he might reveal just what South East Containers had been doing because he wasn't carrying the can for it all.

Chambers had worked out his rage, eventually retreating to his car and driving off, leaving Kepple to survey the damage before using his cell phone to summon a taxi to take him home. His vehicle had been destroyed in the explosion and Kepple didn't think he had much chance of getting Chambers or Canfield to replace it.

He questioned the wisdom of the outburst as he rode home, but his resolve to not be made the scapegoat for Cooper's attack stayed strong. Later, alone in his house, drinking heavily, Kepple admitted to himself he had been careless. Chambers would do his best to shrug off responsibility, leaving Kepple high and dry. Hugo Canfield worried Kepple more than Chambers. He had only met the man once when Chambers had brought him to look over the site. That had been enough. The man frightened him. He didn't like Canfield but he respected the man's power and influence. Someone like Ray Kepple was unimportant to Canfield. Simply an employee paid to do a fairly menial task in Canfield's eyes. And someone who could be disposed of without much concern.

Kepple sat up. He was sure he had heard a noise outside the house. Moments later he sank back in the armchair, waving a dismissive hand. He had imagined the noise. If he hadn't it was most likely a stray cat or dog nosing around the trash can. He decided another glass of whiskey would send all the noises away. Before he had time to fill his glass he heard the noise again, and this time he didn't dismiss it. He placed the bottle and glass aside and hauled himself up out of the chair, swaying unsteadily.

"Bloody strays," he muttered, the words slurred. "I'll fix you bastards."

He stumbled toward the kitchen door, pushing it open and reaching for the light switch. As light flooded the kitchen Kepple realized two things.

The back door was open. And there was a dark-clad figure facing him.

Kepple's vision was a little blurred but he felt sure he knew the man. He tried to focus. When he managed to bring the figure into sharp relief he saw he had been right. He did know the man.

Canfield's minder. The one they called Sergeant Gantley. Ex-military copper. A big, powerful man. Broad across the shoulders and chest. Walked as though he was still on the drill field.

Gantley stood there and reminded Kepple of some immovable statue. He wore a black coat over a thick black sweater. And there were thin black leather gloves over his large fists.

"What are you doing here?" Kepple asked.

The question sounded superfluous. But Kepple didn't want to admit he knew what Gantley was there for.

Kepple turned, seeking refuge away from the man. His alcoholic stupor slowed him.

Gantley, moving swiftly for a man of his size, reached out and caught hold of Kepple by the collar of his shirt. He pulled the wriggling, sobbing man to him, and spun him around.

Kepple didn't even see the first blow coming. He just felt it as Gantley's massive fist smashed into his face. The powerful blow drove his head back, knocking his skull against the door frame. The black-leathered fist began to repeatedly pummel Kepple's face, crushing bone and tearing flesh. It didn't stop until Kepple, unconscious, hung from his hand.

Gantley let Kepple fall to the kitchen floor, turning him over onto his stomach with his foot. Then he bent over the inert form, took Kepple's head in his gloved hands and wrenched it savagely, hearing the neck snap.

When Gantley straightened up there was a contented smile on his face. It had been some time since he had killed a man with his bare hands. It was a satisfactory act for him. Any fool could kill with a gun or knife. He preferred this way. It still gave him a thrill.

Crossing the kitchen he rinsed the blood off his gloves under the faucet. Then he left the house by the kitchen door, closing it behind him. He returned to his car the same way he had approached the isolated house, crossing a field and walking through a small stand of trees. He climbed into the car and drove away from Kepple's house, using only his side lights, along the quiet lane, following it until he reached the main road. Forty minutes later he merged with the freeway traffic heading in the direction of London. When he reached the city he drove directly to his apartment block. Inside he changed his clothes, throwing what he had worn into his washing machine and switched it on. While the clothes were washed Gantley made himself a mug of tea, into which he poured a generous slug of whiskey. He watched a couple of hours of TV, then turned in for the night.

WHEN HE ENTERED Hugo Canfield's office the following day, around noon, at the Canary Wharf headquarters, Gantley saw that his employer had a visitor.

Canfield glanced across the office, over Paul Chambers's shoulder, meeting Gantley's gaze. Gantley merely nodded. It was all Canfield needed in the way of explanation.

"Sergeant Gantley," he said, "would you have the car ready for me in ten minutes? I want to go direct to the airfield. Make sure the plane is ready for takeoff."

"Of course, sir."

Gantley stepped out of the office and closed the door, leaving Canfield to deal with Chambers.

16

As soon as Gantley closed the door Hugo Canfield picked up his conversation.

"When I said back off, Paul, I didn't suggest taking everyone away and leaving the place wide open."

"It wasn't like that," Chambers protested. "We always scale things down at weekends. It would have looked odd if there had been extra activity. The site was well covered by the security system. How was I to know Kepple would let that bastard just waltz in and take a look around? I mean, we hadn't seen or heard from him since that last incident in Rotterdam. I figured he'd up and moved on."

"Too bloody right, Paul. He moved on here. You made a bad call, don't you think? Not the first you've made recently. Rotterdam. Bickell dead. The fucking farm. You handled it all carelessly. If Cooper had died the day he was supposed to we wouldn't be having our current crop of problems. Kepple was your responsibility. You hired the man. Not me."

"Now wait a damn minute. I hope you don't hold me responsible for everything that went wrong over there. The farm getting hit, van Ryden, DeChambre. Bloody hell, Hugo, I'll hold up my hands as far as Kepple is concerned but not for things that were nothing to do with me. I can't be expected to be in every place at the same time."

Chambers was almost shouting at the end of his protest,

then saw the hard expression on Canfield's face. He had gone a step too far.

Chambers became aware of the tense atmosphere in the room. He felt Canfield's animosity toward him and the first feelings of apprehension began to make themselves known. In the past he had always felt comfortable being around Canfield, despite the man's reputation. Canfield was all-powerful, almost arrogant in his dealings with others. That had never worried Paul Chambers. Since joining Venturer Exports his own standing had risen and he moved in wealthier circles, being introduced to a number of Canfield's associates. Now, doubt manifested itself and Chambers's nervousness showed as his hand trembled slightly, the contents in his glass shaking.

If Canfield noticed he said nothing as he crossed the room and refilled his own tumbler, savoring the aroma of the aged whiskey. In fact, he was enjoying the moment—letting Chambers sweat. The man deserved to be upset. His stupidity had cost the Organization dearly, and that was something Hugo Canfield could never forgive. It was bad enough they had lost cargo, money and facilities. With the multinational task force still hovering in the wings, just waiting to pounce, anything that drew their closer attention should have been avoided. Chambers had jeopardized Venturer Exports. He was going to have to pay for that.

"Hugo, let me put things right," Chambers said in an attempt to smooth things over. "I made mistakes. I've lost out, as well. South East Containers was my business, too. How do you think I feel about that? I'll make sure Kepple doesn't get away with what he's done."

His words had the sound of desperation. Chambers was floundering. He was aware he had committed a grave error and was eager to try and make reparation. He had no chance of doing that. In purely financial terms the cost of replacing the truck fleet was far beyond his means. Canfield could have made good the loss, but that was not the problem. It was less about the money, more about the damage to Canfield's reputation and his standing in the eyes of his influential friends. He would, of course, play down the events for his contacts. It would take some doing but Hugo Canfield was confident he could overcome the recent setbacks.

Chambers was another matter. His failure left Canfield only one course of action. Chambers could not be trusted any longer. The man had to be eliminated. Just as Kepple had been dealt with. More work for the dependable Sergeant Gantley. There, at least, was a man Canfield could depend on. There were never any doubts in Canfield's mind once he sent Gantley out. His decision made he moved on mentally, turning his attention back to Chambers in order to dismiss the man.

"I need to consider how to handle things, Paul. I need to get to Banecreif. I'll call you tomorrow. Go back to your apartment and stay put until you hear from me."

The dismissal was final. Chambers knew not to argue. He emptied his glass and stood. Canfield was already concentrating on another piece of business, as if Chambers had already left the room.

In the elevator on his way to the ground floor Paul Chambers went over the meeting. He was left with no doubt that any decision Canfield made would not be pleasant—for Chambers.

Outside the building Chambers saw Canfield's Bentley parked close by. The solid figure of Gantley was standing beside the car. Chambers had always found the ex-military cop slightly menacing.

When Gantley caught Chambers's eye he inclined his head, watching closely. There was a hint of a knowing smile on his lips.

Chambers walked to his own car, searching for his keys and actually fumbling them from his pocket. He pressed the button that unlocked the door and slid behind the wheel, jamming the key in and firing up the engine. Without looking back he knew that Gantley was still watching. Chambers pushed the stick into first, let out the clutch too quickly and stalled, the car jumping. Swearing Chambers restarted the car, managing to pull away on the second attempt. He didn't let out a breath until the office block had vanished from sight among the other tall Canary Wharf buildings.

He had a twenty-minute drive across the city to his apartment and Chambers felt every minute of the trip. The sheer volume of traffic forced him to drive slowly, stopping and starting every few yards. He hated driving in London. The place was becoming gridlocked. Worse every time he visited.

Still a distance from his destination Chambers's in-car phone rang. He pressed the hands-free button.

"Yes?"

"Paul, it's Greg."

"If it's more bad news I'm not really interested."

"I think you need to hear this, Paul. It's about Ray Kepple."

"Kepple? What's he fucking done now? Burned down the village pub?"

"He's dead, Paul. Someone broke into his place last night and beat him to death. Really did a job on him. He was barely recognizable. Face was caved in. He actually died from having his neck snapped."

Chambers was driving on autopilot, his gaze fixed on the car in front. He was recalling Canfield's cold attitude toward him during their office meeting. The indifference. The curt dismissal. And then the glimpse of Gantley outside the building. The quiet look that spoke volumes.

Gantley.

Hugo Canfield's minder.

Gantley looked after Canfield and also handed out punishment to anyone stepping out of line.

Canfield would have wanted the ultimate price for

Kepple's misconduct. Damn the man. He had allowed Chambers to ramble on about how he would discipline Kepple even while he had known Gantley had already done the job. And he hadn't even considered letting Chambers in on the matter.

"Paul, are you still there?"

The moment passed. Chambers took a breath.

"I heard, Greg. I don't suppose anyone saw or heard anything?"

"Nothing. Not surprising with Kepple living where he did. His closest neighbor was a quarter mile away."

"Local police handling it?"

"Yeah."

"Okay. We have to stay out of it. Let them screw around all they want."

Chambers severed the connection.

A cold sweat broke out on his forehead as he found himself reliving that moment when Gantley offered him that hint of a smile. He knew now exactly what it meant. Gantley had him on his list. Kepple's error had earned him a painful death. Now he was on the list. With everything falling down before his eyes Canfield was cleaning up loose ends. Making sure his surviving team was composed of strong people. He wanted the defaulters out of the picture. Weakness in one area could lead to weakness in others. Canfield would want to make sure there were no loose mouths left open.

The sound of someone hammering on a car horn startled Chambers. He snatched at the wheel and brought his car back into its own lane. He had let it wander. He hit the air-conditioning button, letting the cool air wash over his face. He realized his hands were shaking as they gripped the wheel.

Jesus, Paul, wake up. Clear your mind. Don't let the bastards do this to you, he told himself.

Chambers almost missed his apartment building. He had to

stamp on the brake, causing other drivers to swerve and give him the finger as he ignored them and swung into the parking lot.

He went into the apartment building and took an elevator up to his floor. As he walked along the thickly carpeted corridor, the cathedral silence of the place made him even more nervous. He had never noticed before how quiet the upper floor was. He looked back over his shoulder a couple of times, shaking his head when he realized what he had done.

Get a grip.

He slid the key into the lock and worked the handle. The door opened and he stepped inside. As the door swung shut behind him Chambers froze on the spot.

He was not alone.

He saw a tall figure, dressed in black pants and a leather jacket.

A lethal-looking auto pistol in his right hand was pointing at Chambers's heart.

"You were out, so I decided to stay around and wait," the man said. "I think you should sit down, Chambers. You don't look too well."

17

Paul Chambers decided his life was falling apart. The mistakes he had recently made, Canfield's loss of faith in him and the unspoken threat posed by Gantley—things could not get worse.

Then he realized he was wrong about that, too.

"I… How the hell did you get into my apartment?"

"You've got more important things to consider," the Executioner said.

Chambers paled at the implication behind Bolan's words. He looked around the room as if he had never been in it before, finally locating a chair. He sat down, rubbing a hand across his very dry mouth.

"What do you want? Haven't you already done enough?"

"You remember how this all started? You, me, in Rotterdam. The last thing you said to me was that I wouldn't get to see the sights. Wrong, Chambers. I've been seeing sights since then. None of them very pleasant. Innocent women and children caged up. Waiting to be sold like meat so you and your partners can turn a tidy profit. So scum like you can stay in an apartment like this. Must make you feel all warm inside."

"It's a business. We supply a hungry market, Cooper. And it's growing. What makes you think *you* can shut it all down?"

"You'll have to wait and see about that."

"So what do you want from me?" Chambers's growing fear spilled over, his voice rising to a high shrill sound. "Damn you, Cooper, your fucking hits against us have put me in the firing line. Canfield has more or less hinted I'm on my way out. He holds me responsible. Remember Kepple? Canfield had him killed. He sent his trained dog, Gantley, to beat Kepple to a pulp, then snap his neck. And it looks like I could be next. Gantley will be coming after me. Canfield is launching a tidy-up campaign. Cutting out what he thinks is dead wood…"

Bolan's face remained impassive. Whatever trouble Chambers had got himself into made little difference to the Executioner. His business pushed him outside the limits for redemption. There was no get-out clause for a man like Paul Chambers. By the very nature of his employment he was already in Bolan's sights.

"Look, I can give you information. But I want protection. I don't give a bloody damn what you think of me. I want to survive. We can trade," Chambers pleaded.

"Trade what?"

"Canfield is moving into something different. To add to his business dealings. A new venture."

"I don't expect it to be legal," Bolan said.

"Drugs. He's struck a deal with a Russian supplier. Opium from Afghanistan. Had a big consignment delivered a few days ago to his place up in Scotland."

"Where?"

"Canfield has an old house. Massive place. Pretty isolated. Up on the northeast coast. House is called Banecreif." Chambers rubbed his dry mouth. "I need a drink."

Bolan gestured in the direction of the bottles on a side table. Chambers picked up a whiskey and splashed it into a glass. He swallowed the contents in a single gulp and immediately poured a second.

"Well? Do we have a deal?"

"I'll let you know when we're in sight of Banecreif," Bolan said.

Chambers laughed and downed his second whiskey.

"You actually think I'm going to Scotland with you in tow? I might be desperate but I'm not suicidal."

"And do I look like I just came off the farm? Your choice, Chambers. You're my point man on this, or I walk out that door and you're on your own."

Chambers did some fast thinking. At least with Cooper at his side he might have a chance of staying alive. On his own, with Gantley hunting him, he had little chance. Paul Chambers had never considered himself a capable man in a fight. He always paid others to work violence for him and watch his back. Like it or not, the tall American holding the gun would seem the most likely man to prevent anything happening to him, and if Cooper managed to put Canfield down Chambers could take his chances. It wasn't foolproof but it was better than being on his own and waiting for Gantley to show, because sooner or later Canfield's trained dog would slip his leash and come looking.

"Okay, Cooper. I can't say it's what I'd choose if I had any other options. Only I don't. So we go together."

AN HOUR LATER Bolan accompanied Paul Chambers from his apartment. They picked up the rental car Bolan had left in the parking garage and drove across the city to London's Euston Station where they boarded the train that would take them to Scotland. The train would terminate in Glasgow and Bolan would pick up another that ran up country, his destination the far northeast of Scotland, taking him closer to Canfield's remote lair.

As they settled in the private compartment Bolan had requested when he had booked their passage, the Executioner was aware of his companion's nervous condition.

"Chambers, sit down and relax."

"Easy for you to say. Christ, I'm a walking dead man. That bastard wants me buried. If Gantley is looking for me the far north of Tibet won't be far enough away."

Bolan stowed his bag on the overhead luggage rack. He wasn't happy having to walk around with a cache of weapons but the situation called for extreme actions. Heading for Hugo Canfield's base he was not going in empty-handed.

"Right now we're ahead of the game. If we can stay that way there's a chance we might come through," he told Chambers.

"That's bloody pessimistic. 'Might come through?'"

"It's called being realistic. I don't guarantee anything, Chambers. Every situation like this comes with a fifty-fifty chance of survival. I accept that."

"Maybe you do. I figure those to be poor odds. Why the hell should I be in a mess like that?"

Bolan moved so fast Chambers had no chance to step aside. He felt a big hand close on his shirtfront. Bolan slammed him up against the compartment wall, the impact making Chambers gasp for breath. He found himself staring directly into chilled blue eyes.

"Quick to forget what you're involved in? Chambers, you trade in human lives. You buy and sell women and kids. Send them into virtual slavery. Into lives of sheer misery. The money in your wallet comes from the depravity some of those people have to endure. One of your own kind has turned on you and now you expect sympathy. Are you expecting me to forget what you do and hold your hand? Be thankful I don't pull out my gun and put a bullet through your head. Now sit down and shut up."

Bolan released his hold, allowing Chambers to shrink away from him. Chambers moved to one of the seats and pressed himself into the corner, staring out the window in cowed silence.

"THEY'RE ON A TRAIN for Glasgow," Canfield's man said from a pay phone at Euston Station. "I sent Breck and Munro after them. If they get the opportunity Cooper and Chambers won't even reach the Scottish border."

"If they do, at least we know they're coming," Gantley said. "Keep me informed, Harris."

Gantley put down the phone and turned to Canfield.

"Cooper's on his way. He's got Chambers with him, sir. They left London on a train for Glasgow. Breck and Munro are on board, as well. They might get the chance to intercept and deal with them."

"Hopefully we could be spared the need to expect them showing up here. If they *do* survive it still gives us time to arrange a welcome for them. Sergeant Gantley, don't bother to get any rooms ready. Cooper won't be staying long."

"Just a quick visit, then, sir?"

Canfield smiled.

"Very brief. Painful and brief. Especially for Chambers. Didn't take him long to change sides."

"I should have got to him sooner, sir. Before he could open his mouth to Cooper."

"One way or another Mr. Paul Chambers is going to find it's a very small world, Sergeant Gantley. One where he can't run away and hide."

"Yes, sir."

The ex-military cop finished pouring the whiskey. He sealed the bottle and placed it back on the wet bar. Without a word he placed the tumbler within Canfield's reach and left the room, closing the door quietly behind him.

Canfield picked up the tumbler, raised it to drink, then paused. His gaze turned hard, eyes gleaming as he struggled with the turmoil inside his head. Too much was happening that was causing him aggravation. When he'd retreated to Banecreif he expected a calm and restful time. Canfield hurled the thick tumbler into the wide stone fireplace. The glass shattered and the whiskey flared as the flames engulfed it.

"Damn you to bloody hell, Cooper," he said. "Damn you for making me feel like this in my own house."

On his feet he strode to the glass-fronted gun cabinet. He opened the doors and reached for a racked Franchi-SPAS shotgun. The weapon, customized for him in London, was finely balanced. The SPAS was a formidable tool in Canfield's expert hands. He liked hunting with the shotgun even though it was not primarily a sporting gun. When he turned it on either Cooper or Chambers there would be no hint of sport in his actions. This time around his targets would have a special significance.

He wanted the pair dead and buried and he cherished the hope that they actually got through to Banecreif. If his men on the train failed to stop them, Canfield could look forward to handling the matter himself.

Especially Cooper, the man responsible for so much death and destruction. He was the reason for the fragmenting of Hugo Canfield's organized and well-oiled machine. Because of Cooper, Canfield had lost merchandise, money and people. His reputation had been tarnished and so had his credibility. If the news spread to his potential new partners it might sour their decision to do business with him. Canfield understood how they might view the attacks on Venturer Exports. The drug business thrived on being able to move its products around with comparative ease, taking any small losses without suffering too badly. The fact Canfield was under the eye of a multination task force looking into his trafficking might not bother them. The blatant strikes against him by Cooper, who ignored the restraints placed on a lawful investigation, might easily do more to scare them off.

The problem was Canfield's and Canfield's alone. He needed to clean up his own mess. Prove to his future partners that Hugo Canfield was capable of maintaining order. Only he could solve it, and solving it meant getting rid of Cooper. The man's sheer audacity was bringing him here to Banecreif. Canfield saw that as Cooper's mistake. If he did survive the rail trip he would be on Canfield's home ground. Here he was the master. His knowledge of Banecreif and the surrounding terrain was indisputable. That gave Canfield the advantage. He would use it to the limit.

And this time Cooper would not walk away so easily.

In fact, he wouldn't walk away at all.

18

Breck waited for his partner to join him in the buffet car. He handed Munro the cup of coffee he'd ordered. Munro ignored his partner while he blew air across the steaming surface of the drink. It was one of his partner's habits that annoyed Breck. He held back from saying anything because it would only encourage Munro to continue doing it.

"Aren't you going to ask me if I found 'em?" Munro asked abruptly. There was a thin smile on his lips. "Pay attention, son, or life is goin' to pass you by."

They had each taken one end of the train, working their way back to the central point, that being the buffet car. Breck had seen no sign of Cooper or Chambers. The smug expression on Munro's lean face suggested he had been successful.

"Have you found them?"

Munro took a mouthful of coffee, nodding. He led Breck away from the counter to avoid being overheard. "Third carriage along. Compartment 12B. Easy as that."

Breck glanced out the window behind him. "Be dark in a couple of hours. Reckon we should wait until then?"

"About right. What do you think? Take 'em down and dump 'em off the train while it's still dark?"

"Makes sense to me."

"That Yank will be armed," Munro said. "And he's not slow to use his gun from what I heard."

"So we'll be careful. Here, you're not going soft on me, are you?"

"Like I would. Anyhow, what sort of a question is that to ask?"

"Since you started going around with that skirt from the club I reckon you have."

Munro wagged a finger at his partner, grinning widely. "Jealous. You are bleedin' jealous, Marty Breck." He swallowed more coffee. "She never did fancy you. Thought you were too rough for her. She prefers the sensitive type like me."

"Says who?"

"Who is she with, partner? Need I say more?"

Breck shrugged as he reached into his jacket and took out his cell phone. "Better let Gantley know we spotted them."

He spoke quietly when his call was answered, finally completing his conversation. He shut the cell and put it away. "Same as before. If the chance comes up we do it. If not we stay on their tail until they reach Banecreif."

"Never been to Scotland," Munro said.

"Sheltered life, son. You need to get out of the smoke more often."

"Right now I fancy a meal. There's a proper restaurant car back that way. Help pass the time."

"Very smart, Sherlock. And what if Cooper and Chambers decide to do the same? Chambers knows us."

Munro accepted the fact grudgingly. "Well, they do sandwiches here. What do you fancy? Chicken? Chicken with salad. Or they do a nice chicken with chicken."

"Just get something, huh?" Breck glanced at his watch. It was going to be a long wait.

NEITHER COOPER NOR Chambers left their compartment. Food had been ordered and was delivered to the door. On watch farther down the car Breck saw an opportunity to get them inside the compartment. Give Cooper and Chambers ample time to eat their meal before they moved. He returned to the buffet car and an increasingly fidgety Munro.

"It's getting dark, Marty," he said. "Time to move?"

"We give 'em a couple more hours. I just saw food being delivered. Let them eat, then we go. Wait until things quiet down."

"That's generous of you."

"No. It gets us a way into that compartment. Knock on the door and say we've come to collect the tray. They open up and we go in hard and fast."

Munro peeled open his sandwich and studied the contents. "Does that look like chicken to you?"

"A couple of hours. We take turns to watch the compartment in case the waiter turns up first. Now eat your bloody sandwich."

IT WAS DARK BEYOND the train windows. No one had gone near the compartment. Breck joined his partner and they made their way along the corridor to 12B. From inside their jackets they pulled out the suppressed 9 mm Glock pistols they carried in shoulder rigs.

"Nice sharp knock," Breck said.

Munro nodded, rapping on the door.

"Restaurant service, sir," Breck said. "Come to collect your tray."

The door clicked after a few seconds. It opened. Paul Chambers stood there. As he recognized the two men he put out a hand as if to ward off any threat.

"No way," he shouted.

"Hey, Paul," Munro said and stepped inside the compartment, his Glock already rising.

Breck tried to warn his reckless partner but he was too late. Sudden movement from just behind the door caught Munro off guard. The dark outline of a fast-moving figure loomed over him. An arm swept down. Munro gave a strangled cry as the solid metal of a pistol smashed across the back of his skull with tremendous force. He stumbled across the compartment, out of control, slamming into the far wall.

Already committed Breck followed his partner over the threshold, aware of the threat behind the door. He moved fast, starting to crouch, angling his Glock to punch a round through the panel. His intention might have been sound, but the execution was not fast enough. The door was driven at him, catching his shoulder, driving him off balance. He hit the compartment floor, the Glock firing as his finger jerked the trigger. Breck rolled, desperation leading his frantic moves. He heard the compartment door slam shut, caught a blurred glimpse of an armed figure. He dragged the seemingly reluctant Glock around to take a shot. He never made it. The muzzle of the other man's pistol winked brightly—once, then again. Breck felt the impact of the pair of slugs as they cored into his chest. The force at close range slammed him to the floor, his arms spread wide as he sucked in air, struggling against the lethargy that was drawing him into a silent and shadowed place.

BOLAN STEPPED BACK, still gripping the Beretta 93-R Len Watts had supplied. It was as if a blanket of silence had cocooned the compartment and it stayed that way until he let out the breath he'd been holding.

Reality rushed back. He could feel the rhythmic cadence of the speeding train. The occasional creak of metal from the gentle sway of the car. Bolan backed across the compartment, moving the Beretta to cover everyone.

That was when he saw Chambers. The man was crumpled in a corner of the compartment, limbs twisted awkwardly. The loose bullet from Breck's pistol had blown in through his left eye and angled up to erupt from the top of his skull.

19

The Executioner collected the Glocks the intruders had carried and dropped them in his bag, along with the spare magazines they had. He knew from past experience that adding to his arsenal was recommended.

His only choice was to leave the train at the earliest opportunity and make alternative travel plans. It wouldn't be the first time he had been forced to rethink a mission. Flexibility in these situations was often necessary. Bolan had made such moves on many occasions before.

He secured his bag by its long strap, swinging it across his back. The Beretta was back in its holster beneath his zipped leather jacket. He opened the compartment door and checked that the corridor was clear. He made his way along until he reached the end. At the junction where the car joined the next one there was an exit door set in the side. Bolan waited until he felt the train start to reduce speed. It was making the pull up one of the long gradients as it coasted through the Scottish lowlands. Working the door release Bolan eased it open until the gap was wide enough for him to push through. He used the grab rail set in the car side, searching for the foot step, and swung clear of the door, slamming it shut once he was secure.

The chill draft caused by the train's motion buffeted him and pulled at his clothing. Bolan hung on to the grab rail, thinking how well it had been named. He peered around. There was enough illumination coming from the train's windows and from the pale moon to show him the terrain. From the tracks the ground fell away in a long grassy slope. Some way ahead he could see clusters of lights, indicating some habitation. A town. That meant people and maybe the chance to gain some kind of transportation.

The sudden shriek of the train's whistle sounded. Following that, the train's speed reduced more. Bolan checked out the slope some feet below his level. It still seemed to be moving by at a good speed but he figured it wasn't going to get better. He was about to take a calculated risk. One that might leave him injured. If he decided to stay on the train he could find himself in the hands of the authorities and, if Canfield learned about it, the man's influence would be asserted. His contacts would home in on Bolan and freedom might become a thing of the past.

As the train reached midpoint along the gradient its speed dropped down another notch. Bolan swung around so he faced the direction the train was moving. He waited for the clearest patch of slope and went for it. He pushed out from the step, relaxing his body and hit the soft surface of the slope with enough momentum to hurl him forward. His feet made contact. He let himself go, loose limbed, skidding across the grassy slope. He slammed facedown, his arms crossed to protect it.

The hard shock stunned him and he was barely aware of being flung downslope. The hard contents of the bag dug into his chest and ribs as he bounced and slithered across the face of the slope.

His wild ride came to a dead stop as Bolan slammed into a thick tangle of thorny bushes. He didn't attempt to move until his senses settled. The first thing he did was check his arms and legs. Then he sat up and dropped the bag. Bolan stood slowly, turning to check out the train. He could still see the faint glow of lights as it continued up the gradient.

The sooner he started to move, the better. Walking would help keep his battered body from stiffening up. He checked out his surroundings. The lights he had seen from the train were slightly west of his position, a couple of miles away. Bolan spotted moving lights below him—vehicles on a road a quarter of a mile distant. Bolan brushed himself off, slung the bag over his shoulder and headed in the direction of the road.

IT WAS CLOSE TO MIDNIGHT when Bolan closed the door of the room he had taken at the roadside lodge. The lodge was the U.K. equivalent of a motel, there to provide accommodation for long-distance travelers. The young man on duty at the desk had processed Bolan's request for a room with barely any interest. He was eager to get back to his viewing the international soccer match on the television set in his cubbyhole behind the desk.

"You have a car?" the young man asked in a Scottish dialect strong enough to almost baffle Bolan.

"No. Local sales man dropped me off. He'll pick me up in the morning. We had a long day."

"So haven't we all." Bolan's key card was slid across the desk. "Straight along the corridor. Room fourteen. You take your breakfast at the diner across the way. It's in the price."

Bolan nodded, but the man had already turned back to his TV, absorbed in the droning reflections from the commentator and his group of former players as they analyzed the match.

The room was comfortable and functional, equipped with a TV and a kettle for making hot drinks from the supply on a sectioned plastic tray. Bolan flipped the switch. As the water boiled he crossed to the room and closed the curtains. He checked the bathroom. The shower beckoned. Bolan made himself a mug of instant coffee, sitting on the edge of the bed as he drank it. He stripped off his clothes and padded into the bathroom. He caught his reflection in the mirror over the sink. His torso was crisscrossed with bruises and the still-healing bullet tear. He had half expected it to start bleeding again. He counted himself lucky that his leap from the train had let him off so lightly. Bolan turned on the shower and stood under the hot water. He soaped himself, then leaned against the tiled wall and let the water ease away some of the aches and pains.

His strike against Canfield's home base would still go ahead. It would take him longer to reach the place, but that might work in his favor. Anticipation of the coming attack would play against Canfield. He might lose some of his confidence. Start to doubt his own safety as he debated where and when Bolan would show. It was a strategy that could give the Executioner an edge. Anything that took the edge off Canfield's force was welcome. Bolan had no idea of the strength of Canfield's security. He was going in blind. It didn't worry him too much. It wouldn't be the first time he had gone up against an unknown force. He had the advantage of time on his side.

Out of the shower Bolan dried himself and wrapped a towel around his waist. He prepared another coffee, stretched out on the bed and checked his phone. He saw the power was in need of charging, so he took the unit from his bag and clicked in place the converter that would allow him to use the U.K. socket. He connected to the cell phone, saw the power indicator rise and hit the speed dial that would link him to Hal Brognola.

"Striker, where are you?"

"A long way from home," Bolan said.

"How close are you to wrapping this up?"

"Close enough. You got anything for me?"

Brognola held back for a moment.

"Good news and bad news," he said. "On the bad side there's no way of making it any easier to say."

"Just say it, Hal."

"A ship on its way to the U.K., the *Orient Venturer,* dumped one of its containers over the side. They didn't know they'd been spotted by a trawler out of a British port. The trawler hove to where the container had been dropped and marked it with a buoy. A British Navy vessel was called and it sent down diving teams to locate the container. When they raised it and got it open they found twenty-five bodies inside. Young women and kids. Later identified as Thai. The call went out and the authorities were waiting when the container ship docked. Captain and crew were arrested. No one will talk but we lucked out when the Bear did some hard probing into the container ship's background. This is the good news. Aaron found one hell of a maze as far as ownership was concerned. Blind alleys and phony registration. But bless that man, he finally pinned it down. Bottom line is that the *Orient Venturer* belongs to Hugo Canfield's organization. He can deny it until hell freezes over but he's the man."

Brognola sensed Bolan's feelings through the protracted silence that followed his revelation. He let Bolan have his moment, knowing how the man would be hurting. If emotion was ever allowed to break Bolan's stoic image, it could be guaranteed when he was faced with more innocent suffering. The facts about the women and children would hurt Bolan more than a 9 mm bullet.

"Hal, how far has this information gone?"

"I haven't spoken to anyone."

"Leave it that way. We started this mission one-to-one. I'll finish it that way."

"No problem. A little more feedback. Aaron's digging into the data he downloaded from van Ryden's computer has paid off, too. Names on Canfield's payroll. High rollers in government positions. Customs. Police. Canfield has connections. Those names covered individuals in Europe, the U.K. *and* the U.S. Looks like van Ryden was hedging his bets by keeping lists. Covering his ass in case he needed protection himself. That's a lawyer for you. The task force will be drooling for weeks when they get their hands on that intel."

"Tell Aaron nice work."

"I'll hold back on this until I hear from you," Brognola said. "I guess Canfield is in for a surprise when you show up."

"That's the idea, Hal."

Banecreif was more than five hundred years old—a sprawling stone mansion with extensive grounds. Isolated—the closest village was over ten miles away—it stood on the coast, the east side of the massive building overlooking the cold gray waters of the North Sea. From the base of the east wall a sheer rock cliff dropped eighty feet to the inhospitable waters.

Since he'd purchased the house Hugo Canfield had invested a great deal of money in the place. He added modern refinements. A powerful generator supplied electricity to light the house and provide heated water for the bathrooms he had built. The kitchen was equipped with professional stoves and freezers. There was no permanent staff. When Canfield was away a local couple kept the house running. If he was expecting business guests he flew in catering staff.

With the current situation Canfield had Sergeant Gantley, plus a five-man security team at the house. His personal helicopter had brought them to Banecreif from the closest airfield. It was standing on the concrete landing pad next to the house.

Sergeant Gantley looked after security and supervised the kitchen. One of the ground-level rooms served as a small but efficient control center. From there it was possible to view the incoming images from a number of security cameras that had been installed around the property. Total security systems had yet to be completed, with motion sensors and infrared detection still to be added. Fortunately the house was far enough off the beaten track not to attract many visitors. Canfield maintained a low profile when he was at the house and his roving patrols were enough to keep any unwitting trespassers away.

Hugo Canfield always felt secure at Banecreif. The peace and quiet allowed him time to think out his problems and plan future enterprises. He had installed expensive communications systems—satellite phone lines, high-speed Internet. Distance was no problem. He could speak to anyone he wanted, anywhere across the globe.

He was on the phone to his Russian contact in Leningrad. Pavel Molenski was head of the drug syndicate Canfield was hoping to do business with.

The conversation was not going well.

"Hugo, I hope you are keeping well? I have heard life is a little difficult at the moment."

"A few local problems, Pavel. Nothing to worry about."

"But that *is* the problem, Hugo. Friends are concerned. Questions have been asked. About your suitability to join us. And as much as I admire your past record, these recent setbacks are starting to give me reason to doubt."

"No need, Pavel. As I said this is a local disturbance. One that I will settle very soon."

"First your setup in Holland. Now your U.K. base. My sources tell me that your organization has been severely hit."

"Nothing that cannot be brought back on-line. Trust me, Pavel, I won't allow this interference to put our deal at risk."

Pavel's strong Russian accent came through clearly. "It has been decided, Hugo, to give you exactly one more week. If nothing has changed by then, if you have not completely cleared up this mess, we will be expecting the return of our merchandise and all future deals will be off."

"Don't do this to me, Pavel. Not now. I've made commitments to my contacts here. I can't renege on my promises."

"Understand me, Hugo. You made a commitment to *us*. We

supplied the merchandise. It seems clear that you will not be able to go through with your end of the deal. We have to protect our interests. If you are compromised we could be drawn into the area of suspicion. One week, Hugo, then we collect our goods. And we can do it peacefully, or with extreme force. Please do not make it that we need to use force. That would be extremely foolish on your part."

The phone went dead. Canfield listened to the buzz of the line. He experienced a growing anger as he recalled the Russian's words. The implicit threat.

"The hell with you, Pavel."

He slammed the phone down and strode across the room, standing in front of the blazing fire in the ornate stone hearth. Canfield stared into flames, his thoughts working overtime. First Cooper. Now the fucking Russians. Whining because they were scared their consignment of drugs, stored in the temperature-controlled cellars beneath Banecreif, was going to be lost. Crying like babies who wanted their toys back. They were pathetic. They were greedy. Wanting everything instantly. Suddenly they were acting as if they were the top dogs. Pushing into every corner of his business. Uneducated, nonthinking thugs. Maybe he had been wrong to negotiate the deal. It was a mistake on his part. They were going to have to wait until he had the Cooper affair handled. Then *he* would show them how negotiate.

He heard a clock chiming at the far end of the large room that served as his office. Canfield turned and crossed to the oak desk and sat down in the huge leather chair. He reached for the internal phone and called for Sergeant Gantley to join him.

The ex-Army cop was there in minutes. He was an imposing figure in his dark military-style fatigues. He carried a SIG-Sauer P-226 in a high-ride holster on his right hip. The pistol, with its stainless-steel parts and wood grips, was Gantley's personal weapon.

"Any sign of Cooper?" Canfield asked.

Gantley shook his head. He had his security detail on roving patrols in and around the massive old house. "Nothing from Breck or Munro, either, sir. I'm trying to get in touch with Harris," Gantley said. "Maybe he can give me an update."

"I've just been speaking to Pavel," Canfield said. "He had the nerve to actually threaten me. This Cooper mess has those Russians wetting their pants. He's ready to go back on the deal. Told me we have a week to sort this out, or they'll demand the drugs back."

"Russians? They couldn't even keep their own country together, sir. Now they all think they're Al Capone. Never met one I couldn't drink under the table, sir."

"Just thought I'd let you know, Sergeant Gantley. First things first. We deal with Cooper, then sort out these bloody Russkies."

"Yes, sir."

GANTLEY MADE THE ROUNDS, checking his team. They were well armed. Two outside. Two more on the roof and one manning the security room, watching the camera monitor screens. Each man was carrying a holstered Beretta 92-F and an HK MP-5A4. The long-established submachine gun still performed well and Gantley trusted the weapon. The MP-5s were loaded with 30-round twin magazines for extended firepower.

He climbed to the roof, walking the stone-flagged flat area bounded by a three-foot-high buttressed wall. From there he was able to look out across the surrounding terrain.

He saw undulating grassland and timber and the thin gray snake of the narrow approach road. Moving around to the east side he stared out across the water. Mist hung over the jagged coastline extending away from Banecreif. Strong currents sent icy waves crashing against the base of the rocky cliff, the spray leaping high up the dark, weathered rock. Gantley felt the touch of rain and saw gray cloud sweeping in off the sea. He made contact with the roof sentries. The men wore thick parkas over their clothing against the chill. It started to rain heavily.

"Anything?" Gantley asked.

"Nothing, sir. If he's coming he's taking his time."

"That could be deliberate," Gantley said. "Trying to make us sweat."

The sentry smiled. "Hardly likely in this bloody weather."

"Well, don't slack off just because he hasn't shown yet. From what I've learned Cooper is no quitter. He'll show."

Gantley started back down into the house. His cell phone rang and he answered.

"It's Harris. You need to hear this. Took me some time. There's been a shut down on information coming from the cops. My contact in the information office finally came through. When the train arrived in Glasgow Breck and Chambers had already been found dead in the compartment Cooper booked. They had both been shot. Munro was found alive but with the back of his skull caved in."

"Cooper?"

"No sign of a fourth man. He could have jumped the train anywhere after it crossed the border. He could be long gone."

"No, Harris, he's not gone. The man is on his way here." Gantley checked his watch. An hour after midday. "He's had plenty of time to make new travel arrangements. Keep me informed of any developments."

Gantley ended the call and put his phone away. He crossed to stand at the wall again, scanning the surrounding countryside, nodding to himself.

"Come ahead, Mr. Cooper. I'm ready and waiting for you."

21

Using the available guest computer Bolan had checked out Banecreif on Google's map site. It was a long drive down a rugged road that would take him to the easterly edge of the Scottish highlands. The road ran along the coast, the North Sea bordering the route. Remote. Isolated, with only a few scattered villages along the way. It would take Bolan the best part of a day to reach his destination. He didn't mind that because the delay in his travel would leave Canfield wondering when his unwelcome guest might turn up.

Checking out of the lodge Bolan asked the young woman behind the desk, the day-shift receptionist, to call him a taxi, explaining that his pickup had been postponed and he needed to locate a car rental agency. The closest agency was in the next town, a forty-minute ride away. The taxi turned up in short time and Bolan settled in the backseat. The journey took just over thirty minutes after Bolan promised the driver a bonus if he could get him to his destination quickly.

At the rental agency Bolan made the necessary negotiations and hired a late-model Volkswagen Toureg SE. The big 4x4 had auto transmission and even a touch-screen DVD navigation system. Its powerful engine would provide Bolan with the kind of horsepower needed to cover the long distance to the Scottish Highlands.

Leaving the rental agency Bolan spotted a convenience store and pulled in. He stocked up on a few sandwiches and bottles of water. Behind the wheel he tapped in the coordinates for his route and watched as the sharp image came on the screen. Pushing the stick into first Bolan settled into the comfortable leather seat and moved off.

LATE AFTERNOON, hours into his drive, Bolan was away from the sprawling bustle of Glasgow and heading north, toward Inverness and the eastern side of the country where he would eventually link up to the coast road that would lead him to Banecreif. He saw that he was heading into rough weather as dark clouds rolled in from the east, gathering into a storm bank the farther he drove up-country. The road ahead stretched across low hills with little habitation save for a few farms scattered across the landscape. His original estimate was that he had roughly two hundred and seventy miles to cover—around six hours' driving. With the weather backing up, threatening rain, Bolan added to that time. However it worked out, it was going to be late by the time he reached his objective.

The realization did little to unnerve Bolan. A strike in the wee hours might work in his favor. It was the time when the most alert opponent lost a degree of his deductive powers. When the body naturally reached that twilight condition, slowing down. Leaving perceptions at a low ebb. Something to be taken advantage of.

When Bolan spotted a truck stop he pulled in. The small restaurant and store was hosting only a couple of drivers from the long-haul trucks parked outside. Bolan picked up a thermos flask from the store section, went to the restaurant counter and ordered a black coffee. At his request the red-haired woman serving filled his flask with more coffee. Bolan allowed himself a leisurely break, downing a second mug of coffee before settling his bill and leaving. He took a few minutes to walk around the parking area before he returned to the 4x4.

As he settled himself behind the wheel, securing his seat belt, the first fat drops of rain hit the windshield. By the time he had driven out of the parking lot and turned back onto the road the rain had increased to a hard downpour. Bolan flicked on the wipers, the built-in sensor determining how fast they needed to operate in order to clear the glass screen. It became gloomy enough that Bolan needed the headlights, as well. He set his speed and activated the cruise control, letting the vehicle take the strain.

Bolan drove through Inverness into a rain-filled night, the road swinging toward the coast. Beyond the town the strip of road ahead was dark and empty, leaving Bolan the opportunity to consider what lay ahead for him at Banecreif.

He had his mission to complete.

Retribution to deliver to Hugo Canfield.

THE UNBROKEN STORM followed Bolan all the way to his turnoff. He lost time negotiating the empty, winding main highway, only the powerful headlights of his vehicle breaking the darkness surrounding him. The navigation system performed its task well, and Bolan easily found the narrow, single-lane road that led to Banecreif. According to the screen readout the road ran for two miles, dead-ending at Canfield's property. He cut the lights as he rolled the Toureg onto this feeder road, taking the first chance he got to turn the vehicle around and reverse into the cover of the trees and bushes edging the road. Bolan killed the engine. The drum of falling rain on the roof matched the distant crash of waves hitting the rocky shore close by.

He pulled his blacksuit and boots from his bag and changed. His shoulder rig held the Beretta 93-R. Len Watts had also provided an Uzi, still one of Bolan's favorite weapons. He slid a sheathed knife onto his belt. Snapping on a combat rig Bolan made sure the pouches held plastic ties and extra magazines for the Beretta and the Uzi. It was basic equipment, but enough for what he intended. He pulled on a black baseball cap to complete his transformation, slipped out of the vehicle and locked it, dropping the key into one of the blacksuit's zippered side pockets.

Using the faint moonlight Bolan headed in toward the dark bulk of Banecreif. Even at the distance he was from the house Bolan could see how it dominated the headland where it stood. Cold and brooding.

HUGO CANFIELD FOUND IT hard to sleep.

The early hours were the worst. Night was still hanging on, reluctant to relinquish its hold to the coming dawn. Canfield hated waking because he could never get back to sleep. This time was even worse. He couldn't get Cooper out of his mind. The man stalked through his thoughts. A spectral figure bringing death and destruction with every step. He had certainly done that to Canfield's operation.

It angered and interested him at the same time. The anger was easily explained. His interest in Cooper another matter. The man intrigued him. Canfield wished he could learn more about him. No getting away from the fact that Cooper was a hell of an opponent. He came through every confrontation ready for the next. Gained his information and acted on it. He had a relentless drive to him that pushed him ever forward, his mind like a guided missile, directing him to the next target. In a perverse way Canfield likened himself to Cooper. In their respective businesses they knew what they wanted and simply went for it, casting aside doubt and uncertainty.

If Cooper had allied himself with Hugo Canfield they would have made a formidable team. They would have been unstoppable.

Canfield pushed that out of his mind as quickly as it presented itself. Cooper was on the side of the good and righteous. No doubt about that.

The mix of conflicting thoughts denied Canfield any

further rest. He left his bed, showered, shaved and got dressed. He made his way downstairs to the kitchen, craving coffee. He found Gantley already there. A mug of steaming black coffee was pushed across the work surface. Canfield took it.

"How did you know?" Canfield asked.

"It's what you pay me for, sir. And I heard you in the shower when I passed your room ten minutes ago."

"So, is everything secure?"

"As we can ever make it, sir," Gantley said.

"Can we stop him? Given his recent record."

"A bloody good try is what we can offer."

"Not the best summation, Sergeant Gantley, but an honest one."

BOLAN WALKED STEADILY, head down against the rain driving in from the seaward side of the track. The unpaved surface of the road had already become a soft morass of dark mud. He had only walked for a few hundred yards before the chill began to penetrate the blacksuit. There was nothing he could do to change that. Bolan kept moving, his mind focused on his objective.

He was there to make sure Hugo Canfield was taken down. That his organization was neutered. Venturer Exports would be reduced to ashes and scattered beyond repair.

That was going to require Bolan going on the hunt.

He had no qualms about that. All he had to do was recall the deaths of two task-force agents and the twenty-five Thai women and children dropped overboard from Canfield's ship while locked inside a steel container.

Bolan wouldn't derive satisfaction from whatever happened at Banecreif, but he would achieve some kind of closure for the dead.

And that would have to do.

22

Faint dawn light was edging away the night. The rain persisted, laying a misty curtain across the landscape. Bolan didn't mind that. It would offer some additional distraction for his approach. With Banecreif looming in front of him Bolan took to the ground, working his way through the wet grass, using every patch of shadow he could find until he was close enough to pick out the sentries.

Bolan studied the sentry as he slogged his way through the heavy waterlogged grass. Even though he was clad in a waterproof coat the man was probably chilled to the bone and hoping to be relieved. Bolan figured this would be the best time to take the man. He had probably been on duty for a long few hours. He would be tired and ready to get under cover.

The man moved by him. Bolan was no more than twenty feet away and was able to see the MP-5 the guard was carrying over one shoulder, his hands shoved deep into the pockets of his jacket.

The sentry paced on, pausing at the perimeter of his patch to look around, before slowly, reluctantly, turning and retracing his steps. By this time Bolan had moved in closer, so that when the sentry drew level with him, Bolan was almost under his feet. As the man reached the ideal position Bolan swept his legs from under him, dropping him flat on his back. Unprepared the guard hit the ground with a hard thump, gasping as the air was forced from his lungs. Before he could recover

Bolan slammed a bunched fist against his jaw. The sentry grunted and lay still, momentarily stunned. It was enough time for Bolan to strip away his MP-5 and handgun, turn the man facedown and use a couple of plastic ties to secure wrists and ankles. He rolled the man back over and as the sentry shook away the dizziness Bolan slid the fighting knife from its sheath and pressed it against the man's exposed throat, applying just enough pressure so that the fine sheer edge cut into flesh, drawing a little blood and creating a prickly stinging sensation.

"Listen good," Bolan said. "You have an easy choice. Give me the answers I want, or I lean on this knife a little harder and open your throat all the way."

The sentry stared up at Bolan, only just able to see his face in the dawn light. But there was enough to recognize the hard, icy gleam in the eyes staring back at him.

"I say anything Gantley will—"

"Gantley isn't the one you need to worry about, friend. It's me you're going to have to deal with. Right now I'm the most important man in the world."

Bolan emphasized his words by drawing the blade a little deeper across the sentry's throat, causing a warm trickle of blood to slide across taut flesh.

"Jesus…"

"I'd suggest it's a little late to start getting religion. Are you ready to answer my question?"

The sentry stopped trying to free his bounds wrists and nodded. "What?" he asked.

"How many more of you are there? And don't make up numbers. I'm going to leave you here. Mess with me and I'll come back and show you just how persuasive my friend here can be."

"Okay, okay. One more on the ground like me. Two on the roof. One inside manning the security cameras. And Gantley."

Bolan took hold of the sentry's collar and dragged him through the grass until he reached the trees. He used the knife to cut a wide strip from the man's waterproof coat and gagged him, propping him against the trunk of a tree. He searched the sentry's coat and found a spare magazine for the MP-5. Returning to the spot where he had taken the man down Bolan picked up the MP-5. He swung the Uzi across his back, moving forward, his eyes searching for the second sentry.

It was the sentry who found Bolan. As the Executioner circled a heavy stand of tangled undergrowth the sentry appeared off to his right, picking up speed as he fixed Bolan's position. The guard called out, raising his MP-5 and let go with a loose burst that chopped at the undergrowth, showering Bolan with debris.

Bolan dropped and rolled, propping himself on his elbows and returned fire. The sentry jerked aside, cursing wildly, and then hauled himself to a stop. His weapon tracked back in Bolan's direction but he was a couple of seconds too late. Bolan's second burst caught the man chest-high, a follow-up adding to the devastation as the 9 mm slugs cleaved into his body, tearing into his lungs and heart. The man uttered a high squeal, falling back and slamming to the ground.

Bolan scrambled to his feet and dug in his heels, angling across the open ground for the cover of the house. In his mind he was calculating how soon the sentries on the roof might respond.

The chatter of concentrated automatic fire answered his question as a pair of MP-5's opened up. Bolan heard the sodden thumps as 9 mm slugs tore at the rain-soaked ground around him. He ducked and weaved, presenting a constantly shifting target, feeling the impact as slugs struck closer than he wanted. The shooters were having to lean over the parapet as Bolan got closer to the house, the angle they were having to deal with making accurate fire difficult.

Bolan reached the rough stone wall, slamming against the unyielding surface and pausing for a moment. Shadows at the base of the wall helped to conceal him but he was aware that some of the 9 mm projectiles were also getting closer to the angle where the ground met the wall. By the law of averages he was soon going to feel one of those slugs. He glanced left and right. He saw a low-sited window a few yards away. He needed access to the house and a window was as good a way of entering as a door. He edged along the wall, taking himself away from the bursts of fire, albeit briefly.

The window was large, the sill no more than a couple of feet from ground level—an old, wooden sash-style window. Bolan pulled away from the window, raised the MP-5 and triggered the remaining magazine capacity at it. The burst of sustained fire shattered the glass from the frame and shredded the wood. Throwing his arms up to cover his face Bolan took a run at the empty gap and launched himself through the window, taking the remaining glass and wood with him. He landed on his feet, glass showering around him.

The first thing he did was eject the empty magazine and snap in his remaining full one. A glance around the room showed it in shadow, devoid of furniture. The door was on the far side. Bolan crossed to it, easing the handle and edging the door open to show the empty passage beyond.

23

The moment the sound of gunfire reached the security room, the guard in charge, Lou Trencher, snapped out of his half-sleep state and hit the exterior lights. Instantly the monitor screens were illuminated by the powerful lamps mounted around the outside of the house.

Damn, I should have had them on already, he thought.

Trencher knew he was in trouble. Once Gantley found out he had been slacking at his post it wouldn't matter if an intruder was out there. The former military cop would kill Trencher himself. Sergeant Gantley had a fetish about running the security team like a small army. And he had no patience with anyone who slipped below his standards.

The first thing Trencher saw was a body stretched out on the ground. He focused in with the camera controls, bringing the motionless form into sharp relief. He couldn't identify the man because he was lying facedown, but he did see the blood oozing from the ragged bullet wounds, being sluiced away by the rain still sweeping in across the grounds.

Trencher keyed the Send button on his internal handset.

"Intruder alert. West wall."

Trencher heard the rattle of more automatic fire. It was coming from somewhere overhead. The roof guards. They must have spotted the man. What was his name—Cooper.

Close by Trencher heard more gunfire. Then the shattering of glass. He realized it was coming from the room just along the passage from his security cubbyhole.

Is Cooper breaking in? he wondered.

Aware he had some making up to do Trencher snatched up his own MP-5, swinging around and stepping out into the passage. He flattened against the opposite wall.

He heard the rattle of the handle, saw the door pulled open. The room inside was dark. Trencher could hear the sound of rain splashing in through the shattered window.

Where was Cooper? *Why didn't the bastard show himself?*

He eased away from the wall, his finger curling against the submachine gun's trigger.

In the distance he heard someone shout his name. He recognized the harsh bark.

Sergeant Gantley.

The angry call drew Trencher to an involuntary halt, head turning in the direction of the sound.

What did the man want now?

Fuck you, Trencher thought, I got more important things to do.

He swung back toward the point of his interest. The empty doorway.

Only it wasn't empty any longer.

A black-clad figure stood there, the muzzle of his own weapon already tracking Trencher.

Oh, shit, Trencher thought.

Second time he had screwed up tonight.

Bolan hit the armed man with a solid burst from his MP-5. The blistering stream of 9 mm bullets cut into and through the guard's midtorso, kicking him back across the passage until the stone wall brought him to an abrupt stop. Trencher's finger squeezed back against the MP-5's trigger and a burst hit the ceiling overhead, flattening and spinning across the passage. Trencher slid to his knees, dropping his weapon and clutching at his wounds. The last thing he saw was the dark-clad figure turning and heading along the passage.

The Executioner had seen the flight of stone steps that led from the ground floor. The steps were set against the wall, steep, and disappeared into apparent darkness. As he sprinted up he felt the flow of chilled air that met him. The stairs curved slightly to the left and as Bolan followed the turn the cold air increased. His initial guess had been correct—the steps led to the roof. Above him now he made out the shape of a heavy wooden door, partly ajar. The last few stone risers were wet from rain that had blown in through the gap.

He drew himself tight against the cold wall, using his foot to edge the door wide, giving it a final hard shove. The door swung wide, banging against something solid.

Bolan went through fast, dropping to a crouch and veering to the left, his MP-5 tracking ahead, searching for targets.

He had two armed men on the roof. Aware of his presence. Now that the high-mounted lights had been activated there was a degree of illumination spilling across the rain-swept flat area.

That light would expose the two guards *and* Bolan.

A hunched shape cut through Bolan's field of vision, firing as he moved. Bolan heard the hard snap of the slugs as they struck the stone behind him, so he changed direction, following the man and also searching for guard number two.

More automatic fire. Bolan felt hot stone chips bite his left cheek. He swung around in response, seeing the still-moving shape. He pushed the MP-5's muzzle around and kept the guard in his sights for a couple of seconds. His finger eased back on the trigger, sending a burst at the man. The guard stumbled, a muffled curse on his lips. He still managed to fire back, his slugs clanging against a metal ventilation duct only a few feet away from Bolan. Bolan dropped, rolled, then dragged himself away from his position, working his way into a stand of heating and ventilation ducts, letting the complex shadows conceal his black shape. It wasn't going to hide him for long, but he needed a moment to check out the relative placing of his opponents.

He was a second away from raising his head when the faintest crunch of a boot against the stone roof slabs reached his ears.

The sound came from too close to his right.

The second guard. Moving in for the kill.

Bolan rolled over on his back, sensing the dark bulk rearing above him. In the fragment of light that fell across the section Bolan saw the rain-slick face, arms extending the man's MP-5, the shiny surface of the waterproof jacket. The light gave his eyes a cold, metallic gleam.

His MP-5 had moved with Bolan, an extension of his body, and he triggered the weapon the instant he locked on to the guard. Bolan kept his finger on the trigger, expending the remaining half of the magazine, pumping the 9 mms into the man's torso. The close range pushed the slugs through, blowing out the spine in a bloody spatter of flesh and splintered bone. The guard gave a strangled groan as he toppled away from Bolan and crashed down hard on the stone roof slabs.

Bolan threw the empty MP-5 aside and pulled the Uzi into position as he turned back to face the remaining guard. He worked his way out from the stand of pipes as the man, ducking and weaving as he sought a clear shot, was silhouetted against the bright glare from one of the spotlights.

The guard realized his error and turned to step out from the light.

Bolan's reflex action triggered the Uzi. He used a tried-and-tested figure eight, stitching the guard from chest to crotch, the man jerking from the impact of the 9 mm burn. He bounced against the stone slabs, his MP-5 slipping from his grasp. A second burst from the Uzi took a section of his skull off, ending the fight.

A moment of calm descended as Bolan eased to his feet, though his left shoulder ached from slamming against something when he had dropped to the roof and he had a faint ringing in his ears from the harsh chatter of automatic fire.

He turned his face to the falling rain, letting the cold water refresh his senses.

He didn't hear the soft footfall behind him. Only sensed that he wasn't alone a split second before something struck him across the back of his skull and he dropped to his knees, the shadows turning even blacker.

24

Bolan felt fingers working his combat rig loose, dragging it off his body, then freeing the holstered Beretta. He struggled against the dark mist fogging his senses, aware that the knife was being stripped from its sheath. The Uzi had gone from his grasp as he had been driven to his knees. He struggled upright, swaying as he gained his feet, turning about at the harsh voice ringing out.

"All right, son, so you're the tough man? Christ, you don't look so hard to me."

The man facing Bolan was his height, broader across the shoulders and chest. His hair was cropped close to his skull, glistening with rain. He wore dark military fatigues, heavy boots on his feet. Bolan saw him unclip the holstered pistol on his hip and place it on one of the exhaust ducts. Then he was flexing massive fists, covered by thin black leather gloves, as he faced Bolan.

This *had* to be Sergeant Gantley. Canfield's minder.

"Fuckin' Yanks. Too much money and fancy ordnance. All that bullshit about being the best."

Bolan didn't reply. He was using every second to recharge his reserves because he was going to need them. It was why Gantley had deprived him of his weapons. The man was ready to use his hands.

They squared off in the predawn paleness. Rain still sweeping in across the slabbed roof of Banecreif.

"Come on, then, Cooper," Gantley taunted. "What is it you arseholes say—give me your best shot."

Even in the low light Bolan could see the perverse smile edging Gantley's thick lips. He realized that the man was anticipating the upcoming conflict and expecting to enjoy it.

Gantley moved forward, impatient because Bolan was refusing to move. In his eyes that would only confirm what he felt about Americans.

All show and no go.

Bolan let him close in, saving his strength for what was to come. Gantley had left him no choice. He was going to have to fight, or allow Gantley to beat him to death.

The Brit swung a powerful fist. His left. A clumsy feint. Bolan eased away from it, his eye on Gantley's right, which was looping around in a blur. He ducked under the powerful swing and leaned in to deliver two hard punches to Gantley's ribs. Bolan concentrated his power into the blows and though Gantley's muscular torso absorbed much of the impact there was enough to make him grunt and step back. Bolan caught the lips peeling back from Gantley's teeth in an angry snarl.

He can be hurt, Bolan thought, and he doesn't like it.

The next attack came swiftly. Despite his bulk Gantley could move fast, his upper body weaving. His long arms enabled him to swing early, still just beyond Bolan's stretch. He didn't feint this time, simply lashed out with both fists. His left caught Bolan across the side of his face, knocking the big American off balance. The blow was hard, not crippling, but left Bolan smarting, blood running down his cheek from a fresh gash.

Bolan pulled away, saw the thin smirk on Gantley's rain-slick face as he retreated. Then he brought himself to a stop, catching Gantley off-kilter for a second. It was enough time for Bolan to slam his fist full into Gantley's mouth. The blow split Gantley's lips, blood blossoming as flesh was hammered back against his teeth. Bolan held his attack, throwing hard punches to Gantley's mouth and cheeks, rocking the man's head from side to side. Gantley took steps back, seemingly confused by the sudden and unrelenting attack. Bolan changed tack without warning, using his booted foot to deliver hard sidekicks to Gantley's left knee. The blows hurt Gantley. His leg was weakening, his reflex blows uncoordinated, missing more than connecting. He could not contain his anger. Gantley was not used to being hurt, even opposed, and he had to gather himself with a great effort, sucking in his rage and concentrating his efforts.

One of his large fists caught Bolan's left wrist, yanking his arm to pull Bolan in close. He batted aside Bolan's free arm, then swung him aside with the ease of a child casting off an unwanted toy. Bolan was thrown across the roof, losing his grip on the wet stone. He went to his knees, throwing his hands out to prevent contact with the solid slabs. He knew immediately that he had to get back on his feet. Gantley would be moving in. Before Bolan could stand upright Gantley's thick arms encircled his neck, closing tight like the coils of a snake as he hauled Bolan to his knees. Bolan could hear him snorting through his bloody mouth as he bore down.

Bolan sucked in a breath before Gantley's stranglehold cut off his air. Knowing his time would be short Bolan reached up and back, getting a grip on Gantley's fatigue jacket. He hauled hard, letting his body drop from the waist. The leverage worked and Gantley was dragged up and over Bolan's head, in a perfect shoulder roll. As he thudded to the stone slabs his grip on Bolan's neck slackened and Bolan rolled free, turning his body and slamming his right boot full into Gantley's face. Gantley's nose simply collapsed under the kick. Blood erupted from the crushed organ.

Rolling again to gain distance Bolan staggered to his feet. He saw Gantley doing the same, and not wanting to give the man any leeway he launched a full roundhouse kick that hammered into Gantley's chest, driving him backward. Continuing his forward run Bolan had almost reached Gantley when the Brit hooked his own right leg around and kicked Bolan's legs from under him.

The drop to the slabs left Bolan struggling for air. He saw Gantley rise over him, fists opening and closing in unison. Bolan drew his legs under himself and pushed upright. He swung at Gantley, drawing blood from the man's left cheek. Bolan didn't see Gantley's left sweep up out of nowhere. It struck him across the side of his face with a meaty thump. Bolan recoiled from the blow, tasting blood in his mouth. He backpedaled and slammed against the buttressed stone wall edging the roof, gasping from the impact.

The man was not going to give him time to recover. Even as the thought crossed his mind Bolan sensed movement, saw the shadow that fell across the stone slabs at his feet. He heard the grunt of exertion as Gantley launched another fist. Bolan yanked his head to one side, the solid knuckles raking the curve of his jaw. Although the full force of the blow was reduced, there was enough energy to spin Bolan off balance. Bolan heard the scuff of Gantley's boots as the man moved to keep up with him. He threw up his left arm and took a solid blow just below his shoulder, then hauled himself around and countered with his right fist, slamming it hard into Gantley's ribs. The blow drew a grunt from the man and he retreated briefly, giving Bolan time to slam a booted foot against the Brit's knee again.

Gantley pulled back, struggling to maintain his balance and Bolan thrust himself forward, driving his shoulder into the man's broad chest, then launching a forearm smash that impacted against Gantley's cheek. The sheer force of the blow fractured the cheekbone. Bolan delivered a second punch, increasing the damage. Flesh tore and a shard of splintered cheekbone showed white before blood discolored it.

The pain he must have felt only increased Gantley's fury. He caught hold of Bolan's blacksuit with both hands and hurled him across the stone flags. Losing his balance Bolan had seconds to throw out his arms to break his fall as he went down for the second time. He landed hard, bouncing and tumbling across the weathered slabs, scraping his face against the rough surface. He felt the wash of warm blood streaking across his cheek and mouth. The low stone wall edging the roof brought him to a bone-jarring stop.

Bolan could hear the heavy crash of the surging tide slamming against the rocks at the base of the east wall behind and below. Twisting his head he saw Gantley advancing. Blood streamed down his face and spattered the front of his fatigues. Gantley still looked every inch the hard man he was. His solid bulk did nothing to hinder his movements and he lunged forward without warning, slamming into Bolan as he pushed to his feet, aware of the low wall at his back. He was too late to move aside and Gantley crushed him against the stonework, massive hands clamping around Bolan's throat. Bolan felt his spine driven against the lip of the wall. He braced his booted feet and pushed back against Gantley's sheer bulk. The man was snorting with the effort he was putting into his attack. Hot breath fanned Bolan's face. He felt Gantley's thick fingers squeezing down on his neck, starting to deny him air.

Bolan sensed déjà vu. Gantley's arms were around his neck again. If he was unable to draw in oxygen his responses would begin to falter. He spun through his options, realizing they were few. Gantley had him pinned against the wall so there was no retreat that way. The man's brute strength, spread against Bolan, held him near motionless. Only Bolan's arms were free. He spread them for a moment, closing his hands into fists, then struck out at Gantley's face—first against the already damaged cheek, then to the other side of the Brit's face. Every ounce of Bolan's not inconsiderable strength went into the blows, delivered without mercy. He maintained the two-sided attack, slamming his knuckled fists against Gantley's face, seeing it turn even more bloody and raw.

Gantley increased his grip on Bolan's throat and it became a simple contest between the two—who would quit first. Bolan centered his whole being on his unrestrained physical assault on his opponent, his fists aching from the contact with Gantley's head. And it was Gantley who jerked back, gasping from the relentless blows slamming into his battered flesh. As his grip on Bolan's throat slackened Bolan planted his left hand on Gantley's chest and accelerated his withdrawal, pulling back his right arm to aim a telling blow that landed square against Gantley's already smashed nose. Blood erupted in bright streams.

Howling with pain Gantley stumbled back, raising his hands to his ruined face and Bolan went directly for his un-protected stomach and ribs, pounding in blow after blow that brought the former military cop to a stop. Gantley let out a shuddering moan, starting to fold. Bolan dropped his hands on Gantley's shoulders, pushing down as he swept his right knee up to smash into Gantley's face. The blow straightened Gantley, his face a caved-in bloody mask. He didn't even see as Bolan stepped in close, turning, then hauling Gantley over his shoulder in a body throw that launched the Brit off his feet. There was a surreal moment when Gantley seemed to hang in the empty air, then a long scream as he vanished over the buttressed wall, out into empty space before the long drop to the granite rocks at the base of the house.

Gantley's scream faded as he fell, ceasing the instant he struck the rocks.

25

The Executioner retrieved his Beretta after he finally located it, then crawled on hands and knees back to the base of the wall where he leaned against the stone, head hanging, dripping blood. Waves of nausea engulfed him. The only way he might have described his condition was as one big bruise. He was aching from head to foot. Bloody and sick. Even his hands hurt. His knuckles were raw and bleeding. He raised his aching head back against the cold, rough stone of the wall, wishing the rain would wash away his pain. He knew he had to move soon. To go find Hugo Canfield and complete his mission.

In the end he didn't need to do even that.

Something told him Canfield would find him, and Bolan was too exhausted to climb to his feet there and then.

From where he sat he could see the door that led back down into the house. A square of light against the graying dawn. He fixed his gaze on the doorway and waited. Something stirred in him, warning that Canfield was going to come to him. Bolan's battered right hand grasped the Beretta, drawing it close to his side where it was hidden by his thigh. He moved the selector lever to tri-bursts.

He waited.

The minutes crawled. When he breathed Bolan felt a stab of pain across his ribs down his right side. He laid his left hand across his body, pressed over the ache. He hoped they were simply bruised and not cracked.

He saw the shadow first, moving against the stone wall just inside the open stairwell. Bolan fixed on it, watched it pause, then rise higher. He could see the head and shoulders. The extended outline of a weapon. The form grew larger. It was the bulk of a tall man carrying an easily recognizable SPAS combat shotgun.

The man chose his weapons well, Bolan thought.

His grip on the Beretta tightened.

Hugo Canfield stepped through the open door, moving quickly to one side to avoid being framed. His searching eyes picked up on Bolan's motionless form, the shotgun coming around to center on the Executioner.

"Tell me you're still alive, Cooper. I want you alive, you interfering son of a bitch, so I can blow you to hell and back."

Bolan didn't respond. He needed Canfield to walk closer so he had a clear shot.

"Just move. Enough so I know you can see who it is putting you down. Damn you, Cooper, fucking move. You hear me? Thought you'd won? I'll get through this. Rebuild. Come through even stronger. Do you bloody well hear me..?"

Bolan heard him.

He showed he had heard by bringing up the concealed Beretta.

He saw the shock on Canfield's face in the instant before he fired.

He placed a triple burst that cored between Canfield's eyes and into his brain. He followed with two more, dropping the man where he stood, his finger frozen on the trigger of the shotgun. Canfield sprawled on the rain-soaked roof of Banecreif, his shattered skull leaking blood and brains across the slabs.

"You talk too much," Bolan said.

He let his gun hand drop to his side. Despite the wet and the cold he was too tired to move for the moment, so he stayed where he was as dawn crept over the horizon.

HAL BROGNOLA ANSWERED his phone and for a moment failed to recognize who was on the other end. It was only when he picked up the word *Banecreif* that he realized it was Bolan.

"Hey, Striker, you sound a little rough."

"It's been one of those days."

"You get your result?"

"The organization is minus its head boy. Banecreif might be open for a new tenant. After some redecoration."

"Do I pass our findings along to the task force now? They are going to think Christmas has come early. I've already had reports of Canfield's associates starting to jump ship and getting lawyered up."

"The whole package. Have a word with Aaron. He should have completed his excavations into the databases we downloaded. I figure the task force will be knocking on quite a few doors in the next week or so."

"Hey, thanks for your input, pal. We can start to pick up the pieces and step in. No doubt there's going to be some raised voices heard but with Canfield out of the frame and most of his major setups out of action...well, I guess you see the situation should work in our favor once we start producing the downloaded data."

"Before I moved out I found the drug stash Canfield had on-site."

"His new venture?"

"Yeah. Hell of a size, too. I didn't like to leave all that white powder lying around in the basement. Anyone could have wandered in and found it."

"I understand."

"Happens that Canfield kept a fuel backup in one of the outhouses with Banecreif being off the track. Diesel and gasoline. I jury-rigged supply hoses to feed in through the extraction vents to the basement. Those storage tanks held quite a few gallons. Made one hell of a blaze."

"Are you clear, Striker?"

"Way down the road. Couple of police cruisers went by a while back, but I'm observing the speed limit and out of uniform."

Brognola sighed.

"Thank God for that. Hey, you sound bushed. You need any help?"

"The final quarter got a little rough. I held my own but took some whacks."

"You fit to drive?"

"Slowly."

"Keep your cell handy. I'll see what I can fix through the U.K. task force. Make a rendezvous for you. Hell, they owe you that much. No, dammit, we *all* owe you."

"Keep an open file on this dirty business, Hal, because it isn't finished yet. If no one else does I'll be coming back to it. Sooner or later I'll be coming back. And that's a promise."

Don Pendleton

WAR TIDES

**America's new killer submarine
falls into terrorist hands....**

It's called FACOS—Fast Attack Covert
Operations Submarine—and it's now in the
hands of an elusive and violent group known
as Revenge of Allah. With this nuclear-
armed-and-powered warship poised to strike
America's eastern seaboard, failure is not an
option when Stony Man is called in.

STONY MAN®

*Available in June
wherever books are sold.*

Or order your copy now by sending your name, address, zip or postal code, along with a check or
money order (please do not send cash) for $6.99 for each book ordered ($7.99 in Canada), plus
75¢ postage and handling ($1.00 in Canada), payable to Gold Eagle Books, to:

In the U.S.
Gold Eagle Books
3010 Walden Avenue
P.O. Box 9077
Buffalo, NY 14269-9077

In Canada
Gold Eagle Books
P.O. Box 636
Fort Erie, Ontario
L2A 5X3

**GOLD
EAGLE**®

Please specify book title with your order.
Canadian residents add applicable federal and provincial taxes.

www.readgoldeagle.blogspot.com

GSM107

Don Pendleton's

Conflict Zone

**Bolan hunts human predators
in Africa's killing grounds....**

Nigeria is rich in oil, drugs and blood rivals — on both the domestic and international fronts — and Bolan is launching a two-phase campaign against the escalating violence. It's the kind of blood-and-thunder mission that Bolan fights best, the kind of war that keeps him in his element long enough to defeat the enemy and, with luck, get out alive.

*Available in June
wherever books are sold.*

Or order your copy now by sending your name, address, zip or postal code, along with a check or money order (please do not send cash) for $6.99 for each book ordered ($7.99 in Canada), plus 75¢ postage and handling ($1.00 in Canada), payable to Gold Eagle Books, to:

In the U.S.
Gold Eagle Books
3010 Walden Avenue
P.O. Box 9077
Buffalo, NY 14269-9077

In Canada
Gold Eagle Books
P.O. Box 636
Fort Erie, Ontario
L2A 5X3

GOLD EAGLE ®

Please specify book title with your order.
Canadian residents add applicable federal and provincial taxes.

www.readgoldeagle.blogspot.com

GSB134

TAKE 'EM FREE
2 action-packed novels plus a mystery bonus
NO RISK
NO OBLIGATION TO BUY

SPECIAL LIMITED-TIME OFFER

Mail to: Gold Eagle Reader Service

IN U.S.A.: P.O. Box 1867, Buffalo, NY 14240-1867
IN CANADA: P.O. Box 609, Fort Erie, Ontario L2A 5X3

YEAH! Rush me 2 FREE Gold Eagle® novels and my FREE mystery bonus (bonus is worth about $5). If I don't cancel, I will receive 6 hot-off-the-press novels every other month. Bill me at the low price of just $33.44 for each shipment.* That's a savings of over 15% off the combined cover prices and there is NO extra charge for shipping and handling! There is no minimum number of books I must buy. I can always cancel at any time simply by returning a shipment at your cost or by returning any shipping statement marked "cancel." Even if I never buy another book from Gold Eagle, the 2 free books and mystery bonus are mine to keep forever.

166 ADN EYPE 366 ADN EYPQ

Name	(PLEASE PRINT)
Address	Apt. #
City	State/Prov.	Zip/Postal Code

Signature (if under 18, parent or guardian must sign)

Not valid to current subscribers of Gold Eagle books.
Want to try two free books from another series? Call 1-800-873-8635.

* Terms and prices subject to change without notice. Prices do not include applicable taxes. Sales tax applicable in N.Y. Canadian residents will be charged applicable provincial taxes and GST. Offer not valid in Quebec. This offer is limited to one order per household. All orders subject to approval. Credit or debit balances in a customer's account(s) may be offset by any other outstanding balance owed by or to the customer. Please allow 4 to 6 weeks for delivery. Offer available while quantities last.

Your Privacy: Worldwide Library is committed to protecting your privacy. Our Privacy Policy is available online at www.eHarlequin.com or upon request from the Reader Service. From time to time we make our lists of customers available to reputable third parties who may have a product or service of interest to you. If you would prefer we not share your name and address, please check here. ☐

GE09

JAMES AXLER

DEATH LANDS®

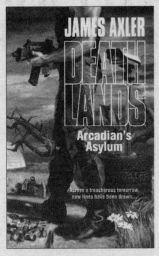

Arcadian's Asylum

Across a treacherous tomorrow, new lines have been drawn.

A lust for power and a strong sec-force are the basic requirements of any Deathlands baron. But brilliant baron Eugene Arcadian has bigger visions than a monopoly on jack and trade—he wants the future. He needs the help of Ryan Cawdor and his warrior group, and for these unwilling participants, a new terror is about to be born....

Available in May wherever books are sold.

Or order your copy now by sending your name, address, zip or postal code, along with a check or money order (please do not send cash) for $6.99 for each book ordered ($7.99 in Canada), plus 75¢ postage and handling ($1.00 in Canada), payable to Gold Eagle Books, to:

In the U.S.	**In Canada**
Gold Eagle Books	Gold Eagle Books
3010 Walden Avenue	P.O. Box 636
P.O. Box 9077	Fort Erie, Ontario
Buffalo, NY 14269-9077	L2A 5X3

Please specify book title with your order.
Canadian residents add applicable federal and provincial taxes.

www.readgoldeagle.blogspot.com

GDL92

ROGUE ANGEL ™

AleX Archer
THE BONE CONJURER

From the ashes of an ancient holy order comes an unholy relic....

Once seemingly blessed by God, the Knights Templar eventually dissolved into mysteries both sacred and profane—creating an object whose power bends to the true nature of its owner. Annja Creed hadn't heard of the Skull of Sidon and is skeptical...yet someone wants it enough to prevent Annja from protecting it. Someone with enough power to kill...

Available in May wherever books are sold.

GOLD EAGLE ®

www.readgoldeagle.blogspot.com

GRA24

He reache
with his hand. As he did so, she caught it and held it
against her cheek, and he watched as a tear fell from
her eye and ran off down the side of his finger.

"Why are you such a special man, David?"

"God, I'm not. I can tell you that straight."

"Oh yes, you are." She paused and looked deep into
his eyes. "I wonder why it couldn't have been me that
you met all those years ago in Oxford." She smiled and
took his hand round to her mouth and kissed it before
returning it to her cheek. "Just the wrong time, the
wrong place, an ocean apart."

She reached over and kissed him gently on the cheek.
Then, putting her arms around his shoulders, she pulled
her face close into his neck.

"But we found a bridge, didn't we, my greatest
friend?" she whispered quietly into his ear. "All these
years later, we found a bridge."

"Warm and readable."

—*Chicago Sun-Times*

"A warm, welcome tale of believable people and places,
told by a born storyteller . . . AN OCEAN APART is
full of beautifully painted characters . . . Though Robin
Pilcher has his own literary voice, it is obvious that in-
heritance has brightened this first long, full tale."

—*The Anniston Star*

"[Pilcher] shares with his mother a warmth that seems
quite genuine, [and] a real fondness for his characters."

—*The Orlando Sentinel*

AN
OCEAN
APART

ROBIN
PILCHER

St. Martin's Paperbacks

NOTE: If you purchased this book without a cover you should be aware that this book is stolen property. It was reported as "unsold and destroyed" to the publisher, and neither the author nor the publisher has received any payment for this "stripped book."

"The Tracks of My Tears." Words and music by William "Smokey" Robinson, Warren Moore, and Marvin Tarplin. © 1965, 1967 (renewed 1993, 1995) by JOBETE MUSIC CO., INC. All rights controlled and administered by EMI APRIL MUSIC, INC. All rights reserved. International copyright secured. Used by permission.

AN OCEAN APART

Copyright © 1999 by Robin Pilcher.

All rights reserved. No part of this book may be used or reproduced in any manner whatsoever without written permission except in the case of brief quotations embodied in critical articles or reviews. For information address St. Martin's Press, 175 Fifth Avenue, New York, N.Y. 10010.

Library of Congress Catalog Card Number: 98-11664

ISBN: 0-312-97184-2

Printed in the United States of America

St. Martin's Press hardcover edition / January 1999
St. Martin's Paperbacks edition / November 1999

St. Martin's Paperbacks are published by St. Martin's Press, 175 Fifth Avenue, New York, N.Y. 10010.

10 9 8 7 6 5 4 3 2 1

For Kirsty,

of course

Acknowledgments

The writing of this book was always a possibility, never an inevitability. For it to have come to fruition, my deepest thanks go to my wife, Kirsty, who was always there to read a chapter, a page, a sentence, a word; to Ros, who constantly encouraged and dug her son out of a literary hole more times than can be admitted; to my sister Pippa and family, who guided a lost Scotsman around Long Island; to Matthew Gloag, Bill Lumsden and Tony Tucker for their infinite knowledge of the whisky industry; to Miranda Lindsay and Charlie Pank, two Oxford students split by a decade or two; to David Nichol, who helped me thrash out the constitutional issues; to Alexander Dundee for keeping me straight on the House of Lords; to Felicity Bryan, my agent, for being on hand always at the right time; and finally to Tom, my editor extraordinaire, who, having encouraged me to write over a period of ten years, gave his all when the time came.

Chapter
ONE

Jane Spiers drove with extreme caution through the pelting rain, her shoulders hunched over the steering wheel as she strained to make out the blurred outline of the road ahead. The windscreen wipers of the old Subaru struggled to cope with the deluge pouring down from the cold grey skies, and the feeble wheezing of the car's hot-air fan was of little help in clearing the steamy fog that had developed on the inside of the windows. That was Arthur's fault. He sat, enclosed in the boot by a large dog rack, soaking wet and panting heavily after his exertion on the moor. Jane opened the window a fraction to see if a little air circulation might help but shut it immediately when she felt the sliver of icy Scottish weather suck the warmth from the car. In all the forty years that she had lived in Scotland, she could not remember a May so cold and miserable.

Turning off the main road through a pair of lodge-gates, newly painted and bearing a sign marked PRIVATE DRIVE, she drove up the long tarmacked avenue, the tall oak trees on either side at last offering some protection against the elements. In this new-found shelter, the windscreen wipers' performance improved, and Jane crunched into a higher gear.

After half a mile, the drive opened out into a gravel sweep that rounded in front of the large Victorian house. Picking up one of her gloves from the passenger seat, Jane wiped the condensation off the windscreen, eager to complete the last few yards of her journey without running over either the trimmed edge of the grass border or one of the three black Labradors who customarily came bounding down the front-door steps.

On this occasion, there was no such welcoming committee, but even as she lurched the car to a halt in front of the house, Arthur sat up in the back and whined, his ears pricked forward and his nose pressed through the square mesh of the dog rack, anticipating a mad tear-around in the garden with his three black friends. Jane looked at his plaintive face in the rear-view mirror.

"Good boy, Arthur—you stay there," she said, pulling up the hood of her Barbour jacket and tightening the draw-string under her chin. "I won't be long."

Holding hard to the door in case the wind took it completely off its ageing hinges, Jane clambered out of the car, then, slamming the door shut, she scrunched her way in a half-run across the wet gravel and up the steps to the front door. With the informality of a frequent visitor, she opened up one of the heavy oak double doors and let herself in.

"Ooooee!" she called out. "Anyone he-ere?"

No immediate reply. She took off her dripping Barbour and hung it on a hook amongst the collection of heavy tweed overcoats and waterproof jackets, then, clearing a space for herself on an old church pew, a dumping ground for fishing-tackle, hats and garden implements, she sat down to take off her sodden walking shoes.

"Hullo-o! Anyone here?" she called out again, and looked around to see if anyone had taken any heed of her call. The hallway of Inchelvie House stretched to the full height of the edifice, and was dominated by a huge central staircase which divided at right angles half-way up, leading to a balustraded landing above. Dark oak-panelled walls were lined with large family portraits intermingled with an eerie selection of crossbows, double-handed swords and shields, and above them, ranging to the highest point of the house, an array of about forty stags' heads, all rather old and moth-eaten. Jane smiled to herself, her own private thought always being that it was a toss-up as to which of these three adornments was the most hideous.

She left the pew and padded in her stockinged feet across the hallway. Approaching the bottom of the staircase, she became aware of a man's voice coming from the drawing-room. It was not a voice she recognized, more the deep, serious tone that might belong to a solicitor or chartered accountant, and instantly she wondered if she had chosen a bad time to call. She was caught in a moment of confusion, whether to try calling out again or just quietly leave, when a door opened in the far corner of the hall beyond the staircase and a small grey-haired lady appeared, precariously carrying a tray of tea and oblivious to her presence.

"Hullo, Effie," Jane said, as gently as possible, so as not to spread-eagle the little housekeeper and her load. Even at that, Effie stopped abruptly, making the contents of the tray shoot forward.

"Oh, Mrs. Spiers, whit a fright you gave me!" Effie said, steadying herself. "I didn't hear ye coming in."

Jane walked around the side of the staircase. "I'm sorry about that, Effie. I did call out twice, as loud as I thought decent." She smiled at the older woman, who was slowly recovering her composure. "I thought the dogs would probably have heard me. It's not like them to miss out on a good bark." She glanced towards the door of the drawing-room. "Tell me, is this a bad time to call? I have a feeling that Lady Inchelvie might have someone with her at this minute."

Effie shrugged up her little shoulders in a display of mousy mirth. "No, no, that's just the television you'll be hearing. Lady Inchelvie always has the volume up pretty high, and that's no doubt why the dogs never heard ye coming in." Effie always spoke quietly, as if everything she said were imparting some hugely private secret. "The snooker's on, ye see, and there's nothing she likes better than to watch the snooker." She moved forward, her eyes sparkling, ready to tell the best part of the tale. "Especially if yon Scottish laddie Stephen Hendry is playing. I think that she must be his greatest fan!"

Effie's face creased into another muted giggle, though it immediately gave way to a frown of concern when she noticed that Jane's jersey and tweed skirt were beginning to steam in the heat of the hall.

"Michty me!" Effie exclaimed. "You're surely awful wet! Dinnae tell me you've been walkin' oot on the moor wi' your dog on a day like this?"

Jane rubbed herself on the arm, Effie's observation suddenly bringing it home to her that she was indeed feeling rather damp. "If I didn't go out in weather like this, then Arthur wouldn't get a walk for about nine months of the year."

"Well, we canna have you standing around here catching your death," she said, bustling her way across the hall. "Let's get you in beside the fire, and then I'll away and fetch you an extra cup. Was Lady Inchelvie expecting you?"

"No, she wasn't. I just wanted to, well . . ." Jane stopped Effie by putting her hand on her shoulder. "Actually, the real reason why I'm here is that my husband asked me to pop in just to find out how everyone is. He's purposely not visited since Rachel . . . well, let's just say he felt that it would be better if I dropped in, sort of in passing, rather than him . . . as the family doctor, so to speak."

"Dinnae say any more," said Effie, flashing an understanding smile at her. "I'll no' tell Lady Inchelvie that you're here just yet. I'll just take in her tea-things and you go through to the kitchen, and we'll have a wee chat before you go in and see her. Does that suit you?"

"That would be just fine. Thanks, Effie."

Jane watched her scuttle off to the drawing-room, knock and enter, then turned and walked across to the door from which Effie had first appeared, and pushed it open.

The kitchen was large and utilitarian, unlike Jane's own, which she herself had lovingly converted into the hub of the house over the years. This was a complete throw-back to the green-baize-door era, all the walls being painted in a sickly yellow and cream easy-wipe gloss. There were no easy chairs, no wall decorations, just a plethora of pots and pans hanging from meat-hooks alongside three blinding strip lights above the enormous scrubbed pine table in the centre of the room, its austere cleanliness reminding her of a Victorian operating-theatre. She walked over to the old cream Aga at the far end of the kitchen and leaned on its spotless surface in order to induce some heat back into her bones.

The door opened behind her and Effie entered. "There we are now," she said, walking towards her. "Let's get the kettle on, and we can have a good natter over a nice cup of tea."

Jane moved to the side of the Aga, so that Effie could put the kettle on the hob. "Can I do anything to help?"

"No, no, you just away and sit down at the table. I know where everything is in this place. Now tell me, how is Dr. Spiers keeping?"

"Run off his feet at the minute," Jane replied, pulling out one of the kitchen chairs from the table and sitting down. "This wretched weather is really keeping the cold and flu bugs flying around. About half the children at Dalnachoil Primary School are off sick, and rather than get them brought into the surgery, he spends most of his day charging around from one house to another in the village."

Effie moved around her familiar kitchen like an automaton, taking cups and saucers from the pine Welsh dresser, then the milk from the fridge and putting everything on the table. "Aye, we're that lucky to have a man like Dr. Spiers around here." She took the steaming kettle off the Aga and poured water into the teapot, then, turning to face Jane, she took up her apron and rubbed her hands on it. "He really has been the saviour of this family over the past six months."

Jane noticed a weary expression had come over Effie's face.

"How *have* things been?" she asked.

Effie carried the teapot over to the table and sat down opposite. "Och, they come and go, up one minute, down the next." She poured out the tea into the two cups. "Lady Inchelvie has had to work like a Trojan this last month, getting all the grandchildren's things together to get them ready for returning to school. Mind, they didn't go back at the beginning of term, it being only a couple of weeks after their mother's funeral; and besides, I have an inkling that Mr. David was in two minds whether he should send them back there at all, thinking that they might be better off closer to him at the village school." She sighed and cocked her head to the side. "However, from what I can gather, it was the children's choice to go back and be with all their friends." She paused, seemingly unconvinced herself by the decision. "I don't know. Maybe a comfort for them to return to some sort of routine."

Jane took a drink from her cup. "I do think that's probably right, Effie. A different environment, yet a familiar one. Sophie has her GCSE exams this term, doesn't she?"

"Aye, she does. She's a grand wee girl—mind you, no' awful wee now, she's nearly sixteen years old, and that well-organized—just like her mother." As she said this, Effie suddenly faltered and swallowed hard, her composure suddenly under threat. "Oh, Mrs. Spiers, it's that hard getting used to not having Mrs. David around anymore."

Jane leaned across the table and patted the housekeeper's hand. "I know. My husband often wonders if cancer doesn't prepare a family better for the inevitable than, say, a heart attack or a road accident, but I don't think so. The loss when it happens is still devastating."

Effie was looking down in her lap, fiddling with her apron, her bottom lip quivering. Jane took a calculated gamble to continue the conversation.

"And what about the other children?"

Effie took a deep breath, and, almost for something to do, replenished both their cups even though Jane's was still three-quarters full. She delved into the pocket of her apron and brought out a handkerchief and wiped her eyes.

"Oh, they seemed to have coped better than any," Effie replied, managing to smile bravely, though her voice still faltered. "Even during the tea after the funeral, Charlie was badgering Mrs. David's brother to go out onto the lawn to kick a rugby ball with him. And wee Harriet, well, Sophie just seemed to take her under her wing. I don't really think the wee lass has taken it all in just yet. It's a blessing that all three are at the same school." She leaned across to Jane and said with a caring look, "Sophie will look after her, you can be sure of that."

Jane smiled and nodded. "Everyone plays a part in the healing process, Effie, not least you. You're as much a part of this family as any, and I know that everyone would have found it hard to cope without your being here."

The older woman went rather pink, not used to being praised quite so openly. She got up from her chair and cleared away the cups and saucers. "Och, we all do what we can under these kind of circumstances." She pulled open the dishwasher and started loading the racks.

Jane picked up the milk jug from the table and carried it over to the fridge, playing for time before asking the next question. "And what about David? How is he?"

Effie closed the door of the dishwasher and turned towards Jane. There was a moment's silence, an expression of concentrated bewilderment on her face as she tried to work out in her mind what to say. Then she just shook her head.

"I really canna tell, Mrs. Spiers. I mean, I have to say that he was wonderful as always wi' his children when they were home, playing tennis and fishing wi' them and all that, but even so, there always seemed to be something missing, as if he was only going through the motions. It was as if his mind was away somewhere else." She smiled at Jane and picked up a cloth from the sink and started to wipe absently at the draining-board. She stopped and nodded her head slowly. "Aye, now I think about it, it was the laughter that was missing." She looked across at Jane. "Maybe he's just finding it awful hard to concentrate properly on anyone but his wife. Dr. Spiers will no doubt have told you that he had nursed her entirely by himself since December." She turned away and looked out the window, and Jane heard her voice once again begin to falter. "I've a wee feeling that he was so devoted to her that some part of him died wi' her."

Jane went over to the little housekeeper and, putting her arm around her shoulder, gave it a comforting squeeze. "I can see that, Effie. I know that it must be really hard for you to talk about it, and I do appreciate you telling me." Jane felt that she had to break the melancholy of the conversation, and looked up at the clock above the Aga. "Heavens, it's half past four. I had no idea it was that late."

Effie turned from the sink, and on reaction looked

up at the clock as well. "Och, Mrs. Spiers, what am I doin'? I shouldn't be going on so." She started to move towards the door, drying her hands on her apron. "Come on, I'll take you through to see Lady Inchelvie."

"Oh, please don't bother to do that," Jane said. "Look, I'll just show myself in. I'm sure that you've enough to do in here."

"Well, if you're sure. I'll have to be gettin' started on the potatoes for dinner. Lord Inchelvie has a meeting in the village tonight, so we'll be eating early."

"Absolutely. I've been enough hindrance to you." She walked over to the door of the kitchen, then turned to the housekeeper. "Keep your spirits up, Effie. You really are one of the mainstays of the household. Just keep being as cheerful as you always have been."

The volume of the television hit Jane as soon as she entered the drawing-room, the usually whispered tones of the snooker commentator sounding as though he were speaking through a megaphone.

"*. . . and if he can get a good angle on the pink ball, that should be the third consecutive frame to Hendry.*"

The three black Labrador dogs, however, heard Jane's entry above the noise, and, looking in her direction, each let out a short bark before realizing that it was a familiar figure. They left their place in front of the blazing fire and trotted over, their backquarters slewing from side to side with delight.

"Hullo, boys," Jane said, reaching down to pat their heads.

At the far end of the room, a figure moved in the high-backed armchair in front of the television. "Is that you, Effie?"

Unable to move any closer due to the keenness of the dogs' welcome, Jane called out, "No, Alicia, it's me—Jane."

Alicia Inchelvie peered round the corner of the chair, bowing slightly to look over the top of her reading spectacles. "Jane! How wonderful to see you! What a lovely surprise!"

She turned the television off with the remote control and rose to her feet, pushing a large ball of red wool onto the ends of two enormous knitting-needles. "Dogs, go and lie down and let poor Jane get into the room!"

Alicia walked rather stiffly towards Jane, her spectacles, now dangling by a cord around her neck, swinging from side to side as she walked. She was a tall and erect figure, dressed in her customary elegance of a tweed skirt and cashmere cardigan, with her grey hair pulled tight and gathered in a comb at the back of her head. It was the first time that Jane had seen her since the funeral five weeks previously, and although Alicia's whole comportment belied her seventy-eight years, it was obvious that even that short intervening period had taken its toll. There was now a drawn look on her face, a look of total fatigue, one that Jane surmised as being brought about by Alicia's own inner conflict to keep her thoughts of loss and anguish under control, so that outwardly she could appear strong and supportive to the rest of her family.

Two of the dogs took immediate heed of their mistress's request to return to the fireside. The other, an old greying boy with opaque eyes and obviously fading hearing, continued to wag his tail and gaze up lovingly at Jane, impeding any attempt she made to move farther across the room. Alicia's voice rose a full tone.

"HORACE!" she yelled in the direction of the dog. "GO AND LIE DOWN BY THE FIRE." She gesticulated like a policeman on point duty, waving on the old dog with one hand and pointing with the other, still clutching the knitting-needles, in the general direction of the fire. Horace looked sideways up at his mistress, her voice now having penetrated his senses, and, unclear as to why she held aloft those menacing objects in her hand, he slunk sheepishly away to join his younger companions.

"I'm sorry," Alicia said. "Horace is almost totally deaf now, rather like me. Can't hear anything unless it's at full volume. How are you, my dear?" She met Jane half-way across the room and gave her a kiss on both cheeks. "Come and sit down by the fire. What a revolting day! Would you like a cup of tea? I've just had one, but let me call Effie—"

"No, don't worry," Jane interjected. "I've actually just had one with Effie in the kitchen."

Alicia looked at her, surprised. "Have you? How extraordinary; I never heard you come in. How long have you been here?"

"Oh, about three quarters of an hour. No, actually I did want to speak to Effie about something." She smiled knowingly at her friend. "At any rate, I didn't want to interrupt the snooker!"

"Ah, so she's been telling you about my secret addiction, has she?" Alicia said, sitting back down in her chair. "I must say I get totally mesmerized by it, and it's such a treat to see so many young Scots being rather good at a sport! Really makes one feel quite patriotic, although I'm sure that being good at snooker reveals a somewhat misspent youth!"

"Absolutely," said Jane. "Who needs exam results when you can make money potting balls!"

They both dissolved into laughter, and Jane immediately felt at ease, any fears of how the overriding gloom of present circumstances might have affected her long-time friend expelled from her mind. They were still very much on the same wavelength, still able to laugh together.

Alicia put on her spectacles again, uncoupled the ball of wool from the end of the needles and resumed her knitting. For a second there was silence, as if her thoughts were taken up on a different plane. Then she looked up and smiled across at Jane.

"It's lovely to see you, my dear. I really have missed

you. As you can imagine, life hasn't been filled with a great many happy thoughts lately."

"I quite understand. I should have popped in before now, but I didn't want to intrude." Jane watched Alicia as she concentrated on her knitting. "What are you making?"

"Oh, just something that Sophie started during the last holidays. It seems to be the rage at her school to have a chunky sweater with huge arms that come down at least six inches over the hands." She looked at Jane over her spectacles. "The waif look, I think. I took her into Inverness to see if we could find one, but they were all dreadfully acrylic, so we ended up buying a pattern and this rather garish wool." Alicia held the shapeless garment up at arm's length and wrinkled up the side of her nose in an expression of uncertainty as to what the end result might look like. "I have a feeling that it might look a little better on a large male gorilla than on Sophie."

"Well," said Jane, "I'm sure that if Sophie doesn't like it, there would be a welcome recipient at Edinburgh Zoo."

"You're not meant to agree with me Jane," Alicia retorted, feigning hurt. "You're supposed to say something like 'It's far too well-made for that!'" She laughed, then abruptly bundled knitting-needles, sweater, and ball of wool into one heap and threw it onto the sofa. "Anyway, I don't know why on earth I'm doing it when you're here. Come on," she said, getting up from her chair and manoeuvring her way through the prostrate dogs to put another log on the fire, "tell me what's going on in the outside world. I don't seem to have been in touch with anyone for so long."

It took Jane all of five minutes to fill Alicia in with the most important topics of local news: how the incessant rain had washed away part of the back road between Dalnachoil and Achnacudden, and how the local Territorial Army Brigade had come to the aid of the already overstretched roads division by erecting a temporary Baillie Bridge over the yawning gap; how Mrs. Mackenzie, the postmistress in Dalnachoil, had also been affected by the weather, bringing on a dreadful bout of arthritis which "literally ballooned up my ankles, Mrs. Spiers, and I have to serve all my customers sitting on a chair behind the counter wi' my bedroom slippers on"; how everyone in the village had been asking kindly after all those at Inchelvie. And finally she told Alicia about how the influenza bug had hit the local school, and how Roger had taken it upon himself to visit all the children at home, rather than risk its spread by treating them in his surgery.

Alicia looked concerned. "You know, my dear, that husband of yours works far too hard. I mean, he really should have retired last year, shouldn't he? Maybe that's a silly thing to say knowing that the prime reason he kept going was to look after Rachel, but now can't he get one of his younger partners to do all these house calls? They really are going to have to start coping without him."

Jane sat back in her chair and sighed. "Oh, I know, and don't think I haven't put that argument forward on more than one occasion. What makes it more difficult is that I do have one of his partners phoning me up every so often to ask if I could gently persuade Roger to call it a day. I'm really caught between the devil and the deep blue sea. Anyway," Jane said, sitting up and looking at Alicia, "we're both in the same boat at the minute, aren't we? Having husbands who should have retired but are still working?"

Alicia smiled. "You're right, but mine are more exceptional circumstances."

"Of course they are. Tell me, how is George?"

"Like everyone else around here—totally exhausted, even though I think he's actually secretly enjoying his return to active duty. Nevertheless, if you've been retired for ten years, suddenly to have to start working again really comes as a jolt to the system. Not that he's hugely overtaxed. The new managing director at Glendurnich, Duncan Caple, is doing a wonderful job running both the business and David's marketing division, but George just feels that as he's the chairman and major shareholder *and* David's father, he should give support where he can, especially as the whisky market seems to be in such turmoil at the minute. I don't really pretend to know that much about it now, but there do seem to be an ever-increasing number of licensed trade dinners and marketing launches that George has to attend on behalf of the distillery."

Alicia paused for a moment, placing her elbow on the arm of the chair and resting the side of her face in her hand.

"But do you know, Jane, what we both find *so* energy-sapping is having to go back to a hectic daily routine we thought we'd left behind years ago! Having to get *up* in the morning, having to get children ready for going back to school, and then having them here all the time meant that one was always on call to entertain them. Heavens, just before he went back to school, Charlie had me out on the lawn operating the clay-pigeon trap! Can you imagine it? I'm absolutely hopeless with mechanical devices, and he kept shouting at me, 'Come on, Granny, you're useless!' as I launched off clays one after the other at about the level of his knees!" She laughed and sat forward in her chair. "Actually, come to think of it, this is about the first time that I've sat down and indulged myself for about a month!"

"Oh, I'm sorry, Alicia," said Jane, "and I come barging in and disrupt your peace."

Alicia waved her hand dismissively. "Don't be silly, my dear. This is exactly what the doctor ordered." She looked at Jane with a quizzical smile on her face. "Well, isn't it?"

Jane gave a surprised expression. "My word, that's intuitive of you." She smiled. "Of course, you're right; Roger did ask me to drop in to see you, just to find out how you all were. That's why I had a quiet word with Effie beforehand, just in case my timing wasn't very good." She paused for a moment. "She said that David is still keeping very much to himself."

"Yes, he is," Alicia said quietly. One of the Labradors had moved from his position by the fire and now lay at her feet, his head resting on her shoe. She bent forward and stroked his sleek black crown. "You know, the appalling thing about this whole affair is that he's going through something which neither you nor I have experienced. He has lost his life's partner. It's just so unfair." Alicia's tone had suddenly changed to one of anger and frustration. "Think of the many friends we have of our age who have lost their husbands or wives. That in a way is expected. But neither you nor I know what it's like, because it hasn't happened to us." She stopped talking and combed a loose strand of grey hair behind her ear with her fingers, her eyes looking at a point somewhere behind Jane's head. "I'm sorry, I didn't mean that. I think that that is the first time I've said it out loud. It's just that it makes me feel . . . well . . . so guilty."

"But that's natural," Jane said caringly. "The pain of losing someone close to you always seems to manifest itself in anger or guilt. But there is a positive side to it, and that is that David is extremely lucky, at forty-three years of age or whatever, to still have both his parents around to give their support. How could he have devoted so much time to looking after Rachel if you and George hadn't been there to pick up all the loose ends? Friends are great, but parents are better. And I'm sure that he's fully aware of that."

"I know, I know, but one just feels so useless. I wish that there was something, well, active that I could do to help him. If only he would let himself talk about it once in a while, but he just seems to bottle himself up. As far as I'm aware, he hasn't mentioned Rachel's name since the funeral. Outwardly, it's as if she never existed, but inwardly, I know he's in turmoil. It's a terrible thing to say, but sometimes I feel like grabbing the poor boy by the shoulders and giving him a jolly good shake." Alicia took a deep breath. "And then giving him a huge hug."

In the moment's silence that followed, Jane was aware for the first time of the wind and rain beating against the four large double-paned windows of the drawing-room. She looked over her shoulder and upwards at the black storm-clouds that spread themselves oppressively across the sky, and thought to herself how cruelly the elements accentuated the tragedy that had befallen this household. Her instincts told her that she shouldn't follow this line of conversation any further. Enough had been said for the moment, and it would serve no useful purpose to either Alicia or herself to continue it. She turned from the window and shook her head.

"Would you believe this weather for May?" She glanced up at the silver carriage clock on the mantelpiece above the fire. "It's only a quarter past five, and it's nearly dark." She did a double take. "Oh, my word, Alicia, a quarter past five! What am I thinking of?" She put her hands on the arms of the chair and pushed herself to her feet. "Poor Arthur has been sitting all this time in the back of my car, and I promised him that I would only be a moment. He'll probably have eaten his way through the dog rack by now."

Alicia rose stiffly from her chair. "My dear, you should have brought him in. The boys would have loved to have seen him."

"No, he would only have caused chaos. He's not as well-behaved as your dogs. Anyway, we had a lovely walk on the moor earlier on this afternoon, and he was soaking wet."

"Well, he's lucky to have such a devoted mistress to take him out on a day like this. I have to admit that I've been totally feeble. The boys' walk today consisted of my going to the front door, opening it and pushing them out for ten minutes. I am certainly not going out in weather like this!" Alicia went over to one of the windows and unhooked the cords that held back the huge room-high damask curtains. "And I really don't think that it is going to improve very much either. Better just to shut it out, don't you think?" she said, pulling the heavy curtains across the window.

Jane walked over to the middle window to do the same. As she unhooked the first cord, she looked out of the window at the darkness falling on the gardens of Inchelvie House. They were, even on this day, quite beautiful. Protected on either side by giant beech- and oak-trees, the long lawns swept majestically down to the dark frothy waters of the fishing-loch, their regularity split by meandering herbaceous borders with azaleas and rhododendrons in the early stages of bloom. Daffodils, still flowering due to the prolonged winter, bravely held their yellow heads high, a small splash of colour in defiance of the all-encompassing greyness of the day. To the right of the lawns, where two parallel paths ran between neat box hedges to the wall garden, Jane noticed that distinct changes had been made to the layout of the garden, the dark rich soil recently dug over to form two new flower-beds symmetrical to those on the west side of the lawn. She was about to turn and remark on this to Alicia, when a movement in the flower-bed farthest to the right caught her eye. She pressed her face closer to the window, cupping her hands around her eyes to cut out the light from the drawing-room behind her.

"Alicia, there seem to be . . ." Jane felt Alicia's arm brush hers as she came to stand beside her. She too cupped her hands over her face.

Alicia continued for her. ". . . two men standing out

in the wind and rain digging holes in the garden and getting extremely wet."

"What *are* they doing?" She screwed up her eyes in an attempt to accustom her sight better to the fading light.

Alicia laughed. "My dear, don't you recognize them? It's David and Jock—you know, Effie's husband. They've been out there all day planting roses in that new flower-bed."

Jane turned and looked incredulously at Alicia. "In weather like this? What on earth for? They could end up catching double pneumonia if they're not careful."

"I tell you, it's more than my life's worth to try to stop them. For the past five months, that garden has been David's greatest therapy."

"Really? In what way?" Jane said, turning back to look out the window to where the two men were working.

Alicia drew one of the curtains across the window. "Do you remember when David gave up work at Glendurnich last December and moved Rachel and the family here from The Beeches after her first course of chemotherapy?"

"Yes, of course," Jane said, standing back from the window to allow the other curtain to be drawn across.

"Well, at that time George thought that it would be a good idea if David had something to occupy his mind, so he asked him to help look after the estate." Alicia moved away from the window and leaned against the back of one of the sofas, her arms stretched out at either side to support her. "Anyway, it became pretty clear to David that the farm manager was coping quite well without his input, and it just happened that while he was looking for some papers in the farm office one day, he unearthed these old plans of how the Inchelvie gardens looked when the house was first built. Apparently, some of the original flower-beds had vanished, I think probably sown out in grass about the time of the Great

War, when manpower was scarce. So, on an impulse, David took it upon himself to reinstate the garden to its former glory, and that is where he has quite literally spent every free minute since. Whenever Rachel was receiving treatment in Inverness or just in the house asleep, David would head out to the garden, pore over his old drawings, and start digging away." Alicia laughed, raising herself from the back of the sofa. "Somewhere along the line, he roped in Jock to give him a hand. I don't think the old boy has ever worked so hard in his life."

They both walked over to the third window. It was now almost totally dark outside, but once again they cupped their hands around their faces to look out the window. The two figures had now moved closer to the house, and were dimly lit by the weak shaft of light that came from Jane and Alicia's window. David, bareheaded, with his hair plastered flat by the rain, stood talking to Jock, who, enveloped in a huge yellow fisherman's raincoat, peered from the shelter of an equally large sou'wester at the plastic-covered paper that David held in his right hand.

Alicia and Jane moved back from the window, both instinctively feeling that they didn't want to be caught looking out at the two men. Alicia turned and smiled at Jane. "The anger that that garden must have absorbed over the past five months has to be immeasurable."

She drew together the curtains of the remaining window and shut out the day.

Chapter
TWO

George Inchelvie closed the file on his desk, put the top on his fountain-pen and clipped it into the inside pocket of his tweed jacket. A squall of wind and rain hitting hard against the office window made him turn around in his chair to look out at the row of young silver birches, planted the previous year to give future shelter to the distillery's new car-park, as they waved their thin branches in submission to the battering that they were receiving.

He glanced at his wrist-watch. It was half past four. He pressed the intercom button on his telephone, and immediately the soft Highland tones of his young secretary lilted through the system.

"Yes, Lord Inchelvie?"

"Mhairi, I'm going to leave the office early today. I have a meeting in Dalnachoil this evening, and I want to get home before the weather gets any worse. Do you have any messages for me?"

"Let me just check, my lord." He heard the sound of turning pages crackle through the intercom. "No, I can't see anything."

"Right. You have confirmed with the Whisky Association that I'll be attending the conference in Glasgow next week?"

"Yes, and I've booked you into Devonshire Place for the Tuesday and Wednesday nights."

"Well done. If you could make sure that it's a twin-bedded room, just in case Lady Inchelvie wants to come down to Glasgow with me."

"Very good, my lord."

"Thank you very much, Mhairi. I'll see you tomorrow."

"Good night, my lord. Make sure you drive carefully, now."

"I will do, Mhairi," he said, smiling to himself at the young girl's motherly concern. He clicked off the intercom and leaned over to pick up the walking-stick that lay at the side of his desk. He rose from his chair, supporting himself both on the stick and on the edge of the desk, and stood for a minute, anticipating the sharp pain that would shoot down his left leg once he started walking.

. He had never given much thought to the wound he had received in Holland during the war, even though at the time the bullet had only been two inches off shattering his spine, but now the incessant cold and wet weather, coupled with his advancing years, seemed to aggravate it more than ever before.

He swung through ninety degrees on his heels so that he was in line with the coat-stand, then, with the fingers of his free hand pressed deep into the base of his back, he took a step forward. It was like a hot knife jabbing into his left side, but he kept moving forward, knowing that it would ease off steadily after each step. He made it to the coat-stand, took down the old tweed overcoat and shrugged it onto his shoulders, and passing the stick from one hand to the other to maintain his balance, he placed the battered homburg on his head and opened the door of his office.

Making his way slowly through the open-plan trading hall of Glendurnich Distilleries Ltd., he headed towards the large glass double doors at the far end which led out into the reception area. He did not like the new layout of Glendurnich's offices but, even as chairman, he had felt that any criticism might be taken as being stuffy and nostalgic. During his more active days with the company, little had changed in the interior of the building since his great-great-grandfather Alasdair Corstorphine had produced the first bottle of Glendurnich Malt Whisky in 1852. Then it had been a rabbit-warren of small oak-panelled offices linked by narrow passages providing direct access to the distillery itself, and therefore constantly bustling with management, secretaries and distillery workers. George had always felt that, by design or default, it was this format that had created the autonomous structure on which the company had built its history of success, one which had been precipitated in 1882 through a chance sampling of Glendurnich's Finest Malt by the Prince of Wales in one of the many London clubs that he frequented. Within a week, the whisky's name had been brought to the attention of the discerning populace through the gossip columnists of every national newspaper. The future king, it was reported, had taken such a liking to Glendurnich's product that "now he feels that there is a worthwhile reason to visit his mother at Balmoral on a regular basis."

By the end of 1889, Glendurnich had doubled its production to 66,000 gallons a year, and in the following year the company was granted a Royal Warrant as purveyors of Scotch Whisky to the Royal Household. Then in 1906, Alasdair's son, Ralph Corstorphine, who found time to be both a Member of Parliament and chairman of Glendurnich, was granted an Hereditary Peerage for services both to government and to industry, choosing the name of Inchelvie after the vast rambling house that he had had built for himself on the moorland estate near Grantown-on-Spey.

Yet these accolades were seen as being achievements of the distillery as a whole rather than those of any individual, and the Corstorphine family never lost sight of that. The hierarchy in the company was built around the workers' knowledge of whisky distilling rather than on the basis of managerial status. One of George's abiding memories was that of his father, himself chairman of the company at the time, leaning against a radiator in one of the passages gleaning information on a point of whisky production from the two young McLachlan brothers, the distillery's stillman and mashman; they would be on the way to the workers' canteen, he on the way to a meeting.

But now the corridors, the individual offices, and the history had been torn out of the building on the recommendations of a London-based architect. George had been shown the drawings by David before the work was commissioned, and the architect, in his accompanying letter, had stated that his design would create *"a workplace in harmony with the requirements of modern technology, where staff could be flexible in utilizing the integrated computer system which in turn would provide an informational network that would optimize Total Quality Management and gear Glendurnich to attain new targets in the next millennium."*

George had thought at the time that the letter and the plans were balderdash. What was more, there had been no provision in the design to allow access by distillery workers to the new building, they having a canteen built nearer to their place of work, so that the turnaround time between shifts could be cut down.

George smiled to himself. Maybe it was a relief to the workers that they didn't have to run the risk of meeting the chairman and losing half their break-time in conversation with him. At any rate, having become involved once more with Glendurnich over the past six months, he had had to admit to himself that the new building, although impersonal, created a fresh and airy efficiency that had been lacking in the old corridors and stuffy offices. More importantly, it was able to accommodate those who held the twenty or so much-valued jobs that had been created by the continued expansion of Glendurnich.

But that didn't mean he had to like it. He walked at his own deliberate pace through the clusters of buzzing work-stations, past accounts, marketing, distribution, aware that his shambling figure must seem a total anachronism to those working on the hi-tech immediacy of the company's new business systems. Nevertheless, young faces looked up from their desks or turned from their computer screens, offering a polite "Good afternoon, Lord Inchelvie" as he ambled slowly past. He reciprocated the greeting to each with a smile and a nod, adding their first names when he could remember them.

George had made it three quarters of the way up the hall when a young man seated at the desk nearest the glass doors jumped up and held one open for him. He waited there for a full fifteen seconds, a smile beaming across his face, until George finally reached him. "There you are, my lord," he said.

"Thank you very much, ah"—George looked at him—"I'm sorry, I don't know your name."

"Archie McLachlan, my lord."

George raised his eyebrows in surprise. "My word, don't tell me you're a relation of the McLachlan brothers?"

"Aye, I am that. Gregor McLachlan was my grandfather."

"How extraordinary. I was just thinking about your grandfather and great-uncle when I came out of my office. They were both quite legendary in this distillery, you know."

The young man's eyes lit up with pride. "I was always led to believe that, my lord."

"Well, it's wonderful to know the family connection

still continues." George glanced at the young man's desk. "You're in distribution, aren't you?"

"At the minute. I'm on a year's training scheme. I've done nine months in the distillery, and now I'm in the office for the remaining period."

"Jolly good, Archie." George put his hand out to the young man. "Let's keep more than one family tradition going here, shall we?"

Archie dived his own hand into the outstretched palm of the old man and shook it once as if sealing a deal. "I'd certainly like to think that, my lord."

George gave the young boy a smiling wink and walked through the door into the reception area. This was the one part of the building that the architect had not been allowed to alter. Four ancient brown leather sofas sat snugly against the panelled walls hung with old sepia photographs of the distillery from the turn of the century. An old, ornate grandfather clock ticked soothingly away between two glass-fronted mahogany cabinets, displaying bottles of Glendurnich specially packaged to mark historic occasions, amongst them the Victory Malts of 1918 and 1945 and the Coronation Malts dating back to 1903. Alongside the bottles stood photographs: a Royal visit; a presentation at a golf tournament; a huge racing yacht keeling at a gravity-defying angle, its ballooning spinnaker bearing the corporate livery of Glendurnich; and flanking the displays were two large silver trophies, spoils won by the distillery's own shinty team.

But probably the most important and invaluable asset of all was Margaret, the receptionist. There had never been any need for security at Glendurnich while she had been guarding the front door. A large and formidable lady, George had always felt that Margaret spoke to humankind as if it were, in its entirety, profoundly deaf.

She had acquired her first job in the typing pool forty years previously with a little help from her father, the distillery's head brewer. Then, five years later, she had been offered the position of receptionist, and thereafter it had been her domain, holding court behind her desk, one eye on the telephone exchange and the other on the front door. Her retirement had been mooted once at a board meeting, but it had been passed over as quickly as any resolution in the history of the company. Since then, it was widely considered that her departure would bear an ill omen for Glendurnich, similar to the ravens leaving the Tower of London. She also happened to be the prime reason why no changes had been allowed to be made to the reception area.

She looked up from her desk as George came through the glass door. "Och, is this you on your way home, then?"

"Yes, Margaret, I have a meeting in Dalnachoil tonight. I thought I'd leave a little earlier, what with the weather being so bad."

Margaret pushed her large frame from her chair and went around behind it to retrieve something from the floor, her enormous tartan posterior momentarily being the only part of her visible over the top of the desk. "Now if you'll just hold on a minute," her voice strained from behind the desk.

She re-emerged, blowing slightly from the exertion of her effort, carrying a large beige mackintosh and a multi-coloured golfing umbrella. "I'll just see you out to your car. We canna have you getting soaked to the skin."

"Now, Margaret, that's very kind of you, but really quite unnecessary—" George was unable to finish, his voice drowned by Margaret's swift rebuff.

"I'll not hear another word, my lord. Let me just get my coat on, and we'll brave the elements together, shall we?"

Margaret placed the umbrella on her desk and began clambering into her mackintosh. "And tell me," she asked in an almost normal pitch of voice, "how is Mr. David keeping?"

"He's all right, Margaret. He still has a few things to get straightened out, but I'm sure he'll be back at work quite soon."

"Well, I hope he will, my lord, because we all certainly miss having him around." She fastened the buttons of the coat and pulled the belt closed around her ample front. "If you could just say that I was asking after him."

"Of course I will. Thank you."

They were almost at the revolving door when the telephone rang on Margaret's desk. She hurried back, picked up the receiver and shouted into it. "Hullo, reception . . . yes, hullo, Mr. Caple . . . No, Lord Inchelvie is still here, but he's on his way home, he has a meeting tonight . . . very good, I'll ask him . . . very good, Mr. Caple." She put down the receiver and turned to George. "Mr. Caple wonders if you could just spare him a few moments. He says he'll be along right away."

George smiled. "That's what happens when one tries to sneak away early. Always found out. Thanks anyway, Margaret. I think you should just take your coat off again. I know how long Mr. Caple's 'few moments' are."

As Margaret went back behind the reception desk, the glass doors leading from the trading hall opened and Duncan Caple appeared. A tall, angular young man in his late thirties, he looked more like an accountant than the driven, dynamic business man he was. It was on these qualities that he had built his reputation, and the reason why David, a year before, had been instrumental in head-hunting him from a Jerez-based sherry company to take on the managing directorship of Glendurnich. However, even though George acknowledged him as being a man of immense capability in business, he also saw him lacking both in personality and social charm.

"George, old fellow, how kind of you to wait," Duncan said, walking towards him. George looked hard at the young man, already rankled by his informality and the way in which he always spoke to him in a slow and condescending manner, as if he himself were in the early stages of Alzheimer's.

Duncan reached him and held out his hand, a gesture that George felt was unnecessary as he had already seen him on three separate occasions that day. Nevertheless, he grasped the proffered hand and squeezed it as tight as he could to show Duncan that his befuddled brain was still capable of sending messages to the muscles in his arm.

"I don't want to be too long, Duncan. I've got to go to a meeting tonight."

"That's fine by me. I won't keep you. Maybe if we could just slip into the boardroom for a moment." He walked over to a door that led off the reception area, opened it and stood aside with his arm outstretched to usher George in before him. He turned to Margaret. "Hold all calls, please, until I'm finished with Lord Inchelvie."

Out of sheer devilment, George thought that he would assert his own constitutional rank over the proceedings from the outset. He walked straight over to the large ornate chair at the head of the boardroom table, hooked his stick on its back, and eased himself down between its two leathered arms, pulling the puckered flaps of his overcoat from beneath him and wrapping them around his body.

"Have a seat, Duncan," he said, pointing to the chair next to him.

Duncan sat down, then slid his back down the chair, stretching his legs out in front of him and crossing them at the ankles. He linked his hands behind his head and smiled, the informality of his actions a wordless snub to George's own small stand for conformity.

"How's David?" he asked abruptly.

George eyed him, wondering whether there was an ulterior motive for leading off with the question or whether it had come out of genuine concern.

He answered slowly. "Well enough. He still has a great deal to sort out at home, what with Rachel's estate and everything, but he's getting there."

Duncan puffed out his cheeks. "Good . . . good," he said, nodding his head slowly. "I'm glad to hear that."

He suddenly untwined his limbs and pulled his seat forward, leaning his elbows on the table and resting his chin on his hands. "Listen, George, we have a problem, and I can't really see a way of getting around it . . . well, the way things stand at the minute."

George was momentarily taken aback by Duncan's unexpected candour. "If I can be of some help . . ."

"Well, I think you can, George." He looked up. "You see, I think we should change our distributor in the States."

George shifted in his chair and looked hard at the young man. "What? You want to change from Lacey's? Why would you want to do that? They've been our agents for the past fifty years. I mean, Jim Lacey's a great friend of mine."

Duncan held up his hands, as if to stem the flow of words. "Maybe so, George, maybe so, but the fact is that over the past year, Lacey's have been slipping further and further behind their projected sales targets for Glendurnich. The latest Morgan-Graz MR report came in last week, and it showed quite blatantly that our market loss in the States corresponds directly with the rise in sales of Glenlivet and Glenfiddich. We simply can't afford to lose market share in this way."

George was silent for a moment, rubbing the side of his craggy face with his hand and staring towards the far end of the boardroom table. "You'll have to hold a board meeting. You can't make that kind of decision by yourself."

"I know, George; I'm calling one for the day after tomorrow. I have to take action on this straight away. I want a new distributor appointed by the end of this month."

"My God, that's the week after next!"

"I realize that, but it's urgent, and that . . . well . . . that is the reason I asked after David."

"What do you mean?" George asked.

"Well"—Duncan leaned back in his chair again—"I want David back at work as soon as possible."

George exploded. "Out of the question!" he said vehemently. "I mean, we can easily handle this ourselves, and David has more than enough on his plate at the minute. Anyway, you said yourself that he could take as long as he needed."

Duncan nodded. "Of course, but that was before all this came to light. Listen, we *can't* handle it ourselves. I'm going to be in London and Europe from the middle of next week, and you're going to be in Glasgow for the Whisky Association conference." Duncan paused, smoothing his hair back from his brow with both hands. "And David is still the marketing director of Glendurnich. I'm afraid it *has* to be his job to appoint the new distributor."

George rested his elbow on the arm of the chair and, closing his eyes, began rubbing his forehead in small circular movements with his fingers, his mind suddenly brought into involuntary conflict over his own instinctive paternal protection of his offspring and the continued well-being of his business. He had a mental vision of his son, who only a year before had himself been a vital and dynamic young man with his whole happy life mapped out before him, and who now spent every one of his waking hours endlessly and mindlessly digging in the garden at Inchelvie, never wishing to end his task lest his brain be taken over with thoughts of his dead wife.

Duncan watched him closely, noticing the colour

drain from his face. He was about to say something when George spoke slowly.

"I do mean it. I don't think that David can take on anything like this just yet."

Duncan thought for a moment. "I was about to say, George, that it may be just what David needs—to get away from Scotland, to go somewhere completely different. I promise you it won't be too taxing. All David will really have to do is . . . well, just be there."

Lord Inchelvie sighed, realizing that for once the wretched man was actually showing some concern. "I know," he said, his voice sounding old and thin, "and I'm grateful for your understanding of the situation. But it's not just that. I'm pretty sure that David wouldn't want to be too far from the children just at the minute."

The smile slid from Duncan's face. He looked at George for a moment, then rose from his chair and started to pace up the boardroom.

"Listen, I quite see your point, but you have to look at it from where I stand. I was brought into this company a year ago to make sure that it grows. So far, I have achieved this. However, I cannot continue to do it without your full support. Right now, I am in desperate need of a marketing director. I cannot afford to lose further market share in our single most important overseas market." He turned and looked directly at George. "I really do need a marketing director right now. I'm sorry to have to say this, George, but if David is not able to fulfil his role, then I'll have to think about replacing him." Duncan had reached the other end of the table. He swung around briskly to face George before continuing. "Regardless of who David is, I'm afraid that I will have to ask the board to give this its full consideration at the meeting."

Duncan looked at his watch. "I hope I haven't kept you too long. Will you still be able to make your meeting?"

George nodded slowly and raised his hand in acknowledgement.

"Well, good night, then, and drive carefully. I think the roads may well be pretty dicey with all this rain."

He turned towards the door, opened it and left the room. George sat for a moment, then rose from his chair and shuffled over to the telephone on the table at the side of the boardroom. He lifted the receiver and dialled.

"Hullo, Hamish? . . . Yes, it's George Inchelvie . . . Listen, I'm afraid that I won't be able to make the meeting tonight . . . no, I'm sorry, but something has cropped up. Can you give my apologies? Thank you, Hamish. All well? . . . Good . . . my love to Christine . . . goodbye."

Chapter THREE

Jock leaned his fork against his body and blew on his hands in a vain attempt to get some warmth back into his numbed fingers. As twilight set in, the rain seemed to come on harder, and the sound of David digging next to him was drowned out by the heavy splattering on his sou'wester and the arctic wind that whisked about his face. Jock winced as he picked up his fork, the dampness kneading at his arthritic shoulders. He looked over to David, who as always continued to dig without break, oblivious to the conditions in which he was working.

"Mr. David."

David straightened up, dug his fork into the ground and looked round.

"Mr. David, it's getting kind of dark."

David snorted a laugh at Jock's morose diplomacy, knowing full well that this understatement of fact was Jock's way of saying that they were both bloody mad to be out digging a garden in the pouring rain, with darkness falling so fast that they could hardly see what they were doing.

But that was Jock. As long as David had known him, and that must be, he thought on reflection, for the best part of his life, Jock had always been miserly with words. He would work away in the garden with such a dark look of solemnity on his face, it was as if he held the world in its entirety responsible for this inability to communicate. Yet under this hard exterior was a kind heart, and it had been Jock himself who had approached David at the outset of his task to restore the old flower-beds with a short, offhand statement to show his willingness to lend support. "Here, man, you've no idea how to handle a fork, do ye?"

After that they had worked together constantly, Jock greeting David each morning with a flick of his chin to the side and a sound emanating from his mouth that was as brief and as incomprehensible as a question mark. It was a perfect partnership. Neither wished to talk about himself or his thoughts; the physical act of digging and raking the new beds, planting the new roses, and watching their efforts take shape was sufficient to create a bond of understanding between the two men.

David looked up at the blackened sky and nodded. "Yes, Jock, I think you're probably right. Sorry about keeping you out so long. I was hoping that we might be able to finish this bed today." He pulled his fork out of the ground, stepped back off the flower-bed onto the grass, and for a moment surveyed their day's achievement. "Come on, we'll call it a day. We'll get the rest done tomorrow."

"Aye, if the Lord spares us," Jock said gruffly. "Gie me your fork, Mr. David, and I'll tak' the tools tae the shed."

David handed over his tool and fondly watched the old boy head off, his waterproof clothing creaking and rubbing as he walked. David delved deep into the inside pocket of his jacket and pulled out the grubby plastic folder that contained the garden plan. He started slowly towards the house, studying the drawings as he walked, then stopped and turned around to look back at the new flower-beds. The project was almost finished. Just that last bit around the variegated holly-tree to reclaim, and then the Inchelvie garden would be as it was before.

Yet he really didn't want the garden ever to be complete. It would break the spell of continuity which had existed since he started the job, his days of work linking the present with the past, linking this very moment as he stood there, rain dripping off his head and running down his face, with Rachel.

He placed both earthy hands on his face and pulled them down to his chin, clearing the water from his face and at the same time wiping away the unwelcome tears welling up in his eyes. "Shit!"

He slapped hard at his face with both hands to clear his head, then turned and began to jog across the lawn. As he rounded the side of the house he broke into an ungainly sprint, his arm movements restricted by his waterproof jacket and his loose-fitting Wellington boots burping out air as he ran.

He threw open the wrought-iron gate which led out onto the gravel sweep at the front of the house, slammed it shut, and heard it miss its catch and bounce open again behind him. He stopped and put his hands on his hips, and as he caught his breath, he heard above the wind the sound of a car going through its gears on the drive. He strained to see if he could make it out, managing only to catch the faint red glimmer of its rear-lights glinting through the trees before losing it to the darkness and the wind.

He shut and snibbed the gate, then, crossing the gravel, took the steps two at a time and threw open the front door, just as his mother was making her way across the hallway in the direction of the drawing-room. She swung round with a start. "David!" she exclaimed, clasping her hands to her heart. "What a fright you gave me!"

"Sorry about that," he said, smiling at her and holding up his hand in apology. He unzipped his jacket and threw it onto the church pew, then proceeded to toe one boot off with the other.

"How are you getting on, darling?" Alicia asked, coming across the hall towards him.

"What?" he said almost defensively, balancing on one foot as he pulled up his sock.

"With the garden, I mean."

"Oh, all right. We'll get that bed finished tomorrow."

"Well, I think that's marvellous, especially doing all that work in those dreadful conditions. You and Jock must be soaked to the skin. Has he gone home?"

"Yup, about ten minutes ago."

"Good, because Effie left half an hour ago to make him his tea. We were going to eat early, but your father has just telephoned to say that he's cancelled his meeting for some reason. So, half past seven all right for you, darling?"

"Yup, that's great." David placed his boots together and kicked them under the pew. Alicia pushed the dripping jacket to one side and sat down, trying to get below David's level so that she could make eye contact with her son. He caught her eye momentarily and gave her a faint smile before turning and walking towards the staircase. Alicia watched him go, and with a deep sigh, rose slowly to her feet and followed him across the hallway.

"I saw a car go down the road just then," David said, without turning.

Alicia stopped, surprised at being given this sudden and rare opportunity to enter into conversation with her son. "Yes, that was Jane Spiers," she said in a bright little voice, immediately being aware of the falseness of its tone. She cleared her throat to cover up for her over-keenness in grasping this slim and unexpected chance of communication, and continued in a more controlled voice. "She popped in for a cup of tea. I had just seen her off when you walked in. She was, well, just finding out how everything was, or is, so to speak."

David turned and looked at his mother out of the side of his eyes. She tilted her head and smiled at him.

"That was nice of her." He paused. "Well, I'll just, erm"—he pointed up the stairs—"go and have a bath."

Alicia nodded. "You do that, darling. Dad and I will see you down here at about quarter past seven."

As he walked slowly up the stairs, Alicia crossed her arms and leaned against the panelled wall, watching him until he was out of sight above her. She heard his bedroom door open and close behind him. She shut her eyes for a moment, shook her head and murmured to herself, "Oh, David." Then, walking back to the door of the drawing-room, she opened it and entered.

David turned off the gush of water that ran from the huge Victorian mixer tap into the bath, and bent over to stir up the peaty-brown water, still in its natural state from the holding tank, being fed by the spring high on the moor above Inchelvie. He threw off his dressing-gown onto the floor and stepped with one leg over into the bath, simultaneously taking his watch off his wrist. As he laid it on the chair beside him, he noticed that its face was misted with condensation. He rubbed it clear with his thumb. It was three minutes to six—just about news time.

He stepped back out of the bath and walked through the bathroom's steaming atmosphere to the mirrored cabinet above the basin. He opened it, took a small transistor radio from the top shelf, and closed the door, its mirror swinging round like a trap to catch the diffused outline of his face. He stood there staring back at his own unrecognizable features, a face that told nothing: not good looks or ugliness, humour or anger, happiness or sadness. It registered neither identity nor emotion, and he felt an obscure sense of comfort just looking at it.

He placed the transistor on the side of the basin and slowly brought his hand up to wipe the mirror clear.

There it was, the face that he knew, its gauntness now accentuated by the muddy streaks left by his fingers when he wiped his face in the garden. Just one year ago, he thought to himself, that forty-three-year-old face had registered the thoughts and cares of a twenty-five-year-old, and now, one year on, it seemed to have doubled its age.

David reached up and threw the door of the cupboard open to break the spell of self-remorse, just catching it before it slammed against the bathroom wall. "Bugger it," he said out loud. "Will you stop thinking of yourself all the bloody time!"

He picked up the radio and turned it on, twiddling the dial to find the news, its speaker screeching a plethora of tones as if in defiance to its rough handling. Somewhere in the middle, he caught the merest sensation of the introductory bars of a song. He stopped and turned the dial backwards. There it was, then a voice-over, ". . . good you could join us this evening. This is Danny McKay on Moray Firth Radio going back in time with a beautiful track from Smokey Robinson and the Miracles—'Tracks of My Tears.' "

He held the radio in front of him as the bars unfolded into the song. "People say I'm the life of a party, 'cos I tell a joke or two." He cradled the radio in his hands as if he were carrying a small injured bird, frightened that if he moved it too much, it would suddenly stop breathing and die. "So take a good look at my face, can't you see the smile, it's out of place." Laying it down carefully on the chair next to his watch, he stepped into his bath and slowly lowered himself downwards, allowing the luxury of the water to flood over his body, and the memories to flood through his mind.

Chapter FOUR

That year, Oxford had uncustomarily shimmered in heat since the first week in May, bringing an early influx of tourists to streets already burgeoning with the youthful, buzzing throng of student life. The weekends were worst of all. On that particular Saturday, the volume of traffic going into town was horrendous, tailing back down St. Aldates as far as the police station. David sat in his stationary car silently cursing himself, realizing that he had been stuck in its baking interior far longer than it would have taken him to walk the distance from the Christchurch College tennis courts to the Kings Arms on Holywell Street.

He drummed his fingers impatiently on the steering wheel of the old Triumph Vitesse, craning his neck out the window to see if there was any sign of movement farther up the line, and then bringing his head back in to glance both at the clock and the temperature gauge on the walnut dashboard. It was ten to one. He was already five minutes late and he could detect light wisps of steam rising from the car's radiator. Dammit, he really *should* have just walked!

Leaning over to the glove compartment, he took out a handful of unsleeved tapes and proceeded to go through them, chucking the rejected ones onto the seat beside him. At that moment, the traffic ahead started to move. He let out the clutch without putting his hands on the steering wheel, and selecting a *Motown Greatest Hits* album, he pushed it into the slot of the new Phillips stereo tape deck, a recent and much valued twenty-first birthday present from his parents.

As the second track was finishing, David eased his car into a space between two rows of bicycles twenty yards from the Kings Arms. Jumping out, he locked the door and hurriedly dodged his way along the pavement to the large double doors of the pub. He pushed at them with both hands, only managing to get them a quarter of the way open, such was the resistance of bodies on the other side. Sliding through the gap into the hot, smoky atmosphere, he slowly threaded his way through the throng of lunch-time drinkers, stretching up to his full six-foot-two height to see if he could locate his friends. A shout rose above the clamour.

"Oi, David, we're over here!"

He looked round and spied Toby, standing on a chair and waving a beer-mat above his head, his square frame silhouetted by the dusty shaft of sunlight that angled through the window of the pub. He pushed his way towards him, eventually extricating himself at the crowded table where his friend now sat, resplendent in cricket whites.

"Look, I've got one in for you," Toby said, pointing to a pint on the table. He looked across to the person sitting opposite him. "Here, budge up, Henry, there's room enough for one more on that bench."

As David perched himself on the small space that Henry had vacated, a brown-haired girl sitting close to Toby's right-hand side on the window bench looked up briefly from the book that she was reading and combed her hair back off her face with her fingers. She picked up her glass and took a drink, her brown eyes catching David's gaze over the rim of the glass. For a split second, they lit up into a captivating smile, before she replaced the glass on the table and returned to her book, her hair once more falling back across her face.

Toby, who had been continuing a conversation with Henry, caught this interchange out of the side of his eye and looked quickly from one to the other. He leaned forward across the table. "Listen, David, if I could possibly drag your attention back here for a minute, I want to introduce you to Jane." He turned to the young blond girl on his left, who grinned inanely at him. David smiled and nodded a greeting at her. No doubt yet another of Toby's attempted first-year conquests, he thought to himself.

"Jane," Toby continued, "this is David Corstorphine—oops, sorry, the HONOURABLE David Corstorphine, second lieutenant-in-brackets-on-probation, I hasten to add, in Queen's Own Highlanders, and owner of one of the only private malt whisky distilleries in the WHOLE of Scotland, thus an extremely good guest to invite to a booze-up—"

"All right, Toby," David interjected, embarrassed by his friend's incorrigible attitude. "That'll do me fine."

"No, come on, let me finish. I'm building you up here." Jane let out a high-pitched giggle, giving Toby ample encouragement to continue with his monologue, and he proceeded to count out David's attributes on his fingers. "Oxford Blue at tennis, erstwhile lead guitarist with that well-known university band, The Tenement Blok, and owner of the most amazing car stereo in the whole of Oxford." He looked across at David. "There, that's it. I'm finished. That wasn't so bad, was it?"

David smiled sardonically back at him and took a drink from his glass, at the same time once more catching the eye of the brown-haired girl, who had again momentarily looked up from her book. She raised her eyebrows and almost imperceptibly shook her head before looking down again.

"So who won the tennis match?" Toby asked.

"We did—just," David replied. "That's why I'm so late. The final set went up to 13-11. What time does your cricket match start?"

"Two o'clock." Toby sucked in a shivering breath and executed a short drum roll on his knees with his hands. "And I'm nervous as hell. Somebody, in their infinite wisdom, has decided that I should open the batting."

"Hell's teeth!" David said, rubbing his hands together in evil glee. "I'm not going to miss that!" He got to his feet. "Come on, you'd better have another one. Build up your Dutch courage. What do you want?"

"Well, it'll have to be quick. Just a half of Flowers." He stretched his arms above his head, then placed one with awkward nonchalance around Jane's shoulder. "And you can get a half of lager for Jane while you're at it."

David pulled his wallet out of the back pocket of his tennis shorts and headed off towards the bar, leaving Toby to continue his somewhat clumsy seduction of Jane. He had only taken a few steps when he stopped and turned to look across the table at the brown-haired girl. "Would you like another drink?"

She continued to study her book, seeming not to have heard him above the general noise. He leaned over towards her. "I wondered if you would like another drink."

She glanced up, starting back with surprise when she realized that David was looming over her. "What? Oh! Well, that's very kind of you." She picked up her glass, drained it and handed it to him. "An orange juice would be lovely! Thank you!" She flashed her smiling eyes once more and immediately returned to her reading.

It took two trips back and forth to the bar to get the whole order complete on the table. Finally he placed the glass of juice in front of the brown-haired girl, and as he sat down she looked up and smiled a thank-you at him. Just then, Toby turned to witness this further exchange. He suddenly picked up his beer, drained it in one gulp and jumped to his feet.

"Right! The time of reckoning is nigh!" He clasped his hands theatrically across his heart and looked down at Jane. "But after the battle is won, I shall return to claim my prize!" Bending down, he delivered a long, loud kiss on the cheek of the giggling girl. Then he turned to David with a sly grin on his face.

"And I think I'll give one to your friend as well!"

Before David could utter a word to stop him, Toby had put his hand on the head of the brown-haired girl and bent down towards her. It had been his intention merely to give her a peck on the forehead, but the unexpected and unsolicited contact made the girl jerk her face upwards to look at him, her mouth open to issue some exclamation of surprise or rebuke. This movement and Toby's forward momentum were so perfectly yet unintentionally synchronized that he found himself administering a kiss not to the planned target, but directly onto her open mouth.

Her reaction to this unwelcome infringement could not have been more immediate. The book left her hands and flew up in the air, and David reached up and caught it with one hand as it sailed over the top of his head. Her arms flailed and her legs kicked out as she freed herself from Toby's embrace, throwing the table violently forward before it crashed back down again on its four legs. Glasses fell over and rolled across the surface of the table, liberally spilling their contents over the people who sat nearby. Warning shouts filled the air as everyone jumped up in the confined space, trying to avoid the cascading flow by opening their legs under the table or pulling their knees round hard against their seats.

In one movement, the girl rose to her feet and gave Toby a mighty open-handed clout on the side of the face. He reeled back from the force and sat down in a pool of beer.

"Sorry! sorry!" Toby exclaimed, holding his hands up in defence against a further attack. "I really didn't mean to do that!"

The girl looked at him angrily, her eyes narrowed. "What the *hell* do you think you're doing? How *dare* you?"

She started to move away, but as an afterthought she turned back and aimed a sharp and powerful kick at his shin under the table before stamping off towards the door of the pub, the packed and silent crowd parting for her as willingly as the Red Sea had parted for the Israelites.

As the door slammed shut, laughter first bubbled, then erupted everywhere in the pub but at their table. Toby sat with a shocked expression on his face, slowly rubbing his cheek with one hand and his shin with the other, while the others around the table, attempting ineffectively to wipe down their sodden clothing with their hands, glared disapprovingly at him.

"Sorry about that," he said defensively, holding up his hand in apology to the assembled company. He looked across at David. "Christ, she's a bit unpredictable, isn't she, your friend?"

Still clutching the girl's book in his hand, David sat shaking his head in disbelief at Toby's actions. "She's not *my* friend, you bloody fool! I've never seen her before in my life!"

"Come on! I saw you buy her a drink!"

"So? I bought her a drink. Doesn't mean you have the right to molest the poor girl."

"I didn't mean to do, well, *that*! It was a mistake!" he whinged, rubbing hard at his face and his leg. "Jesus, I hurt all over."

David got up from the bench. "Serves you bloody right, you twit." He took a deep breath. "Look, I've still got her book. I'll go and see if I can catch her and try to apologize for your . . . lunatic actions." As he turned and started to make his way through the crowds, Toby called after him in a disappointed voice.

"Does that mean you won't come to watch me bat?"

David stopped and looked back at him, shaking his head. "Listen, I'll try, but I think she's the priority right now, don't you?"

He pushed his way through the doors of the pub and stood blinking on the crowded pavement, trying to get his eyes accustomed to the bright sunlight. There was no sign of the girl. He moved ten paces to his left and caught a glimpse of her as she made her way purposefully along the Broad, dodging through the mass of pedestrians. He jogged along the pavement, clutching the book in his right hand, every so often jumping up to keep sight of her bobbing brown mass of hair amongst the mêlée of hatted heads and sunglassed faces. Then, finding it too hard to navigate through the crowd, he stepped out onto the street and started to sprint along the gutter.

He caught up with her just as she passed the gates of Balliol College, and slowed to a fast walk beside her, matching her pace. "Listen, I'm sorry about all that."

She looked sideways at him, then, without speaking, turned eyes front and kept walking.

"I just wanted to apologize . . ."

She stopped and turned to look directly at David. "Look! Let's just leave it, shall we?"

David held up his hands in an act of appeasement, the right still clutching the book. She took off again, taking David's lead in stepping off the pavement and making her way along the gutter. He sighed resignedly and watched her go, her long legs, clad in a pair of faded Levi's, stretching out and away from him, his eyes focusing on her neat denim-clad bottom as she walked down the street. It was only when he saw her veer across the Broad and disappear around the corner into Cornmarket that he was brought abruptly to his senses.

"Shit! Her book!" He took off at full tilt, dodging through the oncoming cars, taking the straightest line to the point where he had lost sight of her. Skidding his way round into Cornmarket, he saw her immediately, twenty yards in front, still striding up the gutter. At last he caught up with her.

"Look, I've got your book for you," he said, exasperated, holding it out towards her.

She stopped and turned to him. He smiled at her, trying to show that he was friend, not foe. "You left it in the pub," he said quietly.

The girl reached over and grabbed the book and was about to make off again when she turned to him, a thunderous expression on her face. "Do you know, there just happens to be one thing I cannot *stand* and that's the taste of beer, and what's even worse than drinking it is being forced to taste it via someone else's mouth!"

For a moment David looked at her incredulously, then felt the overpowering urge to start laughing. He stuck his hands in the pockets of his tennis shorts and glanced down at his feet so that she wouldn't see his reaction to her remark. When he eventually did look back up at her, his face still bore the merest hint of a smile.

"Well, I'm glad *you* think it's funny," she said sharply, and turned to walk off.

David quickly jumped in front of her, and held up his hands to halt her passage. "Please listen, just stop for a minute . . . erm . . ." He looked around, desperately trying to work out his next move. The shop immediately adjacent to them was an off-licence. "Look, would you stay here, *please,* just for a minute."

He moved sideways towards the off-licence, watching her warily in case she decided to bolt off again. He dived into the shop and reappeared thirty seconds later clutching a half-bottle of Veuve Clicquot champagne.

He blew out a sigh of relief when he saw she was still there.

"Look," he said, holding out the bottle towards her, "this is just a small peace offering to say I'm sorry for what happened in the pub. It was unforgivable, and I hope . . . well, I just hope that this'll help you get rid of the taste of beer!"

As they stood there, bumped and jostled by the passing crowds, David watched her closely. She started to bite at her bottom lip, and his heart sank as she half turned away from him. For a moment, he thought that this last chance to make amends had flown out the window when she looked back at him, her eyes creased into the same captivating smile that she had given him in the pub. Suddenly she broke into a laugh, and eyeing the bottle in his hands, slid her hands into the back pockets of her jeans.

"Well, that has to be the most expensive bottle of mouthwash I've ever been bought!" She paused for a moment, then, pushing her fingers through her hair, took a deep breath. "Look, what happened in the pub really doesn't justify you buying this." She paused and pulled an embarrassed face. "I think that I probably over-reacted a bit. Anyway, it's not really for you to apologize."

David smiled at her. "Well, I think someone has to." He offered her the bottle. "Okay, if not an apology, then let's just call it—an introductory offer."

After a moment's hesitation, she slowly took the bottle and clasped it in her arms next to the book. "Well, in that case, thank you, it's more than generous." She held out her right hand towards him. "And by way of introduction, I'm Rachel Devereux."

David took hold of her hand. "Hi, Rachel," he said, overwhelmed with relief that the whole incident was apparently finished with. "It's a pleasure to meet you. I'm David Corstor——"

"I know you are," Rachel interjected, a huge grin on

her face. "Oxford Blue at tennis, titled, lieutenant in the army, what else was it? Oh yes, rock star . . ."

David felt himself blush. "Ah, of course, Toby's wretched introduction!" He looked up at her and smiled. "I think we'd both be better off if we forgot about that little interlude, don't you?"

Rachel smiled and nodded. "Maybe for the best."

"Good! So, which way are you heading now?"

"Back the way we came." Rachel flicked up her wrist and looked at her watch. "I was meant to be at the science buildings at two o'clock for a tutorial, but I don't think I'll make it."

David put his hand on her arm and turned her in the direction of Broad Street. "Come on, I've got a car back at the pub. Even in this infernal traffic, I think we've more chance of making it on wheels than on foot. At any rate, I'm going up that way." He glanced apprehensively at her as they walked. "Maybe I shouldn't really say this, but I'm meant to be watching Toby play cricket this afternoon."

Rachel looked sideways at him, a rueful smile on her face. "Yes, you're right. Better left unsaid."

They walked briskly up Cornmarket and around the corner into the Broad, sometimes divided and at other times pushed together by the crowds coming towards them. "So how does it work, you being here at Oxford and being in the army at the same time?"

"Well, I'm not really in the army yet. I'm what Toby quite rightly termed a 'second lieutenant-in-brackets-on-probation.' I joined up after leaving school, the army pay my way through university, and then, if all goes well with my finals, I do six months at Sandhurst and five years with the regiment."

"Right. So when *are* the finals?"

"God, I wish you wouldn't ask that question." He looked over to her, pretending to chew on the finger-nails of his right hand. "Next month!"

"Yeah, same as me."

"Really? I can't believe that. Which college are you in?"

"Hertford. Why do you say you can't believe it?"

"Well . . . because . . . well, I just thought that I might have met you before now. I mean, Oxford's not that big a place."

Rachel turned and smiled at him, but said nothing more until they had turned the corner of the Broad and were nearing the car. David took the keys from his pocket and Rachel walked out into the street to stand by the passenger door.

"Actually, I have seen *you* around," she said, looking at him over the roof of the car.

David stopped as he put the key in the door and glanced at her, a puzzled expression on his face. "Really? Whereabouts?"

"I don't know. Just around."

"Then why haven't I seen you?"

Rachel shrugged her shoulders. "I don't know. Maybe you just haven't been looking in the right direction."

The remark was laced with such possibly seductive innuendo that David felt an involuntary shiver of excitement course its way up his spine. He looked directly at her, catching the physical intent of the statement in her eyes.

"Obviously not," he said quietly to himself. Unlocking the car, he climbed in, and having bundled the pile of cassettes back into the glove compartment, he reached over to open the passenger door. Rachel threw her book onto the back seat and jumped in, wedging the bottle of champagne between her feet.

"The science building, then?"

She thought for a moment. "No, I don't think it's worth it. My tutorial will have started by now." She looked across at him. "Anyway, what the hell! I haven't had a break from my books in weeks. Maybe I'd be better doing something relaxing, like watching cricket."

David was taken aback by her suggestion. "Are you sure?"

"Why not? As long as I don't have to make physical contact with your friend Toby again!"

David let out a short laugh and, pushing the car into gear, he pulled away from the kerb and manoeuvred a tight U-turn on the junction of Broad and Holywell Streets, then headed back up Parks Road towards the university grounds.

He counted five cricket matches in progress as he drove the car as unobtrusively as possible around the periphery of the grounds, straining his eyes to see if he could make out any familiar figure on the pitches. He passed by the first game, and on to the second, and there caught sight of Toby standing in the crease at the bowler's end, one hand leaning on his bat, the other placed firmly on his hip, an air of confidence about his person.

"There he is!" he said, pointing Toby out to Rachel. "We'll park here, next to the sight-screen, and hope we don't get moved along."

"What's the sight-screen for?" Rachel asked, looking at the large white board that stood beside them.

"Well, it's positioned in direct line with the bowler and the batsman, so that the batsman can get a clear sight of the ball when it comes at him." David looked over at the score-board. "God, the jammy devil! He's only three runs off his half-century! No wonder he's looking so cocky!"

Rachel sighed. "If he's only got three more runs to make his half-century or whatever, why is he standing around doing nothing?"

"He's not facing the bowling at the minute."

"I've never understood the stupid game. When you're in, you're out there, and when you're out, you come back in here again."

Leaning forward, she picked up the half-bottle of champagne and pulled off the foil top. She rolled down the window and, twisting off the wire, exploded the cork towards the sight-screen, quickly putting the top of the bottle to her lips to catch the first frothing mouthful. She handed it over to David.

"It's over," he said, taking a swig and pointing towards the game.

"What, already?"

"No, not the game. 'Over' just means it's time for someone to bowl from this end. It's Toby's turn to face now."

Rachel shook her head. "It's a very stupid game." She reached over for the bottle and took another sip.

David watched the new bowler walk back towards where they were sitting in the car, turn twenty-five yards from the wicket and set off like an express train towards the crease. The first ball was a vicious outswinger at which Toby attempted to play a forward defensive shot, but missed it by a foot. He straightened and strutted up the wicket, tamping with his bat at various spots on the ground, obviously feeling that they were the major cause for his missing the last ball by such a wide margin. He returned to his crease, played a practice shot identical to the one that had just failed him, flexed his knees, and readied himself for the next ball.

"Wow, I'm not used to champagne!" Rachel said, leaning back in her seat. "I can feel it going straight to my head!" She rolled her head back and forth against the head-rest, then something on the dashboard of the car caught her eye. She leaned forward and pointed to the cassette player. "So, this is the famous stereo system that Toby was on about?"

David nodded. "Yeah, that's it."

"Can we put it on?"

"Don't see why not—as long as we play it quietly." Reaching forward, he pressed the on/off button and pushed the present cassette into the player. As the fadeout of Martha Reeves and the Vandellas hissed through the speakers, David watched Toby steer a ball off the edge of his bat for two runs.

"Come on, you fluky bastard," he said under his breath, "one more like that and you've got your fifty!"

As Rachel was tilting back another measure of champagne into her mouth, the muted, mellow guitar introduction filled every corner of the car. She suddenly sat upright, her body taut as she waited to hear the next bar. The instrumental gave way to the close harmony of the backing vocalists.

"Oh my God! It *is*! It's Smokey Robinson and the Miracles!" She reached forward and turned the volume button full on. "Oh, David, this just has to be the most beautiful, sexy song that has *ever* been written!"

The sound of the music was deafening within the small confines of the car, and instinctively David put his hand forward to turn it down, realizing that it could be no doubt heard by the players on all five of the cricket pitches.

"I think that that's just a bit lou——"

"Oh, please don't touch it!" Rachel said, reaching out and catching his hand to stop him. "Oh, *David*, this is just too fantastic for words!" She pushed open the door and jumped out, leaving it wide open.

"What *are* you doing?" he laughed.

But Rachel never answered him. Taking another drink from the bottle, she kicked out each foot to rid herself of her shoes and began dancing on the grass, moving slowly but steadily away from the car towards the sight-screen. David watched her for a moment, then dragged his attention back to Toby, who by this time was becoming increasingly agitated at the speed of the bowling. It was then that it suddenly dawned on him what was about to happen.

"Oooooh, hell's teeth!" he exclaimed out loud. He threw open his door and leaped out. "Rachel, you can't——"

He didn't go any further. Suddenly the visual impact

of the cricket game became a stark and uninteresting antithesis to the spectacle that he was now witnessing. He swallowed hard as he watched Rachel gradually approach the sight-screen, her movements liquid as she danced, her rhythm perfect, her body picking up every sensuous particle of the song, and he found himself transfixed by the combination of the words, the music, her beauty and her motion. She turned, mouthing the words of the song directly at him, using the bottle as a makeshift microphone, "So take a good look at my face, can't you see the smi-ile, it's out of place," then again turned away from him, moving farther into the danger zone, gently swinging her hips and hands in complete symmetry and unison with the song.

A shout from the cricket pitch broke David's trance. He turned to look towards Toby's game. Everyone was gawking in their direction—all except Toby, who stood at the crease, waving his hand and yelling something at him.

"What?" David called back.

"I — said — get — her — away — from — the — bloody — sight-screen," Toby called out at the top of his voice. "She's—a—bloody—distraction!"

"You can say that again," David said to himself, and held up his hand in apology. He ran over to Rachel, who was now dancing directly in front of the huge white board.

"I think you'd better move," he said. "You're right behind the bowler's arm."

"No, I'm not. I'm miles away from him," she replied, continuing to dance, her voice now slightly fuzzy from the effects of the champagne.

David swept back his hair and scratched at the back of his neck. "Listen, I don't think we're going to be very popular with Toby."

Rachel said nothing but smiled wickedly at him.

"Come on, are you going to move, or am I going to have to carry you?"

Her reply was immediate. "All right."

David shook his head. "Oh, hell's teeth!" he said under his breath as he walked up to her. Putting one hand behind her back and the other under her knees, he picked her up off her feet, and as he half-walked, half-ran towards the car, Rachel linked her arms around his neck.

The whole episode had a dramatic effect on Toby. He was finding it hard enough to deal with the pace of this new bowler without the distraction of a sudden burst of music and the appearance of a girl in front of the sight-screen. As he held his hand up to signal his state of unreadiness to the bowler, he recognized David's car, and realized immediately that this was the girl who had given him such a hard time in the pub. It was, to Toby, an ill-fated omen. As David carried the girl away, he took up his stance once more, but when the umpire dropped his arm and allowed the bowler to start his run, his eyes were distracted from their normal line of concentration to watch David and the girl move towards the car. He never saw the ball. He only heard the thump and clink as it cart-wheeled his middle stump out of the ground and knocked the bails clean over the wicket-keeper's head. The fielding side erupted in delight and ran to the bowler, slapping his hands and patting him on the back in congratulations.

As soon as they reached the car, David dropped Rachel onto her feet and dived inside to switch off the stereo. When he reappeared, she was looking out towards the cricket game.

"Toby seems to be walking off the pitch. Does that mean he's out or in?"

David glanced over to the score-board in time to see the number 49 taken off the main display and relegated to the "Last Man" position, then turned back to view the dejected figure of Toby as he slumped his way back to the pavilion, slamming his bat into the ground as he went. David looked across at Rachel, who was biting at her lip, a cringe of embarrassment on her face.

"Oops, was that my fault?" she asked quietly.

David laughed. "I wouldn't worry too much about it. Anyway, I think he probably more than deserves it, don't you?" As Toby reached the steps of the pavilion, he turned to glare in their direction. David hastily opened the door of the car. "Nevertheless, I think the best thing we could do right now is get the hell out of here."

Rachel seemed to heed the suggestion immediately, but instead of climbing in, she reached over to the back seat and retrieved her book. She straightened up and stood directly in front of him, looking up at him. "I'll think I'll walk from here," she said.

"You don't have to."

"I know, but I need to clear my head. That champagne has just made me feel like going to sleep."

"Well, why don't you?"

"Because I have a mountain of work to get through this weekend, and because of today's . . . well . . . circumstances, I haven't even started." She clutched the book in her crossed arms and looked down at her feet. "But anyway, it was lovely to meet you—and thanks for the champagne. It was delicious."

She suddenly reached up and gave him a light kiss on the cheek, then turned away and walked off towards the gates of the cricket park.

"Do you want to meet for a drink sometime?" he called after her.

Rachel turned and smiled. "No, I don't think so."

"Why not?"

"Because I've only got a month before my finals, and I really don't want any distractions."

"I wouldn't be a distraction."

"I think you would."

"Well . . . er . . . what about after the finals?" David asked, desperate to prise even the faintest hope of commitment out of her. A thought came into his head. "I tell you what. Christchurch have a Commem Ball this year. Would you come with me?"

"When is it?"

"The twenty-third of June."

Rachel thought for a moment and nodded slowly. "All right, I'll come, but only on one condition."

"What's that?"

"You wear your kilt."

"Okay."

Rachel swung herself gently from side to side. "AND you bring your car and Smokey Robinson with you."

"That's two conditions."

Rachel smiled at him. "Well, that's the deal."

"Okay. Sounds good enough to me!"

Chapter FIVE

Effie pattered her way across the hall to the drawing-room door, knocked quietly, and popped her head around the corner. There was no conversation in progress, only the sound of the fire crackling in the hearth and the contented snoring of one of the dogs lying out in front of it. Lord and Lady Inchelvie sat opposite each other at the far end of the room, he snoozing gently in his large, threadbare armchair, a glass of whisky precariously balanced on one of its sunken arms beside him, while she, clicking away with her knitting-needles, watched the muted screen of the television.

"Excuse me, Lady Inchelvie," Effie said, almost in a whisper.

Alicia turned and dipped her head to look over the top of her spectacles at the little grey-haired head that peered round the door at about the same level as the handle. "Yes, Effie?"

"That's the dinner through in the dining-room now."

Alicia bundled up the knitting and placed it on the table beside her, then rose from her chair. "Thank you, Effie. I'm afraid that we're still waiting for David. I don't quite know what he's up to. I called up the stairs about a quarter of an hour ago, but he obviously didn't hear me. I think I'd better just nip up to his room to see if everything's all right."

"Och, don't you bother yourself about that," Effie said, appearing in full around the door. "I'm just away upstairs now to turn down the beds, so I'll give him a wee knock on his door." She looked across at Lord Inchelvie and smiled. "That'll give you time to wake up his Lordship."

"Oh, Effie, could you? That would be most kind." Alicia glanced over towards her husband. "I'm afraid the poor man's had a pretty tiring day at the office."

Effie paused for a moment. "Everything's all right, is it not, Lady Inchelvie?" she asked tentatively.

"Yes, of course. Why do you ask?"

"Oh, it was just that I was hoping that his Lordship was feeling quite well, what wi' him not going to the meeting tonight."

"No, nothing to worry about, Effie. Just something quite important has cropped up which he has to discuss with David over dinner."

"Well, I'm glad to hear it, then." She gave a quick smile in the direction of Lord Inchelvie and then waved her index finger in the air, as if conducting herself back into action. "Now I'll just away and see where Mr. David has got to."

Effie closed the door of the drawing-room and made her way to the staircase and, readying herself for the ascent by placing one hand on the banister and the other on her left knee for extra leverage, she began to climb the stairs, gently humming to herself as she went. Having made the half-way landing, she stopped long enough to catch her breath and to make a mental note to remove an over-conspicuous cobweb that floated high up on the large dark portrait that loomed above her before continuing on her way.

The door of the bathroom was open wide and the light off, but the steamy air that emanated from within still carried on it the smell of soap and after-shave. She hesitated, wondering whether she was a little premature in knocking on David's door. Her fist was about to come into contact with it when it flew open and David emerged, unaware of Effie's presence on the landing. They both started back in surprise.

"Oh, I'm sorry to disturb you, Mr. David," Effie said breathlessly. "It was just that your mother and father have gone through to the dining-room, and they were wondering if everything was all right with you."

David, dressed in a clean pair of jeans, an open-necked shirt and bedroom slippers, smiled lightly down at her. "I'm sorry, Effie. I dozed off in the bath. I'm heading down now."

"That's fine, then." She stood there uneasily, her hands clasped together in front of her apron. "Well, I'll just away and turn down the beds."

David closed the door behind him as Effie scuttled off around the balconied landing. He walked to the top of the stairs and stopped, looking across the high divide of the hallway to the other side of the balcony where she was just about to enter his parents' bedroom.

"I'm afraid that I kept Jock out in pretty horrible conditions today. I hope he's not suffering any ill effects?"

Effie turned, her face briefly registering a look of surprise at David's concern over her husband before it broke into a smile. "Och, he's fine, Mr. David. He aye moans a bit when he's working out in the rain, but then again, he does the same when the sun shines. Jock has never been able to extract much pleasure from the weather, I'm afraid." She let out an affectionate sigh. "That said, you'd have a hard task keeping him away from the garden, whatever the weather!"

David did not reply, but simply nodded and smiled. He turned and took the stairs two at a time, his slippered feet creating loud flat echoes in the hallway as he descended. He crossed over to the dining-room and entered, and his parents, already seated at the top end of the large polished table, both looked up towards him.

"Sorry about that," he said, nodding a silent greeting to his father. "I fell asleep in the bath."

"Not surprising," Alicia said, getting up from her chair and walking over to the sideboard. She began to ladle a savoury-smelling stew onto a plate. "You must be exhausted after working out there in that dreadful weather."

George put his knife and fork down on his plate and sat back in his chair, chomping on his mouthful and pointing over to the far corner of the sideboard. "I brought the whisky through from the drawing-room for you, my boy, so help yourself to one."

"Thanks. I will."

He poured himself a sizeable whisky and added as much water to it again before sitting down at the table. While he settled in his place, his mother hovered at his side before placing the steaming plate of food in front of him. "There, that should be restorative."

"Thanks," David mumbled quietly, pulling his napkin from its ring and laying it on his lap.

Alicia returned to her seat and continued her meal. Over the past months, she had come to dread their dinners together, every night the mood of the whole proceedings being orchestrated by David's sombre and silent presence. Previously, it had been the time of day that both George and she had enjoyed the most, sitting quietly together uninterrupted, talking about their respective days and making plans for future ones. Now, if there was any conversation at all, it was still mostly between George and herself, but it was inevitably an exchange of words that sounded as thin and as falsely happy as a Linguaphone lesson. She knew that George understood this, and both came to prefer an uneasy silence to their chirrupy sentences, the three of them sitting together as if observing some monastic vow of quiescence, the high-vaulted ceiling of the dining-room amplifying the irritating sound of cutlery scraping against plate.

But she knew that tonight had to be different. In the drawing-room beforehand, George had told her of his meeting with Duncan Caple, and she knew that sometime during the meal the subject of the States would have to be broached. She therefore gave a small involuntary shudder of trepidation when she saw George put down his whisky glass and turn toward David.

"How are you getting on in the garden?"

The sudden break in the silence took David by surprise. He took a drink of whisky and wiped his mouth with his napkin. "Getting there," he said, his voice sounding croaky through lack of use. He cleared his throat. "I reckon that we'll have finished the whole thing by this time next week."

"Well, I think it looks pretty wonderful. You and Jock have really done a terrific job. I never thought that we would see the day when the garden would be restored to its former glory."

He took another mouthful of food, and silence once again fell over the proceedings, all three continuing their meal without looking at the others. David put down his knife and fork and turned to his father. "I thought that I might have a look at that bit of rough ground down by the loch next and see if I can't come up with a plan for that."

Lord Inchelvie stopped chewing and looked across at his wife. She was caught with her fork in her mouth, her eyes anxiously darting back and forth between her husband and her son. David picked up on the exchange.

"Is something wrong?"

His father sighed deeply and sat back in his chair, resting his elbows on its carved arms and linking the fingers of both hands together on his lap. His brow was furrowed deeper than usual, the loose skin on his thick neck creating a series of double chins as he looked down at his hands. He began to flick at one thumb-nail with the other.

"Well, in a word, my boy, yes."

A worried look came over David's face. "What is it?"

George Inchelvie looked back at his wife, who gave him the lightest of nods. "Well," he said, slowly, trying to pick his words carefully, "we have a slight problem in the marketing department at the distillery."

David paused for a moment, glancing back and forth between his parents. "Duncan should be able to sort it out, shouldn't he? That's what he's there for."

"Well, it's a little bit more complicated than that," his father continued. "There is only so much that Duncan can do, and he's finding himself a little short of human resources at the moment." He looked over at his son, realizing that he'd better just come out with it. "Listen, David, I know that you find it hard right now to give much thought to work." He paused for a moment. "But the fact is that we have this problem which I don't think we are going to be able to solve . . . well . . . without involving you." He watched as his son let out a deep sigh and began scratching at the back of his neck with both hands. "Duncan brought it to my attention today that our sales have slipped dramatically in the States. He was quite blunt about the fact that he wants to hold an extraordinary board meeting within the next few days so that we can appoint a new distributor over there as soon as possible."

George glanced over to his wife, who smiled reassuringly at him.

"I'm going down to Glasgow next week for the Whisky Association meeting, and, well, Duncan is heading off to Europe at the same time, so"—he began pulling at his ear-lobe with the thumb and forefinger of his right hand—"it's really just a question of who is going to be able to go over to the States." He quickly picked up his whisky glass and took a mouthful as a way of giving himself the excuse to be silent while his son came to terms with what was being said.

David leaned back in his chair and folded his arms. "What about Robert McLeod?" he said softly. "What's he doing at the minute?"

His father let out a short laugh. "Well, you know Robert better than any. He may be financial director, but he's hardly ever been out of this country, let alone to the States! He'd end up in Alabama or somewhere, and we'd have to send out a search party!" He smiled, but became serious once more when he realized David had not reacted to the light-hearted remark. "Anyway, like everyone else on the board of Glendurnich, Robert's getting a bit long in the tooth to be able to cope with something like this."

David shut his eyes and nodded slowly. "So, what you're actually saying is that Duncan wants me to go."

Alicia, who had been sitting quietly listening to her husband explain the situation, cut in. "Darling, the last thing we want in the world is for you to go out there, especially when we know that you don't feel up to it. We, of all people, understand this, David, but you also have to realize the predicament your father is in."

David rubbed at his forehead with the fingers of his right hand. "It's not only that I don't feel particularly up to it. It's just that I don't want to be too far away from the children at this precise time."

George paused for a moment, then reached out and placed his hand on his son's arm. "Listen, David, I do realize this, and I actually mentioned this very point to Duncan. However, he did say that he would make it fairly painless. Really, all you will have to do is to go over there for a couple of days to make the appointment. It will be a very simple operation and you'll be back almost immediately." He paused and looked once more at his wife for her silent support before continuing in a calm and reasoning voice. "Your mother and I also think that it might be a good opportunity for you to get away from here for a bit. I know that at the moment you might not think this is right, but I have a feeling that once you've made the break, it could be of benefit."

David picked up his napkin from his lap and threw it on the table and, pushing his chair away, he began to get to his feet. "Right—well, I'll give it some thought."

Alicia put up her hand, stopping him half-way out of his chair. "David, please . . . just sit down for a moment." She gathered her thoughts while he settled down once more. "David, your father and I are trying our best to do everything to help you at the minute . . . and it's very difficult . . . because we know how much you are bottling up inside yourself. We watch you every day becoming more and more introverted, and . . . well, it really is becoming too much of a strain on us old things." She looked at her husband, who sat silently in his chair, his face grey with fear of overstepping David's gossamer-thin tolerance level. "You see, life has to go on—not only for us, but for you—and, most important of all, for the children. We have to try to get back to some sort of normality, and everyone in the household is making the hugest effort to achieve this, even though the immediate past has been so damaging." She stopped and cleared her throat, her voice beginning to quiver with emotion. "I don't mean to be hard, David, but you have to come some way to helping us—and to start talking to us, otherwise I don't think that your father and I will really be able to cope with the situation much longer."

David glanced across at his parents, noticing the look of sheer sadness on his mother's face, while his father, issuing a gruff cough to cover for his emotions, took a handkerchief from his top pocket and loudly blew his nose. Somewhere deep in the turmoil of his brain, the sight of them showing their despair so openly pin-pricked at a sense in David which had been hitherto anaesthetized. He chewed slowly on his bottom lip before eventually speaking.

"For eighteen years of my life . . . I shared it . . ." He stopped, wrestling with his brain to get the word out, like someone who had suffered a massive stroke and was going through the agony of learning how to talk again. ". . . with Rachel."

He looked around the room and therefore didn't catch the slight movement that his mother made as she reached over to hold the hand of her husband under the table. David continued, his voice coming out in spasmodic phrases.

"We . . . were . . . one. We thought the same things . . . we laughed at the same things . . . we lived the same . . . we *were* the same . . . and . . ." He paused and took in a choking breath. ". . . now that she's no longer here . . . I feel lost . . . and empty . . . and I don't have any feelings any more. I find it difficult to show gratitude, because . . . my powers of being able to notice even the smallest kindness . . . seem to have been purged from my body." He wiped roughly at each eye with the back of his hand. "There is now . . . this huge void in my life . . . I have no senses . . . my emotions are gone . . . my self-confidence is gone . . . everything is gone." He glanced briefly at his parents. "But even if I can't feel anything, I do *know* . . . that you two have both been wonderful over the past six months . . . and I also *know* that I haven't shown my full appreciation for what you have done . . . but I do . . . appreciate it, that is."

"Darling, you don't need to—" his mother started.

"No, please," David interrupted, "let me finish." He got up from his chair, stuck his hands in the pockets of his jeans, and again gathered his thoughts before continuing slowly and methodically. "I guess I've shut out everything in the world . . . because my own world no longer matches with it. For most of the time, I walk around existing as if nothing has happened to change my life . . . ever . . . then suddenly it's there, reality, right bloody there in front of me." His voice crescendoed as he angrily spat out the words through clenched teeth. "And just as I think, right, now you stupid bugger, this is where you can stand up and face it"—he paused and sat back down on his chair again before continuing almost inaudibly—"the shut-off valve cuts in again."

His mother looked across at him tenderly. "Darling, I know it might sound a bit of a cliché, but I really do think that this has to be nature's way. I would imagine it's a bit like losing an arm or a leg. To begin with, the mind numbs the senses, but eventually the reality, the pain, does catch up with you. It will catch up with you, David, and you will be able to face it . . . and you will come through it all right and begin to build your life again . . . I *know* so."

George and Alicia watched as their son stood up from his chair and walked up to the far end of the dining-room. He turned to face them. "You're probably right. Maybe I should go away, because I don't really want to be around here when it all does catch up with me." He stopped and began tracing a line down the pattern of one of the heavy damask curtains with his finger. "Because no matter how hard I try, I cannot . . . physically . . . move one step around here without thinking of Rachel. Everything and everybody reminds me of her . . . and I resent that . . . so I end up feeling . . . sad, depressed . . . even embittered towards those who are closest to me . . . like you two . . . and Effie . . . and, God forbid, even Jock sometimes!" He breathed out a shallow laugh and stuck his hands back in his pockets. "You know, I really thought that by staying out of our own house, it would make it easier. But it doesn't work. Rachel is everywhere."

He turned and walked back down the room towards his parents, giving them a forced smile of reassurance. He breathed out heavily. "Pretty hopeless, huh? Pretty bloody hopeless!"

Reaching across the table for David's empty whisky glass, George rose slowly to his feet, took his stick from the back of the chair, and picking up both his and David's glass with the fingers of his free hand, made his way to the sideboard. "I think that we could both do with another one, don't you, my boy?" he said with false cheerfulness in his voice. He poured two large whiskies, added a splash of water to each, placed one on the table, and slowly pushed it across to David with his stick. "One good thing, I suppose—there's plenty more where that came from!"

David looked at him and smiled and took the glass off the table. His father plumped himself heavily back down on the chair. "David," he said slowly. "There's never going to be a good time for you to make this trip, but I'm afraid that it really does look as if you will have to go. If you could bear to, I think that it would be a good idea if you came into work with me tomorrow, just to have a quick word with Duncan. Then, as soon as he's briefed you, you can bring the car back afterwards, and I'll get a ride back." He lifted the tone of his voice in an attempt to inject a tinge of light-heartedness into the overriding oppression of the conversation. "I was just telling your mother that I met a charming young boy in the distillery today by the name of Archie McLachlan. Turns out he's the grandson of Gregor McLachlan."

David smiled and nodded. "Yeah, I know Archie. I took him on for work experience just before I left."

"Well, he seems to be a very willing young man. I'm sure that he won't mind giving me a lift." He paused and looked across at his son. "Rest assured, David, that while you're away, your mother and I will give every support that you might need—with the children and everything. You'll only be away for a short period, and then, when you return, we can take it from there. If you feel you need a bit more time, then you can certainly have a look at that bit of the garden down by the loch."

He looked across at David. "How does that suit?"

David didn't reply immediately, but bent forward and picked up the glass of whisky off the table. "Well, whatever plans Duncan comes up with, I don't want to leave without seeing the children."

"No, of course. I quite understand that."

David nodded slowly. "Right." He held up his glass to his parents. "Well, if you don't mind, I think I'll just take this up to my room."

He began making his way across the room, then, as an afterthought, turned back and walked over to his mother. He put his arm around her neck and gave her a kiss on either cheek. " 'Night."

"Good night, darling/my boy," his parents said in unison, and watched him walk to the end of the dining-room, open the door and leave. For a moment they sat there wordlessly, their eyes fixed on the door, both lost in their own private thoughts, before the movement of one broke the trance of the other.

"Well done, old girl," George said quietly, smiling across at his wife. "At least you started to get him talking."

Alicia did not reply immediately, but sat fiddling with an unused spoon on the table. "He's on a knife-edge at the minute, Geordie. He could go either way."

George leaned across and squeezed his wife's hand. "I know he is. I also know what he's talking about, this thing of being devoid of all feeling. I remember being like that during the war, seeing friends and comrades killed in battle, and just having to carry on." He took another drink of whisky. "I'd really forgotten until he started to speak about it."

"He will be all right, won't he?"

"Yes, I'm sure he will"—he slowly nodded—"but I'm afraid he's yet to suffer that cold hard shock to his system."

"You didn't say it all, did you?" Alicia said quietly.

"What? About Duncan's ultimatum?" He shook his

head. "No, I couldn't. I think it's best to leave it as it is, and see how it works out." Pushing himself laboriously to his feet, he picked up his stick and walked round to his wife's side, placing his hand on her shoulder. "Come on, old girl, I think we're both pretty well emotionally drained. Let's turn in as well."

Alicia got up and linked her arm through her husband's. They walked together to the door, and as he opened it, she pressed the bell to signal to Effie that the dining-room was clear.

Chapter

SIX

For a moment, David stood motionless in his bedroom, his eyes closed, allowing its soothing quiet to envelop him slowly and gently ease the clamour in his mind. Putting his whisky glass on the dressing-table, he walked over to his bed and sat down heavily, leaning his elbows on his knees and rubbing at his face with both hands.

"Oh, *bugger*!" he said softly.

He fell back on the bed and lay looking up at the ceiling, wishing that there were an easy way to refuse his father's request. But there wasn't. Too much had been said over dinner, too many things had to be considered. He swung his legs over the side of the bed and sat up again. His parents were right. He did have to start getting some sort of perspective into his life, and even though the prospect of flying over to the States and having to conduct business once more with people that he had never met filled him with trepidation, he realized now that ending his closeted and protected existence at Inchelvie was inevitable—and that forcing himself into contact with others would, in the long-term, be healing.

Yet it really did terrify him. He got to his feet and

walked over to the dressing-table and took a gulp from
his whisky glass. In pouring it, his father had been over-
generous with the whisky and less so with the water,
and he coughed involuntarily as he felt it burn its way
down deep into his stomach. He was about to turn back
to the bed when he stopped, his eye caught by the photograph that stood propped up against the wall at the
back of his dressing-table. He reached forward and
picked it up. It was one that he had taken himself about
two years previously—of Sophie, Charlie and Harriet
in a boat on the loch, the soft evening light gently
bouncing off the mirror-calm surface of the water and
accentuating the glowing smiles on the children's faces.
Sophie was pulling hard on the oars, her giggling face
tipped up towards the sky as she tried her hardest to
get the heavy craft on the move, while Harriet sat in
the stern, looking open-mouthed over the side of the
boat in the belief that she would soon pull out a fish
with the help of her bamboo cane with string attached.
Charlie meanwhile balanced precariously on one foot
on the seat in the bows, his outstretched arms tipped to
one side like the wings of a banking jet, as he half-
heartedly fought his compulsive desire to fall overboard.

Smiling to himself, David opened up the top drawer
of the chest and took out a pair of socks and gave the
dusty glass of the photograph a wipe before placing it
carefully back in its position. He took a pace back and
stood looking at it for a moment, then his eyes dropped
to another picture that had been concealed in the
drawer. He hesitated, then took it out and, without
viewing it, carried it to his bed. Falling back on the
faded yellow eiderdown, he lay there looking up at the
ceiling, the picture face-down on his chest. After a moment's meditation, he held it up.

It was a photograph of a wedding group—its colour
almost faded out from having stood too long in direct
sunlight—of himself and Rachel, flanked by an undis-

ciplined gaggle of little bridesmaids and pages who strained at the leash, wanting to be anywhere else at that time but in the picture. To David's left, dressed in a black morning suit and looking somewhat out of place amidst the profusion of kilts, stood his best man, Toby, who leaned forward looking along the line at Rachel, a beam of sheer delight on his face. The photograph was one that had not been initially selected by the mimsey little wedding photographer, who had stated categorically that he didn't want to use the photograph as "it does not meet with my general high standards of portraiture." However, David had clandestinely saved it from the outtakes, as it was the only one that he really liked of the wedding, the reason being that as he looked towards Toby in admonishing seriousness, Rachel was looking directly at the camera, her face overflowing with laughter, having just secretly undone the buckle of his sporran, the shutter of the lens only managing to catch the image as a streaked blur as it fell to the ground.

David dropped the photograph back down to his chest and closed his eyes, suddenly cradled in the enveloping warmth of humorous nostalgia. He remembered now that he had chosen the photograph because at that time he had realized that it encapsulated every facet of Rachel's character. Direct, funny, incredibly beautiful. He felt his face break into a smile and he crossed his arms over the picture, hugging it to his chest, his pain gradually fading out of focus.

"Tell me again why Frank was called Frankie Push-Push?"

"What?"

"Frankie Push-Push. You remember—your friend at Oxford. Why was he called that?"

"God, what made you think of that?"

"I always think of things like that. They're all very precious memories—things like that."

David looked across at his wife on the bench beside him and reached over and tucked the tartan rug around her neck. Even though they were in the relative warmth of the old summer-house, he knew that she really shouldn't be out of her bedroom—not when it was this bloody cold.

"This is mad. You should be in bed."

"Come on, don't fuss. I'm all right. I just looked out of the window and saw you working, and I wanted to be with you."

Giving a shrug of resignation, David got up and walked over to the corner of the dark-pined room. He picked up an old paraffin stove and gave it a shake to check if there was any fuel in it.

"Should be enough," he said, removing the funnel and delving in his pocket for a box of matches. He lit the wick and watched as the thin yellow flame worked its way around each side to meet, then, replacing the funnel, he adjusted the flame until it glowed blue through the little window. Instantly, the summer-house was filled with its heady, comforting smell.

As he sat down again, Rachel unravelled her hands from the rug and pulled her woolly hat farther over her ears. "Well?"

David frowned at her for a moment before remembering her question. "Ah, yeah, Frankie Push-Push." He put his arm around his wife's shoulders and eased her gently towards him, ever conscious of her now constant pain. "Well, it was all a bit naughty really. He just happened to turn up at the flat one evening with a girl who turned out to be, well, somewhat loud when it came to love-making, and we all just happened to hear her yell out. 'Push! Frankie, Push!' probably at rather an important moment. Anyway, the next morning, I happened to call him Frankie Push-Push, really just as a passing remark, and he was so taken aback that he sort of blew out his mouthful of cereal across the table. After that, the name just stuck; actually, as it turned out, to his own egotistical pride and joy!"

Rachel's face broke into a wide smile. "I always loved that story."

"You knew it all along, didn't you?"

She turned towards him. "Yeah, but I still love hearing it." She moved awkwardly on the bench and let out a deep sigh. "It all seems so long ago."

"Twenty-one years, to be exact."

"I know. I'll never forget it."

For a moment, they sat together in silence, looking out onto the partly frozen loch, the opaque rays of the weak February sun glinting off the surface of the icy water. It was so quiet that even with the doors of the summer-house closed and the background hiss of the stove, somewhere, out on the lower reaches of the snow-capped hills, the distinctive and haunting sound of a single grouse could be heard, calling out its panicked chuckle. Rachel pulled the rug closer about her and let out a shiver, despite the heavy pine-tanged heat that filled the now fuggy interior of the summer-house.

"Do you remember how warm it was that morning after the Commem Ball?"

"That whole summer was boiling."

"That's right. It was, wasn't it? We had the roof of the car down—and then we tried to have breakfast with the Duke of Marlborough at Blenheim Palace."

David laughed. "Well, sort of. It was a pretty half-hearted attempt. I don't think he would have been too happy to be woken at five o'clock in the morning."

"No, maybe not. But then if we *had* seen him, we would never have ended up in that hayfield near Woodstock, would we?" She pushed herself in beside him to get the warmth from his body. "I can remember so vividly the smell of the hay—and the quiet. It was just like this. And then that fox appeared right beside the car—and he just stood looking at us." She let out a shuddering sigh. "My God, that was a magical morning."

David kissed her lightly on the side of her woollen hat. "Yeah, but there was something else, wasn't there?"

Rachel turned her head to look at him. "You mean Smokey Robinson?"

"Yup."

She grinned and nodded lightly. "Can you remember how many times you recorded that same track for me?"

"Not offhand, no."

"Twenty times. Ten each side. We must have played it about three times right through that morning—and we just danced—you in your kilt, me in my ball gown."

She swallowed hard, and David felt her body grow taut with effort.

"And still Smokey sang." She let out a short laugh. "You know, that was the one year of my life I kept a diary, and that was the sole entry for that whole week— 'And still Smokey sang.' I wrote it diagonally across the page in big black letters. It said it all, really."

David could now feel the vibrations of her shivering against his body. "Come on, I think it's time that we got you inside." He put his arms around her to lever her gently to her feet.

She pushed his hands away. "No, not yet," she said, shaking her head. "I'm loving this—being outside again. It's just—*so* beautiful."

David held up his hands resignedly and sat down again, pulling her close in beside him once more. At that moment, they both became aware of a new sound, the faintest fluttering reverberation against the window-pane. A butterfly, having lain dormant in some dusty crevice of the summer-house, had been tricked by the heat of the stove into waking, and was now vainly attempting to make its way though the invisible screen into the open air. Rachel took a hand out of the rug and, leaning across, closed her fingers gently around it. For a moment, David heard the soft whirring of its wings against her palm before it stopped, content to rest itself in the moderate darkness of its shelter.

"Poor thing," she said, squinting through her fingers at the rich orange and brown of its colouring. "Doesn't stand much of a chance, does it? Either it stays in here and dies of starvation, or we let it out and it freezes."

David pulled her hand towards him and looked in on her little captive. "Yeah, the odds are pretty much stacked against it, aren't they?"

Rachel got to her feet and shuffled over to the door and opened it. She slowly uncurled her hand, but the butterfly seemed reluctant to move. She lifted it to her mouth and gently blew on its wings, encouraging it to fly. After a moment, it took off and was borne away on the frigid air. Rachel closed the door and stood watching until it disappeared.

"At least it will get the smell and taste of the world," she said, almost inaudibly, "even if it is only for a short time." She turned and shuffled back to the bench. "Better than being cooped up inside for the rest of its days."

David stared straight ahead, not wanting to catch her eye, understanding the simile that she was making and frightened by its direction. He felt her hand on his knee.

"We don't talk about it, do we?"

"What's that?" he said unconvincingly.

"Come on, my darling, you know—the inevitable."

David took in a faltering breath. "Darling, we don't . . ."

Rachel turned to him. "Yes, we do, David, we do. Because I really want to tell you that I'll be all right. I want to tell you that so that you can tell Sophie and Charlie and Harriet that I'll be all right—that I'll be safe—and that I'll be with you all wherever you go." She reached up and stroked the side of his face. "You know, you were without doubt the most handsome boy in Oxford." She let out a weak laugh. "I just could never quite believe that you would turn out as nice—and that it was me that caught you."

David leaned his face against her woolly hat, secretly

using it to brush away the tears from his eyes.

"I'd really like to go back to Oxford, darling."

He cleared his throat before replying. "Would you?"

"Yeah. Very soon. Very, very soon." She pushed herself away from him. "But right now, I'm absolutely bloody freezing. Let's go back to the house."

Needing no further encouragement, David jumped to his feet and turned off the stove, then, helping her to her feet, he opened the door and put a supporting arm around her waist. As they walked close together across the frost-hardened lawn towards the house, David's leg bumped against a hard object in her coat pocket, making her wince with pain. He stopped.

"Are you all right?"

Rachel smiled bravely at him. "Yup."

"What have you got in there?" he said, feeling the side of her coat.

Rachel pushed her hand deep into her pocket and brought out a Walkman.

"It's my music."

"What is it?"

She stopped. "Here." She reached up and pushed one of the ear-plugs into his ear, then, standing close to him, she placed the other in her own, and pressed the "play" button. "It's the tape."

The song cut in immediately, filling his head with the words. "So take a good look at my face, you'll see the smi-ile, it's out of place."

He looked at her and smiled, shaking his head, incredulous. "You still have it?"

"Of course. All twenty recordings of it."

David linked his arm around her shoulder, and as they walked across the lawn, around the side of the house and up the steps to the front door, still Smokey sang.

Yet they never made it to Oxford.

———

The photograph fell onto the floor with a clatter, and even though he had been fast asleep, David sat bolt-upright, swung his feet over the side of the bed and stooped down to pick it up. He checked the glass. Nothing broken. He laid it on the bed beside him and bent forward, leaning his elbows on his knees, and rubbing his eyes with his knuckles. He glanced over at the clock. It was twenty to two in the morning.

He turned round, picked up the photograph and sat looking at it.

It had never been any different—from the moment they met to the moment they were married to the moment that she died. They had loved and laughed through life and through the procreation of life, and their children had loved and laughed with them. He was she, and she was he, their true bonding not having been made during the pageantry of the wedding, but three years before in that vast open Oxfordshire hayfield under the burning blue sky, witnessed only by the birds, the fox, the Triumph Vitesse—and Smokey Robinson and the Miracles.

He pushed himself off the bed, walked over to the dressing-table, and carefully stood the photograph up beside the one of his children. Then stripping off his shirt, he unbuckled his belt and kicked off his jeans, and fell into bed to sleep more soundly than at any time since the night that Rachel died.

Chapter

SEVEN

The next morning David woke early and immediately became aware of an ache of anxiety gnawing deep in his stomach, a different and more frightening sensation than the cold realization of solitude which normally settled like a leaden weight around his heart. He pushed himself up quickly from the bed, as if fast action would help to shed this unwelcome feeling, and hurried out across the landing and into the bathroom. Turning the shower tap full on, he entered the cubicle before the water had a chance to heat up, and tilted back his head so that his face took the full force of the invigorating flow.

Yet the thought was still with him. Today he would not be going back out into the garden to work alongside Jock. Today, without option, he was having to return to a way of life for which he knew he was still both physically and mentally unprepared.

He bent down to retrieve the bar of soap which spun haphazardly above the outflow of the shower, and started to scrub hard at every part of his body, trying to scourge the cowardice from his being and revitalize the drive which he knew was locked away deep within him. In his mind, he went back over the conversation he had had with his parents the night before, remembering that for the first time he had suddenly understood their own feelings of anguish and vulnerability, feelings which lay just beneath an outward show of strength and support.

He shut off the water and stepped out of the shower, his skin tingling and his mind clearer. Still with the same sense of urgency, he shaved quickly and returned to his room. He put on a clean pair of boxer shorts and slipped into them, then, without thinking, pulled on his work jeans and started to do up the buttons. He stopped in mid-action.

"Oh, come on, get your bloody act together!" He pushed his jeans hard to the ground and, with a swing of his foot, kicked them back onto the chair, then, walking over to the wardrobe, he slipped his dark blue suit off its hanger and laid it on his bed. He stood back and stared at it blankly.

Somehow, he hadn't been able to bring himself to wear a kilt at the funeral. It was just too tangible a link with Rachel, and in some irrational way he had wanted to distance himself as far as possible from her on that day, hoping that it would make it easier for him to cope with the whole thing. So he had worn the suit—and he hadn't worn it since. He shook his head, his mind suddenly thrown into turmoil by an overpowering sense of rejection both to wearing it again and to his new routine. In one quick movement, he picked it up and threw it onto the chair next to his jeans. He pushed his fingers through his hair and glanced over to where it now lay, its pressed perfection standing out in powerful and self-assured contrast to the honest simplicity of his earth-streaked denims.

"Jesus, I'm not ready for this," he said quietly to himself.

He turned back to the wardrobe and took out a pair of fawn chinos and a navy-blue double-breasted blazer as a compromise both to conformity and to his feelings.

He put on the trousers, along with a blue open-necked shirt and cashmere jersey, and pulled on a pair of socks before slipping his feet into a pair of dark brown boating shoes. Then, with one last huge intake of air, he strode over to the door, threw it open and walked out onto the landing.

They left the house at eight-thirty, David behind the wheel of the Audi Estate, with his father sitting hunched in his tweed overcoat next to him. Although it was David's own company car, his father had been making use of it while David himself had been working at home, and being more used to driving the garden tractor and on occasion his mother's small Renault, he found himself spinning the wheels on the gravel as he took off, being unused to the power of the big fuel-injected engine.

George looked across at him. "How are you feeling this morning?"

David nodded briefly. "Okay."

His father reached over and gave him a hard but reassuring smack on the leg. "You'll be fine, my boy. Don't worry."

The old man pressed the on/off switch of the radio, having become accustomed to listening to it on his way to work each morning, and thinking it better for David's sake that there be some form of diversion from conversation during their journey. The news programme *Good Morning, Scotland* blared from the speakers, and he quickly adjusted the volume and settled back to listen to the twangy tones of a sports correspondent discussing strategy with the manager of Glasgow Rangers Football Club.

As soon as David turned out through the gates of Inchelvie and onto the main road towards Dalnachoil, the clouds broke for the first time in about a month, allowing a fleeting splash of pale blue to push weakly through from above, followed almost immediately by a meagre ray of sunshine which glinted briefly on the windscreen of the car. By the time the Audi had reached the top of the main street of Dalnachoil, the streaks of blue had lengthened and the sun began to dart in and out through the clouds, bursting forth its unfettered light onto the houses of the village and casting swift-moving fluffy shadows onto the sides of the surrounding hills. As they drove along the main street, George raised his hand continuously to wave at acquaintances on the pavement, and David glanced in the rear-view mirror at the querying faces that followed the departure of the car, the villagers being unaccustomed of late to seeing both himself and his father driving off together.

Once out of Dalnachoil's speed limit, David felt a light unexpected surge of excitement slip its way through the barricades of dullness in his mind, almost as if he was at last managing to make a break from the confines of his small, sad world. He had never ventured farther than the village in the past month, and his visits there had been brief and only out of unavoidable necessity, always fearing that he might be caught up in understanding and comforting conversations with the locals. But now, driving out in his own car along the familiar road, he sensed almost a feeling of well-being as they wound their way southwards through the glen, flanked on either side by green sunlit fields which stretched away to clash against the brown blanket of heather moorland that rolled down from the hills above. He glanced over at his father, and for the first time in a long while was able to feel a sudden burst of intense love for the old man who sat with his eyes closed, his hand cupped around his ear to help him pick up the low tones of the radio. David reached forward to turn up the volume, and his father looked round and smiled.

"Thanks—that's a bit better," he said, dropping his hand to his lap. "Forgot to put in my bloody hearing-aid this morning."

At the bottom of the glen, David edged out at the T-junction, then pulled away in the direction of Aberlour, pushing the car hard so that he could feel the power of the engine press his back into the seat. The narrow road followed the contours of the Spey River, running swollen and brown after the spring rains. David took it fast but warily, being forced to slow from time to time to avoid hitting a variety of obstacles that he met on his way: first an ageing Massey-Ferguson tractor, which came hammering up the road towards him, black smoke belching from its punctured exhaust-pipe, while a large round bale of hay, bouncing wildly on its front loader, successfully impeded its driver's vision of the road ahead; next two blackface ewes that were lying in the middle of the road, soaking up the warmth from the tarmac, their heads thrown back as they cudded, like a couple of haughty old ladies complaining disdainfully to each other about this unscheduled disturbance to their peace; and finally a flashy new four-wheel-drive vehicle parked haphazardly at the side of the road, the empty fishing-rod holder on its roof indicating that its driver was somewhere down on the banks of the river, plying its pools and eddies for salmon.

Two miles before Aberlour, David turned right and crossed a high iron-latticed bridge that spanned the river, then immediately swung left past the large brown sign which bore the name GLENDURNICH DISTILLERIES LTD in gold lettering. The road had at one time twisted down the hill to the riverside in a series of hairpin bends, but had had to be re-routed to allow easier access for the long and unwieldly triple-axled lorries that delivered bulk malt from the maltings at Inverness and took off the casks of mature whisky to the bottling plant near Glasgow. Now it descended in one huge sweep, yet so designed to still leave the distillery completely hidden behind the screen of densely planted fir-trees, save for the two pagoda-style chimneys, the characteristic emblem of all Scotch malt distilleries, that sat over the old kiln-house and jutted their arrowhead-shaped tips above the cover.

Rounding the bend, he left the shelter of the trees and at once the distillery came into view below him. Set in a fifteen-acre site, it stretched out on a plateau twenty feet above the river, bounded by a series of tarmacked roads which, in turn, were bordered by a wide expanse of newly mown banks and lawns interspersed with bright well-kept flower-beds. The road dropped down the incline, so that David began at the same level as the dark grey metal roofs of the four identical maturation warehouses before descending to the plateau and driving alongside the original stone-built still-house and mash-house with their small white irregular windows, and then on past the malt silos to the new office block at the far end of the complex.

He pulled the Audi into the car-park and picked a space as close as possible to the main reception door. He turned off the ignition key, silencing both the engine and the radio simultaneously and, unclipping his seat-belt, he opened the door and got out. For a moment, he stood looking over towards the offices and found himself almost immediately stretching his arms high above his head to counteract an almost puerile sense of nervousness. He shook his head at this idiocy and walked around to the other side of the car where his father was already pushing himself to his feet with the aid of his stick. Putting a hand under his tweedy armpit, David gently heaved him upright, and the old man stood for a minute preparing himself for the first step.

He looked at David. "Ready?"

David smiled and nodded.

"Right. Well, let's make an entrance."

Margaret looked up from her reception desk as the revolving door swung round, and a huge grin spread across her face as she saw David follow in after his father. "Oh michty, michty me!" she said, pushing up her stout frame from the chair. "It's yourself, Mr. David!"

She bustled over towards them and grasped hold of David's hand even before he had time to offer it. "Och, it's wonderful, wonderful to see you." She looked him up and down, still clutching his hand. "My, I have to say that you're looking a wee bit on the thin side," she said, and then, after a short pause for reflection, "but I dare say it makes you look as handsome as ever!" She threw back her head and shrieked out a laugh that could no doubt be heard throughout the building.

"Jolly good, Margaret, jolly good," George cut in, "but David is only here for a short period today."

"Of course, of course," Margaret said quietly, suddenly embarrassed by her own over-ebullience. "I quite understand. But nevertheless, it's a pleasure to see you looking so fit and well, Mr. David."

David smiled at her and nodded. "Thanks, Margaret."

"Did Mr. Caple say at what time he would like to meet this morning?" George asked.

"Now he did that." She trotted over to her desk and picked up her spectacles and a piece of paper. She shook open the legs and placed the spectacles squint on her nose. "Right," she said slowly, holding the piece of paper out in front of her, "it says here could you all meet at ten o'clock in the boardroom."

"That's fine, Margaret. Many thanks. Just let him know that we'll be there." He took hold of David's arm and, turning him away from Margaret, glanced over at the grandfather clock.

"Look, it's twenty past nine now. I suggest you make yourself scarce until then, otherwise you'll only get press-ganged into doing some work. Go and have a walk around the distillery and we'll meet again in the boardroom at ten."

David smiled. "Right. Good idea."

Giving his son a gentle nudge in the back, George

then stood watching as David hurried his way out through the revolving doors, almost as if he couldn't wait to be free of the building.

Arriving in his office, George was somewhat taken aback to find Robert McLeod there, standing with his hands clasped behind his back and looking out of the window. He swung round as George entered the room.

"Ah, George," he said in his extruded Edinburgh voice. "I hope you don't mind me waiting for you here. Mhairi told me that you had half an hour free just now, and I was really wanting to see you quite urgently."

George made his way over to the coat-stand. "Well, all right, Robert," he said, shrugging off his overcoat. "If you could just give me a second while I get myself organized."

As he hung his coat on the stand, he glanced out of the side of his eye at the neat, diminutive figure of Glendurnich's financial director and found himself smirking in mirth at David's desperate suggestion of the previous night that this man should undertake the United States trip. He walked over to his desk and sat down heavily in his chair.

"Ever been to the United States, Robert?" he asked, dropping his walking-stick to the floor beside him.

"No, I can't say I have."

"Didn't think so." Smiling broadly, George opened the top drawer of his desk, took out a pad of paper and unclipped his pen from the inside pocket of his jacket. Robert meanwhile had pulled across a chair from the far wall and placed it close to the other side of his chairman's desk, then, with a deft flick at each well-honed trouser crease, he sat himself down.

"Come to think of it, though," he said, a look of studied recollection on his face, "my wife and I nearly did take the two girls to Disneyland—I think when they were about fourteen and fifteen." He looked pensively over George's head and brushed minutely with his forefinger at the centre of his neatly clipped moustache, as if affectionately stroking a mouse. "That must have been about ten years ago. I think I cancelled the holiday because the exchange rate suddenly dropped." He came out of his remembrances and looked back at George. "Anyway, we much prefer the south-west of England for our holidays. There are so many wonderful golf courses down there."

"I'm sure there are," George said, glancing across at this pedantic little man who could be nothing but an accountant, so much so that he was quite happy to cancel plans to take his family on the holiday of a lifetime simply because the dealings of the international money markets meant that he would forfeit a few measly cents to his own precious pound.

Nevertheless, Robert was an excellent financial director. Having joined Glendurnich from a small firm of accountants in Edinburgh twenty years previously, he had handled the company's accounts with shrewdness and meticulous care ever since. Even so, he was a stickler for punctuality and time-keeping, never erring from his regular hours and always being the first away from the office exactly on the dot of five-thirty in the afternoon—which meant, in the summer at any rate, he would be heading straight for the golf course.

Yet for some time now, George had had a suspicion that Robert's interest in the company had been waning and he put it down to the fact that Robert may have had his nose put out of joint by Duncan Caple's own considerable financial expertise. Nevertheless, he felt it worthwhile to make a note on his jotter to remind himself to ask Robert at the end of their meeting about Duncan's concern over Glendurnich's United States sales figures.

"Well, Robert, what did you want to see me for?" he asked, putting his pen down and starting to glance through some of the morning's letters that Mhairi had marked for his attention.

Robert sat back in his chair and coughed once into his clenched hand to clear his throat. "Well, George, it's just that I think the time is right for me to take early retirement."

"What?" George looked straight up at him, a surprised look on his face. "For what reason?"

Robert crossed his legs and flicked away some specks of dust from his trousers with the back of his hand. "Because," he began slowly, "I think that I'm getting a little bit old for the job. I am very aware that the board of directors is now considerably younger than myself, and I am also beginning to find the whisky industry of today far too cutthroat."

George kept looking at him, waiting for him to continue. "Anything else?"

"Well, er, actually yes." He hesitated for a moment. "You see, I've been offered the job of club secretary at Drumshiel Golf Club, and I feel that it's such a wonderful opportunity that I just don't want to turn it down."

George sat back in his chair and swung it round to look out the window. For a moment he said nothing. "When are you thinking of leaving?" he eventually asked, his voice sounding thin.

"In a month's time," Robert replied jauntily, relieved that he had managed to break the news without receiving instant rebuke or mutterings about repercussions to the company. "That should give me enough time to get last year's accounts finalized. The new incumbent will then be able to start afresh without having to sort out any of my idiosyncrasies."

George continued to gaze distantly out the window, then, closing his eyes, he began to shake his head almost imperceptibly from side to side as a feeling of anger began to rumble away within his mind. Thanks, Robert, he thought to himself, this is exactly what I need right now! Not only do I have Duncan breathing down the back of my neck with regards to David's future with the company, but I also have David to deal with. He's not in any fit state to handle himself at present, let alone this American trip, and now you come traipsing into my office and tell me that we have to find a new financial director. So you think it's time you bloody retired, do you? Well, *bully for you*, because I'm meant to have been retired for the past ten years, but here I am back again having to sort out everybody's damned problems.

Robert watched him closely as he turned back from the window, noticing that the usual ruddiness had drained from George's face, suddenly making him look extremely old. Concerned, he leaned forward in his chair and was about to ask the old man if he was feeling quite well when George took a deep breath and slapped the arms of his chair purposefully.

"Well, I suppose we'd better start looking for a replacement for you, Robert," he said in one expulsion of air. "You'll be a hard act to follow, you know."

"Thanks for saying so, George," Robert said, sitting back again, "but I really don't think it will be that difficult. I believe Duncan has already got his eye on the present financial director of the malting company in Elgin."

"Has he, by heck!" George barked out. "How long has he known of your plans?"

"I told him last week," Robert answered meekly, somewhat taken aback by the vehemence of George's retort. "He was very sad that I had decided to go, but felt that it was a good move for me."

Resting his elbows on the arms of the chair, George linked his hands together and chewed pensively at the side of his mouth. "What's his constitutional remit?" he asked abruptly.

"What do you mean, George?"

George glowered at Robert across the desk and repeated the question. "Is Duncan allowed to hire and fire employees of Glendurnich Distilleries Limited without consultation with the board?"

Robert nodded slowly. "Yes, I believe that that was one of the conditions to which we agreed when he joined the company."

George rested his elbows on the desk and began rubbing at his forehead with his fingers, suddenly realizing that not only could Duncan appoint whom he liked as financial director, but also that if this remit was taken to its extremes, it could have implications on his son's own future on the board of directors.

"God, why the hell did we agree to that?"

"I think," Robert replied timidly, aware that George was becoming quite irascible, "that we were all very keen to get Duncan as managing director."

George sat back in his chair. "Yes, I suppose so." He paused for a moment, looking back out of the window. "Robert, he didn't . . . erm . . . Duncan didn't ask you to leave, did he?"

Robert shook his head briskly. "Oh, no! Nothing like that. It really was all my idea. Heavens, no! I don't think even Duncan would have the nerve to do that!"

George smiled across at him. "I'm sure not, Robert. I'm sorry I had to ask you that, but I just wanted to make sure that things weren't going on behind my back."

Robert stood up, taking George's climbdown as an opportune point at which to end their meeting, and replaced his chair against the wall of the office. "No, not at all, George. Duncan can be a little, well, self-centred sometimes, but he's a good business man, and looking at the first draft of last year's accounts, I would say he's doing well for the company."

George looked across at him and nodded. "I'm sure, Robert . . . and thanks, I value your opinion."

"I'm happy, as always, to give it, George, and now if you'll excuse me, I must get on with those accounts." He grinned nervously at George. "Now that time is of the essence, so to speak."

"Of course, and Robert, thank you for all you have

done for the company over the years. You've been a real stalwart."

With a fleeting smile, Robert turned briskly on his heel and left the room. For a moment, George stared at the closed door, then pressed the intercom button for his secretary.

Ten seconds later there were two small knocks on the door. Without waiting for a bidding, Mhairi entered the room, carrying a notepad and pen in her hand. The young secretary came over to George's desk and stood in front of him. He looked up at her and smiled.

"Right, Mhairi. I wonder if you could confirm with Devonshire Place that both Lady Inchelvie and I will be staying on Tuesday night?"

Mhairi began to scribble on her notepad. "I take it that Lady Inchelvie won't be going to the conference?"

George shook his head. "No, no, she won't. She's really just taking the opportunity of the lift so that she can go on to Perth to visit the grandchildren at their school."

"Very good," Mhairi said, making a final full stop on her notepad. "Is that it, my lord?"

"Not quite. Could you telephone British Airways and book a return flight from Glasgow to New York for Tuesday morning?"

"This coming Tuesday morning, my lord?"

"That's right." He paused for a moment. "And I think you should make the ticket open-ended, Mhairi."

She waited, her pencil poised above the notepad. When George didn't continue, she asked, "And whose name should be on the ticket?"

George lifted his hand in apology. "Ah yes, sorry about that. It's for Mr. David."

Mhairi nodded and scribbled on the notepad.

"That's it, Mhairi. I'd be grateful if you could confirm all that."

"Certainly, my lord." She turned and walked briskly to the door. As she left the room, George swung his chair round to face the window and, picking up his pen, he began to turn it top to base, over and over, each time bringing it down harder on the surface of his desk. After a moment, he took the top off the pen and, with two heavy strokes, scored out his memorandum for Robert. He threw the pen on the desk and sat back in his chair, an exhausted expression on his face.

"I hope you're not up to anything, Duncan my boy," he murmured under his breath, "I just hope you're not up to anything."

Pushing open the door of the still-house, David was immediately met with the hot, heady smell of whisky distillation in progress. He climbed the four well-worn stone steps and walked out onto the steel-meshed floor that ran the full length of the high building, fifteen feet above the base of the still-pans. The still-house hissed like a pressure cooker, drowning out the clanging resonance of his footsteps on the grid flooring as he walked to the far end of the room past the four huge highly polished copper stills. He climbed the metal staircase and made his way along the narrow gantry that ran level with the highest point of the stills. Half-way along, he stopped outside a door newly painted in bright green and stencilled in white with the word CANTEEN. He hesitated a moment before pushing it open and entering.

Despite the overpowering smell of cigarette smoke, the workers' new canteen was bright and airy, having been converted from an old sky-lighted sack-loft when the old canteen was swallowed up in the refurbishment works. At one end, a loading door had been knocked out and replaced with a full-length window, so that from where he stood, David could see all the way down to the river below. At the other end, a modern Formica unit housed a stainless-steel sink, a refrigerator, and a microwave oven, while a brand-new Cona coffeemaker sat, still boxed, on the worktop, a marked indication that the work-force preferred their own vacuum flasks of hot sweet tea. The whole place might have resembled a smart well-appointed kitchen had it not been for the fact that the men, in illogical but pointed rebellion against their eviction from the old canteen, had voted to bring their furniture with them. The centre of the room, therefore, was strewn with an ill assortment of rickety, broken-backed chairs, gathered haphazardly around a long wooden table, its surface stained with mug rings and the dark brown, pitted lesions of cigarette burns. Above this was hung the wall's only adornment—a large calendar still turned to the month of March, which showed a blonde, well-developed young girl pretending to undo the wheel-nut of a lorry without the protection of a single stitch of clothing.

Around the table sat three men, all dressed in T-shirts and coveralls, drinking steaming mugs of tea and reading tabloid newspapers that were spread out in front of them. They looked across to where David stood and rose slowly to their feet, mumbling indiscernible greetings in his direction while casting embarrassed and uneasy glances both at each other and at the clock above the sink.

"Don't get up, please!" David said, also feeling embarrassed at their reaction to his entry. He looked across at one of the men. "How are you, Dougie?"

Pulling a fully laden ashtray towards him on the table, Dougie Masson stubbed out the butt of a self-rolled cigarette and walked over to David, wiping his hands on the back of his dungarees. He was as wide as he was tall, a little terrier of a man in his early fifties who had the sides of his head shaved down to a grey stubble to lessen the contrast with its polished dome. For twenty-five years, he had served in the army, at first with the Seaforths and then finishing off a proud and unblemished career as a colour sergeant in Queen's Own Highlanders in the same platoon as David. During that time, David, as a young and very green second lieutenant, had come to trust and rely on the experienced and much-respected little man, so much so that when they eventually demobbed together, he had felt strangely honoured when Dougie asked him if he might be able to pull a few strings with his father to get him a job in the distillery. Within a month, he was taken on as a trainee still-house operator, and since then their relationship had developed, not into a close friendship, but into an alliance built both on mutual respect and their ability to talk straight with each other.

Dougie grasped David's hand in a vice-like grip. "Good tae see ye back, Mr. David," he said in a voice that was as deep and as gruff as a gravel-pit. "Are you keeping yourself well?"

"Yup, I think so."

"Glad tae hear it." Dougie stood back and scratched at the taut thick muscle of his tattooed forearm. "The lads, well, we were all very sorry tae hear about your wife. That was a real bugger, sir."

David folded his arms and looked down at the ground, pushing a cigarette end under the table with his foot. "Yuh, I'm afraid it was."

Dougie glanced at him, then back to his workmates, who had meantime gone back to reading their newspapers. He walked up close to David, gave him a brief wink, and nodded his head sideways in the direction of the door. "I'm just awa' back tae work, sir."

Understanding his message, David turned to follow him out, but not before raising his hand in silent farewell to the other two men. They looked up momentarily, reciprocating the gesture with a brief flick of their heads before returning to their reading.

"How're things with you, then?" David asked, leaning his elbows on the gantry barrier next to Dougie, as he looked down with a frown of concentration onto the still-house floor.

"Och, no' bad. Could be worse. We've been havin' a real bugger of a problem with that number three still over there." He pointed a stubby finger down to where an oxyacetylene welder stood amongst a cluster of tools. "Only just managed to get it sorted. That's why we're all a bit late in taking our tea-break."

"What was up with it?" David asked, looking down on the still.

"Och, it developed a leak in the steam kettle yesterday afternoon." He chuckled. "Bloody good thing that Jimmy has a big nose. It was him who picked it up in the condensate going to the boiler. Anyway, we had to empty the still overnight so we could isolate the steam valve, and we've just finished spot-welding the leak about an hour ago. We should be able to get the thing refilled this afternoon."

"Ah. Well done."

Dougie turned and grinned at David, knowing full well that a technical engineering fault in the distillery was not something of which he had great knowledge. However, when he noticed that David's eyes were focused blankly onto the still-house floor, the smile vanished from his face and he began slowly shaking his head.

"Och, Davie lad, ye're a wee bit distracted at the minute, aren't ye?"

David looked at him and nodded. "Yup, you could say that," he said with a long, heavy sigh. He turned round and leaned his back against the rail.

"So," Dougie asked quietly, "what have you been doing with yourself since, well, then?"

"Gardening, mostly."

Dougie rubbed abrasively at the side of his head. "Aye, well, it's good tae keep yourself occupied somehow." He turned to take up the same position as David. "So what brings you in here today?"

David reached out and took hold of the handle of a brush that stood against the wall opposite. He put his foot heavily on its head so that the bristles splayed out on the floor. "Well, I've got to go out to New York to

do some business—and—as you can imagine, it's the
last thing I bloody well feel like doing!"

Dougie crossed his arms and looked glumly down at
his boots. "Aye, I can understand that." He let out a
long sigh and began picking at a callus on his finger.
"Will ye be seeing Lieutenant Eggar when you're out
there?"

David stopped fiddling with the broom handle and
looked quizzically at Dougie. "What do you mean?

"Lieutenant Eggar? Was he no' a friend of yours?"

"Of course he was. But why do you think that I
would be seeing him?"

"Well, he's in New York—or somewhere's about.
I've just read a wee bit about him in this month's regimental news. Hang on a minute"—Dougie pushed
himself off the rail—"I've got it in my locker." He went
back into the canteen, re-emerging a few seconds later
with a copy of the magazine in his hand. "It came yesterday in the post. I just stuck it in my piece-bag last
night to have a look at over the tea-break." He licked
at a dirt-engrained thumb and began to leaf clumsily
through the glossy pages. "Now where the hell—aye,
here it is!"

He bent the magazine in half at the penultimate page
and handed it to David. It was a small paragraph at the
bottom under the column "Other News."

Richard Eggar (2nd Lieut. QOH. 1973–1976) recently organized a reunion of Queen's Own Highlanders who, like himself, have put down roots in
the United States of America. Now a vice-
president of Dammell's Bank in New York, Lieutenant Eggar said that he was well pleased with
the attendance figure of fourteen, especially as
three of the attendees had made the effort to fly
over from the West Coast specifically for the occasion. Lieutenant Eggar, who is married and lives
on Long Island, said that he would be delighted

to meet with any QOH who might be visiting New York in the future. He can be contacted on 001 516 357 4298.

David raised his eyebrows and turned back to Dougie. "Do you mind if I borrow this?"

"That's nae bother. Just get it back tae me sometime."

"You'll have it by lunch-time," David said, placing the broom back against the wall and rolling the magazine into a scroll in his hand. "I just want to get that telephone number." He glanced at his watch. "Hell, it's five to ten. I'd better go. I have a meeting in five minutes."

As they began walking along the gantry together, Dougie turned to him with a kindly grin on his face. "Well, I hope I've brightened up your day a wee bitty."

"Yeah, you have, actually. Listen, sorry if I'm seeming a bit distant at the minute."

Dougie slapped him on the back. "Och, dinnae worry yourself about it. I think we know each other well enough. Just look after yourself, laddie, and dinnae do anything that I wouldn't do."

David let out a short laugh. "That's leaving me a wide margin." He descended the stairs, holding up the magazine. "I'll make sure this gets back to you."

"Aye, well, I'll be here or hereabouts."

The grandfather clock in the reception area had just whirred laboriously to a close after striking the hour of ten when David entered the building at speed and hurried across to the boardroom. Margaret, who was talking loudly on the telephone, swung round with a thunderous look on her face, but on seeing David the frown turned into a wide lipsticked grin and she simply waved heartily at him without interrupting her conversation.

His father was alone, sitting in his high-backed chair

at the far end of the table and stooping down to suck the first mouthful from an overfull cup of coffee. He looked up when David walked in.

"I don't know how the hell she does it!" he said, his voice bordering on grumpiness.

David laughed. "Who's she and what does she do?" He walked up the room towards his father, pulled out the chair next to him and threw Dougie's magazine onto the table.

"Margaret! You ask her for a cup of coffee, and she comes in at the speed of light, dumps it down in front of you without one spilt drop, and look at it!" He gesticulated towards his steaming cup. "The wretched thing has a meniscus on it, it's so bloody full!"

He bent forward and slurped at his cup, then, pulling a large paisley-patterned handkerchief from his top pocket, he leaned back in his chair and wiped his mouth. "Did you go out to the distillery?"

"Yes, I ran into Dougie Masson."

"Ah, right. I haven't seen him for a bit. How is he?"

"Seems to be fine," David said, reaching forward to pick up the magazine. "He showed me this bit about an army friend of mine." He flicked through the pages to the article. "Seems he's working in New York and living out somewhere on Long Island." He pushed the magazine towards his father. "Thought I might give him a call to see if he has a spare bed for a couple of nights. Better than sitting in some hotel by myself."

George raised his eyebrows as he reached forward to pick up the magazine, not so much in interest at the article but more in pleasure at his son's seeming willingness to try to make the best of the New York trip. He gave the magazine a cursory glance before sliding it back up the table. "That's a terrific idea. Give him a call once we've finished . . ."

As he spoke, the door of the boardroom was thrown open and Duncan Caple appeared, bearing an armful of files and walking backwards as he continued to speak to someone outside the room.

"All right. Well, tell him I'll return his call in about half an hour." He turned and back-heeled the door closed. "Sorry I'm a bit late. Got held up." He walked towards them, plunked down the files with a thud on the table and pulled out the chair opposite David. "Would it be all right if we kept this meeting quite brief? I'm expecting rather an important call from Japan at any minute." He looked across at David. "David, sorry, how *are* you?" he asked, a condescending tinge to his voice. "Apologies for having to call you in for this trip, but there really was no alternative. Anyway, as I said to your father, it'll probably do you the world of good to get away for a bit."

George began chewing quickly at the side of his mouth, furious at the crassness of Duncan's last remark. He caught the eye of the young managing director and fixed him with a steely glare.

"I think we'll just get the briefing over and done with as soon as possible, Duncan. David still has quite a bit to sort out at home."

The rebuke went straight over the top of Duncan's head. He glanced at David. "What? Are you going straight back after this? I thought you might be able to make a few telephone calls for me, seeing that you're back into the—"

"No, Duncan," George interjected pointedly, "David is going straight back after this!"

Duncan was silent for a moment. He was beginning to get fed up with having to carry the work-load of both David and himself, and fed up with the way that the Corstorphine family always seemed to close ranks on him whenever he was trying to achieve something for the company. He shook his head, taking on an air of truculent resignation.

"Oh, well, if that's what you've agreed between yourselves, then we'd better crack on with the briefing."

He picked up one of the files, flicked off the elastic holder, and opened it in front of him.

"I won't go into huge detail on this, David, as I'm sure your father has filled you in on the reason why I feel it necessary to appoint a new distributor in the States. Anyway, it suffices to say that it is essential that we improve or at least maintain our sales in the U.S. This simply has not been happening with Lacey's. Now, I managed to get hold of profiles on four different distribution companies, and from those have selected one which will go before the board on Tuesday."

George leaned forward in his chair. "I won't be here on Tuesday, Duncan. I'm traveling down to Glasgow for the Whisky Association conference."

The managing director sat back, resting his elbows on the arms of the chair with the palms of his hands held upwards at either side of him.

"It really is only a formality, George, as we discussed here yesterday. It has to be done." He turned towards David. "So, I've arranged your meeting with the new distributor for the Wednesday at ten A.M."

The lack of response from David made George glance along the table to his son, immediately noticing that, after his brief spark of excitement over the article in the magazine, he had returned to his own introverted normality, gazing as if mesmerized at the palm of his hand and rubbing it slowly back and forth with the opposite thumb.

This was too much for Duncan. Come on, man, he thought to himself, so okay, you're mourning your wife, but it doesn't mean that you have to show such a blatant disinterest in what's going on.

"Excuse me, David," he said sharply, "you may not think it, but actually what I'm saying is quite important."

David snapped his head up to look at him, fury suddenly flashing in his eyes. George saw it immediately and held up his hands.

"Okay, let's calm this all down, shall we? Duncan, you have the briefing document there. Just give it to David. That's all he really needs."

Duncan let out a resigned sigh. "Very well." He slid the document across to David. "The name of the company is Deakin Distribution. It's relatively new, but has had excellent results in promoting the sales of a couple of English gin companies over the past two years. They're based on Madison Avenue, I'm not sure where, but the address is in the file." He slapped his hands on the table and, pushing back his chair, got to his feet. "Well, I don't suppose there's much more to be said." He turned to George. "What about flights?"

"That's in hand. Mhairi's fixing it."

"Good." He picked up his remaining files and began to walk towards the door. As he passed behind David, he stopped. "Ah, just one more thing. I thought yesterday that it might have been an idea for you to pay a visit to Lacey's, just so that we finish with them in good grace. However, in retrospect I believe you should just leave it. I'll handle it from this end."

He went forward and put a reassuring hand on David's shoulder, but removed it immediately when he felt him flinch at the contact. For a moment, his hand remained hovering in mid-air, then, with a brief nod in George's direction, he turned on his heel and left the room.

A heavy silence enveloped the boardroom until George finally pushed back his chair, picked up his stick and began levering himself upwards. "He may be a good business man, but by God he can be an insufferable little devil sometimes."

David jumped up and helped his father to his feet. "Christ, I thought I was only a hair's breadth from thumping him."

George chuckled. "Yes, I realized that." He winced with pain as he took his first step forward, then began to shuffle his way towards the door. "Listen, old boy.

I've booked you on a flight from Glasgow on Tuesday morning, and I've actually told Mhairi to make the trip open-ended. It's just that I thought that it might be, well, remedial or even beneficial for you if you stayed over there for a bit. Do some travelling or something. I mean, I shall leave it entirely up to you."

David shook his head. "No, I don't think so. I reckon I'll come straight back. The children will want to see me—and anyway, I'll have to be thinking about coming back to work quite soon. I can't have you filling in for me for ever." He smiled at his father. "About time you continued your retirement."

"Oh, goodness' sakes, don't worry about me! I'm perfectly all right! In fact, I'm actually rather enjoying myself!"

David laughed. "Yeah, I can see that." He paused. "Look, it's a really kind thought—and I might consider it just for a short while, but I'll need to speak to the children first. I'm going down to see them on Saturday at any rate, just to explain what's happening."

"Damned good idea." George stopped and walked back to the table and reached over for the telephone. "Now before you head off, just let me make sure I can get a lift home." He dialled a number and waited for a second. "Ah, Margaret, would you be kind enough to get that young man Archie McLachlan to come into the boardroom? No, he's in distribution at the minute . . . yes, that's him . . . thanks, Margaret."

He replaced the receiver and looked up at David. "Listen, I wouldn't worry too much about Duncan. He was making a meal of it, just because that's the way his mind works. You just handle this trip in your own way and at your own pace. I'll make sure you get all the backing you need from this end without your having to have any contact with him. All right?"

David nodded. "Yeah, probably the best idea under the circumstances."

There was a quiet knock on the door.

"Come in, Archie."

Archie McLachlan slowly opened the door and put his head round the corner, his eyes wide with uncertainty. "Did you want to see me, my lord?"

"Yes, Archie, come on in. You know Mr. David, don't you?"

Archie came forward and shook David by the hand. "Hullo, sir, nice to see you again."

"Archie," George continued, "Mr. David is heading back to Inchelvie right now, which leaves me without a car. Would it be going very much out of your way if you were to give me a lift back there this afternoon?"

"Not at all, my lord," Archie said, his voice lifting with the thought of this important assignment. He paused for a moment. "The only thing is I'm afraid that I've only got an old Ford Fiesta."

George let out a single loud laugh. "I don't mind what we go in, Archie, as long as it has four wheels and it moves."

Relief spread across the boy's face. "Oh, well, in that case, certainly, my lord." He began to edge his way back to the door. "If you would just like to let me know when you're thinking of going, and I'll get the car up to the reception door."

George held up his hand. "Now, don't go quite yet. I have something else I want you to do."

Archie stopped in his tracks and looked intently at Lord Inchelvie.

"Mr. David is going to the States next Tuesday, Archie, to appoint a new distributor, and I'm going to be in Glasgow on that day and the following one, while Mr. Caple will be in London and Europe from about Wednesday onwards."

"Right, my lord," Archie said, his brow creased in concentration at what his chairman was saying.

"I want you to be Mr. David's contact here for the time that he is away. If there is anything he wants, you deal with it yourself. You don't have to clear anything with anyone else in the company; is that understood?"

"Yes, my lord."

"Good. And Archie, check with Margaret each morning for any faxes that might come through from Mr. David. I shall tell her that they are for your eyes only. Everything must be carried out in the strictest confidence. All right?"

"Of course, my lord," he said.

"Very good. You head off now, and I'll get Margaret to give you a call when I'm ready to leave."

Archie nodded, and smiling briefly to David, he walked to the door and left the room.

David looked at his father. "You sounded like 'M' just then, giving James Bond his orders. What's up?"

George frowned. "I'm not sure. It's just that I have this sneaking suspicion that things aren't what they seem." He shook his head and smiled. "Maybe age is making me a trifle paranoid—I don't know." He glanced at his watch. "Look, you head off now. That'll give you time to get back out in the garden with Jock this afternoon."

David shook his head and flicked through Duncan's brief in his hand. "No, I think that I'd better start reading up on this. I've got to start sometime."

"Yes," George replied, putting his hand on his son's shoulder. "I'm afraid that you do."

Chapter

EIGHT

As he turned the car in through the gates at Inchelvie, David saw Jock head towards him on the lawn tractor, carefully manoeuvring his way around the trees as he cut the grass verges of the drive. Feeling a sudden deep pang of envy for the old man and for the hard, yet undemanding simplicity of his job, his immediate impulse was to stop the car and tell him that they would continue immediately with the work on the flower-bed. But he checked himself and simply raised a hand in greeting as he drove past. No, he thought, you really do have to start sometime.

Parking the car at the front door, he ran up the stone steps and entered, then made his way across the hall to the drawing-room. Sitting down at his father's desk, he opened the document and found, stuck to the first page, the yellow Post-it on which he had written Richard Eggar's telephone number. He glanced at his watch. It was half past twelve. That would make it half past seven in the morning in New York. Maybe he could catch Richard before he left for work.

He picked up the receiver of the fax/telephone on the desk and dialled the number. The line cracked and whistled as it connected, followed within seconds by the single long ringing tone of the American telephone system. It rang four times before someone answered.

"Hu-llo?"

It was a man's voice, his vocal cords breaking as he spoke, so that the two syllables of the word ranged from base to falsetto, respectively, making David think immediately that whoever had answered the telephone was either suffering from a bad cold or had just woken up.

"Hullo, is that Richard?" As he spoke, he heard the man cough and clear his throat.

"Yeah, this is he." The voice was English, but tinged with an American slant.

"Richard, this is David Corstorphine. I was in Queen's Own—"

"David!" The voice, in its drowsiness, lifted a tone. "Hang on!" David heard a rustle of movement at the other end of the line. "Bloody hell, David Corstorphine! Where are you calling from?"

"Scotland."

"Scotland? Well, would you believe it? David! How the hell did you get my number?"

"It was in this month's regimental news. Something about you organizing some sort of get-together?"

"Oh, right." David heard a stifled yawn at the other end of the line.

"Sorry, Richard, have I woken you up?"

"No, not really . . . well, actually you have, but I should be up anyway. Just me being lazy. We were out at Montauk last night, and didn't get back till three o'clock this morning. Anyway, what am I talking about? This is crazy. I'm being phoned up at seven-thirty in the morning by a man I haven't seen in years. Could you give me a minute, David? I'm going to put you onto the cordless, so that I can get out of the bedroom."

The line went dead for a moment, and David sat twiddling the telephone cable around his finger.

"Hi, are you still there?" Richard asked, his voice sounding through the interference of the cordless phone.

"Yes, I'm still here."

"I'm in the kitchen now. Just bear with me while I put on the kettle. I'm dying for a cup of coffee." The interference swished as he moved around. "Right, that's it. So, David, how are you? It's great to hear you from you. What's the reason for the call?"

"Well, I was just wondering if—"

"No, hang on, let's get first things first. Tell me, how is the wonderful Rachel?"

David felt his mouth go dry. He tried to speak but nothing came out. For some reason, he had been totally unprepared for the question. All he had expected to do was to ask Richard if he could stay with him.

"Hullo, David, are you still there?"

"Erm . . . yes . . . sorry, Richard, sorry . . . I'm still here. Could you just hold the line a minute?"

Without waiting for a reply, he put his hand over the receiver and sat with his eyes tightly closed, a look of pained concentration on his face. Dammit, it had completely slipped his mind that Richard knew Rachel. Then of course he would have, because they'd been married for a year before he left the army. Now, thinking back on it, Richard had been with them on that mad skiing trip to Verbier. He could always press the "disconnect" button and call back later. No, what the hell good would that do?

"Hullo, Richard, sorry about that. Someone . . . er . . . just came into the room."

"Hey, that's all right. So, how is she?"

"Rachel . . ." David cleared his throat. ". . . died last month, Richard."

He heard nothing for a second except the continued crackle on the line, followed by the sound of a coffee-cup being knocked over on the sideboard or dropped to the ground. When Richard spoke again, his voice sounded distant and weak.

"Shit, David . . . shit . . . what . . . I mean, what happened?"

"Cancer."

"Oh my God . . . I'm so sorry. Did she . . . I mean . . . how long ago was this?"

"It was only diagnosed in October, and then by December, well . . ."

"Christ . . . what a *bastard* of a thing! Poor Rachel."

"Yeah."

"How are *you*, my friend?"

"Not . . . brilliant."

"Christ . . . I don't really know what to say . . . I mean, how are you . . . sort of . . . coping?"

"Not . . . particularly well. I'm staying with my parents at the minute."

"Right . . . and you've got children, haven't you?"

"Yup. Three. They've only just gone back to school."

"Jesus, I'm so sorry, David, for you all. I mean . . . shit! I'm so glad you telephoned to tell me."

David took a deep breath and cleared his throat again, realizing that Richard had given him the briefest opportunity to get away from the subject. "Look, Richard, that's not actually why I'm calling. It's just that, well, I have to come over to New York on business for a couple of days, and I was wondering if—"

Richard cut in. "Great! Can you come and stay?"

"Would that be all right?"

"Of course it would be. The only thing is that Angie is going back to Boston for a couple of weeks to visit her parents—but that's no problem, we'll just have to cope for ourselves. When are you coming over?"

"On Tuesday. I haven't got the tickets yet, but it'll be the morning flight from Glasgow, which gets into Kennedy at about twelve-thirty P.M., if my memory serves me correctly."

"And what are your plans for that day? Do you have a meeting?"

"No, it's not until the Wednesday at ten."

"Right, and have you any idea where the meeting is?"

"Somewhere on Madison Avenue."

"Okay, just hang on a minute while I get my diary. It's through in the sitting-room." David heard him move off through the house and then a frenetic rustle of papers before he spoke again. "Right, tell you what I'll do. I have an account with Star Limos here in Leesport, so I'll get a car over to Kennedy to pick you up. It's just over an hour's journey out here, so you can get the whole of Tuesday afternoon and the night to unwind, and then I'll take you in myself on Wednesday morning. My office is on Madison as well, and I'll bet you're only three or four blocks away from where I'm going to be anyway."

"Are you sure? I don't want to be a nuisance—"

"No way, José! Don't be stupid! I'm actually working summer-time hours at the minute, so I'm usually out here Friday through to Monday and then head off to the city for the remainder of the week. But while you're here, I'll just come back every night. That's no problem at all! Anyway, I've a mountain of paperwork to catch up on and the office can always E-mail me stuff if need be."

"Well, if you're sure, Richard, that really would be great. I can't tell you what a weight that is off my mind. It'll make my trip a great deal easier."

"It's a pleasure. Look, see you on Tuesday, okay? And, David . . . well, just *shit,* I'm so, so sorry about Rachel."

"I know. It's just one of those things."

"No, it's not. I know for you it's probably everything. Look, if you want to talk about it when you get out, I have really good ears. Anyway, enough said at the minute. Have a good flight, my friend, and look after yourself."

David dropped the receiver onto its base and sat rubbing his hands up and down his trouser legs, realizing they were trembling from the sheer effort of talking about Rachel. Taking a deep breath, he picked up the document, then immediately threw it back on the desk without opening it.

"Oh, bugger that!" He jumped to his feet and made his way out into the hall and upstairs to put on his work clothes.

Chapter
NINE

"This is meant to be the summer term!" Sophie said, pulling her blazer around her and tucking her hands under her armpits. "Summer terms are meant to be warm!"

The clonking contact of cricket ball against bat floated out on the chill breeze from the centre of the pitch, and a light ripple of applause sounded from the brave but sparse audience that encircled the game. The boys, who were fielding out on the ground, pulled their sweater sleeves down over their hands and jumped up and down to keep warm.

"Is it like this up at Inchelvie?"

Resting up on one elbow, David plucked absently at the daisies that carpeted the grass at the edge of the boundary. "No, it's been worse, actually. Last Thursday was about the first time that the sun broke through—but there wasn't much heat in it."

"I wish there was a switch we could turn on for summer," Harriet said, rocking herself back and forth as she perched on her father's hip-bone, "and then everything would become, well, summery just like that."

"Ow, Harry, don't do that! It's quite sore!"

Harriet let out a giggle and stopped momentarily,

then, fixing him with a grin of wicked intent, began rocking again in short spasmodic bursts, testing out her father's resilience.

"Right, you little devil!" he exclaimed, swinging his arm round and pushing her down onto the grass. "War is declared!" He tickled her fiercely, making her shriek out in hysterical laughter.

"Dad, stop it!" Sophie said in an embarrassed whisper. "Mr. Hunter is watching us from the cricket pitch!"

David sat up, pulling a face at Sophie's reprimand, but continued to keep his younger daughter at bay by darting his hand back at her every time she tried to make a move.

"I don't think we need to watch the *whole* match, do we?" Sophie asked, pulling her knees up under her chin.

"Probably not." He looked over at the score-board. "That's the last batsman in for their team anyway, so they'll all be coming off quite soon. I think we should keep watching just in case Charlie *does* get the chance to bowl."

Sophie sighed. "It's just such a boring game, cricket."

She reached her hands behind her neck and pulled the elastic scrunchie on her mousy-brown pony-tail tight against the back of her head. David looked across at her and clandestinely studied her face. Tiny smile lines, creasing the olive skin at the sides of her mouth and eyes, were now the only indication that the hardened, unemotional glare which she had adopted since her mother's death was alien to her character. She wore it like a mask, as if in some way smiling or laughing might be construed as being disloyal to her mother's memory. On her upper lip there blossomed two small but angry spots, blemishes that in the past would have caused her as much anxiety as a smallpox outbreak, but which now were left untreated and uncared for. It was like looking at an incomprehensible abstract painting—

textures of unhappiness, longing and dogged bravery all mixed together on a canvas of incipient beauty.

"That's exactly what Mummy thought," David said eventually. "She had absolutely no time for the game either."

Harriet sat up from her supine position at the mention of her mother and leaned across her father's body.

"What games *did* she like, then?"

David thought for a moment. "Well, you *know* she liked tennis—and—she was quite good at fishing. What else?"

"I know!" Harriet said, jumping across his legs and coming to sit between them both. "She liked cooking!"

Sophie sucked her teeth. "That's not a game, Harry!"

"It could be, though, couldn't it, Daddy?" She turned her face up to David, pressing her curly mop of jet-black hair against his arm, a pleading look in her eyes, willing his support in her argument.

"Well, I suppose you could fry eggs against the clock."

Sophie flicked up her head in disdain. "You would say that, Dad, just to agree with teeny-weeny."

Harriet kicked her foot against her sister's leg. "*Don't* call me teeny-weeny, Sophie!"

"All right, you two," David said, catching Harriet's foot as it flashed out for another strike.

Sophie turned, resting her cheek on her knee, and smiled lightly at her sister. "Teeny-weeny," she teased in a high-pitched voice.

"Sophie!" David laughed, "that's enough. Leave your extremely grown-up younger sister alone." He glanced across to the cricket game and saw with relief that at last Charlie was about to start bowling. "Come on, there's Charlie on now! Let's watch him."

Out on the distant pitch, Charlie sped into the wicket as fast as his spindly young legs would carry him, and with a somewhat over-complicated bowling action sent a looping ball towards the batsman. It was given a solid, yet sadly deserving blow, and as the young fields-man chased off after it towards the boundary, Charlie stood watching him, hands on hips and disappointedly kicking the toe of his shoe into the ground. Taking this all as a sign for immediate congratulations, Harriet began clapping heartily and David grabbed her hands before her badly timed applause could be heard by her brother.

She tilted back her head and looked up at David. "Wasn't that any good?"

"No, not really."

Sophie let out a long sigh. "If he keeps bowling like that, we'll be here all day!"

Charlie's next ball was identical to the first, only this time the batsman, lulled into a false sense of security by the snail-like pace of Charlie's bowling, bounded down the wicket to take another fearsome blow at the ball—and missed. The diminutive wicket-keeper fumbled the ball into his oversized gloves and knocked off the bails, and an immediate unison cry of "Howzat" rang out from the pitch. The umpire raised his finger to signify the batsman's dismissal and the fielding side descended both upon Charlie and the wicket-keeper in a frenzy of excitement.

"Thank goodness for that," Sophie said, clambering to her feet. "Let's go into the school now."

"Hang on a minute!" David laughed, getting up and dusting off the damp grass clippings from the seat of his trousers. "Wait for Charlie. He's coming over."

They stood watching as Charlie ran towards them, his sweater thrown over his shoulder and his loose shirt-tail flying out behind him. He arrived in front of them, a grin spread across his freckled face, and blew upwards at the long string of auburn hair that fell in front of his eyes.

"Did you see that, Dad?" he asked excitedly.

"I certainly did."

"Not bad for second ball!"

David walked over to him and tousled his hair. "Not bad at all!"

"Can we go in now?" Sophie asked, running rapidly on the spot.

Charlie took no notice of his elder sister. "Dad, I'm not batting until number ten and they're going to have tea first, so Mr. Hunter said that we could go off for a bit."

"Where would you want to go?"

"McDonald's in Perth! Please, Dad! I'm famished."

The idea was greeted with an immediate shout of approval from Harriet. David looked across at Sophie.

"Is that all right by you?"

She shrugged noncommittally. "I don't really mind, as long as we go somewhere warm."

A quarter of an hour later, following a speedy drive around the Perth ring road, they sat in the car-park outside McDonald's with the tangy, sweet smell of fast food wafting about the fuggy interior of the Audi.

"Are you sure you don't want anything more than that?" David asked Sophie, who sat beside him picking at the smallest bag of fries that she had been able to order.

Sophie shook her head. "No, I'm not that hungry."

"Dad!" Charlie exclaimed from the back seat between slurps at his milk shake. "Harriet's just dropped a piece of gherkin on the floor."

"I don't like them," Harriet retorted quietly.

"Doesn't mean you have to throw—"

"All right!" David interjected. "It couldn't matter less." He turned in his seat and, picking up the offending object, jettisoned it out of the window. The children sat without speaking, munching loudly on their meals. David took in a deep breath.

"Listen . . . erm, I've got something to tell you. I'm going to have to go to America next week on business."

Sophie glanced round, a chip half-way to her mouth. "For how long?"

"Well, it should only be a couple of days. It depends really on how long it takes."

Charlie leaned forward between the front seats, licking ketchup off his fingers. "Does that mean you won't be coming down next weekend?"

"I don't know, Charlie. As I said, it all depends."

Charlie let out a moan of disappointment. "But we're playing Clevely Hall on Saturday."

"I know you are. But if I'm not back, I'm sure Granny will come down to watch you play."

"Granny doesn't understand cricket," Charlie whined. "She just spends her time talking to people and not watching."

"Oh, do stop moaning, Charlie!" Sophie said sharply. "It's really kind of Granny to come at all. Anyway, Dad will probably be back by next weekend." She looked round at her father, a flash of uncertainty in her eyes. "Won't you?"

David smiled reassuringly at her. "Well, it depends, but I'll certainly do my best." Stretching across, he took an over-cooked chip from Sophie's bag and, crunching on it, eyed the glum faces of Charlie and Harriet in the rear-view mirror.

"Listen," he said after a pause. "I know that we discussed this all before, but, well, now that you've been back at school for a bit, I wondered if you had any second thoughts about being away from home. It's just that I spoke with Mr. Hunter this morning and he says that he would quite understand if you did want to come back to Dalnachoil."

Sophie was shaking her head even before he had finished his last sentence. "No, I *really* don't think it would be a good idea."

"Can I ask why not?"

Sophie let out a long sigh. "Because we did discuss it, Dad, not just with you, but between ourselves as well. We all agreed that we didn't want to leave our friends, and well, since we've been back, Mr. and Mrs.

Hunter have been really kind. We go up and see them every night and they, well, just talk to us."

"They don't play cricket *or* rugby at Dalnachoil," Charlie interjected quietly.

"We are really all right here, Dad," Sophie continued, "unless . . ." She stopped and looked across at her father.

"Unless what?"

"Unless you want us to come home."

David put his hand on her head and smoothed back her sleeked hair. "No, please, I really want what you want. It's just that, well, I thought it was worth asking the question again."

"*I* want to go home." The voice sounded so distant and so diminutive that everyone turned to look at Harriet. She was sitting contentedly munching on her hamburger and staring out of the window at a screaming child who had just covered the car-park with chocolate milk shake. Seeing everyone staring at her, she grinned broadly and readied herself for another bite. "Not now, though—in the holidays."

Everyone let out a groan of relief, then burst out laughing. David reached forward to turn the ignition key, but stopped when he felt the light touch of Sophie's hand on his arm.

"Dad?" A serious expression had suddenly come over her face.

"Yeah?"

"Are *you* all right?"

David paused for a moment, then smiled and slowly nodded. "Yeah, I'm all right."

"Good." She sat back in her seat. "Then we're all all right."

David looked round at the faces of each of his children in turn. "Yeah, we are, aren't we?" He fired up the engine. "Come on, let's get back to school before our master batsman misses out on his big moment!"

Chapter

TEN

Despite having left Inchelvie at six o'clock, the journey down to Glasgow Airport on Tuesday morning took one hour longer than planned, due to the endless stream of temporary traffic lights set up for roadworks between Perth and Stirling. Consequently, when David pulled the car to a halt outside the terminal, he had only time to bid a fleeting farewell to his parents before grabbing his cases from the trunk and hurrying into the building. At the check-in desk, the taut-faced girl glanced at his ticket, then told him, with acid delight spread across her over-made-up face, that the flight was due to leave in an hour and that she was only accepting late arrivals for Business Class passengers. Silently cursing the fact that he had the last seat on the plane, and that it happened to be in Economy Class, David had to use every ounce of his guile and charm to persuade the girl to allow him to proceed.

"Departure gate two then, sir," she said without a trace of a smile as she handed him back his documents, "and as fast as you can. The flight has just about finished boarding."

Returning her lack of animation with a flashing grin, David rushed through passport control and sprinted the full four hundred yards to gate 2 before thumping his way noisily down the telescopic bridge onto the plane. He was immediately the star attraction, The Man Who Dared Arrive Late. Every seat was taken and every eye turned towards him as he walked up the aisle between the rows of disgruntled passengers.

His boarding pass did say that he was in seat number 21F, but when he arrived beside it, all three in the aisle row seemed to be already taken. A young woman in a garishly purple nylon shell suit sat in the seat nearest to him, clutching the pudgy fist of a baby girl who occupied the middle seat, while a hyperactive five-year-old boy, sporting a Celtic football strip with matching nylon track-suit bottoms, bounced energetically on the third seat, playing peekaboo with the elderly couple behind. David delved his fingers into the top pocket of his blazer for the stub of the boarding pass, finding it just as a stewardess approached him.

"Have you not found your seat yet, sir?"

"No, not yet." He handed her the stub, and she studied it for a moment before turning to the woman.

"How many seats did you reserve, madam?"

"Only twa," the woman replied in a broad Glasgow accent. "The wee yin is meant to be sittin' on my knee, but I wis hopin' this one wis free."

The stewardess smiled at her. "I'm afraid not. This seat is reserved for this gentleman."

David expected the woman to sigh heavily at this last-minute inconvenience, but instead she grinned up at him. "Och well, it wis worth a try." She unbuckled her seat-belt and, picking up her daughter, moved into the next seat. "C'mon, Tracy, you come onto my knee, darlin', and you, Darren, sit doon and dinnae be such a pest!"

Smiling a thank-you at the woman, David slumped down into his seat, buckled up, leaned back against the head-rest and let out a long sigh of relief.

That was cutting it far too fine. In fact, the past

twelve hours had been cut too fine. He had really done very little to prepare himself for the trip over the previous two days, preferring to try to finish off the work in the garden with Jock and do most of his organization and packing on Monday evening. But then on Monday afternoon he had picked some daffodils from the garden at Inchelvie and had taken them to the small churchyard in Dalnachoil to put on Rachel's grave. Once there he hadn't wanted to leave, and consequently he had sat for hours, talking quietly to her until the sun eventually dipped away behind the hills.

The engines of the plane rose in volume and it edged slowly away from the terminal building. David turned his head to stare past the occupants of the window-seat as the plane taxied out onto the runway. He remained in that position until they had risen far above the river Clyde and had begun the ascent through the low cloud base. Once nothing was left in view below, he turned away, only to find himself being eyed with uncertainty by his three travelling companions. He gave them a smile, then suddenly realized that he was clutching tight to Darren's hand. "Oh, God, I'm sorry about that!" he said, letting go immediately and looking over at Darren's mother. "It's a natural reaction, I'm afraid. I always seem to grab hold of one of my children's hands during take-off."

The woman's face broke into a smile once more. "How many do *you* have?" she asked.

"Three."

"Jeez, twa's quite enough handlin' for me. You must be a glutton for punishment." She let out a throaty laugh which ended in two rasping coughs, and instantly David wondered how on earth she was going to survive the long non-smoking flight with the tantalizing sight of the pack of two hundred duty-free cigarettes protruding from the basket at her feet.

Darren, meanwhile, had not taken his eyes off David.

"Mum's takin' us tae Disneyland," he said in an un-animated monotone.

"Is she?" David replied. "Well, you're a pretty lucky boy, aren't you!"

"Dae ye like Mickey Mouse?"

"Yeah, I think he's great! Is he your favorite?"

"No. I think he stinks."

"Darren!" the mother exclaimed, a look of embarrassed horror spread across her pasty features. "Dinnae be so cheeky tae the man."

"I'm no' being cheeky, Mam. You think he stinks too."

"Darren, that's ENOUGH, laddie!"

David smiled a fixed grin at the happy little trio, and as a form of diversion to return to his own company, he opened his brief-case and took out the Glendurnich document.

"Mam," Darren piped up again, "I'm needin' the bog."

His mother leaned across and whispered angrily at him. "How many times dae I have tae tell ye? It's no' called the bog, it's called the toilet."

"But, Mam, you call it the—"

"Darren!"

She undid her seat-belt and stood up, not noticing that the "Seat-Belt" sign was still on. A young stewardess came along the aisle towards her. "I'm afraid that you will have to sit down again, madam, until the captain has switched off the 'Seat-Belt' sign," she said, pointing up to the little illuminated light above the seat.

"My wee lad's desperate for the toilet. Can I no' tak' him?"

The stewardess, uncertain as to what to do, looked along the aisle for guidance from her superior, who was in the galley at the back of the plane. Hand gestures were exchanged, and she turned back to the woman.

"That's fine. I'll take you along with him, but the

senior stewardess has indicated that it would be safer if you didn't carry the little one along."

The woman was beginning to get flustered, darting worried looks at the baby on her hip. "I canna leave her here by hersel'. Could you tak' Darren along for me?"

It looked as though a solution had been found until the stewardess put her hand out to Darren. He resolutely stuck both hands behind his back and began to wail loudly. "I want to go wi' you, Mam."

"Please, Darren," the woman pleaded in exasperation with her son. "Go wi' the nice lady."

David looked up at the scene, and wondered how it could possibly resolve itself. He didn't particularly want to become involved, but realized that if drastic action wasn't taken soon, young Darren would begin to flood the plane.

"Excuse me," he said, leaning across the seat towards them.

They all looked at him.

"I'm quite happy, if you want, to hold her until you come back."

The woman smiled at him. "Och, thanks, mister, but dinnae you worry yoursel'."

"I promise you, I don't mind. As I said, I've three of my own, so I'm quite an expert."

"Do ye really no' mind, mister? I'm afraid she's got an awful dose of the cauld."

"Come on, don't worry about it." He shoved his papers into the seat pocket in front of him and stretched out his hands to receive his charge.

The woman handed over the little girl. "There you go, Tracy. You stay with the nice man. Thanks, mister, you're a gem. I'll no' be a minute."

As the "toilet" party headed off up the aisle, Tracy sat on David's knee, staring at him in astonishment, her large brown eyes as round as the pacifier in her mouth, which thankfully was doing its job in preventing any

outburst of protest. David gave the snuffling child a reassuring smile, then, thinking it better if she didn't have
to suffer such a blatant reminder that she had been
abandoned with a complete stranger, he turned her
around so that the back of her head rested on his chest.
He pulled in his chin to glance down at her, and
thought that, for all the earthy coarseness of her
mother, Tracy was beautifully turned out. Her tiny feet
were tucked into a pair of cheap white plimsolls, and
through the lace at the top of her short white socks were
woven yellow strands of ribbon, matching exactly the
colour of her little acrylic dress. Her soft, wispy hair
was caught up in a white elastic band, making it sprout,
like a tiny fountain, from the top of her head. David
leaned forward to retrieve his document from the seat
pocket, and with that, caught a whiff of the warm,
sweet smell of baby, a cocktail so addictive, yet its in-
gredients so indescribable, save for the liberal sprinkling
of Johnson's Baby Powder. It was a smell he had known
so well in the past, a smell so powerful that, at one time,
it had made him think that he could never live without
a baby in the house.

Leaving the document where it was, he pulled Tracy
close into his chest, the gentle movement of the little
girl's body against his supporting hand seeming to calm
his mind and dust away cobwebs from long-stored-
away memories of his own children.

It was surprising that, during his first three months of
working at Glendurnich, he hadn't been given the boot
for sleeping on the job, as it seemed to be the only time
that he could catch up on much-needed rest. This was
all because of a small, vulnerable bundle of humanity
called Sophie Rosemary Alicia Corstorphine, an angel
during the day, who metamorphosed into a screaming
scrap of unconsolable wretchedness in the early hours
of the morning. Waking hours at night suddenly
matched those of day, and even though it quite often

resulted in a gritty-eyed tetchiness on the part of both himself and Rachel, she never lost patience with the baby. She would take it into bed in the middle of the night and, gathering up all the pillows behind her, would sit cross-legged gently rocking the baby, until its violent sobs receded to a gulping contentment as it sucked from her nipple. He, meanwhile, would be forced to lie pillowless, wedged into an eight-inch width of bedspace, with a hand and a foot stretched out to the floor to stop him from rolling out.

"Try singing to her," Dr. Spiers had helpfully suggested, and, not realizing that it all mostly took place at two in the morning, "or maybe take her for a walk in her pram to settle her."

So they tried one and then the other, only to find that Sophie would respond solely to a combination of the two. Consequently, the lights of The Beeches were often seen to burn brightly in the night, while David walked up and down in the hallway like some destitute busker, bleary-eyed and unshaven, singing soothing lullabies to his first-born child.

And then four years later, when Sophie had grown into a constantly happy, lovable child, thus making more than enough atonement for her ignominious start in life, Charlie appeared, live and kicking, with all the clichéd remarks about a future football star in the making. They battened down the hatches, prepared the pram in the hallway and the guitar at the ready, but it was as if he had been conceived by a different formula of genes (or, more likely, that he and Rachel had ironed out all their inexperience on Sophie), because the baby slept by night and grinned by day. By the time that Harriet appeared, there was enough baby-care knowhow in the household for Rachel to afford to take a back seat while her eldest daughter, just turned seven years old, took control with an accomplishment and dedication that surpassed by far the efforts of any of the morose, disinterested au pair girls that had been employed in the past to look after herself and Charlie.

And as they grew, they became a unit within themselves, independent and content with each other's company in the games that they played: Sophie the organizer, Charlie the stuntman, and Harriet the cook, the chief bottle-washer, the alien from a different planet, but ultimately the baby. Yet their relationship with each other was not one of sugary-sweet perfection, their individual strength of character quite often being the cause of fervent disagreement, and games, on occasion, would culminate in vicious fights between the two elder siblings. While they ran to their mother to get first word in for comfort and mediation, Harriet would for a moment cast an uncomprehending look after them and then return happily to their now-abandoned game—to wash her teacups or to send her spaceship into warp five.

"Sorry we were so long, mister."

David looked round sharply from the window, his hand tightening instinctively on Tracy's stomach in the immediate thought that he might have unconsciously lessened his grasp on the baby. The woman was edging her way back into the seat, pushing a much-relieved Darren in front of her.

"Darren needed more than a pee. Och, would ye look at that! She's fast asleep."

David glanced down at Tracy. Her face was turned to the side, one flushed cheek squashed hard against the front of his shirt, her eyelids flickering, her pacifier hanging loosely in her mouth.

"My, she's lookin' awf'y hot. I hope she's no' comin' down wi' the flu or anything like that. Anyway, thanks again for your help, mister." She reached over and relieved David of his charge, and at once he felt the coolness of the plane's air-conditioning hit the warm little area which Tracy had occupied.

"Not at all. It was my pleasure," he said, smiling

across at the woman. Then, pulling his blazer around him, he took the Glendurnich document from the seat pocket and at last settled down to read it.

Alicia stuck her spectacles on the end of her nose and looked up at the latest school photograph that hung on the wall outside the headmaster's study to see if she could pick out her three grandchildren amongst the other two hundred or so faces. Across the hall from her, the headmaster's nervous little secretary tapped ineffectively on the door for the second time.

"Come in!" a muffled voice bellowed out.

The secretary flashed a brave smile at Alicia before slowly opening the door and putting her head round the corner. "Mr. Hunter, I have Lady Inchelvie here to see you."

Without waiting for a reply she jumped back from the door, and within a second it flew open as if caught in a whirlwind, to reveal a tall, spindly young man in his mid-thirties with wild bushy hair and half-moon spectacles, the combination of which would have made his age indeterminable to Alicia if she hadn't come to know him so well over the past six months.

"Lady Inchelvie," he said, stretching out a long, bony hand. "I'm so sorry, I had no idea you had arrived. I've just been having to reschedule a boys' cricket match to another venue, because the girls are going to be using the athletics track around the one out there"—he waved airily with his hand in the direction of the front of the school—"and I do rather want to prevent them from coming under fire from one of the big hitters in our team." He smiled down at her from his lanky height. "Nevertheless, I do apologize for not springing up to meet you immediately."

"Not at all, Mr. Hunter," Alicia said, smiling at the dishevelled young man. "It's actually I who should be apologizing to you for being extremely disruptive and insisting that I should visit the children during the week.

It's just that my husband was coming down to Glasgow for a meeting, and I thought that I would take the opportunity of a free ride!"

The young headmaster held up his hand. "Of course you should visit. Please, never think that you might not be welcome. It really is no imposition." He swung himself round to stand at the side of his study door, his gown billowing out as he did so. "Now let's go and have a seat in my office. Can I get you a cup of tea or coffee?"

"No, thank you very much," Alicia replied as she passed him. "I had an interesting cup of tea on the train over from Glasgow which tasted as if it might be a combination of coffee, tea and hot chocolate, so I think I've probably had my fair share."

Mr. Hunter let out a short, almost manic chuckle, then, having seen Alicia settled on the sofa, he slumped down with a *boing* of a loose spring into an armchair and almost disappeared from view. Alicia stifled a smile, realizing that he was built like a young giraffe—all legs and no upper body. He placed his elbows on the arms of his chair at about the same level as his chin. "I hear that Mr. Corstorphine is flying out to the States today."

"Ah, you're being kept abreast of the news, then."

Mr. Hunter smiled. "Yes, Sophie told us on Saturday night. She said that he wasn't too sure if he would be back by next weekend, but that he certainly would be for the leave-out. She was actually quite excited to talk about it."

Alicia paused for a moment, a worried expression coming over her face. "Mr. Hunter, how do you think they are? I mean, do they seem to be, well, bearing up all right?"

The headmaster pushed himself forward on the chair and, stretching out a long tentacle of an arm, momentarily touched Alicia's elbow.

"Firstly, Lady Inchelvie, I must tell you that they are never alone for a minute. Every member of my staff is looking out for them at all times and are under strict instructions to bring them straight to myself or my wife if there are problems. Then, as far as they are individually, all three are coping admirably. Of course, they all handle it differently. I think Charlie blots the whole thing from his mind, which might mean that there could possibly be a relapse at a later stage, but we'll cross that bridge when we come to it. He is as lively as ever, and a great asset to the Under-Thirteen cricket team. As for the girls, I really have to say that I am filled with admiration for Sophie in the way that she handles Harriet. For a girl of such tender years, her whole manner and decorum have been exemplary, and I have to say that she's one of the most resourceful, responsible and, without doubt, bravest girls I have ever had the honour of knowing . . . but . . ." He continued slowly, carefully picking his words. "I do know that the emotional upheaval within herself must be extreme, not only because of her mother, but also because she is at that chrysalis stage, Lady Inchelvie, and I have experience enough of being a headmaster of a mixed school to know that it is an extremely vulnerable time." He paused for a moment to change direction, noticing a slight quiver in Alicia's bottom lip, despite her upright and steadfast comportment. "Harriet is also fine. I know this because she is relying totally on her sister as a mother figure. Of course, one realizes that Sophie can never be a replacement, but there is still an order and sense in Harriet's life. However, I'm afraid that Sophie does realize this and that only increases the burden that she is carrying on her shoulders. Now, by telling you this, I don't want to appear alarmist, but only explain to you that I do understand everything that is going on, and that I do, I assure you, have it all under control."

Alicia smiled at the headmaster, feeling an urge to get up and hug the man for his kindness and the intuitive understanding he had of both the situation and her feelings. He rose from his chair, unravelling his legs like a couple of elasticised magic wands.

"Now let me see if I can locate them all for you. If you would just like to wait here, I'll quickly pop down to the classrooms. Will you be taking them out for lunch?"

"I don't think I'll get away without doing something fairly special with them."

"Well, you do whatever you want." He walked towards the door, then suddenly stopped and turned, hitting his head lightly with his hand. "Ah, dash, I almost forgot. I actually do need Charlie back here at two-thirty this afternoon. We have an inter-house cricket match on, and I'm afraid that his team would be quite bereft without him. Is that all right?"

"Of course. Sounds much more fun than lunch with stuffy old grandmother."

The headmaster raised his eyebrows. "As the boys would say, Lady Inchelvie, *don't you believe it*!" He turned and swept out of the room.

Alicia sat for a moment absently playing with a button on her cardigan, then, pushing herself to her feet, she walked over to the window to look out. Mr. Hunter was kind and understanding and in the nicest way persuasive. But she still worried. About the children, about David, and increasingly more about her husband. George was working too hard, taking too much on, yet she knew that he felt that there was no alternative at the minute. If she were to tell him that he had to stop going into the office every day or cut out the business meetings, he would just turn round and say that he was fine. But she had noticed him becoming more pale and tired as the weeks of his working progressed, and that really worried her more than anything. She shook her head slowly and looked out onto the cricket pitch that stretched across the vast lawn in front of the house. Near its centre, two boys were standing twenty yards apart, playing Gaining Ground with a cricket ball, straining every muscle in their skinny arms to see who could outthrow the other. A male voice sounded down below the window. "Come on, you ruffians, get to your class."

"Sorry, sir," they said in unison and ran off in the direction of the scolding voice, laughing and shouting as they went.

The door of the study opened behind her, and before she could turn around, a girl's voice shouted out. "Granny!"

Sophie rushed forward to greet her, circling the head-master's desk and throwing her arms around Alicia's neck. She hugged her tightly, almost making her grand-mother lose her balance.

"Hullo, darling, how are you?"

"I'm fine," Sophie said in a muffled voice, her face still buried in her grandmother's neck. She relinquished her hold and stood back looking at her grandmother. "I didn't know you were visiting today! Dad only said that you might come down at the weekend! How did you get here?"

Alicia studied her granddaughter's face, noticing that her smile did little to cover the look of sad exhaustion in her eyes.

"I've just taken the train over from Glasgow. Grandpa and I dropped off your father at the airport early this morning, and then he left me at the station. Grandpa has some meeting today and tomorrow in Glasgow. I thought that I might have stayed with him tonight, but seeing I'm quite literally on the road home, I thought it would be as well to catch the train from Perth to Carrbridge this evening." She paused. "So, tell me, how's everything been?"

Sophie levered herself up onto Mr. Hunter's desk and swung her bare legs over the edge. "Oh, all right, I suppose. Harry seems to be okay. I see as much of her as I can. Charlie's a pain most of the time, though. I go up to him every now and then at lunch-time to say hullo, and he gets all stupid and embarrassed in front of his friends." She let out a long sigh and turned to look out of the window. "Granny, do you think Dad's all right?"

Alicia walked over and took hold of her granddaughter's hand. "I think so, darling. Didn't he seem so to you on Saturday?"

"Yes. Well, in a way. It's just that he seems so . . . different—sort of distant. But I suppose it's understandable. I think he misses Mummy *so* much, Granny."

Alicia put her hands on Sophie's shoulders. "Of course he does, as you do, and all of us too. Grieving is the most terrible, painful thing for everyone, so one can only imagine what it must be like for people as close as your parents. But you mustn't start burdening yourself with his sorrow as well. You must think about *you*, Sophie. You've got your own life to lead, and, well, you've got exams and things very soon, so *please* don't worry. Your father will heal, I promise you—it might take a little time, but he will heal." She took Sophie's face in her hands and tilted it up to her. "Look, let's strike a bargain. Mr. Hunter has told me how wonderful you are being with Harriet, so you continue to look after her, and I'll make sure that Dad is all right. Okay?"

Alicia held out her hand, palm upwards. Sophie looked at it and, smiling, gave it a slap with her own. "Okay."

At that point, the door flew open and Harriet and Charlie burst in. Alicia turned, only having enough time to open her arms before the little girl jumped up from a distance of about three feet and circled her arms and feet around her grandmother.

"Watch out for Granny's back, Harry!" Sophie scolded.

"No, it's all right," Alicia said, kissing the top of her younger granddaughter's head. She looked across to Charlie, who had come to stand beside Sophie and was running a toy vehicle up and down the surface of Mr. Hunter's desk while at the same time surreptitiously trying to read one of the many letters that were strewn across the top.

"Charlie? How are you, my darling?"

"Fine," he replied, at first not breaking his concentration away from the letters. Then he swung round to face his grandmother. "Granny?" He had a look of such questioning seriousness on his face that Alicia thought that she was about to be asked her own personal views on "the meaning of life."

"Yes?"

"Have you got any sweets with you?"

"Charlie!" Sophie exclaimed, astounded at her brother's mercenary tactics. "You really are insufferable!"

Charlie's face creased into a wide grin, and they all broke into laughter. Putting Harriet down, Alicia walked over to the sofa where she had left her handbag, Charlie and Harriet following close on her heels. Alicia took three bars of Cadbury's chocolate from the depths of the bag and gave one to each of them, and they immediately started ripping away at the silver paper. Alicia held the third forward towards Sophie. "Darling, do you want one?"

"No, thanks, Granny. I don't feel like it."

Alicia moved forward and slipped it into the pocket of Sophie's dress. "Well, keep it for later. Share it with your friends or whatever. Now," she said, turning to them all, and at the same time looking at her watch, "Mr. Hunter says that I can take you out for lunch."

Charlie's eyes went wide with delight. "Can we go to McDonald's? We went with Dad on Saturday. It's really terrific, Granny!"

"Yes!" Harriet shouted in approval. "*Pleeeease*, Granny."

"Oh dear, I don't think that we can do that. For one thing, I don't have a car, and anyway, Charlie, Mr.

Hunter has asked me expressly to get you back here by two-thirty this afternoon for your cricket match."

There was a groan of disappointment from the two younger children.

"We could go to the village pub," Sophie suggested. "I went there once with a friend of mine and her parents. It's only three hundred yards from the school and they do pretty good chips."

Alicia smiled across at Sophie and mouthed a relieved "thank you" in her direction. "Right," she said, "the pub it is!"

Charlie punched the air with his fist. "Yesss!" he said, darting towards the door. "Come on, let's go!"

"Just a minute," Alicia called after him, picking up her handbag from the sofa. "Let's get organized and all, go out together, so that we don't disturb any of the classes." Taking hold of Harriet's hand, she moved towards the door. As Charlie opened it, Harriet looked up at her grandmother.

"Granny?" she said in a quiet voice.

"Yes, darling?"

"I think Daddy's gone away like Mummy."

The procession to the door stopped abruptly, and Alicia felt her face tingle with shock at the unexpectedness of the statement. She bent down and put her arm around Harriet's shoulders. "No, he hasn't, darling. He's just off to America for a short time to do some work. He'll be back soon. Didn't he say that he'd be back in time to take you home for leave-out?"

"Not that, Granny," Harriet continued, in a matter-of-fact way. "Daddy doesn't really seem to be in his body any more. He's somewhere else."

Alicia glanced up at the other two. Sophie stood looking at her sister, biting hard on her lip, while Charlie pushed the door shut with a sigh, his eyes focused on the door handle as he pulled it back and forth on its loose-fittings.

"Let's just go and sit down for a minute, shall we?"

Alicia said, guiding Harriet back to the sofa. Sophie came over and sat on the arm, while Charlie stayed where he was, continuing to play noisily with the door handle.

"Now," Alicia said slowly, as she settled herself beside her granddaughter, "you tell me exactly what you mean."

"Well, it's sort of opposite to Mummy."

"I'm sorry, darling?"

"Mummy's spirit is all around us, but her body's not. That's what Sophie says. And Daddy's body is around us, but his spirit's not. So really it's opposite."

Alicia sat for a moment in silence, stroking the top of Harriet's head, trying to work out what to say. "Listen, darling," she said eventually, "I know that Daddy has been a little distracted over the past few months, and it must be really hard for you to understand why he *is* like that. But he is most definitely still with us, and I know that he thinks so much about you and loves you all very much. Now, I'm pretty sure that his trip to America will do him the world of good, and when he returns he'll be the way we have always known him." She peered round at Harriet's face. "All right?"

Harriet nodded, quite content with the explanation.

"Can we go now?" Charlie asked, opening the door.

"Good idea!" Alicia said as brightly as she could. "To the pub, then!" She gave Harriet a final squeeze and rose to her feet. "I didn't get any breakfast, so I'm looking forward to a great big plate of chips!"

Harriet ran to the door and followed Charlie out into the hall. Sophie, however, held back and stopped her grandmother by placing her hand on her elbow. "Granny?" Alicia turned to her. "I have a feeling he won't come back."

"Of course he will. He'll be his old self very soon."

"No, I mean, I think you're right about him needing to get away from Inchelvie and needing time to heal. I don't think he actually *should* come back for a bit."

Alicia patted the small slender hand that held her elbow. "We'll see, darling. But remember our deal. You look after Harriet, and I'll make sure Daddy comes back as the man we all know. All right?"

Sophie nodded, forcing a smile onto her face. Alicia took hold of her hand and kissed her on the cheek.

"I'll let you into a secret, Sophie. Mr. Hunter said that you were one of the most special girls he has ever met. Of course *he* didn't need to tell me that, but it's good for me and for you to know that you have a real ally here. And I'll tell you something else, my darling, and that is that I think you're turning into a very beautiful young lady, and I am so very proud of you." She pulled Sophie towards her and gave her a final hug before turning towards the door. "Now come on, let's catch up with those other two before they start disrupting the whole school."

Chapter

ELEVEN

As the plane pulled up to the terminal building at Kennedy Airport, David watched with interest as his neighbour leaped to her feet even before the "Seat-Belt" sign had been switched off. She busily began to organize her children and to pull bags and jerseys from the overhead locker, eager to get off the plane and get on with her holiday. Others immediately followed her lead, but after ten minutes of muttered complaints about slowness in opening the doors and craning of necks to try to see why those in Business Class weren't attempting to make any obvious moves, most of them had sat down again, bags on knees, shaking their heads and raising their eyebrows at those who had shown similar impatience.

Two minutes later there were signs of movement farther up the aisle, and immediately the little Glaswegian family was on the move, Darren in the lead, pushing his way resolutely forward while his mother followed hard on his heels, with baggage and baby in arms.

David waited until the line from the rear of the plane was moving steadily towards the doorway before retrieving his brief-case and pushing himself out of his seat. He made his way down the aisle, stretching out his back and legs as he walked, stiff from having been crammed into such a small space for so long. He stepped out of the plane and relished for a fleeting moment the rush of warm air that squeezed its way through the gap between the fuselage and the air bridge before being met full-on by the chilling blast of air-conditioning that swept its way down the tunnel from the terminal building.

At the top of the air bridge he joined the herd of passengers emerging from other arrival gates and strolled leisurely down the long glassed-in corridor towards Immigration. As he went, he began to feel a quietening sense of relief come over him, realizing that amidst the massing throng of people on the move he was simply a statistical entity, anonymous, totally without history. He was of no interest to anyone, each person cocooned in his or her own thoughts and worries, as opposed to the one common, suffocating cloud of sadness that had come to hang over everything and everyone at Inchelvie.

He chose not to use the moving walkway and kept himself to the uncrowded side. Half-way along, his eye was caught by a flash of Celtic green on the walkway next to him and to his horror he saw Darren's head come bobbing along, a wide grin on his face as he delighted in his new-found game of running up the moving belt in the wrong direction, causing havoc with the flow of oncoming pedestrians. With that, the undecipherable pronunciation of his name rose high above the general noise of footsteps and chatter, and David caught sight of the boy's mother at the far end of the walkway, Tracy on her hip and her bags cast forlornly around her feet.

Once inside the Immigration hall, he took his place in the queue that snaked through the roped-off barriers to the line of fluorescent-lit booths. People fumbled nervously with passports and immigration forms, affording edgy smiles to one another as if they felt that they were about to be subjected to an intensive interrogation before being allowed into the country. Slowly, the queue shuffled forward until it was David's turn. He stepped into the booth and handed his papers to the young immigration officer.

"Are you here on business or pleasure, sir?"

"Business," David replied.

"And how long?"

"I'm not sure. Probably no longer than a week."

The young man nodded his head slowly. "Okay, and might I ask what your business is?"

"I'm in the whisky industry."

The young officer raised his eyebrows, a look of interest registering on his face, then stamped part of the immigration form and slipped it into the passport before handing it back. "Well, just keep it rolling in over here!" he said with a laugh.

"I will." He gave the young man a smile and was about to walk out into America when the officer spoke again.

"Just before you go, I wonder if you had a moment to explain something."

For a moment, David stood without replying, a frown of concern on his face as he tried to work out what the question might be.

"Surely," he said eventually, returning to the desk. "If I can."

The young man noticed his disquiet and smiled reassuringly at him. "There's nothing wrong. It's just that I'd like to know what 'The Hon.' means in front of your name? I'm new at this job and though I *have* seen it before, I've no idea what it means."

"Nothing much, to be quite honest. It stands for 'The Honourable.' It's just a courtesy title."

"Ah, and how'd you get it?"

"Well," he said, moving closer to the desk, embarrassed that someone might overhear their conversation, "it's just because my father is, well, a lord."

The young man's eyes opened wide. "Really? Does that mean you're related to royalty?"

"No, far from it!" David laughed. "As I said, it's just a courtesy title."

The young man cocked his head to the side. "Well, there you go. You live and learn. Thanks for the lesson, Mr. Corstorphine." He turned and called in the next person.

David recovered his suitcase from the carousel, cleared customs and strode out into the Arrivals hall. A sea of expectant people greeted him, some appearing immediately dejected on seeing that his wasn't the face for which they were looking, whilst others, with name cards held out in front, grinned hopefully at him. He picked out his driver, a small knuckle-headed man in a short-sleeved white shirt, black tie, and impenetrable Rayban sun-glasses, bearing a "Star Limos" sign with his name spelt phonetically underneath.

David approached him. "Hullo."

"You Mr. Costawfin?" the driver asked, chewing open-mouthed on his gum.

"Yup."

"Okay, I'm Dan, sir." In one swift movement, he grabbed David's suitcase and shook him firmly by the hand. "Car's just outside the building. If you don't mind, we'd better move fast before I get towed."

They made their way out into the glaring sunlight, and Dan aimed his remote at a black Lincoln Town Car. He threw the suitcase into the trunk and, having seen David into the back, leaped into the driver's seat and took off at speed, his tyres squealing on the hot asphalt.

Fifteen minutes later, they were heading east along the Southern State Parkway, the surrounding country-side changing with every mile that they drove away from New York City. Far from being the endless sub-urban sprawl that he had envisaged, the parkway was bounded by a screen of tall hardwood trees, which eventually gave way to dense, tangled expanses of spindly pines that stretched off into the distance on either side of the road. These, Dan informed him, were the pine barrens of Long Island, a haven for mosquitos and "a helluva fire risk."

Exactly fifty minutes after leaving Kennedy, Dan took an exit next to an enormous swivelling sign that said: LEESPORT OUTLET CENTER. At the top of the ramp he turned right and headed south along a wide stretch of road before clattering across a railway line and past a sign that welcomed visitors to Leesport. David gazed out the window at the houses, some with white picket fences enclosing gardens with neat, orderly beds of brightly coloured flowers while water sprinklers played on the lush green, mower-striped lawns. Beech-trees and native pines stood tall and leafy, wrapping their branches protectively around each house, granting it seclusion from its nearest neighbour. No two were the same, some gleaming white clapboard, others with brown cedar shingles, still others a mixture of the two. Wide-pitched roofs hung like stern eyebrows over shuttered windows while others, four-pitched and prim in their perfection, looked like wimpled nuns. Every hundred yards, bright yellow fire hydrants stood like sentries on the clipped, nurtured strip of grass that ran between the black asphalt sidewalk and the roadway, strategically placed to keep guard over the tinder-dry houses.

At the bottom of the road, Dan just made it through the traffic light and swung the car to the left. He glanced back at David. "Okay—so this is Leesport Village now, sir."

The thoroughfare was spotlessly clean, bordered by wide, white-lined parking spaces and fronted by a line of small shops, all in regulation-white clapboard, with paned display windows and flower-urns brimming with pansies, marigolds and petunias at their doors. The sidewalk was busy with pedestrians, old couples walking arm-in-arm, young mothers carrying babies on their hips, all dressed in summer clothes and all moving at an easy, unhurried pace. As Dan accelerated along the street, David looked out and caught some of the names on the small multi-coloured signs that hung above the shops: The Leesport Deli, Danby Real Estate, Helping Hands, Leesport Liquors, Jo-Ann's Fitness Center and, at the end of the street, the local sports shop, Lar Sport.

Two hundred yards farther on, Dan turned the Lincoln left up a narrow leafy street, past a green-and-white sign which read NORTH HARLENS, and pulled to a stop beside a letter box with "52" written on it in black lettering. The two-storied house stood back from the street, up a short concrete driveway bordered by wide strips of coarse zoysia grass, its frontage dominated by a high wooden sundeck, on which a table and chairs were neatly arranged. A couple of faded oars had been nailed to the wall like crossed swords. To the left of the deck, David could just make out, through a screen of shrubs, the shimmering blue of a swimming pool. There was nothing to set the house apart from any others that he had seen so far in Leesport, save for the network of scaffolding that jutted out from its farthest side and the heavy tarpaulin, flapping gently in the breeze, that covered a third of its roof.

Dan turned off the engine and pressed the switch for the trunk. "Here we are. The Eggars' house."

They both got out of the car, and as Dan took the suitcase from the trunk, a voice boomed out from the direction of the house.

"David, you old bugger!"

A tall, slim, blond-haired man came bounding down the drive towards him, his arms outstretched, and without seeming to slacken off his pace, he met David with a thump of chests and threw his arms around him, then gave him a bone-shaking slap on the back. "It's great to see you, my friend!"

"And you, Richard."

Richard stood back and eyed him up and down. "Christ, you haven't changed much." He stepped forward and roughly tousled David's hair. "Just a few grey hairs sneaking in there!"

He skirted round David and relieved the driver of his load. "So, you managed to track down the mad Scotsman, did you, Dan?"

"Yeah, no problem, Mr. Eggar." Dan turned towards David. "Have an enjoyable stay, sir, and if you want to get back to Kennedy at any time, just get Mr. Eggar to call the office."

David smiled and slipped him a twenty. "I will. Thanks, Dan."

They both stood in silence, watching as the car pulled away from the house, then David let out a long, relieved breath and looked up and down the street. "Well, you seem to have found a nice place to live. It's all so . . ." he paused, trying to think of an adequate word to describe what he had seen so far of Leesport, ". . . pristine!"

"Virginal, my boy," Richard replied in a mock Cockney accent as he walked back up the drive with David's bags in hand, "that's how I describe it—vibrant and virginal! Now come on, let's go crack open a few bottles of beer."

Richard led the way up a flight of steps onto the deck and crossed over to a wire-meshed screen door. He pushed it open with his shoulder and David followed him into a large, airy kitchen, its centre dominated by a long scrubbed pine table across which were spread Richard's work-papers. The whole room was aflame with dancing splinters of light that reflected off the open French doors as they gently swung in the breeze.

"Listen, I hope you don't mind roughing it a bit, old boy," Richard said. "You've slightly caught us at a bad time. We're in the throes of doing a major conversion job to the side of the house, so I'm afraid the roof is off the two guest-rooms." He opened the door and David followed him into the carpetless hall, their feet making imprints in the building dust that lay thick on the floor. Richard started up the stairs. "Just bloody typical of Angie, though. She starts something like this and then buggers off!" He walked along the narrow passage and pushed open a door with the suitcase. "So I hope you don't mind sleeping in here. It's my office. Not very salubrious, I'm afraid."

The room itself was only about eight-foot square, but was reduced in size still further by the wide shelf that extended round two walls, stacked neatly with filing trays and books. At one end, amidst a cat's-cradle of different-coloured wires, sat Richard's laptop computer, laser printer, fax machine and telephone. A single bed had been jammed in behind the door, the bottom half of which extended under the shelf. There was no wardrobe, but the jangle of clashing metal when the door was initially opened indicated that there must be a number of wire coat-hangers hanging behind it. Any daylight that might have entered through the two small windows was closed off by impenetrable roller blinds, which only added to the cell-like qualities of the room. Everything in the room was coloured light-brown with dust.

Richard put the cases down and looked around, his hands on his hips. "Hope it's all right."

"Yeah, fine," David said, trying to sound buoyant at the prospect of sleeping in what resembled an executive broom cupboard, "really fine. All I need is somewhere to lay my head."

"Good, well, the bathroom is right next door when you want it." He turned to leave. "Look, I've got a couple of calls to make, so get yourself organized and then come down and we'll have that drink."

He left the room and David stood for a minute surveying his filthy quarters. Jesus, maybe this hadn't been such a good idea and he'd be better off in a hotel somewhere. He felt an involuntary shiver run through his body and, putting his brief-case on the shelf, he began rubbing hard at his legs to try to relieve the aching that had suddenly developed. Putting his hand to his forehead, he wiped away a bead of sweat. Oh, no, don't say he'd gone and picked up a bug from that child in the plane! That was all he needed! He slumped back onto the sagging bed and stared up at the ceiling, a sudden sense of depression and uneasiness coming over him, and for the first time since leaving Scotland he felt the familiar dull ache of loneliness return to his body. Yet this time it was worse, the reality of his situation beginning to take a numbing grip on his ill-sorted and fevered mind—that now, in these characterless and unfamiliar surroundings, he was truly alone—an ocean apart from the children, and an ocean apart from Rachel.

Chapter

TWELVE

By dinner-time that evening, there was little doubt in David's mind that he had caught some fast-acting and virulent bug from the child in the plane. His whole body ached and his head thumped as he sat with Richard at the kichen table, eating rubbery, undercooked pasta and drinking too much wine, hoping that as soon as possible he would be able to excuse himself and go to bed. However, Richard hardly drew breath as he recounted endless stories and anecdotes of their time in the army together, and David, feeling duty-bound to play the polite guest, sat listening with a fixed smile on his sweating face.

At the end of the meal Richard stacked the plates in the dishwasher, then, without offering David an alternative, opened up a kitchen cupboard and took out two glasses and a bottle of whisky. Having poured two powerful measures into each glass, he sat down again and, after a moment's hesitation, broached the subject of Rachel, and David, not feeling in the mood to go into any great detail, proceeded to give him only the broadest outline on what had happened. However, as he talked, he noticed Richard's interest in the subject quickly wane, and almost imperceptibly the topic of

conversation was guided away from Rachel and on to
Angie. Soon David found himself in the role of sym-
pathetic listener, as Richard, drinking two whiskies to
his one, slurred on in an endless monologue about the
problems they had encountered in their seven-year mar-
riage—how she couldn't have children and how she
made up for it by spending money as if it grew on trees,
and now the final straw being this latest conversion,
which she had started without his prior knowledge.

Until midnight David sat and listened, his face burning with fever and his eyes heavy with lack of sleep and
jet lag. Then, unable to restrain himself any further, he
let out an enormous yawn and pushed himself to his
feet, an action which brought about an abrupt halt to
Richard's outpourings. Mumbling abject apologies to
David for burdening him with his problems and for
keeping him from his bed, he too rose unsteadily to his
feet and together they weaved their way upstairs.

With a sense of relief David shut his bedroom door
and sat down heavily on the narrow bed, leaning his
elbows on his knees and rubbing at his smarting eyes.
He flicked his wrist over to look at the time. Half midnight. That meant he had been on the go for almost
twenty-four hours. He let out a sigh of exhaustion and,
heaving himself to his feet, made his way to the bathroom.

He gave his teeth a revitalizing brush and splashed
cupped handfuls of cold water onto his face in an attempt to relieve the stinging in his eyes and the thickness
clutching at his head, caused both by the flu and the
overconsumption of wine and whisky. Then, returning
to his bedroom, he undressed and jumped into bed,
pulling the covers up around his chin to stop the uncontrollable shivering. He tried shutting his eyes, but
his head seemed to be taking off in different directions,
whirling in circles from Richard's endless chatter, and
at the same time sinking in and out of the pillow with
too much booze. He needed something to settle his

mind, even just for a moment. He turned and scanned the small room for a magazine or a book to read, but there was only a shelf-full of company business plans propped up by a large legal encyclopaedia. He thought that he might have kept a newspaper from the plane journey, so he clambered out of bed and sprang open the catches of his brief-case. No luck. Only the Glendurnich distributor report. Better than nothing, he thought to himself. He took it out, closed the brief-case and got back into bed.

The next morning he was awakened abruptly by a clatter of coat-hangers as the door swung hard against his bed, and he looked up to see Richard's bleary-eyed and colourless face hovering above him.

"Richard? Whatsamatter?" he asked, bewildered.

Richard rubbed at his hair with his fingers: "Look, David, I'm sorry, but I'm afraid we've slept in. We'll have to get a move on. I'm going to telephone Star Limos right now for a car, 'cos I don't think I'm in a fit state to drive."

He hurried out of the room, and for a moment David lay in his bed while the throbbing in his head and the aching in his limbs began to register in his brain. He looked at his watch. It was half past eight. "Oh, *shit!*"

He threw off the bedclothes and jumped to his feet, the sudden movement exacerbating the overpowering feeling of nausea. He stood for a minute concentrating hard to bring it under control, goose-pimples pricking the surface of his shivering body.

"Oh, for crying out *bloody* loud! Why now?" He grabbed his sponge-bag and made his way through to the bathroom. There was no time for a shower, only a quick wash and a shave, before he was back in his room to riffle through his suitcase for clean underpants, shirt and socks.

"Dan'll be here in three minutes," Richard's voice sounded up the stairs.

A host of butterflies suddenly invaded David's stomach, and his fingers started to shake as he fumbled with his tie. Christ, he thought to himself, this is all I need. Bloody late for the meeting and a dose of flu to go with it.

He pulled on his trousers and, pushing his feet into shoes while still on the move, he grabbed his jacket and brief-case and ran downstairs.

Richard was already in the kitchen, flying around the room picking up bits of paper off different surfaces and stuffing them into his brief-case. "Sorry about this, David. Listen, grab a cup of coffee. It's in the percolator. I'm afraid it's left over from last night, but at least it'll be strong." A car horn sounded outside the house. "Christ, no time! That'll be Dan now! Come on!"

He ushered David out onto the deck and locked the door, then hurried down the steps, his guest hard on his heels. Dan was waiting for them on the street, holding open the back door of the Lincoln. They both bundled themselves in, and as the car powered off down the street, Richard slumped back against the head-rest. "Bloody hell, I feel rough! How're you doing?"

"Not too good. I think I've got the flu as well as a hangover."

"Christ, you poor bugger! You should have said something!" He paused. "Look, I'm going to come back tonight, but you'll probably be finished way before me, so I suggest you get yourself to Penn Station and just take a train to Patchogue. You can get a taxi from there." He delved in the pocket of his jacket, at the same time flicking open his brief-case. "There's the key of the house, and"—he took a mobile phone from the case—"I think you'd better call ahead and tell them that you're running about half an hour late." He shook his head and looked sheepishly at David. "I really am sorry about all of this."

The journey thereafter was completed in silence. Richard, green-faced in his sufferance of the mother of all hangovers, sat snoring loudly with his mouth open and his eyes closed, while David pulled his jacket tight around himself to try to curb his interminable shivering. Dan drove as fast as the speed limit and the traffic would allow, but by the time they reached the queue for the toll at the Midtown Tunnel, Richard's projected half-hour delay was already five minutes over schedule.

Dan looked round from the front seat. "Do you know where on Madison you're going, Mr. Costawfin?"

"Yes, somewhere between Forty-fifth and Forty-sixth East."

Dan nodded. "Right—that's easy enough. Just along Forty-second and up Madison. If it's all the same with you, Mr. Eggar, we'll drop off Mr. Costawfin first."

"Certainly, Dan," Richard agreed. "Without question."

The horn-blowing Manhattan traffic was heavier than Dan had anticipated, with the result that it took a further ten minutes to reach the block of Forty-fifth and Madison. Bidding Richard a cursory farewell, David jumped out of the car, then proceeded to take another ten minutes of frantic searching to find the building in which the offices of Deakin Distribution were situated. By the time he came out of the creaking lift onto the fifteenth floor, the clock on the wall opposite read five past eleven. He looked up and down the corridor. At the far end, a polished brass plaque bearing the company's name hung on the wall beside a pair of large glass doors. He ran towards them and burst into the reception area so forcefully that the young blonde receptionist, her mouth open with fright, pushed her seat back from the desk, as if she felt that her office had suddenly come under siege from an Armed Response Unit.

David turned to catch the hinged glass door as it swung wildly back and forth following his forceful entry. "Sorry about that," he said almost inaudibly, trying to calm the situation by talking quietly.

The girl never took her eyes off him, but warily drew her chair back to the desk. "Can I help you?" she drawled, an annoyed slant to her voice.

"Yes," David said, trying to catch his breath following his exertions of the past quarter of an hour. "I'm afraid that I was meant to be here at ten o'clock, but I was held up. I'm from Glendurnich Distilleries Limited."

"And you are . . ." The girl ran her finger down the appointment book on her desk before looking back up at him with a sudden light and happy look on her face. ". . . Mr. Corstorphine?"

"That's right."

"If you would like to follow me, sir, the directors are waiting for you in the boardroom."

David followed her as she teetered along the narrow, newly carpeted corridor, her feet splayed out in stiletto-heeled shoes which made her tight-skirted bottom swing unnervingly from side to side in front of him. She stopped outside one of the doors, knocked and, without waiting for a reply, opened the door and stepped aside to allow David to enter.

A group of five or six men sat slouched in their chairs around a long boardroom table, some with their hands linked behind their heads. As he entered, they pulled themselves upright and swung round to look at him, then jumped to their feet in unison. A silver-haired man who had been sitting up at the far end made his way down the side of the table to meet him.

"David," he said, approaching him, his hand outstretched and a wide, beaming smile on his face. "Charles Deakin, managing director of Deakin Distribution."

. David took his hand, and Deakin clenched it in his powerful grasp, giving it a shoulder-dislocating shake. He let go and clapped his hands together, as if wanting to start proceedings immediately.

"So you eventually found us," he said, pulling out a

vacant chair for David and making his way back to his own at the head of the table. "I must apologize for not having sent you directions. I thought that you must have been to New York before and knew about our morning traffic!"

Charles Deakin had reached the top of the table as he finished his sentence and, turning to face David with a sardonic smile on his face, was joined in his moment of amusement by a rippling murmur from the rest of the assembled company. David smiled weakly. Apart from their managing director, all of those around the table were at least ten years younger than himself and dressed as though they were following a strict company code of attire—in razor-creased shirts, muted silk ties and brightly coloured gold-slided braces. He became acutely conscious of the fact that his own dark grey worsted suit looked old and dull, not only standing out in stark contrast against the vibrance of his companions' dress, but also perfectly reflecting the way that he felt within.

As Deakin sat, everyone around the table immediately followed his lead. David moved quickly to his own chair, realizing that he was in danger of getting completely out of step with the meeting. God, he thought to himself, what am I doing here? I should be in bed. Anyway, this was destined to be a mistake. I should never have agreed to come out here in the first place. His head pounded mercilessly, perspiration soaked the back of his shirt, and he became aware that his cheeks were shivering uncontrollably. He leaned forward in his chair, thinking that he should try to offer some explanation for his being late, but as he opened his mouth to speak, Deakin cut in.

"I'm afraid that we'll have to press on, David, as some of the guys have other meetings scheduled for mid-day. Alex here"—he held out his upturned palm in the direction of the young man beside him, who leaped to his feet and went to stand by the flip-chart in the corner of the room—"will be carrying out the presentation, and will introduce you to each of my colleagues in turn as he explains their individual involvement in the marketing and distribution strategy that we have laid out for Glendurnich." He opened the presentation document in front of him. "So, gentlemen, if you will all turn to page one, I'll hand over to Alex."

Deakin swung his chair round to face Alex, and there was a sound of acetate scraping against paper as the men opened their files. David, trying to keep up with proceedings, leaned over the side of his chair, picked up his brief-case and opened it up. The document was not on the top. It must be below the pad of paper. It wasn't there. He slid his hand to the bottom of the pile of papers and flicked his thumb through them. Nothing. He pulled open the flaps on the lid of the brief-case and stuck his hand down inside, but they were empty. A cold, terrifying sense of realization overcame him as his frowning concentration began to clear away hazy memories of the night before, and he remembered that he had taken it out to read in bed. Oh, no, he'd never put it back! It was still on his bed.

Alex, who had started the presentation, halted when he noticed David still scrambling inside his brief-case and stood looking in his direction, turning his black marker over and over and tapping its end impatiently on the palm of his hand. Charles Deakin, following the eye-line of his young colleague, swung round in his chair and looked down the table towards David. There was silence. David glanced up and saw that everyone was looking at him.

"Are you all right, David?" Charles Deakin asked.

David pushed his fingers through his hair and scratched at the back of his head. "Erm, I'm sorry—no—I don't seem to have the paperwork. I think I've left it behind."

"Not in Scotland, I hope!" Charles Deakin said with

a chuckle, and his colleagues once more dutifully joined him in his amusement.

"No!" David said, a little too loud, thinking that he had to defend what little credibility he had left with the assembled company. "I mean, no, I've left it in my bedroom where I'm staying."

Charles Deakin nodded and smiled down the table at him. "No problem," he said slowly, as if he were about to explain a point to a classful of primary-school children. "If you would like to take Jack's copy and Jack, you share with Curtis."

Jack slid the document down the table, and David smiled an embarrassed thank-you at him. Deakin swung his chair back to face Alex. "Right! Let's get going."

Everything, from that moment on, came in a blur. Alex's voice sounded as if it were being played back through a slowed-down tape recorder, as the young man waarp-waarped his way through the presentation. He introduced each of the men in turn, and one by one they stood up, grinned in David's direction, and sat down again, their movements as slow and as fluid as the motions of weightless astronauts, without David's catching either their names or what roles they would be playing in the future marketing of Glendurnich in America. His mind drifted, a bizarre continuity in its train of thought. It started with his father, and how he had let him down so badly by making such a fool of himself at this meeting; then he thought of meeting his father in the boardroom at Glendurnich and how delighted he had been that he was to be staying with Richard; Richard, his friend, caught in a spiralling whirlpool of discontented unfulfilment with Angie, his wife; his own wife, Rachel, and the turmoil in his mind suddenly abated as he returned to Scotland with her, to long summer evenings down at the loch with their children, Rachel lying spread eagled with laughter on the bank, while he, his jeans rolled up to his knees, waded into the loch to catch on camera the mad and uncoordinated antics of the children in the boat.

The last of the men around the table had sat down again, and the sudden break in activity penetrated his senses enough to make him realize that Charles Deakin was talking to him. He screwed up his eyes to clear his head.

"Sorry?"

Deakin repeated his question. "Are you married, David?"

"Yes."

"Great," the managing director continued immediately, "because we think that it would be opportune for your wife to accompany you on these PR trips. We Americans prize family tradit——"

"NO!" David yelled out.

Everyone sat back, startled at the sudden outburst. David clamped his hand over his mouth.

"I beg your pardon?" Deakin asked.

"No," David said, his voice choking. He had never said it before. No one had ever asked him that question. Everybody knew. "I'm sorry, I meant to say no—I'm not married."

There was a slight shifting of body weight in chairs, as the directors shot uncomprehending glances at one other.

"You're—not—married," Charles Deakin said slowly.

David looked along the table at him, feeling a tear suddenly trickle down his cheek and onto his hand. He shook his head once in the direction of them all, then, pushing out his chair, he jumped to his feet and, slamming his case shut, ran towards the door.

"You'll have to excuse me. I'm sorry, you'll have to excuse me."

He threw the door open and walked hurriedly along to the reception area. The girl smiled as he approached, then her face went expressionless as she saw the look on David's face. He strode past her without speaking, pushed open the glass doors, and left the offices of Deakin Distribution.

There was a stunned silence for thirty seconds following David's departure from the boardroom, broken only when Charles Deakin rose slowly from his chair. He cleared his throat.

"Well, gentlemen. I'm not quite sure what happened there." He turned and walked over to the window, the faces of his young executives following him as he went. He stuck his hands into the back of the waistband of his trousers and looked out at Manhattan. After a minute he returned to his place, gathered up his papers, and thumped their ends once on the desk.

"I think the best course of action would be for me to speak immediately with Duncan Caple at Glendurnich, and thereafter I'll circulate a memo to you all which will include the outcome of this meeting." He reached the door and turned round. "Thank you all for being in attendance." He pushed open the door and left the boardroom, leaving a crescendo of discussion behind him.

Tears welled up in David's eyes as he thumped at the elevator button with the palm of his hand. The panel showed lights on the fourth and twenty-third floors, but neither car seemed to be moving. He stood close to the door, his head bowed, willing one of them to reach the fifteenth floor before someone came out of the offices of Deakin Distribution to question him about his behaviour. A bell pinged once and the door farthest from him opened. He glanced in. It was empty, thank God. He dived into its haven of solitude, pressed the ground-floor button, and slumped back against the steel panelling. As the doors closed on him, he knew he was alone and, dropping his brief-case to the ground, he covered his face with his hands and broke into convulsive sobs, at the same time sliding down the panelling until he squatted on the floor.

Never before had he been so exposed to the reality of losing Rachel. Never before had he been so unable to control his emotions. But it seemed that, over the past twenty-four hours, fate had hit on a systematic plan to break down his defences, battering at his endurance, his emotions, his self-confidence, before delivering the final coup de grâce in the boardroom. It had worked. He felt no semblance of self-respect, no measure of ability, and now felt no inclination to suppress the one thing that he wanted to fill his thoughts with day and night—the memory of Rachel. He pulled his knees close to his chin and stared out in front of him, letting her name run through his mind over and over, like a jumping needle on a scratched record.

The doors clunked open on the third floor, and a black girl with a laden mail-cart held them back with one hand as she manoeuvred her vehicle in with the other. She looked down at David, leaned across to push the ground-floor button on the panel, and as the doors closed and the lift set off again, she squeezed herself back behind her trolley. She took a pack of chewing-gum out of her pocket, pulled a stick out with her teeth, undid its wrapper and pushed it into her mouth. She looked down at David again. "Hard day, huh?"

David continued to stare directly in front of him, his eyes vacant yet his mind focused on his thoughts. The girl shrugged her shoulders. "Never mind, friend," she said, looking up at the floor indicator just as the ground-floor light lit up. "By the looks of you, I don't think things could get much worse."

The doors opened and, with a hefty push, she rolled out her cart. David remained where he was, making no effort to move, not caring what happened to him and not really wishing to go anywhere else. He watched as the doors began to close on his solitude once more, but before they shut completely, a hand shot in and pushed them back. The girl leaned into the lift, her hand out-stretched. "Come on, it'll do you no good goin' up and down the building all day. Just make you sick. Any-ways, I might end up pushin' my cart in here again, and that'll only get me feelin' as depressed as you."

David looked up at her beaming face and slowly stretched up and took her hand. Effortlessly, she pulled him to his feet. "Let's go, friend," she said, guiding him out of the lift. "You'll feel better with some fresh air."

She walked him over to the doors of the building and took him outside onto the sidewalk. "You okay?" she asked, a concerned look on her face.

David looked at her and nodded, forcing a smile onto his face. He held up his hand in thanks and started to walk south down Madison, for no good reason other than that was the direction in which he was facing. The girl watched him for a moment, then, shaking her head, went back into the building.

He walked slowly, concentrating his sludged mind on moving one foot in front of the other, his legs feeling as if they were filled with a mixture of cement and jelly, the combined effect making him weave like a drunkard from side to side. He started to cross over Forty-fifth Street without noticing the signal and a cab screeched to a halt inches from his right hip. The driver slammed his hand on the horn and yelled something at him out of the window. He ran the remainder of the way to the sidewalk, finding that even that small amount of exertion had left him feeling exhausted, and leaned his back against the spindly trunk of a street-side tree, its thin branches waving in the blustering breeze that whirled through the shadowed streets. Despite the warmth in the air, he felt freezing cold, and with one hand pulled together his suit jacket and fastened the buttons. He tilted back his head to see at what point the skyscrapers ceased to cast their shadows onto the streets below, then continued his gaze on upwards until he was look-ing directly above into the unshielded warmth of the deep blue sky. Little things, he thought to himself, little things please little bloody minds.

He pushed himself off the tree and continued to walk aimlessly down Madison Avenue, on collision course with the side-stepping masses that approached him. Fifteen minutes later he had reached the block between Thirty-first and Thirty-second Street and stopped outside the open door of a pub, its glass window bearing the name FLANAGAN'S in gold crescent-shaped lettering. He looked in at the long bar, stretching thirty feet back into the depths of the building, every inch of it occupied by early lunch-time drinkers, and after a moment he entered and began to sidle his way through the crowd to the far end. A young barman in a white shirt and green bow-tie caught his eye and came down towards him, running a cloth over the bar as he walked. "What can I get you, sor?" he asked in a strong Irish brogue.

David looked around to see what others were drinking. The young suit next to him was drinking Budweiser from the neck. "Budweiser."

"Would that be bottle or tap?"

"Tap—and I'll have a Scotch malt as well."

The bartender held the beer glass under the gurgling tap. "Any particular brand?"

"I don't suppose you have Glendurnich?" he asked, almost sarcastically.

The barman looked over his shoulder at the mirrored display shelf half-way up the bar, then, leaving the beer-tap running, hurried his way up to check his stock, expertly judging his return just as the beer had begun to trickle over the top of the glass. He flicked off the tap. " 'Fraid not. Only Glenlivet and Glenmorangie."

David grunted derisively at himself. Stupid question. There it was, the proof of the pudding. That's why he was bloody well meant to be here, to get Glendurnich onto the shelves alongside its competitors.

"Would you be wantin' one then, sor?"

David let out a long sigh. "One of each."

As the bartender headed off to pour him the whisky, the young suit next to David vacated his bar-stool. Taking a huge mouthful of beer, he pulled the stool towards him with his foot and sat down, ready to numb his pain with alcohol.

Two hours later he lurched out of the pub and stood unsteadily in the middle of the sidewalk, his befuddled brain trying to decipher the barman's garbled instructions on how to get to Penn Station. More by good fortune than by better judgement, he had ended up only three blocks east of his destination, but nevertheless it took him thirty minutes of concentrated staggering before he found the station in his inebriated state.

The place was bustling with people even though it was only two-fifteen in the afternoon, and David, keeping close to the wall in fear of bumping into someone and losing his balance completely, skirted round the terminal until he saw the ticket office. He walked up to a vacant window and slumped forward, resting his arms on the shelf, his head only inches away from the glass partition. "One way to Patchogue."

The clerk pressed a button on his machine and shot out a ticket into the steel recess in front of David. "Eight-fifty."

Steadying himself against the window, David pulled his wallet out of his pocket, took out a ten-dollar bill and slid it into the recess. "Could you please tell me when the next train is?" he asked, trying not to slur his speech.

The ticket salesman looked at his timetable. "Two twenty-seven to Babylon, track seventeen. Change at Jamaica for Patchogue."

"Thank you," David said, this time hearing himself sound as if he had a severe speech impediment.

By the time he reached track 17, the train was already waiting. He clambered into the first car and sat down opposite a minute wizened albino man who wore a pair of blue-tinted spectacles and whose white hair poked through the plastic mesh of his red-and-blue baseball cap. He seemed to be working simultaneously on two crosswords, obviously photocopied from newspapers onto one piece of paper. David blinked at this near-surrealistic encounter, thinking that his imagination had become distorted with drink. But the little man was definitely there, checking the clues on each of his crosswords in turn and scribbling down the answers without once stopping to ponder the questions.

The train took off with a jolt and slid away from the platform, picking up speed as it entered into a pitch-black tunnel. David shut his eyes and tried to concentrate on synchronizing the natural swaying of his body with the movement of the train, but it made him feel sick, so he laid his head back against the seat and focused on an AIDS-Helpline poster that was stuck on one of the partition windows. With that, the train shot out of the tunnel and into Queens, the sun suddenly bursting so brightly through the window of the car that he had to put up his hand to shield his eyes. He tried shutting them again, but once again was overcome with nausea. He leaned forward, resting his elbows on his knees, and placed his hands over his face, finding it a bearable compromise—being able to cut out the glare, yet maintain his equilibrium by squinting through the gaps in his fingers at the chalk-faced dwarf opposite him. He remained in that position until the train conductor's voice crackled over the intercom.

"Jamaica. Change for Patchogue."

As the train drew into the station, about half the passengers rose from their seats. David grabbed his brief-case and followed, but once out on the platform he realized that he had no idea in which direction he was meant to go. He therefore tagged on to the larger of the groups as they made their way up and over the railway bridge.

It was the right decision, the Patchogue train pulling

in just as he came down the staircase. Doors opened
and a few passengers disembarked before the Penn
crowd began to push their way in. David found a seat
to himself in the corner, and for a moment wondered
why others had chosen to squeeze themselves together
so far from where he was sitting. His question was answered almost as soon as the train pulled out of the
station by the sound of a flushing toilet from the door
opposite him, followed by the sour, overpowering smell
of urine. He put his hand across his mouth and nose to
stop himself from gagging and turned to see the whole
partition of the lavatory swing back and forth on its
loose brackets as someone inside wrestled with the door
handle. It eventually flew open and a gaunt middle-aged
man appeared, dressed in a pair of coveralls and clutching a plastic bag in one hand and a can of beer in the
other. He crossed over and sat down opposite David.

"Fuckin' lock's busted," he said, gesticulating with
the side of his head towards the lavatory and taking an
almost dainty sip of beer from his can.

David silently nodded and looked around, hoping
that if he didn't make eye contact with his travelling
companion he would be spared further revelations
about his visit to the lavatory.

In comparison to this train, David realized that he
hadn't quite appreciated just how clean the previous
one had been. The imitation leather seats had at one
time been two-toned, but now their fading colours were
indistinguishable under years of grease-stains, and the
windows were so smeared with engrained dirt that it
was difficult to see out. He looked down at the floor
and noticed a suspect trickle of liquid, originating at the
rest-room door, which wound its way down the central
passageway, its meandering course governed by the
constant side-to-side swing of the train.

His travelling companion tilted back his head to
catch the last drops of beer in the can and placed it
neatly on the floor at his feet. Then, putting his hand

in his plastic bag, he took out a second can, flicked open the ring-pull, and took another dainty sip. David thought about moving, but then simply shut his eyes and leaned his head against the hard metallic edge of the aluminium windowsill. He felt the feeling of nausea spread over him once more, this time made more acute by the smell coming from the lavatory. Why the hell should he move? This was exactly where he was meant to be, stuck in the corner of this filthy, seedy train with his chain-drinking companion, two losers together, the perfect theatrical scene for his own complete self-degradation.

He clenched his teeth and screwed up his eyes in an attempt to stop himself from sliding over the edge of the emotional abyss, but this time there was nothing to hold him, every saving foothold of pride and self-esteem at which he had grasped so many times in the past having been chipped away by the events of the day. He felt the first of the tears force their way through his tightly closed eyes and run in parallel lines down the side of each cheek before falling, their sly, discreditable work finished, onto the lapel of his suit jacket.

It was some time before he noticed that the beer-drinker had quietly moved away from him to the opposite end of the car.

Chapter
THIRTEEN

Having only gone through the motions of working that morning, owing to his unabating hangover, Richard decided that he could be of no further use to Dammell's Bank that day and slipped discreetly out of the office at two-thirty. He knew that it would take his last ounce of fortitude to suffer the tedious train journey back out to Long Island. Two hours later, he pushed open the unlocked door of the kitchen—an indication that David was home—and, chucking his brief-case onto the table, went over to the sink to fill up the kettle. As he plugged it in, a slight movement on the sofa in the corner of the room made him turn around abruptly.

"David? Jesus, what a fright you gave me!" He walked over to the sofa. "What the hell . . . ?"

He knew something was wrong immediately. David lay, his back turned towards him, making no move to acknowledge his arrival. He clutched a cushion tightly in his arms and his legs were drawn up into his stomach. Richard leaned across him and looked down on his ashen-white face. His eyes, swollen from crying, focused blankly into the fabric of the sofa.

"David," he said quietly, "what's up, old boy? Christ, you look all in."

David swung his legs round and sat up and rubbed hard at his eyes with his fingers. "Sorry, Richard. I'm so sorry."

"For what?"

David shook his head. "I don't know. Just being here. I shouldn't be."

Richard sat down next to him. "Christ, of course you should be here. What do you mean?" He bit hard on his lip, not understanding quite what had happened. "What is it, David? Is it . . . Rachel?"

David fixed his gaze out the window and slowly nodded.

Richard put a hand on his friend's shoulder. "Christ, David, I really am so sorry." He glanced around the room as if trying to search out an answer to David's problem. "Would you like a whisky or something?"

David shook his head. "No, I've already had a skinful." He pushed himself to his feet. "Listen, if you don't mind, I think I'll just get out of your way and go to bed. I'm not feeling too good."

Richard jumped up. "Yeah, of course. Do you want me to get a doctor or anything like that?"

David shook his head. "No, I just need to sleep." He walked to the door and turned round. "I'm sorry, Richard."

"Look, you really don't have to apologize, my friend. Just go to bed and sleep as long as you want. I'll be leaving pretty early tomorrow morning, but . . . er . . . listen, I'll tell you what. Angie's sister, Carrie, lives here in Leesport. She's always popping in, so I'll get her to organize something for you to eat, okay?"

David shook his head. "You don't need to bother—really."

"It's no bother, old fellow. Carrie won't mind at all. You just get to bed—and sleep." He paused for a moment. "Listen, Angie's got some pretty lethal sleeping pills. Do you want one?"

"No. I'll be fine."

"Okay." Richard walked over and patted him on the back. "But try to clear your mind, David."

David smiled and let out a shuddering sigh. "I doubt I'll ever be able to do that again, Richard."

"Yeah," Richard said quietly, "I know."

He waited until he heard David's door close before letting out a long, relieved breath. He walked over to the kettle and made himself a cup of coffee, then leaned his back against the sideboard as he tried to work out what he should do.

Carrie. He should call her first. No, maybe not. He went across to the table and opened his brief-case and took out his telephone book. He flicked through it to the correct page, then, picking up the telephone, he dialled the number and stood scratching at his cheek while waiting for an answer.

With a hot-water bottle tucked under her arm, Effie had made it to the half-way stage on the staircase when she heard the sound of the car scrunching to a halt on the gravel outside the house. She stopped, a puzzled expression on her face, then turned and descended the staircase and went over to the door of the drawing-room, knocked and entered. Alicia Inchelvie glanced up from her book at her, then swung round to look at the clock on the mantelpiece.

"Effie? Have you not gone home yet? It's half past nine!"

"Not quite. I was just going to put a hot-water bottle in your bed before I went—but—well, I was wondering if you were expecting someone. It's just that I'm sure that I heard a car stop at the front door."

"No," Alicia replied, putting her book down on the side-table and heaving herself up from the chair. "I can't think who would be coming at this time. Let's go and have a look."

As she walked across the drawing-room, the sound of the front door opening made the three dogs jump up from their place by the fire. Barking furiously, they skidded their way past her and out into the hall, their claws scraping on the polished wooden floor as they developed wheel-spin in their eagerness to find out who had entered their house. Alicia glanced inquiringly at Effie, then together they followed the dogs out into the hallway.

Surrounded by bouncing and panting animals, George Inchelvie slowly took off the scarf from around his neck and hung it on one of the coat-hooks.

"Good boys. That's enough now." He looked up as his wife and the little housekeeper came out of the drawing-room.

"George!" Alicia exclaimed, a concerned expression on her face. "What on earth are you doing home? I thought that you were spending another night in Glasgow."

George took off his coat and laid it on the pew. "I was meant to be." He steadied himself on his stick before starting to walk across the hall towards them. "Duncan Caple telephoned me at the hotel at about five-thirty. He said that he'd been on the point of leaving the office for his European trip when he'd had a call from this new distributor fellow in New York. Anyway, I had a fairly intensive conversation with him for about half an hour, after which I decided that I didn't particularly feel like staying away for another night—so I just drove home."

Alicia watched him closely as he spoke. If the economy of his slurred words was not enough to register his exhaustion, the colourless features of his face, its shadowed lines accentuated by the dim lighting in the hall, gave her the strongest indication that her husband had just about used up every reserve of energy.

"What's happened, George?"

He hesitated before replying, and Effie, realizing that her presence was no longer required, backed away towards the staircase. "Right, well, I'll just away and put the hot-water bottle in your bed, Lady Inchelvie." She bustled off, then stopped and turned back. "Would you be wanting a wee something to eat, my lord? There's a bit of the stew left over in the fridge, which I could heat up, or maybe a cheese sandwich?"

George shook his head. "That's kind, Effie, but no, I'm quite all right." A glimmer of a wry smile crossed his tired face. "I think I'll probably just make do with a whisky."

Alicia moved towards him and took his arm. "Come on, let's go and sit in the drawing-room." In silence they walked together across the hallway and into the drawing-room, where George sat down heavily in one of the chairs, grimacing in pain as he did so. "Bloody back is bad at the minute," he said, his voice croaking. "Too much driving."

"Too much of everything, Geordie," Alicia said, looking down at him and shaking her head. "Now, I'll get you a whisky and you tell me what's happened."

She went over to the corner cabinet and took out a glass and a half-full bottle of Glendurnich.

"Has David telephoned?" George asked.

"No," Alicia replied, pouring out a double measure and replacing the cork in the bottle. "Were you expecting him to?"

For a moment, George looked at his wife as he gathered his thoughts. "I'm afraid that David's meeting in New York didn't go too well."

Alicia handed him the whisky, then sat down on the edge of her chair, resting her elbows on her knees and eyeing her husband intently. "What happened?"

"I'm not sure. David apparently walked out half-way through, much to the surprise of everyone present. At any rate, that's what Duncan told me." He took a drink from his glass. "Anyway, that's only half the problem."

Alicia did not speak, but waited for her husband to continue. He chewed pensively at the side of his mouth before resuming. "Duncan feels that David's mysterious behaviour at the meeting is proof enough that he needs a complete break from his job. He says that he cannot operate Glendurnich without a marketing director, and he wants to appoint a new one as soon as possible."

Alicia sat back in her chair and closed her eyes. This was it. The worst had happened. She had never thought that it would come to this. "What did you say to him?"

"What *could* I say?" George retorted almost defensively. "I mean, even though the company belongs to the family, I can't exercise my own nepotistic muscle if David is not up to fulfilling his role. I know it's not his fault, but I have to understand Duncan's position as well." He drained his glass and took in a deep breath to compose himself. "Anyway, that's what I was negotiating with him on the telephone. What has been agreed is that Duncan *will* appoint a new marketing director, but I have managed to limit it to a one-year contract for the time being, and hopefully by then David will have managed to get himself together. If, at the end of one year, there is no change to the situation, then the contract will be extended at Duncan's discretion."

There was complete silence in the room, except for the rhythmic thumping of one of the dogs scratching at its neck with its back paw, and the ticking of the clock on the mantelpiece.

"What is happening with our lives, Geordie?" Alicia said eventually in a quiet voice. "Everything seems to have gone haywire. I mean, we have never had so many worries as we do now, and here you are, having to work harder than ever before." She paused and sat back in her chair and began brushing her hair over the top of one ear with her fingers. "I was so hoping that this trip might be the turning point for David." She looked across at her husband. "I really could not bear it if we found ourselves back to stage one with him, because I can't see how either of us will cope."

George nodded slowly, as if in submission to what his wife was saying. "I know. It's not good, and I just wonder where on earth he is at the minu——"

The telephone trilled noisily on his desk, and Alicia pushed herself to her feet and walked across the room to answer it.

"Hullo, Inchelvie . . . yes . . . yes, of course, Richard, how are you? . . . Why, what's happened? . . . Oh, no . . . oh dear, this was something I always dreaded taking place . . . Flu as well! . . . Oh, my word! . . . Oh, Richard, I'm so sorry . . . Yes . . . yes . . . but can you cope with all that? . . . I see, but does Carrie have time to do that? . . . Right . . . well, that is most kind, Richard. . . . Yes, I think you're right. The sooner he gets back here, the better . . . on the Monday-evening flight? . . . Yes, that would be fine. I'll arrange for someone to meet him at Glasgow on Tuesday morning . . . of course, and many thanks for letting me know, Richard . . . bye."

She replaced the receiver, keeping her hand on it for a moment before turning back to her husband to answer his unfinished question.

Knowing that the reception for his car telephone was better on the A9, Duncan Caple waited until he was south of Aviemore before punching in one of the three autodial numbers he had for John Davenport, chairman of Kirkpatrick Holdings Plc. The hands-free speaker crackled out three ringing tones before being answered.

"Hullo?" a female voice replied.

"Could I speak to John, please?"

"Yes, one minute, please."

Duncan heard the receiver being clunked down on the table, followed by the female voice calling out John's name. There was the sound of footsteps, the receiver being picked up again, and a man's voice spoke. "Hullo?"

"John, it's Duncan Caple."

"Where are you, Duncan?"

"In the car. Sorry to call you at home, John, but I

thought it better if we were both out of our respective offices."

"Good idea. How did you get on? Manage to get hold of that information?"

"Yup, and it's exactly as you thought. Glendurnich *did* set up a stock-purchase plan specifically for distillery employees about twenty-five years ago, I think actually at the instigation of Inchelvie himself. Quite forward-thinking of the old boy, but he's always been a great one for boosting work-force loyalty. Anyway, the way it works is that if an employee wants to take up the company share option, he or she contributes fifty per cent of its value and the company forks out for the rest. However, to protect shares going out of the company, it was written into the original plan agreement that if any employee left and wanted to realize the capital value of his Glendurnich shares, he had to resubmit them to a pool system to allow existing company employees the chance of purchasing them. If they were not taken up by them, the family would then step in to purchase them. I also found out something else quite interesting: In the past twenty-five years, the Glendurnich work-force has expanded by thirty, mostly all within the office, but surprisingly only eight have left across the board."

"Which means?"

"Which means that, at this moment in time the family's shareholding in Glendurnich is quite seriously eroded."

"By how much, Duncan?"

"Well, I've found it bloody difficult to find out anything without causing suspicion. For some reason, Robert McLeod, the financial director, has never shown it in the accounts, but from what I can gather, I'm pretty sure that thirty-one per cent of the Glendurnich shares are now in the hands of the work-force."

"Excellent! I mean, it's not a majority shareholding, but it's a real arm-twister as far as we're concerned.

And you reckon that the family are unaware of this?"

"They may very well be, but I don't think that they have an iota as to what the possible implications might be. Anyway, they don't seem to know if they're coming or going at the minute. My idea of sending David Corstorphine out to the States seems to have killed two birds with one stone. I spoke with Charles Deakin in New York earlier this afternoon, and not only have we managed to engineer his company's appointment as the new distributor, but also David seems to have suffered some sort of breakdown during the meeting and ended up by storming out of the building."

"Not the kind of behaviour one would expect from the marketing director of a bespoke malt whisky company."

"Exactly. So I immediately called old Inchelvie in Glasgow to break the news to him, and told him that we needed a new marketing director in place immediately. I actually felt quite sorry for the old duffer."

"And?"

"He agreed to it on a one-year contract. So you can tell Giles Barker to get up here straight away. He's got a new job!"

"Well done, Duncan. So what have we got? Deakin in the States, Giles taking on marketing. What about Robert What's'isname, the financial director?"

"That's fixed too. Robert McLeod is off to run some golf course at the end of the month, so I've appointed Keith Archibald of Northern Maltsters as financial director."

"Brilliant. So we're just about ready to start the campaign. When do you think that you'll be ready to begin dangling the carrot in front of the work-force?"

"Not just yet, John. I reckon I'll have to do some pretty heavy spadework on the old man first. He's so damned protective of his son, and judging from Charles Deakin's description of his behaviour at the meeting in New York, I'm pretty sure that once David's back in this country, Inchelvie will have to come to terms with the fact quite quickly that neither of them is capable of running Glendurnich. At that point I'm sure he'll be more than willing to negotiate with us, especially if the work-force are on our side. That's how I read the situation anyway."

"So, what's your plan of action?"

"Well, I'll get together a sale proposal with the help of Giles and Keith over here, and Charles Deakin in the States, and once I feel the time is right to approach Inchelvie, I'll coincide it with circulating the proposal to all the worker shareholders. It's a two-pronged attack, but it is imperative that Inchelvie and the work-force come to the same decision at exactly the same time. That about sums it up. Timing is of the essence."

"Well, if you say so. But don't leave it too long. You know how important it is for Kirkpatrick to get hold of Glendurnich as soon as possible. It's the missing link."

"Yes, I know."

"All right then, and by the way, I have had words with the Kirkpatrick board, and they have agreed on your fee note of half a million pounds, but that obviously depends on the successful outcome of the deal. Nevertheless, you could let me know sometime whether you will be wanting that as a straight fee payment or whether you want a proportion paid in Glendurnich shares."

"Right, I will do."

"Okay—well, keep pushing it as hard as you can. I'll contact you in a week to see how things are progressing."

"No, don't do that. Let me contact you. It's just that the old battleaxe on the reception desk at Glendurnich is as fiercely loyal to the Inchelvies as any, and I'm just not too sure how confidential telephone calls are when they pass through her switchboard."

"Maybe a replacement is in order, then, Duncan?"

"Maybe. In time. Trust me, I'll play it right. There's too much at stake here."

Duncan pressed the "end" button on the telephone and sat back in the BMW's plush leather driving seat, a smile of deep satisfaction on his face. Then, letting out a loud whoop of elation, he slammed both hands down on the steering wheel and pressed the accelerator to the floor, letting the powerful machine blast its way down the empty road, only easing back on the throttle when it had peaked at exactly twice the sixty-miles-per-hour speed limit.

Chapter
FOURTEEN

Although his influenza bug had virtually burned itself out within the first twenty-four hours, David felt no desire to leave the haven of his room during the next few days. Time became an unimportant entity in his existence, and the hours were only registered by the sound of Carrie who, at his own request, would simply leave a tray of food or a cup of tea outside his door, without venturing into his room. Through his window, light gave way to darkness, then back to light, but he never attempted to coincide any form of living pattern with it. He tried to sleep as much as possible, desperate to break away from the repetitive thought process that constantly gnawed at his mind, but much of the time he found himself lying awake on the bed or pacing the floor into the early hours of the morning.

Since Wednesday, he had left his room only to use the lavatory, returning immediately so that he might avoid coming into contact with either Carrie or Richard. All pride in his own personal appearance had become as unnecessary as any form of daily routine, and he now constantly scratched at his face, which itched with two days' worth of stubble. Yet obtusely, it satisfied his frame of mind, accentuating his self-induced penance and in harmony with his own deep lack of self-respect. Self, self. That was all it was now. Self-respect, self-disgust. In the past, to think constantly of Rachel had been acceptable to him, but somehow everything had become distorted, and his thoughts now were only of himself—no, probably *for* himself, his mind relentlessly churning over and over a catechism of words that helped to prove just how miserable and hopeless a human being he had become.

That evening, as he had done countless times before, he rose slowly from the unmade bed and walked over to the shelf and leaned his hands on its rough surface, his head, feeling like a leaden weight, drooping so that his chin rested on his chest.

Christ, what was it? What the hell was it? He had been all right when he came over from Scotland, and then somehow everything had gone wrong. Why? He had to try to reason it out. He pushed himself away from the shelf and continued to pace the floor, then stopped abruptly at the window, his actions frozen as he looked out at the darkening day, the merest splinter of enlightened thought breaking through the throbbing dullness in his brain.

That's it. You *were* all right when you came over from Scotland. You had felt quite happy being one of the crowd in the airport, because no one knew you, no one cared about you, no one had any idea of your past, present or future. You were a carefree nonentity. But that all changed the moment you walked into this house, because Richard *knew*. It's not just that you screwed everything up over here. You're frightened, aren't you? Frightened of your own identity, frightened to go back to Scotland, frightened to re-enter that tight claustrophobic environment where everyone knows you and everyone cares about you, and everyone looks at you with sad eyes, and talks about you in low whispers.

He walked over to the bed and fell back on it, gazing

up to the ceiling. Keep thinking—that's it—keep thinking. What the hell *do* you want, David?

"I want to be—*alone*!" he said out loud, "just—*unknown*! I don't particularly want to be—David—fucking—Corstorphine—any bloody more!"

He turned over on his side and clutched his knees up
to his chest. Free from responsibility, free from identity.
It sounded like the song of a protest march. He snorted
out a weak laugh and shook his head, the action amplifying in his ear the scraping sound of his stubble
against the pillow. It was an impossibility, he knew
that, but at least it was something on which he could
concentrate his mind, something on which he was quite
happy to expand his thoughts. He closed his eyes, and
for the first time in two days the tightness in his head
slowly abated.

He was awakened the next morning by a burst of
sunlight shining through the window and onto his face.
Blinking, he turned his head towards the door to avoid
the brightness, and in his drowsy state suddenly became
aware of an overpowering smell. He opened his eyes
and found that he was lying with his hands linked
above his head, his nose resting about six inches from
his armpit.

"Bloody hell!"

He pushed himself up from the bed too quickly, and
for a moment weaved unsteadily about in the centre of
the room while his headspin subsided. He pulled off his
T-shirt and forcefully discarded it onto the shelf, knocking over a small vanity mirror onto the floor in the process. He froze momentarily and stared down at it,
wondering whether he had just condemned himself to
a further seven years of bad luck. Slowly, he bent down
and picked it up. It was unbroken. With a sigh of relief,
he replaced it carefully on the shelf, and in doing so
caught a fleeting glimpse of his new self. He held it up
close to his face. His hair stuck up in punkish peaks
from his head; his face, under its dirty cover of stubble,

was pale and drawn, and the dark brown rings that surrounded his eyes seemed to sink them back into the depths of his skull. What did he look like? What single word could possibly describe this disgusting apparition?

A slug.

That was it. He was a slug—hiding away under its stupid, bloody stone.

The deep anger that suddenly built up within him seemed to trigger off a defence mechanism in his brain. That's it—no more. He glanced at his watch. It was seven-thirty. Right, you stupid prick, time to get your act together.

He grabbed a towel, picked up his sponge-bag and and walked out across the landing. He stopped. The door to Richard's room was still closed and he could hear him quietly snoring from within. He scratched at his head. God, what day was it? Richard must either be working from home that day or it was Saturday. In either case, he didn't want to be seen in his present state. He tiptoed into the bathroom and turned on the shower.

At first the water was cold, but it suited him, invigorating his mood as he scrubbed hard at his body with the sweet-smelling soap. Then, as the stream of water began to heat up, he poured out a dollop of shampoo and gave his hair the same purging treatment, repeating both operations before turning off the shower and stepping out of the bath, clean and renewed in body, if not in mind.

Five minutes and one and a half disposable razors later, he had rid himself of his stubble, finishing off by splashing stinging handfuls of after-shave onto the uncustomary softness of his face. Lastly, he gave his armpits an extra-long spray of deodorant before gathering up his belongings and heading back across the landing.

His room smelt so dank and airless when he returned to it that he immediately opened the window as wide as it would go, instantly feeling the warmth of the early-morning sun on his bare chest. He took a clean pair of jeans, shirt and boxer shorts from his suitcase and, having dressed, sat back on his bed and looked around. He didn't want to be there any longer. Its atmosphere had become too oppressive, too reminiscent of depression. He wanted to get away from it. In fact, right away from the house, away from where he was known.

He jumped up, galvanized into action by this thought. Picking up his wallet from the shelf, he put on a pair of boating shoes, then opened the door and quietly made his way downstairs and into the kitchen. He unsnibbed the French doors and let himself out onto the deck, carefully closing the door behind him.

He stood for a moment gulping in deep, reviving breaths of the fresh warm air before taking the wooden steps two at a time and walking down the driveway. He stopped at the bottom, looked up and down the street, then, with a decisive nod, turned right towards the main street.

The slug had made it.

It was too early for any of the shops to be open, so he strolled along the sidewalk looking in the windows at the goods on display. There were already a number of people about, walking dogs or carrying newspapers under their arms, and many of those who passed him smiled and said "Good morning." He reciprocated the greeting, each time feeling his spirits lift more.

Half-way along the main street, David came across the highest concentration of people outside the Leesport Deli. Men dressed in shorts and T-shirts leaned against large pick-up trucks parked at the side of the road, discussing their forthcoming day's work over bulging rolls and huge Styrofoam cupfuls of steaming coffee. The sight and the smell suddenly made David feel ravenously hungry, so he entered and joined on the back of the queue at the far end of the shop, filling in time until it was his turn by studying the menu on the long pegboard that hung above the counter. A continuous banter went on between those in the queue and the three young men in white aprons that served behind the counter.

"Who's next?" one of the young men called out, wiping his hands on his apron.

Already waiting for their order, those in front of David stood aside to allow him through to the counter. "How can I help you?" the young man asked, smiling at David.

David looked up at the list above his head. "Can I have an egg-and-bacon roll, please?"

"Okay, coming up."

The deli-man turned and bumped into one of his colleagues. "Lose some weight, Joe!" He let out a raucous laugh and ducked as Joe swung a mock punch at his head. He turned back to David. "How would you like your egg?"

"Er, fried please," David replied.

A ripple of laughter spread around the deli. The young man grinned at David.

"They all come fried, sir. That's about all we know how to treat an egg. Do you want it sunny side up or easy over?"

David smiled, embarrassed. "Er—sunny side up will do me fine."

The young man went off whistling and clattered some pans out of sight behind the freezer display before returning to the counter. "Anything else?"

"Yes, a large black coffee."

The young man worked like a trained cocktail barman, taking a Styrofoam cup from the dispenser and spinning it once in the air before pouring in coffee from a Cona pot. He snapped on a lid and, flicking open a brown paper bag, placed the cup carefully inside, just as a young, spotty-faced youth appeared from behind the freezer display, holding the roll wrapped in white greaseproof paper.

"Egg-and-bacon roll?"

"That's mine." The deli-man snatched it from the minion's hand and placed it in the paper bag alongside the coffee.

"Right, that's three-eighty."

David took his wallet from his back pocket and handed over a five-dollar bill. The young man rang it up on the till and gave him his change. "A dollar-twenty change. Enjoy, and have a nice day!"

"Thanks," David said, his face breaking into a smile at the all-American cliché. "I think I might just do that."

"Next?" the young man called out.

David turned away from the counter as the next customer moved forward to fill his place. He stopped and turned back to the young man. "I wonder if you could tell me how to get to the harbour?"

"Do you mean the marina?"

"Yeah, sorry, the marina."

"Turn right out of here, take the first on the right—that's Pearl Street—and just keep walking. If you walk about three hundred and fifty yards, you'll get your feet wet, so stop at about three hundred."

"Thanks," David said, grinning at the young comic.

"No problem," he said, and turned to the old man who had taken David's place. "Okay gramps, what's it to be today?"

David walked out of the deli into the sunlight with a smile on his face, his whole being lightened by the exchange. He decided not to indulge himself in the contents of his bag until he had reached the marina, so he took off at a brisk pace, following the young man's directions.

Pearl Street was like any other that he had seen in Leesport, a wide thoroughfare with secluded houses tucked away in their own grounds, separated from the sidewalk by fences. The road was criss-crossed with smaller streets leading off to rows of similar dwellings, yet, as he walked, he realized that the village was not in any way overbuilt, every so often coming across a grassed area on which there might be room for at least three more houses, this lending a healthy and clean openness to the surroundings.

The street eventually came to an end, opening out into a broad expanse of tarmac that led into the marina. David approached the small gatehouse at the entrance, and the old man who occupied it threw a cursory glance in his direction before looking away again. As there was no one else about, and heartened by the open friendliness shown towards him by the people in the deli, David decided to break the ice and engage the old man in conversation.

"Good morning." He stood purposefully beside the man's window, holding his paper bag in one hand and shielding his eyes from the glare of the sun with the other as he looked out over the marina. "Lovely day."

The man looked up and cocked his head to the side. "Sure is." With that, he leaned forward to turn up the volume of a television that was hidden below the wide ledge of the window.

David felt his face prickle with embarrassment at this blatant shun, but was immediately overcome with a devilish urge to persevere with the conversation, a reaction that was as much a surprise to himself as it was to be of a further nuisance to the old man.

"Is that the Atlantic over there?" he asked, a light-hearted innocence to his voice as he stared out across the marina. "Seems very calm."

The old man rose begrudgingly from his seat, realizing that he would have to respond before being left in peace again and, leaning out of his little window, jabbed a finger in the direction of the water. "That ain't the Atlantic—that's the Great South Bay." The action of his finger now changed to an up-and-over motion. "Atlantic's further over, beyond Fire Island."

David looked out to the long strip of land that lay

about four miles across the bay. "Can you get over there?"

"Ferry goes from the marina every half-hour."

The old man, feeling that he had said enough, turned away from the window and sat back down in front of his television, effectively terminating the conversation. David pulled a face at the nape of his bristly little neck to acknowledge his gracelessness and moved away from the gatehouse. He headed off parallel to the marina, alongside a small public garden secluded from the road by a hedge of wild dogrose which fell untamed over a heavy two-rail fence, as simply fashioned and as rustic as a nursery rhyme. Twenty yards farther on, the hedge formed an archway over an iron gate on which hung a small brass plaque bearing the inscription THE LEESPORT RESIDENTS MEMORIAL GARDEN. He pushed open the gate and walked in.

The lawns and flower-beds of the little garden were beautifully kept, laid out in circular sweeps around the centre-piece of a large concrete plinth on which an old grey naval howitzer perched, pointing its flaking barrel out towards the bay. Beside it, the Stars and Stripes fluttered in the sea breeze atop a tall white flagpole. David walked around the side of the gun to the far end of the garden and stood for a moment gazing into the brackish waters of the bay as they lapped lazily against the vertical wooden pilings that protected the garden from erosion. He stepped back and looked around for somewhere to sit and spied an old wooden bench tucked under the barrel of the gun. Taking the cup of coffee and roll out of the paper bag, he sat down to enjoy both his breakfast and the view across the marina. All was tranquillity that morning, save only for the plaintive scream of gulls overhead, and the sound of the steel hawser-lines clinking like cowbells against the masts of the swaying yachts drawn up tight against each other along the wooden walkways that divided off the moorings.

This is perfect, he thought to himself, this is bloody perfect.

He didn't particularly want to move from the garden, but glancing at his watch, he was surprised to find that he had been sitting there for over an hour and a half, and realized that he should be heading back to the house to see Richard. He jumped to his feet, throwing his breakfast wrappings into the litter-bin beside the bench and, making his way across to the gate and out into the street, he waved heartily as he passed his grumpy friend in the gatehouse before starting back up Pearl Street.

The main street of Leesport was now filled with cars and bicycles, the sidewalks bustling with shoppers. As he weaved his way through them, David had the thought that he should buy Carrie a small token for her kindness in feeding "the invisible man" over the past few days. He caught sight of a flower shop on the opposite side of the street, and quickly crossing over the road, he entered in.

Half a minute later he reappeared, clutching a huge bunch of carnations in his arms while at the same time attempting to stuff the change from his purchase into his wallet. He took a couple of paces and half a dozen coins fell from his hand and clinked onto the sidewalk, rolling off in different directions. Swearing quietly to himself, he bent down to pick them up.

The last to be retrieved was a quarter which had rolled into the edge of the sidewalk, nestling under a flower-box attached to the wall of the next-door shop. Having recovered it, he straightened up to find himself facing a window display board covered with small white cards. He glanced up at the name. It was Helping Hands, the small employment agency that he had seen on arrival in Leesport.

As he turned to walk away, his eyes swept with casual interest across the job cards on the notice-board. He stopped in his tracks. Something had registered. He took a pace back and bent down to read the card in the bottom left-hand corner.

TEMPORARY HANDYMAN REQUIRED
for general garden work
experience preferred but not necessary
apply within

He stood up slowly, his eyes transfixed on the card, then stepped back from the window, his mind whirring with thoughts and ideas. Then suddenly, reason took over and he shook his head derisively at such an impractical thought. He walked away from the shop, but almost immediately came to a halt once more, and a young woman, who had been pushing a pram along the sidewalk behind him, bumped it heavily into the backs of his legs.

"Oh, I'm so sorry," she said, holding up a hand in apology.

David jumped aside to clear her path. "No, it's me who should apologize," he said, smiling at her. "Just having a moment of indecision."

The young mother laughed. "Yep, I just had one of those in the supermarket, but I put it down to postnatal syndrome."

David raised his eyebrows. "Yeah, well, I'm afraid I don't think that I could use that excuse."

The young woman pulled down the corners of her mouth and looked at him out of the side of her eyes in mock contemplation of this suggestion. "No—maybe not. But hey, I just thought, well, it's a beautiful day, why not go for it!—you should maybe do the same!"

Beaming a smile at him, she gave the pram a hefty push and continued on her way. For a moment David remained where he was, watching after her. She was right, he thought to himself, what the hell, and, turning briskly on his heel, he headed back to the shop and pushed open the door.

Although the office was only sparsely furnished with a sofa and coffee-table, two desks and a filing cabinet, David was immediately struck by the way in which it had been decorated, the soft pink of the walls picked out in the patterned loose covers of the sofa and in part of the zig-zag design of the fitted-carpet. One of the desks was occupied by a young girl, a pair of huge round spectacles balanced precariously on the end of her snub nose, whose fingers moved like lightning across the keyboard of her computer. At the other sat a large smooth-faced man of about sixty dressed in a brightly coloured loose-fitting shirt, its collar turned up to protect his neck from the two heavy gold-link chains from which were suspended a pen and a pair of horn-rimmed spectacles. His thick grey hair was combed back across his head, held immaculately in place by glistening quantities of styling-gel. As David entered, they both looked round in his direction, and the man jumped lightly to his feet and came around his desk to greet him.

"Hi, I'm Clive Hanley," he said, holding out his hand to David. "Can I be of assistance?"

David shook his hand. "Well, er, it was only an inquiry, really, about one of the cards in your window?"

Clive smiled at him. "Certainly, of course. Now what would you be particularly interested in?"

"The handyman."

"Okay—so—you want a handyman, is that right?"

"No—I was wondering about getting a job myself."

Clive paused, furrowing his brow, and looked David up and down. "I see . . ."

"Maybe I should explain a bit," David said, realizing that the man seemed a little non-plussed by his request. "It's just that I'm just over here from Scotland staying—"

"Scotland!" Clive interjected with a flourish. "I *love* Scotland! It's just so . . . *barren*!"

David waited for him to continue with his eulogy,

but that seemingly was all he had to say on the subject of Scotland.

"Yes, well," David continued, "as I was saying, I'm over here staying with friends, and—well, I'm just hanging about the house at the minute, getting under everybody's feet, so I came out for a walk and just happened to see your sign in the window. I do have some experience, and well, it does say temporary."

"Right, okay," Clive said slowly, nodding his head. "Let's think about this for a minute. How long do you expect to be over here? You see, I would really need at least a month's commitment before I can put you on my books, otherwise it's just not fair to my clients."

David bit at his lip for a moment before replying. "Yeah, that should be all right," he said, taking instant decisions on his future as he went along.

Clive clapped his hands together conclusively. "Well, let's take some details, shall we? Come and sit down on the sofa, and I'll go get a form from my desk. Would you like a cup of coffee?"

"No, thanks," David said, holding up a hand, "I've just had one."

While Clive rummaged around in the drawers of his desk, David walked over to the sofa and sat down, casting a look around the office once more. Clive noticed this as he approached him, form in hand and, plumping himself down on the sofa next to him, he joined David in his appraisal of the décor.

"Not what one would expect of an employment agency, is it? I mean, I was quite happy with the yellow walls and green linoleum that were here already, but my friend insisted on doing the whole place up. He said that I couldn't possibly work in a place that didn't inspire me. Of course, I think he's done a wonderful job, but I sometimes wonder if it's not just a little bit like a beauty salon!"

With a laugh, he pushed himself forward to the front of the sofa and put the form on the coffee-table in front of him, then, placing his spectacles on the tip of his nose, he pulled his pen from its holder around his neck.

"Okay! Let's get started. Your name is?"

"David Corstorphine. C-o-r-s-t-o-r-p-h-i-n-e."

"And your address?"

David thought for a moment. "Uh, well, right at this very minute, it's Fifty-two North Harlens—but I think that I might be looking around for somewhere else to stay."

For a moment Clive held his pen above the paper while he contemplated this. "So, no problem." He started to write again. "How would it be if I just used this as your contact address, and if you do happen to move, you can always let me know."

"That's fine. Thanks."

"Okay—now, what's the next question? Ah, yes— are you married?"

David took in a deep breath. "No—no, I'm not. I'm not married." He exhaled with a sigh of relief. He had done it. The moment had passed.

"Now, what else?" Clive continued. "Ah yes—hobbies."

"I'm sorry?"

"Hobbies. Have you got any hobbies?"

Seeing that David was a little mystified by the question, Clive put down his pen on the table and leaned back in the sofa.

"I know that it might seem a little strange to ask a question like that, but it's just one of my eccentric little rules to try to learn as much as I can about a prospective employee. I just think that finding out about an individual's hobbies gives such a wonderful indication of his or her character." He pulled a face and placed both hands theatrically across his chest. "I mean, can you imagine how dreadful it would be if I ended up employing a serial killer!"

David smiled at the man, warming to his cosy antics.

"Okay. Right. Hobbies. Well—I play tennis and a bit of golf—and I shoot."

Clive, who had resumed his writing, stopped, and looked slowly round to David, a startled expression on his face.

"No, sorry," David said, shaking his head, realizing that Clive had thought that his worst nightmare might have been fulfilled. "Forget that. It was rather a stupid thing to say. What else do I do?—Oh yes, right, I play the guitar rather badly."

"Classical, folk or pop?"

"What?"

"Sorry! My turn to be silly." Clive let out a short laugh and squeezed his hands self-consciously between his clenched knees. "It's just that I have been known to strum a little myself, though I'm far from contemporary. I'm really most partial to Peter, Paul and Mary, because they use such easy chord changes."

There was a moment of silence while he waited for David to make some sort of comment, but none was forthcoming.

"Anyway," he continued airily, bending forward once more over the questionnaire. "Let's get on with this. I think that's just about it." He gave it a final check-through, put his pen back in its holder, and jumped to his feet.

"There! So much for the formalities. Now let's go over and see what Dotti can come up with on her screen of wisdom."

David got up from the sofa and followed Clive over to the girl with the computer.

"Okay, Dotti," Clive said, leaning over the girl's shoulder. "As you are now no doubt aware, this is David."

The girl looked up at David, pushing her spectacles as far up onto her nose as possible with an index finger, and gave him a shy smile before returning to her screen. Clive put the completed questionnaire in front of her.

"These are his particulars, which you can enter later. Now we want to find David a job as a handyman, so let's bring up that file and see what we've got."

Dotti slid her mouse around the desk, clicking furiously. As the information came up, Clive scanned the screen while Dotti flicked down the list.

"We need to find something in this neck of the woods, don't we . . . okay. . . . Stop there, Dotti! That's it there! Newman." He turned to David. "They're new clients, David, I haven't yet supplied them with anyone." He turned back to the screen. "Where are they, Dotti?"

"Barker Lane," Dotti said.

"Yeah, that would be just perfect. Judging from the address, I reckon that their house would be somewhere down on the waterfront, along the marina? Do you want to give it a go?"

"Of course!" David said.

"Okay, Dotti, let's print out the address!"

Dotti set the printer whirring, and the Newman data sheet appeared on the print-out tray. Clive picked it up and handed it to David.

"Here you are, then. I'll phone Mrs. Newman and tell her that you'll be there first thing Monday morning, okay?"

David nodded.

"Now you'll need to know where the street is," Clive said, turning back towards his desk. "I have a map of Leesport somewhere . . ."

"No, honestly!" David said, stopping him in his tracks. "I haven't got much else to do over the next couple of days, so I'll just go and look for it myself."

"Well, if you're sure." He took hold of David's arm and guided him to the door, and as they passed the sofa, David bent down to pick up his bunch of flowers.

"Clive?" Dotti's sugary voice sounded out.

Clive turned to his assistant. "Yes, Dotti?"

"You haven't mentioned pay to David," she said quietly.

Clive brought both hands up to his cheeks and a look of horror lengthened his face. "Oh my God, what *must* you be thinking, David? I cannot imagine!" He began to walk back to his desk, but David put up his hand to stop him.

"Listen . . . erm . . . this may sound a bit strange . . . but I'm actually quite happy just to do the job . . . rather than get paid . . ."

Clive looked at him, not quite understanding what he was saying.

"You see," David elaborated further, "I only have a visitor's visa. I don't actually have a work permit. But I would really rather do the job and not get paid. I mean, I don't want to get you into any trouble."

Clive stroked at the side of his cheek with his hand and nodded slowly.

"Ah, so I get paid and you don't. Doesn't sound very fair to me." He turned to Dotti. "What do you think, Dotti? Any bright ideas?"

Dotti swung around in her chair, her nose wrinkled up to help secure her spectacles, her brow furrowed in thought. "Well," she said slowly. "I suppose what we could do is that if David does manage to find a place of his own, we could cover his expenses for food and rent. Then he would just be earning his board and lodgings."

Clive looked at David, a brighter look on his face. "How does that sound to you?"

"That sounds fine to me. I really don't need that much," David replied, relieved that the idea hadn't fallen foul at the last hurdle.

Clive looked over to his secretary, who was sitting with a huge grin on her face, seeing that her plan had been accepted. "You never cease to amaze me, Dotti," he said proudly. "You keep coming up with such wonderful ideas!" He ushered David to the door. "Now, give me a call on Monday evening and tell me how it went, and if you happen to have a new address by then, let me know."

David nodded and shook his hand. "I will—and thanks again."

As he headed off down the sidewalk, Clive remained standing at the window, watching him as he went.

"What a nice man," Dotti said, a smile in her voice.

"Yes, he is," Clive said slowly, "But quite a mystery, methinks."

Dotti got up from her desk and came over to stand beside him. Together they watched David's distancing figure. "What do you mean?"

"I don't really know." He turned from the window and walked back to his desk. "One could have quite easily taken him for a banker or some high-flying executive, but I don't know if you noticed his hands, Dotti. They're all calloused and as hard as leather. I mean, that man really has been a labourer." He sat down with a thump and let out a long sigh. "I hope we've made the right decision, Dotti. Do you think he's all right?"

"Yup, I think he's great," she said, making her way back to her own desk. "But I don't think he's Scottish, Clive. I mean, does he sound Scottish to you?"

David took his time walking back to North Harlens, trying to work out in his mind whether his recent action was prompted by fateful inspiration or whether it was quite simply irrational stupidity. On a number of occasions, he stopped and thought about turning back there and then to cancel the job, as his mind churned through considerations of duties and responsibilities that he held for both his children and his parents. And then, on the other hand, if he did take the job, he would have to tell Richard of his plans fairly promptly, something made more difficult by the fact that his behaviour over the past few days could not have qualified him for The Perfect House Guest award. As he walked, he eventually came to the decision that it would be best not to say anything to anyone for the time being. He would go to the new job on Monday, and if it didn't work out, he would just pack up and return to Scotland midweek, without anyone ever being the wiser.

But then, he really didn't want to go back just yet. No. Again that wasn't true at all. Of course he wanted to go back—he wanted to see the children more than anything, and he knew that he couldn't expect his father to fill in for him at Glendurnich for ever. Nevertheless, a return to Inchelvie at that very minute, with all its inherent connections with Rachel, would be a retrograde step, and even now, as he walked along the sidewalk, he felt his stomach knot tight with apprehension and foreboding at the thought of it. He was quite simply not ready for it, and he knew deep within himself that he *could* mend right here in Leesport, with its quiet, sunny surroundings, its gentle pace, and its friendly inhabitants who could take him at face value, without constantly having to make allowances in the way that they treated him.

That was, of course, everyone except Richard. Even though his friend could not have been more kind or understanding, he knew too much about him, and as such would always represent a link to his past and a threat to his anonymity in the future. If he were to stay, then he needed to get away entirely, to find a place or even just a room to rent to allow himself the space and time to get his mind straight again.

Having made a number of unnecessary detours in order to collect his thoughts, he arrived back at the house to find an old convertible Volkswagen Beetle parked haphazardly in the driveway. Its faded hood was folded down as far as the rusting support struts would allow, disclosing an interior that was littered with paint tubes and brushes, free-offer leaflets, chocolate-bar wrappers and empty Coca-Cola cans, while the steering wheel and gear-shift were freckled with tiny irregular twin grooves cut deep into the plastic, making it look as if both had been subjected to attack on numerous occasions by an inebriated rattlesnake.

As he skirted round the car, studying the assortments of dents and scratches that adorned its orange bodywork, a loud splash sounded out from Richard's swimming pool, followed by the manic barking of a small dog. He climbed the stairs to the deck and, walking over to the side rail, looked down onto the pool. A girl in a fluorescent yellow swimsuit was swimming lengths in a rapid overarm crawl, her long streaked-blonde hair flowing out across her back as her powerful strokes created a wake that washed against the side of the pool, soaking the orangy-brown miniature poodle who, barking incessantly, accompanied her length by length.

As she turned at the shallow end, the dog realized that it was caught up in a hopeless endeavour and sat down panting, continuing to watch her mistress through woolly eyes as she swam up to the deep end. David turned away to go into the house, but his movement was caught by the dog, and it came running round the edge of the pool and took up position at the bottom of the steps, squinting up at him and yapping furiously. Hearing the commotion, the girl, who by now had made it back to the shallow end, stopped swimming and stood up, wiping away the water from her face with the flat of her hands.

"Dodie! For goodness' sakes, be quiet!"

She blinked a couple of times to clear the sting of chlorine from her eyes, then, visoring them against the glare of the sun, she looked up at him. "Hi! You must be David. At last we meet! I'm Carrie."

"Oh, hi!" David replied, holding up his hand to acknowledge her greeting, a sign which the dog immediately took as a threatening gesture to its mistress, and resumed its high-pitched bark.

"DODIE!"

The dog turned and jumped up onto one of the sunbeds and sat there, scratching at its tight mat of untrimmed curls and yawning loudly.

"Sorry about the dog," Carrie said, sinking down into the pool and slowly breast-stroking the water away from her body. "She gets quite protective. Not that she could do much. She's only got two teeth!" She looked back up at him. "So, how're you feeling now?"

"Much better, thanks." He held up the bunch of flowers. "I bought these for you, just to, well, thank you for supplying me with all that food over the past couple of days—and to apologize for being so antisocial."

Carrie waved her hands in the air. "Oh, that is so *sweet* of you! God, you mustn't think anything of it! I just, well, feel so sorry—you know—for what happened to your wife. That was such a terrible thing."

David nodded and glanced down at his feet for a moment, before turning towards the house. "Listen, I'll go and put them in some water. Is Richard in?"

"I think so. I haven't been inside yet. I only just arrived before you and jumped straight in here, so I'm really not that sure. But hey, I'm only going to do another couple of lengths and then I'll be right in."

"Well, please don't hurry because of me."

"Okay!" Carrie said, and with a flourish of her hand she turned and duck-dived into the water and resumed her swim. Dodie, obviously feeling restored after her brief respite on the sun-bed, let out another of her high-pitched yelps and took up position once more at the side of the pool.

David had just finished putting the flowers into a jug of water on the draining-board when he heard the sound of Richard's footsteps on the upstairs landing.

"David?" he called out, as he came down the stairs.

"Yeah?"

He walked into the kitchen. "God, where the hell have you been? I was about to send out a search party."

"Sorry, I should have left a note. I decided on the spur to go out for a walk—see a bit of Leesport."

Richard smiled at him. "Good for you. So—how are you feeling?"

David nodded. "Better, thanks. Kicked off the flu, anyway."

"Right. And, er, how about, well, sort of in yourself?"

"Okay—I think."

"Good." They stood, an uneasy silence between them, the reservation of their male emotions making it difficult for either to know how to react to the other. The moment was broken by Carrie, who appeared through the French windows, rubbing her hair dry with a huge blue bathing-towel.

"Hi, Richard!" she said in a singsong voice. "What a nice friend you have! Look what he brought me!" She walked over to the jugful of carnations and took a deep inhalation of their sweet smell before turning back to David. "That really was the *nicest* thought!"

She was wearing a pink cheesecloth dress pulled over her wet swimsuit which made it cling to the contours of her slightly overweight body. Not a classically pretty girl, David thought, her nose was too pointed and her front teeth protruded a little. Nevertheless, she had an inexplicably attractive aura. Her skin was clear and un-wrinkled, belying her age, which David reckoned as be-ing not far off his own, her mouth seemed to be set in a permanent smile and her eyes sparkled with life.

However, all this ethereal beauty was more than off-set by the appearance of her constant companion, Do-die. Seen close up, she looked as though someone, heavily under the influence of an hallucinatory sub-stance, had set about her coat with a pair of curling tongs, so that she resembled more a discoloured old powder puff than a poodle. Only she didn't smell like one. Having jumped up onto the sofa, she now sat pant-ing, looking directly at her mistress, and a doggie odour filled the room of which all except Carrie seemed to be aware.

"Jesus, Carrie," Richard said, wrinkling his nose up in disgust, "do we *have* to have Dodie inside? Can't you leave her in the car?"

"No, I can't," Carrie retorted, bending down to the dog. "Can I, Dodie-wodie? Last time I was cruel to you like that, you ate my steering wheel, didn't you, my little darling."

The dog responded by giving Carrie's face the once-over with its tongue.

"Jeez, Carrie, that is quite *revolting*! Her breath stinks!"

"Oh, well, you get used to it!" Carrie said light-heartedly as she straightened up. "Say, I'm kinda thirsty after that swim. Any chance of a beer?"

Richard glanced up at the wall clock. "Are you being serious? It's only eleven o'clock!"

"Well, it's Saturday, so there's nothing doing, and it's a beautiful day, and I want to get to know your friend."

Richard gave this a moment's contemplation before shrugging his shoulders and glancing at David. "She's right, of course. Always is." He made his way over to the refrigerator. "Three beers coming up then!"

They spent the rest of the day together by the pool, talking only when they felt like it and at odd intervals heading off into the house to bring out food and more beer. During the course of their intermittent conversation, David found out that Carrie was an artist whose itinerant lifestyle had, in her own words, resulted in her being "more successful at capturing scenes on canvas than men in matrimony." Yet there was not an ounce of bitterness or self-pity in the way that she said it. Both she and Dodie were free spirits, she said, living totally for themselves in their little house down by the marina.

That evening Carrie prepared a meal for them that was the complete antithesis to the inedible mess that David had had to endure on his first night in the house. They ate outside on the deck, the light of the setting sun bathing them in a warm red glow which seemed to match the spirit of the occasion. Carrie then succeeded in reducing both men to tears of laughter by recounting stories of her hippie days in San Francisco and her brief involvement with Hare Krishna.

"I was chucked out! I mean, I thought I was so *cool* at it! Then one day, I was out on the street and no one, I mean *no one* was interested in what I had to say about reaching the higher echelons of pure life enhancement, so, well, I had these big Doc Marten boots on, and I just sort of levelled a kick at this guy who was passing—and, er, I caught him between the legs. By mistake, I promise! I didn't mean to—sort of not, anyway!"

As night closed in around them, David sat back in his chair, a smile on his face, quite happy to allow the good-humoured, laid-back atmosphere flow over him, while Carrie continued to dominate the conversation, her scatty, disconnected monologues now directed towards giving a full account of her past painting trips abroad and the "true fulfilment" that each had brought her.

"Talking of which," she said, glancing at Richard, a sudden look of trepidation on her face, "do you have any idea when Angie's getting back?"

"Well, I spoke to her last night at your mother's and she thinks Wednesday. I hope to hell it is because I want to get this wretched conversion finished." He let out a deep sigh. "In her infinite wisdom, she decided to put off all further work until she returned."

"Uh-huh," Carrie replied absently.

"Why do you ask?"

"Well, it's just that, well, I'm heading off to Florence to paint for a couple of months, and she *did* say that she wouldn't mind looking after Dodie."

Richard groaned. "Oh, God, yes, she did mention that. I thought life was looking too good. When are you heading off?"

"Well, the flight's tomorrow evening."

"Oh, for heaven's sakes! What's going to happen to the dog between then and Wednesday?"

Carrie bit at her lip to stifle a laugh. "Well, I thought she could have just stayed—"

"Oh, not in the house, Carrie!"

"Why not?"

"Because she'll stink the place out! Anyway, I'm going to be at work all day, so there'll be no one to let her out. She'll just pee and shit everywhere!"

"She will not either! I've left her all day in the house. She just sleeps. I promise you, Richard, she has a constitution of a camel—or is it a hen? *Please,* Richard, all you'll have to do is let her out into the garden in the morning and when you come home in the evening." She paused and looked pleadingly at Richard. "It'll only be two and a half days."

Richard glanced a long-suffering look towards David, then took a long gulp from his wineglass. "Oh, what the hell! Okay, I'll agree to it on one condition."

"Which is?"

"That you give me full permission to attack her with a bottle of shampoo and some toothpaste every now and then!"

"Sssh!" Carrie held her index finger to her mouth and looked round through the fly-screen to where Dodie lay prostrate on the sofa in the kitchen. "Don't say it too loud or she'll hear." She turned back to Richard. "You can certainly try, but it never seems to make any difference!"

"Well, I'm going to give it a go, anyway." He tilted his head in the direction of the dog. "AREN'T I, DODIE?"

Dodie immediately lifted her head and pricked up her ears, then letting out one single bark, she flopped once more onto the sofa.

"Richard!" Carrie exclaimed in open-mouthed horror. "That is *so* cruel! You promise me you won't make her into a nervous wreck while I'm away."

"What is she now?" Richard laughed, then seeing his sister-in-law on the verge of rising to the bait, he leaned across the table and patted her arm in mock reassurance. "Don't worry, I'll look after her as if she was my own."

"Yeah, I bet!" Carrie gave him a distrustful look which she immediately managed to convert into one of sweet seduction. "Could you keep an eye on my house as well? Just when you're around, that is."

"Okay," Richard replied resignedly, leaning forward

and pouring out more wine into their glasses.

"Thanks . . . and, Richard?"

Richard's face broke into a smile at the persistence of her requests. "Yes, Carrie?"

"There wouldn't be a chance," she said slowly, as if already expecting a negative answer to her question, "that you could get Star Limos to take me to the airport?"

"On my account, I suppose!" He laughed. "What time tomorrow?

"About four-fifteen?" ·

"Okay, I'll organize that," he said, leaning back in his chair. "Just a pity it's not Monday. You could have shared a car with David."

"Oh, are you going back to Scotland on Monday, David?" Carrie asked, and the sound of her voice resounded out loud and clear into the evening as a sudden profound silence descended upon the table. Her two dining partners eyed each other in turn, the smiles no longer on their faces.

Richard eventually cleared his throat and rubbed at his chin nervously. "I hope that's all right, David. I actually, er, spoke to your mother on Wednesday just to say that you weren't, well, quite up to scratch, one way and another, and I thought that you'd probably want to get back to Scotland as soon as possible. So I thought the Monday-evening flight would probably be the best one. Your mother said that there'd be someone to pick you up at Glasgow on Tues——"

He tailed off at the end of this explanation, realizing that David was not really listening to him. He leaned forward in his chair and rested his elbows on his knees, clasping his hands in front of him.

"Listen, my friend," Richard continued quietly, "I'd hate you to think that I'd gone behind your back. It's just that, well, I was actually quite worried about you, and I wasn't quite sure what I was meant to do."

David smiled and shook his head. "No, it's me that

should be apologizing—not you. You've both been brilliant over the past few days, and I know that I haven't really shown you much appreciation for everything you've done." He shifted his weight on the chair, sticking his hands under his thighs. "It's just that . . ." He released one of his hands and scratched at the back of his head. ". . . Look, I have something to tell you which will no doubt come as a bit of surprise to you. I actually went into the little employment agency in Leesport this morning and lined up a job for myself as a gardener, and I'm, erm, starting Monday."

There was a complete silence, and David looked up to find both Richard and Carrie staring at him with looks of disbelief.

"But what about going home?" Richard asked eventually. "I mean back to Scotland?"

David let out a long breath. "To be quite honest, Richard, I . . . really . . . don't think . . . that I could face being back in Scotland just yet. I was walking around Leesport today, and I don't know quite what triggered it off, probably just the atmosphere of the place, but for the first time since Rachel died, I started to get everything into perspective, and I realized that heading back right now would just put me back to square one. I *know* that I have commitments, but well, I have a feeling that I've just reached rock bottom over the past couple of days, and I'm pretty sure that I'm on the way up again. So, in every way, I don't want to waste it—not only for myself but for my children and parents as well."

He took in a deep breath again before continuing.

"What you probably don't realize is that since Rachel became ill, I haven't been at work. I took time off to nurse her, and then, really as a form of, well, escapism, I suppose, I started to reinstate part of the gardens at my parents' house, and that's what I've been doing ever since . . . and I love it. I came over here on business because there was no one else in the company able to make the trip at that precise moment and . . . well, you know the rest of that story. Anyway, it was a complete fluke that I saw the job advertised today, and, as I said, I start on Monday."

David looked across to Richard and Carrie, who sat in silence, their sad eyes fixed on him. He let out a quiet laugh to try to break the gloomy atmosphere that he had created.

"I mean, I don't think that it'll be for very long," he said light-heartedly, "but it'll just give me time to get things in order, and I promise you, Richard, I won't burden either you or Angie with my presence. I'll get somewhere to stay as soon as I can."

"Hey!" Carrie suddenly exclaimed, making both Richard and David straighten in their chairs with surprise.

"Hey! Hey! Hey!" she said again, waving her hands in the air, looking as if she was trying to say something but couldn't work out how to put it.

"What's the matter, Carrie?" Richard asked, scowling at his sister-in-law for being so ebullient at a time when joyous reaction seemed totally inappropriate.

"It's obvious!" she said, jumping up from her chair and starting to dance around the deck in excitement. "David can stay in my house! That's it! He can stay in my house, and look after it. He can use my car, and well . . ." She stopped and grinned at the two men. ". . . Isn't that just a great idea?"

Richard raised his eyebrows and cocked his head to the side. "Well, it's an idea." He turned to David. "What do you think?"

David rocked forward in his chair, an excited look on his face. "Are you sure about that, Carrie?"

"Of *course* I'm sure!" Carrie said, resuming her dance around the deck. "Isn't it the greatest idea? You'd be doing us all a favour by looking after the place, because Richard wouldn't then have to be checking it out the whole time, and the battery wouldn't go dead on the car. Oh, it's great! I'm so pleased with myself!"

They broke out laughing at Carrie's flighty celebrations, and Richard reached for the bottle and began pouring out great splashes of wine into their glasses.

"Great thinking, Carrie!" he said, picking up his glass and raising it high in the air. "Well, I think we should all drink a toast to the newest resident of Leesport Village!"

Carrie sat down again and grabbed her glass, and all three clinked their glasses together at the centre of the table before taking huge mouthfuls of wine. Then, almost as if a huge black cloud had been lifted from their little gathering, they sat back in their chairs and breathed out huge sighs of relief.

"Well, it's all right for you, David," Richard said, turning to him. "You're all sorted out, but Angie and I are still going to be left to look after the dreaded Dodie!"

"Richard!" Carrie exclaimed, reaching over and hitting him on the arm, "you said you wouldn't be horrible to her. She's not the dreaded Dodie, anyway. She's the delightful Dodie!"

"All right, then, the delightful Dodie," Richard moaned, "but I still think we've got the rough deal!"

"Listen," David said, a pensive expression registering on his face, "if you want, *I* could quite easily look after the dog. In fact, the more I think about it, the more sense it makes. She'd probably be much happier at her own house, and anyway, she can quite easily come with me when I'm gardening. It really would be no problem, and I mean, I really like dogs. I've always had dogs."

He looked across at the others, expecting his offer to be accepted unconditionally, but was confronted by two very surprised faces, and for a moment he wondered if he had made completely the wrong suggestion.

"You don't mean that, do you, David?" Carrie asked quietly.

"Of course I mean it. I'd be quite happy to look after

her—anyway, for as long as I'm over here. She'd actually be doing *me* a favour by keeping me company!"

Carrie let out a yelp that wasn't unlike one of Dodie's and, jumping out of her chair, leaped towards him, engulfing his head in her arms.

"Oh, I think you're just the best!" she said, repeatedly kissing him on the top of the head. "Oh, how I cherish the day you walked into our lives!"

The ensuing commotion was loud enough to catch Dodie's attention. She let out one of her high-pitched barks and, jumping off the sofa, pushed her way through the screen door and locked her two teeth into one of the legs of David's jeans. Growling ferociously, she shook her head from side to side, as if determined to end the life of his Levi's.

"Come on, Carrie!" Richard laughed, suddenly feeling quite left out. "Give the guy a break! He's only said that he's going to look after Dodie!" He paused for a moment and looked down with little feeling of affection at the small, motley animal as it pulled hard on its quarry. Then he too slowly raised himself to his feet. "Actually, come to think of it, you're right! He's a bloody hero!"

With that, he threw himself forward to join Carrie in her adulation of "the saviour of the day," binding them both in tight with his arms, as if scrummaging down in a game of rugby. There was a loud crack as his extra weight was added to David's chair, and its legs slowly began to spread-eagle underneath him. With a crescendo of screams, the dissembled company pitched backwards and fell in a heap to the deck, allowing Dodie, amidst loud protestations and uncontrollable laughter, to have a field day in licking the faces of her incapacitated victims.

Chapter

SIXTEEN

Headaches were plentiful in the Eggar household the next day, the celebrations of the previous night having gone on well into the small hours of Sunday morning. Consequently, the plan to shift David and his belongings down to Carrie's house was delayed until the afternoon, a time when Richard felt he might be brave enough to venture out into the bright sunlight.

David, however, chose to clear his head by taking a walk midway through the morning, wanting at any rate to find out where he was meant to be working the following day. He made his way into Leesport, stopping to pick up a much-needed cup of black coffee at the deli, then, having asked directions to Barker Lane, he headed off in the opposite direction to the one he had taken the previous day.

Barker Lane was the last turning on the left before the Leesport Country Club, which lay just beyond the village boundary. He walked the full length of the road, eventually coming across the house in the bottom corner, opposite to where the road swung hard left through ninety degrees to run parallel to the bay, leading onto the marina half a mile away. The property was hidden completely from the road, the driveway descending in a bend through a screen of tall leafy birch-trees and high laurel bushes. For a moment, David stood at the head of the drive, spinning his empty Styrofoam cup around his finger while he considered taking a closer look. However, at that point a car came round the corner from the direction of the marina, and not wanting to give the appearance that he was loitering with intent, he decided to head back to North Harlens the way he had come, leaving his appraisal of the house until the next day.

Richard eventually managed to get his act together at four o'clock in the afternoon. Having bundled David's meagre belongings into the back of his car, they drove the four hundred yards down to Carrie's house, which happened to be situated right next to where he had eaten his breakfast the previous morning in the Leesport Memorial Garden. Both Carrie and Dodie were there to greet them at the gate, Carrie holding hard on to the end of a gushing hose, having been busy giving the plants one final watering before leaving. She opened the gate, then rushed away to the side of the house to turn off the tap. David took his two cases from the trunk of the car and followed Richard into the garden through the opening in the head-high, neatly clipped yew hedge.

If anyone wanted to look in on the property, the only unrestricted vantage point would have been from a boat positioned out on the Great South Bay. The easterly boundary was protected by a bank of high, waving pampas-grass that rustled and whispered in the warm afternoon breeze, while the dogrose hedge that ran around the periphery of the Memorial Garden encroached over onto the westerly side, spreading its weight across the collapsing picket fence that lay beneath it. Borders alive with flowering rhododendrons and azaleas, their heady scent brought out by the recent watering, skirted the lawn of springy zoysia grass which ran forward to the heavy wood pilings that jutted down into the waters of the bay. Still carrying his cases, David walked across the lawn to where it had been cut away into a steep gradient. Rough wooden steps had been sunk deep into the sandy soil to afford access to a small wooden jetty, where an old rowing-boat, its dark blue paint peeling away from its bows, nudged gently against its rubber-tyred mooring-post.

Richard and Carrie seemed to have disappeared inside by this time, so David made his way back across the lawn to seek them out. The house was nothing more than a tiny dark brown shingled shack tucked up into the farthest corner of the garden, next to the dogrose hedge. Yet it was far from shabby, its windows and shutters, downpipes and gutters all newly painted in brilliant white, its shingles giving off a strong aroma of newly applied creosote. The main entrance door was at the side of the house, while at its front, a screened veranda extended out from the French doors, its only furnishings two faded deck-chairs that were turned to face out over the waters of the Great South Bay.

There was a sudden scream from inside the house and Carrie appeared at the door lugging a huge suitcase and a folded-down painting easel, closely followed by Richard who, still suffering from his overindulgence of the night before, was making a half-hearted attempt to wrest some of the burden from his sister-in-law.

"Oh my God, David!" Carrie said, seeing him and dropping the suitcase heavily onto Richard's foot as he took it from her. "I've just realized what the time is! Star Limos will be at North Harlens right now, so I'm afraid I'm going to have to leave you to fend for yourself." She delved into the pocket of her dungarees and pulled out a set of keys. "Everything you need is on that. The saltbox, the car, and the little one is the key for the boat's outboard motor, which is in the sunporch. By the way, there's a fax-cum-phone in the house which just use whenever you want."

Putting his cases on the ground, David took the

bunch of keys from Carrie, giving her a puzzled look. "Right—and where might I find this saltbox, and what the hell do I use it for?"

Carrie flashed him a wide smile of enlightenment as she pointed towards the house. "You live in it, David! That's a saltbox, albeit a pretty small one. Don't ask me why they're called that. I don't know." She smiled and shrugged her shoulders. "I've never thought to ask." She turned and hurried towards the gate, against which Richard was now leaning, rubbing his sore foot.

"Oh my God!" she said, turning back to David, "I haven't said goodbye." She threw her arms around his neck and gave him a kiss on either cheek. "Look after yourself, David, and . . . well . . . start afresh—make this your new beginning."

David put his arms around her waist and gave her a long, tight hug. "Thanks, Carrie, I think I will."

Carrie pushed herself away and smiled up at him, her cheeks lightly flushed. "Wow! Go on squeezing me like that, and I may just decide to stick around," she said in a Mae West voice.

"Come on, Carrie," Richard called out.

"Coming!"

She turned and made her way out through the gate. Richard gingerly put weight on his foot and looked across to David. "Listen, you will telephone your mother, won't you? I feel slightly guilty about sticking my oar in on your business."

"You haven't at all—and I promise you I'll call her and explain what's happening."

Richard smiled at him. "You all right, old friend?"

"Couldn't be better."

"Well, if you need anything or want a swim in the pool, either give us a call or just come over."

"I will—and Richard—thanks for everything."

Richard waved his hand dismissively, then, holding both hands up in Al Jolson mode, he sang out, "That's what friends are for!"

There was yet another scream from outside the garden, and Carrie came rushing in once more.

"What the hell's wrong now?" Richard asked, exasperated.

"I haven't said goodbye to Dodie!" Carrie wailed. "You must have shut her in the house!"

Richard sighed impatiently. "Oh, come on, Carrie. Dan will get fed up waiting."

Carrie opened the door and Dodie appeared, jumping up and down in excitement. She scooped up the dog in her arms and planted a kiss on its head. "Bye, bye, my darling. You be good now, and look after David."

She bundled Dodie into David's arms and rushed out to where Richard now waited for her in the car. David followed her through the gate and stood waving as the car turned with a squeal of tyres and headed up the road. As soon as it was out of sight, Dodie let out a wheak and tried to escape from David's clutches so that she could catch up with her mistress.

"Come on, dog," he said, getting a firmer hold on his charge, "you can show me round your house."

Dodie gave him a bewildered look and started to pant vigorously, an action which made David hurry back through the gate to release her from his grasp as quickly as possible into the safe confines of the garden.

The fact that Carrie treated her car as if it were a dustbin had no bearing on the way in which she organized her house. David stood in the doorway and looked around the small, lovingly furnished dwelling, warm with the sun that flooded in through the windows, each of them hung with red gingham curtains tied back with matching strips of ribbon. In the centre of the room, a round polished mahogany table, piled with magazines, sat between two armchairs with brightly coloured slipcovers, which faced a wood-burning stove whose blackened chimney stuck straight up through the roof.

To his left, on one side of the French doors, a high

row of shelves, made out of bricks and planks, stretched up to the ceiling, each fully stocked with art books and paperback novels, while space had been made on its top shelf for an old turntable stereo system and Carrie's sizeable collection of records. On the other side of the doors, a roll-top desk lay open, its cubby-holes crammed with papers, while its leather writing surface was taken up completely with the telephone/fax machine.

To his right, lined against the back wall of the house, was the kitchen. Space for preparing a meal was minimal, but it still comprised all the necessities of a cooker, a fridge, and a sink. Above these, balanced precariously on nine-inch nails that had been driven into the wall, were four wooden storage shelves, their contents hidden behind curtains that matched those on the windows.

David dropped his cases to the floor and walked over to the heavy damask drapery that hung at the far end of the room. Behind this, he found a small double bed, which Carrie had sweetly made up for him with fresh linen, the corner having been turned down in a welcoming gesture over the top of the patchwork quilt. The only other furniture in the room was a pine chest of drawers, a bedside table with a lamp, and an up-ended packing case which served as a hanging closet. At the bottom of the bed, a door led off into a tiny bathroom into which was crammed a shower, a basin and a lavatory, the close proximity in the positioning of the latter two making David wonder whether the room hadn't been designed by, or even for, a minute contortionist.

He pulled open the drapery, hooking it back against the wall with the heavy sisal-rope loop, then, sitting down on the edge of the bed, he surveyed the whole scene in its entirety, noticing for the first time that every spare inch of hanging space on the walls was taken up with vibrant oil paintings: of beach scenes, of faces and figures, of streets, of exotic castles—all painted in the same distinctive style. He looked up at the one above his bed, and saw that it bore the signature "CL" in the bottom right-hand corner. They were all Carrie's work.

David grinned broadly to himself, then, falling back heavily on the bed, he gazed up at the ceiling, shaking his head in sheer contentment. This is perfect, he thought to himself, this is just perfect. He let out a chortle. Just a pity about the smell. The smile vanished from his face. Oh, Christ, the dog! Where the hell was she? He jumped to his feet and ran towards the door, hurdling over his suitcases on the way. He flung it open and was preparing to let out a loud whistle when Dodie scuttled in between his feet, bounced straight up onto one of the armchairs, and sat looking at him, her head cocked to one side.

"Good girl," he said, breathing out a sigh of relief. He shut the door and picked up his cases. "Right, come on. Let's get unpacked."

By the time the sun had shed its last dying rays on the day, he had everything in order, his belongings put away and his empty suitcases pushed out of sight underneath the bed. Not knowing if Dodie had been fed, he took out a half-used can of dogfood from the fridge, at the same time selecting a couple of eggs for himself. He spooned the meat into a plastic dish, which he had located under one of the armchairs, and gave it to Dodie who, judging by the speed with which she wolfed it down, seemed to suffer little from her lack of dental power. Then, while his eggs boiled furiously on the cooker ring, he pulled down Carrie's collection of records and, holding them in the crook of his arm, he began to flick through the covers.

They were magical, every one of them of his vintage: Jefferson Airplane, The Beatles, Bob Dylan, Joni Mitchell, The Velvet Underground, The Rolling Stones. He selected Dylan's *Nashville Skyline,* and placed it on the table, then, pushing the remaining sleeves back together again, he carried them back to the shelf. As he reached up, the bottom record slipped from his grasp and fell with an ominous clatter to the floor. Swearing to himself and grimacing at the thought that it might be broken, he picked it up and slid the record out of its sleeve. It was undamaged. Blowing out a puff of relief, he reached up to replace it on the pile when the title on the cover suddenly caught his eye. *Motown Greatest Hits*. He paused, holding the sleeve in his hands, then slowly, as if tempting providence, he turned it over. It was there. Smokey Robinson and the Miracles. He looked at it for no more than three seconds, then, quickly and decisively, he returned it to the shelf, sliding it in as far as it possibly would go at the bottom of the pile. "Start afresh," Carrie had said, "make this your new beginning."

To the strains of Bob Dylan he ate his boiled eggs, seated in one of the sagging deck-chairs on the veranda, while Dodie, perched on the other, willed him with plaintive looks to share his food with her. He peeled the shell off the top of one of the eggs and threw the contents to Dodie, who missed it with the first snap of her jaws, but then consumed it voraciously once she had worked out where it had landed. Later, having washed up his plates, he left them to drip-dry on the draining-board, then, wiping his hands on the seat of his jeans, he walked over to the desk and turned on the little light above it. He shifted the fax machine as far into the corner as it would go, then, opening up his brief-case, he took out a sheet of paper and a pen, and settled himself down to write a long, clarifying fax to his parents.

Chapter

SEVENTEEN

"Oh, do get out of the way, boys!" Alicia shouted out, as she nearly tripped over the dogs on her way to the breakfast table, making the two brimming coffee-cups that she carried clatter unsteadily in their saucers. She was not in the best of humour that morning—she knew this, and it was so unusual for her to feel this way that it only seemed to aggravate her mood. Certainly the telephone ringing in the middle of the night hadn't helped, and although it had cut off almost immediately without even giving her the chance to lift the receiver, it had been enough to wake George. She had consequently spent the rest of the night with little chance of sleep, as he moved about restlessly in the bed, pulling the covers away from her, trying to find a position that would give him some relief from the nagging pain in his back. She was sure it was getting worse, and what's more, he now complained about—no, complained was the wrong word—remarked on other aches which seemed entirely unconnected with his war wound. She was worried—worried about this, and worried about the increasing demands put on him by the changes at Glendurnich. He had spent the whole weekend in the office with Duncan Caple, and now, on Monday morning, he couldn't even spare the time to come to have his breakfast.

She put down the cups on the table and walked over to the door and opened it. "Geordie!" she called out, her voice echoing around the hall.

"Yes?" George's distant voice sounded out from the drawing-room.

"What are you doing? Your breakfast is getting cold."

"Just coming," he replied.

Alicia returned to the dining-room and walked back to the far end of the table, sitting down heavily in her seat. She took a brittle piece of toast out of the rack and began to butter it, but only succeeded in making it break off into numerous shards on her plate. Sucking her teeth, she put on her glasses and picked up the newspaper and, giving it an annoyed shake, began scanning through the headlines just as George walked into the room.

"What have you been doing?" she said, looking at him over the top of her spectacles. Folding up the paper, she rose to her feet and walked over to the sideboard. "Your sausages are more like burnt offerings now."

"Sorry about that, old girl," he said, coming over to stand beside her. She gave him the plate, and he exchanged it with a long, handwritten fax. "This came in last night. I thought it must have been a fax when the phone cut off. It's from David."

"Ah, right!" Alicia said, a lighter tone in her voice, as she walked back to the table and sat down. "It'll probably be about his arrival time at Glasgow."

"Er, no, it's not," George said. "Just read it."

He took his plate over to the table and sat down next to his wife, and to avoid making eye contact with her while she read the fax, he picked up the paper and made a show of reading it, at the same time carving away at his over-cooked sausages. Alicia looked at him warily, understanding every one of his actions too well, and therefore realizing that the news was probably not going to be to her liking. She began to read.

George had laid his knife and fork together on the plate by the time Alicia folded up the fax and put it down on the table. She took off her spectacles and sat back in her chair without saying a word. George watched her, waiting to hear her reaction.

"Well?" he asked.

"Well," Alicia replied, shaking her head slowly. "I don't really know what to say. On one hand—yes—I can understand his point about getting away, and—well, if he comes back something like his normal self, then—yes, it's a good idea. But then he's talking about a month, I would say, at the least! So, for a start, he won't be back for the children's leave-out, which he said he would be, and then there are all these sweeping changes at Glendurnich." She paused. "I mean, I'm delighted that he seems to be better, but—well—my thoughts are now that if that's the case, then maybe he should come home, and start taking some of the pressure off you." She picked up the fax and unfolded it, starting to read it through again. "It really *does* seem that he's much better, wouldn't you say?"

George took a slice of toast and began buttering it, only to have as little success as his wife, a piece shooting off the side of his plate and onto the floor. He bent down laboriously to retrieve it.

"I don't think that he should come back just yet," he said, his voice strained from the exertion of his quest.

"What do you mean?" Alicia said. "Geordie, just leave the toast. Effie's going to be hoovering in here later."

"Dog's got it anyway," George said, straightening up.

"Listen, Geordie, I'm afraid that I have to disagree with you, because I simply cannot allow you to continue to work at this pace much longer. It was fine to begin with, when you were only just standing in for

David, but now so much is happening, and I really don't think it's doing you any good at all. He has got to come back and help you."

George took a drink of his coffee and looked across at his wife.

"No, Alicia, I want him to stay out there. I was going to suggest it anyway before he left, that he should go to spend some time with the Richardsons in Massachusetts or the Penworths in Virginia, and that's why I bought him an open-ended ticket. So I'm quite happy that he's found this job." He paused momentarily. "I really do think that if he comes home right now, my dear, there is every chance his recovery would be short-lived. I grant you that he does appear to be better, but remember, it was only three days ago that his prognosis was entirely the opposite. I would think that the mending process has only just begun, and I want to make damned sure that when he does return, he's as near back to his old self as possible, so that he's quite ready to take over his position as marketing director once more. I mean, to put it bluntly, the future of the family involvement with Glendurnich depends on him."

Noticing the frown of concern registering on Alicia's face, George laid his hand reassuringly on top of hers. "Look, don't worry about me. I'm fine, I promise you. Anyway, today we have this new marketing director coming up from London, and even if it's not the ideal situation, at least he'll be taking some of the work-load off both Duncan and myself. To be quite honest, I've been feeling a bit guilty about some of the harsh words I've said about Duncan lately. He also expressed concern about my well-being over the weekend, and really he's as adamant as you that, once this new chap has settled in, I should take things a bit easier and not bother going into the office quite so frequently. And as far as the children are concerned, we'll just have them back here for the leave-out. These are all temporary measures, my darling." Draining his coffee-cup, he stood up and walked round behind Alicia, putting his hands on her shoulders. "Listen, David has given us his fax number. I suggest we write back a really positive message to him, saying that we stand full square behind him and that he should go ahead with his plans. Do you agree?"

Alicia looked over her shoulder and, placing her hand on his, she smiled bravely up at him and nodded. "All right, agreed. But as long as you really do start taking it a bit easier, Geordie. I don't want anything to happen to you."

George leaned over and planted a kiss on the top of his wife's head. "Nothing is going to happen to me." He let out a laugh, and started to walk towards the door. "I'm not ready to kick the bucket yet!"

He turned round and gave her a wink, at the same time leaning heavily on his stick and jauntily kicking one heel up behind him.

Chapter EIGHTEEN

The next morning, David was awoken both suddenly and prematurely by Dodie, who, having ventured onto his bed sometime during the night, felt that six o'clock was an apt time to give his face an unscheduled and somewhat unwelcome wash. With a start, he pushed her off the bed, then lay for a moment dazedly working out his new surroundings and listening to the birds noisily airing their dawn chorus outside in the garden.

From the other side of the room, the dog let out a wheak, and he turned his head on the pillow to see her standing hopefully by the door. He threw back the bedclothes and got to his feet and went over to open the door for her, and with two short barks, she slipped through the narrow gap and sped outside into the garden.

Having made himself a steaming cup of instant coffee, he was about to head to the bathroom when he stopped with a click of his fingers. He glanced at his watch and worked out what time it would be in Scotland. Exactly 11:05 A.M. He went over and sat down at the desk and, picking up the telephone, dialled a number.

He was midway through a gulp of coffee when a

female voice answered. "Good morning, Hatching's School."

"Ah, hullo." He put the coffee-cup down on the floor beside him. "Would it be possible to speak to Sophie Corstorphine?"

"Who's calling?"

"It's her father—from America."

"Ah yes, Mr. Corstorphine. Now if I'm quick, I might just be able to catch her after break-time. Could you hold for a minute while I check her whereabouts?"

"Certainly."

A light scratching on the front door heralded the return of Dodie. He pressed the "monitor" button on the telephone and went over to let her in, just as Sophie's voice sounded through the speaker.

"Hullo, Dad? Hullo? Hullo?"

David dived for the receiver and turned off the monitor. "Hullo, Sophie?"

"Hi, Dad!"

"That was quick! I wasn't expecting you to be found so fast."

"No, well, I was just walking along the corridor on my way to a class when Miss Jenkins caught me. She says that you're still in America."

"Yeah, I am."

"What time is it over there?"

"Erm"—he looked at his watch—"precisely seven minutes past six in the morning."

Sophie laughed. "Isn't it ridiculous! We've had French, Biology and Maths already today, and you've only just got out of bed!"

"Yeah, it does seem a bit unfair, doesn't it? Hang on a minute." He paused long enough to hurl a cushion at the dog, who had just deemed his bed a suitable place to carry out her morning's ablutions. "So, how's everything going? Did Granny come down on Saturday?"

"Yes, she did *and* she was able to watch me playing tennis, seeing that Charlie's cricket match was cancelled. Clevely Hall had something like chicken-pox going round."

"Right. So did you win?"

"No. Mr. Hunter thinks it's because Rosie Braithwaite and I chatter too much on court."

"And do you?"

"Well, it's very difficult, Dad! If we suddenly think of something really important to say to each other, we have to say it straight away, otherwise we'll just forget!"

"So what was so important to say on Saturday?"

"Er," Sophie giggled, "actually, we were wondering what kind of shampoo we should recommend to one of our opponents, because she had terribly greasy hair!"

David laughed. "Well, that sounds *really* important, Sophie. Worth throwing the match for!"

"We *didn't* throw the match! We just, well, got rather hysterical and we couldn't hit a ball! Anyway, Dad, I'll have to get back to class."

"Okay, but don't go just yet. I, er, want to ask you something."

"What?"

"Well, it's just that . . . well, what would you honestly think if I said that I was going to stay over here for a short while?"

"What? In America?"

"Yes."

"Why?"

"Well, I suppose for a short holiday."

Sophie was silent for a moment. "How long's a short holiday?"

"I don't know. About a month, maybe."

He heard her tut down the line. "That isn't a *short* holiday, Dad!"

"Yes, I know. It's just that, well, I've sort of lined up a temporary job for myself, and a month is the least time that I can do. But I really don't need to do it, Sophie, if you would much rather I came home."

Sophie let out a long sigh. "No, I think it's a good idea, Dad. I said to Granny last week that you should stay out there for a bit, and anyway, I'm going to be revising for my exams all through leave-out."

"Did you really say that to Granny?"

"Yeah, I did! I think you need a change-of-scenery sort of thing."

David felt a sudden lump rise in his throat, hearing his young daughter say such reasoned words of understanding.

"But you will write, won't you?"

"Of *course* I will!"

"And you will be back before the holidays start?"

"I promise you."

"Well—no real objections, then. Do you want me to tell Charlie and Harriet?"

"I don't know. Maybe it would be better if I spoke to them myself."

"No, just write them a letter and I'll tell them. It'll probably go in one ear and out the other with Charlie anyway, and Harriet seems happy enough, so I won't go on about it too much to her. Listen, Dad, I'd better go. Write really *soon*, won't you, and whatever you do, don't forget my sixteenth birthday if you're not back for it, okay? Bye. Love you lots!"

David put down the receiver and sat for a moment staring at the wall, his mind torn between feeling relieved at her acceptance of the plan and sheer guilt at the impulsiveness of it all. He rose slowly from the chair. Well, it may be a complete disaster, anyway, in which case, as he had decided before, he would just go home. He took his towel from the tail-board of the bed and walked into the bathroom. Just play it by ear, that's the best thing.

He didn't really need to take the car to work that day. The Newmans' house was well within walking distance, and thanks to Dodie, he had more than enough time. However, he did want to go via the deli to get himself breakfast and something for lunch, and after work, he planned to stock up with provisions at Hunter's SuperSaver, before calling in at Helping Hands to tell Clive of his change of address.

He left the house at twenty past eight, stepping out into a day that promised to be as hot and as clear as the one before, the sky a glaring blue, with the morning sun sitting like a burning globe atop the waving bank of pampas-grass. He toyed with the idea of putting down the hood of the Beetle, but being unsure of how Dodie behaved in the car, he thought better of it. He opened the door and the dog jumped in, pushing herself between the two front seats into the back, where she sat panting with excitement. David climbed in after her and, putting the key into the ignition, went to fire up the engine. However, it was immediately apparent that Carrie's lack of automotive interest was all-encompassing, as it took at least a minute of fruitless cranking, accompanied by numerous backfires, before the engine eventually spluttered to life and he was able to start lurching his way up the road.

By a quarter to nine, he sat parked outside the Newmans' house, drinking coffee and eating the proverbial fried-egg sandwich, and smiling wryly to himself as he wondered what the workmen outside the deli must have thought of him with his little hippie vehicle and the poodle bouncing around inside. He drained the Styrofoam cup and, having stuffed his litter back into the brown paper carrier, he once more coaxed the engine to life and pulled into the driveway.

It was by far the largest and most opulent property that he had seen in Leesport. The gravelled drive, which led down to the rear of the house, was flanked by a wide expanse of well-kept lawn and overhung by the leafy branches of oak- and birch-trees that alternated on each side of its one-hundred-yard length. The house itself was a long Colonial-style building, the cedar shingles on its upper and lower stories being finished in different stains, giving it a two-tone effect. To the west of the house a large glass conservatory topped by a white balustraded veranda extended out to trap the evening light, while at the east end a passageway, subtly blended into the fascia, joined the old stable on to the main block of the house. A clematis montana bursting with pink flowers climbed over the entrance porch and meandered its way upwards to cover part of one of the dormer windows on the top floor, while flower-beds alive with azaleas and dwarf rhododendrons in bloom ran the full length of the house.

David drove slowly down the drive, trying to make his arrival as unobtrusive as possible, and pulled the Volkswagen to a halt next to a metallic-blue BMW 318 parked at the front door. Then, immediately thinking that this might be somewhat presumptuous of a mere gardener, he reversed and parked under the trees next to a long wooden shed, its sides and roof strewn with a tangle of trumpet-vine. He cut the engine, and Dodie, eager to get on with her new adventure, jumped forward onto the front passenger seat and sat blinking hopeful looks up at him.

"Stay here for now, Dodie," he said, putting up the window and leaving several inches open at the top for air. "I'll come and get you in a minute."

He stood looking at the house, trying to work out where best he should go. Two dustbins sat beside the banistered steps that led down from the door in the stable, and presuming this to be the kitchen, he made his way towards it. He climbed the steps and knocked on the door, and as he waited, a muffled yelp sounded out from the Volkswagen. He turned to see Dodie's face peering longingly at him through the side window.

"Sssh! That's enough!" he said in the loudest whisper he could muster.

This seemed only to act as further encouragement to the dog, and she now followed up her muted overture with the main performance, throwing back her head and letting out a long, plaintive howl. David took a quick glance at the back door, and seeing that no one had yet answered his knock, he ran down the steps and started back towards the car, waving his hand in a downwards movement at the dog.

"Dodie!" he called out, much louder, "get down and shut up!"

Dodie looked at him quite surprised, as if unused to being addressed in such harsh tones and, sliding her paws down the window, she slowly disappeared from sight. David turned back to the kitchen door, only to find that the whole episode had been witnessed.

"Oh, sorry!" he said, running back to the bottom of the steps. He looked up at the black woman who stood at the top, a grin stretched across her face.

"You havin' a bit of trouble?" she laughed.

David smiled and looked back at the car. "Sort of, yes. I've got a dog in the car who thinks she can order me around."

"Ah," the woman said, nodding her head slowly, "I'm glad it's a she. Obviously knows who should be the boss then!"

She was a large, happy-looking person, dressed in a strikingly bright pair of cotton trousers, a voluminous T-shirt and blue Reebok training shoes. David thought initially that she must have been in her early fifties, because of the faint wisps of grey that had begun touching at the edges of her tight black curls, but then, seeing her close up, he realized that it was almost impossible to guess her age, her face being as smooth and unlined as polished ochre.

"My name's David Corstorphine, and I—"

"Oh, of course," the woman cut in, her voice lifting in recognition of his name. "You've come from Helping Hands to do the garden."

"Yeah, that's right. Are you, erm, Mrs. Newman?"

She threw back her head and laughed heartily. "Heaven's sakes, no!" she said, putting forward her hand. "I'm Jasmine, Mrs. Newman's housekeeper."

David shook her hand. "Hullo, Jasmine, nice to meet you."

"Nice to meet you too, David. Come on in."

She stood aside and ushered David into the house, closing the door behind them. He had been right—it was the kitchen, a long, airy room with open rafter beams from which tracks of spotlights hung, its black-and-white tiled floor stretching the full length of the place. He was standing at the business end of the kitchen, from where he took in the custom-made units of reconditioned pine fitted with ultra-modern stainless-steel cooking hobs, deep freeze, refrigerator and eye-level oven. Dominating the centre of the room was a long refectory table with bentwood chairs pushed in around it. Its surface was scattered with open newspapers, cereal packets and plates, and in the middle stood a flourishing cactus, with a touch of surrealism added by a bicycle pedal, its chrome stalk pushed deep into the earth of the flower-pot.

Beyond the table, two sofas were grouped around a television, the space between them taken up with two enormous beanbags. The whole area was bathed in light from the three full-length French doors that extended the complete width of the far gable end, each being open to allow the warm breeze to blow into the room from the front garden.

"So," Jasmine said, walking over to the sideboard and flicking on the switch of the electric kettle. "Where you from? I love the accent."

"Scotland."

"Oh?" she said, leaning back against the unit and folding her arms. "You sure don't sound like any Scot I ever heard talk."

David smiled at her. "Well, it depends where you come from."

"Yeah, I guess it does." She pushed herself away from the unit and reached up for two mugs from one of the top cupboards. "Would you like some coffee?"

"Well, if you don't mind," David replied, putting his hands into the pockets of his jeans. "I don't want to hold you up."

"You're not," she said, picking up the coffee pot from the hob. "How you take it?"

"Black, please."

As Jasmine poured the coffee into the mugs, the urgent click-clicking of high-heeled shoes on stone flooring crescendoed towards them from the main part of the house.

"Jasmine!"

"In here!" she called out and walked out of the door in the direction of the voice.

David picked up his mug and, taking a cautious sip of the piping-hot coffee, started to move towards the French doors so that he could look out at the front garden.

"Listen, there's an old car out there with a dog in it that's going ballistic. Do you know who it belongs to?"

David stopped abruptly and swore quietly to himself.

"Yeah, it's all right. It's David, the new gardener from Helping Hands."

He turned and hurried over to the back door and craned his head against the window to see if he could catch a glimpse of the car.

"Oh, God, I forgot he was starting today. Look, I am so late, and I really need to get Benji to school, so maybe you could tell him what to do."

"Well, he's here in the kitchen."

There was a short pause before the click-clicking of the footsteps started again. David moved quickly away from the door and stood with his hands thrust into his back pockets, an inexplicable feeling of nervousness in the pit of his stomach at the prospect of meeting his new employer. Jasmine came back into the kitchen, followed by a tall, strikingly attractive woman in her mid-thirties. She was dressed in a fawn linen business suit worn casually over a cream silk blouse, its collar opened wide to reveal the full length of her slender neck. Her honey-blonde hair was pulled back from her lightly freckled face and gathered at the back of her head in a large gold clasp. She wore no make-up, save for the merest touch of pale lipstick on her mouth, and her only jewelled accessory was a pair of tiny diamond-studded earrings. In her hand she carried a brief-case, and across her shoulder, slung by a long strap, was a large crocodile-skin handbag.

"This is David," Jasmine said, grinning at him. "He's from Scotland."

"From Scotland, huh?" the woman said, coming no farther than where she had stopped next to Jasmine. "And do Scotsmen know more than Australians about gardening?"

David frowned, not understanding the context of her question. "I'm sorry?"

"Our last gardener was Australian. Actually he wasn't a gardener, he was a butcher. He could mow the lawns, but he treated everything in the flower-beds as if it were a weed. Do you know the difference?"

"Yes, I think so. I mean, yes, I know so." He inwardly kicked himself at the uncertainty of his reply.

"Good," she said, glancing briefly at Jasmine as if seeking approval that she had said enough to the new gardener. She looked back at him. "Well, I'm sure that Jasmine will show you where to find everything, and then you can, well, just get on with things." She caught sight of the clock on the wall. "Oh, God, Jasmine, look at the time! Where the hell is Benji? Could you find him and say I'll meet him in the car?"

"Okay." Jasmine disappeared off through the house.

"Oh, and Jasmine!" she called out after her.

"Yup!"

"Make sure that Germaine picks him up on time today. Benji said that he had to wait for at least half an hour outside the school last Wednesday."

"Okay, will do."

The woman turned and made her way towards the back door, and David, who still stood close by, quickly stepped forward and opened it for her. She glanced at him as she passed, a brief smile being the only acknowledgement of the gesture, and hurried her way down the wooden steps and along the path. David leaned forward out of the door to watch her go. As she approached the BMW, she began to talk urgently to a young boy who had emerged from the front door of the house and now walked unhurriedly towards the passenger door. He threw it open, slung in his school-bag, and got in. The woman revved up the engine and, with a spatter of gravel, reversed round in a tight arc and sped away up the drive.

David turned and walked back into the kitchen just as Jasmine entered through the other door.

"What a hassle!" She picked up her mug from the sideboard and took a sip. "Monday mornings are always like that." She made a face at the lukewarm contents of the mug, and throwing the remainder into the sink, she walked over to the table. "Give me a minute while I clear this up, then I'll show you where everything is."

"I suppose that that was Mrs. Newman?" David asked.

Jasmine turned from the table, her face aghast. "Oh, for heaven's sakes, I forgot to introduce you!" She picked up a stack of plates and carried them over to the dishwasher. "Yeah, that was Mrs. Newman. Jennifer, actually, she don't really like being called Mrs. Newman. She always moves like a whirlwind, so sometimes formalities just fly out the window."

"She obviously works, then."

"Yup, and how. She's what's called an account eexecutive with an advertising company in Manhattan, so she's away mostly during the week, usually Mondays through Wednesday or Thursday. She and her husband have an apartment in the West Village."

"Ah, right."

He paused for a moment, wondering whether it was preferable to remain silent or continue asking questions that might be considered inquisitive. Silence sounded like the wrong option. "And Mr. Newman? What does he do?"

"Oh, he's some big shot with a computer company. He was here for the weekend but left earlier this morning. He's away most of the time." She pushed the cereal packets into one of the cupboards and put her hand on the top of the unit, letting out a sigh of concern. "Hard on them both, I think. Don't manage to see much of each other, only on weekends, sometimes not even that." She supplied the dishwasher with detergent, shut the door and switched it on. "But it's really hardest on Benji."

"So what happens to him?"

"Benji? He stays here with me." She picked up a cloth, and giving it a quick rinse under the tap, set about wiping the surface of the table. "Right now, it's just three or four nights a week, depending when Jennifer gets back, but during the winter, I'm here for the whole week."

"Right."

She finished the table with a flourish and hung up the towel on a hook beside the oven. "Okay, so that's done. Come on, I'll show you the garden."

She began making for the French windows at the front.

"Er, Jasmine, would you mind if we went out the back? It's just that I want to let the dog out of the car."

She looked at him warily. "I'm not usually very good with dogs. It's not some kinda guard dog, is it?"

David snorted. "No, it's a poodle."

"A poodle?" She raised her eyebrows in surprise. "What in heaven's name are you doin' with a poodle?"

"It's not mine. I'm only looking after it for some-one."

Jasmine shrugged and walked towards the back door. "Okay, I think I can handle a poodle."

Dodie was delighted to see them, leaping up and down on the front seat of the car as she watched them approach. David let her out and instantly forgave her for having had yet another obvious gnaw at the steering wheel, in that she immediately gave Jasmine a rapturous welcome before endearing herself still further by picking up a piece of wood that was twice her own body weight and hauling it in circles around them.

Jasmine unlocked the door of the wooden shed next to his car and showed him where to find everything, then together they walked round to the front of the house. The garden was much larger than he had envis-aged, the trees on either side of the lawn running down to the edge of the bay. Over to the right, sheltered from the wind on all sides by a high evergreen hedge, was the swimming pool, a section of its sparkling blue water just visible through the white picket gate, and beyond this still, David made out the high wire-netting of a tennis court above the hedge. The uniformity of the lay-out was cleverly offset by the almost random position-ing of brightly coloured herbaceous borders, although the sparsity of vegetation in some was proof enough of the brutal treatment they had received at the hands of the last gardener.

"Pretty good, huh?" Jasmine said, surveying the gar-den with him.

"It's beautiful. It's so, well, peaceful."

"Yup," Jasmine said, nodding. "Sometimes too peaceful." She took a deep breath. "Okay, well, I'll let you get to work. You want anything, I'll be in the house."

She smiled and turned to make her way back to-wards the kitchen, then stopped and looked back at him. "Have you got anything for lunch?"

"Yeah, I stopped in at the deli on the way here."

"Okay, but come and eat it with me, and in future, don't bother with the deli. *I'll* give you lunch."

"That's very kind. Are you sure?"

Jasmine laughed and shook her head. "Of course I'm sure. Do I *look* unsure or somethin'?"

She turned and David watched her as she walked over to the French doors and back into the house. He looked down at Dodie, who was sitting at his feet staring up at him, her head cocked to the side, a twig now sticking out the corner of her mouth like a twisted cheroot.

"Right, Dodie, let's get started."

He reversed the sit-on mower out of the shed and started on the lawns that bordered the drive, and from the moment that he set the cutters in motion, he felt an instant and overwhelming sense of release. It was like a coming home, his return from the wilderness, and immediately the broken lines of communication and thought that he had had with Rachel in the garden at Inchelvie seemed reconnected. He smiled to himself, relishing the sweet smell of the newly cut grass, realizing now that this had been all that he needed since leaving Scotland, his whole spirit being further uplifted and revitalized by the heat of the sun on his body as he worked.

It took him the whole morning and the first part of the afternoon to cut all the lawns. Dodie ran alongside him for the first half-hour, but then, suffering from the heat and the sudden increase to her exercise regime, she chose to retire to the shade and lay watching him from beneath one of the blue awnings that were hung over the kitchen doors. David joined her and Jasmine for lunch at one o'clock, and the three of them sat together on the paved area outside the kitchen. They talked initially about Dodie, David explaining how his charge had come as a job lot, with a house and car attached. He only took the story back as far as Carrie, never mentioning Richard or Angie, and although to Jasmine his story seemed light and unconvincing, leaving many a question unanswered, she thought better than to ask them. She liked him; she liked his polite and unassuming manner, and his natural ability in displaying a genuine interest in herself. She talked easily about her employment with the Newmans, how she had started seven years ago as a domestic help, and how it had then evolved into her becoming their housekeeper, at the time that Jennifer decided to go back into full-time employment. Lunch went on much longer than it should have, and at two-thirty, accompanied by exclamations of horror at the time, they both jumped up from their chairs. David took off once more across the lawn on his mower, while Jasmine went into the house to continue with her work upstairs.

Having spent two hours giving Benji's room a much-needed clean, Jasmine was in the process of carrying the vacuum cleaner down the stairs when she heard the sound of a car pulling away on the front drive, followed by the sound of the back door slamming shut. She put the cleaner away in the cupboard under the stairs and walked through to the kitchen to find Benji helping himself to a carton of chocolate milk from the fridge.

"Hi, darlin', how's school today?"

"Gross," Benji replied.

"Did Germaine turn up on time?"

"She was five minutes late." Benji poured too much chocolate milk out into the glass, and it overflowed onto the sideboard. Jasmine picked up the cloth from beside the sink and was making her way over to clear up the mess, when Benji picked up the glass and deliberately flicked his hand across the spilt milk so that it sprayed over the floor.

"Benji!" Jasmine said, "Why'd'ya do that?" She bent down to wipe it up.

"Why'd'ya do that?" Benji said, imitating her voice, his mouth turned down at the corners. He carried his glass over to the television area, put it down on the floor and, flumping into one of the beanbags, he turned on the television with the remote control.

Jasmine finished wiping up the mess and rinsed the cloth under the tap, then, leaning her back against the sink, she folded her arms and watched him silently. He had really changed so much in the past year. He always had been such good fun, so full of crazy and wicked ideas, but now, ever since moving up to middle school, he had gotten all moody and uncommunicative, something she could understand of a kid in his mid-teens, but not for one of eleven years old.

Of course, it hadn't helped being kept back a year in elementary, because now all his friends were in the class above him, and he'd told her that none of them wanted to be seen around with him, because he was one year lower. And then, of course, the fact that he had put on quite a bit of weight over the past six months didn't help matters. Not that he was hugely fat, and since he was tall for his age, he didn't look out of proportion. But he certainly was unfit-looking, and it had been enough for him to be excluded from any of the school teams. However, she couldn't really understand why this had happened in the first place. He didn't eat that much at home, and the only explanation that she could come up with was that he might well be heading off to the candy shop in Leesport at lunch-break, much against his mother's every wish.

But then again, she never felt like questioning him about it. She walked over to him and bent down and patted him on the shoulder. "Want a swim?"

"I'm all right," he said, not taking his eyes off the television.

"Suit yourself," she said, raising her eyebrows in defeat. She turned and was about to walk away when she heard above the noise of the television the sound of Dodie barking in the garden. Benji heard it too, and he raised his head and looked out of the French doors, craning his neck to see where the noise was coming from. "What was that?"

"That's Dodie. She's a poodle. She belongs to David, the new gardener. He's from Scotland."

Benji got to his feet and slumped over to the French doors and looked out to where David was working near the swimming pool. Jasmine followed, and standing quietly behind him, they both watched Dodie dancing around on the lawn with an old tennis ball, desperately trying to get David to throw for her. He turned from his work in the flower-bed and gave it a kick across the lawn. Dodie headed after it as fast as her legs would move and, having retrieved it, she made her way laboriously back to him, the ball slipping out of the side of her mouth every so often. Then, dropping it at his feet, she would let out another yelp, and David, in his own time, would start the process over again.

Benji leaned against the French door, his hands thrust into the pockets of his long baggy shorts, rocking himself back and forth against the doorpost as he watched this happen three or four times. "He's not wearing a skirt," he said glumly.

"What d'ya mean, a skirt?" Jasmine asked, perplexed by his statement.

"Scotsmen are *supposed* to wear skirts, Jasmine," he replied with a sigh of impatience at her ignorance.

"Now, for once you're wrong, Benji, 'cos I know they're called kilts."

"Skirts, kilts, what's the difference? All seems pretty girly to me. *And* he's got a girly dog."

Jasmine smiled and shook her head in despair at his mood. She turned away from the window.

"What do you want for supper?"

"Don't care much."

"Okay, I'll give you fried flies on toast, then."

"Jasmine?"

"Yuh?"

"Do you think what's-his-name knows anything about bikes?"

Jasmine turned back to look at him. He was still leaning against the doorpost, gazing out into the garden. "David? I dunno, Benji. Why?"

"Do you think he could put the pedal back on my bike?"

Jasmine smiled to herself. "I reckon he probably could. That is, if you ask him politely and start to remember his name properly."

Benji remained where he was, so Jasmine, thinking that a little active encouragement was in order, walked back towards him, pulling the pedal out of the flowerpot as she passed the table.

"Tell you what. If you put on your swimming trunks, then go get your bike and ask him to put the pedal back on, you can have a swim while he's doing it, okay? But you'd better hurry, 'cos I think he'll be headin' home pretty soon."

"Okay!" With a sudden air of excitement, he grabbed the pedal from her grasp and ran through the kitchen into the house. Jasmine watched him go, then, tilting her head to the side at this unexpected hint of hopefulness, she went to make a start on his meal.

It was Dodie who first alerted David to the boy's approach, suddenly rushing off across the lawn, yapping loudly. David turned from his work in the flowerbed to see what the commotion was about, and recognized the young boy he had seen earlier in the day getting into the BMW. He was dressed only in a pair of surf shorts, and was slowly pushing a bicycle across the lawn towards him. As Dodie reached him, he turned his bare legs in towards the bicycle in an attempt to protect them from her claws as she jumped up to greet him.

"Dodie!" David called out sharply. "Come here!"

For once, the little dog did as she was told, racing back to stand guard over her tennis ball, while the boy, eyeing her every inch of the way, continued warily to-

wards him. David put down the hoe and stepped out
of the flower-bed, wiping his hands on the back of his
jeans. The boy stopped in front of him.

"Hi! How are you? I'm David." He walked forward
and put his hand out to the boy, who tried desperately
to free his own by juggling with the pedal that he was
carrying, and in the process letting go of the bike. David
lurched forward and grabbed hold of the handlebars
before it hit the ground and laid it down carefully. The
boy looked at him and smiled.

"So whom have I the pleasure of meeting?"

"Benji."

"Hi, Benji." He stuck out his hand again, and Benji
stepped forward and shook it. "So what's been happening to your bike?"

"The pedal came off."

"Right—and you're about to fix it, are you?"

Benji looked at him and began scratching embarras-
sedly at his forehead. "Well, I was wondering—well,
me and Jasmine were wondering if you could, well,
maybe have a look at it, 'cos I've tried to fix it, but it
just keeps coming off." He squatted down beside his
bike and made a half-hearted attempt at putting the
pedal back on.

"Right, well, if both you *and* Jasmine want me to do
it, then I'd better get on with it, hadn't I? I'll need to
go back to the shed for a spanner, though. Okay?"

Benji looked up at him, squinting into the sun. "A
what?"

David bent down and took the pedal from Benji's
grasp. "You'll see. I'll be back in a minute," he said,
starting to walk back across the lawn. "Maybe you
could keep Dodie occupied by throwing the ball for
her."

When he had first entered the shed that morning,
David had realized immediately that, even though the
last gardener may have been lacking in horticultural
skills, he certainly knew how to organize his workshop.

Everything had its place, the garden implements hanging neatly from wooden dowelling-pegs stuck into the side beam of the shed, while the hand-tools were mounted in metal clips above the work-bench, the outline of each being traced on the mounting board, both for easy replacement and for recognition of what was missing. He chucked the pedal onto the bench and reached over and took down a 13-millimeter wrench, which, more by luck than better judgement, fitted the nut perfectly. He picked up the pedal and walked back out of the shed, and as he was sliding the bolt across on the door, he heard a distant splash coming from the swimming pool. He laughed to himself. Typical boy. Got bored with the game.

It took him just under a minute to get back to where the bicycle had been left. There was no sign of Dodie, either. He bent down to start fixing the pedal when he heard Dodie let out a yelp from beside the pool. He stood up and walked to where he could glance in through the gate to see why she was barking. Something was strange. There was not a ripple on the pool, and yet he was sure he had heard a splash. Dodie barked again. He turned and moved quickly through the gate to see what was happening. Dodie was sitting, a bemused expression on her face as she stared at its smooth, ripple-free surface. Benji was nowhere to be seen. He turned to walk away, and as he did so, his eyes happened to follow the line of Dodie's vision, and a sudden surge of adrenaline and alarm coursed through his body as he made out the dark outline of a figure, foreshortened by the refraction of the water, lying on the bottom of the pool at the deep end.

"OH, NO!" he yelled out, running around the edge of the pool, pulling off his deck shoes as he went. "OH, MY GOD, PLEASE NO! *JASMINE!*"

He dived in and swam down to the bottom, reaching out and grabbing the inert figure of the boy under the armpit. He pulled hard, expecting to have to drag the dead weight of the body upwards, when suddenly the boy seemed to come to life, kicking out with his feet, and they shot to the surface of the pool at the same time. Benji pushed the hair off his eyes and looked at him, spluttering out water.

"What's the matter?" he asked innocently.

David swam over to the side of the pool and grabbed hold of the edge as he caught his breath. He turned round to face the boy, who was now swimming sedately up the pool.

"What the *hell* do you think you were doing?" David shouted at him.

Benji climbed up the steps at the shallow end and received a rapturous welcome from Dodie. He turned to face David, a look of bewilderment on his face. "What d'ya mean?"

David swung himself out of the pool and turned round to sit on the edge, looking at Benji and shaking his head in disbelief. "What *do* you think you were doing? Christ, I mean, I thought you were drowned! I've never known anyone to do such a stupid, idiotic thing in my life!"

"I was holding my breath," Benji said, looking at him, his bottom lip beginning to quiver. "I can do it for a minute and a half."

"Well, it's a bloody stupid thing to do, and I don't give a damn what you do when other people are around, but you sure as hell don't do it with me. Okay?"

At that point, Jasmine came running in through the gate. "What on earth is going on?" she said breathlessly, looking at David and Benji in turn.

Benji stomped past her, a furious and mortified expression on his face. "He's stupid. He's just a—" He turned and looked at David, anger and tears burning at his eyes. "STUPID GARDENER!"

He ran out of the gate and headed for the house, and in the silence that followed, David could hear him sobbing his way loudly across the lawn. Jasmine threw her arms in the air and looked across at David. "Could you *please* tell me what's going on?"

David shook his head and kicked his feet in the water. "I'd just been getting a tool for his bike from the shed, and came back and found him lying in the deep end of the pool. I thought he was bloody drowned!"

Jasmine closed her eyes and slapped the top of her head with her hand. "Oh, David!" she said quietly, moving around the pool towards him, "I'm so sorry! That's Benji's ridiculous game. He's not supposed to do it. He's been warned so many times by his mother and me. Oh, good Lord above, I am so sorry."

David shook his head and waved his arm. "No, it's my fault. I've obviously over-reacted. It's just that, well, I was so bloody scared."

Jasmine crouched down beside him and put her hand on his shoulder. "Not surprisin'."

They remained in that position without speaking for more than a minute before David swung round and jumped to his feet. "I'm sorry, Jasmine. I didn't mean to shout at him like that."

"You've no need to be sorry, David. I just think it's pretty wunnerful that you reacted that way. I mean, you could have been so right, in which case you might have saved his life."

David glanced at her. "Maybe I should apologize to him?"

"No," Jasmine replied, shaking her head slowly, "I'll have a talk with him. Anyway, I think we should let the whole incident heat up in his brain. It'll be a real good lesson to him." She took hold of his arm. "Come on, I'll get you some dry clothes, and then I think you should be gettin' yourself home." She smiled up at him and gave a wink. "I reckon you've done enough for a day."

Clive and Dotti first stared unbelievingly at him when he walked into Helping Hands, before both burst out into fits of laughter. David raised his eyes heavenwards, not particularly wanting to share in their joke. However, he did realize that he must cut quite a comic figure, standing there with his little dog on its lead and dressed in a garish Hawaiian short-sleeved shirt and a pair of chinos whose cuffs ended three inches above his ankles.

"Yeah, well, I've already had some pretty strange looks in Hunter's SuperSaver."

Clive came round the side of his desk theatrically wiping non-existent tears of mirth from his eyes, and stood looking David up and down. "Oh, David, this is wonderful! So—Mrs. Newman insists that you wear livery, does she?" He burst out into fits of laughter again, and David smiled and shook his head at the ribbing.

"Oh, no, no, I must stop!" Clive continued. "It's just too cruel. Oh dear, oh dear!" He patted himself on the chest to regain self-control, then, bending forward and placing both hands on his knees, he looked down at Dodie. "And who may I ask is this?"

"Er, her name's Dodie," David replied guardedly, expecting Clive to make yet another of his humorous observations. "I'm afraid that I had to bring her in, otherwise she's quite likely to eat the interior of the car."

"Oh, aren't you just a bootiful creature?" Clive crooned as Dodie jumped towards him and started to lick at his hands. He straightened up fast as Dodie's powerful breath reached his nostrils. "Oh, my word! She does have a little problem, doesn't she?"

"That's putting it mildly." He reined in Dodie as Clive moved close up to him.

"Garlic pills," he whispered in his ear.

"What?"

"Garlic pills. Wonderful for canine halitosis!"

"Ah, right! Thanks for the tip. I'll get some for her."

"So, how'd it go today? And whose clothes *are* those?"

David recounted his day's experiences, getting more than a horrified reaction from Clive when he eventually explained how he had come to be wearing such bizarre clothes.

"Jasmine did point out that Mr. Newman was a little shorter than me, but it was either this or nothing. Anyway, that reminds me." He stood up, digging his hand into his pocket and bringing out the sodden piece of letter-head which he had picked up that morning from Carrie's desk. He opened it up carefully and handed it to Clive. "I managed to salvage this from my jeans. It's really why I dropped in. It's my new address."

"Oh, wonderful, so you found somewhere?"

"Yeah. It came with dog and car attached."

"Shore Road!" Clive said, reading the piece of paper. "That's pretty fancy, isn't it?"

"Not really. I'm in one of the little saltboxes."

"Oh, that's perfect for you! Now"—he started to pat at his pockets—"what did I do with that envelope?"

"It's here, Clive," Dotti said, turning from her computer screen, the envelope in her hand. "You gave it to me for safekeeping."

Clive tutted and raised his eyebrows in disgust at himself. "I'll be forgetting my own head next." He walked over to Dotti's desk and took the envelope, handing over David's address at the same time. "Be a gem, Dotti, and stick this on the machine."

He approached David and handed him the envelope. "I thought you should have some spending money, so I've made up a week's wages in advance for you."

David shook his head and made to hand the envelope back. "Clive, you don't—"

Clive stood back and held up both hands in refusal. "No, I insist. Really." He laughed. "If it makes it any easier for you to accept, I should maybe tell you that I do this for all my employees—just a little ruse I have for buying loyalty! And in future, all you need to do is drop in at the end of every week, and we'll settle up then. Is that okay?"

David slipped the envelope into his back pocket. "Yeah, perfect—and thanks again."

"Not at all," Clive replied, putting an arm on his shoulder and walking him to the door. "And for goodness' sakes, don't go saving kids from swimming pools every day. I don't want to have to start paying you danger money as well!"

Heavily laden down with the two carrier-bags filled with groceries, David fumbled the key into the lock of the saltbox and pushed open the door with his shoulder and, giving Dodie a whistle to get her inside, he kicked it shut behind him. Putting the bags down on the draining-board, he rooted around in one for a can of beer and made his way towards the veranda, taking a healthy swig as he went. He had just undone the bolts on the door when he noticed that a fax was sitting on the machine. He walked over to the desk, and instantly recognizing his mother's writing, he tore off the sheet and walked out into the veranda, plumping himself down in one of the deck-chairs.

My darling David,
Dad and I were delighted to get your fax and to hear that you are feeling so much better. I always had the notion that getting away completely from Inchelvie would do you the best good of all. Accordingly, we discussed your plan this morning over breakfast, and we are both of the opinion that it is an excellent idea for that period of time, and I am sure that it will enable you to eventually return to Scotland afresh and renewed.

What may come as a bit of a blow to you (yet in a way a mixed blessing to ourselves), is that Duncan Caple has felt it necessary to appoint a temporary marketing director in your place. Of course, it is not the

*ideal solution, but now that we know of your plans, it
does allow you a breathing space, and also takes much
of the pressure off your father. The new man starts today
and Duncan has insisted that Dad should begin to take
things much easier from now on, so let's hope!*

*I have no doubt that you will have already spoken to
Sophie or even all the children about this, and of course,
we are quite happy for them to come back here for their
leave-out. By the way, when I visited them the day you
left, Sophie said that she knew that you wouldn't be back
straight away. She's turning out to be a very intuitive
young girl, that one! Knows her father better than his
mother does!*

*Do keep in touch. Faxes are wonderful—that is, as
long as people on the other side of the world send them
during our daytime! (A little hint!)*

*All my love,
Mama.*

David folded up the fax and placed it beside him on the
floor. He leaned back in his chair and closed his eyes,
and instantly his mind was filled once more with
weighty feelings of guilt and self-reproach for taking the
job. Okay, so it had been a snap decision, but he would
never have been able to afford the luxury of making it
if he hadn't had his parents on hand to step into the
breach.

Maybe he should just pack up and go home now.
But there again, what was the point? This new marketing director had just started, so his job would be taken,
albeit on a temporary basis, and the appointment would
certainly take the onus off his father and allow him to
return to his retirement. So what would *he* do? He certainly didn't want to go back to work in the garden.
Well, not that one, at any rate. That would be a retrograde step, and he was past all that. But then again,
he would have nothing to occupy his mind, and he

would just open himself up to the danger of slipping back to where he had been before.

But what about the children? Were they now not only deprived of a mother, but a father as well? But in a way that was just a negative thought, because even though they probably had not given an enormous amount of reasoning to their decision, their instincts also had been to get away from Inchelvie and return to the different but happy environment of their school.

He pushed himself out of the chair and walked out into the garden, and stood looking out across the bay. No, they had *each* made the right decision, and their respective changes *would* help to start the long healing process. And at the end of term, that would be the time when they would get back together, refreshed and renewed.

He turned and made his way purposefully back towards the house, a plan beginning to form in his mind. Right, so he would return to Scotland at the end of June, a week before the children broke up for their summer holidays, and he would immediately take them off somewhere exciting and new, somewhere they could all make a fresh start at being a family once more.

He went into the living-room and, sitting down at the desk, he scribbled off half a dozen lines to his mother, laying it on top of the fax machine to send the following morning. Then, taking a piece of stationery from one of the cubby-holes on Carrie's desk, he set about writing a long letter to his dear, sweet, intuitive Sophie.

Chapter
NINETEEN

Benji sat on the bench outside Leesport Middle School, listening to the shouts of his fellow pupils fade off into the distance as they made their way down the road towards main street. He got up and kicked at his schoolbag that lay on the sidewalk, and looked at his watch. Come on, Germaine, it was twenty past four. He was the last one *again*.

He heard the main door of the school bang shut behind him and turned to see two boys come running down the path towards him. Recognizing one of them as Sean Dalaglio, his best friend in elementary school, he walked over to the end of the path to meet him.

"Hi, Sean! How're you doing?"

Sean walked past without looking at him, acknowledging his greeting with only a surly grunt. Benji watched them tittering secretly with each other before heading off down the road, now roaring with laughter and trying to push each other off the sidewalk.

He walked back to the bench, scraping his shoes along the ground, feeling the horrible and uncontrollable sensation of imminent tears build up inside him. He hated school. He hated everyone in the school, because he knew that they hated him. He sat down with a thump on the bench and opened up the side pocket of his school-bag and took out a candy bar. Why did his mother have to make him get a lift every day from that dumb Germaine? Everyone else walked to and from school, and they were all right. It was only 'cos *she* thought it wasn't safe. He even had to pay one of the boys to go down to the shops for him at lunch-time to get him his treats. It cost him twice as much as it should do for a candy bar, and because his pocket money didn't cover the cost, he had to sneak into his parents' bedroom at a time when Jasmine was busy downstairs to search the drawers of his father's desk for loose change. He felt guilty every time he did it, but then it was *their* fault. If they allowed him a bit more freedom, then he wouldn't have to do such a dishonest thing.

He glanced at his watch again. It was half past four. Come on, where *are* you, Germaine?

Adults were so . . . selfish. They only did what *they* wanted to do, what suited them best. Why did both his parents have to work? He *knew* his father must be pretty well off, because he always had big cars and quite often he had someone to drive them for him, and their house was one of the biggest in Leesport. He had lived there all *his* life, so it must have been bought when his mother wasn't working and was at home looking after him. It was so stupid. If she were home all the time now, then maybe she would see for herself that it was quite safe for him to walk to school.

Oh, come on, Germaine! Where *are* you?

What it all boiled down to was he only had one real friend and that was Jasmine. She could be pretty bossy sometimes, but she always played games with him if he wanted to. But it wasn't the same with her as it had been when Sean used to come round to his house. Anyway, she was probably going to get all pally with that idiotic Scottish gardener. Well, he *was* pretty dumb thinking that he was drowning, and then he had started yelling at him. How did he think he could get away with that? He'd only just started working for his parents. He was both stupid and rude—but then, that was probably why he was only a gardener. He didn't have brains like his own father, who was able to run a huge computer firm. Jasmine didn't have a boyfriend, though. Ugh, he couldn't *stand* it if they started dating each other!

He looked at his watch again and gave his schoolbag another hefty kick. He stood up from the bench and started to walk up and down the sidewalk.

If only he could do something at school that would make everyone realize that he was all right. If only he could prove himself in some way. But how? He had tried his hardest at football, but he was much slower than the other guys on the team and could never keep up with the game, and as far as baseball was concerned, he was always striking out or dropping the ball. He had thought about entering this talent competition for poetry and music that the teachers were running, but they were putting each entry out over the school PA system every morning, and he *knew* that everyone would just laugh if he did something. It was all just so . . . hopeless!

He looked at his watch again. It was ten to five. He went back to the bench and picked up his bag. He was *not* going to wait any longer for stupid Germaine. If he walked home, then she would have to come looking for him, and that would serve her right, and hopefully Jasmine would chew her out. He slung his bag onto his shoulder and, glancing once more up the road to make sure that Germaine's car wasn't in view, he set off towards the village.

He enjoyed every minute of his illicit freedom, taking time to gaze into the shop windows in the main street as he passed by, eventually ending up buying himself a chocolate milk and a blueberry muffin in the deli. He munched his way to the top of Barker Lane and considered going on to the country club to watch some tennis, but thought better of it, knowing that Jasmine would be wondering where he was. Anyway, more than likely there would be some of his fellow pupils there being coached, and he certainly didn't want to see *them*. He turned down Barker Lane and headed for home at a slow, meandering pace.

He had walked far enough down the driveway of the house to see that the gardener's car was still parked by the shed when he heard the scrunch of gravel at the head of the drive as a car turned in. He turned and watched as Germaine's green Jeep came roaring in, coming to an abrupt halt beside him. Without turning off the engine, Germaine jumped out, a look of fury on her weaselly face.

"Where in God's name did *you* get to? I have been waiting for you outside that school for the past quarter of an hour, and I tell you, my boy, that I have one hundred and one better things to do than to hang around for *you*!"

"But you were very late, Germaine," Benji said quietly.

"It doesn't matter if I'm late. Your mother pays me to pick you up every day, so you just wait until I get there. Is that understood?"

"Okay," Benji said, looking down at his shoes. He heard the back door of the kitchen open and raised his eyes high enough to see Jasmine running along the path towards them.

"So don't you *ever* leave there again without me. Is that understood?"

"What's all the commotion about?" Jasmine asked as she reached them.

"This stupid boy walked home today," Germaine said, her teeth gritted in fury. "I have been sitting for *at least* fifteen minutes outside that wretched school waiting for him to come out, only to find that he's taken it upon himself to walk, *expressly* against the wishes of his mother, and I think you should give him a real good talking-to."

"Oh, do you?" Jasmine said, folding her arms and nodding slowly, "and what time, Germaine, did you arrive at the school to pick him up?"

Germaine started to bite at her lip. "*That* is irrelevant! He's *supposed* to stay there until such time as I decide to arrive."

"And what time did you *decide* to arrive today, Germaine?" Jasmine asked again quietly.

The frown on Germaine's brow deepened visibly as she became increasingly more angry. "I got there in plenty of time to pick him—"

"Okay, if I can't get a straight answer from you," Jasmine interjected, "I'll ask Benji." She put her hand on his shoulder. "Benji?"

"I left at ten to five, Jasmine, because I didn't think that—"

"Ten to five!" She glared at Germaine, her eyes like thunder. "Ten to five! That's thirty-five minutes late! Where *on earth* were you? You know he comes out at quarter past four."

"How *dare* you speak to me like that? Who do you think you are, you black—"

"I think you have said quite enough!" The voice came from such an angle that no one saw him approach. They all turned to see David walking across the lawn, a rake in his hand, with Dodie skipping along at his heels. Germaine looked at them both, a quizzical sneer on her face.

"And who the hell might you be?" she asked.

"It doesn't matter who I am," he said, his voice low and controlled. "I think you've said quite enough, so probably the best thing you can do right now is just get back in your car and leave, all right?"

Germaine looked from one to the other, then, turning on her heel with a yell of anger, she jumped back into her car, slamming the door behind her. She let down the window. "I'm going to make damned sure that Jennifer hears about this. I'll call her at the office."

"You do just that," Jasmine said slowly.

Germaine let out another cry of frustration, and having executed a noisy three-point turn, she threw up a middle finger as a parting gesture and roared back up the drive, spraying gravel onto the lawn as she went.

Having watched in silence as the car disappeared around the bend in the drive, Jasmine turned to Benji and put her hand on his shoulder. "Are you all right?"

"Uh-huh."

"Well, I think you acted real grown up, darlin', and I'm proud of you, so you've gone and done nothin' wrong as far as I'm concerned, okay?"

Benji looked up at her and smiled.

"Now, why don't you go and get yourself some chocolate milk out of the fridge, and I'll be in right after I've had a word with David."

Benji's face fell visibly, and giving a sullen glance in David's direction, he walked off towards the kitchen door. They stood silently watching him until he had entered the house.

"Oh, *goddammit*!" Jasmine exclaimed, slapping her hand hard against her thigh. "That really takes the cake!"

David shook his head. "Who *was* that, anyway?"

"*That* was Germaine. She takes—or should I say, *has* been taking Benji to and from school every day. She is always late for him, and today she was *so* late that Benji walked home. That was what all the shouting was about. What a *b* she is! Oh, hell, now what are we going to do?"

"Look, if you want, you can always borrow my car and take him," David suggested.

Jasmine raised her eyebrows. "That's very kind of you, David. It would be a great idea if I could drive!"

"Ah," David said, nodding in realization of the problem in hand. "Right. Well, in that case, the other alternative is that I could take him to school and pick him up—that is, if you agree with it. I mean, I'm here anyway, so it would seem to make sense—wouldn't it?"

Jasmine focused her eyes up the drive for a moment as she pondered the proposition, then turned to him, a smile on her face.

"Would you mind doing that?"

"Not at all. I'd be delighted."

"We'd have to clear it with Jennifer."

"Of course." He paused for a moment. "Actually, thinking about it, Jasmine, I wonder if we should consider clearing it first with Benji? I mean, I'm not exactly the flavour of the month right at this minute."

"Yup, I think that's a great idea." She grinned. "Just wish I'd thought of it. C'mon, let's go inside and ask him."

David stayed where he was. "Jasmine?"

"Yuh?"

"I wonder if you would mind if I did it. I really would like to clear up the misunderstanding that we had yesterday."

Jasmine nodded and moved off towards the house. "Okay. C'mon then."

They walked back along the path and up the steps to the kitchen door. As Jasmine opened it, she paused for a moment before turning back to David. "Listen, thanks for what you did back there."

David waved his hand dismissively. "Och, it was nothing. She was just a very stupid woman!"

"No, it meant a lot to me and I think probably to Benji as well. So thanks from both of us."

She started to go into the kitchen, but then stopped and turned to him once more. "Och!"

David looked at her. "What?"

"You said 'Och!' Now I know that that *is* Scottish!" She let out a laugh and entered the kitchen, leaving David to shut the door behind him.

Although there were tell-tale signs of Benji's having

been there, like the open chocolate-milk carton being still on the table, he had obviously thought of something other to do than watch television. Jasmine walked over to the French doors and scanned the garden, but seeing no sign of him, she turned and motioned David to follow her through to the house. They went into the hall and stood at the bottom of the stairs, and Jasmine called out for him. Benji's muffled voice replied from somewhere above.

"He's in his bedroom," Jasmine said quietly. "If you go upstairs, turn left on the landing and it's the furthest room on the right, okay? Tell me how it went when you're through, so's I can give Jennifer a call. Good luck!"

David gave her the thumbs-up and headed up the stairs. He walked along to the end of the landing and hesitated for a moment outside Benji's door, working out how best he could eat humble pie before finally knocking.

"Yeah?" Benji's voice answered from inside.

"Benji, it's, erm, David. Would you mind if I came in for a moment?"

There was silence.

"Benji?"

"If you have to."

David pulled a face at this less than hopeful response and walked into the room. The boy was lying on his stomach on the bed, playing intently with a Game Boy, never raising his eyes for a second to acknowledge David's entry.

David stood in the centre of the floor and pushed his hands into the back pockets of his jeans while surveying the room, trying to find some talking point with which he could break the ice. It was wallpapered throughout with images of Superman carrying out gravity-defying stunts with an assortment of beautiful women held close under his Lycraed armpit. Light flooded into the room through the large dormer window, and he walked over to look out at the unimpeded view of the Great South Bay and over to Fire Island beyond. To the left of the window, a row of shelves was stacked high with a vast array of technological toys and plastic models of grotesque comic-book heroes, and underneath these, covering the whole surface of Benji's desk, was a computer system that looked complex and powerful enough to launch a rocket into space, its screen saver blipping out repetitive images that floated out to the surface of the screen before vanishing.

"That's pretty impressive," David said, nodding at the computer. He turned to see if Benji had reacted in any way, but he was still engrossed in his Game Boy, pushing hard at its controls as it sang out little tunes to register his rate of success and failure. David decided to persevere by trying out some inbred knowledge.

"I'm surprised you're still playing with a Game Boy. You've got CD-ROM over here."

He walked over to the desk and picked up some of the CD games that were lying beside the computer. Benji sighed deeply at David's unwelcome disturbance and pressed even harder at his controls.

Realizing that he was getting nowhere, David decided that the only option left open to him was the direct approach. He was just about to turn round to speak to Benji when his eye was caught by a small ukulele, tucked away forgotten on the top shelf, its small body emblazoned with the words "Hi from Hawaii!" He reached up and took it down and plucked at the strings. It was completely out of tune. He began fiddling with the wooden tuning-pegs, twanging the strings, and once he had it reasonably in tune, he strummed off a couple of chords before reaching up to replace it on the shelf.

"How d'you do that?".

He swung round to find Benji watching him, his mouth open, the now silent Game Boy held limply in his hands.

"What?"

"I thought that was only a toy. You made it play a tune."

David looked up at the ukulele. "Well, I don't suppose that one was specifically designed for playing." He took down the ukulele once more. "Probably just a souvenir, but it's got all its strings and it seems to work all right."

He played a number of quick chords, strumming hard and fast on the instrument, then, finishing with a flourish, he held his hands out at each side as if willing applause and gave Benji a quick bow.

"Where did you learn to do *that*?" Benji asked, his eyes wide. He slid off the bed and, discarding his Game Boy onto the bedside table, came across the room towards him.

"Well, I had this rather eccentric uncle who used to come to stay with us when I was a boy. He always brought his ukulele and made up silly songs for me. He taught me how to tune it first." David twanged the strings, singing out a word for each pitch. "My—Dog—Has—Fleas."

Benji laughed and, snatching the ukulele from David's grasp, plucked clumsily at the strings, singing out the tuning-ditty at the same time.

"There you are," David said. "You've just had your first lesson."

Benji's eyes shone with delight at his new-found skill.

"And then, once you've mastered that, you can start on the guitar."

Benji's eyes grew wider by the minute. "Wow, really! Can *you* play the guitar?"

"Well, I haven't for some time, but yeah, I reckon I could again. It's rather like riding a bicycle." David paused for a moment, realizing that this was a perfect entrée for his apology. "Speaking of which, Benji, erm, the incident that happened yesterday when I was mending your bicycle . . . well, I'm sorry that I shouted at you over the swimming-pool thing. I didn't realize that you were an expert at holding your breath."

Benji smiled and shrugged. "Aw, that was nothing. Say, did you ever play in a group or anything?"

David laughed and shook his head at the boy's fickleness. "Yes, as a matter of fact, I did—at university."

"Wow! And did you write songs and stuff like that?"

"Sure. Not very good ones, but if the group played them loud enough, they didn't sound too bad."

"Wow! That's incredible! I thought you were just a gardener!"

David chuckled. "Well, I have just a few hidden talents."

Benji looked down again at the ukulele. "How old were you when you started playing this?"

"Oh, about eight."

"Eight! But I'm eleven," he said excitedly.

"Well, then, it's time you started to learn how to play, isn't it?"

"You mean you'd *teach* me?"

"If you want."

"Yay! And would you teach me how to write songs and things? I mean, I can write poetry. Would that be a help?"

"Well, you've got it made then. If you can do that, you can write songs."

Benji forgot to say "Yay!" this time, instead only letting out a high-pitched sigh that seemed to signify utter contentment. He looked up at David, a pleading look on his face. "Could you maybe start to teach me now?"

David shook his head and looked out the window. "No, not now. I think the evening's too good to sit inside teaching you how to play the ukulele."

Benji's face lengthened with disappointment.

"So I thought that we might go and play some tennis."

Benji looked up at him, his mouth open. "What?"

"I want to play some tennis. Is something wrong with that?"

"You can play tennis *too*?"

"Sure, why not?"

"*All right!*" Benji paused for a moment, his look of excitement suddenly dropping from his face, and he began fiddling with the pegs on the ukulele.

"What's the matter?" David asked. "Don't you want to have a game?"

"Yeah!" Benji replied. "It's only that . . ."

"Only what?"

"Only that I can't run very fast, 'cos I'm kinda . . . you know. . . . fat." He started turning the pegs of the ukulele round and round.

David slanted his head to one side and made a show of studying his physique. "I don't think you're fat. I would say you're more, well, powerfully built."

Benji looked up at him, an expression of sheer hopefulness on his face. "Do you really mean that?"

"Of course I mean that. I tell you what, in four years' time, I wouldn't like to meet you down a dark alley."

"What?"

"Well, you'd probably beat me up."

Benji's mouth broke into a wide grin. "No, I wouldn't! I'd beat up an enemy, but not a friend!" He laid the ukulele down carefully on his bed, then turned and raced towards the door. "Come on, let's go play some tennis."

"Benji," David said, staying where he was, his eyes fixed on the ukulele. Benji turned to see David beckoning him back with his finger.

"Yes?" he said quietly, looking at the instrument and trying to work out what he had done wrong with it.

"I watched you put that ukulele out of tune."

"Oh, sorry," he said humbly, going over to the bed and picking it up.

"No, it's all right. Only I want you to get it in tune for me by tomorrow, okay?"

Benji's face once more broke into a wide grin. "Okay!!" He put the ukulele down and ran back to the door. "Now can we go play some tennis?"

"Just one more thing."

Benji turned back again, this time letting out a groan of impatience. David smiled at him.

"Look, as you no doubt heard, Germaine is not going to be taking you to school any more, and—well—Jasmine and I were wondering if you would mind if I started to take you."

"What? In the Volkswagen?" Benji gasped.

"Well, if you don't mind."

"Wow! That's so cool! Can we have the top down?"

"Yeah, I'm sure we can. Why do you want the roof down?"

" 'Cos it's so cool, and . . ."

"And what?"

"Well, it's just that I was playing with Dodie yesterday and I bent down to get the ball, and she licked my face, and her breath is real lousy. That's why I stopped playing with her."

David laughed. "Okay, it's a deal." He walked over to Benji and held up his hand and they sealed the arrangement with a slap of palms. "Right, *now* let's go and play some tennis."

Benji threw open the door and ran off down the landing, and David reached the top of the stairs in time to witness him making it to the hall in four leaps, yelling out Jasmine's name as he did so. Jasmine came running through from the kitchen.

"Jasmine! David's going to teach me tennis, and then he's going to teach me how to play the uke——the uke——" He looked back up the stairs towards David.

"The ukulele."

"Yup, that's it. He's going to show me how to play the . . . *ukulele*. He's taught me how to tune it already!"

As he ran off towards the kitchen, David descended

the stairs to find Jasmine standing with an incredulous expression on her face. "For heaven's sakes, what did you *do*?"

"Oh, we just had a bit of private men's talk, and, well, he seems to be pretty *cool* about me taking him to school, so I think you're probably quite safe to make that telephone call now."

He blew on his finger-nails and waggled his hand to signify his own self-excellence, then, giving her a wink, he headed off after Benji.

Chapter
TWENTY

Sam Culpepper chucked the briefing document onto the boardroom table and sat back in his high-backed leather chair. He glanced down the table at the pensive looks on the faces of his two main account directors, who, in turn, stared at him in silence.

"Okay, so it's not that big, but I really want us to win this contract." He bent forward and picked up the cigar that was smouldering in the ashtray, and took a deep inhale of smoke. "Why? Because there are rumours that both Bates and Young and Rubicam have also gotten hold of this." He slapped his hand down on the document. ". . . And it would be one hell of a feather in our caps if we got it. I'd make damned sure that Media Week found out about it anyway!" He let out a loud laugh which immediately gave way to a crackling cough.

Russ Hogan was the first to comment. "To be quite honest, Sam, I don't think we stand a chance. We've never handled a liquor account before, let alone one based in the UK. I mean, the amount of research that we're going to have to put into this is enormous. I really wonder if it's worth it."

Sam slowly nodded. He could have bet a hundred

bucks down flat that it would be Russ who'd come out with such a statement. Granted he was a good account director and excelled in smarming up his clients, but more often than not this was counteracted by his ability to sound off on a subject without giving much thought to what he was actually saying—and here was a perfect example.

Sam pushed himself out of his chair and walked over to the window, dragging on his cigar as he stared down at the clogged traffic far below on Fifth Avenue. He turned and looked at Russ.

"I think you're wrong, Russ. I think it *is* worth it." He returned to the table, flicked ash off into an ashtray, and leaned on the back of his chair, swinging it from side to side. "It took us over twenty years to build up Culpepper Rowan to the size that it's now, but I think we've hit a peak, and for the first time I'm concerned about the underlying strength—or should I say, lack of strength—of the company. Now, I may be wrong, but I think that we may have become just a little too complacent with the work that's ongoing. Our accounts may be numerous, but the majority are small. We don't have one big fish to fry."

"You're not trying to tell us that you think Tarvy's Gin is a big account?" Russ interjected, rankled by Sam's slanted accusation, and too thick-skinned to realize that it would be more diplomatic to allow his CEO to finish making his point. "I mean, you read out the UK sales figures just then, and I wouldn't say they're over-impressive. Okay, I grant you, these are probably indicative of the fact that it *is* a fairly new product in the UK, but there again, Sam, it's going to be totally new over here, and we'll be running up against the likes of Gordon's and Beefeater."

Sam held out his hands in exasperation. "But don't you see, Russ? Come on! What else did I read out?"

Russ leaned on the arm of his chair and bit at a finger-nail, not sure what his managing director meant.

Sam looked at both his account execs. "Don't either of you see what I'm getting at?"

There was a moment's silence, broken eventually by the sound of Jennifer Newman's pen hitting her pad as she lobbed it onto the table.

"What you're saying—I think, Sam—is that it's not simply Tarvy's Gin that is important, more the fact that it is the new house gin for Gladwin Vintners, who also have Glentochry Blend Whisky and Valischka Vodka as house brands. You were saying that both of these command fairly sizeable market share in the UK, even though they are not prestige products. The gin is a relatively new product for them, so they give us the chance to push this one on a low promotional budget, and then, if it takes off, they might consider doing the same with their whisky and vodka products over here, hopefully through the same company. That means whoever wins the Tarvy's contract could eventually end up with the complete brand range of Gladwin Vintners."

Sam clicked his fingers and pointed at Jennifer. "Exactly. And that's what all the other top agencies in Manhattan would be thinking, and that's what they would be going for." Sam smiled at his female executive. "Thanks, Jennifer."

Russ chewed noisily on his gum and glanced across at Jennifer, giving her a look of light-hearted disdain at being upstaged. He turned back to Sam.

"Come on. There's nothing to back up that theory. It's pure supposition."

"Okay, so it is. But I really think we're going to *have* to start taking a few risks and spend a bit more time and resources on R and D, otherwise we could quite easily be brought down by our own complacency. I mean, we need something to put fire in our bellies, and I reckon that this account is as good a way as any of achieving that—and, as I said beforehand, the publicity would be terrific!"

Russ shrugged his shoulders in resignation. "Okay, so we do it. Who's going to handle it?"

Sam pointed his finger down the table. "I want you to do it, Jennifer."

She raised her eyebrows. "Why not? What's the timetable?"

"A month, to be precise." He watched tentatively her reaction to this, seeing her eyes widen as she began to understand the implications of his remark.

"Are you saying this proposal has to be completed in a *month*, Sam?"

"Yup, 'fraid so. This document has already been out for about three weeks, and I've only just got my hands on it." He opened up to the first page and began reading. "Proposals have to be submitted by Saturday, the fourth of July, at the latest, and Gladwin's will be announcing the successful agency on the seventh. So I'm afraid no Independence Day break for any of us this year."

Jennifer let out a long whistle as Sam looked up from the document at Russ.

"Okay, so it may be a long shot, but let's go all out to get this goddamned account!"

Half an hour later, Jennifer left the boardroom, cradling the papers and her notepad, laden with action points, in the crook of her arm. She walked along the corridor and was about to enter her office when her secretary appeared from the room opposite. "Jennifer, that's Jasmine for you on line two."

"Ah, right, thanks. Oh, Mandy, here," she said, handing her secretary the notepad, "could you type this up ASAP?"

"Sure thing."

"Thanks."

She walked into her office, and throwing the document onto the desk, she picked up the receiver and pressed the flashing button on the set. "Jasmine?"

"Hi, Jennifer."

"Nothing's wrong, is it?"

"No, not really."

"What does that mean?" Looping the telephone cord over her desk lamp, she walked around behind her desk and sat down. "Is there or is there not something wrong?"

"Well, there's nothin' wrong with Benji, which I guess is what you're meanin'. It's just that Germaine was real late in pickin' him up—I mean, all of thirty-five minutes late—and, well, Benji did the right thing and walked home."

"Oh, for Chrissakes, Jasmine!"

"Now don't start gettin' on your high horse, Jennifer! He did right. He couldn't go on waitin'. He didn't know if she was goin' to turn up or not!"

"Okay, so what happened?"

"Germaine came here just as Benji arrived home and started to tear strips off the poor boy, and er, I kinda got angry with her, I'm afraid, Jennifer, and she headed off, saying she was goin' to get in touch with you. She obviously hasn't yet."

Jennifer scanned her desk for a message. "No, I don't think so. I've been in a meeting for the past hour, so I wouldn't know. She probably won't at any rate. She knows she's in the wrong."

"Yeah, well, she sure as hell was out of line." Jasmine paused. "The trouble is, Jennifer, she's not goin' to do the run any more."

"Oh, God," Jennifer sighed, brushing her hand over head. "What on earth are we going to do now? I am *not*, repeat, *not* going to allow him to walk to school, Jasmine."

"Yup, that's what I thought you'd probably say. Okay, in that case I think that I may have come up with an alternative."

"What's that?"

"David has offered to take him."

"David? Who's David?"

"The gardener, Jennifer."

"Jasmine!" Jennifer leaned forward heavily on the desk. "You cannot be serious! We don't know him from Adam! I mean, he could be a—a child molester or something! I mean—"

"He is *not* a child molester, Jennifer. To be quite honest, I don't think I've ever met someone less like a child molester. He's a decent guy."

"Oh? And how can you tell that after he's only been there for two days?"

There was a pause at the other end of the line.

"Well," Jasmine said at last, "because Germaine called Benji stupid and then started in on a racial, and David came across the lawn and cut in and told her to go!"

"Ah—I see." Jennifer swore quietly at herself for being so one-track-minded. "I'm sorry, Jasmine. I didn't realize. What a bitch! How *dare* she?"

"It don't matter. Anyway, I can really vouch for David, Jennifer. I mean, he's here with Benji right now, out on the court teaching him how to play tennis."

"You're joking!"

"Nope, I am not! *And* he's going to teach him how to play the guitar."

"We don't have a guitar, Jasmine."

"Well, that other thing then. The uke . . . something."

"The ukulele?"

"Yeah, that's it. There's one in Benji's bedroom."

Jennifer sat back in her chair. "That's incredible! And is Benji quite happy with all this going on?"

"Jennifer, I haven't seen that boy look so plumb happy for the longest time!"

The door of her office opened and Jennifer turned in her chair to see Sam and Russ enter. "Hang on just a minute." She put her hand over the receiver, but Sam waved his hands at her to indicate that she should carry on with the conversation. Jennifer smiled and took her hand away from the receiver.

"Jasmine? Right, okay, if you think it's all right. I mean, it *sounds* all right, so yes, let David take Benji to school."

"That's great! I tell you truthful, Jennifer, I think that David could be the making of your boy."

"Well, let's not go overboard."

Jasmine laughed. "Okay, but you wait and see. I'll go tell them now."

"All right, and give Benji a big kiss from me." She put down the telephone and looked across at Sam and Russ who, by this time, had pulled up chairs opposite her desk.

"Everything all right at home?" Sam asked, a concerned look on his face.

"I guess so," Jennifer replied, nodding. "We've got a new gardener who seems to be something of a Superman. He's teaching Benji how to play tennis right now."

"That's great! Hey, speaking of which, we must get a game sometime! I haven't played this season yet."

"Well, come on out," Jennifer said, flicking open her desk diary. "Maybe not this weekend, because I want to get started on this." She pointed to the document. "But what about the one after?"

Sam put his hand in his inside pocket and pulled out his diary and began to leaf through it. "No, nothing on. Molly and I would love to do that."

"Okay, then that's a date!"

"Is Alex going to be around?" Russ asked, taking his own diary out of his pocket.

Jennifer smiled. "I could try to get hold of him and ask. Do you want to give him his yearly thrashing?"

"Well, he's about the only guy who can give me a decent game."

Jennifer and Sam gave each other a knowing look, and noticing this, Russ raised his hands in innocence. "It's true, I tell you!"

"Okay, I'll give him a ring." Jennifer jotted it down on her desk-pad, then dropped her pen on the desk. "Now why I am being honoured with this visit from you both?"

Sam pushed himself out of his chair and stretched his hands above his head. "No reason, really. Only that we're going out for a quick drink and wondered if you would like to join us. Probably be the last opportunity that we'll all have for some time."

Jennifer smiled at both men, then shook her head. "That's sweet of you, but I'd better not." She picked up the document on the desk and started leafing through it. "I really want to get started on this."

Sam's face broke into a broad grin. "Great! I'm glad to hear it!" He took a pace over to Russ, who sat with a disgruntled pout on his face, and held out his hand. "That's what I call commitment, don't you, Russ?"

Russ looked round at him, and after a brief moment made a reluctant show of pulling a ten-dollar bill from the top pocket of his jacket and thrusting it into Sam's open hand. Jennifer's mouth fell open and she threw the papers back onto her desk, shaking her head in disbelief. "You two! You were betting on me coming with you, weren't you?"

"No, get it right!" Sam said, giving her a wink. "*Russ* was betting on you coming, while I, as always, had total confidence in you, and subsequently . . ." He folded the bill in two, placed it in his top pocket and gave it a little pat ". . . the outcome of our bet!"

"You men are such *babies*!" Jennifer jumped to her feet, and picking up her pen from the desk, made to throw it at them both.

"Uh-oh!" Russ exclaimed, ducking out of his chair and moving fast after Sam who, laughing loudly, had managed to beat a hasty retreat to the door. The two men pushed and jostled each other outside into the corridor, then Russ turned and stuck his head round the corner of the door. "Don't forget to call Alex!"

The pen hit the door a foot to the right of his nose. He glanced surprised at the point of impact, then, sticking out his tongue, closed the door quickly before further retribution could be administered.

"Goddamned schoolboys!" Jennifer said, smiling to herself. She walked over to retrieve her pen, then, returning to her chair, fell back into it and reached forward to pick up the telephone receiver. She pushed a button for one of the stored numbers and opened the document in front of her, closing it immediately when she heard an answer.

"Hello?"

"Hi, darling! It's me!"

"Oh, hi! Hang on, Jennifer, it's too noisy here. Just keep talking, though."

"Where are you?"

"San Francisco airport. I'm just about to catch a flight to Houston. Okay, is that better?"

"Yes, much."

"So, how're things?"

"Great! Sam's just given me a new contract to work on. Could be the big one for us."

"Glad to hear it. Listen, can you be quick 'cos I'm going to have to go."

"Oh—okay. In that case, could you just check your calendar and see if you're going to be back in Leesport the weekend after next? I've invited Sam and Molly out for tennis, and, well, Russ wants to come out to get his game of singles with you."

"Oh, hell, do I have to play him? It's just one big ego trip as far as he's concerned. I mean, he beats me every time."

"I know, darling. But can you make it anyway—for me?"

"Look, I don't have my calendar here, but I'll do my best to keep the weekend free. Okay?"

"Yeah, that's fine."

"All right. Well, I'd better be off."

"Okay. Have a good flight."

"Will do. See you."

"Yeah, see you."

Jennifer replaced the receiver and sat staring at the phone, suddenly feeling low at the lack of spontaneity in their conversation. "Love you," she said quietly to herself.

There was a knock on her door and Mandy entered the room and came across to her desk. "Here are your notes."

"That's great, Mandy. Going home now?"

"Yup, if that's okay?"

Jennifer lifted her head from her notes and smiled at her. "Yeah, fine. I'll see you in the morning."

As the door closed, she glanced back at the telephone, wondering if she should try calling Alex again. No, he'd said he was in a rush—it would probably just be a nuisance to him. She shook her head to support her decision, then pulled the file towards her and ran her hand down its centre to crease it open.

Chapter

TWENTY-ONE

There had been all-round improvement at the Newman household by the time the day of the tennis party came round. Firstly, Benji's tennis had now reached the stage that he could hold an extensive rally with David, even though David had to make sure that he kept hitting the ball to his forehand, otherwise it was quite likely to end up in the swimming pool. His ukulele playing likewise went from strength to strength, the only times that he was ever seen without the instrument being when he was playing tennis or at school, not yet having the confidence to show off his newly discovered prowess to his fellow pupils.

Despite this, he had decided that he would try entering a little song of his own for the school talent competition, his motivation for this being derived from the fact that David had himself written a little ditty about Dodie, specifically for Benji to play on the three chords that he had learned. However, throughout its first recital, Benji had criticized the song endlessly for its lack of accuracy and bad rhyming.

"So the chords are just straight G, C and D-Seventh—like that. Okay?"

"Yup. Can I do it now?"

"Hang on! You don't even know how it goes yet!"

"Okay. But I'll do it next time."

"All right. Now, are you listening?"

"Yup."

> *"Life is filled with such wonderful things*
> *Like beer and hot apfelstrudel—"*

"What's apfelstrudel?"

"It's a sort of a German apple-tart."

"Do you always eat it with beer?"

"No, I don't think so."

"Well then, why beer and hot apfelstrudel?"

"Because it rhymes, Benji."

"With what?"

"Just hold your horses! We haven't got there yet.

> *"But it's beaten by far*
> *By a ride in the car*
> *With Dodie the fun-loving poodle—"*

"That's ridiculous! Can't you think of anything else to rhyme with poodle?"

"Hey, give me a break! It only took me an hour to write this!"

"An hour! But it's only five lines long!"

"Just wait, Sir Tim Rice, I haven't finished yet!"

"Who's Sir Tim Rice?"

"Listen, do you want me to go on or not?"

"Okay."

> *"We ride around the town*
> *With the top folded down*
> *And in Leesport I tell you that's freezin'—"*

"No, it's not!"

"Not what?"

"It's never freezing in Leesport. Well, not in summer, anyway. In winter, it sometimes goes down to minus—"

"Benji!"

"Okay, I suppose you only used the word to rhyme with—"

"Look, do you want me to go on or not?"

"Sorry."

> *"Then the air becomes thick*
> *You think Dodie's been sick*
> *But it turns out that she's only breathin'."*

"Hey! I like that!"

"Thank goodness! I've made an impression at last."

"Only *freezin'* doesn't rhyme with *breathin'*."

"Oh, forget it then!"

"No, please, David, do it again!"

"No. Couldn't be bothered. Anyway, I haven't finished it yet."

"*Please*, David, sing the whole thing! I promise I won't interrupt again."

"Promise?"

"Yeah, promise. Go on, how does it start?"

> *"Life is filled with such wonderful things*
> *Like beer and hot apfelstrudel*
> *But it's beaten by far*
> *By a ride in the car*
> *With Dodie the fun-loving poodle.*
>
> *"We ride around town*
> *With the top folded down*
> *And in Leesport I tell you that's freezin'."*

"*Though it's not!*"

"You said you weren't—"

"Sorry!"

> *"Then the air becomes thick*
> *You think Dodie's been sick*
> *But it turns out that she's only breathin'."*

"Right, all together now!"

> *"Life is filled with such wonderful things*
> *Like beer and hot apfelstrudel.*
> *But it's beaten by far*
> *By a ride in the car*
> *With Dodie the fun-loving poodle.*

> *"Well, she sits in her seat*
> *Growls at all that she meets*
> *'Cept the boy, and her boss who's a*
> *navvy."*

"Is the boy me?"
"Yeah."
"Great! Er, David?"
"What?"
"Can I ask another question?"
"What?"
"What's a navvy?"
"A workman. That's me."
"Oh. Okay."
"Can I go on?"
"Okay."

> *"But although she goes wuff!*
> *She's just a bundle of fluff*
> *And you can use her to clean out the*
> *lavvy!"*

"A lavvy?"
"A loo—a toilet. I don't know what you call it."
"Hey, that's really *rude*!"
"Well, those are the lyrics."

"I think it's great! But I bet I could do just as well!"
"Well, do it then!"
"Okay, I will. But can I do that one now?"

It soon became their constant anthem, both of them singing it out loud as they drove back and forth through Leesport on the school run, with Dodie, ever present in the back seat, lapping up every moment of reflected glory.

June had also brought out an abundance of new colour in the garden, which helped to create a fresh and exciting vibrancy to the already perfect setting of the house. Roses of every hue bloomed majestically, while flocks and Japanese irises, encouraged by the warm weather, stretched their spindly necks above the hydrangeas and spicy-smelling geraniums, splashing their pin-points of colour against the blue backdrop of the bay. The trumpet-vine that grew at the front of the house and climbed high onto the veranda above the conservatory broke open its flowers, spreading them outward so that they licked like tiny incandescent flames at the white wooden railings and the shingles around the upper windows.

This all helped give David even greater impetus in his work. He had found a small garden centre five miles out of Leesport on the Montauk Highway, where he had bought an abundance of herbaceous shrubs and bedding plants to fill in the gaps that had been left by the previous gardener. However, his eccentric appearance whilst shopping, pushing his laden trolley along the paths with a poodle attached by its lead to the handle, soon drew the attention of the young couple who owned the place, and subsequently, during his third visit, they introduced themselves and asked him into their office for coffee and muffins. Visits thereafter gradually lengthened in time, and even though they became firm friends, he eventually had to try stockpiling his lists in order to cut down both on the time he spent away from the garden and on his intake of caffeine.

Nevertheless, it was these friends, really genuine friends, that he had made during his short time in Leesport who helped him prove to himself that his own healing process was well under way. No longer did he wish to head home each night to sit alone in the house. He actively sought company, and when he was not having supper with Jasmine and Benji, he either dropped in at the Leesport Bar for a beer and a chat with the locals, or he was being invited out for dinner with new-found acquaintances. On one such occasion it had been at the house of Clive and his friend Peter. While David was made to sit at the kitchen table, the two men accompanied the preparation of the meal with a hilarious and obviously well-rehearsed two-man act, each singing and dancing around the other, saucepan and mixing bowl in hand, to the strains of an old recording of *My Fair Lady*.

But the closest relationship he had of all was brought about by his daily contact with Jasmine and Benji, the bond that he had now formed with the young boy helping to bring thoughts of his own children constantly to the surface of his mind. Every second night he would sit down to write each a letter, starting always by knocking off the number of days left to the end of term with the words "Then Holiday Time!!" written after the scored-out figure. He really missed them so much, and although he felt apprehensive about eventually having to return to Scotland, there was also a profound excitement at the thought of being with them again.

Yet at present it was the environment of the Newman household which gave him the strongest indication that he was returning to normality, both the simplicity of his own existence and the innocent, uncomplicated chemistry engendered by his two friends helping to reduce the tangled mess of barbed wire in his brain to a smooth, straight line of clear thought.

Consequently, life for him revolved around his work in the garden: the tennis matches with Benji, for which Jasmine, at Benji's insistence, had now been made to perch on a step-ladder at the side of the net, calling out what was invariably the wrong score, but all adding to the authenticity and importance of the occasion; the ferry trips to Fire Island with Benji, who, more often than not, was allowed to demonstrate his nautical skills by taking over at the helm; the evenings in the kitchen or on the terrace, drinking wine with Jasmine whilst Benji interrupted them constantly to sing Dodie's song or yet another line of his own "hit" single; and then Jasmine's driving lessons up the drive, which numbered only one and a bit, Jasmine having stormed off halfway through the second, leaving her passengers bent double with uncontrollable laughter at her total inability to master clutch control.

However, despite their ever-deepening friendship, David never mentioned anything about his past, unprepared to start revealing any of his innermost thoughts. This was not through any lack of trust or opportunity in confiding in Jasmine, but more that he was frightened of the reaction that he himself might have to his own revelation, knowing that it could so easily open up healing wounds and allow the infection of unwelcome sorrow to penetrate his mind again.

Friday had been such a beautiful day, with the sea breeze picking up enough to blow away the sticky humidity which had hung about since the previous weekend, that David had picked up Benji from school and, with Jasmine's permission, they had gone straight to the marina to catch the ferry to Fire Island. There they had spent the late afternoon and early evening, happily playing football on the beach and swimming in the sea, making it back across the boardwalk just in time to catch the last ferry home. Because it was too late to complete the work that he had scheduled for himself that day, David decided to return to finish off his tasks on the Saturday.

He arrived at the house at his usual time of eight-fifteen in the morning, to be met by Benji, who came running out of the kitchen still wearing his pyjamas. He proceeded to rattle off a garbled explanation about why he wouldn't be able to keep him company until later, seeing that his father was home and he wanted to play him his new song. David excused him, secretly relieved that he would now be allowed to complete the rest of the mowing without interruption.

By mid-day, the lawn tractor was back in the shed, and he had moved down to the flower-bed at the far-thest end of the tennis court to plant the rest of the shrubs that he had purchased from the garden centre two days beforehand. He was in the process of digging in a new dwarf rhododendron when he heard voices coming from around the side of the hedge and turned to see five figures dressed in tennis whites slowly make their way towards the small summer-house at the other end of the court, chatting as they walked. Dodie let out a short bark to warn him of strangers in their garden.

"Dodie! That's enough!" he said quietly, watching them long enough to see Benji careering around the corner on his bicycle before turning back to his work.

"Benji! Watch out! You nearly ran over Sam!"

"Sorry, Sam! Sorry, Dad! HI, DAVID!"

David looked up and gave him a brief wave before returning to his work.

"Who's that, Jennifer?" David heard a female voice say.

"That's David, the new gardener. God, look, I'd better go and have a word with him. I haven't spoken to him since he first arrived. Listen, Alex, darling, why don't you play with Molly—no, that's not fair—Russ, you play with Molly, and Alex, you play with Sam."

"Christ, Jennifer, I *still* think it's too hot to play. I mean, it's the middle of the day!"

"Come on, moaner, you've been sitting on a plane all week. It'll do you good, and anyway, it might sweat off some of those extra pounds that total inactivity has put on your middle!"

There was an outburst of laughter.

"Thanks for nothing!"

"Can't I introduce Dad to David, Mom?" Benji asked.

"Yeah, why can't I meet Superman?"

"Sssh, Alex! For God's sakes, he might hear. Just go play some tennis."

There was the general mumbling of voices and the sound of tennis-racket covers being unzipped, and David had just heard the clink of the bolt being slid across on the court gate when a voice spoke at his side.

"Hi."

He turned in his bent position to look at a pair of long brown legs, his eyes following them upwards to the fringe of a short white tennis skirt. He stood up quickly, not wishing to make it look as if he was lingering on the sight, to find Jennifer standing beside him. He'd had only had a fleeting glimpse of her since their first meeting, that being on the previous Saturday, when he had come over especially to give Benji a tennis lesson. She had come out onto the veranda above the conservatory to watch them play for five minutes before going back into the house. Benji had said something about her being busy working on a new contract.

"Hullo. I hope you don't mind my coming over today. It's only that—"

"No! Not at all!" she cut in. She looked down at the rhododendron that he had just dug into the ground. "Are you putting in new plants?"

David followed her eye-line downwards. "Yeah, I'm afraid that the last gardener *did* leave a number of holes, so I thought I'd fill them in." He looked back up to her. "I hope that's all right."

"Of course it's all right. Where did you get them?"

"Oh, I found a small garden centre out on the Montauk Highway. They've really got good stuff out there."

"How much have you bought?"

"Oh, well, it's all right," he said, realizing that she might be thinking that a huge bill was imminent. "I just thought one or two here and there might help."

"But how are you paying?"

"No, I mean, that's all right. I just thought it would look better."

"But you must give me the bill. I can't expect you to pay for them."

"Well, I—"

They were interrupted by a ball coming high over the back netting of the court and landing on the lawn ten yards from David. He walked over and picked it up and lobbed it back over the netting.

"You must tell me how much I owe you, David."

He smiled, embarrassed, rubbing his hands together to rid them of the loose soil. It was the first time she had mentioned his name.

"Okay."

"And in future, if you go there, open an account, okay?"

"Right."

She turned and gazed around the garden. "It looks wonderful."

"Well, it's getting there."

"No, it's not. I think it looks wonderful now. I mean it. You really do know how to garden, don't you?"

David scratched at the back of his head. "Well, I have had a bit of experience."

They stood looking at each other for a moment, and David, unsettled by their lengthy eye contact, picked up his spade and made to start digging again.

"David?"

He straightened up again.

"I, er . . . well, I just want to say how much I appreciate what you're doing for Benji. He really loves his tennis with you, and his ukulele . . . and er, I'm quite happy to pay you extra for what you're doing, especially for taking him to school."

"For heaven's sakes, no!" David said, almost too forcefully. He smiled to mollify his tone. "I mean, no, I really don't want to be paid for that. It's a pleasure, believe me. He really is a great boy."

The remark had the most staggering effect on Jennifer, suddenly unleashing the full natural beauty of her face. Her mouth broke into a wide grin which wrinkled her cheeks into smile lines that had been imperceptible beforehand, her lips drawn back to reveal the perfection of her glistening white teeth. David was so taken aback by his own reaction to her that he looked down at the ground and started to kick nervously at the blade of his spade.

"Thank you for that." She let out a resigned sigh. "Well, at least promise me you'll open an account at the garden centre."

He looked up at her and smiled. "Okay, I'll do that."

"Jennifer!" Alex's voice called out from the court.

"What?"

"Are you all right?"

"Yes, fine."

"What're you doing? Gerry's arrived. Come and see him."

Both Jennifer and David looked to the other end of the court where a tall, thin young man was sitting down on the bench outside the summer-house. He was dressed in tennis whites, his hair sleeked tight to his scalp and gathered in a pony-tail at the back of his head.

"Okay, I'm coming!" She turned and gave David a smile. "See you."

"Right."

He watched her for a moment as she walked back up the side netting of the court, then turned back to his work in the flower-bed.

The players had just started on the second set when

Jasmine came out from the house and called Alex to the telephone. David glanced out the side of his eye to see him leave the court immediately, asking the pony-tailed young man to take his place. As he ran towards the house, Jennifer, who had been knocking a ball back and forth with Benji on the lawn, watched him intently. After a brief discussion as to the score, the game continued, with the older man called Sam serving to the athletic and fiercely competitive Russ, who partnered Sam's dumpy little wife, Molly, at the end nearest to where David was working.

The first ball of the new game had hardly been hit across the net before Russ was jogging over to Molly to whisper urgent words of encouragement and new tactical ideas in her ear. The effect on her game was immediate, and of the next two balls that came to her, one was missed completely and the other dribbled harmlessly into the bottom of the net. Russ turned round and stood looking at her, hand on hip, his tennis racket over his shoulder and his head cocked to one side.

"Come on, Moll, what the hell's gotten into you? You were doing better than that before!"

"Sorry," Molly said meekly, returning to the backhand court and trying to give her partner the impression that she really was trying by crouching in concentrated readiness for the next ball to come to her. Sam wound himself up for the serve and it winged its way down to Molly's backhand. This time she made perfect contact, so much so that it sailed clean over the back netting of the court, landing at Benji's feet on the lawn.

"Oh dear!" she said, her voice faltering slightly. "I do apologize, Russ."

"That's game!" Sam called out from the other end, and proceeded to hit the balls down to Molly's end of the court. They finished in a clump against the back netting beside David.

"Right, your serve now, Moll," Russ said, his voice

sulky at the thought of inevitable defeat. "Try and get them in."

Molly walked over to retrieve two balls from the back netting next to David, talking to herself as she did so.

"Oh dear! Oh dear! What *am* I doing wrong, I wonder?"

David tilted his head slightly towards her, never stopping his work in the flower-bed.

"Nothing," he said quietly.

Molly, being in the process of picking up a ball, glanced up at him. "Sorry?"

"You're doing nothing wrong. Just play to your husband's backhand. It's very weak."

"But I can't even get the ball over the net!"

"That's because they're playing to *your* backhand. Just run round the ball and play it on your forehand. You hit *them* well enough."

Russ turned round from his position at the net. "Molly! What's holding you up?"

"I'm coming." She looked at David and smiled.

David did not watch the next point, but listened to the ball being hit hard and often across the net. The rally ended with a shout of frustration from Sam, and a whoop of joy from Russ.

"Great shot, Molly! That's a helluva lot better!"

David smiled to himself in satisfaction as he dug his fingers into the ground to loosen the roots of a particularly stubborn dockleaf. He heard the squeak of tennis shoes approach him, and Molly bent down to pick up another ball.

"Thank you so much," she said quietly, and he turned to see her upside-down head grinning at him. He gave her a wink just as the weed came away in his hands.

Jasmine waited for Alex by the door that led into the hallway, and watched as he bounced his way up the steps at the side of the terrace.

"It's the phone in the study," she said, standing aside to allow him into the house first.

"Okay, thanks."

He walked down the hall and entered the drawing-room, closing the door carefully behind him, while Jasmine returned to the kitchen to finish putting the bottles of beer and iced tea into the cooler. She was just pushing the door of the refrigerator closed with her backside, a bowl of mixed salad in one hand and a plate piled high with tuna sandwiches in the other, when Benji ran into the kitchen.

"Have you seen Dad?"

"He's in the study, darlin'."

"Great! I want him to come and meet David," he said, running back the way he had come.

Jasmine called after him. "Just leave him be, darlin'. He's on the telephone right—"

"Dad, come and meet David!" Benji's voice carried through the house, as he yelled into the study.

She smiled and shook her head, and transferring the plate and bowl to one hand, she picked up the cooler in the other, and walked back through the hall.

The door of the study was slightly open, Benji obviously having failed to close it properly before running back out into the garden. Jasmine tutted and put down the cooler and walked over to the door. She was about to put her hand out to close it, when she heard Alex laugh quietly into the telephone.

"That's wicked!" he said in a hushed voice. "You shouldn't say those kind of things over the phone! Are you sure there's no one there that can hear you?"

Jasmine drew back her hand, wondering if she should close the door or just leave it as it was.

"Look, I really don't know if I can make it. I promised Jennifer that I'd be here this weekend." He laughed again. "I know you are. I'm horny too. But we'll just have to wait until next week."

Jasmine clasped her hand to her mouth and turned

slowly away, feeling a sudden flush of panic burn at her cheeks.

"When are you off? . . . *Monday?* . . . Christ, you didn't tell me you were going away . . . yeah, and I want to see you too . . . goddamn it! . . . Okay, listen, I'll get out of this thing today . . . no, no, I'll just say I've been called away on business . . . no, just leave it with me. I really want to see you before you go . . . okay, meet you at your place in a few hours . . ."

Jasmine had heard all that she wanted. She tiptoed over to where she had left the cooler and, picking it up, hurried out of the door into the garden.

Alex put down the telephone and sat for a moment drumming his fingers on the surface of the desk. He turned to look out the window and caught sight of Jennifer and Benji hitting a tennis ball to each other on the lawn. Pushing back the chair, he rose and walked over to the window, where he stood watching them as they counted out the number of shots in their rally. It ended with Jennifer lobbing a ball high over Benji's head and he threw his racket up in the air in a desperate attempt to intercept it. He leaped to pick up the racket and the ball, then directed a yell towards the new gardener at the other end of the court. Jennifer looked round and laughed at the remark, as the man straightened up from his task and smiled in their direction, acknowledging whatever it was that Benji had said with a wave of his hand. As Alex watched this, he felt an unexpected pang of jealousy course through his body, as sudden and as powerful as an electric shock. He shook his head and turned from the window, giving the chair at his desk a kick as he walked towards the door.

"*Shit!* What a *fucking* mess you've made of this!" he said, slamming the door shut behind him.

Jasmine was on her way back to the house when he passed her on the terrace. Alex smiled at her, but she kept her eyes low and hurried past. He turned to watch her enter the house, then, pulling a face at her odd,

unfriendly behaviour, he walked down the steps of the
terrace and around the side of the hedge, arriving at the
summer-house just as the players were coming off court.
Jennifer and Benji had brought their own game to an
end and were moving across the lawn to meet them.

"Hey, Alex," Russ called over to him as he approached. "You really should have seen that! Molly
played like a woman possessed! She won that match
single-handed!" He turned to his blushing partner and
gave her a kiss on the cheek.

Alex smiled and stuck his hands into the pockets of
his shorts.

"Yeah, I wish I had," he said in a flat voice.

Jennifer looked at him, a worried expression on her
face. "Are you all right, darling?"

"Yup." He glanced down at his feet and rubbed the
toes of his tennis shoes together. "Listen, Jennifer, I'm
afraid I've got some bad news. I've got to go."

Jennifer let her tennis racket fall limply to her side,
and Benji ran over to his father and grabbed hold of
his hand.

"You can't go, Dad. You haven't met David yet, and
I want to show you how well I can play tennis now!
Please, Dad!"

"I know, Benji, it's a real pain. I want to see you
play tennis as well, and meet David, but this is sort of
an emergency."

"How much of an emergency?" Jennifer asked.

"I'm not sure. That was Harry. Something's not
good with the contract in Dallas. I have to meet him at
the office in two hours. He says we can't afford to leave
it until Monday."

Jennifer threw down the racket. "Oh, for heaven's
sakes! Can't they manage without you for once?"

"Doesn't look like it. I may have to fly out there. I'm
not sure."

Jennifer turned to the rest of the tennis party and
held up her arms resignedly. "Sorry, folks."

Alex nodded. "Yeah, sorry about this, everyone. I'm afraid it's just the nature of the job!" He walked over to his wife and took her by the arm and led her around the hedge towards the terrace steps. "Look, I really *am* sorry about this."

Jennifer smiled and shrugged. "It's not your fault. It's only that sometimes I wish that we had the weekends to be a little more like a normal family—if not for our sake, for Benji's."

"I know." He paused. "Listen, I don't know if I will be going to Dallas, but I'm certainly heading back to San Francisco Wednesday night. So I was wondering if we might have an early dinner together?"

For a moment, Jennifer held off giving an answer, thinking about the work she still had to do on the Tarvy's proposal. Then she nodded. "Okay. Where?"

"We could try the new fish restaurant on Forty-eighth between Lex and Park. I think it's called the Ocean Floor. Supposed to be good."

"What time?"

"Have to be early, I'm afraid. Can you make it seven o'clock?"

"Yup, okay."

"Good. Well, look, I'd better be off. Apologize to Russ for not giving him a game."

"Oh, I think he'll survive," Jennifer sighed. "As will we all."

Alex smiled without looking at her directly. "I'll see you Wednesday then." He turned and began running up the steps.

"Alex?"

He stopped and looked back. "Yeah?"

"Could I have a kiss?"

Alex came down the steps towards her and gave her a peck on the cheek. "See you Wednesday."

He took the steps two at a time and, without a backwards glance, headed along the terrace and went into the house. Jennifer stood where she was, her arms folded, looking up towards the empty terrace. Then, with a shake of her head, she turned and walked slowly back to join the others at the tennis court.

"That's a goddamned shame," Russ said, taking a swig of beer from the bottle. "I'm not going to get my game now."

"Well, I sure as hell ain't going to take you on!" Sam laughed, sitting back in his deck-chair and taking a drag on his cigar. "I'm not going to risk spoiling an enjoyable afternoon by having a coronary."

"You don't need to play tennis to do that, Sammy," Molly said in a matronly voice. "You smoke too many of those things for your own good."

"Oh, don't start on that, Moll! Hey, Gerry"—he turned to the pony-tailed man—"why don't you give Russ a game?"

Gerry shook his head. "No, I'm really not into tennis as a competitive sport," he said in the mildest of Irish accents. "I just like to have myself a gentle run-around."

"Mom?" Benji had been sitting cross-legged on the ground, pulling up clumps of grass.

"Yes, darling?"

"Can I whisper something to you?"

Everyone turned to look at Jennifer, raising their eyebrows in intrigue.

"Okay."

Benji jumped up and walked over to his mother's chair, and putting his arms around her neck, he whispered in her ear.

"Oh, I don't think so, Benji."

"Why not? It's a great idea."

"I know, darling, but he's busy right now."

"Well, can't we ask him? Or at least ask Russ."

"Oh, this involves me, does it?" Russ said, moving towards Benji with his hands held out in strangle formation.

Benji screamed and sought refuge behind his mother.

"Go on, quick, Mom, ask him before he gets me!"

Jennifer laughed. "Okay—Russ. Benji has suggested that you play David."

Russ stopped and looked at her inquiringly. "David? Who's he? I heard his name mentioned earlier."

Jennifer leaned sideways in her chair to look past Russ and pointed to where David was working.

"The gardener." She watched as he tamped at the ground around a newly planted shrub with his hands. "Look, Benji, I don't think he'll want to be disturbed. He's extremely busy."

Russ turned round and looked to the other end of the court. "Can he play?"

"You bet he can!" Benji said, moving quickly to stand by Russ so that he could convince him of the idea. "He's really good, Russ, 'cos he's teaching me how to play, and he can hit the ball real hard!"

"I think it's a good idea," Molly said quietly, and everyone turned to look at her.

"Now why would you say that, Moll?" Sam asked in a surprised voice.

Molly smiled. "Let's just say that he had a hand in turning my game around during that last match."

Russ looked at Jennifer. "Well?"

She shook her head. "Okay, Benji, you win! Go and ask him."

And with a whoop of joy, Benji ran off round the side of the court to fetch David.

Dodie, who had been sniffing around the pine-trees next to the shore of the bay, let out a short bark as she saw Benji approach, and ran past David at a gallop to greet him. David looked up from his work. "Hi! How are you getting on?"

"Great!—David?"

"Where's your father? I thought you were going to introduce me to him?"

"Yeah, I know," Benji said in a disheartened voice. "He had to go off to work."

"Oh, I'm sorry to hear that. Maybe I'll meet him next time."

"Yeah—but, David?"

"What?"

"Russ usually plays Dad at tennis, and Dad's gone now."

"That's a pity."

"Yeah—but Russ . . . well . . . David, would you play Russ?"

David pushed himself off his knees and stood up, and glanced to the other end of the court where everyone was looking in his direction. He turned back to Benji. "No, I don't think so."

"Why not?"

"Well—for a start, I'm not wearing any of the right clothes."

"You can play in those, can't you?"

"Well, then, I don't have any shoes."

"You're wearing shoes!"

"I know, but—well, I don't think I should, Benji. I've got work to do."

"Mom says it would be all right. Please, David, I think she wants you to, otherwise she'll have to listen to Russ grumbling all afternoon!"

David smiled at him and, after a moment's thought, nodded slowly. "Why not?"

Benji's face lit up. "You mean you'll play?"

"Yeah, if your mother doesn't mind."

Benji let out another whoop. "He's going to play you, Russ! He says he's going to play you!" He grabbed hold of David's hand and began pulling him as fast as he could around the side netting of the court.

Jennifer got to her feet and walked a few paces towards the corner of the court to meet them.

"I'm sorry about this, David. I hope you don't mind. It was Benji's idea."

"Yeah, I guessed that. Look, I'm afraid that I don't have proper shoes to wear."

"I told him that the shoes he's wearing would be okay, Mom," Benji cut in, still holding on to David's hand. "Dad's would be too small for him."

"I expect they would be." She looked down at David's battered pair of boating shoes. "They'll do fine, David." She turned and started to move back to the others. "Well, come on, you'd better meet your opponent."

Jennifer introduced David to Russ and the rest of the assembled company, Molly giving him the biggest smile as she shook his hand. Gerry jumped up from his chair and spun his racket round in his hand, offering it, handle first, to David.

"You'll be needing a weapon."

David bent down and cleaned his hands by rubbing them hard on the grass, then took the racket with a smile. "Thanks." He turned to look onto the court, where Russ was already hitting booming and faultless practice serves down to the far end. "Well, I'd better go and start doing battle."

After a brief knock-up, during which Russ had David running from one side of the court to the other in order to gauge the weaknesses of his new opponent, Russ felt confident enough in his appraisal of David's game to knock all the balls down to his end.

"Okay, we won't toss. You just serve." He walked over to the forehand court, giving Jennifer a smile and a wink before settling himself in readiness for the first ball of the match.

He made no contact with the serve at all. Not with the racket at any rate. The ball came over the net like a bullet, swinging straight in towards his body. The spin kicked it up viciously from the service line causing Russ to throw his head to the side to avoid being hit in the eye, and the ball struck him with a resounding *thwack* just above the left cheek-bone. There was a gasp from the spectators, followed by a muffled grunt of pleasure from Sam and a much less subtle yell of joy from Benji.

"Shit!" Russ exclaimed, standing stock-still and looking down the court at David.

He held up his hand in apology. "Sorry about that!"

Rubbing at his painful cheek, Russ made his way slowly across to the backhand court, and, giving his racket one quick spin in his hand, he readied himself for the next serve.

This time, the ball slammed down into the backhand corner of the service box, without a trace of the spin that had been put on the first serve. Having expected it to slew back in towards him once more, Russ found himself having to lunge sideways to try to reach it, doing so with such force that he continued on into the side netting. Dropping his racket, he spread-eagled his hands against it to prevent his face from being shredded through the wire.

As he turned to pick up his racket, there was a silence from the audience, save for a few throats being cleared. He walked back to the forehand court, glancing at Jennifer as he went.

"Where the hell's this guy from?" he whispered to her out the side of his mouth.

"Scotland," Jennifer said quietly.

"Hey! I didn't even know they *played* tennis there!"

He whacked at the soles of his shoes with his racket, more to vent his anger than for any constructive purpose, and once more settled himself down to face both the power of David's serve and the ignominy of his task.

By the time that four games had been played, Russ realized that he was no match for his opponent, never once being able to premeditate what he was going to do. If he powered a serve down towards him, David would take all the speed off the ball and plant it at such an angle across the net that Russ was invariably left stranded somewhere in the middle of the court. If he relied on his slower spin serve, then David would come in like an express train to hit the ball so early that it would be thumping hard against the back netting before he'd even had the chance to move off the baseline. Swearing in frustration to himself at being four games down and avoiding now the looks of the hushed spectators, he hit the balls hard down to David's end to prepare himself for the coup de grâce.

At that point, things started to go very wrong with David's game. Serves began to go inches wide or whack against the white tape of the net, and his returns either ballooned over the baseline or hit the side of the racket and skidded off to the edge of the court. Russ, encouraged by his sudden change in fortune, began to play once more to his audience, winking at them when he managed to win a point, or yelling out "Yes!" every time that David double-faulted. Within twenty minutes, Russ was poised at match point, victory and vindication for his earlier inabilities within his grasp. He swung a service down to the backhand court, and David, moving to the wrong side, missed the ball completely. Russ threw his racket in the air and ran to the net, and stood with his hand outstretched, happy to end the match at that point. David approached him and grasped his hand.

"Well played, Russ, that was good fun."

"Yup, good game. Damned lucky I began to read your game right. I thought you had me there for a minute."

They both walked off court to applause and many congratulatory comments on the standard and enthralment of the game. Benji, however, approached David with a profound look of disappointment on his face.

"We thought you were going to beat him, David, but you started to play like me!"

David laughed. "That's what happens in tennis, Benji. Things go right for a time, and then suddenly, *whoosh*! everything goes wrong."

Russ threw his racket on the ground and went over to the icebox and took out a beer. "Do you want one, David?"

"No, thanks. That's very kind, but if you don't mind, I think I'll just finish off what I was doing."

"You won't go brooding on defeat now, will you?" Russ said, flipping off the bottle-top and taking a mouthful of beer. "It was pretty evenly matched throughout."

"No, I won't do that."

Jennifer looked up at him from her chair. "You really don't have to go back to work, David."

"Well, actually, I do. I really need to get the rest of those shrubs in by this evening, otherwise there's every chance they won't last."

"Okay—but thanks again for giving Russ a game."

David nodded, then walked back around the court to continue his work in the flower-bed.

By five o'clock, the final shrub was in place. He gave each of the new plants a final watering, then, gathering up his tools, he made his way back around the side of the court, giving Dodie a whistle as he went. There was no one left at the summer-house, the tennis party having finished an hour before.

As he reached the corner of the hedge, Jennifer appeared around it, accompanied by Gerry. They stopped as he walked towards them.

"All done?" Jennifer asked.

"Yeah, they're all in."

Jennifer smiled. "David, I don't think you've been properly introduced to this mad Irishman, Gerry Reilly."

David stepped forward, and transferring his tools to one hand, stretched out the other. "Hullo, Gerry, pleased to meet you."

"David," Jennifer continued, "Gerry has a recording studio here in Leesport, and he's just had a . . . what is it again?"

"A new mixing console."

"Right—well, he's just had a new mixing console delivered, and he can't manage it into his studio by himself, so he was wondering if you might be able to give him a hand. That is, if you haven't got any other plans."

"No, I'd be delighted. I've got nothing at all on this evening."

"Oh, that would be great, David!" Gerry said, rubbing his hands together. "It's just that I've got to get it ready for this group coming in tomorrow, and I'd be struggling by myself. Look, I'll go and get my things from the house and meet you round at the back. Have you got a car?"

"Yeah."

"Okay, so you can just follow me. Are you sure this is no imposition?"

"Not at all. As I said, I'm doing nothing else."

"Great—well, see you at the cars, then!" He turned and ran back up the steps onto the terrace and disappeared into the house.

Jennifer made a move to follow him, then stopped and turned back to David. "You could have beaten him, couldn't you?"

"Sorry?"

"Come on, you know what I mean. You could have beaten Russ, couldn't you?"

David smiled and began to waggle his head from one side to the other. "Well . . . maybe."

"Why didn't you?"

"Well, I just thought that it might not be, erm . . ."

"Diplomatic?"

"Yeah, that sort of thing."

Jennifer flicked at a piece of grass with the toe of her tennis shoe. "Well, it's totally un-American, but nevertheless a very kind thing to do. My life would've been hell on Monday morning if Russ had lost."

David nodded. "Yes, well, I guessed he might not take it in the best spirit."

Jennifer laughed quietly. "You guessed right." She folded her arms and once again looked down at her feet as she smoothed over the grass with her shoe. "Well . . . I suppose I'll see you next week then."

"Yeah, okay."

She turned and made her way back to the steps, and David watched her as she stretched her long legs out to take them effortlessly two at a time. Then, giving Dodie a whistle, he set off across the lawn towards the garden shed.

Chapter
TWENTY-TWO

It was apparent from the outset that Jennifer's "mad Irishman" description of Gerry Reilly could not have been more apt. As David sat in convoy behind Gerry's ageing Maserati at the top of Barker Lane, Gerry suddenly pulled out into a non-existent gap in the traffic, causing a Chevrolet pick-up truck to slew dangerously to the side of the road and the driver to thump the heel of his hand on the horn. He then put his foot down so hard on the accelerator that smoke belched from its squealing tyres, and by the time David eventually managed to turn out himself, the car was a mere speck of red at the far end of the main street. Consequently, David found himself having to drive the Volkswagen harder and faster than it probably had ever been driven before in his vain attempt to catch up.

Two miles east of Leesport, David had practically given up all hope of ever seeing Gerry or the Maserati again, but racing round a tight right-hand corner, he came across the car parked at the side of the road, and he reckoned that it had probably been just good fortune that Gerry had actually looked in his rear-view mirror and realized that there was no sign of the Volkswagen. As he slowed, Gerry took off again, this time at a more

gentle pace, and within one hundred yards he signalled
to the right and pulled off the road. David followed him
down an overgrown and rutted driveway, eventually
coming to a halt outside a large weather-beaten barn.
Gerry jumped out of his car and came round to open
up David's door.

"This is very kind of you, David. I had a go at putting the console in myself last night, but just about did
in my back and the bloody equipment at the same
time!"

David got out and pulled up the top without securing
it in order to prevent Dodie from jumping out, and followed Gerry towards the double doors at the front of
the barn.

"Two of us should manage fine, though. It's just a
question of slotting the new one in and connecting up."

He unlocked the small door that was set into one of
the larger ones, and ushered David inside.

The front half of the barn had been converted into
a huge open-plan room, the centre of which was
adorned with a clutter of old sofas and chairs gathered
round a large rough-hewn oak table. To one side, a
kitchen stretched along the wall, separated from the
sitting-room by a long breakfast bar, while the dining
area was tucked away at the back of the room underneath a balustraded upper deck, upon which David
could just make out the top of an enormous double bed.
The whole place smelt strongly of old cigarette smoke
and beer, as if it had been the scene of a wild party the
night before.

Gerry went over to the refrigerator and took out two
bottles of beer, and levering off the tops with the handle
of a spoon, held one out to David.

"No use getting hot and bothered over the task, is
there?"

He took a swig from his bottle and gestured with his
hand for David to follow. He walked over to a door
behind the dining-table and pulled it open, then pushed

open a further door and flicked on a bank of switches, flooding light into the recording studio. It was only half the height and three quarters of the width of the living area, the front part being divided from the smaller back section by a soundproof wall, in the centre of which was a large double-glazed viewing window. The room that they stood in was filled with musical equipment: two keyboards, a set of drums and a variety of guitars haphazardly strewn about on metal floor-stands, each of these being connected to a large input box below the viewing window by an entanglement of leads.

Through the window, two large Anglepoise lamps cast a speakeasy light over the gaping hole in the middle of the desk.

"Sorry about the mess everywhere," Gerry said, picking his way through the equipment. "The boys were in rehearsing last night, and didn't leave till about three this morning. They're not what you call very house-proud."

David followed Gerry's path through the instruments. "What kind of recording do you do?"

Gerry laughed. "Anything that makes a bit of money. Generally groups, but we do a few jingles for radio stations and the like, just to fill in the downtime." He held open the two doors that led into the control room. "That's how I met Jennifer, actually. I've done a couple of things for her company over the past year."

He walked over to the corner of the room and carefully pulled away a dust-sheet to reveal the new mixing console. "There she blows." He stood back to admire it. "Isn't she a beauty?"

David nodded, not really knowing if she was a beauty or not, but reckoning that if looks were dependent on the number of knobs and LCD screens that this machine had, then it certainly would be worth a wolf whistle or two.

"Right, David," Gerry said, squeezing his way in behind the console and edging it out from the wall. "If you could just get your hands in below, we'll get it up into its place."

David rid himself of his bottle of beer and bent down and levered up the console, and with a few manoeuvres around the room to get into the right position, they slotted it down on the desk.

"That's it! Perfect! Thanks a lot, David." He walked round to the back of the desk and picked up a handful of leads. "Now all I have to do is get all these bloody wires stuck into the right holes."

Retrieving his beer, David leaned against the ledge on the viewing window and watched as Gerry began pushing jack-plugs into their corresponding ports. "So, is it all different types of music that you produce?"

"Yeah, suppose so. I mean, I'm lucky enough to have been in the business for some time now, so I get groups seeking me out to produce for them. That's really why I moved out here to Leesport." He grinned at David. "Actually, to blow my own trumpet a bit, I've come to be known as the Pied Piper in the trade, seeing that I'm luring all the groups out here away from the studios in the city!"

"Seems a pretty good position to be in. Where were you beforehand?"

"I had a small place in the Village, but it just got too expensive, so I bought this place about a year ago. I thought at first it might be a bit of a white elephant, because I found out after I'd bought it that no insurance company would cover me for putting all this equipment into a wooden building." He gestured with his hand around the room. "So I had to brick up the bloody lot in the inside. That's why it's so much smaller than the other part of the barn, that and the soundproofing, of course. It cost me an arm and a leg, I can tell you."

"And obviously the bands are quite happy to make the trip all the way out here?"

"Well, it was a bit of a gamble, but yeah, they seem to love it! They book into a bed-and-breakfast in Leesport, and then, because most of the work is done in the evening or at night, they head off to the beach during the day, or the more sporty ones play tennis or golf at the country club." He looked across at David and raised his eyebrows. "It's quite funny, actually. The club has a strict dress code, and you can imagine the kind of clothes these guys turn up in to play their games."

David chuckled. "And they get away with it?"

"I've never actually witnessed what happens. I think it's better if they don't know who the culprit is who's bringing them here in the first place, but yeah, usually there's someone there who knows of the band, or their children know of the band, and they get to bend the rules a little. I think they try to get them out on the course or onto the courts before the old duffers come along and get the chance to complain." Gerry juggled with a handful of leads, shaking his head from side to side as he made a silent calculation as to where they should go. "Look, would you mind just holding on to these for a minute?"

David pushed himself off the ledge and took hold of the leads, while Gerry went round the other side of the desk and squatted down on his haunches to study the confusion of inputs on the patch-bays below.

"So most of the groups that you produce are quite well-known?"

"Yeah, you could say that. The lads here at the minute are popular on the sort of rock/folk circuit over here. Dublin Up, they're called. Ever heard of them?"

"No, can't say I have. I'm afraid that I gave up my musical career some time ago."

Gerry looked up at him. "You played, did you?"

David made a noncommittal gesture with his head. "Well, sort of. I had a group at university, but I've really done little since then."

"What instrument?"

"Lead guitar."

"Good for you!" Gerry said, swapping round two

inputs on the lowest patch-bay and straightening up in front of the desk. He flicked a couple of switches on the console and feedback screeched through the two massive speakers behind David. Gerry quickly twisted two knobs and the noise subsided to a loud hum. He pointed through to the recording floor next door.

"That's the Gibson live. Do you want to have a go?"

David turned to look through the window at the bright blue guitar in the centre of the floor.

"Would you mind?"

"Not at all. Just give me a second, and I'll join you."

David laid down his handful of leads on the desk and pushed open the two doors. He picked up the guitar from its stand, slung the strap over his neck, and pulled out the plectrum that was stuck between the strings, creating a tuneless thwang that rang through the speakers as he did so. He played a couple of chords to make sure that it was in tune, then went through a couple of lead runs to get his fingers accustomed to the feel of the guitar. At that point, Gerry pushed open the doors and came through.

"Bert Jansch, yes?"

David smiled at him. "Oh, well, couldn't be that bad if you recognized it."

"Bad? I tell you, there's many a lead guitarist nowadays who couldn't do better!" He picked up a semi-acoustic Ovation from one of the stands and sat down on a leather-padded chrome stool. "Christ, you're some man for a gardener, aren't you? First tennis, then the guitar. What else do you do?"

David shook his head. "That's about it, I'm afraid. You happen to have witnessed the sum total of my talents in one day!"

"Thank God for that!" Gerry exclaimed, plucking at the strings of the guitar and adjusting the knobs on the machine head. "It's quite enough. Any more and you'd be making me feel humble." He played three quick chords. "Right then, David, that's it! The night is young, so let's get stuck in."

Chapter
TWENTY-THREE

Duncan Caple walked across the empty car-park at Glendurnich, turning his key-ring over in his hand to find the one that unlocked the front door of the office. It was seven o'clock on Monday morning, and even though the distillery throbbed with activity, having been in operation throughout the weekend, the office was completely deserted. He pushed the key into the lock and opened the door, and walked briskly to his office.

Placing his brief-case on the desk, he shrugged off his jacket and draped it over the back of his chair, at the same time pressing one of the autodial numbers on his telephone. While waiting for it to connect, he clicked open the locks of the case and took out a thick typed document. He sat down and began leafing through it as the distorted ringing sounded out from the telephone speaker.

After the tenth ring, he leaned forward with a silent curse, and was about to end the call when it was answered.

"Hullo?"

Duncan quickly picked up the receiver. "John? It's Duncan."

"Duncan! You just caught me. I was on the way out

to the car. How are you getting on? I was going to call you today, but I never quite know when to ring."

"I know. Sorry that I haven't been in touch, but I just wanted to get this document ready before I made contact."

"So you've got it then?"

"Yup, and it looks good, though I say it myself. Giles has done a wonderful job in selling the idea, as has Keith with the figures. It all looks very convincing, even though it is fairly simplistic, but there again, it has to be put in such a way that all the distillery workers can understand what's going on. Having read it through in its entirety, I would have thought that we'd more than a fair chance of pushing this thing through to fruition."

"Bloody wonderful, Duncan! Well done! You'll let me have a copy?"

"Yes, I'll get one couriered down to you today."

"Great! So have you any idea as to when you're going to move on to the next stage?"

"Well, where are we today?" He pulled his desk calendar towards him and flicked over the page to look at the next month. "Right, it's the fifteenth of June, so . . . I think to be on the safe side, John, I would really like a month to get everything ready. I want to make damned sure that this whole thing succeeds, as I'm sure you do, and I just don't want to push it any harder than I need to. So . . . let's see now . . . how does Friday, the seventeenth of July, sound to you?"

"No earlier, huh?"

"No, I really think that if we left it until then, it would give me the best chance to make sure that it went through without a hitch."

"And you're pretty confident that there won't be one?"

"John, I've been up here for a year now, and I've seen how this place works. The Inchelvies pride themselves in having built Glendurnich on labour relations, almost to the point of extreme. Even though they hold only thirty-one per cent of the shareholding, if, to a man, the workers back our proposals, then the Inchelvies will go along with them. I can honestly vouch for that. And once you've had a chance to look at this document, you will see that the terms laid down will be more than attractive to the family itself."

"Right. And have you heard anything at all from Corstorphine?"

"Not a cheep. As far as I can gather, he's gone to ground somewhere in the States. Wallowing in his sorrow, no doubt. I don't think we'll have much bother on that account."

"Okay, well, you know what's going on. I'll put Friday the seventeenth of July in my diary, then. Now I want you to do just one thing for me, Duncan."

"Yes?"

"I really need to get in touch with you over the next month on a much more regular basis, so I want all lines of communication to be opened up between Kirkpatrick's and Glendurnich. That means telephone, fax and E-mail. I cannot be expected to keep tabs on what's going on through these hit-and-miss telephone calls."

"Fair enough."

"Well, as you know, it's impossible at the minute while your old battleaxe has control over the switchboard."

Duncan slowly nodded his head. "Ah."

"You'll have to get rid of her. It's important. As you said, you need time to set the wheels in motion, and we can't afford to have it being leaked out before the designated date. What's her name, anyway?"

"Margaret."

"Right. How difficult *would* it be to give her the push?"

"Well, I wouldn't like to give a firm answer on that one. She's well over retirement age, but she does wield a great deal of clout both here in the office and with old Inchelvie himself."

"Can't be helped, Duncan. Just keep Inchelvie at bay for a month by keeping him in touch on a more than regular basis from his house. Visit him if needs be, but just keep him so well informed on how the business is going that he finds no reason even to telephone the place. All right? And as far as Margaret is concerned, give her a substantial amount more than the redundancy due to her, and if you have to, let everyone know that she's been given a handsome ex gratia payment. Don't lose sleep over it. Just do it. Okay?"

"All right, John."

"Good! Well, I'll look forward to receiving the papers, and say well done to the boys."

Duncan put down the receiver and swung his chair round to look out of the window. He sat for a moment, rubbing at the side of his cheek as he worked out his memorandum to Margaret. Then, with a thin smile curling up the edges of his mouth, he turned back to his desk and, unclipping a pen from his inside pocket, he pulled forward a pad of paper and began to compose the receptionist's retirement order.

Chapter

TWENTY-FOUR

Catching his breath as he rushed into the kitchen, Benji threw his tennis racket down on the table and turned triumphantly to David as he entered through the French doors.

"Beat you!"

"Okay, but you had a head start."

"But you're faster than me."

"Not much. I think it'd be fairer if you gave me a start."

"Oh yeah, right!" He walked over to the refrigerator, and pulling open the door, took out two cans of Coke.

"Here, catch!"

He threw the can erratically towards David, who lunged forward to catch it, but the condensation on its surface made it slip from his grasp, and it struck hard against the corner of the table and fell to the ground punctured, fizzing Coke in every direction. Jasmine, who had been in the process of taking a hot casserole dish out of the oven, turned to witness the sticky liquid spraying out across her polished floor.

"Oh, for Chrissakes, Benji, what the hell do you think you're playin' at?" She banged the casserole dish down on the sideboard, and shaking off the oven gloves, took a cloth from the kitchen sink and walked across to the table. "Just go and put your racket away where it belongs. Go on—do it now!"

Benji, taken aback by Jasmine's uncharacteristic reaction, glanced warily at David, who flicked his head to the side to indicate that he should do what he was told. David bent down and picked up the can, and covering the puncture with his finger, walked over to the sink and poured away the remainder of its contents.

"Sorry about that. It was more my fault than his."

"Well, you should have caught it, shouldn't you!" Jasmine sniped at him as she knelt down to wipe up the mess.

David pulled a face at Jasmine's mood, as surprised as Benji at her outburst. He walked over and squatted down beside her. "Look, let me do that."

She pulled her arm away from his outstretched hand. "No, I am perfectly capable of doin' it myself."

David straightened up and stood watching her as she wiped furiously at the mess.

"Jasmine?"

"What is it now?"

"Is something wrong?"

She stopped wiping for a second, then continued, rubbing harder on the floor. "Nothin's the matter with *me*."

She stopped again, and letting out a loud sniff wiped her eyes with the back of her hand. David went back down on his haunches and put his hand on her shoulder. "Look, there is something wrong. What's happened?"

She turned to look at him, tears in her eyes. "It's nothin' really. I just overheard something on Saturday during the tennis party, and . . . well, I could use some advice from you." Her eyes focused beyond David's left shoulder. "But not right now." She returned to her task.

David followed her line of vision to see that Benji had come back into the kitchen and was walking towards them. "I'm sorry," he said quietly, "I didn't mean to do it."

Jasmine laughed as she wiped at one of the legs of the table. "I know you didn't, and I didn't mean to yell at you. Just me being real bad-tempered. As David said, just as much his fault as yours."

The boy ran forward, and throwing himself on her back, kissed the top of her wiry hair over and over again. Jasmine spread-eagled her hands to stop herself from being flattened on the ground by the extra weight. "All right, Benji! You can get off now! I accept your apology."

"Great!" Benji said, slipping off the side of Jasmine's back. "Can we do it now, David?"

"In a minute. Just go and do a bit of practising. I want a quick word with Jasmine."

"Okay." He turned and raced upstairs.

Jasmine pushed herself to her feet and studied the floor just to make sure that she hadn't missed any of the Coke. "So what have you two got cooked up now?"

"Oh, it's his song. The school told him today that he has to have it ready for tomorrow morning. D-day has arrived! He has a slot on the public address system at a quarter to nine."

Jasmine smiled and walked over to the sink and began rinsing out the cloth.

"So . . . what do you want my advice about?"

Jasmine shook her head. "Nothin' that can't wait." She draped the cloth over the tap and turned to face him. "We'll get a chance to speak sometime when Benji isn't around. I don't want to risk havin' him hear what I gotta say." She picked up the casserole dish from the sideboard and placed it back in the oven, twiddling at a couple of the dials on the control panel. "Anyway, I think you've got a more important job on your hands than listening to me."

With a shrug, David turned and made his way through to the hall and up the stairs to Benji's bedroom.

As he walked in, Benji looked up from where he sat playing the ukulele on his bed, the piece of paper bearing the words of the song spread out on his knees.

"This is soppy!" He threw aside the ukulele and scrumpled up the word-sheet, and letting it fall to the ground, he slumped back onto his bed.

David walked over to the bed and bent down to retrieve the ball of paper. "It is *not* soppy!" he said, carefully unravelling it and pressing it between his hands to iron out the creases. "Listen, I think this song is great. What don't you like about it?"

"It's all about *love*," Benji said quietly.

"So? That's what all the good songs have been written about. What would you rather write about? Playing tennis?"

Benji looked at him, a sulky expression on his face. "Don't be silly. Who'd listen to a song about tennis?"

"Exactly. The words are great—and they're a bit different too. I mean, you've got a really good rhythm going in that first line—'I do love you, but you're breaking my heart, breaking my heart in two'—I think that's really great. It's very catchy."

"But everyone's going to laugh at me when it comes out on the PA system."

"Why? You know the tune, you can play it well enough and you sing it just fine. So why would the others laugh at you?"

" 'Cos they'll call me a sissy for singing about *love*."

David pushed himself farther onto Benji's bed and leaned back against the wall, his arms folded. "Okay, how much is it worth?"

"How much is what worth?"

"Well, let's say I'm your record producer and I say, 'Right, Benji Superstar, I'll give you ten dollars if they laugh at you, and twenty if they don't, would we have a deal?"

Benji looked hard at him, his brow creased with

thought. "That's not much of a deal. You lose out both ways."

"Well, maybe I just know that they won't laugh at you. Okay, so I'll have to pay you out twenty dollars, but then I'm pretty sure I have a hit single on my hands, otherwise I wouldn't have made you the offer."

Benji was silent for a moment. "Do you really think it's that good?"

David nodded. "Yeah, I actually do."

"Gee!" Benji's eyes focused on open air as he contemplated his impending fame.

"So, do we have a deal?"

"You bet!" He leaped up from the bed, and picking up the ukulele, proceeded to play the first few chords of the song. "What do we do now?"

David pushed himself off the bed. "Well, we need to find a tape recorder."

Benji thought for a moment, then, placing the ukulele back on the bed, he leaped towards the cupboard at the far end of the room. He threw open the doors and rooted around inside, ejecting long-unused toys from its depth, eventually reappearing with an old plastic Fisher Price recorder. "How about this?"

David walked over and took it from him, and having given it a quick appraisal, chucked it dismissively onto the bed.

Benji's shoulders dropped visibly. "No good, huh?" he said, profound disappointment in his voice.

" 'Fraid not. The thing is, if we want to make a hit single, we're going to have to call in the professionals."

Benji swallowed hard. "What d'you mean?" he said quietly.

"C'mon. I'll show you."

Twenty minutes later, Benji stood half-hidden behind David in the centre of Gerry's recording studio, his ukulele held firmly behind his back and his mouth open in amazement as they listened to the ear-blasting music being played by the four musicians present. David felt the young boy tug at the back of his shirt, and he turned and bent down so that he could hear him above the noise.

"David, I think those guys are Dublin Up. They're *really* well-known!"

David nodded and gave him a wink, and Benji's mouth fell even farther open.

Inside the control room, Gerry looked up from his console and caught sight of them. He got to his feet and came through the double doors, then flicked a switch on the wall which immediately cut all sound from the instruments.

"What the f——"

Gerry held up his hand to the long-haired fiddler. "Watch it, boys. Kids present." He approached them and sidled a glance at Benji, who was trying to get in as close as possible to David's back. "So, Benji, I understand you've got a song you want to record."

Benji did not reply, but gave David an anguished look and shook his head.

Gerry winked surreptitiously at David. "A bit nervous, huh? No worries, everyone's like that." He turned to the group, who by now had rid themselves of their instruments and were lounging around on easy chairs and lighting up cigarettes. "Patrick, what were you like when you first went into a recording studio?"

"Shi——" Patrick grimaced. "I mean, pretty scared."

Gerry shrugged and looked back at Benji. "There you are, then. Even the lead singer of Dublin Up was scared. Would you believe that?" Putting his hand on Benji's shoulder, he guided him forward to the microphone in front of the viewing window and pulled forward a high stool. "Right, you get your backside up on there, and I'll adjust the microphone for you."

Benji did as he was told, but still tried to keep his modest instrument out of sight of the group. One of them, a lanky youth with a fierce Mohican haircut and a silver ring in his eyebrow, noticed this and suddenly let out a whoop of recognition.

"Hey, you've got a ukulele!" He walked over and took it from him. "Great machines! I learned to play on one of these." He stuck it under his arm and ran off some chords, and a smile slowly spread across Benji's face as he realized that the guy was only playing G, C, and D7.

"I know those chords, too," he said proudly.

"Well, in that case, you know as much about the ukulele as I do." He smiled and handed the instrument back to Benji. "So let's hear what you can do then."

Having placed an enormous pair of earphones on Benji's head, Gerry went into the control room, with David following hard on his heels. He flicked a couple of switches on the console. "Can you hear me, Benji?"

Benji nodded.

"Right, well, when you're ready, just sing a couple of the lines, so that I can get the balance right."

The boy gave David a look of sheer terror through the window. He leaned forward to Gerry's microphone. "Just take a deep breath and do it, Benji. Doesn't matter if you make a mistake. Gerry can do it as many times as it takes."

And with a brave smile, Benji began to strum.

On the initial take, he managed to get through the first verse without fault, but then, as he started the second, he played a wrong chord and doubled up with embarrassment. Gerry flicked the switch on his microphone. "Don't worry, Benji. That sounds great. We'll do it again, only this time, keep an eye on me, 'cos I'm just going to beat out the time with my hand. You seemed to speed up a bit at the end of the verse."

Benji's voice sounded through the speaker. "You'll throw me."

Gerry smiled at him. "No, I won't. Just watch my hand out of the corner of your eye. Are you ready?"

Benji nodded.

"Right, let's go again."

This time, Benji went through the whole song without fault. At the end, Gerry held his finger to his lips to indicate to everyone to keep quiet, then, after a few seconds, flicked off all the switches and gave the thumbs-up. Immediately, the muted sound of clapping came through the soundproof divide and Gerry and David watched as the group gathered around the grinning boy, giving him slaps of congratulations on the back.

They went back through into the recording studio. "Well done, Benji!" Gerry said, giving his head a light cuff. "All done in two takes! Not many professional singers can do that"—he turned to the group's lead singer—"can they, Patrick?"

The singer laughed. "I hope you're not implying anything by that remark!"

"Can I hear it now?" Benji asked excitedly.

"Sure you can." He went back into the control room and patched the song through to the massive speakers in the recording studio. Benji sat with an incredulous look on his face throughout, and at the end the assembled company once more broke into applause.

Gerry came back through from the control room. "Right then, Benji, you can either take it away as it is, or, if you want, I can add a few things to it."

Benji was silent for a moment. "What sort of things?"

"Well, we could put a drum beat to it and maybe a bit of bass."

Benji bit at his lip, a look of uncertainty on his face. Gerry smiled reassuringly at him. "Benji, it's your song. You wrote it and you played it. I'm just the mechanic, and I can, well, sort of fill it out a bit if you want."

"It won't sound stupid, will it?"

Gerry laughed. "Well, if it does, I'll have to pack up doing what I do and get another job."

Benji grinned and jumped off the stool. "Okay! Will you do it now?"

"Not quite now," he said, holding up his hands. He flicked his head towards the group. "I've got to get this lot sorted out first, but if David returns later on this evening, I'll give him the finished tape, so you'll have it first thing in the morning. Would that suit?"

Benji nodded.

"Okay, then!" Gerry said, giving him a slap on the shoulder. "You've done pretty well, my lad. You've a bright future in front of you!"

Outside the studio, Benji's excitement seemed immediately to diminish, and he ambled slowly towards the car, glancing thoughtfully at his feet. David eyed him as he spun his key-ring around a finger. "What's up?"

"David?" He paused. "You don't think I'll look stupid, do you?"

David shook his head. "Benji, I promise you that by this time tomorrow, you'll be a superstar at school"— he jumped into the car and started the engine—"and twenty dollars better off!"

He arrived at the house the next morning a quarter of an hour earlier than usual to ensure that Benji had plenty of time to hand in the tape at the school office. He sounded his horn twice, then repeated it a minute later when there was still no sign of the boy. The kitchen door opened, but it was Jasmine who appeared, giving him frantic gestures to come inside.

David got out of the car and ran over to the steps, taking them in two leaps. Jasmine was waiting for him in the kitchen, a look of humorous foreboding on her face, and pointed to where Benji lay face-down on one of the beanbags.

"What's up?" David whispered.

"Stage fright," Jasmine mouthed at him.

David raised his eyebrows and walked over to him. "Okay, Benji—you ready to go?"

Benji let out a groan and slowly pushed himself to

his feet. "I feel as if I'm going to be executed."

David tried hard to suppress a laugh, but hearing Jasmine snigger behind him, he snorted it out through his nose.

"Sorry, Benji. I don't mean to laugh." He put his hand on the boy's shoulder and steered him towards the door. "Come on, let's go. It's going to be fine."

Benji shuffled towards the door, and as he passed Jasmine, she bent down and gave him a kiss on the top of his head.

"Go for it, maestro. Give 'em your best shot."

He thumped his feet down the steps and mouldered down the path towards the car. "More like they'll give me their best shot."

Jasmine picked up his school-satchel from the sideboard and handed it to David. "Is this going to work?"

"God, I sincerely hope so!" And with crossed fingers raised, he leaped down the steps in one and ran to join Benji in the Volkswagen.

Even though it was half an hour before school was due to begin, there was already a crowd of pupils milling around the main doors when they arrived. David pulled the car to a halt at the end of the path, and opening up the glove compartment, took out the tape and handed it to Benji.

"There you are, all ready for you. Now listen, there's a piece of paper in the cover. Make sure that you tell whoever takes the tape from you that they must read what's written before playing the song. Okay?"

Benji acknowledged him silently and climbed slowly out of the car. He walked round to the driver's door and David handed him his satchel.

"Will you wait?"

David nodded. "Okay, I'll wait right here until ten to nine."

Taking a deep breath, he turned and made his way up the path to the main doors. As he was about to enter the building, a boy, being hotly pursued by another, came storming out and careered into him, making the tape fly out of his hand. As if in slow motion, he watched it hover in the air then threw himself forward to try to catch it, but there were too many bodies around for him to get anywhere near it. He let out a strangled yell as he watched it fall towards the ground, but just as it was about to make contact with the concrete doorstep, a hand stretched down and caught it.

Sean Dalaglio straightened up, a grin spread across his face, and held out the tape to him.

Benji breathed out a sigh of relief. "Gee, thanks, Sean."

"Is that the song you wrote?"

Benji swallowed hard. "How d'you know about the song?"

"It's been announced out on the PA system already. Did you write it?"

Benji nodded.

"Is it good?"

Benji did not know how to respond. He turned to look down the path to the Volkswagen. The car was there but David was not. He looked around and saw that he was slowly walking Dodie up the sidewalk. He turned back to Sean.

"Well?" Sean asked.

"I don't . . . know." He pushed his way past Sean and ran along the corridor to the office and knocked on the door. Miss Trimble, the school secretary, opened it.

"Hello, Benji."

Benji held out the tape to her.

"Ah, this must be your song." She glanced round at the clock on the wall. "Well, your slot's in five minutes. We're just about to put on Chester Todd's poem, 'Seagull Over the Great South Bay,' and then it will be your turn, okay?"

Benji nodded and turned to go, then suddenly remembered what David had said.

"Miss Trimble?" he asked just as she closed the door. She opened it a fraction.

"Yes, Benji?"

"There's a piece of paper in the cover of the tape. It has to be read out before it's played."

Miss Trimble smiled at him. "All right. I'll be doing the announcement today, so I'll make sure to read it out beforehand. Is that all?"

He nodded and Miss Trimble closed the door behind her. He stood staring at the mottled glass for a moment, then, with a sigh of resignation, walked down the corridor to his locker. As he turned the key in the lock, the PA system crackled and Miss Trimble's voice sounded out.

"Good morning, boys and girls. The first of our entries for the talent competition today is from Chester Todd. It's a lovely poem called 'Seagull Over the Great South Bay.'"

There was a crackle as the tape recorder cut in and Chester's voice began reading.

> *"Over the bay the seagull flies*
> *Then on a flagpole he does sit*
> *The trouble is he cannot fly*
> *When he wants to have a shit*
>
> *"The seagull strains his—*

The tape was suddenly cut off, as the whole corridor erupted into uncontrollable laughter. Boys leaned against their lockers and slid their backs down to the ground, clutching at their knees to suppress the aching in their stomachs, while girls clustered into tight groups, sniggering into cupped hands. Then they heard Miss Trimble's quivering voice again.

"I think that's enough of that. Chester Todd, please go immediately to the principal's office. Now, without further ado, I think we'll go on to the next entry. This is a song written by Benji Newman entitled 'I Do Love You.' "

Immediately there was a loud whooping noise from the boys in the corridor, and they all ran to crowd around him, letting out loud wolf whistles and wiggling their hips and blowing kisses at him.

That was it! He'd really screwed up this time. Why had he bothered listening to David? He should never have done this. He slammed his locker door shut and ran down the corridor to the lavatories and pushed open the door. Oh, no, there was a speaker in here as well! He darted round into an empty cubicle and pushed the door closed and locked it, and sinking down on the seat, he stuck his fingers in his ears and shut his eyes tight. Yet even in his silenced world, he could still hear the muffled tones of Miss Trimble's voice rambling on. What *was* she going on about? It had to be something to do with that note in the tape-box. He pulled a ream of lavatory paper off the roll and stuffed it into his ears, then, screwing up his face, he cut out all remaining sound with his fingers.

As he sat there, his elbows resting on his knees, he suddenly became aware of a powerful, rhythmic reverberation coming up through his feet. He looked up at the door of the cubicle and saw it rattling violently against the lock on the partition wall, as if someone were trying to get in.

"Go away!" he yelled out, momentarily unblocking his ears.

There was no one there. The reverberation was not man-made, but came from the speaker high up on the wall in the corner of the lavatory, blasting out the introduction of a funky, up-tempo song. He stood up and pulled the paper out of his ears, just as the vocals of the song began. "I do love you, but it's breaking my heart, breaking my heart in two." He pushed open the door of the cubicle and walked out, and stood for a minute listening to *his* song.

It was fantastic! It was like . . . real! There were drums and a deep thumping bass and something like a trumpet breaking in every now and then. But other than that, it was all *him*—with his ukulele! He had to go and tell David about it—he had to go see him outside, right now! He began to chew apprehensively on a finger-nail. But how? He would have to get past all those boys again. He walked over to the door of the lavatory and, after a moment's hesitation, pulled it wide open and stood back. The first thing he saw was a black boy from the class above him moon-walking past the door in time with the music. He moved forward and peered round the corner. The whole way along the corridor, kids were dancing around to the song. He edged out and walked towards the main door, trying to make himself as inconspicuous as possible by staying close to the wall.

Sean Dalaglio was the first to spot him.

"Hey, Benji!" he yelled out, running towards him. "That's a great song! How d'ya get Dublin Up to play session with you? They're my favourite group! Can you get their autographs for me?"

Benji looked at him wide-eyed. "You mean, Dublin Up are—" He gulped. "I gotta go, Sean."

He broke into a run and headed towards the main doors, and as he passed through the throng of dancing pupils, he was greeted with countless voices calling out "Great song, Benji!" and "You're sure to win with *that* one, man!"

He raced outside and saw David at the other end of the path, leaning against the side of the Volkswagen, a grin stretched across his face, and between the fingers of his right hand was held the twenty-dollar bill.

Benji started to run down the path towards him, but David suddenly held up his hand to halt him in his tracks and, at the same time, pushed the bill into the breast pocket of his shirt. Benji stopped and looked at him, a puzzled expression on his face. David flicked his hand at him, motioning for him to return back the way he had come. For a moment, Benji stood where he was, then, with a look of utter disappointment, he turned round, only to be faced by a crowd of pupils who had silently gathered on the wide step outside the main doors. At the front stood Sean Dalaglio. Benji glanced round and gave David the broadest of smiles before heading back to school to run the gauntlet of congratulations from his friends.

Chapter
TWENTY-FIVE

As the taxi edged forward in the solid Park Avenue traffic, Jennifer glanced at her watch. Five to seven already, and the restaurant was still another twelve blocks away. There was no way she was going to make it in the next five minutes. She leaned sideways, feeling the dampness of her shirt becoming unstuck from the dirty plastic of the seat due to the overpowering humidity outside and the lack of air-conditioning within, and looked past the driver to see the jam stretching up as far as Grand Central. She pushed herself forward in the seat and knocked on the partition glass. The driver reached back and slid it to one side.

"Ye, leddy?" he said in an accent that gave Jennifer little confidence in his ability to find the Empire State Building, let alone the Ocean Floor restaurant.

"Can't you cut across to Lexington or Third and try going up there? This is hopeless."

The driver smiled at her and nodded in agreement, at the same time holding up his hands and slapping them down hard against the orange acrylic steering-wheel cover.

"Yez, hopless!" he said, and remained where he was.

Jennifer stared at the back of his head, waiting for

him to spin the steering wheel and make an attempt to cut off to the right, but he seemed happy to sit and wait for the traffic to start moving again, rocking his head from side to side in time to the strangled tones of the Middle Eastern singer that blared from his stereo.

She turned and looked around her in every direction to see if there was another taxi free anywhere nearby, but every one had its light off. Anyway, it would probably be out of the frying pan into the fire. She pushed her hair back off her forehead, feeling the dampness of it clammy on her hand, then, picking up her handbag, she took out her mobile phone and dialled Alex's number. It was engaged. She turned it off and threw it back into her handbag, and leaned forward once more to the open partition glass.

"Can't you at least turn on the air-conditioning?" she said angrily.

It was seven o'clock. Alex would be there by now. He was never late. She knew that, and that was why she had left the office in good time so that she could be there before him. But now it had been a full twenty-five minutes that she had been stuck in this taxi. She rolled down the window, only to be hit by a blast of air that was as hot as a hair-dryer and which only exacerbated her present discomfort. She rolled it up again and sat back to wait.

She hadn't seen him since the tennis party. He had left a message on the answerphone at the apartment, saying that he'd had to go to Dallas after all. "Unavoidable" was the word he had used. What was new? It was always unavoidable as far as Alex was concerned. Not that it mattered much. She had been working every hour that God had given her on the Tarvy's contract, so they probably wouldn't have seen much of each other at any rate. She shook her head. The bloody contract. Nothing she had produced so far gave her overwhelming confidence that they would secure it.

Maybe Russ had been right. Maybe they were trying to bite off more than they could chew.

For no apparent reason, the traffic suddenly began to move again, and the driver turned and grinned, obviously thinking that theirs was now a well-bonded relationship following their brief but mutually misunderstood exchange of words.

"Ye, leddy, we move now!" He nodded contentedly and slowly the car began to roll forward up Park.

By the time they made it to the Ocean Floor, the time was edging towards twenty past seven. Having paid her budding linguist, Jennifer jumped out of the taxi and ran across the sidewalk into the restaurant.

The place was only half-full, with the consequence that she was greeted by three white-aproned waiters, obviously eager for any passing trade that they could muster. At that point, she spied Alex sitting over at a table in the corner of the room, laughing as he talked into his mobile phone. She cut a path through her welcoming committee, leaving them with frowns of resigned disappointment on their faces.

Seeing her approach, Alex quickly pressed the "end" button on the phone and tucked it away in the inside pocket of his jacket.

"Sorry I'm late, darling," she said, slinging her handbag over the back of the chair. "The traffic was lousy."

Alex got up and reached over the table and gave her a peck on the cheek.

"You looked happy just then on the phone," she said, pulling out the chair and sitting down. "Do I take it that all went well in Dallas, then?"

"Not really. That was just a social call to, er"—he faltered for a second—"to John. Now listen." He picked up the menu and made a show studying it. "I didn't know when you were going to arrive, so I've ordered you mussels and swordfish. I hope that's all right?"

"Fine." She reached forward to pick up her napkin,

but was outmanouevred by a waiter who quickly plucked it away from her outstretched hand and, flicking it open, placed it on her lap.

"Good eat!" he said, smiling broadly at Jennifer.

Jennifer watched him turn and walk away. "Does no one speak English in this city any more?"

"What?" Alex asked.

"Oh, nothing," she sighed, shaking her head. She leaned on the table and cupped her chin on the back of her linked hands. "So Dallas wasn't a success, then?"

"No, not really." He reached over with the wine bottle and filled her glass. "I mean, I think it'll work out in the long run, but the company we're dealing with seems pretty edgy about the new system. It's just a question of earning their confidence."

Jennifer nodded slowly, understanding the implications. "Meaning that you're going to have to hold their hand for the time being."

Alex let out a long sigh. "Yeah, I'm afraid so. I'm heading straight back there after San Francisco." He glanced around the restaurant to see if there was any sign of their food, then pushed back the sleeve of his shirt and looked at his watch. "I hope they're quick. I can't be too long." He turned back to Jennifer. "So how's the new contract going?"

Jennifer leaned back in her chair. "We haven't got it yet, Alex. I'm just doing the proposal at the moment, but the problem is that it's completely new ground for me. I'm not really sure if I've hit it quite right so far, but . . ."

She tailed off, realizing that he wasn't listening. He was looking at his watch again and turning round to see if their food was arriving. At that point, a waiter came backwards through the kitchen doors and headed for their table with two plates held high in his hands.

"Mussels?"

Jennifer nodded and the waiter placed the steaming bowl in front of her.

"I get you finger-bowl, madam—and for you, sir, seafood salad."

"Thank you." Alex looked up at the waiter. "Could you see if we can get our second course as quickly as possible? I have a plane to catch."

With a smile and a bow, the waiter turned briskly on his heel and hurried off back to the kitchen.

"That looks good," Alex said, picking up his knife and fork. He looked across at Jennifer, who sat staring at him, making no move to start her meal. "What's the matter? Isn't that what you wanted?"

She shook her head slowly. "Alex, how long have we been married?"

Alex had taken a mouthful of salad as she asked the question, and stopped with his fork in his mouth. "Whop?"

Jennifer didn't reply, letting the question sink into Alex's brain. She picked up one of the mussel shells and tilted it back to her mouth.

"What was that supposed to mean?"

"We've been married thirteen years now," she said quietly, "just in case you've forgotten, but I could bet you that anyone here who just happened to witness how we're acting with each other would think that we've hardly ever met before. I mean, we're like total strangers! What have we talked about so far? Your business and mine." She leaned over the table towards him. "We have a life together, Alex. Thirteen years' worth of it, for Chrissakes!"

Alex let his knife and fork fall with a clatter to his plate and he raised his eyes to the ceiling. "Come on, Jennifer," he said in a whisper. "Don't start making a scene here. People will hear."

"I am not—making—a—scene!" she hissed at him between clenched teeth. She paused to compose herself. "It's just that every time we see each other, we seem to drift further and further apart. We don't seem to have anything in common any more—or do we? What's gone wrong? We did—no, that's not right—we *do* have a really good life together, Alex. You're my best friend. You're my lover, though one might not have thought it of late, and you also happen to be my husband and the father of my child. But nowadays, it seems to be all too much like a . . . a business arrangement."

Alex cocked his head to the side and continued to eat his meal. "Well, it was you who chose to go back to work. I didn't make you."

"Alex, I am not trying to fix blame. I just want for us to be . . ." Jennifer was interrupted by the waiter, who placed a finger-bowl down in front of her.

"Is our main course on the way?" Alex asked him.

"Yes, sir. On the way." He turned and left the table, and Jennifer continued. "I just want us to be together more, even if it's only on weekends."

"Well, you could always give up your job. You don't need to work. I'm successful enough."

"And how does one measure success, Alex?" Jennifer said, louder than she meant. Alex looked round the restaurant to see if anyone was looking in their direction. "Is it the number of zeroes that's on the paycheck at the end of each month? Or is it how much fun you have with your child, and how much you are involved with his upbringing? Does that count for anything? I mean, right now Jasmine and David seem to be the ones most involved with Benji, especially David, who—"

Alex picked up the napkin from his lap and threw it onto the table, and slapped down his hands hard onto its surface.

"Jennifer, are you comparing my contribution to Benji's upbringing with that of some . . . unmotivated good-for-nothing who just walked in off the street? Because if so, I resent that! Okay, Jasmine does a lot for Benji, but that's what she's paid for, but don't start giving me all that crap about this guy David. Anyway, Jasmine works in order that *we* can work, so—come on, you tell me—how much time are *you* spending with

Benji, O perfect mother? It cuts both ways. You do realize that, don't you?"

Jennifer finished off the last of the mussels and dipped her fingers into the bowl and wiped her hands on her napkin, then let out a long, resigned sigh.

"Okay . . . I know . . . you're right, it does cut both ways. The difference is that I have the whole thing going through my brain all the time. Do you?"

Alex didn't reply, knowing that whatever he said would be taken in the wrong light. The pause was long enough for Jennifer to realize that what she had intended to be a reasoned discussion was now turning into a heated argument. She reached over and put her hand on his.

"I'm sorry, darling, I didn't mean for this to happen. It's just that . . . well . . . I just want us to be together more—as a family. I know that might sound like a cliché, but the whole thing seems so hopeless right now!"

The waiter came over and placed their main courses in front of them. Alex glanced at his watch. "Christ, it's eight o'clock. I haven't got time to eat this. I'll have to go, or I'm going to miss the plane."

Jennifer nodded. "Okay," she said quietly.

"Are you happy to eat by yourself or do you want to leave it?"

"No, I think I've had my fill. Anyway, I don't know how good this place is. Those mussels tasted a bit strange."

Alex smiled at her and called back the waiter. "I'm afraid we're going to have to leave. We've run out of time."

"But you order food!"

"I know, but we have no time to eat it!"

"But you have to pay for food."

"Fine!" Alex snapped at him. "Just get the check!"

The waiter pulled a long face and stomped off, and Alex and Jennifer looked at each other for a moment before bursting out into fits of subdued laughter.

"You see what I mean?" Jennifer said. "It's catching!"

He bent down and picked up his brief-case, then paused before rising to his feet and looked across at Jennifer. "We'll work it out, darling. I promise you. But it just might take some time, okay?"

Jennifer nodded. "Okay."

He pushed back his chair. "Come on then. I'll get a couple of cabs."

The traffic was by this time much lighter, and Alex had no trouble in flagging down two empty taxis. He walked over to Jennifer and made to give her a kiss on the cheek, but she tilted her head round so that his lips came into contact with her mouth.

"I love you, Alex," she whispered.

He smiled at her. "Yeah, I know. Look, I'll give you a call when I'm back, okay?"

"Sure. Have a good trip."

He nodded, then turned and walked over to the cab and got in. It sped away from the kerb before he had time to close the door, and Jennifer stood watching until it had crossed over the lights on Park Avenue. Oh, Alex, you could have said it too. Not just "yeah." She put her hand to her forehead, feeling the first pangs of a headache coming on. It must be the humidity, or maybe just the after-effects of their stupid argument. That's exactly what it was—sheer stupidity, on both their parts. She screwed her eyes tightly shut to try to relieve the pressure building up in her head, and despite the heat she suddenly began to feel cold, with an involuntary shudder at the realization.

"You comin', lady?" the taxi driver called out to her.

Jennifer hugged her arms around her body and walked over to the car and jumped in the back.

"Where to?"

"Barrymore Street, please."

"West Village?"

"Yeah."

The cab sped off and took the lights on Park Avenue at yellow. By the time he had stopped at Fifth Avenue, Jennifer was shivering uncontrollably and her head felt as if it were undergoing a rhythmic pounding from a sledge-hammer. She tapped on the dividing glass, and the driver flicked it open.

"Yup?"

"Would it be possible to turn down the air-conditioning, please?"

"Hell, lady, it's roasting outside!"

"I know, but I don't think I feel too good."

The driver shrugged his shoulders and reached forward and turned a knob on his dashboard. The lights changed to green and he slewed the car round into Fifth Avenue, throwing Jennifer sideways in the seat. She put her hand to her mouth, feeling bile rise from her stomach and a choking sensation at the back of her throat. She reached forward and banged on the glass.

"Stop, please—now!"

The taxi pulled over to the side of the street and Jennifer pushed the door open before it had time to come to a complete standstill. She leaned out and threw up violently into the gutter, the whole scene witnessed by some passers-by, who instinctively withdrew to the far side of the sidewalk, uttering muted groans of revulsion. She closed the door again and fell back in the seat. The driver turned round slowly and eyed her.

"You been drinking, lady?"

Jennifer shook her head weakly.

" 'Cos if you been drinking, I won't have you in my cab."

"I haven't been drinking. I think I've eaten something."

"Well, for Chrissakes, don't throw up in my cab," he said, thumping his foot hard down on the accelerator, desperate to get her back home before she had a chance to do just that.

By the time they reached the traffic lights on Forty-third Street, Jennifer had had him pull over two more times, each session more violent than the one before. Her head now felt as if it was going to burst and she had to bend forward to try to relieve the unbearable ache in her stomach. Christ, she felt ill—it must have been the . . . she felt a sudden rush of pressure building up in her bowels—oh, no, please, God no, not that as well!

In her crouched position, she bent forward and knocked on the glass, and with a shake of his head, the driver immediately pulled over to the sidewalk again.

"No, no, don't stop. I just want to know where we are."

"Just coming up to Forty-second, lady."

"Well, could you turn left here, please."

"Left? But I thought you wanted to go down to the West Village."

"No, please, turn left. I want to go out to Leesport."

The driver spun round in his seat. "Leesport? You mean Leesport on Long Island? I can't go all the way out there. This is my busiest time!"

"Please. You have to. That's where my home is. I'm ill. Please. I'll pay you double the fare, I promise. Just take me there."

She slumped back in the seat, and for a moment the driver stayed where he was, staring at the ashen face of his passenger in the rear-view mirror. Then he pressed down his foot and sped away from the kerb, taking a left onto Forty-second Street towards the Midtown Tunnel.

Jasmine placed the cup of coffee on the table in front of David and sat down opposite him. He stared at the steaming cup, then slowly looked up at her.

"You see why I couldn't tell you when Benji was around," she said quietly.

David let out a long sigh. "Yeah, I certainly can. Just as well that he's staying with Sean tonight."

"Exactly. Mind you, I reckon it'll do him a lotta good staying with Sean again. You kinda pulled off something of a mini-miracle turnin' that one around, didn't you?" She took a sip of her coffee. "So what should I do about this goddamn mess?"

David shook his head. "I don't know, Jasmine. I really don't. I mean, I don't honestly think that we, or should I say you, can become embroiled in something that's not really your affair."

"Well, it *is* my affair, because I don't want to see Benji hurt."

"Yes, I understand that, but . . . well, Jennifer and Alex are adults. They have to sort it out for themselves. I mean, have you any idea whether Jennifer suspects anything?"

"No. As far as I know, she thinks everything's pretty much hunky-dory. Not that I ever talk about that kinda thing with her."

"Well, that's it, Jasmine. You've hit the nail on the head. You don't talk to her about that kind of thing, because it's really not your job. No, that doesn't sound right." He paused. "Look, you are probably the most loyal friend that she has, but this is her own very personal relationship." He pushed his chair away from the table. "I don't know. Maybe I'm barking up the wrong tree here. It's just that regardless of how well I knew a person, I wouldn't have ever wanted them to give me advice on something that concerned only myself and . . ." He tailed off, suddenly realizing what he was saying and, feeling his face instantly flush, he cast a quick glance at Jasmine.

"And what, David?" Jasmine asked quietly, her coffee-cup half-way to her mouth.

David looked at her stony-faced, struggling desperately to try to think of a way of diverting their dialogue away from the trap that she had inadvertently sprung on him. At that precise moment, the front doorbell rang three times in quick succession, and both turned simultaneously to look at the clock on the wall.

Jasmine frowned. "Who on earth would be callin' at a quarter to ten?" She got up from her chair and hurried off through the house. David stayed where he was, watching until she had left the room, then let out a long sigh of relief. Jesus, he'd nearly blown it that time. That was the past unconsciously weaving its way into present circumstances, and he had been caught completely unawares.

"DAVID! COME QUICKLY!"

The urgency in her tone made him jump up violently from the chair, making it fall with a clatter to the ground. He ran quickly to the hall to find Jasmine and a red-faced overweight man gently placing Jennifer down on the bottom stair and leaning her limp figure against the banister. She was ashen-faced, her pale shirt spattered with a yellow liquid that made it stick to her skin, and a nauseating smell permeated the whole area.

"What's happened?" David asked, glancing from one to the other.

The man turned and started walking back towards the door. "The lady's sick, sir, that's what's happened, and she's made one hell of a mess inside my taxi. Jeez, I didn't want to do the run, but she said she'd pay me double, and now I've gotta clean out the inside of—"

"All right," David cut in, holding up his hand. "Let's get one thing at a time. Just tell us what happened first." He looked over to where Jennifer sat slumped against the banister, clutching her arms around her stomach, a look of near-delirium set in her eyes. Jasmine had sat down beside her, a frightened look on her face, her arm around Jennifer's shoulders.

"Picked her up outside a restaurant opposite the Inter-Continental. New place, I think, so can't remember the name. Said first that she wanted to go to the West Village, then she was as sick as a dog about three times, and then made me bring her out here. She said she'd eaten something that didn't agree with her."

David looked at Jasmine. "Sounds like food poisoning. You'd better get the doctor fast, Jasmine."

"I can't leave her sittin' here, David. I gotta get her to bed."

"And I gotta get back to the city," the taxi driver interjected. "I gotta clean out the mess in the back of the car, and that's gonna take the best part of the night."

"How much is the fare?" David said, taking his wallet from the back pocket of his jeans.

"A hundred bucks, and that only covers the fare. As I said, I gonna have to—"

Jennifer let out a groan and keeled forward, throwing up a stream of liquid yellow vomit so forcefully that it covered her skirt and three feet of the floor in front of her, making Jasmine jump to the side to avoid being hit.

David had a shiver of recognition at Jennifer's plight, the whole scene sparking off a vision of instant déjà vu, as if a window, hitherto closed tight within his brain, had suddenly been opened.

"You must be prepared for the worst with chemotherapy, David," Dr. Spiers had said to him. "It can have some pretty unpleasant side effects. She'll be depressed, frightened and very sick, but you must just give her your support, David, all the support and all the love and all the gentleness that you can."

This was all too familiar to him, and God, he'd had enough experience of it to know exactly how to act. It was like a switch being turned on in his brain, and he moved forward to take control of the situation, his actions as if on autopilot.

He handed his wallet to Jasmine. "Pay him two hundred, then get hold of the doctor as fast as you can."

Jasmine rose to her feet. "But what about Jennifer, David? I gotta get her to bed."

"I'll do that."

She looked at him warily.

"Don't worry," he said, putting his hand reassuringly on her arm. "I know exactly what I'm doing." He turned to the taxi driver. "Thanks for bringing her out. We really do appreciate it."

The taxi driver dolefully grunted his acceptance of David's thanks and headed towards the front door followed by Jasmine, who still wore a look of worried uncertainty on her face. David skirted round the liquid on the floor and squatted down beside Jennifer.

"Listen," he said quietly to her. "I'm going to get you upstairs now. Do you think you can manage?"

Jennifer raised her head to look at him, her eyes barely focusing on his face. He placed his hand under her armpit and gently raised her to her feet, but her legs seemed too weak to carry her weight and she slumped forward against his chest. Wrinkling his nose at the smell of her clothes, he pushed her limp body away from him, and placing one hand round her back and the other behind her knees, he lifted her up in one swift movement and carried her up the stairs as fast as he was able.

Once on the landing, he suddenly realized that he had no idea in which direction her room was. He called down to Jasmine. "Which room is it?"

"Turn right and second on the left. Are you sure you can manage, David?"

"Yeah." He walked along the corridor and pushed open the door and, having pressed the light switch with his elbow, he carried Jennifer over to the bed and laid her upon it.

"Not down," Jennifer said weakly, trying to get herself back into a sitting position. "Feel sick like that."

David helped her back upright and felt an involuntary retch shudder through his body, caused by the putrid smell of vomit.

"Okay, try and stay like that for a moment. I'm just going to run you a bath, and then we'll get you out of those clothes." He looked over to a door that led off the bedroom. "Is that the bathroom?"

Jennifer nodded weakly, too ill to complain, and followed him with her eyes as he walked across the room to the bathroom.

Having turned on the taps, David grabbed a towel and returned to the bedroom to find Jennifer holding tight to the front of her blouse, a look of helplessness on her face. David leaned forward in front of her, resting his hands on his knees.

"Jennifer, you're going to have to trust me. I promise you, all I'm going to do is get you into the bath. Jasmine can take over after that, but I don't think she can manage to do the lifting work by herself."

The kindness in David's voice was too much for Jennifer. Her face suddenly creased up and she burst into tears, leaning slowly forward so her face rested on his arms.

"This is so . . . degrading," she said between sobs.

"No, it's not, Jennifer," David said, putting a hand under her chin and turning her face up so that she was looking straight at him. "There's nothing to worry about."

"It's not that," Jennifer said, pulling her face away from his hand and looking down into her lap. "I think that it may not be just the sick."

David squatted down on his haunches so that he could look up into her face. "Look, I promise you, I couldn't give a damn. I've seen a lot worse than anything you can show me." He paused. "I don't mind, Jennifer, if you don't mind."

Jennifer sniffed and nodded her head.

"Come on, then, let's get those clothes off."

Jennifer let go of the front of her skirt and put her hands to the side, and David calmly began to undo the buttons. He pulled the shirt off round her shoulders and let it fall to the ground, then, undoing the clasp and zip at the side of her skirt, he lifted her up enough to slide both that and her half-slip down over her legs.

At that point, he heard Jasmine's voice talking to him as she came up the stairs and along the corridor.

"I called the doctor, David. Thank God he lives just down the street. I reckon he should be here any min——" She walked into the room to find Jennifer sitting on the bed in her bra and pants, with David standing in front of her. "David! What are you doin'? You shouldn't be——"

David looked over to her and held up a hand. "Jasmine," he said in a quietly controlled voice, "could you just go and turn off the taps? The bath will nearly be overflowing by now. I'm going to get Jennifer into the bath and then you can take over."

Jasmine looked quickly at Jennifer, who turned enough to give her a brief nod. She went into the bathroom and turned off the water, swirling it around with her hand to check the temperature. Then, standing back from the bath, she found a position from where she could get a clear view of what was happening in the adjoining room.

"Right, now I'm just going to put the towel round you and get everything else off, okay?"

David flicked open the towel and wrapped it round Jennifer's shoulders, then, reaching round her back, he undid her bra strap and pulled the bra free, letting it drop to the ground beside the shirt. Having inched her forward enough to slip the towel underneath her bottom, he gently rid her of her pants, and wrapping everything up into the skirt, he threw the soiled bundle over towards the door. Then, pulling the towel tight around Jennifer's body, he hoisted her up from the bed and carried her towards the bathroom.

Jasmine stood aside as David entered, dumbfounded at what she had just witnessed. It had been a scene of such gentleness and caring that she felt instantly ashamed for ever considering that there might have been any other motivation behind David's actions.

Every movement that she had seen him make was as if it had been rehearsed many times before—from the way he knew how to shift Jennifer's body weight with little or no effort to how he wrapped her in the towel and tucked it neatly into its own folds.

"You've done this before, haven't you, David, my boy," she said to herself as she watched him lower Jennifer's feet into the water. "Yessir, you sure done this before."

"Is the temperature all right?" David asked.

Jennifer nodded, and he turned to Jasmine, still with an arm around her waist. "Can you manage from here?"

"Yup, I reckon so," Jasmine said, coming forward and taking Jennifer's weight on her arm.

"Right, well, I'll just go downstairs and clean up that mess. Give me a call when you're finished and I'll come back up and get her into bed."

Jasmine nodded slowly and watched him as he left the room. Then, turning to Jennifer, she removed the towel and gently lowered her into the bath.

The front doorbell rang fifteen minutes later, as David made his way down the stairs after having helped Jennifer back to her bed. He walked across the hall and opened the door, letting in a young man whose dishevelled appearance was indicative of the fact that he had obviously done more than his fair share of work that day.

"Sorry I couldn't be quicker. I was already out on a call when you phoned. So where's the patient?"

David pointed up the stairs. "Go right at the top and it's the second door on the left."

The young man took off up the stairs, then turned back to David. "Has she been sick since you called?"

"Yeah, once at least. Jasmine would know better. She's up there with Mrs. Newman."

The doctor nodded. "Good. Better to get it all out."

He turned and continued his way up the stairs.

David stood in the hall until he heard the bedroom door shut behind the doctor, then, thrusting his hands into the back pockets of his jeans, he walked through to the kitchen and put on the kettle. He shook his head. He needed more than a cup of coffee. A large whisky would be better. He made his way over to the refrigerator and took out a can of beer, then, walking to the table, he picked up the chair that he had knocked over and sat down, pulling off the ring of the can and taking a long drink.

A flood of emotion suddenly coursed through his mind. Never had anything that he had done over the past few months brought back such vivid memories of Rachel. No, that wasn't right. She was constantly right there at the surface of his thoughts, but until this time it had been the happy, carefree memories of her that had occupied his mind, never the bad ones. Now he began to remember the countless occasions on which he had comforted his wife, gently stroking the soft patchy bristle on her head, being all that remained of her shining brown hair, while she, contorted in pain, bent over the basin at the side of her bed. Once she had finished, he would lay her down carefully, wiping her face clean with a wash-cloth. Then her hand would feel for his, and he would hold it, carefully so as not to hurt its thin covering of flesh, and she would open up her eyes and they would sparkle at him, exactly the same way as when they had first met, all those years ago in Oxford. And they never lost their sparkle. Never, until the day that she—

He heard the door of the kitchen open and, giving his eyes a rub and clearing his throat to rid it of the lump that had formed in his gullet, he turned to look at Jasmine. She smiled at him and walked over to the kettle.

"It's just boiled," he said, his voice still choked.

Jasmine looked at him and nodded and, taking a cup

from the draining-board, she spooned instant coffee into it.

"How is she?" he asked.

"She'll be fine. The doctor gave her something to make her sleep. He reckons though that she'll have to get rid of it all herself. He doesn't know how long it will take. It can go on for some time, he says."

She poured water into her cup, and walking over to the table, she pulled out a chair and sat down beside him.

"You all right?"

David nodded.

"You look as if you've seen a ghost."

"No, I'm all right."

"Reckon now I can't say much to her about what we were talking about."

David sat back in his chair and shook his head. "No, I don't think so."

For a moment, Jasmine was silent, turning her coffee-cup round in circles on the table. "Can I ask you somethin'?"

"Yeah?" he said, picking up his can of beer.

"Are you a doctor or a nurse or somethin'?"

David stopped and looked at her, the lip of the can pressed against his mouth. "What?"

Jasmine leaned forward on the table towards him, an intent expression on her face. "David, you knew what you were doing up there. You said as much yourself. I saw it all. You've done that before—many times, I'd say. How come?"

David continued to look at her.

"Are you married, David?"

He said nothing.

"Because you were about to say something about you and someone else when we were talking earlier, just before Jennifer came back. Are the two things tied up, David? Is that why you're lookin' like you do right now?"

He turned and stared out of the window into the darkness.

"David? Do you want to talk about it?" Jasmine asked quietly.

He looked back at her, then began in a faltering voice. "Yeah, I was married. For eighteen years, actually. That was until April." He took a deep breath. "Rachel"—he paused and wiped at his eyes with the back of his hand—"had ovarian cancer. It was not detected till too late, and she underwent treatment for about six months. I nursed her the whole time—no one else—hence what you might call my expertise in the job. But she died in April." He turned and looked out the window once more. "And that's it, really. Now you know the whole story of David Corstorphine."

Jasmine sat with her hands clasped over her mouth. "Oh, Lordy, I didn't know, David. I'm so sorry. I didn't mean to . . ."

David shook his head. "No, you didn't do anything wrong. I was going to tell you sometime, but didn't really feel I was quite ready yet. Hadn't quite exorcized the ghosts of the past. That's really why I took this job—so that I could get away from it all. I didn't want to think, let alone talk, about it."

"And here's me puttin' my big foot in it. Oh, I feel awful. I didn't mean to get that out of you."

He smiled at her. "You know, Jasmine, you've been more help to me than anyone else. That's the truth. Both you and Benji. You've taken me at face value. You haven't once asked me about where I come from or what I've done. I really mean that, Jasmine, you couldn't have done more good for me. And as for Benji, well, just being with him has helped me realize just how much I've missed my own children."

Jasmine let her hands fall with a thump to the table. She sat with her mouth wide open. "Children? You have children?" she asked incredulously.

David nodded. "Three. Sophie, Charlie and Harriet."

"But where *are* they?"

"At school."

"Yeah, I guessed that, but who's looking after them at nights?"

"They're at a boarding-school."

"At a boarding-school? You mean they *live* in?"

David nodded.

"Do you mean to say that their mother died last April, and you have them at a boarding-school?" Jasmine exclaimed, shaking her head in disbelief and slowly rising from her chair.

"Yes, but—"

"That is . . ." She paused, trying to think of the right word. ". . . unforgivable, David! How could you do that? I mean, how old is the youngest?"

"Nine."

"*Nine?* But that's younger than Benji, David! *Nine?*"

"Listen, Jasmine, it may be difficult for you to understand this, but the children were all away at school before their mother was ill, and when the time came to choose whether to continue with their present school or find somewhere nearer home, it was the children themselves who chose to go back. You see, they have all their friends there; they're happy and secure; and for me, that is absolute. Even though *I* wanted them nearer home, I couldn't go against their wishes, because *that* would have been both cruel and self-indulgent."

Jasmine stood eyeing him, her arms folded and her head on a tilt.

"That's as may be, but what I can't understand is how you've felt able to . . . gallivant around having fun with Benji when your own children are . . . locked up in some boarding-school."

The remark hit a nerve, a painful one. He jumped up from his chair, banging his fist down on the table.

"That is neither fair nor true, Jasmine! I love my children, more than you can ever imagine! I have been in constant touch with them since I've been over here, and they with me. And if it's any of your business, I'm going back to Scotland at the beginning of next month, and we're all going off on holiday together. Anyway, I was only meant to be here for a couple of days, but then I realized that I couldn't go back, because . . ."

He slumped back down in his chair, his anger having worked its way deep into his mind to batter at the defences that had been hitherto holding so strong against his grief and sorrow.

". . . because I found that I just couldn't cope without my wife."

Fighting hard to control his emotions, he rubbed at his forehead with his fingertips, pressing them in hard to cause enough pain to act as a distraction. He took a deep breath. "I'm sorry, I didn't mean to shout at you."

He hadn't heard her walk round the table to stand beside him, but suddenly felt her hand resting on his shoulder.

"It's not you who should apologize. It's me. I'm too darned stupid to understand all that's gone on in your life. It's not for me to pass judgement on what you do and don't do. You know and understand your children much better than me, and I *know* that you love them better than I could ever imagine. I'm sorry. I should never have opened my big mouth."

David sat up and took a deep breath. "No, your reaction was quite justifiable. It does sound pretty harsh when you hear it cold like that. Just shows up all too clearly our difference in culture. What is it you Americans say about us Brits? Keeping the animals at home and sending the children off to kennels?" He let out a short laugh. "I can't make excuses for it, Jasmine, but I think you know me well enough when I say that it *was* the best thing for them under the circumstances."

She sighed and raised her eyebrows, then sat down heavily on her chair again. "Yeah, I guess so." She paused. "It's just a pity we won't get to meet them. How old are they?"

"Sophie's coming up to sixteen, Charlie's twelve, and Harriet—well, you know how old she is."

Jasmine nodded slowly. "Charlie's twelve. How about that? Pity we couldn't get him and Benji together."

"Yeah, they'd hit it off pretty well, too. Both born enthusiasts. Problem is Charlie courts disaster wherever he goes. That's why I over-reacted so, the time that I found Benji lying at the bottom of the pool. It was really Charlie I saw there, you know."

"For heaven's sakes, yes. God, you must have been scared some."

David gave a brief shake of his head. "You can say that again!"

She smiled. "So where are you taking them on their vacation?"

"Don't know yet. I'll fix it up when I get back."

She looked at him, her eyes bright. "I have an idea! Why don't you bring them out here?"

David gaped at her. "What?"

"Bring them out here to the States, to Leesport! I mean, why take them anywhere else? You know the place. You now have us and all your other friends over here. There's the sun and the sea, and the pool and the tennis here. Go on, David, it would be so much fun for them."

He smiled at her and shook his head. "No, Jasmine, I think not."

"Why not? Give me *one* good reason why not?"

"Because . . ."

"I know what you're going to say. Because no one knows about you and what's happened to you all, and you want to be able to guard your privacy. Is that it?"

"Well, in a word, yes."

"Well, in that case, bang goes your argument, because I know. So what other excuse do you have?"

David shrugged and scratched at his head. "I don't know, Jasmine. Maybe it would be better if I just finished off out here and went back to start again."

"No, it wouldn't," she said, her tone so sharp that it made David start back in his chair. She picked up a pencil that happened to be lying on the table and began to roll it over and over in her fingers. "Listen, David, I'm goin' to tell you something. This house has never been filled with so much happiness and laughter than since you been around. We really want to keep you here as long as we possibly can." She paused. "And I can tell you, that don't just go for me and Benji."

He looked at her quizzically. "Meaning?"

"Meanin' that I was with Jennifer just after the doctor left. I gave her the sleeping-pill, but she kept tryin' to sit up. She was pretty delirious, but she kept asking me, 'Where is he? Where is he?' over and over again. I said that I didn't rightly know, thinking that she meant Alex, but then she shook her head. 'Where's David?' she asked. I said that it was all right, you were downstairs, and with that, she kinda slid back against her pillow and went to sleep—just like that—with a big smile spread across her face." She let the pencil fall to the table. "The pill sure as hell couldn't have worked that fast!' "

David sat in silence, staring at her.

"David, you're right on two counts. First, we couldn't tell Jennifer about Alex. It's not our business. The other thing is, yeah, I *am* her best friend. I know her like a kid sister. Goddamn it, I *treat* her like a kid sister! And I sure as hell could not cope myself with this thing with Alex if it came out, and neither could she, especially not right now when she's sick. Whether you like it or not, you have gotten under all our skins. You've become our security, our—what was it Jennifer called you?—yeah, our Superman! You make things happen that ain't ever happened before in this household. And if you went right now, and Alex then decided to head off, I think the whole ship would sink."

David shook his head slowly. "I can't be around for ever, Jasmine."

"I'm not asking you to be around for ever. I realize that you have a life over in Scotland with the children an' everythin'. But if you bring the kids over here, it would at least keep you here too another week or two, and maybe by then, things might have gotten sorted out between her and Alex—or maybe not." She stretched out and put her hand on his. "Please, David, think about it, and think of all the fun the kids would have together."

He smiled at her. "My house isn't very big."

Jasmine grinned, realizing that the discussion was turning in her favour. "It doesn't matter! Kids love sleeping rough! Anyways, they could always come and stay here. Jennifer wouldn't—"

"No!" David cut in.

"Why on earth not?"

"Because I want no one else to know about my past, that's why."

"For what reason?"

"Because it would, well, just change everything. It would mean . . . that people knew about me . . . and that's what I couldn't deal with back in Scotland. I am quite happy with this identity of simply being David-the-gardener. I don't want to be known as David-whose-wife-has-just-died. Am I making any sense to you?"

Jasmine raised her eyebrows.

"I know it sounds quite underhanded, Jasmine, but what difference would it really make? I promise you I will tell Jennifer when the kids arrive, and then everyone else in my own time." He smiled at her. "As it happens, I was going to tell you first. Only you found out earlier than I had planned."

Jasmine slowly nodded. "So when d'you think the kids could come?"

"In about two weeks."

She looked at David, the excitement returning to her eyes. "Gee, that's wonderful! I could give you a hand to get some beds put up in your house. Hey, I can't wait to meet them! And to think of all the fun we'll have with Benji and with Dodie an' all." She suddenly sat bolt-upright. "Speakin' of which, where is she?"

Slapping his forehead in forgetfulness, David jumped up from his chair and looked around the kitchen, his sudden movement disturbing the dog, who had been lying, hidden from sight, deep within one of the bean-bags next to the television. She stretched her woolly head up towards the ceiling and let out a loud yawn.

"Never far away," he laughed. He stuck his hands into the pockets of his jeans and arched his back, suddenly feeling very tired. "I think I'll go home now, Jasmine." He walked round behind her and put his hand on her shoulder. "Thanks for the talk, and for the great idea—and also for being a friend. I really appreciate it, you know."

Jasmine put her own hand up to her shoulder and patted the top of his. "Goes for both of us, David, I can tell you."

He gave Dodie a whistle, and Jasmine turned in her chair to watch him as he walked across the kitchen to the back door. "Be here usual time tomorrow?"

"Of course," David replied, and with a fleeting wave, he let himself and Dodie out into the warmth of the night.

Chapter

TWENTY-SIX

Seeing that Benji was staying with Sean overnight, which let him fulfil his golden wish of walking to school, David did not need to leave the house quite so early the next morning, and consequently he decided to use the extra time to make some initial arrangements for the children's visit. Having called the airline in Glasgow and booked their flight, he realized that he might have been a little preemptive in doing this without first consulting the children, so he immediately put a call through to the school.

Mr. Hunter was delighted with the idea, saying that a trip to America would be a wonderful experience for the children and a fully deserved break for them all, especially Sophie, who had worked like a Trojan during the term, making him feel more than confident about the outcome of her GCSE exams. David heard him call through to his secretary to ask her to bring the children up to his study, and while she went off to search for them, the headmaster talked enthusiastically about how well each was faring, and how proud he had been not only of them, but also of their friends, who had given them all so much support. He had just begun to describe Charlie's latest endeavours on the cricket pitch when David heard the door of the study being opened in the background and the sound of voices approaching the telephone.

"Right, Mr. Corstorphine, that's them here now. I'll put on the speakerphone so that they can all hear you."

There was a click and David heard the sounds of their breathing coming down the line.

"Are you all there?"

"Hi, Dad!" David smiled to himself at the familiar enthusiasm in their voices.

"Hi, you lot! How're things going?"

"Great! Fine!" Charlie and Harriet replied in unison.

"Is everything all right, Dad?" Sophie asked, a worried edge to her voice.

"Yes, darling! Couldn't be better! In fact, the reason I'm calling is that I've just had this idea which I want to put to you all. You know that I said in my letters that we would all go off on holiday when I got home?"

"Yes," the three voices replied.

"Well, I just thought it would be quite fun if you all came out here."

"What, to America?" Charlie gasped.

"Yeah, to America."

"Wow! That's *amazing*! Do you get cowboys and things where you are?"

David laughed. "Not around here, I'm afraid, Charlie. I'm over on the East Coast, quite near New York. It's a place called Long Island. I'm sure if you asked your geography teacher, she'd show you where it is on a map." He paused. "Well, what do you think?"

"Would you be around, Dad?" Sophie asked uncertainly. "I mean, you wouldn't be working all the time, would you?"

"No, not at all. It would be *our* holiday, and, I tell you, there is so *much* to do out here. Swimming, tennis, windsurfing."

"I haven't got my swimming-costume here," Harriet's disappointed voice piped up.

"Don't worry about that, darling. I'm going to be telephoning Granny straight away, so I'll get her to send your stuff to the school, okay?"

"Yess!" he heard Charlie and Harriet yell out.

"Sophie? What do you think?"

"Yes," Sophie answered, a hint of excitement now in her voice. "I think it would be a great idea."

"Well, in that case, I can now tell you that I've already booked your flights, and I'm going to ask Mr. Hunter to arrange for a car to take you to the airport, and then I'll be in New York to pick you up. This is really exciting! I really can't wait to see you all again! Now listen, you'd better get back to whatever you were doing, okay?"

"Okay, Dad! We'll see you in America!"

There was a moment's pause as they left the room, then a click as Mr. Hunter picked up the telephone. "Well, you couldn't have wished for a better reaction than that!"

"No, you're right! Sophie, er, seemed a bit unsure to begin with."

"She's fine, Mr. Corstorphine, believe me. Maybe your reassurance was all that she required, because she certainly went off with a beaming grin on her face."

"Thank goodness for that. Now, Mr. Hunter, I'd be most grateful if you could arrange the car for them. I've booked them on a flight on the first of July . . . tell you what, I'll fax you all the details. That would be simpler."

"Very good, and I'll just go ahead and fix it up at this end. Well, I hope you all have a wonderful holiday. I think it's just what they all need."

"Yeah, I'm sure it's what we *all* need. Thank you again, Mr. Hunter."

David pressed the "disconnect" button and immediately dialled his mother's number. It was she who answered, and from the instant she spoke, he was aware of a happiness in her voice that had been so acutely lacking over the past months. Her reaction to the idea was as enthusiastic as the children's—"tickled pink" was the phrase she used—and she went on to say how everything now seemed to be turning out for the better. His father hadn't been required to go into work at all over the past two weeks, really due to Duncan, who had completely come up trumps by keeping him so well-informed with what was going on, quite often actually taking the time to come out to the house to see him. She asked David when he thought he might return, and he replied that he would leave it open-ended, but he reckoned that they would all be back sometime in the early part of August. Then, having asked her to collect the children's passports from The Beeches and to send them, along with some summer clothes, to the school, they ended the call with a final jocular comment from his mother about him beginning to sound quite American.

He drove to Barker Lane that morning with a sense of excitement and elation tingling in his mind, not simply with the thought of the children's coming out to see him, and how positive his mother had sounded during their call, but also with the relief of realizing that his secret was out, that Jasmine knew everything about him. It was like a weight lifted from his mind—no reason for pretence, no reason for keeping his guard up in front of her.

He entered the kitchen to find her laying out a breakfast tray for Jennifer.

"It's all fixed, then!" he said almost triumphantly, pouring himself some coffee. "They're flying out here on the first of July."

Jasmine took a sharp intake of breath and, with a yell of delight, hurried over and threw her arms around him in an all-enveloping bear-hug. "Oh, David, that's wonderful!" She clapped her hands together in readiness for imminent organization. "Listen, as soon as everything gets back to normal here, I'll help you find some foldable beds and sleepin'-bags. I'm sure we've got 'em stuffed away somewhere upstairs in the loft."

David smiled at her obvious excitement. "That really would be great, Jasmine." He leaned back against the sideboard and took a drink of his coffee. "So how's the patient this morning?"

"Much better. I slept in the next-door room last night just in case she needed me. Heard her get up once, but besides that, I'm pretty sure she slept through. Anyways, right now she's sittin' up in bed and sayin' that she might get up later on this morning. I told her just to stay where she was, and if I saw her down here, I'd chase her so fast up those stairs again that her feet would hardly touch the ground." She laughed and, turning to pick up the tray, which was set with cup and saucer, a pot of tea and some toast and marmalade, she handed it to him. "I was just going to take this up to her, but seein' you're here *and* she's already asked to see you, I think we could kill two birds with one stone, don't you—nursey?"

She gave David a wink, and with a shake of his head at her gibe, he turned and walked upstairs.

Balancing the tray on one hand, he knocked on the bedroom door and, receiving a mumbled response, he entered in time to see Jennifer stuff something under her bedclothes and glance towards him with a flushed look of guilt on her face. She was dressed in a white, short-sleeved cotton night-dress, her hair hanging in loose strands against her washed-out cheeks, and the whole scene gave David the impression that he had just caught some impish child doing something that was very much against the rules.

She let out a sigh of relief on seeing him. "Oh, thank God it's you!" She retrieved a large acetate-covered document from under her bedclothes. "I thought it was Jasmine. She'd have given me hell if she'd caught me with this."

David laughed and carried the tray over to her bedside. "Where do you want this?"

"Hang on," Jennifer said, pushing back the bedclothes, "I'll just put this back in my brief-case." She scrambled on all fours across the double bed to the side nearest him, then tilted her head up, a grin on her face. "I went downstairs and got it early this morning before Jasmine was up, so I've had to hide it under the bed. Wicked, huh?"

David put the tray down across her knees. "So, how are you feeling this morning?"

"Okay. A little woozy, but the headache has gone and I haven't been sick again, thank God!" She took a piece of toast from the rack and crunched on it.

"Glad to hear it." He took a deep breath and turned to go. "Well, I suppose I'd better be getting to work."

"No, dom'p yep!" Jennifer exclaimed, her mouth filled with dry toast. She swallowed. "I mean, can you stay and talk for a minute?"

He stood for a moment, indecisively scratching at the back of his head. "Well, okay, if you want."

She reached forward as far as the tray would allow her and patted the bed, and out of habit, David found himself dusting off the seat of his jeans before he sat down. Jennifer poured herself a cup of tea and put down the pot, then for a moment just stared at the tray, lost in thought.

"David," she said eventually, still looking down at the tray. "I just, uh . . ." She let out a short embarrassed laugh. "I actually don't know what I want to say . . . no, I mean, yes . . . I do know. I just want to say . . . that what you did last night . . . was one of the kindest things I think that anyone has ever done for me in my life." She glanced up briefly and a smile flashed across her face before she looked back down to the tray. "So thank you." She looked up again and took in a deep faltering breath. "It sounds pretty inadequate, I know, but—"

"No, look, it was nothing," David interjected with a wave of his hand. "I tell you, we were all pretty worried about you. I think Jasmine's probably right. You should just take things easy for a day or two."

Jennifer nodded. "Yeah, I will." She took a long drink of her tea, then held her hand up mid-mouthful and gulped it down. "I know what I wanted to talk to you about. Benji's song. Jasmine says it's wonderful."

"How come you've heard about that so quickly?"

"Well, I sneaked along to Benji's bedroom on my way back from picking up the brief-case, and he wasn't there, so it was my first question to Jasmine this morning. She said that he was staying with Sean, and I said that I didn't think that they were friends any more, and then she told me the story of the song. How on earth did you pull it off?"

"God, I did nothing! Benji wrote and performed the whole thing himself, and Gerry added a bit of arrangement—with some help from this mad Irish bunch called Dublin Up. All I did was hang around in the studio looking spare!"

"Oh, come on, that's nonsense! It's just like the tennis. All this Scottish modesty infuriates me! I'll spell out exactly what you achieved, David, though I know I don't need to, because you know damned well yourself. Benji being accepted by his friends again, that's what. And you orchestrated the whole thing, didn't you?"

David rolled his eyes. "Now, listen, you've not been very well, and I don't think you should get quite so over-excited—"

"Oh to hell with you, you condescending brute!" With a cry of laughter, she whisked out a pillow from behind her and dealt him a blow on the side of the head. "Don't try to change the subject! Come on, SAY IT!" She whacked him again with the pillow.

"All right! All right!" David yelled out, covering his head with his hands in mock protection against the feeble blows that were now raining down on him in quick succession. "I give up! I admit it!"

"Good," Jennifer said quietly. She leaned back, panting from the exertion, the pillow still held poised for the next blow. "That wasn't so hard, was it?" She suddenly gritted her teeth, building herself up for another blow. "But I think you deserve one more for good measure."

As the pillow struck David on the side of the face, the bedroom door opened and Jasmine appeared.

"What's all the noise ab——? What on *earth* d'you two think you're doin'?"

Jennifer sprang back under the bedclothes as Jasmine approached the bed, giving David a reprimanding cuff on the side of the head as she passed.

"Honestly!" she scolded, fussing over Jennifer like a clucking hen, pulling the duvet cover up to Jennifer's neck and smoothing it down with her hand. "I can't leave you for a minute and you're revving yourself up. And as for you, David, you know how sick she's been. You should know better than to encourage her." She straightened up and looked at the two smirking faces.

"Sorry, miss," David said in a high-pitched voice.

It was enough to set Jennifer off. David looked up at Jasmine, trying desperately to offset the infection of Jennifer's reaction, and to his relief a huge grin spread across her face, and now they all burst out laughing.

"Okay, that's it! Enough's enough!" Jasmine said eventually, wiping a tear from her eye with the back of her hand. She walked to the end of the bed and put her hand on David's shoulder. "You—outta here!" She pushed him to his feet and guided him to the door and out into the corridor, then stopped just inside the room and looked back at Jennifer.

"Now, you get some rest, d'ya hear me? And no gettin' out of bed."

David stuck his head back round the corner of the door and winked at the trussed-up figure in the bed.

"And no more scrabbling under the bed!"

Jennifer let out another snort, and Jasmine pushed him out of the door and closed it behind her. "What's that supposed to mean?" she said, a puzzled expression on her face.

"One day, Jasmine," he said, putting his arm around her shoulders and slowly walking with her along the landing, "all will be revealed."

Jasmine pushed herself away and gave him a hard punch on the arm. "Oh, git on with you! I don't know if I like you any more! You're behavin' way too happy!"

Chapter
TWENTY-SEVEN

It only took three days of cosseted convalescence before Jennifer was deemed fit enough by Jasmine to be allowed downstairs, despite having had a relapse during the afternoon of day one. Jasmine had at first blamed the shenanigans of the morning, but then later on that day, when Jennifer was having a bath, she had found the secreted brief-case whilst making the bed and, with many a moaning protest from Jennifer about being treated like a ten-year-old, she had removed it to the safekeeping of the kitchen.

David also came under fire from Jasmine's dictatorial leanings, something which he found quietly amusing. She had banned him from visiting Jennifer without her being in attendance, not so much that she felt that he would hinder her recovery, but rather because she had a sneaking suspicion that he had been in cahoots with Jennifer in smuggling the brief-case up to the bedroom in the first place.

Nevertheless, by Saturday the curfew had been lifted, and during a short handing-over ceremony in the kitchen, Jennifer was reunited with her brief-case, and given full permission by the "boss" to continue her work in the study. However, a combination of her illness, the break from work and the fact that Benji was at home made Jennifer feel lackadaisical about giving any immediate thought to Tarvy's, and she decided to postpone any further work on it until Monday, when she would return to the office.

Consequently, she was able to devote the entire weekend to Benji. Taking him out in the rowing-boat, watching from the shoreline at his ever-improving attempts at windsurfing on the bay, and of course listening to "the song" over and over again, during each rendition of which Benji gave her a running commentary of every sound that had been introduced into the final mix.

But above all, she enjoyed the moments when David was around. At first she couldn't even explain it to herself, but then, on the Saturday afternoon, while sitting high on the umpire's ladder, giving out loud and biased judgements in favour of her son and killing herself laughing when David approached her and complained in true McEnroe style about unfavorable line-calls, she realized that this was all she strove for with Alex. This was family. This was happiness. For a moment, she wished that Alex could be there to be part of it. Then, almost guiltily, she understood that his being there would more than likely be a dampener, for David would no doubt see his own presence as an intrusion, and if she insisted on his joining in, it could quite easily lead to resentment from Alex.

That evening, having successfully exercised a bit of arm-twisting on Jasmine, she arranged a lunch-time barbecue for the following day, primarily as a thank-you to Gerry Reilly for his part in helping to produce Benji's song. As it turned out, Dublin Up were still in the process of recording their album, so the invitation was extended to include them, much to the delight of Benji, who saw a way to add to his already burgeoning reputation at school by inviting half of his class to the party.

It turned out to be an afternoon of riotous fun, precipitated by the fact that at last Jennifer had found something at which David was quite useless. His attempts at barbecuing were a complete disaster, and Benji and his friends spent most of their lunch-time running down the lawn with armfuls of charcoaled hamburgers and chucking them Frisbee-style into the bay. However, such was David's obstinance in giving up his post—"I'll get it right next time" he kept saying—that Jennifer, armed to the teeth with skewer and spatula, finally had to drive him away from the barbecue. Thereafter the women of the household took over, Jasmine cooking everything to perfection, ably assisted by Jennifer, who used the water-squirter not only to keep the flames dampened down, but also to ward off David's sneaky efforts to return for another attempt.

The party stretched on through the afternoon into the early hours of the evening, with tense games of doubles on the tennis court, crazy antics in the swimming pool, and hotly disputed games of soccer, alternated with periods of indolent slouching both on the lawn and on the sun-beds around the pool. Age became immaterial as adult partnered child, and child conquered adult, with fierce rivalry developing between each team, for the most part engendered by the adult members.

There was only one occasion during the whole proceedings on which Jennifer had call to be momentarily concerned, this being brought about by a young female classmate of Benji's who had developed an obvious crush on the lead guitarist of Dublin Up. Having subsequently ensconced herself on his knee as he lay on the sun-bed next to Jennifer, the girl asked him quite pointedly why his cigarette was such a funny shape and why it smelt so strange. However, much to Jennifer's relief, and before there was need for her to exercise responsibility as the hostess, the young man snuffed out the suspect cigarette between thumb and forefinger and stuck it behind his ear. Then, in order to divert his young suitor from asking any more leading questions, he sprang to his feet, gathering her up in his arms, and lobbed her with calculated precision into the middle of the swimming pool.

As she heard Benji loudly bid farewell to the last of his friends at the front of the house and the sound of a car taking off up the drive, Jennifer walked slowly down to the bottom of the garden to retrieve an article of clothing left abandoned on the lawn. After picking it up she continued on down to the shore of the bay and stepped out onto the wooden jetty. She stood there hugging the shirt to her chest and listening to the cacophony of crickets that broke the quiet of the evening air, and watching the final rays of the setting sun as it shimmered pink across the gently undulating waters.

The perfect end to a perfect day, she thought to herself. No, it hadn't been just the day. The whole weekend had turned out to be the most relaxed, happy and—she consciously stopped her train of thought there, wondering if she dared admit it even to herself—yes, why the hell not—*intimate* time that she had experienced in years. She suddenly shuddered, despite the warmth of the evening air and, closing her eyes, she drew in the heady aroma of the pine-trees mingled with the tangy freshness of the salt water. Then, disregarding the mosquitos biting ferociously at her ankles, she walked slowly back up onto the lawn and meandered her way to the house, kicking out her bare feet in time with the chorus of a Lou Reed song that had begun to play over and over in her mind.

> *Oh it's a perfect day*
> *I'm glad I spent it with you*
> *Just a perfect day*

By the time that David arrived at the house the next morning, Jennifer had already left for work, and Jasmine remarked with a delighted gleam in her eye that, for almost the first time in living memory, she had done so reluctantly. Nevertheless, whereas she had been morose about starting the new week, it was immediately heralded with a new buzz of excitement by the others in the Newman household, as David and Jasmine began to make plans for the children's arrival.

Benji was naturally irritated by their clandestine chats, so David decided to bring him in early on the plan, and sitting around the kitchen table after school that afternoon, he told him from the beginning about Rachel and the children, and about their imminent visit.

At first the young boy had mixed feelings about the whole affair. He couldn't believe that David had children of his own and hadn't told anyone, and at the same time there was a funny low feeling of resentment in his stomach when he thought about their coming out to the States and David spending all his time with them, and not with him any more. He also found it difficult to understand why David didn't want to tell his mother straight away, because he *knew* that she would be both amazed and excited that David had children.

David explained to him as concisely as possible that of course he would tell his mother, but that he wanted first to get the chance to explain things in full, as he had done with him. At first, Benji appeared despondent at not being allowed to break the news himself, but when Jasmine happened to mention Charlie's age, the boy's face suddenly lit up with intrigue.

"He's twelve?"

"Yup."

"About the same age as me?"

"Just a bit older, I'd guess."

"Do you think we might be friends, David?"

"I'm relying on it!"

"Wow! When's he coming?"

"Thursday of next week."

"Fan-tas-tic!!"

Thereafter, Benji was won over, and he joined in

with as much enthusiasm as David and Jasmine in searching out the loft for the sleeping-bags and rummaging around in the rafters above the garage for the foldable beds and tent, the latter thrown in by Jasmine for good measure, just in case the walls of David's house couldn't cope with the sudden expansion in numbers of its inhabitants.

David realized quite early on in his organization of events that he was not going to be able to rely totally on Jasmine as a back-up, especially when Jennifer and Alex were around. Also he wanted his children to have a free run in Leesport, to come and go as they pleased, and if he were to take a few of his friends into his confidence, they would always act as a focal point for a visit from the children, or as a refuge if something went wrong. Consequently, he telephoned both Gerry Reilly, even though he lived a bit out of Leesport, and Billy, the joke-cracking young man in the deli, and after work that afternoon, he went up to the main street to see Clive and Dotti. Although he had thought it only necessary to disclose the more general facts to Gerry and Billy, he felt comfortable in telling the whole story to Clive, who appeared suitably moved with emotion throughout, every so often dabbing at his eyes with a large paisley-patterned silk handkerchief.

The night before the children arrived, David felt as if it were he himself who was coming to the end of term. He woke constantly during the night to glance at his alarm clock and carry out mental calculations as to how many hours were left until it was time to get up, as well as working out what point the children might have reached on their journey. At six o'clock, he decided that he was not going to be able to go back to sleep and, jumping out of bed, he showered and dressed quickly and took Dodie out for a walk down to the marina. There he killed time by standing out on the farthest walkway, watching the sun rise over the horizon beyond the eastern reaches of Fire Island, making a deal with himself that he would only turn back when its lower tip had broken clear of the far-off sand dunes.

Having shared a breakfast of three shredded wheat with Dodie, he carried out a final check of the store cupboards to make sure that he hadn't forgotten any of their favourite foodstuffs, and gave the house one last look-over to see that all the beds were ready and made up—two in the screened sun-porch and the other in the corner of the sitting-room next to the desk. He then locked up the house and headed off to the garage to fill up the Volkswagen.

Benji and Jasmine were waiting outside the front door of the house when he arrived, both holding on to the ends of an old sheet that was stretched out between them. On it was written in big black blotched letters: WELCOME SOPHIE, CHARLIE AND HARRIT, with a blobby insertion caret adding the omitted E to Harriet's name.

"We're going to hang it outside your house, so that they see it when you get there," Benji said proudly, craning his neck over the side of the banner to admire his handiwork. "What d'ya think of it?"

"It's a work of art, Benji!" David exclaimed, standing with his head at a slant and giving it as much scrutiny as if he were admiring a van Gogh. "I reckon that that'll just make the start of their holidays."

"C'mon, Benji," Jasmine said. "Let's get this put away before it starts catchin' dirt." She turned to David as she pulled the sheet into tight folds. "You wantin' a cup of coffee before you leave?"

"No, I don't think so, thanks. I'll just take my time driving into Kennedy, and I can always grab a cup there if I arrive too early. You never know with these transatlantic flights. Sometimes they arrive an hour ahead of their time."

"When's it due? Just so's I know when to be down at the house."

"Twelve-ten. But then they'll have to get through Im-

migration and pick up their luggage, so I don't think
that we'll be clear of the airport much before, say, quarter past one. There shouldn't be that much traffic on
the parkway at that time of the day, so I reckon we'll
be back by a quarter to three."

"Okay. We'll try gettin' there by two-thirty." She
paused and smiled at him. "You excited?"

He nodded. "And how!"

"Well, in that case, I reckon you'd better jump to it!
I'll see you later—and good luck with the kids. I got all
kinds of butterflies workin' away in my stomach!"

"That makes two of us, then," he laughed, as he
moved off towards the car.

As it turned out, it was just as well he had given
himself so much time to get to the airport. There had
been an accident on the Belt Parkway which caused a
traffic jam that stretched all the way back onto the
Southern State in Malverne. For an hour, he had remained in a stationary line of traffic, drumming his fingers impatiently on the steering wheel and glancing at
his watch, while Dodie had amused herself by growling
incessantly at the bearded truck driver whose vehicle
edged forward alongside.

By the time that he found the most shaded place in
the parking lot nearest the terminal, it was just after a
quarter past eleven. Having opened the front windows
an inch or two, he pulled up the canvas top of the
Volkswagen and clipped it shut, leaving Dodie to feast
herself on the knob of the gear-shift, and ran across the
road to the terminal building. Pushing his way through
the crowds as they stood in a series of zigzagging queues
leading to their respective check-in desks, he glanced up
at the information screen, only to find that he was on
the Departures floor. He scanned around for a sign saying "Arrivals," eventually seeing it at the bottom of a
flight of stairs twenty yards farther along the hall. Moving as fast as the thronging masses would allow, he

made it to the steps and took them, two at a time, to the upper floor.

It was far less crowded than the Departures area, but nevertheless, there were already a cluster of expectant faces gathered around the chrome rail at the Customs door, watching and waiting for the first signs of their opening. The information screen indicated that the plane had just touched down, half an hour ahead of time, so he walked over to stand at one end of the barrier. Then, realizing that they still had to come through Immigration and Customs, he turned away and sought out a coffee bar. Ordering himself a black coffee and a muffin, he pulled out a bar-stool and sat down, and turned to watch for the doors to begin disgorging the passengers from Glasgow.

Twenty-five minutes and two coffees later, the doors eventually opened and the first shrieks of welcome resounded around the domelike hall. A young child was pushed under the chrome rail by encouraging parents and walked apprehensively forward to greet an old couple who struggled bravely to co-ordinate the welcome that was expected of them while still trying to keep their overladen luggage trolley on its designated course.

Thereafter, the newly arrived passengers came thick and fast through the doors, some being welcomed by friends and families and whisked off to waiting cars, while others, casting lost looks around the terminal building, traipsed unsurely away in different directions, like sheep in desperate need of a sheep-dog to nudge some order and guidance into their lives.

Charlie and Harriet appeared first through the door, both coming out in reverse as it happened, Charlie shrugging up his haversack onto his back as he yelled to Sophie to hurry up. David slid off his bar-stool and made his way slowly towards the barrier, content to remain at a distance, quenching the deprivation that he had felt over the past month by savouring those few seconds in which they were unaware of his presence.

They turned, suddenly shy as they stood scanning the smiling faces gathered round the barrier, then Charlie caught sight of him, and with a loud shout of "Dad!" ducked under the rail, getting his rucksack caught up in the process, and ran towards him. David stayed where he was, watching his son approach, strangely lean and lanky compared with Benji, his tight jeans and cotton gingham shirt making him appear unaccountably British.

Charlie hit him at speed and threw his arms around his waist. "Dad! We had a great time on the plane. I was allowed to go up with the pilot and watch him fly it! They wouldn't allow me to touch anything though!"

"I'm glad to hear it!" David laughed.

David pulled him in close to his body and leaned forward to give him a kiss on the top of his head, relishing the slightly musty smell of his hair. Charlie immediately pushed himself away and ran back to collect Harriet, who still stood where he had left her, having become entirely captivated by the sight of a young girl lying screaming on the floor of the terminal, kicking out her little legs in temper at her parents' luggage trolley as they tried their ineffectual best to calm her down.

"Harriet! Quick! Here's Dad!"

Harriet immediately broke out of her dream-world and an expression of yearning agitation came over her face as she looked around for her father. Then seeing him, she broke into a run, taking the long way round the barrier. As she came towards him, David bent down and gathered her up, feeling her arms and legs clamp around his body like some deliciously formed octopus.

"Hello, darling!" He nuzzled his face deep into the mop of thick black curls and kissed the nape of her smooth soft neck. "How are you?"

Harriet lifted her head off his shoulders and looked at him, her face a mere six inches away from his own. "Daddy?"

"Yeah?"

She glanced back towards the door. "That little girl is behaving *so* badly."

David laughed. "I know she is. I hope you behaved better than that on the plane."

Harriet turned back to look at him, a grin on her face. "Of *course* I did!" Her smile slid into a frown. "Except I was frightened quite a lot."

"Why?"

" 'Cos Charlie kept saying that the plane was *bound* to blow up!"

David raised his eyebrows and began walking with her towards the Arrivals door. "Oh, yeah, that sounds like him."

He stopped next to his son, who was leaning against the barrier, breathing on the chrome to make it fog up, then rubbing it hard with his hand to clear it.

"Where's Sophie got to, Charlie?"

"She's coming out with the stewardess. We had to have someone with us everywhere we went, 'cos they said we were too young to go by ourselves. It was really embarrassing, 'cos they put tags on us with our names. I pulled mine and Harriet's off when we landed."

"And I wanted to keep mine," Harriet whined.

"No, you didn't! You thought it was stupid, too. Here she is. Come on, Sophie, Dad's here!"

David moved to the side so that he could see her approach, and from the moment that she appeared around the corner, chatting animatedly to the stewardess as they helped each other with the luggage trolley, he felt a smile broaden across his face and a feeling of unbelievable pride rise up in his heart. She had changed so much, not only having grown upwards, but—well, sort of everywhere. Her long auburn hair was drawn back and gathered loosely behind her head with a clip, which seemed to accentuate the contours of her face. God, it had only been a month since he had seen her last, but it was enough for him to be aware of the meta-morphosis that had taken place within her—no longer the gawky, self-conscious teenager, but a young fledgling fast breaking into womanhood. David let Harriet down onto the ground without taking his eyes off his eldest daughter, watching as she and the stewardess came round the barrier towards him, and noticing out of the side of his eye that a young boy, standing with his parents at the rail, also followed her progress with interest.

Leaving the stewardess to push the trolley the last few yards by herself, Sophie walked quickly towards her father, and just as she reached him, her face broke into a wide smile and her eyes sparkled, and in that brief, mind-shattering instance, David realized that it was as if Rachel had been re-incarnated.

"Hi, Dad," she said quietly.

For a moment, David stood entranced, shaking his head slowly at this incredible apparition, then moved towards her and pulled her in close to him.

"My God! You look wonderful!" he said, rocking her from side to side in his arms and kissing the side of her head. "Oh, it's so lovely to see you! I really cannot begin to tell you how lovely it is to see you!"

There was a loud tutting noise from beside him, and he looked down to see Charlie eyeing the stewardess and scuffing his feet across the floor.

"C'mon, Dad, this is embarrassing. Can't we go now?"

"Okay!" David exclaimed, giving Sophie a final kiss on the cheek. "Let's grab ourselves a horse and get the hell out of Dodge!"

Thanking the stewardess for her help, he took over at the helm of the luggage trolley and steered it towards the door of the terminal, his two daughters holding on to the handle at either side of him while Charlie ran ahead.

"Is this America now, Daddy?" Harriet asked as she jogged alongside David, trying to keep up with his brisk pace.

"Yup, this is it, darling, home of hot dogs, hamburgers and er . . . can't think of anything else that begins with *h*."

"And heat!" Sophie added with almost pleasurable relief, as they left the coolness of the air-conditioned building and walked out into the throat-searing swelter of the mid-day sun.

"Yeah," David laughed, "heat! And there's plenty of that, I can tell you!"

They walked across the road into the parking lot and made their way towards the Volkswagen. David had already given detailed descriptions of the car in his letters, and consequently both Charlie and Harriet spotted it at the same time and raced ahead, only to recoil sharply on reaching it, as Dodie suddenly jumped up at the half-open window and yapped fiercely at them.

"Is that Dodie?" Charlie asked, laughing uncertainly.

"Yup."

"She sort of suits the car."

"Why do you say that?"

" 'Cos they both look, well, battered."

"Well, for goodness' sakes, don't let her hear you say that! Dodie is very sensitive about her looks! I once suggested that she should consider having a fur-lift and she wouldn't speak to me for a week!"

"Really?" Harriet gasped, her mouth open as she stared at Dodie through the window.

"No, stupid!" Charlie retorted. "He's only joking!"

David unlocked the car, and pushing Dodie into the back seat, he reached over to release the catch for the front trunk.

"Can we have the top down, Dad?" Charlie asked, grabbing hold of a suitcase and dragging it round to the front of the car.

"Yeah, well, I guess we'll have to, otherwise I don't think there'll be room for all your stuff."

"Great!"

David squeezed Harriet's haversack into the last re-

maining space in the trunk and carefully shut the lid.
Then, unclipping the roof, he folded it down, thus re-
leasing Dodie's aromatic wonders to the world.

"Phew!" Sophie said, wrinkling up her nose. "What
a niff! Bags I don't have her on my knee!"

David grinned at her. "Yeah, I'm afraid that she does
have a bit of a problem. Someone suggested that I give
her garlic pills, but I think she's built up some sort of
immunity to them!"

"I'll take her!" Charlie said, reaching over the side
of the car and ruffling Dodie's woolly fur. He turned
and gave his elder sister a narrow look. "But only if I'm
allowed to sit in the front."

The bargain was struck, and once the remainder of
the luggage was jammed into the small compartment
behind the rear seat, they set off on their journey back
to Leesport.

Once they reached the Southern State Parkway, the
traffic eased considerably, and as they bumbled along
eastwards, David decided that this was the perfect opportunity to teach them the words of "Dodie the Fun-
Loving Poodle." Three times through it, and Charlie
and Harriet had picked it up completely, singing along
with enthusiasm and rocking themselves side to side in
time with the tune. Sophie, however, seemed reticent to
participate, and as he accompanied his two youngest
children through the verses, he eyed her in the rear-view
mirror, as she sat leaning her elbow on the sill of the
car and gazing absently at the passing scenery.

They eventually arrived at the traffic lights on Leesport's main street at exactly two-thirty, and thinking
that Jasmine and Benji would have yet to complete their
work on the welcoming banner, David pulled to a halt
outside Helping Hands, giving the horn two quick
beeps. He watched through the window of the shop as
Clive and Dotti looked up from their desks and, on
recognizing the car, both jumped to their feet.

"Why are we stopping here?" Charlie asked.

"I just want you to meet a couple of my friends."
With that, the door of the shop flew open, and Clive
came rushing across the sidewalk to the car, followed
closely by Dotti.

"Well, for heaven's sakes!" he said, putting a hand
to his cheek and surveying the incredulous looks on the
children's faces. "Oh, David, they are simply wonderful! All so good-looking!" He grinned, giving his shoulders a cosy shrug, before offering his hand to each of
the children in turn. "Hi, my name is Clive. You are?
Sophie—hello, Sophie, and—Charlie, and—Harriet.
Well, I can't tell you how fantastic it is to meet you all!
Oh, and by the way, this"—he turned and put an arm
around his assistant, who smiled shyly, pushing up her
spectacles onto her nose—"is Dotti." He sighed, surveying the children with a look of sheer delight on his
face. "So where are you off to now? Straight to the
beach, I'd guess."

David looked around at the children, who had not
taken their eyes off Clive, riveted by his boisterous enthusiasm.

"Well, we'll go back to the house first and get the
car unpacked, but then maybe a cool-down might be
the order of the day."

"I think that sounds like a great idea!" He leaned his
hands on the side of the car. "Now, any time you kids
want to drop into the shop, you're more than welcome.
Dotti has already got some Coke in the refrigerator, so
come soon, won't you?"

The children smiled, mumbling a thank-you, and David turned the key and started the engine.

"We'd better be off, Clive. We're meeting Jasmine
and Benji at the house, so we'd better not be late."

"Okay!" Clive said, jumping back from the car. "Remember now, any time you want, kids, just drop in!"

The white tip of the welcoming banner was clearly
visible, fluttering high above the hedge, as David turned
the car into Shore Street. He pulled to a halt outside

the house, hearing immediately Benji's voice shout out excitedly from the garden.

"Jasmine, they're here!"

The gate flew open and he came running out onto the sidewalk. Then, stopping at a distance from the side of the car, he stood grinning and shifting his weight self-consciously from one foot to the other, as he was scrutinized by the new arrivals. David jumped out of the car and came round to the sidewalk.

"Right! Introductions!" He pointed to each of his children in turn. "Sophie—Charlie—Harriet. This is Benji."

There were a few uncertain murmurings as they acknowledged one another's existence, and David watched the whole scene with quiet amusement as he leaned over the side of the car and pulled the trunk lever.

"All out and we'll get the cases inside. Where's Jasmine, Benji?"

"I'm here!" a voice called out from behind the hedge. She appeared through the gate, a hammer under her arm as she wiped her glistening forehead with the back of her hand. "My goodness, you nearly caught us nappin' there!" She scanned the children, and her face broke into a huge smile. "Hi, everybody, I'm Jasmine. Now, Benji, I heard you bein' introduced, so you can go ahead and tell me who everyone is."

As the children clambered out of the car, Benji went through their names faultlessly, and Jasmine stepped forward to shake the hand of each in turn.

"Right!" David said, unloading the suitcases and putting them on the sidewalk. "Everyone grab something!"

Scooping up the two largest suitcases in an immediate test of individual strength, Charlie and Benji struggled with them through the gate into the garden.

"Hey, Sophie! Harriet! Come quickly!" Charlie's voice sounded out. "Come and have a look at *this*!"

The two girls picked up their haversacks and hurried through the gate to find Charlie standing in the middle of the garden, looking around in sheer wonderment.

"Isn't this great? Look, we're right by the beach! And look at the sign on the house! Benji says he made it himself!"

"You missed out the *E* in my name," Harriet said, disappointed.

"Harry, don't be so tactless!" Sophie scolded her.

"Yeah, sorry about that," Benji said quietly, pushing his hands deep into the pockets of his shorts. "I sorta got mixed up with the spelling—but I did put it in at the end."

Sophie smiled at him. "Well, I think it's great, Benji. It's really well done!"

Benji looked down at his feet, his face colouring with embarrassment.

"And I think so too!" Charlie said, grabbing Benji by the arm. "Come on, let's go and explore!" The two boys turned to run off together down to the jetty just as David came into the garden, carrying the last of the suitcases.

"Hang on, you two! Where are you heading off to?"

"We're going to explore, Dad!"

"Not just yet. We'll get the suitcases inside first, and I'll show you where you're sleeping."

"Yesss!" Charlie shouted out in excitement, and he and Benji ran back across the lawn towards the house.

It turned out that Jasmine had not only busied herself in putting up the banner, but had also gone through the house plumping up the cushions on the sofa and clearing away the cups and plates that David had left to dry on the draining-board. Harriet and Charlie were delighted with their bedroom out on the screened porch, both throwing themselves onto their beds and looking around to see what views were afforded them from their supine positions. However, Sophie showed little emotion at what the house had to offer, having placed her suitcase on her bed in the sitting-room and begun to unpack it with quiet and methodical efficiency.

"Okay!" David said, clapping his hands to assemble the company in the sitting-room. "Let's forget about unpacking for now. What do you think, Jasmine? The ferry to Fire Island?"

There was a whoop of joy from Benji, immediately echoed by Charlie and Harriet, who hadn't a clue what or where Fire Island was, but if Benji thought it was a good idea *and* it needed a ferry to get to, then it must be an idea worth agreeing with.

"Looks like you've hit on a good plan there!" Jasmine said with a laugh.

"Okay! Fire Island it is! Let's get your swimming things out of the suitcases, and we'll be off!"

Charlie and Benji ran through to the porch and began tearing at the contents of his haversack, while Jasmine gave Harriet a hand to sort through her belongings to find her swim-suit. David went into his bedroom alcove and took a pair of trunks from the top of his chest of drawers, and came back to find that Sophie had made no move to find her own.

"Can't you find yours, darling?"

Sophie looked up at him, her mouth lifting into a light smile. "If you don't mind, Dad, I don't think I'll come."

"Oh," David said, disappointed, "do come, darling. It really will be good fun. It's a beautiful beach, and—"

"Dad, I just don't want to!" She picked up a shirt from her suitcase and threw it down on the bed. "Do you really mind *that* much?"

For a moment, David stood staring at her, taken aback by the razor tone in her voice. He was about to answer her when he felt a hand on his arm, and turned to find Jasmine and the other children standing silently behind him. She walked towards the door of the house, gesturing with her head for him to follow.

"Come on, you lot," he said, waving his hand at the

children. "Let's go out into the garden for a minute."

As soon as they were all outside, Benji, Charlie and Harriet ran off down to the jetty, yelling with enthusiasm as they went.

"Do you want to stay here for a while?" Jasmine asked quietly.

"Yes, I think I'd better. Would you mind taking them off for a bit?"

"Not at all! Tell you what, I'll bring them up to the house to swim in the pool, and then you two can join us later. How about that?"

"That would be great, Jasmine."

They walked down to the edge of the garden where Harriet stood watching Benji and Charlie competing with each other in a pebble-throwing contest off the jetty.

"Right, you lot! Slight change of plan! You're all going along to Benji's house to swim in the pool."

Letting out yet more whoops of excitement, the two boys ran back up the steps and headed straight past them to the gate. Harriet's return journey to the garden, however, was more laborious, pushing on her knees to give herself extra leverage as she climbed the steps.

She stopped beside her father. "Aren't you and Sophie coming, Daddy?"

"Not just yet, darling." He bent forward, his hands on his knees. "But if you go with Jasmine, Sophie and I will be with you very soon, okay?"

Harriet nodded and without a hint of shyness, slipped her hand into Jasmine's.

"Okay, Harriet!" Jasmine said, raising her eyebrows in delight and giving David a wink, "let's go catch up with the boys, then we'll have some fun!" They walked together across the garden and out through the gate, and as David headed towards the door of the house, he heard their voices on the other side of the hedge fading off down the street as they engaged each other in conversation.

David opened the door and walked back into the house. Sophie still stood beside the bed, unpacking her belongings. He picked up the kettle as he passed the sideboard and filled it up from the tap.

"Well, I'm going to have a cup of tea. How about you?"

Sophie shook her head without turning.

"No?"

She turned and flashed him a light smile. "No, thanks."

David leaned against the sink, folding his arms. "When I spoke to Mr. Hunter, he said that you'd done really well in your GSCEs. They went all right, then?"

"I suppose so."

Perplexed by the offhand reaction to his questions, David walked over to Sophie and put a hand on her shoulder. "Are you feeling all right, darling?"

She turned to him. "Not really," she said quietly. "I've just got this really bad tummy pain."

"Oh, darling, you should have said! Something you ate on the plane, d'you think?"

She raised her eyebrows at his misunderstanding of events. "No, Dad, not that kind! It's, well, you know—my time of the month."

David was silent for a moment as the realization of what she was saying dawned on him.

"Oh, for heaven's sakes, of course. I'm sorry, Sophie, I should have understood. No wonder you're feeling mouldy. Have you got, well, everything you need?"

She smiled at him as she continued to unpack. "Yup, I do, thanks." She stopped as she carefully laid a pair of trousers in the drawer. "It's just that, well . . . oh, never mind."

"No, go on, darling—please."

"Well, it's just that I'm still not very sure of myself, you know, dealing with all this, and sometimes I get panicky, and I find it difficult to cope—with swimming and things like that." She glanced at her father and bit hard on her bottom lip, then let out a faltering laugh. "I don't suppose it's the kind of thing that a girl discusses with her father. It's just that I haven't got Mummy any m——"

It was as far as she got. In that brief moment, the vulnerability brought on both by nature and by the long flight's disruption to her own body's time-clock broke through her steely resolve, allowing her emotions to burst through to the surface.

"Oh, Dad, I miss Mummy *so* much."

She ran towards him and circled her arms around his chest, her body heaving convulsively with shuddering sobs as she began to rid herself of the grief that she had been storing up deep within her for so long. For a moment, he held her in silence, kissing the top of her head over and over again, and feeling her tears slowly seep through the front of his shirt, wetting the skin beneath.

"I know you do, my darling, I know you do," he said eventually, tears welling up in his own eyes as he rocked her gently against him, "and I do too—so much so that it hurts, and I don't think that it ever will stop hurting. There is not one second of the day goes by when I'm not thinking about her." He pushed her gently away and, cupping his hand under her chin, he raised her face to look at him. "But listen, darling, I'm here for you now, I'm here for you all. Things were different for me back in Scotland, but they really have changed now, and they will keep changing—for the better, I promise you. I'm afraid we won't ever get Mummy back, no matter how much we wish and pray, but the most important thing is that we all have each other, as a family, and that's what Mummy would want—that we keep going and have more happy times, and laugh and joke just like we used to." He paused and looked around the room. "Do you know, she's here right now. I know she is. Right here in the room, and she's saying to us, 'That's it! Go ahead, you guys, do it for me! I'm cheering you on! Just keep laughing and joking and be happy, because if you're sad and down-hearted, you won't be like me any more, and I want to leave you my wit and humour and love of life and—beauty.' "

Sophie's face slowly broke into a sad smile and she pulled her face away from her father's hand and turned to look around the room.

"Do you really think she's saying that?" she asked quietly.

David smiled. "Well, something like that, only she's probably being a bit more forceful in the way that she says it."

Sophie snorted out a laugh, immediately following it by a hefty sniff, and David walked over to the draining-board and took a great wodge of paper tissue off the kitchen roll. He handed it to her. "Here, 'gie yersel' a tidy-up,' as Effie would say!"

Sophie laughed again, and taking a deep breath, she gave her nose a hearty blow and wiped away the tears from her face.

"All right?" David asked, putting his arm around her shoulder and giving it a quick squeeze.

Sophie nodded and handed the sodden mass of paper back to him. He turned and threw it into the waste-paper basket.

"Listen, I had a thought the other day that, well, seeing I missed your sixteenth birthday at home, we should have a party out here for you." He gave her a wink. "It's a pretty important birthday, you know, sweet sixteen and all that. We should celebrate it in style."

Sophie let out a long sigh. "Oh, I don't know, Dad."

"Why not? It would be great fun! We'll have it here and invite Jasmine and Benji—"

"Dad, it's a really kind thought, but, well, I feel a bit old to have a birthday party." She walked back to the bed to continue with her unpacking. "What would we do? Play games and things?"

David slowly nodded his head. "Yeah, I do know what you mean. So, what kind of party would you like? Sort of . . . a discotheque or something like that?"

"I suppose," Sophie replied, shrugging her shoulders noncommitally.

"Okay, right, how about this for an idea? First, we'll have a small get-together out here—nothing too formal and certainly not childish—and we'll invite a few of my new friends who would love to meet you, and then, when we get back to Scotland, we'll have a real blow-out of a party, either at The Beeches or Inchelvie, depending on how many friends you want to invite. And we'll make it the happening of the year—no, what the hell!—the century! What do you think of that?"

Sophie's eyes lit up with excitement. "Do you really think we could?"

"Yeah, too right we could!"

"And can I invite a whole load of friends from school?"

"Of course you can—and they can stay on as long as they like after it!"

Sophie ran forward and threw her arms around his neck. "Oh, Dad, that would just be so *cool*!" She reached up and kissed him on the cheek. "When can we have it?"

"Well, I think it would be best if we work all that out when we get home—but I promise you, we certainly will have one!" He pulled her to him and gave her a kiss on the neck. "But in the meantime, let's decide on a day for our Stateside hooley." He freed himself from her embrace. "No point doing it this weekend, because it'll be the Fourth of July and there'll be parties enough going on around here. So, how about next Tuesday? That should be enough time to get things organized!"

"Okay—so, what kind of party should we have?"

"How about a barbecue? I'm lousy at doing them, but you and Jasmine could help me with the cooking. Then afterwards, we'll head off to Fire Island on the ferry and veg out for the rest of the afternoon on the beach." He paused. "Actually, the best idea would be for you and Jasmine to organize all the shopping and everything, and I'll do the inviting. How does that sound?"

"Sounds good." She looked dubious for a moment. "But, Dad, I would rather it was a party for *all* of us. I mean, don't make a big thing about it being my sixteenth, because, well, there really won't be many others there of my age, will there?"

He nodded. "Okay, message understood. It's a deal, then?"

Sophie smiled at him. "Yeah, it's a deal!"

She spat on her hand and held it out, and for a moment David stood looking startled, suddenly remembering that this was the exact way in which he and Rachel used to strike their bargains. He slowly raised his hand to his mouth and, spitting on it, placed it in Sophie's hand.

"Right now, how about going to join the others? We'll finish the unpacking when we get back."

They turned towards the door, linking their arms around each other, and as David opened the door, Sophie stopped and glanced over her shoulder.

"Do you think Mummy's coming?" she asked quietly, looking up at him.

David smiled at her and turned round to look back into the empty room.

"Yup, she's with us all the way."

Chapter
TWENTY-EIGHT

Jennifer pushed the rear-view mirror of her BMW to one side to stop the glare of the setting sun from hitting her face, then switched on the radio to listen for the traffic report, wanting some guidance as to whether she should just stick to the Long Island Expressway or cut down the Grand Central Parkway, pick up the Van Wyck Expressway and take the southern route out to Leesport.

However, judging by the traffic build-up that she was presently experiencing in Queens, it was probably going to be a case of just sitting it out either way. It was a pretty dumb idea, at any rate, trying to get out of Manhattan on the eve of the Fourth of July weekend. All the world and his dog seemed to be on the road, but really she had no choice. Sam Culpepper had specifically asked her to be in the office on Saturday so that they could give the proposals for Tarvy's just one more look-over before it was overnighted to London. Her initial plan had been to head out to Leesport after that had been finished with, but then when Russ asked her to attend a meeting first thing Monday morning with some new clients, she felt that it would be better to spend the whole weekend in the apartment in the West

Village, rather than having to face the start-of-the-week rush.

Nevertheless, she hated the idea of not being able to see Benji at all over the holiday weekend. So, on the spur of the moment, she had decided to head out to Leesport, so that she could at least spend a couple of hours with him before returning to the city early the following morning.

As she sat in the queue of cars, she glanced over at the thick typed proposal that lay on the passenger seat. She reached over and picked it up, letting the pages run across her thumb from beginning to end as if she were carrying out some form of superhuman copy-editing. She shook her head and chucked it back on the seat, lightly touching the accelerator to edge the BMW forward a couple of yards.

God, she hoped they'd get this contract. Sam had really set his heart on it, yet she still couldn't help but feel slightly apprehensive about its final content. Of course, the few days off last week hadn't helped. It had completely broken her flow, and consequently, over the past four days, she had found herself having to work well into the night in order to get back into the feel of it *and* to get it completed. Well, not quite completed. There were still a couple of statistics that she wanted to include in the report, but she had all the information with her, and she could just add them in on her laptop at home and take it into the office for printing the following day.

She let go of the steering wheel and linked her hands behind her head, stretching out her tired back.

But my goodness, those few missed days at work had been worth it, even though the reason for them had been thoroughly unpleasant, and the fact that she had had to work those long hours as a result. Having been with Benji for such an unbroken period of time, she had realized just how much he had changed, not only in the way she acted, but in himself, his whole body. Those mornings when he had come to sit on her bed before going to school and she had held him, she had felt no longer the soft flabbiness of his plump little body, but rather the beginnings of a fit young frame.

Yet she could take no credit for this change. It had been entirely David's doing, generating a renewed self-confidence and an almost tangible vibrance in the energy and enthusiasm of her son. David. She said his name again, feeling an unpremeditated buzz of excitement run through her, tingling her senses so much that a juddering shiver ran down her spine. She smiled and shook her head. No, it wasn't *that* kind of feeling. On the other hand, maybe it was. She couldn't work it out. It was just that being with him made her feel happy and relaxed and, well, almost tranquil without him having to do anything particularly special. Yet that was probably what made *him* special. There was no pretence with David. She knew exactly where she stood with him. He was kind, spontaneous, funny and totally trustworthy, and—come on, Jennifer admit it—attractive as hell, and, without doubt, one of the main reasons that you happen to be making this ludicrous trip out to Leesport.

The driver behind her blew hard on his horn, making her jump up in her seat and bringing her mind immediately back to concentrate on matters in hand. A gap of thirty yards had opened up in front of the BMW, which, at that moment, was being filled up fast by others who jumped lane in the vain hope that they could speed up their journeys in the process. Jennifer glanced to her right and saw the sign for the Grand Central Parkway. She flicked on her indicator and, turning round to beam a smile at the adjacent driver, she pointed to the exit, and within a minute she had used her charm to cut across three lanes of traffic, leave the LIE and begin heading southwards at a steady thirty miles per hour.

By the time that she descended the driveway to the

house, it was just coming up to nine o'clock. She pulled the car to a halt, and picking up her papers and laptop from the back seat, she got out and hurried across to the front door.

"Hi, everyone!" she called out as she entered. She walked through to the study and dumped her stuff on the desk, then turned and made her way back into the hall, just as Jasmine appeared from the kitchen.

"Hi, Jasmine," she said brightly.

"Hi! Didn't think you was comin' home this weekend."

"You're right! I'm not supposed to be here, but I just couldn't bear not seeing Benji over this weekend. We've never spent a Fourth of July apart before. Is he around?"

"Not yet. He's still with David, but they should be home any minute now."

"So, how's everything been?"

"Really couldn't be better! And how are *you* feeling?"

Jennifer smiled at her. "Still a bit washed out, but I should be able to take things a little easier once this proposal's finished."

Jasmine nodded. "Do you want anything to eat?"

"Oh, Jasmine, that would be great. Just a sandwich or something would be fine. I've got some work to finish off, so if you could just bring it to the study . . ."

Jasmine turned to walk back to the kitchen. "Okay. One sandwich coming up."

Jennifer made her way to the study, and having laid out her work on the desk, she had just managed to bring the Tarvy's proposal up onto the screen of her laptop when Jasmine reappeared with a plate of ham sandwiches and a glass of beer. "Here you are," she said, putting it down on the table next to the desk.

At that instant, the front door opened and Benji's voice called out excitedly. "Mom!"

"In here, Benji!"

Bursting through the door, he ran over to his mother and threw his arms around her neck.

"Hi, darling! Where have you been until now?"

"We've been on the beach *all* afternoon. We only just caught the last ferry home, and then we went into Leesport to watch them get the firework display ready for tomorrow night. They set some off just to make sure everything was working. Didn't you hear them? Anyway, David said that we—"

He stopped when he heard the door of the study open. David entered the room, and Benji broke away from his mother and ran over to him. "David, can I tell Mom now?"

David ruffled the boy's hair. "Would you mind if I did it, Benji?"

Benji let out a disappointed moan, but before he could remonstrate still further, Jasmine walked over and put her arm around his shoulders. "Come on, Benji, I think we should leave Mom and David to talk, don't you?"

"Okay! As long as you tell her though." He ran from the room, with Jasmine following hot on his heels.

Jennifer watched them go, then turned to David, a smile on her face. "Hi!"

"Hi!" He put his hands into his pockets as he walked over to her desk. "Sorry about not getting Benji back here earlier. I didn't realize you were coming home this weekend."

She leaned back in her chair. "Well, I wasn't going to. We have to get this proposal off tomorrow, but I just wanted to see Benji, so I thought I'd come back for the night." She sighed. "Not that it'll be much of a night. I'll have to leave at about five-thirty tomorrow morning."

David nodded. "So, how are you feeling?"

"Great! Only I've probably undone all the good that I got out of the rest Jasmine made me take last week.

I've had to work pretty long hours on this damn proposal, just to catch up."

"How's it going?"

Jennifer looked at the computer screen. "I don't know really. The trouble is I have nothing to judge it by. I *hope* it's all right, because Sam is really counting on me pulling this one off. It would really give the company *such* a boost if we managed to land it."

"Who's it for?"

"Oh, it's just a gin company in London. Tarvy's. You ever heard of it?"

"Yup, I know them well." He paused. "What I mean by that is, ah, I know the brand well enough."

"Oh, well, thank God for that!" Jennifer laughed. "At least *you've* heard of it." She reached over and picked up the market research report. "Tarvy's name doesn't even appear in this, but at least it gives me an idea as to what kind of sales figures we should be looking to achieve, and I tell you, it's pretty awesome!"

She tossed the report back onto the desk and let out a sigh. "Anyway, I can't really do much more. If we don't get it, well, that's that, but for Sam's sake, I sure hope that we're in with a glimmer of a chance." She smiled up at him. "Do you want a beer or something?"

"No, don't bother. I don't want to interrupt you."

"You're not," she said, getting up from her chair and walking towards the door. "I'll go get one for you from the kitchen." She turned back to him. "Anyway, I want to hear what the big secret is all about."

As her footsteps faded off down the corridor towards the kitchen, David turned and picked up the Morgan Graz market research report from the desk. Heavens, he hadn't looked at one of these for ages! In the past, he had read them as often as he had the daily newspapers. He shook his head and turned the pages, stopping abruptly as the familiar name of Glendurnich caught his eye. He glanced up at the top of the page. It was the top-ten world-wide sales listings for single-malt

Scotch whisky brands. He scanned through the figures, a puzzled frown beginning to crease his forehead.

This wasn't right. Glendurnich was listed as being number four, exactly the same position they had occupied the year before. He looked down at the bottom of the page to check the date. It was the June issue. Okay, so they were world-wide listings, not specific to the United States, but the country was their single biggest customer, so they must reflect the sales over here. He scratched at his head, trying to work out if there was an alternative explanation. Maybe he was wrong. Maybe Glendurnich *had* reached a higher position while he'd been absent from the company, in which case, if sales had been on the slide, then Duncan was right in registering concern. But there again, he just didn't know.

He raised his eyebrows at the anomaly and quickly flicked through the remaining pages of the magazine. He was just about to close it when yet another name bounced out at him from the inside back page, making him shudder just in reading it to himself. Deakin Distribution. For a moment, he found his mind flashing back involuntarily to that appalling day in Manhattan, when every event that occurred and every action that he took seemed to be orchestrated to hasten his downfall. He blew out nervously at the very thought of it, then once more focused his eyes on the article. It was only a small piece in the bottom right-hand corner of the page, listed under the "Management and Appointments" column.

UK's third-largest drinks company **Kirkpatrick Holdings Plc.** has announced the recent acquisition of New York–based distributors **Deakin Distribution Inc.**

Kirpatrick's chairman John Davenport said that he welcomed the announcement, and that Deakin's had the proven ability to spearhead a new and aggressive sales drive in the USA, promoting their ever-expanding list of brand names.

David grunted derisively to himself, wondering if Deakin Distribution knew what they were letting themselves in for. "Aggressive" was a complete understatement as far as Kirkpatrick's were concerned, especially with that corporate shark, John Davenport, at the helm. He bit hard on his lip as it suddenly occurred to him that, as a result of his abortive meeting, Deakin's could now quite easily be Glendurnich's distributor. He closed his eyes in concentration, trying to work out in his mind what possible repercussions this might have on Glendurnich. No, it should be all right—for now, anyway. He knew for certain that Kirkpatrick's didn't have a malt whisky as part of its portfolio, so there shouldn't be any immediate conflict of interests. Nevertheless, he didn't like to think that Glendurnich was giving anything away to that company.

Just as he made a mental note to himself to check the whole scenario thoroughly when he returned to Scotland, he heard the sound of Jennifer's footsteps moving quickly back across the hall. He closed up the report and replaced it on the desk, turning round just as she came through the door.

"Sorry I was so long," she said, coming over and handing him the glass of beer. "Would you believe it, a woman selling cosmetics came to the door? I mean, not only at nine-thirty but also the night before a damned national holiday?"

David raised his eyebrows and took a long drink of his beer, while Jennifer sat back down at her desk. "So when do you expect to hear about the Tarvy's contract?"

"Tuesday. Ridiculous, isn't it? I don't know how they can expect to really study all the proposals in that short space of time. Nevertheless, that's what they want."

David looked at his watch, his mind still distracted by what he had read in the market research report and conscious that he had left the children alone in the saltbox. He drained his glass and put it down on her desk. "Listen, I'm going to have to go."

Jennifer looked up at him, a surprised expression on her face. "Hang on, what was it you were going to tell me?"

David scratched at his head. "Are you going to be back here on Thursday?"

"Yeah, I guess so. I was hoping that Alex would be here, but he telephoned last night to say that he has to be in Dallas for the next two weeks."

David nodded. "Would you mind if we left it until then? It's sort of quite important, so I'd rather take time to explain."

Jennifer shrugged her shoulders resignedly.

"Okay. In that case, I shall await the disclosure with bated breath."

David smiled at her and walked over to the door, turning back as he opened it. "Listen, best of luck with the account. Judging by the amount of work that you've put into it, I'm sure you'll be in with a shout."

"Thanks." She paused for a moment and squinted a rueful smile at him. "I don't suppose you'd be able to fix it, would you?"

David looked at her inquiringly. "Sorry?"

"No, don't worry. I was only joking. Just thought that you might have been able to cast a magical spell over this one as well!"

She gave him a wave with her hand, then turned back to her desk and resumed her work.

An unnatural quietness seemed to be radiating from the little saltbox when he got back to Shore Street, making David think immediately that something *had* to be wrong. He hurried from the gate to the door of the house and threw it open, breathing out a sigh of relief when he saw the children sitting cross-legged in the centre of the floor, gathered around a Monopoly board.

"Heavens, this is all very harmonious," he laughed.

Charlie looked up, a disgruntled look on his face. "Well, there's no telly and we were getting bored waiting for you. Where've you been? We thought you were only going to be five minutes."

"Yeah. Sorry about that. Benji's moth——"

"Hey, Harriet!" Charlie yelled out. "You can't do that! You're meant to be in prison!"

"All right, Charlie!" Sophie said sharply. "She didn't know!" She reached across the board and pushed Harriet's top hat back a square. "You'll have to wait until your next go, Harry!"

"Oh, pig's whistles!" Harriet exclaimed at being caught out. She rolled backwards onto the floor and bicycled her bare legs in the air, showering off the sand that had accumulated on them during the day on Fire Island. She turned her head and looked up at her father. "Daddy, do you want to play? You can be the ship."

"Not just at the minute, darling." He cast a caring eye over his children, noticing in the subdued light that each was beginning to show signs of a healthy tan following just two days on the beach. He walked over to Harriet and gently pressed his foot into her stomach, making her squeal loudly. "I've just got to make a quick telephone call, okay?"

He squeezed his way sideways past Sophie's bed to the desk and took his address book from his brief-case. Then, sitting down on the edge of the bed, he opened it at the correct page and scanned down the list of numbers until he found Gladwin Vintners. He was sure that he had William Lawrence's home number. Yup, there it was.

He picked up the telephone and dialled, turning to watch the game of high finance in progress while he waited for it to connect.

"Hu-llo?" a man's voice answered.

"Will, it's David Corstorphine."

"David, you old devil! What the hell are *you* doing phoning at two o'clock in the morning?"

David glanced at his watch, and then clapped his hand on the top of his head. "Oh, God, Will! I'm sorry! I'm in the States. I forgot totally about the time change. Jesus, I'm sorry! Look, I'll call you in the morning."

Will laughed. "Don't worry about it. We've just been out at a dinner party which turned into something of a marathon, so we're not long in anyway. So how are things? Are you out there on business?"

"Yeah, sort of. Listen, are you sure it's all right to talk now? I can always—"

"No, I promise you. I'm not even out of my clothes yet. So go on, what can I do for you at this ungodly hour?"

"Well, this may seem a ridiculous question to ask under the circumstances, but I was just wondering whether you were still handling the international sales of Glentochry?"

"Yup, I am."

"Right. You, er, don't happen to have anything to do with Tarvy's Gin as well, do you?"

"Yeah, funnily enough, I do. More by default than anything else. Gladwin's have recently set up a new marketing committee for the product, specifically to target the States, and I've been called onto it, ostensibly for my knowledge of the U.S. market. Why do you ask?"

"Well, it's only that I heard through the grape-vine that Tarvy's are looking to appoint a new advertising company over here."

"Christ, how the hell did you hear about that? I only just learned about that this week!"

"As I said, my ears were flapping the other day, and I just happened to hear word of it at a sales conference."

"Yeah, well, you're right. Gladwin's seem to be in

an almighty hurry to get Tarvy's into the U.S. market, so they're looking to appoint a new agency ASAP. In fact, I'm going to have to spend the first two days of next week going through about five bloody proposals." He paused for a moment. "So what's your interest in Tarvy's?"

"None at all, I promise you. It's only that . . . well, listen, I know of one company that is putting in a proposal, and I can tell you that they're building up quite a reputation as being a pretty smart and up-and-coming lot."

"What are they called?"

"Culpepper Rowan."

"Yup, that name rings a bell. Have you got a vested interest in *them*, then?"

"Absolutely none! It's only that I know a couple of the directors quite well. From what I can gather about the company, it's extremely successful, but they're in need of a major international client to help them break into the big time, and I think that if they happened to be appointed, they would pull out all the stops for Gladwin's to get Tarvy's positioned as fast as possible."

There was a moment's silence at the other end of the telephone. "Well, I can't promise you anything, David."

"Oh, I quite understand that, Will. But if you could give their proposal just a little more than passing consideration."

Will laughed. "Yeah, okay, you pushy bugger, I'll do that!"

"Thanks, Will."

"Hey, listen, David, while you're on the phone, and talking of grape-vines and all that, is Glendurnich being attacked at the minute?"

David frowned. "What do you mean?"

"No, obviously it's not. Only I had lunch with Fraser Campbell of Dunmorran Malt the other day, and he said that one of the corporates had been snooping around his company."

"Christ, that's all we're needing in the industry! Which one was it?"

"Kirkpatrick's."

David felt his mouth immediately going dry. "Did you say Kirkpatrick's?" he asked quietly.

"Yeah. Word has it that they're trying to acquire a malt whisky for their portfolio, but if you've heard nothing about it, you should be safe enough."

David did not reply, but stood staring at Carrie's painting above the desk. He heard Will yawn at the other end of the telephone.

"Listen, mate, I'm knackered. Is there any more information I can give you, or can I go to bed?"

David shook his head to break his line of thought. "No—sorry, Will. That's all, and apologies for ringing you at such a ridiculous time."

"Don't mention it. And I'll keep Culpepper Rowan in mind."

Putting down the telephone, David sat back heavily on the bed and ran his fingers through his hair. Jesus, Kirkpatrick's couldn't be after Glendurnich, could they? Surely he would have heard. His father or Duncan would have been in touch with him.

"You all right, Dad?" Sophie's voice asked quietly.

He turned round to find the three children staring at him with concerned expressions on their faces.

"You've gone completely white," Sophie said.

David smiled and pushed himself up from the bed. "No, everything's fine." He clapped his hands together. "Right! Come on, Charlie and Harriet, time for you to get to bed!"

Ignoring their synchronized groans of protest, he reached down and scooped his youngest daughter up in his arms and, carrying her through to the porch, he dumped her down on her bed and tickled her stomach, and amidst screams of playful torture, she shot her legs up to her chin to protect herself.

"Daddy?"

"Yup?"

"Will you play Monopoly with me tomorrow?"

"Course I will."

"Can I be the top hat again?"

"Sure you can. Now get ready for bed!"

He bent over and planted a kiss on her forehead and walked back into the house, giving Charlie a pat on the top of his head as he passed. He pushed Sophie's bed over into the middle of the room to make way for a seat in front of the desk, then, taking a piece of paper out of his brief-case, he sat down to try to make some order of the jigsaw of events that were swimming disconnectedly around in his mind.

There was really nothing to go on. Any pattern that he worked out was based purely on supposition and hypothesis. The only real concrete line of connection was Duncan's recommendation that Deakin's should take over the distribution of Glendurnich in the States, and that Deakin's had been acquired by Kirkpatrick's. Then again, Duncan's insistence in appointing them as the new distributor had come about because of a fall in U.S. sales, and he didn't have any solid information to hand proving whether they had or not.

He closed his eyes and scratched hard at the back of his head with both hands. You're probably reading too much into this, you bloody fool. Lack of brain usage over the past eight months has begun to make you paranoid. Anyway, Kirkpatrick's surely couldn't touch Glendurnich. It was a private company, shares held by his father and himself. And, hang on, yes, there would now be a few in the hands of the workers as part of the stock-purchase plan that his father had set up. But they wouldn't account for much. No, Glendurnich was undoubtedly safe from predatory attack.

But then again, how could he make sure that nothing had been mooted within the company? Whom the hell could he contact? Not Duncan anyway—if there *were* any firm pointers to connect Glendurnich with Kirk-patrick's, then they would most certainly be directed at him. Nor his father. There was no reason to worry him unnecessarily over something that was probably highly speculative.

Margaret was the obvious person, being without doubt someone on whom he could truly rely for her loyalty. But there again, he wasn't sure that her normal ebullient manner would be best suited for such detective work. Nevertheless, through her, he could get a fax safely into the right hands. But whose? He suddenly began clicking his fingers over and over. What about the young man his father had called into the boardroom just after the briefing? He thumped his head with his hand, trying to knock the boy's name back into his mind. What in God's name was it? Come on, his grandfather had worked in the distillery. Mc, Mc-something-or-other, Mc-McLachlan! That was it! Archie McLachlan!

"Dad?"

David turned to find Sophie standing beside him, dressed in her pyjamas.

"Yes, darling?"

"Are you going to be long? I'm feeling a bit zonked. I wouldn't mind turning in."

He glanced round at her bed, which stood hopelessly marooned in the middle of the room.

"Oh, hell, I'm sorry! Look, I promise you I'll only be five minutes. I just want to send a fax back to the office. Would you mind using my bed until I'm finished, and then I'll get yours sorted out. If Dodie's on the bed, just push her off, okay?"

With a shrug, Sophie turned and pushed through the curtain into his bedroom. There was an immediate growl from the dog, followed by a resounding thump as she was dispatched from the bed onto the floor. David picked up a pen from the desk and began to write.

Fax to: Archie McLachlan (VIA MARGARET)
Glendurnich Distilleries Ltd

From: David Corstorphine

Dear Archie,
I wonder if you could do a bit of investigative work for
me. I have just heard through a friend of mine in London
that a company called Kirkpatrick Holdings Plc. are
looking to purchase a malt-whisky business. I know that
there is probably nothing to worry about on Glendur-
nich's part, but could you just have a few discreet words
with some of your associates to see if they have heard
anything along these lines?

Also, I would be grateful if you could keep this be-
tween ourselves, and please do not approach anyone on
the board of directors. If you do manage to find out
anything, please fax me back immediately at the number
on the confirmation slip. If I don't hear from you, I'll
take it that all is well!

With best wishes,
David Corstorphine

David inserted the paper into the machine and dialled the Glendurnich fax number. Then, as it began to
go through, he turned and picked up the chair, pushing
back Sophie's bed into its customary position with his
foot.

"Sophie?"

"Yes?" a sleepy voice replied from behind the curtain.

"Your bed awaits you."

Chapter

TWENTY-NINE

Since getting her job at Glendurnich Distilleries, Doreen McWhirter had arrived at the office every morning at eight-thirty sharp, even though she was not expected until nine, along with the other office workers. However, in order to assert the control that she felt befitting her newly appointed position as receptionist, she thought it necessary to be at her station to greet the directors of the company when they walked through the door, and also to show herself as a figure of dedication and responsibility to her fellow workers when they traipsed in at the scheduled arrival time.

Consequently, on that Monday morning she was both surprised and somewhat miffed to find that she was not the first to arrive, the main door having swung gently open when she had placed her key in its lock. She clipped her way across the reception area to her desk and studied the lights on her telephone.

Mr. Caple was in, the red light corresponding to his office telephone being the only one that shone out from the console. Doreen smiled coyly to herself and, picking up her handbag, walked around the desk and with a dainty jaunt to her step made her way over to the ladies' room. Placing the handbag on the shelf in front of the mirror, she took out her compact and lipstick, then, removing her winged spectacles, she began to give her face the gentlest of touch-overs.

She really liked Mr. Caple. She had known that from the moment she had met him at the interview. It was so pleasant to encounter a young man who was so organized, so particular in the way he liked things done, and she was sure that he had given her the job because he had recognized similar attributes in herself.

She snapped shut her compact and placed everything back in her bag. Then, having given the sides of her neatly cropped greying hair a quick flick with her fingers, she walked back out into the reception area and over to her desk. Pulling open one of the larger bottom drawers, she carefully laid her handbag on its side and slid the drawer slowly shut, making sure that no part of the soft leather would catch on its runners. Then, straightening up, she clapped her hands together once to signify that, for her, work was now under way.

She began her routine by walking across to the front door and picking up the newspapers that had been pushed through the letter-box. She placed them in order of size on the coffee-table that was positioned between two of the leather sofas, uncreasing each as she laid it out with two quick wipes of the side of her hand.

Having stepped back from the table to make sure that the newspapers appeared symmetrical also from the front angle, she made her way over to the fax machine to check if anything had been sent through over the weekend. There was only one message. She picked it up and walked back to her desk, reading it through as she went. At first, her face registered incomprehension, then, having read it through again, she looked up in thought, her eyes narrowed and her newly glossed lips pursed tight in disapproval.

Glancing down at the switchboard, she saw that Mr. Caple's light was now off. She strutted across the reception area and made her way quickly up the stairs and along the corridor to his office. She knocked and cocked an ear to await his reply.

"Yes?" his voice called out.

She opened the door and put her head around the side.

"Ah, Doreen! How are you this morning? Come on in!"

The receptionist smiled at his bright manner and entered. "You're up with the lark this morning, Mr. Caple," she said playfully, feeling a glow come to her cheeks as she said it.

"Work to do, Doreen! Nothing should stop for work!"

"Absolutely not!" she replied, letting out a merry little laugh. "I couldn't agree with you more!"

"So what can I do for you?"

She walked over to his desk, clutching the fax to her bosom. "I hope you'll agree with me that I'm doing the right thing. It's just that I found this fax on the machine this morning, and, well, in my opinion, I do not think that its contents seem to have the best interests of the company at heart."

The smile on Duncan's face was replaced with a quizzical frown, and he reached out his hand for the fax. "Then you'd better let me have a look at it, Doreen."

Doreen handed it over, quickly clasping her hands back to her bosom as she stood waiting in trepidation for his reaction. As Duncan read it through, he felt his stomach begin to tighten into a knot, and he had to make a conscious effort not to swear out loud. Looking up, he forced himself to smile at the receptionist before reading through the fax once more.

"Right!" he said eventually, tossing the page down onto his desk. "You did exactly the right thing in showing me this." He turned his chair to the side and stared thoughtfully out of the window.

"Well, I think that it's bordering on being a criminal

act, Mr. Caple!" Doreen snipped tartly, pleased that he had agreed with her and thinking that this now granted her the right to speak her own mind on the subject. "I mean, fancy trying to go over the heads of the directors! And who, may I ask, does this man"—she leaned forward and spun round the fax on the desk so that she could read it—"this Mr. Corstorphine think he—"

"I'll tell you what we'll do," Duncan cut in, turning his chair round to face her again. "Until I've been able to make some inquiries into this, I think we should keep it entirely between ourselves. Tell nobody, especially this"—he glanced at the fax—"this Archie McLachlan." He looked up at her inquiringly. "I don't think I know him, do I?"

"Well, he's presently working in distribution. As far as I can gather, he's on a year's training scheme, so he's not a full-time employee of the distillery."

"Ah," Duncan said, slowly nodding his head. "Well, as I said, Doreen, we'll keep this to ourselves; but in the meantime, could you do something for me?"

"Certainly."

"Could you find out how much longer young McLachlan has to serve before he completes his training scheme?"

"Of course." Doreen smiled knowingly at Duncan. "A very shrewd move, if you'll allow me to say so."

"Okay, well, let's leave it at that, and thank you for bringing this to my attention. I have a feeling that it might turn out to be an invaluable piece of information."

"I sincerely hope so," she replied smugly and, turning sharply around, she walked smartly over to the door and left the office.

Duncan waited until he heard her footsteps descending the stairs, then he jumped to his feet, making his chair shoot backwards. He turned and caught it before it banged against the back wall.

"*Damn!*" he said under his breath.

He picked up the fax and paced up and down the floor as he read it through again. He stopped and slapped the top of his head.

"Damn! Damn! Damn!"

He scrumpled up the paper into a ball in his fist and went to stand by the window, his eyes fixed blankly on the tall pines that stood beyond the car-park.

How the hell had David found out about Kirkpatrick's? Nobody else knew about it! And how long had he been keeping up clandestine contact with this guy Archie? Maybe more faxes had passed through the office without his knowing while old Margaret had still been here. Damn it, he had underestimated David. He thought that he was going to be away from the business for a hell of a lot longer than this! He turned and walked back to his desk, unscrumpling the fax as he went. He pulled in his chair and sat down, reading through the fax once more.

He wasn't definite, though, was he? "Probably nothing to worry about on Glendurnich's part" he wrote. But, on the other hand, he must think *something* was up if he had expressly asked this guy McLachlan not to approach the board of directors.

He shook his head and pressed the automatic dialling code on his telephone, leaving it on speaker mode. He sat back in his chair, still trying to work out the connotations of the fax as the telephone rang.

The nasal tones of a female telephonist sang out from the speaker. "Good morn-ing, Kirkpatrick Hol-dings!"

"Mr. Davenport's office, please."

"May I say who's call-ing?"

"Duncan Caple, Glendurnich."

The telephone clicked, giving way to ten seconds of electronic Mozart before John Davenport spoke. "Hullo, Duncan. How are you this morning?"

"Not good, I'm afraid, John. We've got a problem. The receptionist here has just brought me up a fax which came in sometime over the weekend."

"And?"

"It's from David Corstorphine in the States."

"Go on."

Duncan leaned forward to the speaker and went through the fax slowly and concisely. At the end, he sat back in his chair and waited. There was silence on the line, save for John Davenport's heavy breathing.

"Christ, I thought you said that he was out of action!"

"Well, I thought he was! On the other hand, I wouldn't say there's any real evidence here to indicate that he's back *in* action."

"Hell, I would have thought that that fax was conclusive enough."

"Not really. For a start, he's based the whole thing on supposition. I honestly think that by coincidence he *has* heard a rumour of your plans to purchase a malt-whisky business, and he's just checking it out—nothing more than that. And besides that, I'm pretty sure the guy's not fit in the brain yet, because I make a point of asking his father about him, and he always replies that he's not ready to come home yet."

"Right." There was a short silence. "Then why do you think that he didn't want the directors to be approached? I mean, why did he not just fax you direct?"

"I don't know. I can't fathom that out either. At first, I thought that it might be that he'd been back in touch with Deakin's, but then we'd have heard from Charles Deakin if that had been the case. The way I read it is that the guy feels the whole thing is *so* improbable that he doesn't want to risk my witnessing him make a complete fool of himself again, like he did in New York."

John Davenport sighed. "Well, let's look on the bright side. Thank God he sent a fax, and thank God we intercepted it."

Duncan picked up his pen and began doodling on his desk-pad.

"So what do you want to do? Continue with the plan or, well, rethink it?"

John Davenport's voice exploded through the speaker. "*Christ* no! Listen, as you said, his whole fax is pure supposition! Kirkpatrick's has great *need* of Glendurnich, Duncan, and I'm not going to throw a whole year's positioning work out the window at this juncture! And remember, you've got half a million pounds coming to you if we succeed in purchasing the company. You don't want to kiss that goodbye, do you? Come on, we go ahead with it, but we'll just have to bring the whole schedule forward. We can't risk leaving it for another two weeks."

"Right. So you want to make it this week, then."

"I'm afraid so, Duncan. What do you think? Can you manage it?"

Duncan threw the pen down on the desk and fell back in his chair.

"Okay!" he said decisively. "We'll bring the schedule forward a week. I'll call a meeting of all personnel in the car-park at five P.M. on Friday, just before they head home, and go through the proposal with them then. That'll give them the weekend to mull it over. Then I'll pay Inchelvie a visit on Saturday afternoon and tell him about the offer."

"All right, but I really think you are going to have to start putting some fairly extreme pressure on him now, Duncan. You *have* to convince him that this really is the only way that Glendurnich will survive in the future, and make sure that he understands implicitly that we have the best interests of both the company and the family at heart. I would suggest you really push your trump card concerning the workers' thirty-one per-cent shareholding as soon as you've heard their decision on Monday, and maybe see if you can't get him to sign over some of his own shares as soon as possible after that. I'd feel happier if we had nearer the fifty per-cent mark before the whole world gets wind of this."

"Yeah, don't worry. I think we've worked out pretty well how to handle this whole thing."

"I hope so. I have to warn you that we *are* sailing pretty close to the wind with Glendurnich. While we're not doing anything strictly illegal, our actions could be classed as being 'over-manipulative.' "

"Yes, I understand that, John."

"Good! Now, what are you going to do about Corstorphine's fax?"

"Well, I thought at first that I might answer it by sending a fax straight from the computer—no identifiable signature or anything. But I think that's too dangerous, inasmuch as it *would* actually constitute an illegal action. No, I think we'll just leave it. I mean, at least he left open that option for us by saying that he didn't expect a reply."

"Okay, well, I agree with that. And what about this chap McLachlan?"

"Don't worry. I'll deal with him."

"Right. Just make sure you cover your back, Duncan, in every way. I've had to do it all my life, so I know what you're about to let yourself in for! And keep in touch on a daily basis from now on, or even more frequently if you want any advice."

"Will do."

"Well, best of luck, then. Just go for it, boy!"

The telephone clicked off before Duncan had time to reply. He switched off the speakerphone, then picked up the fax and slowly tore it into pieces and threw it away. He pressed the button on his intercom. "Doreen?"

"Yes, Mr. Caple?"

"What did you find out about McLachlan?"

"His apprenticeship terminates at the end of next month."

"Okay. Well, I'm afraid that I have no option but to bring it forward, Doreen, so could you ask him to come to see me right now, please?"

"Very good, Mr. Caple."

"And, Doreen?"

"Yes?"

"Thanks again for your assistance over this matter. I really think that that fax could have been very hurtful to the future of the company."

"That's exactly what I thought. I shall contact young McLachlan straight away."

Chapter
THIRTY

The atmosphere in the offices of Culpepper Rowan on Tuesday morning was one of tense expectancy, the whole place seeming to have taken on the air of a legal-appeals office that was awaiting word of a reprieve from execution. There was little laughter or chat, the executives choosing to stay in their own offices behind closed doors, and those employees who passed in the corridors did so in silence, exchanging only a fleeting nervous smile with each other instead of the customary light-hearted greeting or teasing remark.

The only contact that Sam Culpepper had made with the members of his staff that morning had been in the form of an internal E-mail, giving express instructions that if Tarvy's were to be in touch, then he should be the first informed. Consequently, every time the telephone rang, Jennifer stopped what she was doing and gazed mesmerically at the light on the panel, nervously biting at a finger-nail until it went out again. Then, with a sigh of resignation, she would set about trying to get her brain back to work on the proposal for Russ's new clients.

However, by mid-day, she had heard nothing from Sam, and realizing that it would now be five o'clock in the afternoon in London, she began to conclude that somewhere in an office, not very far away from theirs, a party was already under way to celebrate the winning of the Tarvy's account. She went back over in her mind every last detail of her proposal, knowing each heading and paragraph as if it might be the most personal record she had ever kept of herself. The more she thought about it, the more new ideas or angles which had been discarded seemed to spring to mind, ones which she now wished she had had the sense to include in the document. And the more consideration she gave it, the more despondent she became.

By one o'clock, the telephone seemed to have stopped ringing completely. That's it, she thought to herself, it's all over. We *definitely* didn't get it. She slumped forward on her desk and rubbed at her face with her hands. What a waste of effort! *Jesus*, why did Sam ever think that they might have a chance against all those big shots? It was like—David trying to take on Goliath! She suddenly snorted out an involuntary laugh, realizing the funny side to her pun, and a mental picture sprang instantly to mind of *her* David standing in front of an enormous Philistine giant armed with a garden hoe and a tennis racket. Knowing him, he'd probably win, too!

She pushed her seat back, and smoothing her hands over her hair and linking them at the back of her head, she swivelled round to focus on a couple of window-cleaners suspended in their cradle from the roof of the opposite office block, seemingly oblivious to their height above Fifth Avenue as they chatted.

The door of her office was suddenly flung open with such force that it crashed against the bookcase behind it, making her jolt round in her chair. No one entered, but she heard muffled voices outside in the corridor.

"Who's there?" Jennifer asked, leaning forward on her desk to see if she could make out what was going on.

"Come on, Russ, get it off!" a voice whispered.

"I can't! It's stuck!"

"Give it a shake!"

"What the hell's going on?" Jennifer got up from her chair and walked round the side of her desk. As she approached the door, there was a loud explosion and a champagne cork cannoned awkwardly off the ceiling, hitting her sharply on the toe and making her jump back with the fright.

"What the *hell* is . . . ?"

Sam's balding head came round the side of the door.

"Who happens to be a genius?" he said, his face set in such an asinine grin that it looked as if he were trying to get used to an oversized set of false teeth. "Who's just won us the Tarvy's contract?"

Jennifer felt her jaw quite literally drop open and she put her hand up to her mouth.

"*What!* But how? When? The phone hasn't rung for well over an hour."

Sam entered the room, shaking a fax above his head. "Maybe it hasn't. But who said anything about them using the phone?"

Jennifer clapped her hands to her head. "Oh my *God*! You mean we *got* it?" she said breathlessly, scarcely believing what Sam was saying.

"No!" Sam exclaimed, pumping the fist that held the fax in the air. "*You* got it, Jennifer! *You* got it for us!"

She staggered unsteadily backwards towards her desk and sat down when she felt its support behind her. "We got the contract?" she asked quietly.

Sam's face took on a look of impatience. "How many more times do I have to say it? Yeah, we got it, we—got—the—Tarvy's contract!"

Jennifer stared blankly over the top of Sam's head. "We got the Tarvy's contract," she stated as if in an hypnotic trance.

Sam put on his madcap grin again and stood nodding his head furiously in front of her. Russ came round between them and, handing her a glass of champagne, he gave her a kiss on the cheek. "What a wonderful woman you are, Jennifer Newman!" he said with a wink.

Jennifer's face suddenly broke into a smile as the news finally began to register, and putting her glass down on the desk beside her, she leaped forward towards Sam, threw her arms around his neck and began jumping up and down.

"We got it, Sam! We *got* it!"

"I *know!* I *know!*" he said, trying to get into step with her bouncing.

Jennifer pushed herself away from him. "Well, let me have a look at it!" She grabbed the fax from his hand, and began to read every word of it out loud.

7th July

FAX TO:	*Culpepper Rowan*
FOR THE ATTENTION OF:	*Sam Culpepper*
	Managing Director
FROM:	*Adrian Thompson*
	Managing Director, Tarvy's Gin Ltd.
RE:	*US Advertising Campaign for Tarvy's Gin*

Jennifer turned and smiled excitedly at her two colleagues before reading on.

Dear Mr. Culpepper,
Having given due and careful consideration to the proposals that were tendered for the above campaign, we have the pleasure of informing you that our marketing committee has unanimously agreed to offer you the above contract.

It should be known that the decision was reached, not only on the basis of your excellent proposals, but

also on a recommendation made to a member of our
committee by an associate within the drinks industry,
namely that yours is a company that would be in the
position to take immediate action in implementing
soonest an advertising campaign for Tarvy's Gin. We
see this as being an integral part of our projected plan
to secure for ourselves a share of the U.S. market within
this coming year.

I have already taken the liberty of booking a flight
to New York for both myself and our marketing director
next Monday. We will be arriving at 2 P.M. U.S. time,
so I would be grateful if you could confirm both accep-
tance of this contract, and also a meeting for 3:30 P.M.
on Monday 13th July.

With best wishes, and again many congratulations on
an extremely well-thought-out campaign!

Yours sincerely,
Adrian Thompson
Managing Director, Tarvy's Gin Ltd.

Jennifer's voice tailed off as she ended the fax, and she looked up with an incredulous look on her face.

"We got it, Sam! We goddamned well got it!"

Sam and Russ held their glasses up to her, and she in turn raised hers.

"To Tarvy's Gin!" Sam said with a laugh. "And long may it pour!"

They drank a long toast, and Russ came forward with the bottle to replenish Jennifer's glass. "So?" he asked, looking at her out of the side of his eye as he filled her glass.

Jennifer gave him a puzzled look.

"So," Russ continued, "who's this secret contact you have?"

Jennifer looked down at the fax again and quickly read it through once more. "I don't know. I—I was going to ask you the same question!"

Sam pulled on Russ's arm and guided the champagne

bottle back to his glass. "Oh, who gives a damn!" He cast his eyes to the ceiling. "But whoever it is, may God look down on him or her at this precise minute, and lay a kiss on his or her brow!"

With a laugh, they raised their glasses up once more.

The combination of fast intake of champagne and a complete mood swing from one of deep depression to flying elation suddenly took its effect on Jennifer. She walked round behind her desk and fell back heavily in her chair.

"God, I feel completely and utterly emotionally *drained*! I have been sitting here all day thinking about it! I never imagined for a moment . . ."

Her voice tailed off and she glanced sideways out the window, picking out once more the two window-cleaners opposite. They were in exactly the same position, still continuing with their idle banter. God, in the last three minutes, right here in *this* office, future direction had been changed, not only for herself, but for Sam, for Russ—in fact, for the whole company! Yet out there, it was like a time warp—as if someone had pressed the "pause" button on a video machine.

She looked round at her colleagues, seeing immediately that their expressions had altered from ones of joy to querying concern. Sam stepped forward to the front of her desk.

"Listen, Jennifer," Sam said quietly, "they're not here until next week. I'm just going to reply to the fax right now and confirm everything. Know what I want you to do? I want you to get the hell out of this office, and I don't want to see you back here until Monday morning."

Jennifer looked at him. "But what about moving ahead with the contract?"

"There's nothing to do until they come! You've done it all already! We'll just be going over the proposals. So, as I said, get out of the office, go home to Leesport, and spend the rest of the week relaxing and spending time with Benji. Jeez, Jennifer, you sure deserve it!"

Jennifer closed her eyes and let her head fall back against her chair, the idea of being away from the office for nearly a week suddenly filling her with a euphoric sense of relief. She opened her eyes and looked at the two men who now both leaned forward on her desk, like a couple of praying mantises eyeing their next meal.

"Do you think I could, Sam?"

"Of course!" He smiled at her. "Just relax and get ready for the meeting on Monday!"

From that moment on, every action that Jennifer took seemed to be in total contrast to the frenetic way in which she normally ran her life. Having taken a taxi back to Barrymore Street, she spent an hour packing a suitcase that would normally have taken her ten minutes, and then, driving back to Leesport, she even found herself taking the unprecedented step of pulling over at a roadside restaurant for a cup of coffee. There was simply no hurry now. She had the best part of a week to herself, and she was going to savour every moment of it.

By the time that she arrived back at the house, it was half past four in the afternoon. Taking her suitcase from the trunk, she walked over to the front door and pushed at it. It was locked. Her immediate reaction to this was one of puzzlement, but then, smiling to herself, she sorted out her keys and unlocked the door. They had probably all gone to Fire Island. Anyway, wherever they were, there was no need either for explanation or for worry. David would no doubt be with them.

She let herself in and for a moment stood in the hall, listening to absolutely nothing, simply relishing the peace and quiet of the empty house. Then, carrying her suitcase upstairs to her room, she put it down on the bed, and crossing over to the bathroom, began running a deep and relaxing bath. As the water cascaded from the taps, she watched it transfixed, allowing her mind to indulge itself happily in the elation over her own success again and again.

The sound of the water beginning to gurgle through the overflow waste-pipe shook her out of the daydream. She turned off the taps and made her way back into the bedroom, and picking up the telephone, dialled Alex's mobile number. While waiting for it to connect, she kicked off her shoes and began to undo the buttons of her shirt, listening to the hissing on the line before the staccato tones of a female voice machine cut in.

"The number you have dialled has not responded. Please try late——"

Jennifer replaced the telephone, and quickly slipping out of her clothes as she walked back to the bathroom, she slowly lowered herself into the steaming water.

An hour and a half later, having indulged herself for longer than she had planned, she stood in the still deserted kitchen dressed in a simple cotton frock, her wet hair pulled back into a stringy pony-tail. She glanced at the clock on the wall. Just before half past six. Well, there was no point in sitting around the house waiting for them to return. If they had gone to Fire Island, they would be taking the ferry back pretty soon. Okay! So why not go to meet them and give them a surprise!

She considered at first walking the half-mile to the marina, but uncertain as to what their normal arrangements might be, she realized that they could have gone their separate ways by the time that she got there—and she really *did* want to tell David about her triumph.

She ran back through to the hall, picked up the keys of the car from the table and let herself out the front door, locking it behind her. Then, jumping into the BMW, she reversed hard round and took off up the drive in a flurry of dust and gravel.

By the time she arrived at the entrance of the marina, she knew for certain that she had made it before them, there being no sign of them either there or anywhere on Shore Street. Pulling the car over to the side of the road, she got out, and leaning on the door, she shielded her eyes with her hand and looked out across the bay to see if she could make out where the ferry might be. Once she had become accustomed to the glare, she caught sight of the little craft about half a mile out from the shore, plying its way towards the marina, the Stars and Stripes fluttering from its mast in the gentle breeze.

As she turned to make her way down to the marina, she glanced to her left and noticed David's orange VW parked farther along Shore Street beyond the Memorial Garden. She smiled and shook her head, never having realized before where he lived. She took a step towards the marina, then stopped. Maybe she could just go and sneak a look at his house. She glanced out towards the boat, and judging that it would take at least another ten minutes to reach the marina, she turned and made her way along the street.

She first became aware of the sound of music and laughter as she walked past the Memorial Garden. Her immediate thought was that it came from the garden, but as she passed the gate she could only see an old man walking slowly around the path with an equally aged dog on a lead. No, the noise was definitely coming from the house farther along the road.

She slowed her pace as she approached the gate adjacent to the Volkswagen, and standing to one side of the hedge, she peered round the corner and looked over the top of the gate. She could see nothing, the action seeming all to be taking place farther over to the right. She stepped across to the centre of the gate, and was just about to lean over to see if she could make out what was going on when a ball came shooting over to land beside her at the gap in the hedge. She took a step back and pushed herself against the hedge as someone ran over to retrieve it.

"All right, Benji," she heard Gerry Reilly's voice call out, a weariness dulling its usual bright Irish tones. "That's it! You boys have won. I think we should call it a day." There was a short pause. "Oh, for crying out loud!" he continued softly, as if talking to himself. "Who the hell's idea was it to start a conga?"

Jennifer slowly stepped forward from the hedge. What was going on? What was Gerry doing here? She moved towards the gate and, unsnibbing it quietly, she walked through into the garden.

The music came from the small house that was set in the corner of the property, the doors of its porch open wide to allow the music to filter out into the garden. A conga line was threading its way down towards a flight of steps at the front of the garden, led by a large, middle-aged man with an abundance of sleeked-back grey hair who wore the gaudiest shirt that Jennifer had ever seen. A man of similar age clung on around his middle, while behind him, Jasmine kicked out her legs to the side and threw back her head in laughter. As the line began to descend the steps, the tail of the conga flicked round, and Benji, who was taking up the rear, was catapulted off and rolled across the lawn with a shout of gleeful annoyance. He jumped up, and was just about to head off to join on the end again, when he suddenly did a double take, seeing his mother standing ten feet away from him. He ran towards her, rubbing his hands up and down the seat of his pants.

"Hi, Mom!" He turned towards the rest of the party. "Hey, David, it's Mom!"

Jennifer looked around. "What's going on, Benji?"

"It's a birthday party for Sophie, Mom! She's sixteen!"

As the line broke up, Jasmine made her way across the lawn towards Jennifer with a grin stretched across her face, but then slowed to a standstill when she noticed the look of utter bewilderment on Jennifer's face. David appeared from the centre of the now-silent melée and walked towards Jennifer, scratching nervously at the back of his head. Jasmine caught this action as he passed and grabbed at his arm.

"You never told her, did you?" she exclaimed, her voice aghast at the realization that Jennifer knew nothing about the children or the party.

David shook his head. "Not yet. I was going to on Thursday."

Jasmine hit her head with the palm of her hand and put her fists on her hips. "Oh, *David!*"

Jennifer stood shaking her head, her brows furrowed. "What *is* going on? Who *is* this Sophie whose birthday it is, anyway?"

David approached her. "Listen, I was going to expl——"

"She's David's daughter!" Benji cut in excitedly. "David's oldest daughter!" He looked around to see if he could find Sophie, but she was nowhere to be seen at that precise moment. He grabbed hold of his mother's hand and dragged her past David and Jasmine to where the others stood. "And this is Charlie!" He pulled his new friend forward out of the crowd, and then did the same with Harriet. "And this is Harriet! They're *all* David's children, Mom. Isn't it great?"

"Is this your mummy, Benji?" Harriet's sweet little voice cut through the commotion like a razor blade.

"Yup," Benji said proudly.

Jennifer could do nothing but stand and stare at everyone, her head suddenly feeling as if it were about to explode beneath the pressure of the countless emotions converging all at the same time. David was married? Her friend David was *married*? And he had children? And he hadn't *told* her? Everyone else in Leesport seemed to know about them, but he hadn't told *her*?

"Listen, this is really all my fault . . ." David started, but Jennifer stepped back, holding up her hand to stop him from speaking further. She cupped her elbow in her hand and covered her mouth, knowing that her bottom lip had begun to quiver involuntarily.

At that point, the door of the house opened, and she

turned to watch a tall young girl appear, carrying a jug that clinked with iced lemonade. She stopped when she saw that everyone was looking at her.

"What's going on?" she asked in a subdued voice. "Why's everything gone so quiet?"

Jennifer looked down at her feet. So, this must be Sophie. She shook her head, suddenly realizing that she didn't care who the hell any of these people were anyway. Oh, she had been feeling so good, so . . . *happy*— and now? She looked up at David, feeling the tears begin to well up and burn at her eyes.

"Yeah, why stop the party?" She began to back off towards the gate. "I'll just . . ." She turned and hurried away.

"Jennifer!" David called after her, but she had gone.

"Oh, for heaven's *sakes,* David!" Jasmine cried out.

"I'm sorry, Jasmine, I didn't think—"

"No, you obviously didn't, did you? Don't you realize that it now looks as if Benji and I were part of some sneaky plan to hide it from her?"

"I know. I'm sorry, but I promise you, I'll explain everything."

Jasmine shook her head slowly and turned away from him. "Ain't it a little late for that?"

David swore to himself, then moved off towards the gate. He turned. "Listen, everyone, I'm sorry about this, but could we just put everything on hold for a minute?" He looked at Clive. "I think it would be a good idea if you and Peter took Jasmine and the children back to Barker Lane for now."

Clive nodded. "Of course."

"What on *earth* is happening, Dad?" Sophie asked.

"It's really nothing, darling," he said, walking towards her. "Just a stupid misunderstanding that's come about through bad timing on my part." He gave her a kiss on the forehead. "But the party will continue later, I promise you."

He turned back towards the gate and as he reached

it, he felt a hand clutch at his elbow. He turned and looked down at Benji. "David," he said, a worried expression on his face, "I think Mom's crying."

David ruffled the boy's hair. "Yeah, I know, Benji, but I'll get it sorted out, okay?"

Benji turned without looking at him and went back to take hold of Jasmine's hand. David threw open the gate and began sprinting as fast as he could along Shore Street. He was moving so fast that he had run twenty yards past the BMW before recognizing it as Jennifer's car. He stopped and loped back slowly towards it, glancing in as he approached. Jennifer sat in the driver's seat staring straight ahead and clutching the top of the steering wheel. He opened the door. "Listen, Jennifer, I just—"

"No," she cut in, holding up her hand. She glanced up at him, a look of deep hurt in her eyes. "I don't want to listen." She fired up the engine and moved off, pulling the car round into the entrance of the marina. David ran after it and opened the door, squatting down on his haunches behind it so that she couldn't reverse away.

"Please, Jennifer. Just give me a chance to explain."

"No! Now would you get out of the way, please?" she said, fighting hard to control her voice.

David did not move from his position. "Not until you've given me a chance to explain."

Realizing that he was not going to move, she took in a deep breath, and pulling the keys from the ignition, she jumped out of the car.

"Please! Just leave me alone!" she said, as she strode off towards the marina.

David stood up and shut the door, then, catching up with her, took hold of her arm. She turned and raised her hand at this unwelcome contact, and he backed off hurriedly.

"Don't you *ever* touch me again, do you hear?" She shook her head in anger as she fought to find her next words. "I thought I could trust you! I thought you were—my *friend*!" She began walking away, then turned back. "I mean, *everyone* seemed to have known about all this except me! Even my own child! How do you think that makes me *feel*?" She spluttered out a gasping sob of anger.

"I was going to tell you on Thursday! I didn't think you were coming back until then."

She crossed her arms and nodded. "Oh, Thursday. That would have been just fine, wouldn't it? Let's keep it all a secret until after the party, then we won't have to invite boring old Jennifer."

"Oh, come on, that's stupid!" David snapped at her, losing his patience. "It wasn't like that at all!" He immediately held up his hands in apology at his tone. "Listen, I'm sorry about the party. It was just that Sophie's birthday was last month, so I thought we'd just celebrate it as soon as possible. There was no subterfuge or malice ever intended by that!"

Jennifer shook her head at the pathos of his explanation and turned and walked past the entrance gate. The same surly-faced little man who had been in the box when David had come down there on that first morning stood up from watching his television and leaned out of the window.

"Hey, you! Is that your car parked up there? 'Cos if so, you can't park it there. It's blocking the entrance!"

David glared at him. "Look, why don't you just— bugger off!"

The man was at first mystified by the retort, but then a thunderous expression came over his face. "Hey, who d'ya think you're talkin' to, you goddamned Brit? Stuck-up bastard. Don't you—?"

"You heard him!" Jennifer interjected with force. "Just *bugger off*!"

She turned and strode off, and David watched as the man, obviously stunned by the fact that an American *woman* could talk to him in such tones, slumped slowly into his seat and turned back to watching his television.

As Jennifer walked out onto the narrow gangway that led to the boats, David pushed past and turned to face her, successfully impeding her from going any farther. She stopped and looked at him, anger blazing in her eyes.

"Why didn't you *tell* me! I can't believe you didn't *tell* me! I wouldn't have minded, David! I just feel so— left out! I don't mind that you have a . . . wife and children, but why did you think you couldn't *tell* me?"

"I don't have a wife!"

"Oh, *right!*" she exclaimed, trying to push past him. "So how do you explain those three kids back there, or are you going to spin me some yarn about you gallivanting around Scotland fathering illegitimate children everywhere?"

"Oh, don't be stupid! Of course not."

"*So where the hell* is *your wife?*"

"*SHE'S DEAD!*"

The two words came out with such passion and anguish that they seemed to hang in the air, breaking immediately through Jennifer's anger to dig themselves deep into her innermost self. It happened so fast, and was so discordant with the preconceived course of her argument, that she found herself swallowing back the angry retort she had intended.

At that point, two yachtsmen, who were walking along the narrow gangway, excused themselves in passing, and both she and David stood aside in silence to allow them through. Jennifer turned and followed them with her eyes, thankful for the interruption to retrain her thoughts. She turned back to David and flickered a half-smile at him, but then, seeing the look of desolation on his face, she lowered her head and closed her eyes, devastated by her own self-centredness in not having allowed him to explain earlier.

"When?" she eventually asked in a quiet, faltering voice.

David remained silent for a moment before answering. "April."

"This April?"

David glanced out the side of his eye at her and nodded.

Jennifer let out a deep shuddering breath. "Oh, David! Why did you—"

"Listen!" David cut in, holding up his hand. "I wanted to explain to you properly. Believe me, I never wanted you to find out like this. It just happened that Jasmine found out, well, really by default, and I asked her not to say anything, because . . ." He stopped and turned to look out across the bay to Fire Island. ". . . because I wasn't ready to tell anyone. That's the reason I'm out here. So I could lose myself, and get away from constantly thinking and having people talk about it."

As he stood, still gazing out across the bay, he suddenly felt a hand slip into his, and he turned to look into Jennifer's upturned face.

"And do you think you could talk about it—with me—now?" she asked softly.

David paused for a moment, then slowly nodded.

"Well, come on then," she said, pulling him by the hand back towards dry land. "Let's find somewhere a little more private than this."

Two hours later, it had all been told and, with nothing left to say, they sat together in silence on the little jetty in front of the saltbox, gently skimming their bare feet across the surface of the water and looking out across the bay as the warming darkness fell about them. Throughout his explanation, Jennifer had continually asked questions with such intuition and understanding that he realized at the end of it that her knowledge of Rachel and the children probably now outmatched that of anyone else but his own closest family. It was at that precise moment that he felt more at peace with himself than at any time since Rachel's death.

The quiet was so enveloping that David caught the

change in Jennifer's breathing as she let out a silent laugh to herself. He turned and looked at her. "What?"

She shook her head and, leaning back on her hands, she straightened out her legs and watched the water drip from her feet. "Nothing. I was just remembering *my* sixteenth birthday."

"God, I can't remember mine! Yours must have been a pretty special occasion."

"Oh, it was!" Jennifer put her head back and gazed up at the stars. "I was at a boarding-school in Richmond, Virginia, and my mother picked me up on the morning of my birthday and said she had a surprise for me. We flew up to New York, and we shopped . . ." She let out a short laugh. ". . . . and we shopped some more. And then, in the evening, we went to my first Broadway show." She paused, pulling her knees up under her chin. "It was *Jesus Christ Superstar*. I have never forgotten it."

David smiled and looked down into the dark waters. "Yeah. I can imagine." He let out a long sigh. "I think that's what I really fear most for my children. They'll miss days like that. They'll never have them."

Jennifer reached across and laid her hand on top of his. "David?"

"Yeah?"

"Would you let me ask Sophie to come to New York with me?"

"What?"

"Can I take Sophie into New York this weekend? I'd love to take her shopping, and then maybe go to a Broadway show."

"Would you really do that?"

Jennifer leaned over towards him, her face lightening up into that same smile she had given him when he had first complimented Benji on the day of the tennis party.

"I don't have a daughter, and I've never regretted it for an instant—except for one thing. And that was that I could never give her a day like the one my mother gave me for my sixteenth birthday. You've been so wonderful with Benji, David, and I would love more than anything to take Sophie."

"Well, I think it's a wonderful idea. We'll ask her. I'm sure she'll be bowled over."

"Good. We'll go into the city on Saturday morning, and we'll shop till we drop; then we can go back to the apartment in West Village, because we'll have it to ourselves, seeing Alex will still be away. Then we'll go to—now what would she enjoy?—I know! *Crazy for You*. That's on at the Shubert!" Her face beamed once more with excitement.

David laughed. "Now *that* will be right up Sophie's street!" He jumped up and, taking hold of Jennifer's hand, pulled her to her feet and then both walked slowly back along the jetty and up the narrow steps into the garden. When she got to the top, she turned as he took the last two steps behind her.

"Oh, by the way, I was going to tell you. We got the contract."

"You did! Well done! You deserved it in every way!" He put his hand out to give hers a congratulatory shake, but she crossed her arms and eyed him closely, as if trying to make out some follow-on to his initial reaction to the news.

He met her gaze. "What's the matter?"

"David, can I ask you something, and would you give me an honest answer to my question?"

"Well, I don't know what it is yet."

"Okay! So here's the question! You said that you gave up work to look after Rachel?"

"Yeah."

"Right! So what I want to know is—what do you do? I mean, what is your normal job?"

"Why do you ask?"

Jennifer turned and began walking nonchalantly towards the house. "Oh, it's just that one reason we got the contract with Tarvy's was because some unbelievably kind person and obviously well-connected with the company put in a good word for us." She turned and looked directly at him. "But neither Sam, Russ nor I have any idea who it could be."

"Ah, right," he said quietly, looking down at his feet to cover for the smile on his face.

"You don't happen, by any chance, to be in the liquor business, do you?"

He looked up and nodded noncommittally. "Well, sort of."

"What do you mean, 'sort of'? You either are or you aren't."

"Yeah, okay, I'm in the whisky industry."

Jennifer walked slowly back towards him. "And have you, by any chance, contacted anyone over the past week who might just happen to work for Gladwin Vintners?"

David stuck his hands in the back pockets of his trousers and looked everywhere except at Jennifer. "Well, sort of, yeah—but it was a social call as well."

Jennifer stopped directly in front of him. "You've done it again, haven't you? I only said it as a joke, but you managed to fix that too!" She gave out an incredulous laugh. "Your name *is* David Corstorphine, isn't it?"

"Yeah, why?"

"It's not anything like, well, Clark Kent or . . . something similar?"

"God no, you're looking at a mere mortal here."

Jennifer shrugged her shoulders. "Well, maybe." She reached up and gave him a slow and gentle kiss on either cheek. "But a particularly special one."

She turned and hurried over to the porch. "Come on, I haven't celebrated yet! Let's have a drink! God, I'm in need of one after this afternoon!"

David thumped his hand against his forehead as he followed her towards the house. "I'm afraid that could be a problem! I know for a fact that I don't have anything. I didn't have much at home, and I think Gerry ended up nicking the last beer. But look, I'll go straight up to the liquor store and get a bottle of wine."

"No, don't worry," she said, disappointed, as she entered the living-room.

"Honestly, it's no problem!" he said, picking up the keys of the Volkswagen off the table. "Give me five minutes, and I'll be back. Just make yourself at home. The place is so small that you'll probably find everything from where you're standing at the minute!"

As it happened, it was a good fifteen minutes before he returned. Having taken a bottle of champagne out of the cooler in the liquor store, he became embroiled in a lengthy conversation with Victor, the old man who ran the place, about the differing qualities of champagne that were now coming out of France. Eventually, he managed to get away, leaving Victor to continue his droning appraisal with some guy who had only come in for a six-pack of beer.

The moment he arrived back at the house, David moved quickly, fearing that Jennifer might have decided to go home. He ran across the garden, and entering through the porch, he found her sitting in one of the armchairs with Dodie on her knees.

"Sorry about that!" he said, beginning immediately to take the foil off the top of the bottle. "I was held up!"

"Don't worry!" Jennifer replied. "Dodie appeared from somewhere and has been keeping me company. Listen, David, I didn't know how long you were going to be, and I was a little worried about the children, so I rang Jasmine. Just as well, as it happens, because she was in somewhat of a state about this afternoon. Anyway, I put her mind at rest, and then got her to ask the children if they minded sleeping at the house tonight. They seem to be okay about it. Do you have any objections?"

"No, that's great—as long as it's all right by you."

"Yeah, sure it is! And anyway, I'd love to have them to stay whenever or for as long as they want! Please treat it as an open—"

She stopped talking, realizing that David was suddenly frozen in mid-action as he prised the cork off the bottle. He seemed to have become aware of the music that Jennifer had put on the record player, and was standing staring at the pile of records that she had taken from the top shelf and had left sitting on the table. She looked across at them.

"Oh, I'm sorry! I hope you don't mind. I just thought that I'd put on a record, but they all seemed, well, either doleful, or . . ." She laughed. ". . . a little too seductive, and I didn't think that I should give you the wrong idea! So I thought that there was no harm in a bit of Martha Reeves and the Vandell——"

Her voice petered out, as she noticed that David's face had drained of all colour.

"David, what's wrong?"

"Could you change the record, please?" he said quietly.

"Why?"

"Could you just please change the—"

It was too late. The song faded out, and the needle crackled unerringly on the spacer towards the next track. Jennifer watched as David shut his eyes, his whole face tightening as if he expected someone to deal him a final, mortal blow.

The quiet guitar introduction of "The Tracks of My Tears" sounded out around the room. David turned away and lowered his head, the bottle held limply at his side as he leaned his free hand on the back of the armchair. Jennifer looked up at the speakers, realizing now that it was the song. She walked over to him and took the bottle from his grasp and placed her hand on his shoulder.

"Is it the song?"

David slowly nodded.

"Was it yours? Yours and Rachel's?"

He nodded again.

Taking a grip on his arm, she slowly turned him towards her and looked into his lowered face, seeing the tears in his eyes.

"Oh, David!" she said quietly, "I didn't know! Come here!"

She pulled him against her, and as he rested his head on her shoulder, she suddenly felt a shudder run through his body and into her own as he broke down, the tears beginning to flow uncontrollably as she held him close to her.

"So take a good look at my face, can't you see the smi-ile, it's out of place."

She pushed him away, and, placing her hand gently on the side of his cheek, she tilted his face up so that he looked at her directly.

"You know, you must be the bravest man I know. You've come out here and you've managed to exorcize all these ghosts by yourself. And on top of that, you've fixed it for Benji, Jasmine *and* myself over and over again. It's my turn now. It's my turn to fix it for you. This is the last ghost, David, and I'm going to be with you every step of the way."

As the track came to an end, Jennifer left him and reached up and placed the needle haphazardly somewhere near the beginning. She turned round and took him again in her arms, and gradually, as the song continued, she felt him begin to move against her in rhythm with the music.

"Since you left me, you see me with another girl, seemin' like I'm havin' fun."

David held himself tight against her, feeling the warmth of her body, pulled close against him, loving the smell emanating from the softness of her neck. He closed his eyes as he felt her lips reach up and caress him below the ear. They moved in sequence across his cheek, eventually kissing at the side of his mouth. Then he felt it, the gentle pressure against his own lips, and he let them part, allowing himself to taste for the first time in what seemed an eternity the essence of all that he had longed for, and all that he had missed since losing Rachel.

Her name. Rachel. It was Rachel he missed.

He pushed himself away from Jennifer and stood, his gaze lowered to the ground.

"I—I'm sorry, Jennifer, I can't! I can't do this so soon after . . ."

Jennifer moved quickly over to the record player, using the opportunity to replace the needle on the record, this time hitting the introduction perfectly. She turned back to him, and gently took hold of both his hands.

"People say I'm the life of a party, 'cos I have a drink or two."

"David, nothing is going to happen, I promise you. I won't let it. We do nothing more than dance. That's all—but there is this one very beautiful and special ghost that we have to exorcize."

She pulled him back towards her, and this time her lips had no need to work their way to his mouth. He was there, waiting for her, ready for her, and together they began moving gently, as one, around the tiny confines of the living-room.

And still Smokey sang . . .

Chapter
THIRTY-ONE

Jasmine really didn't know what had hit her over the next couple of days. The house had suddenly lost its usual airy tranquillity and been turned into a place of vociferous mayhem. The route leading from the hall through the passageway and into the kitchen had come to resemble more the Indianapolis Speedway, and she would often find herself having to jump clear of a gaggle of screaming children as they burst through the kitchen like a litter of unruly puppies. And even though they spent most of their time outside in the swimming pool or on the tennis court, there always seemed to be a child at her side, either asking advice as to where something had been left, or where somebody was, or what time the next meal was going to be.

But she didn't mind. In fact, she revelled in it. Not only because she loved having so many children about her, but also because of the sheer relief she felt in not having to be party to any further clandestine fibs or secrecies. Jennifer was now part of it, wholly integrated into this new uproarious way of life that Jasmine herself had been enjoying, though somewhat guiltily, over the past week.

Furthermore, Jennifer seemed to be a changed person, having almost an aura of serenity about her that Jasmine had never before witnessed. Gone was the rushed and, at times, offhand formality of the business woman, replaced by a more gentle, relaxed character who appeared totally content in giving her complete and undivided attention to the new household. Yet despite being happy about this inexplicable change, Jasmine found herself becoming increasingly concerned about what effect Alex's wrongdoings might have on this new, more vulnerable, Jennifer if she were ever to find out about them.

A further change was that, without any hint of favour or encouragement, she had acquired a constant shadow in the form of Harriet. The child was always there at her side, either asking if she could help her cook or bake a cake, usually at a time when she was attempting to prepare yet another gargantuan meal for the troops. Jasmine eventually concluded that one of her main assets in attracting so much attention from the little girl was the colour of her skin, in that whatever they did together, Harriet would just stare up at her, her eyes wide with fascination, as she moved her head from side to side, quite unashamedly studying every pore on Jasmine's face.

David, meanwhile, had found it impossible to do any further work in the garden, not because he didn't want to, but because, on making his first appearance with a hoe and fork in hand, he was met with such a derisive cry of *"Boooriiiing!"*—for the most part orchestrated by Jennifer herself—that he was left with no option but to return his tools unused to the garden shed. Feeling almost heavy-hearted about it, he shut the doors and locked them up, knowing that he was probably doing so for the last time.

Nevertheless, there was now no excuse or covert reason for not devoting himself entirely both to his children and to Jennifer, Benji, and Jasmine. Moreover, as the week unfolded, it became apparent to him that, right here and now, he was in the company of those with whom he most wanted to spend his time. There were trips to Fire Island, excursions into Leesport in the Volkswagen, disruptive visits to the huge multiplex cinema in Sayville, always returning at the end of the day to Barker Lane, where tennis matches and swimming competitions continued well on into the evening.

After their first night in Jennifer's house, the children quickly came to the conclusion that it had far more to offer in terms of comfort and amenities than the saltbox in Shore Street, and it was therefore agreed, to a man, that they would prefer to stay there. Sophie at first felt a little guilty in letting her father return to the saltbox by himself, and subsequently cajoled Jennifer into asking him if he too wanted to stay. However, Jennifer secretly understood David's wish to return to the haven of his own house every night, knowing that he was still in need of a private space. She therefore immediately accepted his somewhat lame excuses that it would be less disruptive for Dodie, and that he was also half-expecting a fax to come in from his office in Scotland.

This distancing allowed David the perspective of standing back and observing his children as they blended, as smoothly as synchromesh, into the way of life of this household—a way of life that had been so much a part of his own over the past six weeks. Charlie and Benji had become an inseparable and independent unit, spending most of their time on the tennis court or out on the bay with the Windsurfer, taking it in turns to man the rowing-boat and yell encouragement to the other as he wobbled his way across the shallows. Harriet, meanwhile, appeared content to be anywhere in the vicinity of Jasmine, always being the first to run back into the house to seek her out if she had been away with the others for any length of time.

But what gave David the most satisfaction was the bond that was forming between Sophie and Jennifer. At first, he'd had fears that there would be a cool reserve on Sophie's part, especially as she might see Jennifer only as the person who had disrupted her birthday party. But he had not counted on Jennifer's intuition in understanding this for herself, and on that very same night when she had returned from David's house, she had gone up to Sophie's bedroom and had sat on her bed until well after midnight, simply talking to her and making plans for their forthcoming weekend in the city.

What was more, in seeing for the first time this woman, who happened to be no part of his family, so closely involved with one of his own children, he became almost imperceptibly aware of his mind creating a direct link between her and Rachel, and instead of banishing it as an invasive and unwelcome thought, he found himself quite at ease not only in accepting it, but also in being able to admit to himself just how important a role Jennifer had begun to play in his life.

Seeing that the promised continuation of Sophie's birthday party had not taken place on the Tuesday, David decided that, on the eve of Jennifer's and Sophie's departure to the city, he would take everyone, including the original guests, out to dinner in the Leesport Restaurant. As they were to number thirteen at the table, and not wishing to tempt providence, he also invited In-Deli-ble Billy (as the children had now christened him), having noticed that, during their countless visits to the deli, Billy had come to direct his wicked and teasing remarks to Sophie, and she in turn had reacted to them with a sparkle in her eyes and a flush to her cheeks.

As it turned out, the party was a wild affair, with all protocol regarding age and status being summarily discarded from the moment it began. Gerry had brought along with him two guitars, one of which he handed over to David at the end of the meal, much to the embarrassment of the children, and thereafter those who were willing stood up to do a party piece.

Of course, Benji was first to take up the challenge. He launched into his own song, then interjected it throughout with excuses about how it sounded much better when Dublin Up were playing with him. Then, amidst shrill protests from Sophie, Billy dragged her up from the table to perform a duet with "You're the One That I Want," and although it appeared at the outset to be a strong contender for The Best Entertainment Award, Billy became somewhat over-suggestive in his Travolta dance routine, and the act came to an abrupt end with Sophie running from the room with an embarrassed scream of "That's absolutely *revooolting*!"

David and Gerry were next to perform, singing a merry little tune which turned out to be slightly bawdy in content, earning them some stern looks of disapproval from Jasmine.

The finale, of course, was the best, coming as the direct result of a request from David. With loud yelps of encouragement from the assembled throng, Clive and Peter were pushed self-consciously to their feet, and after a few furtive whispers to each other in deciding which way they should initially face, they set about performing, in perfect sychronization of both voice and foot, their well-polished rendition of "Wouldn't It Be Lovely."

The next morning, David was up at Barker Lane at half past eight, eager to make sure that Sophie had everything she needed for her trip. However, he found himself more of a hindrance than a help, the two citybounders already seeming to have everything in hand, so much so that Jennifer had told Sophie only to pack her night-things, seeing that the main reason they were going to the city was to shop! Feeling slightly embarrassed by this, David managed to catch Jennifer for a fleeting moment by herself, and stuttered his way around the subject of money. Jennifer, however, stopped him mid-sentence by simply reaching up and placing the tip of her forefinger on his mouth. Then, walking away from him, she began to reel off a string of expenditures, relating to the garden and to Benji, which he himself had incurred without reimbursement. Thereafter, David felt it best not to make another approach, but eased his conscience instead by slipping one hundred dollars into Sophie's purse.

At nine on the dot, the two girls (as Jasmine had begun to call them) were sitting champing at the bit in the BMW. Sophie gave an excited wave first to David and Jasmine and then to the three very tired-looking faces who peered out of an upstairs window, before turning round and pointing her finger à la "Wagons Roll!" up the drive. With a flick of her hand in a final gesture of farewell, Jennifer powered the car away from the house.

Exactly two hours later, they arrived in the West Village, and having parked the car in a space in Barrymore Street and deposited overnight bags in the apartment, they walked the short distance to Spring Street. There, Sophie spent the rest of her morning in a bemused trance, as Jennifer led her up from one shop to another. All the names that she had heard of, and had talked about with her friends at school, were there. Agnes B, Replay, Guess, and they went into every one and bought something for her, and for her alone.

They then took a taxi uptown and ate a late lunch in a restaurant on Madison Avenue. At the end of the meal, Jennifer ordered coffee for two, and being for the first time in the relaxed privacy of their own company, she broached the subject of Rachel. With almost a frightened reticence to begin with, Sophie suddenly found herself being able to open up to this woman whom she had come both to like and trust over the past week.

Having been allowed to leave their shopping bags at the restaurant, they took a taxi to Central Park. There the conversation continued as they walked side by side along the path by the lake, Sophie's arm linked through Jennifer's, only stepping away from each other to allow for the occasional erratic Rollerblader or single-minded jogger to pass unhindered. The more they talked, the more admiration and love Jennifer felt for this young girl at her side, realizing that she herself had never experienced such devastating loss and emotional upheaval in her own life.

When they eventually left the park, Jennifer decided that there was not enough time to go back to the apartment before the show. Consequently, they took a taxi straight to Broadway, stopping off to collect their bags on the way. Then, having ensconced themselves in a welcoming pub called the White Lion, they sat drinking Coke and eating chips, while studying the faces of the people who entered and, giggling uncontrollably, comparing their looks with well-known people.

They walked the remaining distance to the Shubert Theatre, arriving ten minutes before the curtain of *Crazy for You* went up. Having entrusted their shopping bags to the little lady who ran the cloakroom, and having stocked up with programmes, they entered the auditorium and sat down in their plush velvet seats just as the overture began.

To Sophie, it was the most magical thing that she had ever seen. She sat transfixed throughout the performance, listening intently to every song and humming the melody over to herself after each was finished, desperate to remember everything that took place during the performance. The man in front of her seemed to be the tallest person in the audience, but she didn't mind, because it meant that she could lean over to the side in order to look around him and, without excuse or self-consciousness, feel the warming comfort of physical contact with Jennifer as she did so.

After the show had finished, they stood on the sidewalk outside the theatre, feeling the sultry heat of the evening blow about their faces and, deciding not to take a taxi, they turned and walked off in the direction of the West Village, swinging their shopping bags to and fro as they jumbled through the words of the songs together.

By the time that they reached Twenty-first Street, their hands ached so much from carrying their bags that they succumbed to the lure of the taxi, and within a few minutes were deposited back outside the apartment in Barrymore Street. Jennifer unlocked the door and flicked on a light switch, then, dumping everything on the hall floor, she walked through to the sitting-room and sat down with a sigh of exhaustion in an armchair.

"So," she said, looking at Sophie, "what shall we do now?"

Sophie shrugged. "I don't know. Isn't it a bit late to start doing something now?"

Jennifer glanced at her watch. "Heavens, it's ten to twelve! I'd no idea it was so late! Maybe you're right. Do you just want to go to bed?"

Sophie wrinkled up her nose in disapproval of the motion. "Not particularly. I'm pretty hungry, though!"

Jennifer slapped her hands on the arms of the chair and jumped to her feet. "Yup, so am I! So what do you want? Do you like pizza?"

"Do I not!"

"Great! Me too! So tell you what we'll do, I'll phone for the best pepperoni pizza that money can buy, and while we're waiting for it to be delivered, we'll get into our night-clothes and you can pick out a video for us to watch. Then we'll just curl up on the sofa and pig out on pizza! How's that for an idea?"

Sophie nodded slowly, a contented grin on her face. "I would say that it couldn't be better!"

Five minutes later, having changed into her night-dress, Jennifer padded into the sitting-room in her bare feet and vaulted over the back of the sofa to sit beside Sophie. The video had already started, the opening credits being accompanied by some seriously eerie music. Jennifer turned slowly to her young companion, a look of complete shock on her face. "Sophie, what on earth are we watching?"

Sophie smiled at her. "*The Amityville Horror.*"

Jennifer's mouth dropped open. "Oh, Sophie, do we really want to watch this? Is there nothing a bit tamer?"

Sophie laughed. "Come on, Jennifer, it's only a *film*! Anyway, I thought we'd had enough sugary sweetness for one night. Time for a bit of nerve-tingling spice!"

Jennifer shook her head slowly. "Ooh, you evil girl!" She grabbed hold of Sophie's hand and squeezed it. "Okay, but if you're going to make me suffer this, I'm holding on to you good and tight. I just *loathe* horror films!"

Sophie let out a wicked chuckle and, pulling Jennifer's arm across her shoulder, tucked herself in against her.

Although they both heard it simultaneously, the noise at the front door was more like a soft scratching than a knock.

"Pizza time!" Jennifer exclaimed, jumping to her feet. "Last one there has to eat the box!"

They both ran for the door, and Sophie, having had more recent practice in the art of outwitting her siblings, sneaked under Jennifer's arm and made it there first. She threw it open, making the bunch of keys that hung in the lock jangle against the metal of the door handle. A couple stood in the corridor, locked together in a deep embrace, being so enwrapped in each other that it took all of two seconds before either of them realized that the door had been opened.

Sophie looked quizzically at them, thinking that neither looked very much like pizza-delivery people, then turned round to Jennifer. She stood behind her, stock-still, a look of sheer horror on her now ashened face, her mouth twitching as if she was trying to say something. Then, in the quietest voice she spoke, her tone registering both total disbelief and unbearable hurt.

"Oh, Alex, no!"

Chapter
THIRTY-TWO

Throughout the day on Saturday, there had been more than a few disgruntled moans from Benji and Charlie about not being included in the trip to the city, so, in order to take their minds off the unfairness of it all and to add some variety to their escapades, it was arranged for them to spend the Sunday with Sean Dalaglio. Jasmine, meanwhile, said that she wanted to take Harriet to visit her mother in North Leesport, so, David found himself to be a free agent for the first time in over two weeks.

Having allowed himself a lie-in until nine o'clock, he took Dodie for a short walk down to the marina, before setting about tidying up the house and ridding it of the clutter of camp-beds and sleeping-bags. He had taken everything outside to put into the Volkswagen, when he found himself consumed with guilt over the state of the car's interior, a week and a half's worth of ferrying children around having left it in a worse condition than when he had taken it over from Carrie. Therefore, having stretched the cable of the vacuum cleaner to its full length from house to car, he proceeded in sucking out a dust-bag's worth of sand and old candy wrappers, all which seemed to have worked their way into the most inaccessible crevices of the plastic upholstery.

As the electronic bells of the little Roman Catholic church on Champner Street began to summon the congregation to eleven-o'clock mass, he made his way to the bottom of the garden, a can of Pepsi in hand, and descended the steps to the jetty. He flicked off his deck shoes and sat dangling his feet over the edge as he watched a windsurfer skim his way across the bay about three hundred yards offshore.

God, this place really *was* perfect. He smiled to himself, realizing just how many times and on how many different occasions he'd said that over the past six weeks. But it was true. Never, for one minute, had it lost the special magic that he had felt that first morning when he had walked down to the marina and looked out across the bay. And now, on top of that, it had succeeded in casting its healing spell, not only over him, but over his whole family. But it wasn't just the place— it was the people as well. Everyone had played a part in his revitalization and in his own children's readjustment to family life, something which was going to make it so much easier for them all when they returned to Scotland.

Scotland. His mind turned to the distillery, and he wondered for the hundredth time if he shouldn't have asked Archie to fax him back regardless, the lack of response having left a niggling doubt in his mind that something untoward might be taking place. But then again, Archie would surely have contacted him.

As he finished off the last remaining drops of the can he started, turning his head quickly towards the house, positive that he had just heard the sound of a door banging.

"Hullo?"

He waited for five seconds, listening for a reply, then jumped to his feet and ran back up the steps. The side door stood ajar.

"Hullo?" he called out again as he walked across the

lawn to the porch. He heard a scuttling noise from inside the house, and Dodie came bouncing out of the screen door, followed immediately by Sophie.

For a moment, David just stood looking at her, her presence there being so unexpected.

"Sophie?" he said, a confused tone to his voice. "What are *you* doing here? I thought you weren't due back until tonight."

Sophie said nothing, but ran over to him and put her arms around his chest, holding herself tight against him.

"Has something happened, darling?"

Sophie looked up at him, a worried expression on her face, and nodded her head.

"What? Tell me."

Sophie took a couple of deep breaths, as if steeling herself to speak, before she finally blurted out her explanation.

"It was so awful, Dad! We'd been to the theatre and then we went back to Jennifer's place and we were watching a video and waiting for the pizza to arrive, and then I opened the front door and there was this man and woman there, and they were snogging each other in the corridor." She pulled herself even tighter against her father. "It was Jennifer's *husband*, Dad!"

David stood with his eyes tightly shut, not wishing to hear the final sentence, knowing already what she was going to say. For a moment, he held his daughter in silence.

"When did you get back to Leesport?" he asked quietly.

"Last night—no, this morning, I suppose, at about three o'clock. We just packed our things and came back. Poor Jennifer, Dad. She was *so* upset all the way home."

David bent forward and kissed the top of her head. "Did you see Jasmine when you got home?"

"No, we were pretty quiet. I don't think Jennifer wanted to see anyone. Then, when I got up about an hour ago and went downstairs, there was no one in the house, but I found a note on the kitchen table from Jasmine saying that she had seen the car and explaining where everyone had gone today. That's why I knew you were here. Then I went into the conservatory and found Jennifer. She's just sitting there by herself on the sofa." She looked up at her father again. "I asked her if she wanted me to get you, and she just nodded without speaking. I was going to ring, but I thought it would be better if I came and saw you, so I borrowed Benji's bike."

David put his arm around his daughter's shoulders and began walking towards the house. "Listen, we'll just leave the bike here for now and go straight up there in the Volkswagen, okay?"

Sophie stopped and looked up at him. "Actually, Dad, I think it would be better if you went alone. To be quite honest, I don't want to go up there now."

"Right. In that case, will you stay here and look after Dodie?"

Sophie nodded.

David gave her a kiss on the forehead. "Look, I'll be back as soon as I can. And don't worry. I'll speak to Jennifer and see if I can help her to get something sorted out."

"She's such a lovely person, Dad, and it's just so horrible seeing her look so sad."

"I know. Well, let's see what I can do, okay?"

As soon as he arrived at the house, David caught sight of Jennifer through the conservatory window, sitting motionless on the sofa. He got out of the car and walked round the side to the French doors, watching her at all times through the glass. Yet her eyes never followed him, even though, at one point, he moved directly through her line of sight. He entered the room and quietly sat on the low coffee-table in front of her. Her legs were tucked up under her chin, her vacant eyes puffy with too little sleep and too much crying, her cheeks streaked with tear-stains. David reached forward and stroked the back of his hand up and down her bare arm.

"Jennifer? Are you all right?"

She didn't look at him, but took in a deep sniff. "That's a pretty stupid question for Superman. Does it look as if I'm all right?"

David glanced down at his hands and began flicking at one thumb-nail with the other. She was right. It was pretty stupid.

"Alex has been having an affair with his bloody business associate for three months, David," she said, her voice choking.

"Yeah."

Jennifer turned to him. "What do you mean, 'Yeah'? Did you know about it?"

David rubbed at his forehead with his fingers. "Well, in a way. Jasmine had an idea that something was going on. She overheard Alex talking on the telephone the day of the tennis party. But she didn't know for certain, Jennifer, and once she'd told me, I didn't really think it was for us to say anything."

Jennifer nodded and looked away. "No, I don't suppose it was. I should have realized it myself."

As she said this, she leaned her face forward on her knees and burst into tears once more. David got up from the table, and squeezing himself down between the arm of the sofa and her back, he pulled her against him and began rocking her gently, as if comforting a distraught child.

"What did I do wrong, David? Was it my fault? What did I do *wrong*?"

"Nothing. You did nothing wrong. You mustn't blame yourself for this. It's totally Alex's fault that this happened."

"But why did he do it? Why did he think he *needed* to do it?"

"I don't know. I have no idea. It's just that maybe,

well, sometimes people lose sight of what they've got, and as far as Alex is concerned, I think he's probably gone fucking blind."

"I thought we were good together, David. Maybe not perfect, what with the jobs and everything, but I thought we were good! And Benji as well. I really did think that we had everything going for us . . ." Her voice grew higher as she fought back the tears once more. ". . . and now I'm talking about it all in the past tense!"

David pushed himself off the sofa and sat down again on the coffee-table, taking both her hands in his and looking straight into her face.

"That's just it, Jennifer! You mustn't speak about it in the past tense! You *do* have it all—still! Listen . . . oh, hell! . . . I can't really explain this properly, but . . . you see, I don't . . . I *don't* have it all any more, Jennifer. I can't *help* but speak in the past tense, and I can tell you, I would give anything for it to be different. You know, when Rachel died, I became, well, self-absorbed and bitter, and I suppose completely selfish, but I realize now that, even though the hurt is still profound, I not only have the obligation of the children, but also the sheer joy of them as well. You still have both Benji *and* Alex. And what's more, Benji has Alex—and he really needs him, Jennifer. He loves him. He's his *father*! You can never lose sight of that. Please don't ever lose sight of that. Okay, I realize that Alex has behaved like a complete moron, but it's worth everything, your happiness and Benji's happiness, to try and get it all back together. You've got to work it out, Jennifer. Please try—even for me, try, because I tell you, I couldn't bear it if I went home knowing that this family, *your* family, which has become so—so important to me, should have suffered the same fate as mine—without it needing to happen."

She turned away from him, sadness expressed in every inch of her face, and slowly shook her head. "But how? Where would I begin, David? I didn't know any-thing was *wrong!* So how would I have any idea where to begin?"

"I don't know. I just don't know. God, we men can be such complete idiots in this way. But we've got to think about doing something." He paused for a mo-ment to gather his thoughts. "I mean, did you say any-thing to him last night?"

Jennifer continued to shake her head. "No, nothing. I was too angry." She sniffed out a brief laugh. "I ac-tually slammed the door in his face, which was really idiotic, since he had his own keys. Anyway, by the time that he let himself back in again, he'd got a taxi for his . . . his woman, and Sophie and I were about ready to leave."

"Why did he come back then?"

Jennifer let out a deep sigh. "Because he *said* he wanted to talk."

"And you didn't?"

"No, of course not! He'd just cheated on me, and I . . . I . . ."

Her bottom lip started to quiver.

"Keep going! And what?"

She blurted out her response. "And I was frightened he was going to ask me for a divorce."

David squeezed her hands to try to keep her atten-tion. "And—did he?"

"No, he just kept saying that he was sorry and that he wanted to talk."

"So—then what happened?"

"Sophie and I left."

"And that was it?"

"No." She paused. "As I was getting into the car, he ran up to me and said that he was going to come out here this afternoon so that we could talk."

"And will you do it, Jennifer? Will you please speak to him? You've got to try! Just talk about what's important—in both your lives—and make him understand it as well."

"But why the hell do you think that I should ever want to?"

"Because in everything that I've asked so far, you've never said no!"

In the silence that followed, Jennifer just stared at him, biting her lip. Then she smiled faintly at him and nodded. "Yes, you're right. I haven't, have I?"

He reached up to give the side of her face a brush with his hand. As he did so, she caught it and held it against her cheek, and he watched as a tear fell from her eye and ran off down the side of his finger.

"Why are you such a special man, David?"

"God, I'm not. I can tell you that straight."

"Oh yes, you are." She paused and looked deep into his eyes. "I wonder why it couldn't have been me that you met all those years ago in Oxford." She smiled and took his hand round to her mouth and kissed it before returning it to her cheek. "Just the wrong time, the wrong place, an ocean apart."

She reached over and kissed him gently on the cheek, then, putting her arms around his shoulders, she pulled her face close into his neck.

"But we found a bridge, didn't we, my greatest friend?" she whispered quietly into his ear. "All these years later, we found a bridge."

David pushed her away from him and held her face in his hands, smoothing away the tears from her eyes with his thumbs. "Yeah, we did. And I'll never, ever forget you for it."

They sat together in silence, their total concentration in each other only being broken by the shrill sound of the telephone ringing. Jennifer slowly let go of David's neck and, with a smile, got up and walked through to the study and picked up the telephone. David listened to her as she answered it.

"Hello? . . . yes, hello, darling . . . yes, I'm fine . . .

where are you? . . . right . . . yes, he's here, do you want to speak to him? . . . Okay, just hang on a minute." She cupped her hand over the receiver. "David, that's Sophie on the telephone. I think there may be something wrong. Her voice sounds a little shaky."

David hurried to the study and took the receiver from Jennifer. "Sophie?"

"Dad, I heard the telephone ring when I was outside in the garden with Dodie, and it just cut off, so I didn't bother coming in, but it was a fax coming through."

David could hear the anxious tone in her voice. "That's all right, darling, don't worry about it. It's probably only from Archie at work."

"No, Dad, it's not!" She paused. "Dad, is a stroke serious?"

"A stroke? Yes, it can be. Why do you ask?"

Sophie's voice faltered at the other end of the line. " 'Cos Grandpa's just had one."

Chapter
THIRTY-THREE

David sat by himself on the jetty below the saltbox, staring out across the bay, the crumpled page held tight in his hand. He took a deep breath and, unfolding it, began reading for the third time the scrawly handwriting of his mother.

Darling David,
I find this terribly difficult to write, but I'm afraid that there is no easy way to break this devastating news to you. Just before lunch-time today, your father suffered a stroke, and I am at this very moment sitting beside his bed in Raigmore Hospital in Inverness. The doctor has just left the room, and he said that he was in reasonably stable condition, but I can see for myself that there is very little colour in his dear old face and he has tubes sticking out of him in all directions. Nevertheless, he is sleeping quite peacefully at the minute, so I am taking the opportunity of this quiet time to write you what I am sure will turn out to be a long epistle, because I think it most important that you understand every detail of what led up to this.

There had been no warning of it happening. He really seemed to have been so well. However, late in the afternoon yesterday, Duncan Caple came to see him. I thought that he was only just keeping your father up-to-date on what was happening at the distillery, but after he had left, I went into the drawing-room to find your father in a complete state of agitation.

It appears that Duncan has not been as straight as we thought, David. Your father explained it to me, but I'm afraid that I was so concerned about him that I didn't manage to take it all in.

Nevertheless, it seems that a company called Kirkpatrick has put in an offer for Glendurnich. I don't know how long Duncan has been planning this, but it must have been for some time. He had already spoken to the workers at the distillery on Friday about it, because it seems that they hold 31 per cent of the shares, and then he tried to put extreme pressure on your father to begin the transfer of his own shares as soon as possible, saying that it was for the best for both the company and the family.

I did say to your father that he should get in touch with you straight away, but he wanted to leave it until today, so that he could go into the distillery to learn the full story—not from Duncan, but from one of the workers—and thereafter, he was going to fax you.

Anyway, as far as the events of today are concerned, I can tell you word for word what happened, because he telephoned me mid-morning from his office in the most frightful tizzy. He had left at nine o'clock (he was actually meant to be reading the lesson in church, but managed to get Roger Spiers to stand in for him), and went into the distillery and spoke to your ex-sergeant, Dougie Masson. Dougie didn't know very much about the ins and outs of Kirkpatrick's plan, but he thought that it must have been brewing up for some time. He also said that, having spoken to the other workers on Friday evening, after Duncan had announced the proposal, they seemed quite excited about the idea, as they realized that they would be making some money out of

*the deal. However, as you can imagine, Dougie was
fiercely loyal, and said that he wanted no part of it.*

*What really hurt your father the most (and I also
think what made him realize that Duncan had been totally dishonest) was that Dougie told him that two people had left the company under what he termed
suspicious circumstances. One of them was Margaret,
and the other was Archie McLachlan, the young man
whom your father said he'd asked to act as a contact
for you in the distillery. At that point in our conversation, he said that he was going to come straight home
and fax you—and that was the last time I spoke to him.*

*The rest of the story I was given by the police ser-
geant who came to the door to tell me the news. Apparently, your father had stopped somewhere on the
Grantown Road to allow a young shepherd to get his
flock across the road. As the boy closed the gate behind
his sheep, he waved to thank him for stopping, but the
car never moved forward. He went over to the car and
found your father slumped over the steering wheel.
Thankfully, the boy then used his wits, and seeing that
there was a car phone, called both the police and an
ambulance. The sergeant did say that it was very lucky
that the phone actually worked in such a remote area.*

*So here I am at his bedside. Jane Spiers kindly gave
me a lift up here, and here I shall stay. But I'm afraid
the doctors have told me that the prognosis is not good,
David, so you must really try to get back here as soon
as possible—not only to see your father, but also to stop
this appalling thing that's going on at the distillery. I
pray you'll be able to rally the troops behind you and
get rid of that dreadful man Duncan Caple and all his
henchmen.*

*I have just read this through again, and realize that
you could be feeling guilty about all this taking place.
You must not. Your father was right in allowing you the
time to heal. If you had been here, you would still be
mouldering around in the garden, none the wiser for*

*what was going on in the distillery, and none the wiser
in yourself. This was going to happen regardless. It has
been planned for ages. But now I know that you are
better, and I know that you will come back fighting—for
your father.*

*I must go down to the front desk now, and ask them
to fax this for me.*

All my love, darling, to you and to the children,

Ma.

David scrumpled the piece of paper back up into his
fist and hit it three times hard against his forehead.

Yeah, but what you didn't know, Ma, was that I *did*
have a bloody clue that something like this might be
going on. Dammit, it was over a week ago that I sent
the fax to Archie!

Jesus, the fax! That was it! Both Margaret and Archie had gone, so it would have no doubt landed right
on Duncan's desk. He knew exactly what he was doing!
The *bastard* knew *exactly!*

"Is it bad, David?"

He glanced round to find Sophie and Jennifer, who
had returned with him to give him moral support, sitting on the steps watching him.

"Yeah, I'm afraid so. We have to go back now."

Sophie let out an anguished cry and Jennifer put her
arm around her shoulders and pulled her to her. As
David ran back up the steps, he bent down in passing
and gave his daughter a comforting kiss on the head,
then hurried off across the lawn into the house. He
picked up his brief-case and, placing it on the desk, he
took out his address book and dialled the number of
the airline in Glasgow. There were four seats available
in business class for the evening flight. He booked them,
and as he put down the telephone, Jennifer and Sophie
walked into the room.

"Jennifer, could you do something for me?"

"Of course."

"Would you take Sophie back to the house and get everything packed up, and then get the others there as soon as you can?"

"Sure I will. Anything else?"

David thought for a moment, trying to get his mind clear. "Yeah. If you could maybe give this friend of mine in Leesport a call. His name's Richard Eggar. I'll give you his number. Explain to him that I have to go home, and ask him if he could pick up Dodie and the car from your house this evening. Also, could you ring up Star Limos in Leesport and get them to send a car around to your house in, erm . . ." In his mind, he quickly worked back from the time of the flight departure. "God, it'll have to be in an hour's time."

"Okay."

Jennifer came across and touched his arm. "Are you all right?"

He smiled. "Silly question."

"Yeah, sorry."

She reached up and gave him a kiss on the cheek, then, putting her arm through Sophie's, they walked together back out into the garden.

David picked up the telephone again and dialled the number for Inchelvie. It rang six times before finally being answered by a very faint, quavering little voice. "Hullo, Inchelvie?"

"Effie, it's David."

"Oh, Mr. David, have you heard the awful news?"

"Yes, Effie, I have, and I'm coming straight home tonight with the children."

"Oh, thank goodness! It's so awful, Mr. David. Your poor father!"

"I'm just so sorry I wasn't there."

"Aye, but you'll be coming home now, Mr. David. That's the main thing."

"Listen, Effie, I need your help. Do you think you can do something for me?"

"Certainly. Will I be needing a piece of paper and a pen?"

"Yes, I think you might."

"If you could just hold the line a wee minute then."

He waited until he heard her voice again.

"I'm ready, Mr. David."

"Okay. I'll go slowly, but if you want to stop me at any time, just say so. First, I want you to go to the top drawer of my father's desk. In there, you will find a black book with the words 'Glendurnich Telephone Numbers' written on it. Now, it has all the home telephone numbers of those who work in the distillery in it. Have you got that so far?"

"Yes, Mr. David."

"Right, I want you to find the numbers for Dougie Masson and Archie McLachlan."

"Dougie . . . Masson and Archie . . . McLachlan. Yes, I have that."

"Well done. Now, our plane gets into Glasgow at seven-ten tomorrow morning. Ring Dougie Masson first and tell him the time of the plane, and then I want you to ask him to hire two cars from Gillespie's Garage in Grantown and to put it on my account. Have you got that?"

"Heavens, what a lot to write!"

David suddenly had a vision of the little housekeeper writing feverishly in her loopy writing.

"I know. I'm sorry, Effie, but you're the only one who can do this."

"That's all right. I have it so far."

"Next, get Dougie to ring Archie. They can arrange with each other for the cars to be picked up and I want them to meet us at Glasgow tomorrow."

"Is that it, Mr. David?"

"That's it. Do you think you have that all?"

Effie went back through the list without fault.

"Well done. Just one final thing. I'm going to get Archie to bring the children straight back to Inchelvie, so they should be with you about mid-day. You will be there?"

"Yes, of course."

"Thank you so much, Effie. I'll see you sometime tomorrow, then."

"Very good, Mr. David."

He put down the telephone and let out a deep sigh, then turned to start packing up his belongings in the little house that had come to mean so much to him.

The limousine had already arrived at Barker Lane by the time he got there, and he felt quite thankful to see that it was Dan himself who was going to be driving them. The children were milling around, all looking a little bewildered by what was happening. As he opened the door of the car, Dodie jumped out to welcome Benji and Charlie, who came rushing forward to meet David.

"Do you really have to go, David?" Benji asked in a soulful voice.

"Yes, I'm afraid so, Benji. Now, come on, you two can give Dan a hand to get my things into the car."

As the two boys began to pull his suitcases out of the back seat, David walked over to the front door just as Jasmine and Jennifer came out.

"You got hold of Richard all right, then?"

"Yup," Jennifer said, handing a child's haversack to Dan. "Everything's arranged."

David nodded sadly. "Right. Well, I really think that we should just get straight off."

"Benji and I are coming too," Jennifer said quietly.

He looked at her, startled. "Are you sure?"

"Yes."

David nodded. He bent down and scooped up Dodie, then walked over and handed her to Jasmine. "Jasmine, could you look after Dodie until this evening?"

"Of course." She sighed deeply. "I was so sorry to hear about your father, David. I'll pray mighty strong for him. But I have to say I'm also real sad 'bout you all goin'."

David moved towards her and wrapped his arms around her ample shoulders, giving her a tight hug.

"Goodbye, my dear friend, and thank you for all you've done—for me and for my children."

"I've done nothin' special."

"Oh yes, you have. More than you can ever imagine. In a way, I feel I owe you my life." He felt himself begin to choke up, and cleared his throat. "And look after Jennifer, won't you? You realize that she now knows all about Alex."

Jasmine nodded. "Mm-mm. She told me."

"Things will work out. I know they will."

Jasmine grinned at him. "Yeah, sure they will—if you've had a part to play in it."

David turned towards the limousine. "All right, everybody in the car!"

The children clambered in, Benji and Charlie letting out a loud exclamation of glee as they simultaneously discovered the television and the drinks icebox. David stood aside to allow Jennifer to get in before him. At that moment there was a sound of crunching gravel at the top of the drive, and a dark blue Mercedes came speeding down towards the house. Jennifer groaned audibly, one foot in the car, and watched it come to a halt beside them.

Alex opened the door and got out, flicking off his sun-glasses and sliding them into the top pocket of his shirt. Benji, on seeing who it was, let out a yell of joy, and pushing his way past Jennifer, ran over and threw his arms around his father's waist.

"Hi, Dad! We didn't know you were coming today, did we, Mom?"

Jennifer smiled at him and shook her head. Alex gave his son a kiss on the top of the head, then looked up at his wife.

"Where are you going?" He directed his question to her alone.

"To the airport. David is returning to Scotland."

"And you're going too?" There was a hint of uncertainty in his voice.

"To see them off, yes." She looked at David and smiled. "David, I don't think that you have had the pleasure yet of meeting my husband, Alex, have you?"

David walked over to Alex and held out his hand. "How do you do, Alex."

Alex slowly took hold of the offered hand and shook it once. "Hi."

"I really can't tell you how much I've enjoyed working here. It's the most wonderful place. You must be very proud of it."

Alex looked at him and then at Jennifer.

"In fact, you must be very proud of everything you've got. I can say quite categorically that I have never before worked for such a wonderful family. So thank you."

Alex smiled bemusedly in acknowledgement of the remark, then looked at Jennifer. "When will you be back?"

"This evening."

Alex nodded. "Great. I'll see you then."

She climbed into the car, and Benji dived his way in after her, shouting out a loud farewell to his father. David glanced over at Alex, and then at Jasmine, blowing her a final kiss before getting into the car himself.

There was little said on the way to the airport, primarily because Charlie and Benji spent most of the journey trying to get the television to work, the reception being so intermittent that they had to press their ears to the speaker in order to be able to hear anything at all. Consequently, whenever anybody tried to talk, they were met by a barrage of hushing noises. Jennifer did ask for further details about what had happened in Scotland, but rather than explain, David simply handed her his mother's now-battered fax and let her read it for herself.

They arrived at the airport exactly two hours before the flight was due to depart. Dan parked directly outside the terminal and found a luggage trolley before taking his leave of them, explaining in his deep Bronx growl to "Mr. Costawfin" that it would be better if he stayed with the car in case he was moved on.

They were lucky in finding a queue for the check-in desk that wasn't too long, and having rid themselves of their suitcases, made their way across the enormous hall to the Departures gate, Benji and Charlie finding enough time on the way to have their photograph taken together in a booth.

Sophie was the first to say goodbye to Jennifer, holding on to her as if her life depended on it, and thanking her over and over again for her time in Manhattan. Then Harriet gave her a kiss, and pulled out from the depths of her haversack a scrumpled-up drawing that she had discovered on the way there, and asked Jennifer if she would give it to Jasmine. Charlie's farewell was more formal, a solid handshake which nearly took Jennifer's arm out of her socket, before he returned to giggle hopelessly with Benji over one particular photograph in which they both had their tongues sticking out.

"It's just me, then," David said, standing in front of Jennifer.

"Yeah, it's just you." She folded her arms and glanced around the huge hall, not really looking at very much in particular. "I'm so sorry that you have to go back like this, David. I really hope your father will be all right."

David smiled at her and nodded.

"Will you write or call?" she asked. "I mean, just to keep in touch?"

He looked down at his feet. "I don't know. Maybe it wouldn't be a very good idea for a while, you know, at least until things are settled down with Alex. Maybe next summer you both could bring Benji over for a visit . . ."

He hesitated, noticing that Jennifer had looked round at him, a pleading look in her eyes.

"Well, just one call," she said, "so that I know that you all got back safely. That would be all right, wouldn't it?"

David nodded. "Of course."

Jennifer took in a deep breath and shook her head. "I really feel shell-shocked! What the hell is *happening*? Everything in my life seems to have gone completely upside down in the past twenty-four hours." Her eyes suddenly brimmed with tears, and she walked towards him and put her arms around his neck and pulled herself close in against him.

"David, I can't accept that I'll never see you again," she whispered into his ear. "I can't believe that you won't be just there—in my garden—in my life, ever again."

"What? Like a gnome?"

Jennifer laughed against his shoulder and he felt her tears wet on his neck.

"Yeah, Supergnome." Her voice choked. "Super, Supergnome! Oh, David, I just don't know how we're all going to cope without you!"

David pushed her gently away from him. "You will." He kissed her on both cheeks. "I know you will."

He smiled and stood away from her, then turned to his children. "Right, you lot, time to make a move."

Benji heard the words, and for the first time the realization of what was happening hit him. He ran up to David and held tight to his arm without speaking. David tilted back the boy's head to look at him.

"Listen, Benji, I want to see you in ten years' time either as lead guitarist for the most famous band in the world, or playing tennis on the Centre Court at Wimbledon; otherwise I'll think all my expert tuition has gone to waste. Okay?"

Benji nodded.

"Good boy. And you never know—we might get you and Charlie together sometime during the holidays."

Benji's expression turned to one of excitement, and turning to look at Charlie, he gave him a conniving grin. David reached down and gave him a pat on his backside that guided him towards Jennifer. "Now, you look after your mother, and tell her not to work so hard!"

He glanced up at Jennifer and gave her a wink, then taking hold of Harriet's hand, he walked with his family through the automatic doors, turning just as they were shutting behind him, to catch his final, fleeting glimpse of the two people who had helped, more than any, to give him back his life.

Chapter
THIRTY-FOUR

"Oh, it's raining, Dad," Charlie said in a depressed voice, his face pressed to the glass of the window, as the plane broke through the clouds to begin its final approach into Glasgow.

David stopped writing and leaned forward in his seat to look out the window past his son. "Yeah, well, it might not be at Inchelvie. It looks quite clear over there to the north."

"But it never rained in Leesport."

David smiled and reached out and ruffled his son's hair, then, flipping over the cover of his writing-pad, he slapped his hand down on it in a gesture of completion. That was it. It had taken him the whole flight to work it out, but that was it. He had every piece of the jigsaw now in place, every one of those seemingly unconnected events linked perfectly together, running in sequence from the time that he had been asked to go out to America by Duncan right up to the present day.

There was no doubt now that it had all been a set-up, all meticulously planned to take full advantage of both his father's age and his own inability to cope with the situation. In retrospect, maybe they had left themselves wide open for such a thing to happen, either through complacency or inefficiency, but nevertheless, the way Duncan and Kirkpatrick's had acted was, quite simply, heinous. But he did know only too well that that was how big business was conducted, slithering its way just above the threshold of legality, and giving scant consideration either to personal damage or to the consequences resulting. And this was now all too bloody apparent, with his father lying so critically ill in hospital.

The plane thumped down onto the tarmac, and the engines screamed violently as the pilot engaged reverse thrust. Harriet, who was sitting in the aisle seat next to him, instinctively reached out and grabbed hold of his hand. He held on to hers tight, smiling to himself as he remembered the last time he had done just that with the little Glaswegian tyke on his way across to America. God, so long ago. But now he was back. He gritted his teeth as he thought about his prepared show-down with Duncan. Yeah, now he was truly *back*, in every blood-sense of the word!

Dougie and Archie were there waiting for them at the Arrivals hall barrier, Dougie dressed somewhat uncharacteristically in a dark suit that accentuated every muscle in his squat frame, and this, coupled with the expression of hooded seriousness on his face, made him look like a highly experienced Russian bodyguard. David smiled to himself, realizing that it was probably exactly what he was going to need that day.

"Hi, Dougie," he said, stretching out his hand.

"Hullo, Mr. David." He took a firm grip on David's hand. "Did you have a good flight?"

"Yes, thanks. No problem at all." He turned to Archie. "Hello, Archie."

The young man gave him a self-conscious smile and a brief nod of his head. "Dougie and I were just saying how sorry we were to hear about your father, sir."

"I know, Archie. It's very sad."

"Aye, it's more than that," Dougie cut in, flicking his

head to the side in a knowing gesture. "I ken fine well what brought it on. It's just bloody criminal." He touched his finger to his mouth, realizing that he had just sworn in front of the children. "Sorry, sir."

David smiled and shook his head. "No, you're right." He took over control of the luggage trolley from Charlie. "So, come on. Let's go and sort it out."

They walked out of the terminal building and splashed their way across the rain-soaked road to the car-park. As they approached the cars, David turned to the younger man.

"Now, Archie, I want you to take the children straight back to Inchelvie, and make sure that you see Effie, the housekeeper, before you leave, okay?"

"Right, sir."

"Then, after that, go straight to the distillery. I want you there when we meet with Mr. Caple, but you must *not* park in the office car-park, understood? I don't want to risk you being seen, otherwise it might spoil the element of surprise. Go round to the loading bay at the back of the maturation warehouses and park over in the corner next to where the empty barrels are stored."

The young man nodded.

"Right. Now we'll go in convoy as far as Aviemore, and there we'll split, because Dougie and I are going to head straight up to Inverness to see my father. Okay . . ." David looked at his watch. ". . . so it's a quarter to eight now. We should be in Inverness by about half past eleven, if those bloody unmarked police cars aren't on the A-Nine. I reckon we'll be back at the distillery by half past one, so make sure that you are there by then, and keep an eye out for us coming down the road. Is that all clear?"

"Yes, sir."

"Okay, then, let's make a move."

He turned to Sophie, Charlie and Harriet, who had

been standing silently beside him, and bent down and gave each a kiss.

"Now, you lot, go with Archie, and I'll see you this evening at Inchelvie."

"Will you tell Grandpa to get better soon, Dad?" Charlie said in a solemn voice. "Because he *did* say that he would teach me how to cast a salmon rod these holidays."

"Yeah, I will," David replied as lightly as he could.

Archie opened the back door of the car and Charlie and Harriet clambered in. Sophie held back for a moment, then took hold of her father's arm and led him away to a safe distance from the car.

"Dad, do you think we could go back to The Beeches tomorrow? I think we all need to go home."

David smiled at her, and putting his arms around her, he gave her a long hug.

"You're absolutely right, darling. We all *do* need to go home—back to where Mummy is."

He gave her a kiss on the forehead, then walked back to the car and opened the front passenger door for her. "Drive carefully, Archie," he said, looking into the car. "You've got a particularly valuable cargo on board."

The journey to Inverness took a little longer than anticipated, even though the weather, as he had predicted, improved as they headed north. The single-carriageway sections of the road were heavy with lorries, each having accumulated a tailback of cars that were boxed so tightly together that it made overtaking almost impossible. Although Dougie was quite adept at driving a half-mile stretch on the wrong side of the road to get clear of the hold-ups, Archie seemed to have taken David's last remark to heart, driving with such care and attention that Dougie had to pull over into a lay-by on two separate occasions to allow his car to catch up, then watch in seething frustration as a recently overtaken lorry and its parasitical line of cars trundled slowly past.

However, once they passed Aviemore, the traffic thinned out, and having seen Archie and the children safely on their way to Inchelvie, Dougie put his foot down, eventually pulling the car to a squealing halt at the main doors of Raigmore Hospital just before midday.

David asked Dougie to wait in the car-park, then walked in through the main doors of the hospital and approached the main desk. An elderly lady, whose gentle smile made it look as if she'd been specifically bred for voluntary services, looked up from where she had been writing on a shorthand pad.

"*Good* morning, can I help you?"

"Yes. I wonder if you could guide me in the right direction. I want to find Lord Inchelvie's room."

David watched as she wrote down his father's name on her pad. "And may I ask who you might be, sir?"

"Yeah, I'm Mr. Corstorphine, his son."

"Oh, I see. Right," she said, getting up immediately from her chair. "If you could just give me a moment while I get someone else to look after the desk, and then I'll take you to his room myself."

She turned and went into the office behind her. David watched through the window as she spoke to a colleague who was sitting having a cup of tea. The woman cast a glance at him through the window, then got up from her chair.

"Mr. Corstorphine," the lady said, as they both came out of the office. "If you would like to follow me, I'll take you up there now."

They walked over to the lift and took it to the sixth floor. David followed her along the spotless corridor, both standing aside to allow an old lady in a pink winceyette nightie to push her drip-stand slowly past them, muttering incoherently to herself as she went. At the end of the corridor, they entered a long ward, and David's guide stopped outside a door next to the nurses' desk.

"You'll find Lord Inchelvie in here, sir. I think Lady Inchelvie should be there as well."

David thanked her and turned to watch her leave the ward. As he put his hand out to push down the handle of the door, it opened and Roger Spiers appeared. On seeing David, he held his finger to his mouth and closed the door quietly behind him.

"David!" the old doctor said, holding out his hand. "How nice to see you! Well done, you getting back so quickly."

David shook his hand. "How is he, Roger?"

Dr. Spiers flicked his head to the side. "Not that good, I'm afraid. Nevertheless, he's pretty comfortable and I know for a fact that he's not in any pain, but, well . . ." He smiled warmly at him. ". . . like all of us of that generation, the old engine begins to get a little weary, and it becomes increasingly difficult to keep it from stalling." He looked round at the door. "Your mother's in there. She's been absolutely marvellous. Hasn't left his bedside since she got here"—he turned back to David—"so I know she'll be delighted to see you home, my boy." He gave his arm a reassuring squeeze, then shambled his way off down the ward. Taking a deep breath, David gently pushed down the handle and put his head round the door.

The small room was mottled with light that bled its way through the gaps in the closed blinds and a thin ray caught the side of his father's cheek as he lay motionless on the bed, accentuating the pallor of his once ruddy complexion. A network of tubes ran upwards from his body to the plastic drip-bottles that hung above the bed. His eyes were closed and his mouth open, but what little sound he was emitting was drowned out by the constant bleeping of the heart-monitoring equipment which flickered out its glowing light into the semi-darkness of the room.

As David watched, his mother stood up from where she sat knitting beside his father, and gently pressed his chin upwards, closing his mouth. Then, stroking her hand over his forehead, she pushed away a strand of hair that had by some miracle displaced itself, and giving her husband a smile that would never be acknowledged, she turned to sit down again, executing a double take when she saw David at the door.

"Oh, my darling, well done!" she said in a whisper, dropping her knitting onto the chair and coming over towards him. As David walked into the room, he noticed immediately the look of sheer fatigue and sorrow in his mother's eyes as she approached. He took her in his arms and held her tight.

"Let me have a look at you!" she continued to whisper, pushing herself away from him, yet holding firmly on to his arms. "You look so well! You're brown!"

David smiled at her and looked over to his father. "I'm so very sorry that I wasn't here, Ma. I really am so sorry."

His mother turned to follow his gaze. "My darling, it is *not* your fault that this has happened, and you must not even begin to think of reproaching yourself for it. I mean it. That was exactly why I made a point of explaining that in my fax. The doctor did say that it could have happened at any time." She turned back to him and reached up and kissed him on the cheek. "The main thing is that you're here."

David made no comment, thinking it neither the time nor the place to tell her that he had worked out what had been going on at the distillery. Instead, he walked past her and went over to stand by his father, reaching down and gently taking hold of his hand, taking care not to knock out the tubes that were protruding from his wrist.

"I've just had a word with Roger Spiers outside in the corridor. He says things aren't looking too good."

His mother walked around to the other side of the bed and stood looking down at her husband. "No, I'm afraid not. There was a marked deterioration overnight.

They very kindly allowed me to stay in the next-door room, and they called me at about two o'clock this morning, because they were so worried about him." She let out a long sigh. "But he seemed to rally again."

David glanced over at his mother, and caught on her face an expression of unequivocal love as she looked down at her husband. "He's always been a fighter, David. He's very weak, but I have a suspicion that he's been holding out until . . . you got home."

David nodded and leaned over and stroked his father's face, feeling a lump tighten in his throat and his eyes begin to smart with tears. "Well, I'm back now. I hope you can hear, Pa, because I'm back now, and everything, I promise you, is going to be just fine."

He bent forward and gave the wrinkled forehead a kiss, wincing at the coldness of his father's skin against his lips. He stood up and looked over to his mother. "Listen, I'm going to go to the distillery right now. I want to get this whole thing cleared up and finished with today. But I'll be back later, once I've been to Inchelvie to see the children. Do you want anything from the house?"

His mother smiled at him. "No, I've got everything I need here."

They both moved to the bottom of the bed, and David gave his mother a hug and a kiss before walking over to the door. He turned to give his father a last look, then, on impulse, returned to the bed and gave the dear, brave old man another kiss.

"We'll get this sorted out. We really will," he said, addressing no one in particular, but hoping that both occupants of the room could take comfort from his words. He opened the door and walked out, closing it gently behind him.

They drove in silence back down the A9, Dougie intent on getting back to the distillery as fast as possible, while David was quite happy to use the time to look through his notes, trying to get all his facts as clear as possible in his mind. As Dougie drove across the bridge over the Spey and turned hard left down the Glendurnich Distillery road, David glanced at his watch. It was half past one. He took in a deep breath. This was it. The show-down.

They descended the hill and turned the corner above the maturation warehouses. Archie was there, his car tucked away between two rows of barrels at the most northerly point of the concrete apron. Dougie flashed his lights, Archie responded, and his car immediately shot out and came round the side of the sheds, pulling in behind their car as they levelled out at the bottom of the hill and following them onto the car-park.

As soon as Dougie had stopped, David jumped out and looked around to make sure that Duncan's BMW was there. It was. He turned round to Dougie and Archie, who had come to stand behind him.

"Right. Archie, has Dougie explained what's been happening here?"

"Yes, he has, sir," Archie replied seriously.

"Good. Well, as soon as things are back to normal here, I just want you to know that you are to be reinstated at Glendurnich. I take it that you don't have another job yet?"

"No, I don't!" Archie exclaimed, his eyes wide with delight.

"Right. That's settled then. Now, I want you two to be present in the boardroom, just in case things get little out of hand, okay?"

They nodded briefly, and David suddenly realized that both were dressed very much smarter than he was, he still being in the clothes that he had worn when he left Leesport. He felt a wry smile come over his face. What the hell! Better wearing old clothes for this kind of job. Blood would no doubt wash out much better from denim.

"Right. Let's go."

As they walked across the car-park, David turned to

see that Dougie and Archie were making up a V-formation behind him. He smiled to himself. Perfect. Just like the Westerns. Everyone had his gun hand clear for the show-down.

They each took a separate door, bursting into the reception area at the same time, making the woman at the desk start back in surprise. David walked over and leaned both hands on the desk, and the woman, her mouth pursed in displeasure at their unmannerly entrance, pushed back her chair to distance herself from the menacing figure that stood in front of her.

"Excuse me, but who on *earth* do you think—?"

"Just be quiet and listen," David said, holding up his hand. "I want you to get hold of Duncan Caple and both the marketing and financial directors, and tell them to meet me in the boardroom *right* now."

The woman looked at him, her right eye twitching with both fear and indignation.

"Don't be absurd! I—"

"I also want you to get in contact with Margaret, and tell her to get herself back here right now. Then, as soon as you have done that, I want you to vacate this desk. Is that understood?" He flashed her a brittle smile and turned and walked towards the boardroom, followed by Dougie and Archie.

"Excuse me!" Doreen called out after David, her voice shaking with anger. "But I have no idea who you are!"

David turned and gave Archie a wink, and as he and Dougie continued on to the boardroom, Archie broke formation and walked back to the desk. He leaned across, his face two feet away from the receptionist, relishing this moment of glory in his young life as he emulated every movement of his boss.

"You have just addressed Mr. David Corstorphine, son of Lord Inchelvie and the principal shareholder of Glendurnich Distilleries Limited. Now, if I were you, I'd get hold of Mr. Caple, Mr. Barker and Mr. Archibald right now, and tell them that they're wanted in the boardroom immediately. And then call Margaret. You'll find her number in the Glendurnich telephone book—probably at the top of the list."

Doreen looked at Archie, her former expression of self-importance now replaced with one of utter fear.

"What shall I say to her?" she asked in a thin, trembling voice.

Archie pushed himself away from the desk and turned to walk over to the boardroom. "Just tell her that Mr. David's back—for good!"

The young man took his time getting to the boardroom door, eager to hear Doreen talk with Mr. Caple on the telephone. In a faltering voice, she made her announcement, then, almost immediately, repeated it, and Archie imagined with almost sadistic glee the horror on Duncan Caple's face as he learned of David's presence in the building. Then, clenching his fist, he punched at the air, expelling through gritted teeth a silent Yesss before opening the door and walking into the boardroom.

When Duncan Caple entered two minutes later, accompanied by Giles Barker and Keith Archibald, David was standing looking out the window, his hands clasped behind him.

"David!" Duncan exclaimed, as he walked across the room towards David. "How nice to see you back. I was so sorry to hear about your fath——"

David turned and pointed to the table. "Sit down, all of you."

Duncan stopped in his tracks and held up his hands, a sardonic smile on his face. "Of course. So how did things go in Ameri——?"

"Just sit *down*, Duncan!" David hissed through gritted teeth, as he turned to face the window once more.

The managing director shrugged, then pulled out a chair and sat, the other two directors having already taken heed of David's request the first time round. Dun can crossed his arms nonchalantly, then suddenly became aware of both Dougie and Archie, who were leaning against the back wall of the boardroom.

"So what have we got here?" Duncan asked, casting a glance at them over his shoulder. "The heavy brigade? Are you going to get them to beat me up, David?"

David turned. "No, Duncan. They're actually here to stop me from beating you up."

Duncan reached forward and brought his hands hard down on the table. "Oh, *come on*! We can be a bit more mature about this, can't we? You know, it's quite easily explained—"

David held up his hand to stop him. "No . . . no, let me see if *I* can explain what's happened. You just sit there and listen for a change, and if I do happen to go wrong at all, *then* you can put me right."

He walked slowly around the table, glaring at the three as he went. They followed him with their eyes, the two directors visibly blanching as they waited for him to begin. David breathed deeply, trying to steady his emotions, and looking at Duncan's thin aquiline nose, he found himself wondering what it would look like pushed flat against his face. He stopped and leaned forward on the table.

"So how much were you going to get paid, Duncan?"

For the first time, Duncan's smile slid from his face. "I don't think that really—"

"Because it must have been a hell of a lot to make it worthwhile for you to do what you've just done."

He stared with such hatred at Duncan that the man began to rub his hands nervously together between his knees. David pushed himself off the table and walked over to the window.

"I don't know the time-scale on this, but I'm not really bothered. What I do know is that you have . . . *used* my father and myself to your own advantage, with the result that he is now lying near death in hospital."

He turned and looked at Duncan. "And I want you to get something clear from the outset—and I'm really addressing all of you now—and that is whatever has happened or *will* happen to my father will be on your consciences for the rest of your lives. Maybe, at this very minute, it will mean very little to you, because I think that you're too pig-ignorant to understand that . . . but Christ, I tell you, it'll eventually catch up with you!"

David surveyed them all in silence. They sat in a row, Keith Archibald now biting at a finger-nail, as they waited for him to continue. David caught Dougie's eye, and his ex-sergeant gave him a wink and a nod of his head in encouragement.

"Right!" David said, turning back to the window. "So let's see how close I can get to your little plan." He paused. "In May, against both my will and my father's, you pulled me back to work, under the pretext that sales figures had slumped in the States. Number-one point. They had not, but you knew pretty well that the only person who might check up would be Robert McLeod, and you managed to slide him away from the company and replace him by—?"

He looked at the two directors, pointing his finger at each one. Keith Archibald slowly raised his hand.

"Right . . . you. Good. So Duncan, you decide to appoint a new distributor in the States. Deakin Distribution, a company run by a Mr. Charles Deakin, who just happens to have recently sold his company to a UK corporation called Kirkpatrick Holdings Public Limited Company." For effect, he spelled out the full name in short, pronounced bursts. "So . . . I am sent over there, and because you have already given Deakin a full briefing on my own . . . personal loss and state of mind, he is able to play heavily on that, to such an extent that he suddenly, quite out of the blue, is able to stress the importance of my having a wife."

He shook his head as he began to take in fully the ruthlessness of Duncan's actions.

"And bang! It works! I fly out of the office, in a worse state than ever before." He took in a deep breath before continuing.

"So that's me out of the way. Deakin calls you and confirms all has gone according to plan. You then contact my father and tell him that you now need a marketing director, because I'm not in a fit state to fulfil my job." He pointed to Giles Barker. "And you were brought in—from Kirkpatrick's, I presume?"

The three directors were by now looking extremely uneasy.

"I take it from your lack of interjections that I'm not doing badly so far."

Duncan shook his head, and blowing out an impatient breath, linked his hands behind his head.

"That only left you with my father to deal with. However, you managed to get him out of the way pretty easily by saying that there was no need for him to come into the distillery any more, and that you would keep him in touch by visiting him at home." He turned and stared directly at the managing director. "How very thoughtful of you, Duncan." He began pacing up and down the boardroom.

"Now, you have the full run of the distillery to yourself." He held up a finger and waggled it in the air. "Ah, but what about Margaret? She commands the switchboard. How can you begin to receive endless telephone calls from Kirkpatrick's without raising her suspicions? Easy! Get rid of her! So out she goes."

He paused for a moment, as he tried to get the next point into his mind.

"Okay, so what about this take-over? What made you think that you could buy out a company that was in the hands of private shareholding? Ah, the workers' stock-purchase plan. You found out that they now owned thirty-one per cent of the shares. Not enough to

swing an outright purchase, but nevertheless, a good-
enough thumbscrew when the time was right . . ." David turned and thumped his hands down onto the table.
". . . to approach my father!"

David took a deep breath.

"So what were you going to say to him? 'Listen, old
boy, you're getting on a bit, and your son has lost all
interest in the company and won't want anything to do
with it, seeing that he's just had a nervous breakdown
in the States. Much better that you realize your capital
from the company now—anyway, thirty-one per cent
of the shares are already owned by the workers, and
they're all for making a bit of money out of the deal,
which I'm sure you will agree is owed to them after *so*
many years of faithful service. So why not *do* the right
thing, *old boy*'!"

David spat out the last words in sheer fury at the
three men who sat in front of him. He turned away and
stood rubbing at his forehead with the tips of his fingers, his eyes tightly shut.

"But then, I found out about Kirkpatrick's, didn't I?
And I began putting two and two together, even though
my evidence was somewhat sketchy. So I faxed Archie
through Margaret, but of course, Margaret wasn't
there, so your . . . tame woman out there"—he pointed
with a thumb over his shoulder towards the door—
"brought the fax directly to you. And that not only
spelt the end of Archie's involvement with the company,
but also made you realize that I had an inkling of what
you were planning."

He turned back and looked directly at Duncan. "But
what gets me is that you continued. I can't believe
that—unless you were being pushed like hell by John
Davenport in London."

Duncan made no move to comment, and David
shook his head. "Christ, I *am* doing well, aren't I? So
you went on. You told the work-force on Friday, and
then, on Saturday afternoon, you began to put the pres-

sure on my father . . . and the consequences of *that* we all know too well."

Giles Barker broke the silence that followed by clearing his throat.

"So what do we do now?" David asked. "You tell me, Duncan: What do you think we're going to do now?"

Duncan pushed himself forward in his chair and linked his hands together, placing them in front of his chin. "Well, we could still go ahead with it. It would still be hugely profitable for your family. If you would just, for one moment, consider—"

David turned, a look of sheer horror on his face.

"*What?* I don't believe you said that! God, you are so *fucking* thick-skinned! Oh, no, Duncan, this is as far as it goes. Not only do I hold thirty-four point five percent of the Glendurnich shareholding, but under the circumstances that surround my father at present, I stand here in proxy of his thirty-four point five per cent shareholding as well! That is sixty-nine per cent, Duncan, just in case your mental arithmetic is not as sharp as your underhandedness. There is no way that you can swing this deal *now!* No, I think you have totally misunderstood my question. What I'm really saying is: What are *you* lot going to do now?"

Duncan was silent. He rubbed at his chin and glanced across to his fellow directors, who in turn looked back at him.

"I don't know," he said eventually. "What do *you* want us to do?"

David pulled out a chair and sat down opposite them, fixing each with a penetrating stare.

"Well, as far as I'm concerned, you have only one option, and that is to leave today, and never, ever set foot in Glendurnich again. But if you feel that you want to go against that option, then I'll tell you exactly what I'll do. Tomorrow morning, first thing, I shall call the Scottish correspondent of the *Financial Times* and the industrial editors of both *The Scotsman* and *The Herald,* and I shall issue them with a news release explaining exactly what has happened at Glendurnich. You'll agree with me when I say that I know the story well enough. And when it is printed, I doubt that you three will ever get a job again in this country." He leaned back in his chair. "I certainly don't think John Davenport will want to know you. He would no doubt put his damage-limitation exercise into overdrive and distance Kirkpatrick's as far as possible from your escapades up here. You'd take the brunt, I'm afraid."

He glanced over to Dougie, who was looking down at his feet, slowly nodding his head. There was a soft scraping on the carpet as Giles Barker and Keith Archibald pushed back their chairs and made their way over to the door. David turned and watched as they silently left the room, then stared over at Duncan, who eyed him with disdain, as if determined to make his final stand of dominance in the company. At that point, there was a knock at the boardroom door.

"Come in!" David called out.

Margaret put her head around the door, and he saw immediately that there were tears in her eyes.

"Yes, Margaret?" he asked in a concerned voice.

"Mr. David. I'm so sorry. Your mother has just been on the telephone." Her voice choked. "I'm afraid that your father died a quarter of an hour ago."

David looked at her and then over at Duncan.

"You fucking bastard!"

The fuse blew in his head and, fuelled by the resultant overload of anger and hatred, he moved so fast around the table that Duncan had no time to get out of his chair. David pulled back his fist as he approached him, and the man cowered away, clamping his hands to his head to protect himself from the blow. He swung with all his force at the side of Duncan's head, but just as he was expecting to feel the satisfying crunch of hard knuckle against soft cheek-bone, his hand was caught inches short of its target in Dougie's rock-hard palm.

"No, Davie!"

David turned to look through his blurred vision into Dougie's face.

"It would'na help, laddie. It just would'na help."

David turned away, and pulling his hands across his head, he walked to the far end of the boardroom and let out an anguished cry.

"Oh, no, Pa! Oh, no, no, no!"

He looked up at the painting that hung above the fireplace and stood, for a time indeterminable, staring into the kind, gentle face of his father. His eyes watched him, his smile enveloped him, and it slowly began to dawn on him that his mother had been right. The old man had picked his time. He had done all that he could, and he had clung on long enough to make sure that his son was there to carry on.

He turned. There was no one in the boardroom. The chairs were left pushed away from the table. It was all over. Glendurnich was unequivocally back in the hands of the Inchelvie family.

Chapter
THIRTY-FIVE

As the haunting strains of "The Dark Island," played by a piper from the First Battalion, The Highlanders, skirled distantly from the hill above Dalnachoil, George, Fourth Lord of Inchelvie, was silently laid to rest in the grave next to his daughter-in-law. Not a sound was heard from the village, not a car driven through, as every one of the inhabitants of Dalnachoil, along with all the employees of Glendurnich Distilleries Ltd., were present at the funeral, packed into every available space in the tiny churchyard.

As the minister finished reading out the final dedication, David dropped the cord into the grave and looked up from where he stood at its foot to give the signal to the other bearers to stand down. With a long bow of his head, he turned and walked back to his mother's side, taking her gloved hand in his and giving it a reassuring squeeze. Sophie, who had been standing behind, holding hard to Charlie and Harriet, stepped forward, so that the Inchelvie household stood in line in front of the grave. Then, each giving a final bow of his head, they turned and made their way through the gravestones towards the path that led down to the gate.

When he reached the path, David stopped and

looked over at his mother. "It's better to do it now," he said quietly. "Much better here than back at Inchelvie."

His mother looked round at the gathering and nodded. "Yes, you're probably right. What about the locals? Do you mind them hearing?"

David shook his head. "They've as much a right to hear what I'm going to say as any." He smiled at his mother. "It'll give them something to talk about at any rate."

He stepped away from her and walked back towards the grave. Everyone was looking at him. "If you could all just bear with me for a minute!" he called out at the top of his voice.

The grave-diggers, who were readying themselves to finish off their task, pushed their spades back into the soil and returned to lean their backs against the churchyard wall. David waited until the querying whispers had died down before he started.

"I had planned to say this to you all back at Inchelvie after the service, and I hope therefore you don't think it improper of me speaking to you here, especially in the context of what has just taken place. Nevertheless, both my mother and I think it apt that this should be said before the final curtain has been brought down on my father's life, because we both are certain that he would have wanted to hear what I am about to say."

He cleared his throat.

"I know that many of you here are not employees of Glendurnich, and even though I am specifically addressing them, I think it only right that everyone knows and understands the implications of what I am going to say and how important it is for the future of our community."

He paused as a gust of wind blew through the churchyard, rustling the leaves on the trees.

"You know, I consider myself incredibly fortunate to live up here in Scotland. We have a way of life, or what they now term 'a quality of life,' which is the envy of many in other parts of this country. But things are not always what they seem, as we all well know. We are a remote nation, especially up here in the north, but that remoteness only helps to strengthen the bond of belonging within our communities. We all look after each other—and we all respect each other, and this could be no more apparent than it is right now, with you all being present here—and I thank you for that from the bottom of my heart, not only for the support you have given my family today, but also for the care and understanding that you have shown towards myself over the past months.

"However, the consequences of remoteness can be fickle. Whereas it can bring us together, it can as easily split us apart, and this is nowadays all too dependent on what employment is available. We do what we can up here, we do with what's available, otherwise there is no option but to pack up and move into the cities where there are more jobs. And that is what erodes our communities. So, it is therefore essential that we protect for ourselves every available source of established employment—and Glendurnich is no exception."

David stopped for a moment and thrust his hands into the pockets of his kilt jacket.

"Last Friday, the employees of Glendurnich were called to a meeting to be briefed on the proposed buy-out of the company by a London-based corporate called Kirkpatrick Holdings Public Limited Company. The reason for this was that the employees, in total, own thirty-one per cent of the shares of Glendurnich, as the result of a stock-purchase plan set up by my father twenty-five years ago. Now I know that, to many of you, the idea of being able to cash in on this might seem extremely attractive, but what I want to put to you is that it could be a very short-lived bonus.

"What you must understand is that Glendurnich is almost unique up here. It is entirely independent, and at present it holds a significant share of the malt-whisky market world-wide. For over one hundred years now, we have never stopped producing whisky. Yet this industry is cyclical, which means that we do have periods of feast and famine, and I can tell you that I have seen what happens to small corporate-owned whisky companies in times of famine. They become a statistic. They become a minus figure on the wrong side of the balance sheet, and because they are only of minor importance to the actual company that owns them, they get closed down. Maybe not for ever—maybe just for a year or two, until demand rises again—but nevertheless they get closed down. And everyone loses his job.

"No one has ever lost his job at Glendurnich through redundancy, and, by rejecting the offer from Kirkpatrick's, I am going to make damned sure that it never will happen. Now, I'm not doing this for any selfish reason, or just for the good of my family, but for you, all of you being the extended family at Glendurnich. Your welfare is as important to me"—he turned and gestured with his hand towards his mother and his three children standing on the path—"as that of my own family, and that is why I could never live with myself if, say in five or ten years' time, I witnessed the closing down of the distillery and the subsequent loss of your jobs."

He paused and looked around the faces, trying to judge from their expression whether he had said enough to convince them.

"Now, I'm not going to say anything further at the moment, and I am certainly not going to ask you for your opinion on the matter right now, because it is neither the time nor place. Nevertheless, for those of you who would like to discuss this further, I am setting up a committee at Glendurnich, and I think it appropriate that that committee should be a true representation of the distillery as a whole. It will therefore consist of myself, Dougie Masson and Archie McLachlan, representing the board, the distillery workers and office workers respectively."

David cast his eyes to the ground for a moment before looking up again.

"That's it. Now, please, I do want you all to come back to Inchelvie where we can have a good few drams of Glendurnich malt and celebrate in style the life of a great man. And talking of which, I think by now you will understand the reason why I chose to speak to you here. Because in everything that I have just said, you would have heard exactly the same from my father."

David watched as sombre heads began to nod in agreement. As they turned their eyes back to the corner of the graveyard where his father had been laid to rest, David nodded briefly to the grave-diggers, and they stepped forward and began to shovel earth into the grave.

He turned and walked back to his mother and put his arms around her. "I'm sorry. That was a bit long-winded. Maybe I shouldn't have done it here after all."

His mother pushed herself away from him and smiled up into his face. "Darling, you were wonderful, and your timing was perfect. You said it all. Only your father could have said it with so much feeling."

She looked back towards the grave where the pile of earth was fast diminishing. "There are two people over there, David, lying side by side, who would be so proud of what you have just done."

David smiled at her, then took hold of her hand and together they walked down to the gate where the children stood waiting for them.

Just before six o'clock that evening, David helped the last of the workers climb unsteadily into the hired coach, and stood watching as the laden vehicle lumbered off down the drive. He turned to make his way back to the front door, but then hesitated, and instead walked across the gravel to the gate that led into the front garden. He pushed it open and rounded the high hedge to view, for the first time since he had returned, the new rose garden. It was in full bloom, every one of the bushes having taken root, despite the appalling conditions under which they were planted. David smiled to himself. Appalling conditions. God, how true *that* was, not only in terms of weather, but of circumstances as well. He walked along the grass path that ran between the borders, every so often reaching over to pluck off a deadhead. It had worked out just as he had planned. Every ounce of effort that he had put into it had come to fruition. And it was all for Rachel. The perfect memorial, representing, in every way, her pure, unadulterated beauty.

He bent down and dug his fingers deep into the earth around the roots of a lone dandelion, feeling the cool stickiness of it against the skin on his hand, so different from the warmth of the light, sandy soil to which he had become so accustomed in Leesport. He threw it onto the grass beside him, then rolled up a lump of earth into a tiny ball between his fingers. Two gardens so different, yet linking two women so alike, and even though one had touched his life for only a fragment of the time of the other, he knew that he would never be able to forget either

Chapter
THIRTY-SIX

The wind and rain drove hard against the windows of the offices of Culpepper Rowan, causing the water to run in diagonal streaks across the tinted glass before settling in the sheltered crevices at the side. Jennifer stood with her arms crossed and her head resting against the cold pane as she gazed vacantly down onto the traffic far below on Fifth Avenue. It was only three in the afternoon, but the sky was so heavy with dark, scudding clouds that the cars were already driving with their headlights on. It all looked so depressing. Thank God it was only two weeks to the beginning of May, and then everything would hopefully transform to sunshine and warmth. Summer would be here.

But there again, it would be only the weather that would change. Not her life. As far as that was concerned, it might just as well be winter all the time—cold, colourless and dismal. It had been that way since November, when Alex had eventually left, and even before that, the effort of trying to work things out with him had been more stressful to deal with than his subsequent departure.

She turned from the window and went over to her desk and, slumping down in her chair, she reached forward and scrolled through the page on her laptop. She laughed scathingly to herself. THE page! That was all she had written. She was supposed to have finished the damned proposal by that evening, but every ounce of creative adrenaline had deserted her. It was as if her brain were swimming in syrup.

She guided the arrow up to the "save" option, then shut down her computer, gently closing the lid and sitting back in her chair. She just couldn't concentrate any more. And it seemed to be getting worse.

She pushed her chair away from the desk and stood up, and as she made her way back to the window, there was a brief knock on her door and Sam entered. "Hi!" he said, clapping his hands together. "Just wanted to find out how you were doing on the proposal."

Jennifer glanced at him, then turned away to look out of the window.

"Not good, huh?" he said morosely.

Jennifer shook her head.

"Well, tell you what, I'll get Russ to have a look at it. I think we should try to get something faxed to them by this evening." He walked over to her desk and picked up her telephone. "Yeah, Russ, it's Sam. Could you come to Jennifer's office? Thanks."

He replaced the receiver and came over to stand beside Jennifer, leaning his back against the window and pushing his hands into his pockets.

"You're not feeling too good, are you?"

"I'm sorry, Sam. I haven't been much use to you over the past six months, have I?"

Sam reached out and took hold of her arm. "Come on, you've said that before. You've done just fine. Things have been pretty difficult for you, and I can live with that. You'll get back into the swing of things soon enough."

Jennifer was silent for a moment, as she continued to stare out of the window. "No, I don't think so. I'm burned out. I have nothing really to offer you any more.

I am beginning to think that it would be better if I just quietly packed up my things and left the company. You can't afford to subsidize my existence here. Anyway, I think that the time has come for me to get my priorities right."

"Meaning?"

"Meaning that I really want to spend more time with Benji and Jasmine at home. I think that's where I am needed the most right now."

Sam let out a long hiss. "Yeah, I suppose I can understand that, but I really don't want you to go." He paused, rubbing at the toe of his shoe with the heel of the other. "I don't, er, suppose you ever heard from Alex again?"

"No. Not directly, anyway. I had a letter from a lawyer in Dallas two days ago, saying that he was going to be representing him in the divorce proceedings."

Sam blew out disparagingly and shook his head. "Christ! What a bastard *he* turned out to be!"

Jennifer smiled sadly. "Well, he wasn't at one time, Sam," she said quietly.

"I know. I'm sorry. I shouldn't have said that."

At that moment, the door flew open and Russ walked in, laughing at a remark that someone had said to him in passing outside the office. "Yeah, Sam, what can I do for—?"

Sam held a finger to his lips to stop him from continuing. He turned to Jennifer. "Listen, I understand your reasons for wanting to leave the company, but I wonder if you might consider just holding fire for a time."

Jennifer looked at him. "For what reason?"

The expression on Sam's face suddenly transformed into a huge grin. "Because—I have just had a phone call from Gladwin Vintners. It seems that they have been *so* impressed with the way we've handled the Tarvy's account that they want us to take on the marketing of Glentochry Blend Whisky and Valischka Vodka over here."

There was a loud whoop from Russ and, stepping forward, he held his hand up in the air and slapped it down on Sam's outstretched palm.

"Goddamn it, Sam, you old son of a gun! You were right! You were absolutely right!"

"Well, I told you we could do it! I knew it was only a matter of time!" He turned to Jennifer. "And that's why I don't want you to go just yet. They have specifically asked for you to handle it."

Jennifer smiled at him, and shook her head. "You know, that's very sweet of you, Sam, and I really am delighted that you've got it, but I'm simply not fired up any more, and I don't want you to risk losing it because of that. Anyway, I don't think that I want to change my mind. You boys can handle it well enough."

Sam let out a groan of frustrated disappointment, then paused for a moment.

"Okay. How about this for an option? Gladwin's want us to fly over to London to meet with them and discuss the schedule. We don't have to produce a document. We don't have to produce anything, just show up for the meeting. Now, I really want you to come over with me, Jennifer, and I also would like you to bring Benji." He threw his hands up in a devil-may-care gesture. "Hell, I want you to bring Jasmine as well! Let's *all* go over! We'll stay at the Ritz, because I think that we damned well deserve it, and once we've had the meeting, *then* you can decide if you want to leave the company. Now, would you consider doing that?"

Jennifer looked at Sam for a moment, then suddenly seemed amused. "Sorry, Sam, I just had this wonderful image of Jasmine being waited on at the Ritz."

"Well, why the hell not?" Sam said, holding out his hands. "She's been through the mill as much as any of you. Come on, Jennifer, *please,* you'd do it for me, wouldn't you?"

Jennifer contemplated the suggestion. "I'd have to get Benji off school."

"Do it!" Sam exclaimed, rubbing his hands together as he realized that he was making some headway with his persuasion. "Come on! It would be great for all of us. And as I said, you can make up your mind one way or the other after the meeting."

"Okay."

Sam slapped his fist into the palm of his hand in triumph.

"But," Jennifer continued, "I couldn't go right away. I mean, I'd have to clear it with Benji and Jasmine first, *and* with Benji's principal at school."

"Yeah, that's no bother. We wouldn't need to go until the beginning of next week. That leaves you three days clear before the weekend." He paused and looked intently into her face. "So we have a definite yes?"

Jennifer smiled at him. "Yes."

"Great!" Sam cried out, pushing himself away from the window. "I'll go fix that up with Gladwin's, and book the flights *and* the rooms at the Ritz." He took hold of Russ's arm as he walked past him. "Russ, would you be good enough to get a copy of that proposal Jennifer's working on, and get something off to the client tonight? Doesn't have to be anything too great. We can stall them for a couple of days."

Russ nodded. "Okay."

"Good." He turned round to Jennifer and gave her a wink. "So, London, here we come!" And giving a little skip, he walked over to the door and left the office.

As the door shut, Jennifer made her way over to her desk and, pushing open the lid of her computer, she turned on the switch. "I'm sorry to load this onto you, Russ. I just couldn't get it going at all."

He shook his head. "Don't worry about it. I'll put something together for them for tonight. Don't forget, I'm a bit of a genius too!"

Jennifer pushed a floppy disc into the computer and

transferred the document across. Then, ejecting the disc, she handed it over to Russ. He stood holding it in his hand, and knocking it nonchalantly against the tips of his fingers.

"How's, er, Benji doing—you know—without Alex around?"

Jennifer let out a long sigh. "Not good. He's really taken it all so hard. In fact, he hasn't really been the same since . . . well . . ."

"Since David left?"

Jennifer looked startled, then smiled. "My, that's pretty intuitive of you, Russ! Yeah. Since David left. He hero-worshipped him, really."

"Have you ever heard from him?"

Jennifer closed down her computer and shut the lid.

"No. Not since the week after he left. He called to say that they had arrived back in Scotland. His father died the day he got back. I haven't heard anything since then. Benji got a bunch of cards and a couple of letters, though, from Charlie, his son."

Russ continued to tap the disc against his fingers. "Listen—maybe I shouldn't say this, but—well—Benji wasn't the only one who kinda liked him, was he?"

Jennifer felt a flush come to her cheeks and she shook her head slowly.

"God, Russ, you've softened some! A year ago, I'd have quite happily laid down a hundred dollars against you noticing anything like that!" She paused as she walked over to the window. "But you're right. I think I can honestly say that he was the most special man I've ever met in my life."

There was a moment's silence.

"Yeah. He was some guy, wasn't he?"

Jennifer turned and looked at him. "How come you say that? You only met him once."

"Once was enough." He paused. "You remember that tennis match?"

Jennifer nodded.

"Well, it just happened that the following week, I went to watch a demonstration match at Flushing Meadows. It was really all put on for the crowds—a mixture of good tennis and good humour. Anyway, in the second set, the better of the two players obviously wanted to make it one set all, so that they could take the match to the third set—and he did it by making his serves and ground strokes go inches over the lines. Okay, so it was planned—but it was so imperceptible that I am sure that most of the spectators didn't realize that it was happening. But *I* knew, because David had done exactly the same thing to me the previous week-end."

He walked over to stand beside Jennifer and began fiddling with the cord of the window blind. "God, I can tell you that it fairly dented my pride. And then I thought to myself, well, hell, what about David? It never made any difference to him whether he won or lost. And then I realized that he hadn't minded humbling himself, because it was all above him, and in that way, he was above me. What was more, he made me understand that without actually having to show me up."

He let go of the cord and looked across at Jennifer, who was standing smiling at him. She walked towards him, and reaching up, gave him a kiss on the cheek.

"He touched everyone, Russ, one way or the other. I know that it sounds like a cliché out of a *Superhero Comic*, but sometimes I just wonder why, of all the millions of front doors stretched across the States, he came to knock on mine." She reached down and unplugged her laptop from the wall socket, then, curling up the cord, she walked back to her desk. "I mean, think of it, if it hadn't been for him, we wouldn't be planning this trip to London!"

Russ watched her as she opened up her brief-case and slid in the laptop.

"Why don't you go to Scotland?"

Jennifer glanced up at him. "What?"

"Why don't you go up and see him?" He walked across to her desk and leaned forward on it, looking directly into her face. "Go on, do it! If you want an excuse, say that Benji wants to see him. Just don't let him go!"

She paused for a moment, then smiled and shook her head. "No, Russ. I can't. I don't know what his life is like. I mean, everything would be completely different. It was just a moment in time, a very happy and unforgettable moment in time."

Russ looked down at the disc that he still held in his hand. "Yeah, maybe. Suppose it's just me being too impulsive. But listen, I'm coming over to London with you, so if you do happen to change your mind, you go and I'll cover for you. Is that a deal?"

Jennifer zipped up her case and nodded. "Yeah, that's a deal, Russ—but I won't be changing my mind."

He pushed himself off the desk and walked towards the door. "Oh, I don't know. There's a good few front doors in the UK as well. Maybe fate will take you to his." He turned and smiled at her, and held up the disc. "Anyway, I'd better get going on this."

"Russ?"

He stopped with his hand on the door handle.

"Thanks."

Russ flicked his hand dismissively at her and walked out of the office.

Jennifer dialled the number of the house in Leesport.

"Jasmine? Hi, it's Jennifer . . . listen, this might come as a bit of a shock to you, but we've got to get you a passport by next week."

Chapter

THIRTY-SEVEN

Narrowing his eyes against the glare of the morning sun, the tall blue-coated doorman at the Ritz moved as agilely as a ballroom dancer around the portly female frame that tried to back out of the newly arrived taxi, finding himself in a quandary as to how best he could be of assistance to the woman without causing obvious affront. He skipped lightly around to her other side and held hard to the hand that was scrabbling blindly for support, and once she had extricated herself, Jasmine turned to him with a beaming smile on her face and blew out a sigh of relief.

"Thank you kindly, sir. Those taxis sure seem to be a lot easier to get in than out."

"Yes, they can be a little awkward, madam," the doorman replied with a diplomatic smile, and briefly touching the brim of his top hat, he glided around to hold the cab door open for the other four occupants.

As they climbed the steps and entered through the revolving doors of the hotel, Jennifer heard Jasmine gasp audibly as she stared in open-mouthed wonderment at the sumptuous interior of the reception area. "Now, this is what I call high-livin'!"

Jennifer laughed. "Well, don't start getting any big

ideas about what we could do with the house in Leesport." She opened her handbag and took out their passports. "Could you just keep an eye on Benji, Jasmine,
just in case he heads off on one of his exploration
jaunts." She walked over to the reception desk, where
Sam and Russ were already booking in.

"So if you could please just fill this in, Mr. Culpepper," the pretty young receptionist was saying brightly,
as she handed Sam a registration form. "And this is
for Mr. Hogan . . . and this for Mrs. and Master Newman . . . and you have a Miss Washington with you?"

"I'll do that," Jennifer cut in, smiling at the receptionist. "She's looking after my son."

"Very good, madam. But you will need to know
Miss Washington's passport number."

Jennifer held up the passports in her hand. "Don't
worry. I have them all here."

Having filled in their forms, the receptionist escorted
them across the hall and left them in the capable hands
of the head porter.

"Right then," he said, taking a number of keys out
of the cubby-holes behind him. "You are all on the
fourth floor. Mr. Culpepper room 410, Mr. Hogan 416,
Mrs. and Master Newman 422 and Miss Washington
427. Now, I'll get someone to take you up, and your
bags will be brought to you directly."

He called over a bellboy and handed him the keys,
and they were led over to the lift in the corner by the
stairs. Jennifer looked around for Jasmine and Benji,
catching sight of them through the glass doors as they
walked slowly towards her along the pink-carpeted
hallway, staring at everyone and everything they passed.
She pushed open one of the doors.

"Come on, you two. We're going up to our rooms."
Realizing that the lift was not going to be able to accommodate them all, Sam took hold of Russ's arm and
stepped out.

"We'll walk up, Jennifer. It'll do us good." He

turned to Jennifer. "Listen, I was thinking on the plane over that maybe we should have a couple of ideas up our sleeves for the meeting tomorrow, so Russ and I are going to put our heads together for the day. But I want you to have the day on your own—take Benji and Jasmine around London or something, and we'll meet down here for a drink at, say, six-thirty, okay?"

"Are you sure you don't need me, Sam?"

He smiled and shook his head. "No. I want you all to enjoy yourselves. If you need anything, though, just give either myself or Russ a call. Room 410 or 416."

"All right. Thanks, Sam." She pushed herself into the lift beside Jasmine.

"Now?" Benji looked up at the bellboy, his finger hovering in front of the fourth-floor button.

"Now," the bellboy replied with a brief nod of his head and Benji punched the button.

Jennifer was allowed only half an hour's respite before Benji began pressing impatiently for her to go out, so, having prised Jasmine from her room, they set off along Piccadilly towards Green Park. Opposite the underground station, they picked up an open-topped tour bus, and despite the blustering coolness of the wind, they succumbed to Benji's insistence that they should ride on the upper deck. Jennifer and Jasmine sat with their coats pulled tight about them, while Benji dived from one side of the sparsely populated bus to the other, as the creamy voice of the tour guide called out each of the sights—Hyde Park Corner, Buckingham Palace, The Mall, Whitehall, The Houses of Parliament—before proceeding along the Victoria Embankment to the Tower. By that point, Jennifer noticed that Jasmine, although pretending bravely to be enjoying herself, looked as if she were in the early stages of hypothermia, so they abandoned the bus and took to the warmer climes of the underground. Taking the Circle Line to Baker Street, they spent the rest of the morning and the early part of the afternoon meandering slowly around Madame Tussaud's, with Benji having his photograph taken with as many of the waxwork celebrities as was possible.

Footsore and weary, they arrived back at the Ritz at two-thirty and, amidst loud protestations from Benji, who was keen to continue with their adventures, they headed off to their respective rooms to recharge their batteries.

"This is going to be boring!" Benji moaned as he threw himself onto the bed.

"You don't have to go to sleep," Jennifer said, taking her wash-bag from the still-unpacked suitcase and making her way through to the bathroom. "Watch TV. But if you don't have some kind of rest, you're just going to flake out tonight."

"No, I won't!" he said, pushing himself off the bed and walking over to the chest of drawers to pick up the remote control. "I'm not tired."

He flicked through the channels, stopping only long enough to give each of the programmes a cursory glance. There was an old black-and-white war film, an Australian soap opera, a cooking demonstration, and something that had just started called "Westminister Today."

"There's nothing on!" he called through to his mother.

"Oh, come on, Benji!" Jennifer shouted back, as she splashed water on her face from the basin. "You've had a pretty good morning. Just make do with what's on."

Benji tutted and threw the remote onto his bed. He pushed his head into the pillow and kicked up his legs, executing a perfect headstand against the back wall and knocking squint the picture of the galloping racehorse that was hung upon it. A woman's plummy English voice sounded out from the television.

"Good afternoon, and welcome to 'Westminister Today.' We are going to begin our broadcast by going live to the House of Lords where a particularly heated de-

bate on the present government's Companies Bill has been in progress for the past two days. We join it now at the Committee Stage where some one hundred and twenty amendments to the Bill have been put forward for discussion."

"Booriing!" Benji said out loud as he flumped down onto the bed, then kicked his legs up once more against the wall. "Mom?"

"Yes?"

"What's the House of Laawds?" He drawled out the last word.

Jennifer appeared at the door of the bathroom, rubbing at her face with a towel, and looked over at the television.

"I suppose the best way to describe it is that it's like the Senate. You know we have Congress. Well, that's like the House of Commons, and the Senate is like the House of Lords. It's what's called the Upper House of Parliament. We went past there this morning on the bus, remember?"

She smiled at his upside-down face and returned to the bathroom.

"Well, it's pretty boring stuff to put on television. I mean, who's going to watch this stuff?"

Benji watched from his inverted position as the camera zoomed in on a man in a long white wig who was sitting on a huge red sofa.

"We pass onto Amendment Twenty-four. The Lord Inchelvie."

"The Laawd Inchelvie," Benji said, with his mouth drawn down at the sides. "The Laaaawd Inchelvie."

"Your Lordships' Committee might wish to consider the aspect of the Bill that is addressed on page fifty-one, line seven. This sets out proposals for the merger between two companies, where it is presumed that the principal of each company . . ."

Benji fell heavily down onto the bed and stared at

the wall, concentrating hard on the voice that was coming from the television.

"*There is, however, an aspect that has been overlooked. Even over a short period of time, the management structure of a company can become obscured. And, my lords, if that is the case . . .*"

Benji jumped off the bed and ran over to the television. That wasn't Lord Inch—what's-his-name's voice! That was David's! He pressed his face against the screen, trying to make out the figure that was speaking from the long shot being broadcast at that moment.

"*. . . e.g. discretion may have been given to a certain family and its members to control events, but it may not be clear to the family concerned which board members . . .*"

The camera cut to a close-up of the speaker's face. It was! It was David! Benji began jumping around, shaking his hands in the air, his voice muted with excitement.

"MOM!" he blurted out.

Jennifer came running through from the bathroom, a white towelling band pulling her hair back and protecting it from the white cream that covered her face. "What's the matter?" she said in a startled voice.

Benji looked at her, an expression of amazement on his face as he pointed at the television.

"It's David, Mom! Look, it's David! He's on TV! He's in the House of Lords! Look!" He ran over to her, and grabbing her hand, which was slippery with cream, he dragged her in front of the television.

"It's David, isn't it? He's all dressed up, but that's David!"

Jennifer slowly turned from her son and stared at the tall pin-stripe-suited figure that stood amongst the red leather seats. Her heart missed a beat as she listened to the familiar voice talking, and Benji watched as her face broke into a huge smile.

"It is," she said quietly, her face registering total dismay. "That's David."

"C'mon, Mom!" Benji said, dragging her towards the door. "C'mon!"

"Where are you going?" she laughed.

"To the House of Laawds! C'mon, we went past there this morning! It's just down the road!"

Jennifer pulled her hand away from Benji's grasp. "Benji," she said, smiling at him and shaking her head. "This must be a recording. David won't be there now!"

"He is!" Benji exclaimed, frustrated. "They said it was live! That means it's coming from there *now!*"

Jennifer turned slowly back to the screen. "It's live?" she said in an astonished voice.

"Yes!! C'mon, Mom, before he finishes! We gotta go and see him!"

Jennifer stood gazing at the screen as the camera zoomed into a tight close-up of David's face. He was sitting now, and she watched as his face broke into a grin over a light-hearted rebuff made by one of the lords on the other side of the house. She knew it so well. She knew that face so well.

"Okay!" She ran through to the bathroom and grabbed a towel, then came back into the bedroom, rubbing the cream from her face. "You go down to reception and get a taxi, darling, and I'll be with you in a minute. I've just got to tell Jasmine and Sam."

Benji rushed from the room, and she heard him running down to the passageway, yelling out "The House of Laawds! The House of Laawds!" over and over again as he went. She picked up the phone and dialled Jasmine's room. A sleepy voice replied.

"Hello, Jasmine here."

Jennifer smiled to herself, wondering if she announced herself that way to everyone.

"Jasmine, Benji and I are going out again."

"Where to?"

"I won't tell you until we get back. But I think it could be a pretty big surprise for you!"

"Oh, okay," Jasmine replied uninterestedly. "I'll just go back to sleep and wait 'till I hear from you then."

"Right." She pressed her finger on the button to disconnect the line and dialled Sam's room number. It was Russ who answered.

"Russ? It's Jennifer."

"Hi! You sound excited. What's going on?"

"It's David, Russ! He's on TV—in the House of Lords. And it's live."

There was a moment's silence at the other end of the line.

"Russ? Are you still there?"

"Yeah, sorry. David's here? In London?"

"Yes!"

"Well, Chrissakes, what did I tell you? Looks like you knocked on the right door! Go for it, Jennifer! Just go for it! Sam and I can handle the meeting. God, what am I saying? Forget us, Jennifer. Just go for it!"

"Will you explain to Sam?"

"Yeah, but he's heard anyway. He's sitting here nodding his head, and if he nods any more, it's going to fall off!"

Jennifer laughed, feeling her eyes prick with tears of elation. "Okay! Okay! I'm going!"

"Good luck, old friend," he said quietly.

"Thanks, Russ."

She put down the receiver and rushed to the door. then turning back to pick up her handbag she took another quick glance at the television. David was standing once more, speaking. She smiled, blew him a kiss, then turned and ran out of the room.

Benji was already sitting in the cab outside the hotel, leaning forward and watching out for his mother coming down the steps. She jumped in and was about to announce their destination when the taxi took off.

"I've told him, Mom! He says he knows where it is!"

"I hope so!" Jennifer laughed. She opened up her bag and took out her make-up, and jammed herself into the corner of the taxi to give some support to her already shaking hand.

By the time they drove down Whitehall, she had finished applying a make-shift covering to her face, while Benji had engaged her in an excited though uncomprehending discussion as to how David Corstorphine had suddenly become Lord Inch—what's-his-name. The taxi drew to a halt outside the Houses of Parliament next to a large statue of a man on a horse, and the driver pulled open the partition window.

"You want to go into the Lords, luv?"

"Yes," Jennifer replied, leaning forward and pulling a ten-pound note out of her purse.

"That's the queue there," he said, pointing to a roped-off section of the pavement. "Not many people. You should get in with the next lot."

"Thanks," Jennifer said, handing him the note. He delved into his pocket for change, but both Jennifer and Benji had jumped out of the taxi.

"Keep the change!" she called back with a smile. "It's worth it!"

"I hope so, luv!" he yelled after her.

As they joined the queue, a man in a uniform came forward and unclipped the white rope and began ushering them into the building. They entered a huge stone-floored hall and followed the line as it moved sedately along between the stone statues of past politicians. At the bottom of the stairs, the usher turned to them and told them in a lugubrious voice that they would have to wait there in the Central Lobby until such times as the last intake of visitors had left the Public Gallery. Undeterred by this, Benji walked to the front and confronted the man.

"Excuse me, but my mom and I know someone who's in the House of Lords, and we want to see him."

There was a murmur of amusement from the other visitors, as the man bent slowly forward to speak to him.

"I'm afraid that you will have to wait, young man, even though you are acquainted with one of the Peers of the Realm."

Benji turned with a disconsolate look on his face and walked back to his mother, scuffing his feet along the floor as he went. He sauntered over to one of the statues and leaned against the base, watching for any movement coming from the stairs.

Five minutes later, the first of the visitors began to descend, turning eventually into a steady stream of people. Benji sighed impatiently, realizing that it was going to take some time before they would be allowed to go up, and turned to read the inscription on the statue against which he was leaning.

"BENJI?"

The voice echoed around the Central Lobby, and everyone, including the usher, turned to look up at the top of the stairs. Charlie was staring down at him, holding hard to the banister and stopping the flow of people who were coming behind him.

Benji's face lit up as he watched Sophie and Harriet thump against the banister beside him.

"CHARLIE! SOPHIE! HARRIET" Benji yelled out, and ran towards the bottom of the stairs as he watched Sophie and Charlie push their way unceremoniously through the crowds towards him.

When they reached the bottom, they stood three feet apart, looking at each other, incredulous grins spread across their faces.

"What are *you* doing here?" Charlie asked in an amazed voice.

"Mom and I saw your dad on television. We've come to see him!"

"Your mother's here?" Sophie asked, looking around for Jennifer. She saw her, still standing in line, leaning sideways and smiling at her. She took off at a run and threw herself into Jennifer's arms, clasping her hands around her neck.

"What are *you* all doing here?" Benji asked. "I thought you were at school in Scotland!"

"We are, but Granny took us off for two days and brought us down here, 'cos she thought we would like to see Dad talk in the House of Lords."

Benji looked past him to see a tall old lady come down the stairs holding on to Harriet's hand. Charlie ran up the first two steps to meet them.

"Granny, this is Benji, my friend from America. He's here—in London!"

His grandmother smiled at Benji as she approached him, her hand outstretched. "Yes, I can see that, darling. How do you do, Benji? How very nice it is to meet you."

Benji shook her hand and turned to find that his mother and Sophie had come to stand behind him.

"Granny," Sophie said excitedly. "This is Jennifer."

Alicia smiled warmly at Jennifer and stepped forward and kissed her on both cheeks. "My dear, I am so delighted to meet you. I have heard so much about you, both from Sophie and from David." She stood back, shaking her head in astonishment. "I cannot believe you're here! What an extraordinary thing!"

Benji walked up to his mother and tugged at her hand. "Mom, can Charlie and I go and see David now? *He* knows where to go."

Jennifer looked down at him. "In a minute, darling. There are still people coming down the stairs."

Alicia looked around. "Oh, I'll see if we can't pull a few strings."

She walked over to the usher at the head of the queue and talked quietly with him. He nodded and accompanied Alicia back to where they stood.

"This very kind gentleman will take you two up to

~ublic Gallery. But remember, Charlie, you have to be very quiet."

"All right, Granny!" Charlie exclaimed and both he and Benji began running up the stairs, squeezing past the oncoming traffic, followed as briskly as he was able by the elderly usher.

Being between intakes, the Public Gallery was completely empty, and all was silent except for the single low voice that droned from the chamber below. The usher showed the two boys to the seats at the very front, and stood beside them as Charlie pointed out his father to Benji. He craned forward in his seat, desperately trying to catch David's eye, then turned to Charlie.

"Can't we call him?" he whispered.

"No, it's against the law," Charlie replied sombrely, pressing his mouth against Benji's ear. "Granny says you're not even allowed to wave."

"How can we get his attention then?"

"We can't. We have to wait until he looks up."

Benji gazed down on the house, looking at each of the lords in turn. "He looks as if he's the youngest person there!"

Charlie put his hand to his mouth to stop himself from giggling. "Granny says that some of them have been sitting there so long that they have cobwebs stretching from their heads to the backs of their seats."

Benji too clamped his hand to his mouth, but not before letting out an involuntary snort of laughter. He turned guiltily around to the usher, who put his finger to his lips.

At no time did David make any effort to look up at the gallery. Benji moved his head fractionally from side to side to try to attract his attention, but it was all to no avail. David didn't know they were there. It was all too much. He had to let him know. He stood up.

"DAVID!"

Charlie grabbed at him and dived below the level of the balcony in embarrassment. Every face turned up to the gallery, each issuing loud murmurs of "Order! Order!" The usher gave Benji a hard pat on the back and pointed to the door. But it was all too late. Benji's call had had the desired effect. David started in his seat, and looked up at the gallery in time to see the beaming-faced boy waving at him as he was ushered out. God, it was Benji! What the hell was he . . . ? Charlie's face suddenly appeared from below the balcony, and as he too got up to leave, he gestured with his hand for his father to come out. David shook his head in disbelief, then turned to look around the chamber. All eyes were on him. He handed his papers to the peer directly in front of him, then stood up and walked as fast as he felt was permissible towards the double doors.

Once outside the Debating Chamber, he hurried across the Lords Lobby, pushed hard at the large swinging doors and entered the Central Lobby, arriving just as Benji and Charlie reached the bottom of the stairs.

Benji picked him out immediately from the crowd. "DAVID!" he yelled and ran up to him, throwing his arms around his waist.

David held hard to the boy and bent down and kissed the top of his head. "Benji," he said, laughing, "what *on earth* are you doing here?"

Benji pushed himself away from him, just as Charlie came to join them.

"We saw you on TV. We're staying in the Ritz, and I turned on the TV and saw you. I didn't recognize your name. You changed it!"

"Yes, you're right. I have. Who's 'we,' Benji?"

"Mom, Jasmine and me."

"All of you? You're all here in London?"

"Yup. Jasmine is still in the hotel, but Mom is here somewhere." He turned and looked around the crowded hall.

"There they are!" shouted Charlie, and he and Benji turned and began running over to the entrance door,

Jennifer stood talking to Sophie and her grandmother.

David walked slowly towards them, his eyes fixed
firmly on Jennifer. As the boys reached them, she
looked around and saw him approach, and her face
broke into a wide grin.

He stopped in front of her and thrust his hands into
his pockets of his jacket.

"Hi."

Jennifer held her handbag with both hands in front
of her, self-consciously swinging it from side to side.
"Hi," she replied quietly.

As they stood in silence looking at each other, Alicia
put her arm around Sophie's shoulders and, giving her
a knowing wink, they followed on after the two boys
and Harriet, who had already run out through the
doors into the sunlight of the afternoon.

"How are things?" David asked, his face still fixed
in the widest of grins.

Jennifer shrugged. "So-so."

"Did, er, everything work out between you and . . . ?"

Jennifer shook her head. "No, it's finished. I did try,
David, but he walked out on us in November."

"What a bloody fool," he murmured, staring down
at his feet in an attempt to disguise his look of sheer
relief. He looked up at her and laughed.

"So . . . how long are you over here for?"

"I don't know."

David acknowledged someone who passed by. "You,
er, wouldn't consider coming up to Scotland, would
you? I mean, all of you?"

Jennifer contemplated this for a minute, before nodding her head slowly. "You know, I think we might.
Nothing else is planned."

They continued looking at each other without either
making a move. Jennifer took in a long breath and let
it out again. "So, you've changed profession? From a
gardener to a lord?"

David nodded and raised his eyebrows.

"Wow!" She gave a little laugh at the incredulity of it all. "That really *is* one for the books!" She pulled a face. "I've never met a lord before. What am I supposed to do? Give a little curtsy?"

David shook his head and moved towards her, putting his arms around her waist and pulling her towards him. "I don't think there's any written law on the subject. So I suppose that we could just make do with a very long and passionate kiss."

And the elderly usher, who had been making his way slowly up the staircase, stopped and cast his eyes around the Central Lobby, wondering why such a profound silence had suddenly descended upon the place.

lebrate Life's Journeys with the
ved Author Whose Stories of Life
and Love Have Touched the World

ROSAMUNDE
❧ PILCHER ❧

FLOWERS IN THE RAIN
"A work of art." —*Los Angeles Times*
_____ 92774-6 $6.99 U.S./$8.99 CAN.

SEPTEMBER
"A jewel of a novel." —*Boston Sunday Herald*
_____ 92480-1 $7.99 U.S./$9.99 CAN.

THE BLUE BEDROOM AND OTHER STORIES
"Breathtaking!" —*Grand Rapids Press*
_____ 92628-6 $5.99 U.S./$6.99 CAN.

VOICES IN SUMMER
"Pilcher displays a perfect touch!" —*Booklist*
_____ 92527-1 $5.99 U.S./$7.99 CAN.

THE CAROUSEL
"Delightful!" —*Publishers Weekly*
_____ 92629-4 $5.99 U.S./$7.99 CAN.

Publishers Book and Audio Mailing Service
P.O. Box 070059, Staten Island, NY 10307
Please send me the book(s) I have checked above. I am enclosing $_____ (please add
$1.50 for the first book, and $.50 for each additional book to cover postage and handling.
Send check or money order only—no CODs or charge my VISA, MASTERCARD,
DISCOVER or AMERICAN EXPRESS card.

Card Number_____

Expiration date_____Signature_____

Name_____

Address_____

City_____State/Zip _____
Please allow six weeks for delivery. Prices subject to change without notice. Payment in
U.S. funds only. New York residents add applicable sales tax.   4PIL 2/98